PRAISE FOR ANNA LEE WALDO'S
NEW YORK TIMES BESTSELLER
PRAIRIE

"A warm, colorful book, weaving all the strands of Irwin's remarkable life into a work of fiction that does not betray its real-life hero."

—*Arizona Daily Star*

"A big American horse and soap opera—the best kind."

—*New York Daily News*

"Notable . . . Conveys the spirit of the times."

—*Missoulian* (Missoula, Montana)

. . . AND PRAISE FOR HER BESTSELLING
SACAJAWEA

"The story of Sacajawea is one of mystery, courage, and remarkable achievement, against an exciting panorama of American history."

—*Seattle Times*

"Exceptional."

—*St. Louis Post-Dispatch*

"A blockbuster historical novel."

—*Fort Worth Star-Telegram*

ANNA LEE WALDO

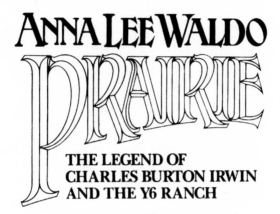

PRAIRIE

THE LEGEND OF CHARLES BURTON IRWIN AND THE Y6 RANCH

AN AUTHORS GUILD BACKINPRINT.COM EDITION

AN AUTHORS GUILD BACKINPRINT.COM EDITION

Published by iUniverse.com, Inc.

For information address:
iUniverse.com, Inc.
5220 S 16th, Ste. 200
Lincoln, NE 68512
www.iuniverse.com

Originally published by Berkley

ISBN: 0-595-14979-0

Printed in the United States of America

DEDICATION

Although Charles Burton Irwin, his family, and many friends actually lived, this novel about him necessitated a few additional fictitious characters to fill in blanks where people probably existed, but have been forgotten. Most of the conversation is made up; most of the stories took place. This work is dedicated to the real people, relatives, and friends of C. B. Irwin, because they left a precious legacy toward the growth of the American West, and should be remembered.

CONTENTS

PHOTOGRAPHS AND ILLUSTRATIONS

(This section follows page 496.)

Etta Mae McGuckin, eighteen years old.

Charles Burton Irwin.

Kenmore Coursing Club group, 1895. C. B. Irwin is in front with a spotted dog. Frank Irwin, well-known jockey, is on the left on a horse. The building in the background is the Sherman County Courthouse in Goodland, Kansas.

Business stationery used by C. B. Irwin.

C. B. Irwin roping an unruly steer, 1906. This picture appeared in the December 1925 *National Geographic*, page 624.

Clayton Danks in angora chaps, and the famous bucking bronc, Steamboat.

Charlie and Etta Irwin's children: Floyd, top; left to right, Joella, Frances, and Pauline, about 1908.

Teddy Roosevelt, Buffalo Bill, Charles Hirsig, and Charlie Irwin, Cheyenne Frontier Days, August 28, 1910.

Joseph Marvin Irwin, Charlie's father, and William H. Irwin, Charlie's brother, about 1910.

C. B. Irwin and Charles Hirsig driving a buffalo team during a Frontier Days celebration, about 1910.

Route cards for the itinerary of the Wild West show.

From left to right: Frances, Pauline, and Joella Irwin, 1914.

The three girls have the same saddles, bits, and headstalls on their horses.

Charlie Irwin in the New York Stampede, 1916.

An advertisement for the Irwin Bros. Cheyenne Frontier Days Wild West Show. *The Wyoming Tribune*, Saturday, June 7, 1913, page 7.

Floyd Irwin on his horse, Fashion, in front of the Sioux camp outside Frontier Park in Cheyenne, Wyoming.

Buddy Sterling, in the driver's seat, and Roy Kivett. Sterling took care of Will Rogers' polo ponies. Kivett was raised as a member of the Irwin family.

C. B. Irwin and the Baron de Rothschild of France, standing beside the Buick touring car and Model T Ford.

Charlie was given his commission and star as an officer of the Wyoming Humane Society and State Board of Child and Animal Protection in 1918 and remained an officer for the rest of his life.

Frontier Days Parade on 17th and Capitol Avenue, Cheyenne, in the early 1920s.

Fire at the Tia Juana Racetrack in Mexico in 1924. All the barns on this side of the railroad tracks were destroyed.

Pablo Martinez, a famous jockey, Will Rogers, and C. B. Irwin.

General "Black Jack" Pershing and Charlie Irwin.

Douglas Fairbanks, Sr., and Charlie Irwin.

Chief Red Cloud and Charlie Irwin with three Sioux women.

A personal letter to C. B. Irwin from General John Pershing.

C. B. Irwin with jockey E. Taplin on Bonnie Kay at the Agua Caliente track in Tia Juana, Mexico, 1930.

Flood at the Y6 ranch, 1935.

Letter to Charlie's middle daughter, Pauline, from one of the Sioux, meant a great deal to the Irwin family.

Foreword

All America loves a Western story. Europe and Japan are enthralled by it. Western clubs are in all of the West European countries. Spaghetti Westerns (made in Italy) are in continuous demand in European and Japanese movie houses. Australia, Argentina, and South Africa, with their own prairie lore, adore the American Western saga. I submit its mystique is *independence*—personal, family, social, and local independence.

Although he heard the news by telegraph and newspaper, the independent westerner paid little heed to Victorian England, Russia's tzars, or Perry in Japan. The discoveries of Madame Curie's radium and the North and South poles were worlds apart from the independent cowboy.

The blacksmith in Chillicothe, Missouri, and Colorado Springs, Colorado, the corn and wheat farmer in Kansas, the rancher in Wyoming, the rodeo rider in Omaha, Nebraska, and Pendleton, Oregon, the railroad man on the Union Pacific, and the racehorse man of Tia Juana paid little heed to these world affairs, even World War I and the economies of the twenties. The West was his life; free and independent.

Such was Charles Burton Irwin. Big in voice and stature, big in deeds and heart, C.B. was also big in the West. As a cowboy, breeder, steer roper, showman, and trader, he loved the open sky, the crops and cattle, and the horse. His life from the 1880s in Missouri to the 1930s in Wyoming epitomizes every modern boy's dream of the Old West. His story crystallizes the dreams of today's man as he yearns for true independence.

Raised by the tough pioneer stock of a Missouri blacksmith and challenged by the horses and men of the Old West, C.B. and his family loved, ranched, rode, and lived the rugged individualistic life of the frontier. He could sit in the saddle for two days at a stretch during roundup time. He could bring in stray calves for branding and deliver feed to cattle during a blizzard, and he could always mend fences. As a rodeo contestant, he set records, but he also furnished livestock needed for first-rate rodeo productions. He sponsored the best cowboys and cowgirls, bringing topnotch contenders to the rodeos. This knight of the corral was always youthful in spirit. Graduates of his tutelage stuck their necks out and developed the Cowboy Turtles Association to increase prize money and to formulate fair rules for the events. The organization today is called the Professional Rodeo Cowboys Association.

He put together one of the top traveling troupes, displaying the popularity of the West. The Irwin Brothers Wild West Show played before tens of thousands each year from coast to coast.

As a livestock agent, general agent, and superintendent for the Union Pacific, he helped ranchers ship cattle to market on schedule. He moved racehorses from one track to another without injury. He contributed to the development of the racetrack at Tia Juana, Mexico, and Ak-Sar-Ben in Omaha, Nebraska. He was able to find consistent winners in bloodlines not previously considered worthwhile. C.B. was a transitional figure in the growth and development of the American West. He was, in fact, a bridge between the Old West and the New, tying them together, in his good-hearted, easygoing, but hard-driving personality of the open frontier. He treated all people the same, regardless of wealth or position, and could be flush with funds one day and broke the next. He loved risk and would as readily step out to stop a runaway team as someone else might jump for safety. No automobile went fast enough, and no horse was swift enough to satisfy him. He was the equal of any in a battle of wits. He never gave up. Persistence was his hallmark.

Warren Richardson, writing in the Cheyenne *Tribune* for March 28, 1934, commented: "If the right man ever writes the life of Charlie Irwin . . . every page will tell of an adventure. If Charlie had lived in Napoleon's day, he would have been a marshal of France in command of cavalry, and like Marshal Ney, would have been always in the front leading the charge." In these few words, Richardson, who knew C.B. for thirty years, summed up that wonderful spirit of the independent man of the West.

—A.L.W.

C.B. Irwin's Family

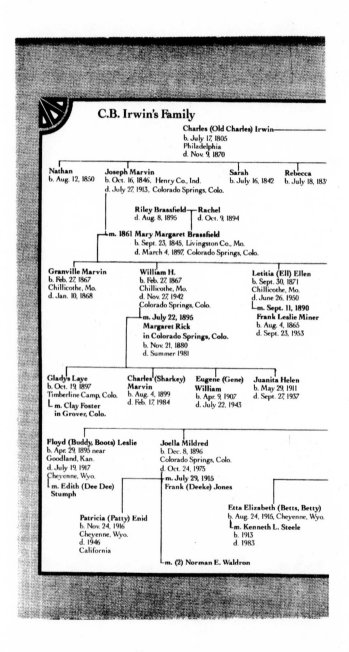

Charles (Old Charles) Irwin
b. July 17, 1805
Philadelphia
d. Nov. 9, 1870

Nathan
b. Aug. 12, 1850

Joseph Marvin
b. Oct. 16, 1846, Henry Co., Ind.
d. July 27, 1913, Colorado Springs, Colo.

Sarah
b. July 16, 1842

Rebecca
b. July 18, 183'

Riley Brassfield ┬ **Rachel**
d. Aug. 8, 1895 │ d. Oct. 9, 1894

└ m. 1861 **Mary Margaret Brassfield**
b. Sept. 23, 1845, Livingston Co., Mo.
d. March 4, 1897, Colorado Springs, Colo.

Granville Marvin
b. Feb. 27, 1867
Chillicothe, Mo.
d. Jan. 10, 1868

William H.
b. Feb. 27, 1867
Chillicothe, Mo.
d. Nov. 27, 1942
Colorado Springs, Colo.

└ m. July 22, 1895
Margaret Rick
in Colorado Springs, Colo.
b. Nov. 21, 1880
d. Summer 1981

Letitia (Ell) Ellen
b. Sept. 30, 1871
Chillicothe, Mo.
d. June 26, 1950

└ m. Sept. 11, 1890
Frank Leslie Miner
b. Aug. 4, 1865
d. Sept. 23, 1953

Gladys Laye
b. Oct. 19, 1897
Timberline Camp, Colo.
└ m. Clay Foster
in Grover, Colo.

**Charles (Sharkey)
Marvin**
b. Aug. 4, 1899
d. Feb. 17, 1984

**Eugene (Gene)
William**
b. Apr. 9, 1907
d. July 22, 1943

Juanita Helen
b. May 29, 1911
d. Sept. 27, 1937

Floyd (Buddy, Boots) Leslie
b. Apr. 29, 1895 near
Goodland, Kan.
d. July 19, 1917
Cheyenne, Wyo.
└ m. Edith (Dee Dee)
Stumph

Joella Mildred
b. Dec. 8, 1896
Colorado Springs, Colo.
d. Oct. 24, 1975
├ m. July 29, 1915
Frank (Deeke) Jones

Patricia (Patty) Enid
b. Nov. 24, 1916
Cheyenne, Wyo.
d. 1946
California

Etta Elizabeth (Betts, Betty)
b. Aug. 24, 1915, Cheyenne, Wyo.
└ m. Kenneth L. Steele
b. 1913
d. 1983

└ m. (2) **Norman E. Waldron**

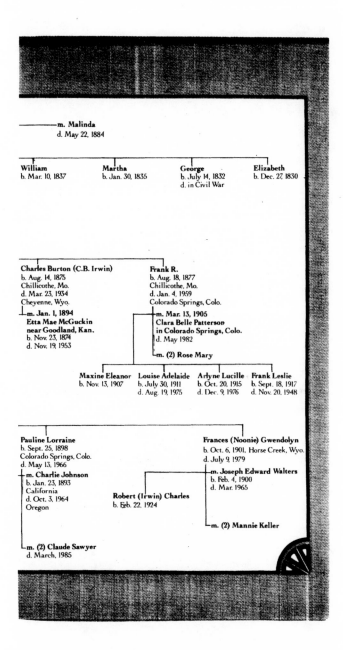

———————m. Malinda
        d. May 22, 1884

William
b. Mar. 10, 1837

Martha
b. Jan. 30, 1835

George
b. July 14, 1832
d. in Civil War

Elizabeth
b. Dec. 27, 1830

Charles Burton (C.B. Irwin)
b. Aug. 14, 1875
Chillicothe, Mo.
d. Mar. 23, 1934
Cheyenne, Wyo.
└─m. Jan. 1, 1894
   Etta Mae McGuckin
   near Goodland, Kan.
   b. Nov. 23, 1874
   d. Nov. 19, 1953

Frank R.
b. Aug. 18, 1877
Chillicothe, Mo.
d. Jan. 4, 1959
Colorado Springs, Colo.
├─m. Mar. 13, 1905
│ **Clara Belle Patterson**
│ in Colorado Springs, Colo.
│ d. May 1982
└─m. (2) **Rose Mary**

Maxine Eleanor
b. Nov. 13, 1907

Louise Adelaide
b. July 30, 1911
d. Aug. 19, 1975

Arlyne Lucille
b. Oct. 20, 1915
d. Dec. 9, 1976

Frank Leslie
b. Sept. 18, 1917
d. Nov. 20, 1948

Pauline Lorraine
b. Sept. 25, 1898
Colorado Springs, Colo.
d. May 13, 1966
├─m. **Charlie Johnson**
│ b. Jan. 23, 1893
│ California
│ d. Oct. 3, 1964
│ Oregon
└─m. (2) **Claude Sawyer**
   d. March, 1985

Robert (Irwin) Charles
b. Feb. 22, 1924

Frances (Noonie) Gwendolyn
b. Oct. 6, 1901, Horse Creek, Wyo.
d. July 9, 1979
├─m. **Joseph Edward Walters**
│ b. Feb. 4, 1900
│ d. Mar. 1965
└─m. (2) **Mannie Keller**

BOOK I

ONE

Chillicothe, Missouri

"Charlie! Charlie Irwin, what in all get out are you doing?" Rachel Brassfield's voice was strident. She was disturbed. Her nostrils contracted as she moved from the fresh air outdoors into the tangy odor coming from the saucepan on her spotless kitchen range. The wood-burning range was a Majestic, cast iron with isinglass in the oven door. Rachel's eyes moved from the empty vinegar bottle lying on her white enameled kitchen table, back to the steaming, eye-stinging liquid in the pan. The room filled with the pungent aroma. Next her eyes settled on the disarray of her white kitchen chairs. One wooden chair was stacked on the wide seat of another in front of her cabinets. The high cupboard doors were wide open, revealing cans of pickling spices, several glasses of strawberry jam with thick paraffin covering the tops, and some of the latest, glass, quart milk bottles.

"Charlie, why do you annoy me? You come into my house and make a mess when I'm not here," complained Rachel. Her eyes watered from the irritating vapors.

"Ma sent me for those eggs you promised her," Charlie said, standing still, trying not to blink his eyes. "Grandma, I looked out the window and saw you out back feeding chickens. I waited for you to come in. I sat in the rocking chair. Then I looked out

3

the sitting room window. You were stringing up pole beans on stakes. I thought you'd be right in. I drank some water and waited. Then I lassoed the kitchen chairs. I pulled them away from the table. Then all of a sudden I got this idea to try the trick Will told me about."

Rachel didn't say a word, but clicked her tongue and looked at Charlie.

Charlie was an average-sized, suntanned nine-year-old with sandy hair that hung over intelligent, deep brown eyes. He took great pride in the fact that he could throw a horsehair rope around his body and do a couple of fancy tricks that opened the eyes of younger boys in the neighborhood Often he would let one of the younger boys try one of his tricks. It was his secret for drawing a crowd. He had learned that it felt good standing in the center of a bunch of wide-eyed kids.

"Don't worry, Grandma. I'll put your chairs back. Look, if I stand in the corner I can pull 'em back without moving a foot. Even the ones stacked together move. Wanna see how good I am using my rope?"

Rachel's lips were sealed as she pulled her four chairs back to the round, drop-leaf table. She motioned for Charlie to sit. She set the empty vinegar bottle upright on the table. She pulled the pan of boiling lachrymator to the back of her range, wiped her eyes on her apron's skirt, and paced across from Charlie.

Rachel Brassfield was in her late sixties, with graying hair braided and wound around her head and held at the back with two tortoiseshell combs. She was short, round-hipped, with large grayish eyes.

"It smells like pickles in here. Why are you boiling my vinegar?" sniffed Rachel.

"Grandma, it's a trick Will told me. It's with eggs and boiling vinegar."

"Mercy! Look at this mess by my range!"

"Can you put an egg in a glass milk bottle?"

"Of course not! No one can, unless it's a pullet's."

"I can. See, you cook this egg, shell and all, in vinegar. Then put it in the milk bottle—right through the skinny neck. Will swore it'd work."

Charlie's older brother, William, was born a twin. The other boy, Granville Marvin, was born first, but he grew listless, then died before he was a year old. After that, Will was pampered and treated as something special. Charlie knew he couldn't always believe what Will told him. But he wanted to show his grandma that he, too, was special and could do tricks.

"Will should have his mouth washed out with soap," said Rachel.

"The egg'd be like that ship in the bottle at Creelin's Jewelry Store. You know, Grandpa's friend."

"He don't count Creelin a friend since the elections." Rachel's breathing quickened and the sides of her neck throbbed.

Charlie's grandpa, Riley Brassfield, was a thick-chested, six-foot farmer and stock raiser. He had three hundred acres in Livingston County's Section 23. Twice he ran for mayor of Chillicothe. He lost both times to Bill Creelin, the jeweler.

Rachel picked up some broken shells, trying not to touch the slimy, raw eggs. "I mopped yesterday! Who's going to mop today?"

"I had to see if an ordinary egg'd go inside the bottle without busting. It didn't! The trick is to cook the egg in vinegar!" Charlie took an egg out of the saucepan with a wooden spoon and tried to push it through the top of the quart milk bottle. Finally he put the egg back in the pan. He looked up at his grandma. "Will told me about this here other trick. You put an egg in lime. Grandpa has lime in the shed. You leave the egg buried about a year and it shrinks so's it looks like a dark green jellybean."

Rachel's nose twitched and she rubbed it.

"Will says limed eggs don't stink and that the Chinese coolies eat 'em. Could I—?"

"Not on your life! That's disgusting! Those slant-eyes live in tarpaper shanties where they're laying railroad ties. What does Will know about that coolie camp and their strange ways?"

"He heard they keep coins in their ears. I'd like to see that!"

Rachel grimaced. "Don't ever put coins in your mouth! You hear?" She shook her finger under Charlie's nose. "Land sakes, you sound like Old Charles. He was always wanting to see, hear, smell, taste, and feel anything new. God rest his old soul."

Charlie looked at her from under his mop of hair and decided not to comment. Charlie never knew Old Charles, his pa's father. Old Charles died of heart failure in the fall of 1870, five years before Charlie was born. But ever since Charlie could remember, adults had looked at him and said he looked and acted like Old Charles.

"Wrench out that vinegar pan. The smell is nauseating."

"Yes, ma'am. But first I want to show you this amazing trick. You know, Frank is still sick?"

"Your poor mother. I suppose she's waiting on these here eggs in my lard bucket. I don't know how she puts up with your foolishness and a sick baby." Rachel pointed to the gallon tin full of eggs, sitting on her kitchen counter. "Charles Burton Irwin! You get going!"

"In a minute," he said. "This trick can't have me stymied. It's too simple. It's a present for you." He blinked to clear his watering eyes and forced a rubbery egg into the milk bottle. It plopped on the bottom.

"Well, I declare! There's an egg in a bottle. I thought you were full of beans, but you were right all along," Rachel said. "That's some trick! I'm going to show Riley. He won't believe it."

Rachel bent a little and put her arm around Charlie. "I'll have more eggs from my hens by tomorrow morning. Would you like some ginger cake?"

"Yes, ma'am!" Charlie smiled. He felt good. He'd found another secret. You get cake when the trick works.

Charlie was careful carrying the eggs home. He passed Orin Gale's Livery and his father's place, Irwin's Smithery, but he did not stop. He cut diagonally through the vacant lot. It was one of those hot summer days of 1884. The wind blew dust into Charlie's eyes and snapped the clothes on the Gregorys' line. Mrs. Gregory had a dishtowel fastened around her gray hair and a clothespin bag tied around her waist. She was taking in dry wash. She waved a handful of straight clothespins. "How's Frank today, Charlie?"

"He's really sick," Charlie said. He stopped a moment, shaded his eyes, and looked up to watch Mr. Gregory crawl stiff and slow on the house roof to replace weather-damaged shingles with new cedar shakes. "Is it hot up there?"

"Yup. Hotter'n hell with the blower on!"

"Hush, that's Joe Irwin's boy!" called Mrs. Gregory with a clothespin in her mouth. "You know, Old Charles's grandson!"

"Yep, I know!" shouted Mr. Gregory. He waved his arms. "Old Charles used to rive all the town's shingles! Look at the boy!" He pointed. "My, oh my! The boy's got a walk just like Joe's pa! You see the way he sort of cocks his head? He's the spittin' image of Old Charles!"

Charlie closed his eyes and felt the sun hot through his muslin shirt. He stood on the wood floor of the Irwin porch, where it was cooler on his bare feet than the dusty paths and sun-scorched boardwalks he'd come over. Through the screen door he could hear his mother talking to his sister, Ell.

"Oh, my dear, it's a scorcher today." Mary wiped the perspiration from her face with her apron. Charlie heard the rustle of the starched cotton material.

"Did Frank drink all the spicebush tea this morning? You know that runs a fever down."

Charlie thought his thirteen-year-old sister talked big, like she knew all about dosing with herbs. He yanked open the screen door.

"Grandma Malinda'd use yarrow brewed in the iron pot for fever," he blurted, coming into the house.

"Don't slam the door!" Ell hissed, holding her forefinger to her mouth. She was slim and light-complected. Her eyes were deep green like the moist spring sassafras leaf. Her long hair was shiny like strained clover honey. Charlie was too young to see that even in her walk was the promise of a vivacious, breathtaking beauty. Ell was hardly aware that she could stare into the eyes of a man and stir his primal urges. She was learning the use of incense, sweet herbal odors, and one day she would be completely adept at keeping a man in a state of desire and constant worship of herself. She took the bucket of fresh eggs from Charlie. "Oh, joy! Now Ma and I can make an egg pie. Charlie, you're an angel," Ell sang. She took the eggs to the kitchen. Charlie followed her so that he could talk to his mother.

"Ma, can I sleep outside tonight with the cheesecloth over me?"

"No! Of course not! The netting is for little Frank so's he can take a nap under the shade oak. Fresh air is good for him and it gives me a chance to redo his bed and sweep his room."

"But—he doesn't use it at night. And it's my room, too." Charlie saw his mother frown, draw in a deep breath, and let it out slowly. He said, "Can't I stay until the egg pie is done?"

"Your big brother is expecting you to help out at the smithery. I think he has a big job this afternoon."

"Oh! Jeems! Where's Pa at?"

"Charlie!" his mother rebuked. "Your pa left only moments ago for the smithery. He's taking the saddlehorse to look for Doc Reed."

Charlie's father, Joe, was the town's farrier, shoeing horses and treating their diseases.

Charlie was shocked. "Can't Grandma Malinda make Frank well?"

Malinda Irwin was distinguished not only for raising eight

children but also for knowing the healing quality of roots, barks, and herbs. She was not more than five feet tall, with nearly cotton-white hair that once had been the color of fine strands of amber. Inquisitive, clear, coffee-colored eyes seemed to see into the center of a person's soul. She competed with the medical physician, Dr. Art Reed, by convincing her clientele that she could foretell the future.

Mary's eyes watered and she swallowed. "No. It was Malinda's idea to get Doc Reed to look at Frank."

"I thought Frank only had summer complaint," said Charlie.

The humidity added to Mary's frustration. The summer sunlight seemed not only hot but oppressive and the air heavy. "We've tried everything to make Frank well." She rubbed her temples.

Charlie went into the bedroom he shared with his younger brother and looked down at the pale face with the mop of reddish-yellow hair lying in the white painted iron bed. Frank opened his eyes. They were luminous in the light from the open door, like the liquid bluing Mary used on wash day.

"Have you ever seen a real angel, Charlie?" Frank spoke barely above a whisper. Charlie thought the freckles on his nose looked like they could be picked off, like fly specks on the wall.

"Nope."

"Me, neither, but I was wondering what one looked like."

Charlie shrugged his shoulders.

Frank pointed to the inside of the doorframe. There were three forged nails hammered in a triangle. "Ell did that to keep witches and spells out. She closed my curtains," whimpered Frank.

"You want them opened? It's awful dark in here," agreed Charlie.

"It's all right. I feel like sleeping anyhow."

Charlie nodded and left the room, leaving the door open. He went to the kitchen and stood by his mother.

Mary said, "There's not only enough eggs for pie, but for rye bread, too." She had put several cups of mashed potatoes into a big bowl with rye and whole wheat flour, sugar, water, and her dough starter. She pushed, punched, and pounded the dough.

All the time Ell stood at the stove repeating charms and superstitions under her breath. They were ones she thought might heal Frank. Ell greatly admired Grandma Malinda and had dreams of also being a famous healer. All her life she'd heard Malinda's stories of the Union soldiers who looked for the "Lady Doc" to sew them together, holding their intestines in their hands. Lately

Ell carried a comb and scissors in her apron pocket because Malinda carried them in her black medical bag. Whenever Malinda performed her medical miracles, she cut the children's hair afterward.

Mary wiped her hands on her apron, divided the dough to fit into several pans, covered each pan, and set them on the oak stump to rise in the hot sunshine. Then she put some bread with thick, hard crust and some dried meat with grains of salt into the lard tin Charlie had brought the eggs in. "Charlie! Take this tin to the smithery quickly. Pa forgot his lunch and he may have to go as far as Brookfield to find Doc Reed. Straight to the smithery! Hurry! That's a good boy!"

Charlie stepped off the porch and saw the cloth-covered pans of rising rye bread dough. He nipped a hunk of dough from one and nibbled it. He enjoyed the mild sour taste. He headed back in the direction of the smithery, kicking rocks and dust. He was careful not to kick the barbed hawthorn hedge in front of the house. He watched a wide, black cricket hop through the dust. Charlie did not step on it, because to kill a cricket was to kill the luck in your house, according to his Grandma Malinda. The cricket sprang into the dry, yellowed grass and Charlie moved on, bucket in one hand, horsehair rope in the other. He twirled a loop in the air and whistled happily. He felt good because the rope didn't catch the side of the bucket as it usually did. He was getting better.

He wished it were he instead of his father riding the red-brown stallion, Flame. That horse had a lordly lift to its head and a dip to its aging back. Charlie liked horses.

The sun was a smidge past midway on the top of the blue sky. Charlie blinked as he walked through the open barnlike doors into the smithery's dusk. He'd finished eating all the sweetish-sour dough ball. He licked the palm of his hand and stood a few moments until his eyes were accustomed to the darkness. He could hear the men talking in the smithery's yard behind him. It was a meeting place where local farmers and itinerant cowboys waited to have a knife sharpened, a horse shod, or a bridle repaired, and they aired views on politics, religion, or stood around gossiping. These men had shown Charlie how to braid a horsehair rope, splice in an eye, and work the end so that it wouldn't unravel. To pass the time they'd shown Charlie tricks with the rope.

Charlie moved toward his father, who was showing Will how to operate the new sling. It had a canvas girth that went under a horse's belly. When it was tightened it raised the horse so that its feet were just touching the floor. Joe rigged this up so that it was easier to shoe the horses that were kickers.

Charlie admired his father, who was about three pounds heavier than an ox, six feet two inches tall, with straight black hair and brown eyes. Today Joe Irwin had his hair tied at the back of his neck with a piece of leather string cut from the bottom of his apron.

When Joe saw Charlie, he removed his apron and hung it on a nail on the wall. "Help your brother all you can," he said, taking the lard tin Charlie held out. "And when you are home, help your ma."

"Yes, sir," said Charlie. "How long you figure you'll be gone?"

"Until I come back with Doc Reed." Joe nodded to Will to continue the shoeing job.

Charlie's father had been gone before. He'd been gone a week burning hickory wood into charcoal. Charlie had practiced a lot of rope tricks then, ridden the saddle horse, and talked Will into letting him hammer out a couple of bucket bails.

"Pa, you suppose I could go down by the covered bridge to fish if Ma don't need me? Could I do some new rope tricks in the vacant lot, if I promise not to lasso Mrs. Gale's picayune?"

"Pekingese, son. Stay at the smithery. Will needs you here in case something big comes in. In the meantime sweep and tidy the place. Stay out of mischief."

Charlie expected that last. He asked, "What about Frank?"

"Pray," answered his father, going toward the back door with his soogan, a couple layers of blankets rolled with a bed tarp on the outside, and the tin pail of dried meat and bread.

Charlie settled himself on a pile of burlap. He could hear his father saddling the stallion, talking to it, then the clop of the stallion's hooves on the packed dirt, as his father rode off.

"Hey! Is the smithy here?" a voice called, startling Charlie. "This here gentle creature sorely needs a forward shoe repaired." The stranger was dressed in a tight-fitting gray wool suit. His face was red and shiny with perspiration. He pointed to the right front foot of his palomino. The horse seemed to sense the awe it inspired. Will stood open-mouthed by Charlie, looking at its flaxen-gold color and the ivory mane and tail.

"That fella looks like a newly minted gold piece, sir," stammered Will, aiming to translate a compliment.

"It is a using horse," said the man in the gray suit. His eyes squinted to get used to the darkness inside the smithery. "It can go over trails that would be highly dangerous to other horses." The man was rather tall and well built, except for the high belly up under his gray vest, out of which his voice thundered deep and slow. "You do shoe horses, Your Excellencies? If so, I have a gold piece for you."

"Oh, yes! I can, sir," said Will, finding his voice. He jerked his father's apron off the nail and tied it over his leather chaps. Will motioned for Charlie to start pumping the repaired bellows.

Charlie threw a handful of wood shavings next to a piece of charcoal that was holding the heat. Instantly they caught fire, and he tossed a couple splinters of dry pine on them, then laid a hunk of charcoal on to catch and glow red. He raked the old, unburned charcoal over the fierce little fire as if he'd been doing this for years. He caught the bellows' lever and pumped a rush of air into the hearth. When the fire was a mound of bright red, he nodded to his brother.

Will told the man to bring in the palomino. The stranger had an auburn mustache, which matched his hair and curled at the corners, like the ends of his long hair curled.

"This your establishment?" The man was inspecting the canvas sling around his horse.

"Why—yes, in a manner of speaking, it is," said Will, without batting an eyelid.

"Put considerable into it for a young man, I see."

"I believe in work and simple living."

"Well put, Your Honor. I say the same myself. No endeavor that is worthwhile is simple in prospect, but if it is right and good, it is simple in retrospect."

Charlie's ears perked up. This stranger sure knew how to use words. He'd try to remember them. He thought, nothing worthwhile is easy, until it's done.

Will's eyes squinted and he blurted, "You looking to sell this here horse? It's a mite flashy, besides its foot's bad with acute founder." Will spit out the side of his mouth. In his anxiousness he added, "I have a younger pony that I could make a trade with, if you'd be willing to judge good horseflesh. The pony has wide hips. They give a horse more power."

Waiting for an answer, Will took up a pair of pliers and pulled the broken shoe from the palomino's hoof. One nail had to be yanked out as the horse pawed the air. Will spoke to the nervous horse, "Whooaa, there now, this won't take long."

The stranger cleared his throat. "Chief, you ain't 'xactly hog-tied when it comes to making chin music." He hesitated long enough for Will to look up and let the words sink in.

Charlie thought he had a perfect way of saying Will sounded like an overblown rooster. He wished he could talk like the stranger.

"This horse of mine's got no more laminitis, nor founder, than I got a malarious poison. Front foot's not even hot. Shoe's broken and that's about the size of it. Nope—I got no intentions of making any trade nor sale."

The stranger winked at Charlie. "Never met such young smiths." He smoothed his mustache. "Unless I'm just getting old. I'm Colonel Johnson." He held his hand out to Charlie.

"I'm Charlie—Charles Burton Irwin. I'm glad to meet you, sir. This here is my brother, William Henry Harrison Faulkner Irwin. We just call him Will and on occasions some other things."

Colonel Johnson shook hands vigorously. "Say, either of you royal citizens ever see a real, honest-to-God medicine show?"

"Nope," said Charlie. "I ain't ever. But I heard they combine some singing and dancing with peddling conjure draughts."

"Nice job," complimented Colonel Johnson, looking at the new horseshoe. "I might have more work. Say, some harness hardware. You two young gentlemen are definitely invited to see Colonel Johnson's Medicine Show, completely free of charge, of course."

"You made the deal for a gold piece," said Charlie, looking Colonel Johnson in the eye.

The Colonel flashed a smile and handed a small gold coin to Charlie.

"Where's the show?" asked Will.

"Right here in this lovely town. At the end of this here main street, yonder on the prairie. Show begins promptly at sundown. Don't miss it!"

A gopher spoke in a thin, sharp squeal two, three times from the vacant lot. It reminded Charlie of the time he'd found a gopher's hole in the center of the tiny mound next to Old Charles's grave in the cemetery. Grandma Malinda filled it, smoothed it, and told Charlie not to say anything to his mother about the gopher digging into the baby's grave. Charlie had asked her who the baby was, but she had closed her eyes and not answered. Charlie looked up Washington Street and saw the emptiness of the land beyond town. The air hung heavy and warm. Suddenly something caught his eye in the last red rays of sunlight. A blue-green-bodied, four-winged dragonfly hung over the foxtails beside the smithery door.

The dragonfly's wings shimmered like liquid silver in the fading burnished light. A dust devil swirled along the road, stopped, started again, and whirled quietly out to the empty land. The breeze felt good on the back of Charlie's neck. He reached out in slow motion for the dragonfly as it hovered over the weeds. He caught a flash of light on its silver wings and closed a thumb and forefinger together. He tried to will the body to be still. Inside the smithery he found a clear Mason jar holding chain links. He dumped the links into an empty Hills Bros. can, then put the dragonfly inside the jar and screwed down the lid. He punched a tiny hole in the metal lid by pounding a rusty nail on the lid's center.

Charlie helped Will pack the forge fire down around a stub of hardwood for the night. A bucket of ashes was mounded over the fire to trap the heat. Will coughed when Charlie exhaled over the heap, blowing ash thick into the air. He made a face at Charlie and lunged as if to grab him by his mop of sandy hair.

Charlie dodged and hung up the tongs, scooped wood shavings back into the box by the wall, and picked up the spent iron shoe and threw it into the box of odds and ends. He looped his coiled rope over his shoulder, checking the end for frays.

Will closed the front doors and fastened the latch by slipping a wooden peg on a leather string through a notch on one of the doors.

"I caught an angel for Frank," said Charlie, holding the jar carefully and shuffling along home beside his brother.

TWO

The Medicine Show

Next morning Malinda showed up early with a basket of blackberries. "Came before it got too hot," she said, preparing to bathe Frank. "Found one of them white cedars in the woods. Rare as a thornless cactus in these parts."

Charlie looked at his grandmother through squeezed-down eye slits. "How could you tell it was white instead of red?"

She chuckled as if half expecting Charlie to check on her. "Its twigs is covered by overlapping scales fitting tight as any snake's skin. But you can tell red cedar in a wink by those small, sky-blue berries and them waxy cones with blue scales that look welded on."

"Where'd you learn all that?" Charlie now watched Will wolf down bacon and eggs in preparation for a day at the smithery.

"Some I got from dear Old Charles and most I learned by looking at the real thing. Not just seeing, but real deep looking and remembering what I see." Malinda's double-chinned face was framed with soft, curling white hair.

"Come on, Charlie, finish your breakfast so's we can open the smithery," said Will. He was looking for his straight razor. "Hey, Ell, you use my razor again to cut heads off clover or some stupid damn weed?"

"I hope Ma washes your mouth," said Ell. She was washing

breakfast dishes and the black iron griddle. "I haven't used your dumb razor. Maybe Pa took it."

"If I shaved I'd have a special place for my razor and things," said Charlie. He was looking out the front screen door. Rachel Brassfield was coming up the walk. She had come in her one-horse shay. Her horse was tied to the iron post beside the hawthorns. "Ma, here comes Grandma Rachel."

"Tell her how much you enjoyed the egg pie, Charlie," called Mary, who was helping her mother-in-law bathe Frank.

"Good morning!" called Rachel. "Think we'll have rain before the week's out? Is Joe back?" Her graying hair was twisted, not braided, back behind her ears and held in place with the tortoiseshell combs. She'd held her long, brown cotton skirt up several inches as she walked across the dusty path from the street to the house. Inside she went right to Frank's room to talk with Mary, not waiting for answers to her questions. "I don't think this sick baby should be taken outdoors. The thermometer Riley has on our porch says eighty-two degrees and it's only seven in the morning! I may have heat prostration by afternoon!"

"It's warm in this room already," said Mary. "I'm going to carry Frank to the cot under the oak; you can put the net over the hoops that Joe built. That'll keep out flies, but not the breeze. Frank always feels better after he's been out. By mid-morning, if it's too hot, I'll bring him in."

"What's this?" asked Rachel, holding up Charlie's Mason jar so close to her face that the dragonfly's blue-green iridescent body reflected in her eyes, making them shimmer.

Charlie paused at the bedroom door. "Grandma Rachel, it's something pretty for Frank to look at. Kind of lights up the room and makes Frank smile. He thinks it's an angel and in the middle of the night I heard him talk to it."

Rachel cleared her throat and looked at Charlie. "Do you want your baby brother to die?"

"Oh, no!" A lump came into Charlie's throat.

"No one talks to angels unless they are in Heaven where the angels live. This is one of those vile insects, darning needles, they're called. Many a time I've heard it said that one can sew a baby's nose and mouth shut tight." She shook the jar, causing the dragonfly to flit back and forth in the confined space.

Mary carried Frank outside. Malinda followed with the folding cot, hooks, and roll of cheesecloth.

"I never heard that," said Charlie. "But I did hear of cats jumping into a cradle and smothering a baby. Frank's too big to be smothered by a cat. He's probably too big to have his mouth sewn. Besides, the dragonfly can't get out."

"I'll make certain of that in a jiffy." Rachel took the jar to the kitchen, pulled the front lid off the range, opened the jar, and turned it upside down. She shook the insect onto the hot coals.

Charlie gasped. His bottom lip trembled and he clamped his top teeth over it. Suddenly he felt the oppressiveness of the new day. He opened the screen door and let it bang shut behind him.

Rachel called shrilly for Charlie to come back. He walked slowly to the front hedge. He heard Rachel, but he didn't turn his head to look at her. He respected his Grandma Rachel, but he was not overly fond of her. Nine-year-old Charlie felt she was picky about cleanliness and jumpy about tiny things, like mice, spiders, and garter snakes. On the other hand she made good ginger cake and was generous with the produce from her kitchen garden and her chickens. He tried to stay on her good side by giving her presents he thought she'd like. But he usually failed in guessing what she'd like. Charlie liked Grandpa Riley well enough. And he knew that Riley respected Rachel, because he gave her a wide berth whenever possible. He let her run the house in town. Riley must be fond of Rachel. He let her have most anything she asked for. Charlie heard a *pad-pad* of running feet and hoped it wasn't Grandma Rachel come to scold about him slamming the screen door. It was his mother. "She called for you to come back. Didn't you hear?"

"I heard. But Grandma Rachel burned Frank's angel—the dragonfly. I'm mad enough to kick Squirt."

"Charlie, the old dog is on its last legs. What good would it do to kick it? Don't let people get you down. You have a long time to live with them."

Mary and Charlie stood by the hawthorn hedge. It was cool in the shade.

"Ma, think. Grandma Malinda gave us Squirt a long time ago. He was a good pet and no one threw him away. That dragonfly made Frank feel good."

"Charlie, think. Grandma Rachel told you about the flying darning needle. She believes there's such a thing. When I was your age I heard the same story. But you and I know there isn't an insect in the world that can perform such a wondrous feat."

"She believed it and she burned it! It made Frank grin when it flew in the jar." Charlie's voice was choked. He felt his nose become stuffy and his eyes water.

"Maybe she is also dead-set against flies and pests and things she calls vermin. She's really trying to help. If it were you sick, she'd worry same as she worries over Frank. She loves us."

"Ma, she's pushy and won't listen!"

"Go back and see. Tell her you are sorry you slammed the door. She'll understand. She'll see that you worry about Frank, too."

"She doesn't have to worry about us. She has her own boys. Can't she worry about them?"

"They are grown and take care of themselves. Go back and say good-bye, then hurry on to the smithery with Will." Mary gave Charlie a hug.

He felt only a little better, and was not yet ready to admit he understood Grandma Rachel's feelings. He wiggled out of his mother's arms. "I'm going to find something else to make Frank feel better and she better not touch it!"

"Then keep it out of sight," Mary said.

They walked back to the house. Charlie lagged behind three, four steps. At the door Mary said, "Grandma Malinda believes Frank'll pass the crisis before your pa gets back with Doc Reed."

"Grandma Malinda told me the Irwins are nonbreakable. So don't worry, Ma. Frank'll get well," Charlie said. He thought his mother's eyes sparkled like a pair of will-o'-the-wisps. Then he blinked and the light was gone from her eyes. She looked tired and sad.

"Indestructible," corrected Mary.

"Yup, that's it. I'm going to take a lunch to the smithery today."

Mary did not go inside, but went to the little cot under the shade oak where Malinda was fussing over the netting. Frank had been ill more than a month. First he had a cough, then a runny nose.

Charlie went to the kitchen. He heard the sizzle as Ell spat on the flat iron to test the temperature. He smelled the freshly ironed clothes. He cut two slices of rye bread and spread on raspberry jam.

"Charlie, make a sandwich for Will, too. Wrap them in a clean dishtowel," said Ell.

Charlie licked off the knife and found the towel.

Ell fixed crystal green eyes on him, shook her head and sighed, then continued to iron.

Charlie called out so that his Grandma Rachel, changing Frank's bed, could hear, "Bye! I won't slam the door!" He rushed out, grabbed the screen, and eased it shut.

Grandma Malinda was coming in. "Slow down, the day is too hot to rush." Her brown eyes crinkled with her smile. "I thought you left a while back."

"I came in for bread and jam," said Charlie, looking for a way to escape. He licked his lips, tasting the sweet jam from the knife.

"Want to know a secret?" asked Malinda in a whisper.

Charlie held his head so that his grandmother could put her lips close to the hair over his ear. She tickled when she whispered, "I'm going to give you Grandpa's old rifle."

"For me?" Charlie's eyes grew wide. "The Henry rifle?"

"Yes. He wants you to have it."

"Did Old Charles say so?"

"Last night he told." She kept her mouth straight. Her eyes sparkled.

"But, Grandma—he's dead."

"I know that. He's an angel now."

"Were you in Heaven?"

"No, he came to visit me in my dream. We all have dreams, Charlie."

Charlie felt as if the pull of gravity had suddenly been divided in half. He could breathe easier and he was lighter on his feet when he walked. "Next time you dream, tell Old Charles 'thanks a lot,'" Charlie said. He not only respected Grandma Malinda and her knowledge of local plants and animals, but he was not continuously on the defensive in her presence as he was with Rachel. He knew he liked Grandma Malinda. "I have to go to the smithery or else Will might wring my neck."

"Next time you come to my place, we'll get the rifle out and look at it. In my time every boy had a rifle by the time he was twelve. It was a symbol of growing up and kept the gopher population in check."

"Grandma, I'm not twelve. Did you forget?" Charlie edged toward the front walk. "You keep the rifle. When I'm twelve I'll look at it with you."

"I'm not senile! Some things I forget, but not your birthday. You are to have the rifle now. It's Old Charles's wish."

They both saw that Rachel was coming out the screen door. Charlie wanted nothing more than to bolt up the street. He took a deep breath.

Rachel came off the porch and swished open a fan she had tied to her waistband with a pink, silk cord. "Is Charlie telling you about the eggs he broke yesterday in my kitchen? Eggs are scarce in this heat. You pay twenty and a half cents a dozen if you buy them at Clem's Groceries."

Charlie looked from one grandmother to the other. "Did Grandpa Riley like the egg in the milk bottle?"

Rachel fanned her face so hard Charlie could feel the breeze. "Well—he was surprised. He couldn't believe it. He wanted to know how it was done."

Charlie smiled and pushed the hair from his eyes. "Did you tell him?"

"I told him about the mess in my kitchen." Rachel looked at Malinda for sympathy. "I remember when Riley gave Charlie thirty cents to help shock wheat. Charlie couldn't keep that money in his pocket. He rode my black mare to town and bought a star candle from Sherman's Merc. I told him not to light it. Why, he'd set fire to my place."

Malinda didn't move an inch. She looked straight at Charlie. "So that's where you got the money to buy me that star candle. I still have it in the bottom of the water glass, just the way you brought it over. It's a pretty sight when I light it. The flame flickers in the bottom of that clear glass like a firefly. Sometimes I have a cup of tea and watch it before I turn on the electric." She put her hand out and pushed the lariat straight on Charlie's shoulder. "Hurry on to help your brother."

"Good-bye—tell Ma we'll see her at supper!" Charlie ran down the dirt path to the street. Then he slowed to a walk. Halfway to the smithery he decided not to tell Will about the Henry rifle. It was a secret. He began to think of his grandmothers. He thought of Rachel as sour and Malinda as sweet. Life was sweet some days, sour other days. If a person let the sour take over, he could become blind to the sweet. He decided to avoid life's sourness any way possible. By the time Charlie got to the smithery he was in good spirits. Life was going to be ruled by the sweet for him.

At the smithery yard were two men sitting on the bench under the tree waiting for something to be repaired. Charlie nodded and smiled to them.

"Hello there, Charlie," said one, putting a wad of tobacco in front of his teeth next to his cheek so he could talk. The other, with gray suspenders, said, "You startled me, son. For a moment I thought it was Old Charles coming along the walk swinging his arms the way he used to do."

"I guess everybody in town knew him," said Charlie, trying to catch a scampering black ant between his toes.

"Yep, and liked him," said the man with the tobacco cud.

"I wish I'd known him."

"Some men are hard to forget. He's one," said the man with gray suspenders. "Everyone was a friend to him. He found something nice to say about the worst. Once a man shot his wife and Old Charles said, 'That man just lost his patience at the wrong time.'"

Charlie stood by the smithery's gaping entrance. Both of the double doors were pulled open to let in air and light. By his feet Charlie saw some gray stones, all about the same size. With a big toe he pushed them in a line. Then he put two of the stones side by side, silently calling them Ma and Pa. He put four smaller stones around the two, naming them Will, Ell, Charlie, and Frank. He stared at the stones. Then he took out the smallest and stared again. He thought, I can see there's a hole. Even the smallest is missed. He spread the stones apart and went inside the shop.

Charlie and Will worked on repairing farm equipment most of the morning. About noon Charlie shared the bread and jam sandwiches with Will. Afterward Will brought a tin can of water from the pump in back, near the horse shed.

"Listen," said Will. "Sounds like fiddle music coming from down Washington."

"Yep, I hear it. I'll go see what's going on."

"Sweep the floor first. Pa could come back while you're gone."

Charlie swept, hung up the broom, and took his lariat off a nail. "You'll tell Pa that you said it was all right for me to go?" he asked.

"You little runt! Don't you trust your big brother?" asked Will.

"Not much reason to," said Charlie, swinging his rope.

"Get that rope out of here. You could knock something over."

"If it's a medicine show, we can all go."

"I was thinking that," said Will back at the forge.

The music became louder and louder. Charlie walked faster and faster. The music made waves that enveloped Charlie. The waves put out invisible strings that made him swing his arms to the beat. He stopped and twirled the rope over his head, trying to hold the rhythm. He continued walking, letting the rope move over his head.

Charlie saw a crowd of kids standing around the back of a

large wagon, freshly painted red and yellow. On a small wooden platform a girl was fiddling "The Old Rugged Cross." She was in her late twenties. Her eyes were glossy gray, like a silver fox fur. Her hair was straw-colored, but dark close to the part down the middle of her head, and she had wound the braided ends to form two coils and fastened them over each ear. Her pink satin dress was none too clean. Charlie could see the dinginess around the high buttoned collar that was not buttoned as high as it could have been. There were dark patches in the material under her arms. Charlie felt the wetness under his own arms. The humidity was high and evaporation low.

She stopped playing as a well-dressed man stepped onto the platform. He took off his wide-brimmed white hat and waved it at the crowd of curious youngsters. "My friends, I am Colonel Johnson, and this medicine show begins at sundown. You saw the dress rehearsal. Now go home and bring your folks back after supper. Bring neighbors, aunts, uncles, grandparents, and a pocketful of change. There's something here for everyone." He pushed the girl through the curtain and he, too, disappeared.

"Are you coming back?" one of the girls asked Charlie.

"Sure, and so's my family." Then he added, "Of course, someone will have to stay home with Frank, who's sick. Boy! That little kid would like a medicine show. I'm coming so's I can tell him about it." The kids left in little groups, heading for different parts of town.

Charlie hurried back to the smithery to tell Will what he'd found. Near suppertime Will and Charlie closed the shop. When the boys were home, they found everyone knew about the medicine show because there were advertising posters nailed to the electric light poles down the main street of town. Ell was going to the show with Grandma Malinda, who had stayed for supper.

Since Old Charles's death, Malinda often stayed for supper. No one ever objected. She was a member of the family and well loved.

Mary asked Will to take Charlie to the show and said she'd stay home with Frank and keep a warm supper for Joe. "He surely will be back with the doctor tonight."

"Don't fret," said Malinda. "Joe'll do what he can to get the doctor. Frank is no worse. Sit by the screen door so you can hear that lady's fiddle music Charlie told about."

*　*　*

There were very few forms of entertainment in Chillicothe, except watching the railroad tracks being laid at the edge of town. A medicine man camped on the outskirts brought out most of the townsfolk.

Charlie twirled the end of his rope until Will told him to put it away. "Do you have to take that blasted rope? Geez, Charlie, I bet you'd take it to church, maybe rope the preacher." Will laughed.

Charlie was looking at the crowd of people in a large semi-circle around the wagon. He waved to Grandma Malinda and Ell standing together and turned to tell Will he was going to move closer so he could see better. Will was talking to a couple of friends, so Charlie squeezed through the crowd and leaned against the wooden platform which was hinged to the side of the wagon and supported by two blocks of wood in front.

Colonel Johnson stepped to the very edge of the platform and waved his hands. "Folks, move up. I am the one and only Colonel Johnson. You are lucky enough to hear this little lady sing. She also plays the fiddle." He pointed a finger at the girl. "The famous operatic star Ophelia."

Ophelia spread out her soiled satin skirt and curtsied. Her feet were as bare as Charlie's, except she had dirty pink ribbon pulled up around each big toe across the top of her feet and wound around her ankles and tied.

"Folks, now, listen. Tell you what I'm going to do! See this here packet of peppermints?" The Colonel took a small brown paper bag from a wooden crate. Ophelia had pulled it through the curtain to the stage. "Young, old, large, small, everybody loves peppermints!"

The sun was below the horizon and the western sky glowed deep crimson. Charlie thought it was the perfect background for the yellow and red medicine wagon.

The Colonel waved his big hat. "Breath sweeteners! Peppermints are the perfect breath sweeteners. They can settle a sour stomach. One packet is worth a nickel, one Indian head, five cents, or one buffalo. Dig in your pockets!

"Now, here's the deal! Tell you what I'm going to do!" His voice carried to the back of the crowd and on across the prairie. It vibrated on the floor of the stage and in Charlie's chest. Charlie had never heard a man talk so well, so loud, so clear. He thought if a man spoke loud he had to be shouting and then his words became garbled, almost incoherent. Colonel Johnson made no effort to get his voice out to the back of the crowd. It was formed somewhere deep at the bottom of his chest and rolled up his throat and out his mouth like fresh, crisp cracklings of thunder. Charlie was fascinated. Suddenly he wanted to do the same thing. He turned from the stage framed in the last pink light from the sinking sun, took a deep breath, held up his head so his voice would go out over the crowd. He waited two, three heartbeats until Colonel Johnson paused, then he called out.

"Colonel Johnson chose the Irwin Smithery to have his faithful, golden palomino's shoe repaired! Irwin's Smithery on Washington. It's the choice of the medicine man. It ought to be your choice. Irwin's Smithery!" Charlie's heart beat fast and hard, as if he'd been running uphill. He saw heads swivel around and eyes look at him. He closed his mouth. He thought the swell of his voice, high and loud, rippled over the crowd. He didn't dare look around again. He'd not realized the extent of the crowd. It seemed everyone from Chillicothe had come out. There were several snickers behind him and he heard someone whisper.

"Chip off the old Irwin block." The voice was Grandma Malinda's.

Will and two friends stood near Charlie. Will wanted to clamp a hand over Charlie's mouth, but he didn't want to start a commotion. Will moved a few feet from Charlie. He was embarrassed and did not want to be associated with a loudmouth for a brother. Yet, he admitted to himself, it was a clever way to draw attention to the smithery. Geez, the customers will razz us tomorrow, he thought.

Colonel Johnson glanced down and glared at Charlie. "Scram! Beat it! You're upstaging the act." He then looked up, ignoring the skinny kid with the sandy hair that nearly covered his eyes. "This is the deal! I'll sell one packet to each customer, for only one nickel. That gives you a real chance to win this here genuine Injun blanket you see behind me."

Ophelia held out a gray blanket with a red and black triangular border design.

"You pay one nickel for a packet of genuine peppermints and in addition you get free a chance to own this real Injun blanket. That's one chance to a customer! 'Course I can't keep track of names, so if you buy two or three of these here peppermint packets, you double or triple your chance to have this beautiful, genuine wool blanket." Colonel Johnson reached out and took the blanket from Ophelia. He shook it out so the people could see the bright-colored design in the center.

"This here is an authentic Navaho blanket. It's hand-woven by

Navaho hands and wove so tight that water can be carried in it for hours. Yes! Carry water in it for four or five hours before it leaks through.

"Folks, it took one Navaho squaw two, maybe three years to complete this one blanket. It will outlast a lifetime. Guaranteed! You can roll it in mud until every bit of color seems gone. Totally muddy! Then, when you wash it in water with kitchen soap, the beautiful colors come back out as bright and clean as new. Ain't no blanket anywhere as good as a genuine, hand-woven, Navaho Injun blanket.

"Tell you what I'm going to do! I have a hat full of numbers to match the ones on your peppermint sacks. Do not destroy nor lose the number on your sack. That is proof positive you bought peppermints and are eligible to match the number pulled from my hat.

"Stick around! Folks, this is one exciting show!"

The Colonel lit two torches that hung on the back sides of the wagon. The flickering light would be welcome in a few more minutes, as the twilight was nearly spent and the now gray sky was darkening fast. The Colonel had on a gray dress vest and pin-striped trousers topped off with a high, black silk hat. He seemed busier than a prairie dog after a rain as he passed out brown sacks of hard peppermints and pocketed one handful after another of nickels.

Ophelia came back in a tight red dress with three rows of ruffles. The bottom ruffle dusted the floor boards. Will whistled, "Wow! Is she stacked!"

Charlie called out, "Pipe down! She's talented, you know!"

Ophelia moved her ribboned feet in a little dance and began to clap her hands. She smiled and it was not long until most of the audience clapped in time with her. She began to sing, ever so soft at first, then it grew until "Skip to My Lou" filled the air between the flickering torches. People in the audience smiled and swayed in time to the music. Some sang with her. She picked up her fiddle. Charlie could not hold back, he sang, raising his voice to match hers. After a couple of songs she laid the fiddle on a beat-up chair near the curtain. She reached inside the curtain and pulled out a small dog, which she held in her arms.

The Colonel used a speaking trumpet to carry his voice into the darkness and to the far edge of the crowd. "Tell you what I'm going to do! Right here, before your own eyes, I'm going to let you see our Wonder Dog! He counts! He sings! He jumps through fire! That's what I said, he counts, sings, and jumps through fire!

He is undoubtedly the cleverest dog in this here county."

Someone shouted, "You mean Livingston County?"

"Yes. Now here's Wonder Dog, the most fantastic dog in Livingston County!"

Charlie felt the surge of the crowd at his back moving in for a better look. He leaned closer and saw that the Wonder Dog was a scrubby, yellow and black, wire-haired fox terrier. He turned to say something about the dog to Will. Somehow he'd lost Will as the crowd moved up. Charlie knew Will was close somewhere. He leaned on the stage for a good look.

"Hey, kid, come on up!" shouted Colonel Johnson, pointing a finger at Charlie. "Yes, you, the loudmouth. Hold this here hoop."

Charlie felt an electric tingle go clear through his chest as someone boosted him up on the stage. The hoop had rags wrapped around it. It smelled funny to Charlie.

"Soaked in alkyhall," whispered the Colonel. "Hang on to it. It's not hot enough to burn nor blister. Hold there. You'll be fine. Not as hot as a forge, you'll see. The tip'll love your show." He motioned out over the crowd with a wave of a hand. "I can't run you off for advertising your business to all these people, so you join my show."

Charlie swallowed and laid his rope on the battered chair beside the fiddle. He hoped his hands stayed steady. His mouth felt dry as dust. He held the hoop high. The Colonel brought one of the torches near and suddenly there was a bright flash and the rags on the hoop glowed an eerie blue, shimmering light. The Wonder Dog jumped clean through on Colonel Johnson's command. Just as Charlie thought the dog was going to run off the stage and into the crowd, it turned and ran back to jump through the hoop again.

Wild applause came through the air. Charlie felt the surge of cheers and heard the call for an encore. He inhaled deeply through his mouth as though sucking in all of it. He felt wonderful. He stepped forward a trifle and held out the smoking, blackened hoop for all to see. He hoped Will, Ell, and Grandma Malinda could see him. Charlie put his left hand to his waist and bowed as he had seen Colonel Johnson do.

Ophelia removed the hoop from his hand and replaced it with a black silk top hat with a false bottom. The motions of the pitchman, Colonel Johnson, were fast. The Colonel kept up a constant patter of words, making the audience remain relaxed and laughing.

Charlie laughed when the Colonel whispered for him to slide the latch on the bottom of the hat. He did this and a huge white rabbit popped up over the top. It was alive. Charlie's eyes were round as silver dollars. He took another bow and popped the hat on his head. The rabbit was bigger and fatter than any Charlie had ever seen. The long pink ears twitched. The rabbit hopped to the edge of the stage and wiggled its nose. Ophelia came behind the animal with a wire cage. She slid the door open and held a limp carrot so that it dangled from the top to the inside. At that moment the Wonder Dog yipped and ran between Ophelia and the rabbit, causing the cage to fall. Ophelia made a fast grab for the rabbit, but tripped over the cage and fell head first with her legs in the air. Her skirt went to her waist, revealing red satin bloomers.

Ophelia picked up herself and smoothed her skirt down over her hips so it covered her slim, white legs. From the corner of his eye Charlie saw the rabbit hopping around the front of the medicine wagon, then he was aware that the Wonder Dog was chasing it. The Colonel cried, "Oh, my Lord! There go the props!"

The crowd hooted back, thinking for sure it was all part of the act.

A voice called, "Bring on the dancing girls!" There were more whistles until someone else called out, "We want the liniment!"

"How am I going to get that fool rabbit and dog back?" moaned the Colonel.

Charlie had already figured that out. He picked up his horsehair rope and stepped down from the stage. He scooted around the wagon, where the crowd thinned out, and ran toward the high-pitched yipping. He prayed the rabbit would not lead the dog into a gully, where the sound would be so blocked that he couldn't follow it. As he ran he could hear the voice of the Colonel buffeting him from behind, "Tell you what I have. It's medicine all right! The show goes on! Step right up here!"

The dog stopped. The rabbit was cornered between two boulders. It was so big and unexercised that it could not quickly squeeze between the rocks, nor run past the panting dog. It was hunched and cowering, scared to death. The Wonder Dog barked in short yips, then longer yaps. The rabbit's breathing was fast. Charlie could see its sides moving in and out like bellows in the moonlight. Charlie was thankful his eyes became accustomed to the darkness, lit only by a pale yellow moon near the horizon, because rocks were everywhere. They were sharp as flint, hidden in the weeds, waiting to twist an ankle. He jumped back from sharp scratches in his knees. Blackberry bushes were in a patch of shadow. He skirted them now and saw the dog, a shapeless shadow that panted and yipped. The dog enjoyed the chase and wanted more. The rabbit, a talcum white in the moonlight, was not going to move.

Don't either of you move, thought Charlie as he steadied his hand. The rabbit's head came up and its ears flicked once in Charlie's direction. He was sure its nose twitched as the wind changed and brought his smell right over into the rocks. His arm reacted automatically. The loop settled over the rabbit and Charlie jerked. He ran to see what was at the rope's end. All had taken place in only a couple of seconds: He was beginning to think he might have jerked the rope too hard. An extra half-pound pull would mean disaster if the rope were directly around the rabbit's neck. Charlie exhaled and shook his head so that the hair was out of his eyes. He picked up the rabbit and hauled in his rope. The dog was by his side barking its head off. His hand felt the rabbit's heartbeat. He nuzzled his face in the warm fur. A hind leg pushed hard against his chest. "It's the cage for you," he said. "Come on, let's get you guys back in show business." The dog ran happily at his heels.

Charlie eased himself against the back of the stage under one of the torches. He patted the rabbit behind its ears and rubbed the dog behind its head. The dog licked Charlie's arm and ignored the rabbit. Ophelia came out with the cage. "Put the rabbit in here," she said, lifting the sliding door. She grabbed the rabbit and slammed the door closed.

Colonel Johnson hustled Charlie out to the back of the stage as Ophelia, in a pink satin dress, began another song. He gave Charlie a dozen bottles of tonic to sell among the crowd.

"I've never—I don't know—" started Charlie.

"You can sell! Damn-tootin'," he called after Charlie. The Colonel was not far behind, relieving Charlie of fistfuls of silver coins he collected. The Colonel had a rope holding a box of tonic bottles slung over his shoulder. He kept passing more bottles to Charlie.

A stranger asked Charlie if he were selling the famous Wizard Oil. Charlie's head came up and his eyes went to the left, where there was a shadowy figure. The figure was Charlie's father! Momentarily Charlie felt a spasm of faintness. It passed quickly and his eye caught Colonel Johnson. The Colonel put a steadying hand on his shoulder. "That rube someone you know, son?" whispered the Colonel.

Charlie swallowed. "Pa, I want you to meet my friend, Colonel Johnson."

"Pleased," said the Colonel, putting a fistful of coins into his pocket before extending his hand. "Fine lad—fine, mighty fine."

"You make a fine spiel yourself," said Joe. "Sounds like you use some tongue oil." Joe stared angrily at Charlie.

Charlie felt his mouth go dry. He rasped, "If you give my pa a bottle of this here medicine, I'll pay for it by selling more of the stuff."

"That's a fair, square deal, pal." Colonel Johnson shoved a bottle into Joe's hands.

"Take this to Frank," Charlie said to his father. "If the medical doctor does no good—this sounds like it cures everything."

Joe pulled Charlie around so they faced each other. "Doc Reed's not coming until morning. Frank's no worse. But your ma's worried about you. Will came in for supper. He said you were working the medicine show. I came in and couldn't believe it!"

Charlie forced a grin. "Tell Ma I'm all right."

Joe seethed. His face was red. "Ell and Malinda went on home, even Rachel and Riley left." His finger pointed in the direction of the Brassfield house. "I'm not keen about you staying! But you made a bargain with that—that colonel. I'll send Will back and when the show closes come home with him. Keep your nose clean!"

"Thanks, Pa. Don't forget, give Frank some tonic!"

Joe turned back and glared, then he was gone, concealed by the crowd.

Charlie held up a bottle of tonic and called in his clear voice, "This here Injun medicine is better'n blood from the amputated tail of a cat to cure a case of shingles!" The bottle sold right away. Charlie called again, "This medicine is more powerful than a calomel purge!" He sold several bottles and felt something rub against his legs. It was the Wonder Dog. He stroked the dog's back and it stuck close to Charlie's heels so as not to miss this rare demonstration of affection.

Colonel Johnson reached out to collect the coins and said, "That's right! Use the long con, slow and deliberate persuasion. Keep these lot lice buying."

Charlie spouted sayings he'd heard from his Grandma Malinda. "A little hair from this ol' Wonder Dog swallowed with your medicine is genuine proof against mad dogs. Or, if you prefer to use just one thin hair in a bread-and-butter sandwich, it will do the trick." Charlie enjoyed diving into his memory for medical hints. "Take one teaspoon of this tonic and put a pan of water under your bed. It will knock out any fever you got." Charlie's voice grew husky.

Colonel Johnson beamed from ear to ear. "We've activated this crowd! We've turned the tip this night." He closed the show down and Charlie helped him stack the empty bottle crates and push up the flimsy stage against the back of the wagon, after the torchlights were doused in water. Charlie stooped to pet the dog as he left, and when he looked up the Colonel was talking to Will. "Say, your brother there is a genuine, natural-born grinder, a medicine hawker par excellence!"

"Thank you and so long, Colonel Johnson!" called Charlie as he and Will turned together and started through the short dried grass for the street and home. Charlie felt as if he were as tall as Will.

Frank was asleep. Joe said the boy's face was cooler. Charlie couldn't tell. Will went to get some rye bread because he felt hungry. Charlie could see better with Will out of the way and thought his father sure used a wet rag because the pillow where Frank's cheek lay was soaked and his hair was plastered to his forehead.

In the living room Ell was telling Mary about the big white rabbit. "The dog chased the rabbit and Charlie chased both of them!" She stretched her arms upward and yawned, and Charlie remembered Ophelia in the pink satin dress. Ell went to bed and Charlie told his mother about the dog jumping through fire and the fiddling. "You would have enjoyed it," he said.

Then Joe asked Charlie to go into the kitchen. "How about a glass of milk?"

"Sure, and a piece of rye bread," said Charlie. "About half the size of the one Will just had."

Joe looked worn out. He slid into a chair at the kitchen table. "Son, there's something important that should be said before the evening is spent."

Charlie felt a soft explosion inside, like the breaking of a glass. The exaltation was gone. He could not get it back. He felt tired and empty even after the bread and milk. He looked at his father, who seemed to be formulating just the right words.

"Charlie, if you ever go into a business, whether it be black-smithing, or even a medicine show, remember these words." Joe looked at his son, who was not quite ten years old. "If you use a hired man, always be honest with him. It's one thing to cheat your equals, as in a horse trade. But don't cheat helpers. That Colonel cheated you. You made him a lot of money. He paid you one bottle of tonic worth fifteen cents. You were worth a man's price, a dollar a day, or fifty cents a half, for all you did."

"Pa, I know he cheated people, But I felt good. I learned I could do something myself. He gave me two bottles—Will has one."

"No matter—be honest with your hired help. Your equals will look out for themselves."

Next morning before breakfast the doctor came riding his horse through a soft, drizzling rain into the yard. Mary wiped her hands on her apron and tucked her hair wisps into the braid circling her head. Her eyes were clear with blue lights in the gray. Charlie went with her out the door. "I'll take his horse to the shed and give it oats," he said.

Doc Reed was a small man, with blond hair and silver-rimmed glasses. He looked tired. Mary told him to go into the house and dry his coat and wide-brimmed felt hat, then have something to eat.

"I would like to eat before I see the patient." Doc Reed washed at the kitchen basin after removing his wet coat and hat. He had biscuits, scrambled eggs, and bacon. After a second cup of coffee he washed his hands again and went to see Frank. Mary followed. Charlie, Will, and Joe stood around to hear what the doctor would say. Ell cleared the table and washed the dishes. Will was ready to leave for the smithery.

"You see those silver-rimmed glasses?" Will said to his mother. "I guess a man can see razor sharp with four eyes." His head ached. He guessed that bottle of tonic hadn't agreed with him last night.

Mary shushed him and sent him out the door.

"Well," said Doc Reed, looking like he had his second wind, "your young man appears to have had an infection in his lungs. I'd say it was pneumonia. But he's outlived the crisis. His fever is broken." He smiled and patted Mary's arm.

"I knew it!" cried Joe. "Charlie and I thought he was cooler last night."

"Well—maybe so. But I gave him an antipyretic that works within minutes," said Doc Reed.

"I've given him willow-bark tea," said Ell. "Grandma Malinda says a fever can be broke by lying on a heap of willow leaves. The fever transfers itself to the leaves. They are warm where the person has lain."

"I've heard of your notorious grandmother," said Doc Reed. He cleared his throat and decided not to say more about Malinda's herbal treatments. "Keep your young man in bed another week. Feed him soft, bland foods."

"If he gets out of bed, his strength comes back sooner," said Ell.

Doc Reed looked at Ell over the top of his glasses. "Young lady, your pa rode clean to Laclede and took me away from a game of cribbage with the postmaster. I give you the best advice I have. You've had several weeks to make the lad well. I've had less than an hour and he's better."

Ell's face turned red. Mary and Joe looked at her with stern faces.

The doctor cleaned his glasses on a snow-white handkerchief. He started for the door. "The boy's blood is thin. He'd catch his death with a relapse. Keep him out of any breeze; one strong enough to blow out a candle is too much."

"I've been letting him rest outside in the cool morning air— when it's not raining. Maybe that was wrong," said Mary.

"Well—I can't be sure. But for now, rest and soft food. Don't do anything that could upset his delicate balance."

Ell could not be repressed for long. Her thirst for medical knowledge was stronger than her fear of reprimand. "Henry Clem broke his leg and I helped my grandma set it. Only the long bone was broken, so it pierced the skin. How should that've been doctored?"

"I don't give out advice on cases handled by another. But if the long bone were actually broken, the man has a limp today. I saw that man last week and he walks as well as you or I!"

Ell's face was red again, but she went on. "If we could exchange information, I could tell you that the fracture was reduced and cedar shingles were tied on each side of the break. To keep the leg straight, a traction apparatus was made with a rope and a flatiron and a couple of horseshoes for weights."

Doc Reed wiped the perspiration from his forehead. He took his coat and hat from the chair, where it dried in front of the open oven. "Is that a fact!" He stared at Ell. "Maybe you and your grandma do know something. My friend, John Pershing, that Laclede postmaster, told me that Joe Irwin knows more about horseshoeing and horse ailments than anyone in the state. Pershing warned me about Joe's mother, saying she'd delivered most of the children hereabouts. But he never said a thing about Joe's daughter." He chuckled.

"Warned you?" said Joe, standing up to help the doctor put on his damp coat.

"Well, yes. He said your boy must have one foot in the grave already or you wouldn't have sent for me. Your mom is the best healer around, according to local opinion. Pershing said if she couldn't make the boy well, I couldn't either. Looks like I owe you folks an apology." His head fell to his chest. He cleared his throat. "Maybe I didn't make the boy better. I think he probably passed the crisis yesterday. The fever broke then."

Charlie looked up, his mouth open. Joe was shaking hands with Doc Reed saying, "Thank you for being honest. I think I know what pulled my youngest through."

Doc Reed, with a wide grin, said, "If you don't mind my saying so—it was the love and concern of this family. Oh, oh, I almost forgot. There's a message from old Pershing. He said, 'Tell Joe to bring his farrier's tools,' because he has horses that need shoes! He'll have you playing a game or two of cribbage also, I'd bet."

The two men settled the medical fee. Joe would put a new rim on the wheel of the doctor's wagon.

Charlie saw that no more was going to be said. He went out to the shed and brought out the doctor's horse. The drizzle had stopped and the sky was clearing in the west.

"Did the Kickapoo tonic work on Frank?" Charlie asked his father when they were back in the house.

"Could have," said Joe with a wink, "but then, there were prayers. Say, Malinda ought to meet that young doctor. They sure have something in common. Honesty! I sure like that in a person."

The thought caused Charlie to think. That's the secret: People like Grandma Malinda because they trust her.

Frank was out of bed in a week, eating meat, potatoes, and string beans.

Joe and Charlie went to Laclede in the farrier's wagon, leaving Will to work in the smithery alone.

On the following Monday morning Joe was telling Mary about the trip. "We would have been back sooner, but old Pershing kept regaling me with stories about his boy's competition for the military academy. And listen to this, his boy taught school to earn enough so's he could go to that normal school in Kirksville."

"Why was that so entertaining?" asked Mary. "Will does not want to teach school and heaven only knows what Charlie wants. Frank is too young to decide anything."

"I was thinking of Ell, Letitia Ellen. If she went to school in Kirksville, she could be a teacher of anything."

"Ell wants to be a healer," added Charlie. "Ma, you should see all the books in the Pershing place. Ell'd go crazy. You know how she irons with a book on the board beside the shirts."

"Normal school takes money," said Mary.

"Charlie!" said Joe. "Your ma and I are talking. Follow Will to the smithery. I'll be along after a while."

Charlie took his rope and let the front screen slam shut behind him. The grass was still damp from the night's dew. The sky was a deep blue. Charlie thought he knew what his father wanted to talk about—sending Ell to school because she was the one who could read. He shrugged his shoulders and thought school could make a slave out of a person, so he craved nothing but books. He wasn't sure that was good. He wondered what old Pershing's boy was like. Probably the boy was pale as paper from reading and soft from staying inside all day. I'd rather juggle a rope or ride bucking broncs, thought Charlie, letting his rope settle on a fence post.

The next morning at the smithery Charlie pumped the bellows so that Will could fire up the forge. A shadow fell through the front door and caused both boys to look up. Auburn-haired Colonel Johnson came in. He let his eyes adjust to the dark interior. Neither boy had expected to see him again.

"Where'd you keep that braided horsehair rope, Senator? A man with a trick rope is a show stopper. What do you think?" The Colonel looked at Charlie but didn't wait for his reply. "If I could learn a few spins, maybe the big loop over my head and around my body—people go for that stuff."

"Sure, they like that," agreed Charlie.

"Here's the broken harness." The Colonel had on a pair of dark wool pants stuffed into black boots, a soiled gray shirt, and a huge, dirty white sombrero on his head. He looked wonderful to Charlie.

Will rubbed his temples and let the intricate network of leather straps, loops, and pads that were held together with iron fittings, such as rivets, rings, lengths of small chain, bolts, clips, and hooks, run through his fingers. "Fifty cents for repairing the fittings. Twenty cents for the leather, if I can fix it."

While Will worked, Charlie took the Colonel to the vacant lot and showed him how to whirl the lariat. Then he showed him how to keep the noose open by turning his wrist as his hand came around to the front, keeping the back of his hand parallel with his head.

Colonel Johnson learned quickly. "Now, where can I buy a rope and some eats?" he asked.

"Clem's Groceries on South Locust will sell you a hemp rope. Get one with a honda-loop; otherwise, you gotta make your own."

Colonel Johnson hurried down the street.

Charlie saw no sense in letting the forge fire go to waste as Will worked on the leather straps, so he tried his hand at mending a large discarded pot. He put an iron bolt in the worn hole. He put a washer over the end of the bolt and heated the bolt close to the surface on both sides. Gingerly he cut the long end off the red-hot bolt and dropped the end in the slake bucket. "I think I'll sell the pot to Colonel Johnson," said Charlie.

Will looked disgusted. "Charlie, he won't buy that. The pot's no good. Been around here a long time and never used."

"It's mended," Charlie said with a smile, "and he'll feel obligated to buy because I taught him how to twirl a rope."

In two, three hours the Colonel was back. The harness was mended. He inspected the work and said, "Uh-uh, I've seen better."

Charlie stepped up. "You've never seen better'n this." With some effort he said the next sentence slowly. "You can see it is worth a dollar." He held out the mended pot.

Colonel Johnson blinked his eyes, then stared at Charlie. He pushed the dirty white sombrero to the back of his head so that Charlie had the thought that his face was like a picture framed in a ring of white felt. The curled ends of his auburn mustache moved up and down as he talked. "Well, Your Honor, I found a nest of bird eggs that would fit nicely in that there pot you wish to sell as a blow-off. I thought to pick them eggs up, but with nothing to carry them in, except my hat, which I need to keep the breeze off my head, I'll take the pot for a half dollar. That will prove your high-pressure salesmanship and liquidate your stock."

"Bird's eggs!" Charlie's eyes were bright. "Really?"

"Have I ever lied to you, my good man?" asked Colonel Johnson.

* * *

Charlie bent a little to watch the Colonel dig at the base of a damp clump of wild honeysuckle. They were at the end of Washington Street, out in the prairie. "Lookee here! The eggs are just as pretty as I remembered. They'll make a fine supper for me and Ophelia," said the Colonel.

Charlie rolled over in his hand one tiny white egg, spotted brown and purple. He said, "You didn't pay for the pot."

"My Lord, I did not forget. I'll pay when I pick up the harness."

Charlie pointed to the mended pot. "It's a half dollar, remember?"

"It's not worth that!"

"All right," agreed Charlie. "Forty-five cents and let me have two eggs."

"Four bits and I'll keep all the eggs."

Charlie rolled the egg from one hand to the other in front of the Colonel. He held the words back until just the right moment. He looked up, squinted one eye against the sunlight. He opened the other eye wide to watch the Colonel. "You're the first person I ever knew that liked to eat snake eggs."

Colonel Johnson stood still. "Snake eggs? Live snake eggs!" He handed the pot to Charlie. He hurried back into the shop and came out with the harness twisted over his shoulder, several leather straps and chains dragging in the dirt.

"Good day, Colonel Johnson," said Charlie, deliberately making his face serious. He put the egg in the pot beside the others. "I hope to see you again. You pay for the smith's work?"

"You owe seventy cents!" called Will.

"Oh, snake spit!" The Colonel reached into his pocket. "Take this you—you Pharisee. He handed Will a single, large paper greenback. He did not look back at Charlie, who stood in the street holding the pot with the late-laid meadowlark eggs in one hand and his side with the other as he suppressed his laughter.

"I have a new present for Frank!" Charlie called out. "I'll make needle-sized holes in the ends and blow the insides out. Then I'll string the eggs on thread. Frank can hang them up wherever he wants for decoration. Aren't they pretty? Too pretty to keep out of sight."

"Better hang them higher than some grandma can reach," Will said and laughed.

"Some grandma don't like snake eggs."
"They don't look like snake eggs," said Will.
"But if I mentioned snake eggs—"
"You wouldn't!"
"Who sez?"

THREE

Catastrophe

In late April the sky was a hazy blue and sunlight shone on the tall, white spire of the Baptist Church, then filtered through trees and glowed on house windows. Early in the morning Malinda Irwin saw a lone pair of whooping cranes flying high overhead toward the Grand River on their northern migration. The cranes dropped low and dipped gracefully as they passed directly over her small frame house. Malinda had not seen cranes since she was a small girl. Her quick mind recalled the old superstition that cranes passing over a house announced a death within that place during the coming year.

She watched the birds' long necks pull straight out like taut clothesline rope as they moved upward to higher altitude. She imagined a sad summoning note in their shrill, prolonged cries. The wailing dirge of the cranes' call caused tears to well in her eyes. She breathed deeply, prepared herself for the final farewell, her last sensations of the glorious Missouri spring. She wiped her eyes roughly on her sweater sleeve and spoke out loud to herself, "I saw the sign and that's that!"

"Grandma! Why are you crying?" said Charlie.

He surprised her. His voice sounded so much like that of her dear, deceased Old Charles. She took a deep breath. "It's nothing. The sight of cranes brought back memories of old times."

"Tell me some," said Charlie, going into the kitchen behind her.

"I remember a day I really cried. Your grandfather and I left our home in Indiana, Henry County, and took off for some place called Chillicothe. It wasn't on no map, because most of the inhabitants were Shawnee Injuns."

"Why'd you choose this place?" Charlie sat at the kitchen table while Malinda poured hot water in two teacups that she'd filled a third of the way with milk.

"Old Charles did the choosing. Stir your cottage tea. Put sugar in it," she said, smacking her lips. "I'll tell you when you have to run to school."

"Did Grandpa rive cedar into shingles then?"

"Land sakes, no!" She blew on her tea. "Old Charles, he learned to make moccasins from them Shawnees. Then on his own he learned to make men's work boots and ladies' slippers. Made his own tools. Bought leather goods from the Injuns with a gunny bag of potatoes, a fat hen, even his home brew. He traded shoes with the settlers for food and livestock. He was Chillicothe's first cordwainer." She pressed her blue-gray lips together, thinking. "He told me this town was named by them Shawnees. In everyday language *Chillicothe* means 'the-big-village-where-we-live.'"

Charlie nodded. He wanted to hear more.

"When did Grandpa sell shingles?" Charlie asked again. He sipped tea from a spoon, copying the habit of his grandmother.

"Later. When the town's settlers wanted frame houses." She sniffed and looked at Charlie. "Did you forget your bath this week? What's that I smell?" She pinched her nostrils.

"I plumb forgot!" Charlie lifted the bottom of his bulky sweater and pulled out a package wrapped in newspaper. "Two catfish I caught yesterday where the Thompson and Grand rivers join. You know that sandbar? Will and I waded out there."

She tore off the paper and pulled away the green leaves that were supposed to keep the fish fresh. She ran her fingers over the broad heads and scaleless backs. "These are dandies. There's enough for two meals, maybe more. Didn't you all go to church yesterday?"

"Nope."

"Time to hie for school. Tell your ma and pa I'll stop by and we'll all go to church next Sunday. Thanks, Charlie." She dropped the fish into the galvanized metal sink.

Charlie hitched his coiled horsehair rope a little higher on his shoulder. "Pa ain't speaking to me."

"For how long?" asked his grandmother.

"Since yesterday when I roped Grandma Rachel's guinea hen on the way home with the catfish. I only wanted to see if I could. She told Pa and I got a whipping. I think she expected to get my catfish."

"Charlie, have you gone clean wacky? You have to realize it is all right to tie a horse to a stob and use the horse as a roping target. But roping things like chickens, cats, dogs, and toddlers upsets their owners." She pushed him gently out the door and off the porch.

"I know. Pa told me." There was a sad, frayed look in Charlie's eyes. "Pa can lay a kid across his knees and whip him harder and faster than any other pa in town."

Malinda did not smile; she gave Charlie a quick hug and waved as he trotted off for school. "Come back and we'll talk more about the olden times," she called.

Charlie figured the sooner he got through school the sooner he'd become a cowboy and own a horse ranch. He dreamed of showing other cowboys how to master roping and how to round up a bunch of wild horses to fill his corrals. Already he had the terse words thought out that would go with these exhibitions. He practiced by giving lessons to some of the young boys at the town's newly built Fair Street Public School. Charlie charged each boy a nickel. He called the group Charlie's Roping Academy. His father put an end to the academy when a neighborhood mother complained that her son's fresh-starched shirts were looking like dust rags after her boy was chosen the academy's roping target for that week.

During the pledge of allegiance Charlie decided to put on an exhibition of his roping prowess. He invited everyone in fifth grade to bring lunch outside in the open field where they played kickball. "Come watch amazing rope tricks for free!"

Every child waited, breathless, to see what Charlie would do with his coiled rope. He kept them wide-eyed with spinning the big loop around his legs, then up, up to his neck. He had good control of the wide open loop and this achievement gave him the confidence to ask the young fifth-grade teacher to come see his show. She came out when Charlie was winding up for the big climax—roping the flagpole.

"Watch me rope the pole! Oh, dear, bread and beer, if I was

home I shouldn't be here!" Charlie called in a loud voice to attract attention. He swung the rope a couple of times to get the loop well opened, then lifted it high over his head and let it sail upward against the clear sky. He felt wonderful. The loop was just shy of the pole when it slowly settled downward and astonishingly slipped around the teacher's head. There was a twist and quick pull and the rope tightened about her waist, pinning her flaying arms to her sides.

Charlie feigned surprise and a sudden muscular contraction of his arm, that was an innocent reflex action, brought screams from the teacher as she went down in the dust beside the flagpole's foot. The applause was tremendous, instantaneous, and short-lived. Charlie quickly apologized and untangled the rope from the teacher and said in a weak, squeaky voice that he needed more practice.

The teacher put Charlie's rope inside her desk and kept him inside the fifth-grade room during recess and lunch for the week. She also walked to the smithery and told Charlie's father. Joe pulled a leather strap from a nail on the wall and waited for Charlie. The moment he walked into the smithery his father grabbed him.

Charlie looked up and saw the dark, piercing eyes, the large nose with nostrils flaring faintly in and out, the slashed, large mouth half open, and the swatch of black hair over the sweaty, red forehead.

Charlie was sick about the whole episode. He thought, when Pa takes the strap to me—I won't sing. I won't open my mouth. He clamped his lips together and drew in a deep breath. He'd die standing up.

"For a week there will be no horseback riding. Understand?" The leather strap hung limp in Joe's right hand, then it was flung up and down, up and down.

Charlie gritted his teeth and held his breath on the down stroke. I'll be gritty as eggs rolled in sand, he thought. He gasped for breath on the up stroke and smelled the acridness of horse-flesh and leather on his father's work apron.

By the week's end everything seemed swell. Charlie had his rope back.

On Sunday, Malinda stopped at Joe's house on her way to church. Mary was slicking back Frank's unruly hair. Charlie and Ell were in their best clothes. "Where's Joe and Will?" asked Malinda.

"Somewheres along the Grand, sawing cordwood," said Mary, letting Frank go put his shoes on.

"A whole family ought to attend church," Malinda said with a sigh. But she knew that Joe thought the outdoors was the best place for worshipful communication with the Lord.

Joe often said, "Alone, close to the earth, a person learns most about his Maker." Whenever he was unstrung he sought the recuperative power of the silent cottonwoods along a riverbank. He didn't want to hear gossip, nor back-biting, nor a preacher's high-flown language. He said that alone in the outdoors he could put his problems in their proper place and find they were always small compared to the Lord's great scheme of things. Nowadays his problems were the drought and hard times.

Will was easygoing and never cared much one way or the other. He could go to church, or work at the forge, or fish, or saw wood without complaint.

Ell ran her hands over her slim hips, making certain her silk skirt skimmed the toes of her gray kid, two-button shoes. "Grandma, I'm going to Teachers' College in Kirksville this fall."

Malinda's brown eyes flew wide with surprise. "How?"

"Quincy, Missouri, and Pacific Railroad."

"I mean, who's going to pay?"

"I can sell herbs. There's no herbalist in Kirksville." Ell smiled as if to add, don't worry about it.

"Maybe I have herbs you can have," offered Malinda, "and maybe a little extra money. I'll look. We'd better not be late for church."

"I've tried talking Ell out of this foolishness," said Mary. Her gray eyes reflected green flecks of light. "We'll leave as soon as I find my purse."

"Pa told us about the Laclede postmaster's son who earned his way. I know I can. I want to be a teacher. And it would be no trouble to heal and study teaching at the same time." Ell's voice turned soft and pleading.

Mary looked down at her homemade shoes, which were the shape of her feet and the color of dust. "Times are hard. Some of the farmers are doing their own smithing now, so Joe loses their work. Ell doesn't realize how much it costs to live away from home!" Mary tucked a strand of loose hair into the braid around her head. She held the screen door open so that the three children could go outside.

Charlie said, "Jeems, Ma doesn't want you to go anywhere, Ell. Can't you tell? Pa's not got enough money for teacher's school in case your stupid herbs don't sell."

"You stay out of it!" snapped Ell.

Charlie stuck his tongue out at his sister. "I'm never leaving. But if I had somewheres to go, I'd take everyone with me."

"You'll never amount to a hill o'beans."

Frank sat on the steps and stared off into space.

"That ain't true!" cried Charlie. "I'll amount to something. I have a secret."

"What's that?" asked Ell, putting her nose in the air.

Frank leaned backward so he could hear Charlie's secret.

"If you want to do something, don't stir everyone up—just do it."

"What if it's wrong and you don't find out until afterward?" asked Ell.

"Say you're sorry, and start over."

"Some secret," said Frank, sitting up and hitting his heels against the riser.

"Maybe when I grow up I'll be Livingston County's most expert rope spinner. That kind of expert don't cost a cent to learn."

"Charlie, that's not funny. You gotta have a real job," said Ell, holding the door for Grandma Malinda and their mother, who'd found her purse on the bureau where she'd left it.

They walked to the Baptist Church, Mary and Malinda leading, the children following one by one.

In the churchyard Ell grabbed Charlie's arm. "Who's that?" She pointed to a tall young man, maybe older than Will, with a firmer chin, but with the same stocky build. He was dressed in the uniform of the United States Military Academy. "He's a dream!"

"I thought you said men around here are stinko."

"Does he look like any men around here?"

"There's old John Pershing," whispered Charlie. "You know, Pa and I went to Laclede to look after his horses. That must be his boy in the army uniform."

"Why'd they come here?" said Ell, following Charlie right up to the newcomers and smiling at them.

"Howdy, Mr. Pershing." Charlie held his hand out. "I'm Charlie Irwin. Remember? Pa and I did some blacksmithing at your place. This is my brother Frank. My sister, Ell. You know my Ma and Grandma Malinda?"

Pershing looked at Ell. "How d'a' do, young lady. My, what pretty eyes. This is my son, Cadet Jack Pershing, home on spring holiday from the military academy at West Point."

Ell grinned and tipped her head coyly.

Charlie thought if she were a cat she'd purr.

"I've heard of your grandmother for years. Jack and I came looking for your father. We need him in Laclede again for a sick horse. I want someone I trust. We stopped in the churchyard to ask directions to your place." He turned. "So, you're Malinda Irwin, the famous lady doctor."

"Come to church with us," suggested Malinda. "Joe ought to be back early this afternoon."

"Well, I'll see what my cadet says." Pershing turned to his son, Jack, who was looking at Ell like she was the only person in the churchyard. "We'd be pleased to accompany you."

After the service, John and Jack Pershing rode horseback to the Irwin home. The Irwins walked home hurriedly. Mary and Malinda worried about dinner, Ell kept talking about the handsome cadet. Charlie thought she was bird-brained and said so. "Your senses have shrunk. Jack puts his pants on same as—"

Malinda put her hand over Charlie's face. "Hush, or I'll wash your mouth with yellow soap."

"Jeems, Grandma! Let me see where I'm walking!" Charlie cried.

At home Will and Joe were back from sawing cordwood and sat at the kitchen table drinking coffee. Joe saw the Pershings tie their horses to the shade oak. He was so surprised he knocked the coffeepot over. Ell cleaned up and told Will to change his sweaty clothes on account of the company they had coming in. "Cadet Pershing would never allow himself to be so grubby," she sniffed.

"I bet you a buck that dude wishes he had on baggy trousers and a flannel shirt," said Will, going to wash.

Joe and John Pershing talked as if they'd known each other for years. Finally they went to the smithery for the farrier's wagon and creosol ointment.

Malinda and Mary made corn pone, rice, beans, and slaw. Ell insisted on making a dried apricot pie. Her face shone and she became even more animated when Jack asked for seconds of pie. "I made—I mean—I like—you know—the pie," she gestured with her hands.

He smiled. "I like fancy apricot pie also," he said easily.

"That's what I meant," said Ell, then, with a playful singsong to her voice, "I heard you rode a mule, each time you went to school."

That made Jack laugh. "Believe me, you can't believe everything you hear."

Ell's eyes sparkled. "What do you know about the Teachers' College in Kirksville?" She bent her head so that her long blond hair spread over the yoke of her dress in front.

"It's small, founded in 1867, on weekends the students go to Columbia if they can find a horse or wagon—or mule."

Ell put out her hand as if to touch his arm, then drew it back slowly. "I'd like to be a teacher."

"That's the place to go, then. But if I were you, I'd start teaching in a rural school and get experience," said Jack. "The state will give you certification if you pass the exam. You can do it, I'm sure. Those one-room schools need school marms as bright as you."

"Really?" Ell was surprised. She took a deep breath and blinked. "You believe I could teach school right away?"

"Certainly. Haven't you been teaching your brothers? Self-confidence is all it takes." Jack looked around as if seeking someone, then he said, "Say, I want to see if your brother will show me how to use a rope." Jack went out the door to the backyard before Ell could take another deep breath or roll her eyes.

Charlie saw him and yelled, "Hey! You wanna see me lasso our dog, Squirt?"

The old brown spaniel got up and wandered out of sight.

"Some tree or post or stob in the ground is good enough. Your pa told my pa that you were real good with a rope."

Mention of being good made Charlie's fingers rush to uncoil his rope. He flung that fourteen feet of horsehair out and twirled the largest loop he could handle. He *kiyi*ed like an Indian and whinnied like a horse, then explained, "It takes both hands to do this, and a long time to get it right." Suddenly he felt wild and cocky, ready to show off all his fancy tricks. "That there eye through which my rope goes is called the honda."

"Doesn't it ever kink?" asked Jack.

"Naw! See, you let the end twist in your hand." Charlie looked at Jack and wondered if his brains were smooth. "Like riding a horse, you let the reins roll so's not to kink."

"Can you rope something high?" asked Jack.

Charlie looked around. He saw his pa's fresh-cut cord of wood; the pile of cow manure had been plowed into the garden.

His eyes moved higher, to the top of the utility shed, where there was an iron weather vane in the shape of a horse that Joe had made one winter at the smithery.

Joe was proud of that roof decoration and could foretell a storm by which direction the horse's nose was pointed.

Charlie lifted his wrist and with a tiny twist the rope settled over the fancy ironwork of the weather vane. With another upward thrust of his left hand and a slight bend forward from his waist, Charlie flipped the rope off the iron horse and to the ground in a graceful curve. "You try once," Charlie said.

The air was warm. Jack took off his dress jacket and rolled up his sleeves. He took the coiled rope from Charlie.

Nine-year-old Charlie began the instruction. He chose his words carefully and showed each move as though he were a ballet master. "Now stand with your feet apart, like this. Your arms should be down below your middle. Helps with the balance."

Twenty-four-year-old Jack listened carefully and followed Charlie's instructions exactly.

"The left hand holds both loop and end. Keep your fingers loose like you were holding the line of a fly rod," Charlie said. "Throw the right hand toward me." He pushed Jack's arm to the proper level. "Now, release the loop with both hands and hold the guilding end with your fingers of the right hand."

This last was as clear as the muddy Missouri River after a hard rain to Jack. He stepped back and laughed nervously. He didn't want the kid to think he was dense. Jack's wrist began to swing loosely and the rope began to whirl. The loop opened and Jack's fingers gripped tensely and the rope slid down over his neck like skin off a roasted snake. "I don't want to hang myself." Jack's face was red and his breath came in puffs.

"You didn't have the rhythm quite right," said Charlie.

Jack coiled the rope, and this time he let his left hand help with the turning, sliding rope. The rope whirled rhythmically by centrifugal force until it flew out of his hands and landed like a spent telegraph wire in the tall grass and bright hollyhocks beside the shed.

"If you could get something in between, you'd have it perfect," said Charlie. "I've taught kids younger than you and they caught on."

Jack set his jaw, flexed his knees, and tried again. The rope spun around as though it had a life of its own. Charlie was ready to whistle his approval. His lips were puckered and he drew in his breath, then Jack threw the loop out from his body and it sailed through the air in a graceful arc to the top of the shed. Jack's right hand jerked and the loop over the weather vane contracted faster than cooling iron in a slack tub. His left hand fell down at his side, putting more pressure on the wood molding at the base of the delicate, skillfully hammered iron horse. The horse bucked off the shingled roof, pulling a huge piece of ridgepole, several shingles, and the hollyhocks down with it as it bit the dust once, bounced up and back, bit the dust again, and then lay in a tangled mess at Charlie's feet.

"Boy! You managed that just dandy!" cried Charlie.

"I'm terribly sorry!" Jack was chagrined. "Can we go up and fix it?"

"Maybe you shouldn't overdo it." Charlie clamped his teeth shut a moment, then said, "Let's put the rope away. Say, do you manage men as well?"

"You mean can I persuade men to do what I want? Give orders?"

"Ya." Charlie looked over the weather vane. He felt better when he found there was no damage to it.

Jack began to pick up shingles and shingle splinters. He stopped all hunched over near the ground and said, "Charlie, I asked a similar question of a colonel, who was my instructor. He looked at me as if I'd come from some wide spot in the road west of the Mississippi that no one in the state of New York ever heard of and least of all cared about. He snapped, 'Cadet Pershing! You manage things! You lead men!'"

Charlie rolled his rope, propped the broken hollyhocks against the weathered boards of the shed, then put the weather vane and loose shingles inside. He crossed his fingers, hoping that his father would not come out before he had a chance to nail everything back on the roof. He was trying to think of something to say in case his father noticed there was nothing on the roof just as he and John Pershing came out the back door. Charlie wished he could sink into the dry ground as if it were quicksand.

"I want to show you my pride and joy," said Joe, strutting proud as a peacock toward the shed and pointing upward. "This weather vane moves with the slightest breeze and it's large enough to see from anywhere in the yard. I made it of cast iron and kept it rustproof with linseed oil. Just look at that stallion, you can almost imagine its muscles flexing as it—it—"

The words trailed off as if carried away by a fierce wind. Joe's face looked flat, as if it had been hit by an unseen force.

"Hey! What happened to my iron horse? Where's the weather

vane?" Joe's words were sharp as a guillotine to Charlie.

"A sudden storm—" Charlie's voice sounded like it was coming from a hollow log.

"I swear to God I saw it pointing southwest this morning!"

"That's the direction of the worst storms! Tornadoes come from the southwest!" Charlie felt as if he were going to throw up.

"We had no storm this morning, young man! What are you trying to say?" Joe's face was dark. His eyes bore into Charlie.

"I was practicing with my rope. A spinning loop—"

"You? You pulled my weather vane off with your rope? Charlie! How could you be so careless? So stupid?" Joe's face turned bright red and his big hands clenched and unclenched.

The Pershings stood at attention, side by side, stiff as boards.

Charlie felt hot tears form in his eyes.

Jack's face was the color of fresh-ground flour. "Sir, if I might—"

"Yes, you might wait until I have this out with Charlie!" said Joe. He pushed Charlie toward the shed.

Jack stepped forward. "Mr. Irwin, sir, wait a moment. It's not all Charlie's fault. I asked him to show me how to twirl the rope. I was all thumbs. The rope was all tangles. It flew out of my hand before I was ready!"

Joe ignored Jack's explanation. He pushed Charlie into the shed and across the wood chopping block and thrashed him with the palm of his hand.

It was a terrible experience for Charlie. He didn't crave witnesses. He felt like a jackass. He could not come out of the shed and face Jack. He hated his father. He wished he'd suffocate right there in the shed beside that damned iron horse.

Thirty minutes later Jack pounded on the door. Charlie didn't answer. Maybe he'll think I've died, Charlie thought. The door opened. Jack was smiling.

Charlie pulled himself off the floor and accidently kicked the iron horse. He jumped backward as if he'd kicked the devil himself.

"I told your pa that it was not fair for you to take responsibility for my transgressions. I told him you managed the rope, but I led you to the weather vane."

Charlie walked out of the shed, blinked in the sunlight, and dug his fists into his eyes to clear the tears.

Inside the house Joe's face was soft. He was telling John Pershing how he'd made the weather vane thin, but strong, on the forge.

* * *

The Pershings said good-bye a short while later. Joe sat in his wagon ready to go to Laclede with them and look after their prize horse. Joe suspected the horse had gavel and needed to be treated with mustard and hot packs. Jack shook hands with Charlie. "So long, friend. We ll get together again. Remember, manage things. Lead men." He winked.

Ell moped around the rest of the day thinking about her conversation with Jack. Suddenly she said, "I'm not going to Kirksville. I'm going to get a certificate and teach in a country school. I have the confidence I can do that right now!"

"That's what Jack said." Charlie made a face.

Ell glared at Charlie so that he felt mad as a rained-on rooster. "He had nothing to do with my decision. He paid more attention to you than he did to me. Charlie, you got all the attention. You took Pa's weather vane off the roof and got a whipping. But somehow, you are still a hero!" she cried.

Etta put down the newspaper she was reading to tell both youngsters to stop squabbling.

Charlie looked at Ell and said, "Crisis is the only thing people remember."

Ell's mouth fell open. Etta dropped the newspaper. Charlie grinned, feeling that he'd said something important. His anger faded.

By April's end school was out. Boys and girls were needed to plow and to seed. School wouldn't reopen until mid-October, after harvest. Charlie couldn't remember when he hadn't done the odd jobs around his father's smithery during the lazy summers, except when he wasn't school age and his family tried farming in Kansas for a couple of seasons.

This morning the *chunk chunk*ing of cardinals in the red cedar at the corner of the house woke Charlie. He got out of bed, pulled denim pants on. He and other youngsters his age called the straight-leg blue denims "shotguns." Charlie went to the back porch and saw that Will had gone. As he went to the kitchen and hunted for syrup to pour over biscuits, he thought of Will going to the dark smithery constantly, morning until night, getting no sun. No wonder Will was pale year-round.

Charlie understood that the smithery was dark so colors of cooling iron could be watched, the subtle greens and blue and the white hot cooling down to yellow, orange, then red. A good striker, and Will was that, knew just the right stage or color for striking. Will suffered from hay fever and the smithery was a kind of refuge from watery eyes, tickling throat, coughing, and sneezing.

Charlie heard Ell in the bathroom. Her bedroom was made from stringing a flowered curtain on heavy wire at the end of Mary and Joe's room. Ell was running the water, probably cleaning her teeth with salt and soda. The Irwins had had their inside plumbing for nearly a year. It was nice not to have an outhouse, not to carry buckets of water to the kitchen sink.

Charlie went to the kitchen where the thin, see-through curtains moved in and out with the breeze.

Mary came into the kitchen. Her hair was combed and her dress was fresh. It was the blue that Charlie liked, with little yellow daisies in the material of the long gathered skirt.

Mary sat down beside Charlie at the table. "Before you go to the smithery, I want you to take a loaf of bread and half a raisin pie to your grandma Malinda. She's not feeling well again."

At the door to Malinda's house, which was clapboard over the original logs, Charlie yelled through the screen, "Grandma! Hey, it's me!"

He was startled to see that her white hair was stringier than usual, and her skin looked paper-thin. She was still short and squat, but this morning, somehow, she seemed fragile. It was the first time Charlie had noticed she might be ill.

She had been drinking a mixture of parsley and willow bark tea to ease her sour stomach and dull her arthritic pains. She took the bread and pie and set them on the counter without taking off the dishtowel wrapped around them. "God bless you, Joe," she said, keeping her first fingers on both hands crossed for luck.

"I'm Charlie."

Her mind had wandered. She thought that this helpless feeling was nothing but age. Age was something everyone felt sooner or later. There was no escape. During her younger days work was done by hand and the old taught the young. Grass was cut with a sickle, dried and cured in piles made with hand rakes. Wheat was threshed on the barn floor. But today, there were mechanical tillers, reapers, and threshers if a person had money to buy. She looked at Charlie and said, "When you become a man, son, have a beard."

"Why'd you say that, Grandma?" Charlie felt she spoke a riddle.

"Look mature right away. Command proper respect. That's

how people know you are wise." This was not a riddle to her, it was good, common sense. "In my day a boy began growing his beard as soon as possible. But today—look, your brother, Will, is clean-shaven. My own son, Joe, shaved his beard when the town got the electric plant. These men resemble hairless boys. What is happening to American men? My dear Old Charles had both a beard and mustache."

"Grandpa Riley has a beard and mustache. They're salt and peppery," said Charlie.

"Riley's a damned fool. He looks old before his time," replied Malinda perversely. "Aren't you cold with no shoes on?"

"No, ma'am. I'd have come without a shirt, but Ma wouldn't let me."

"There'll be another drought. And the dry spell will be worse than in seventy-three or seventy-eight. Someone will find a way to use the Grand River water. Mark my words. Then this dryland farming will be about as popular as a pig's tail."

"Pa says the same thing." Now Charlie was beginning to feel unusually warm in the kitchen. "Grandma, why do you have the range loaded with wood? You fixing to do some canning? It's too hot for a big fire. That's why Ma sent you bread and half of our pie—so you wouldn't have to cook nothing."

"You're right. Women are the best thing that ever happened to men. Joe knows Mary is the sweetest thing in his life, same's Old Charles felt about me. Some men don't appreciate women. Hanging's too good for that kind." She got up from the table and seemed to forget what she was up for. She sat down. "Get yourself a cup and put some tea in the strainer, and pour in hot water. I'll read your tea leaves from those that slip through the strainer."

Charlie poured hot water into his grandmother's cup also. She took a spoonful of sugar and dipped it into her weakened herb tea. She sucked the liquid from the sugar and dipped the spoon into the cup again. It was something that many of the old-timers did. Charlie tried it.

"You sip tea just like my Old Charles," his grandmother said with a sigh.

When the tea was gone Malinda picked up Charlie's cup and looked at him. Then she bent her neck to study the bottom of the cup and the arrangement of the tea leaves. "Huumm—you want to be as big and good-looking as your brother Will?"

Charlie wondered if she could read his mind. He ran a bare foot down the calf of his leg. "Yes, ma'am."

"It will come to pass. You will be a big, handsome man. But

you won't be like Will. He had a twin, you know. The twin was in a bad fix with fever. He lived about a year. Cried day and night. Made your ma ragged. He's the baby buried in the cemetery near Old Charles."

Charlie pondered his grandmother's words. They sounded like a family secret. "I had a brother who died?" Charlie couldn't believe it. "You mean the baby buried in the cemetery was my brother?"

"Prexactly! A long time ago your pa bought Nash's barn for the blacksmith shop on Washington Street. Then he married the prettiest girl in Chillicothe. They had twin boys first."

"Tell me about that time," he said, holding his breath until she spoke again. Malinda laughed. She lowered her voice. "I laugh because if I didn't I'd cry. There were good olden times, and there were bad olden times."

Charlie could feel his grandmother wanted to go on. When she got going she was about as easy to stop as a raging prairie fire. Charlie sat still, his feet not moving off the chair rung. "What was his name?"

"Your ma called him Granville Marvin. Your ma's favorite brother is your Uncle Granville, and your pa's middle name is Marvin. About that time there was gossip about a no-good cousin of your ma's with the same given name. I told her the name could be changed. She was stubborn. I told her the name was cursed."

Charlie saw that the left corner of his grandmother's mouth had a droop even when she smiled. "What do you mean?"

"I mean the first Granville M. Brassfield was a traitor. He would do anything to get information to help the Confederates at Wilson's Creek during the War Between the States. Why, he got hold of a smart Chillicothe lad about your age, George Pepper, and tortured him with near hanging more than once. Pepper was stout-hearted, closed-mouthed, even though he got scars round his neck from rope cutting across his windpipe. Pepper was a Union Army hero the rest of his life. Your ma's cousin Granville was branded a bully and marked for treason for the rest of his life. The rascal was forced, by public opinion, to move west somewheres."

"Jeems! I never heard that! Why did the baby die?"

"I remember the day, like it was yesterday, that he drew his last torturous breath." She closed her eyes, but not her mouth. She talked on as though she were seeing what took place under her eyelids. "I dosed him with peppermint and put mustard and boiled onions in a little sack on that frail baby's chest to draw out congestion, and once I dared to blow mullein smoke into his tiny nostrils so he could breathe easier. Eventually I dosed him with red pepper in whiskey and it brought him out of his lethargy a while. Then he wouldn't eat a flummery of oatmeal gruel. Your brother Will ate everything his pudgy hands could push into his mouth, even the lucky charms on his flannel bellyband.

"The sick baby died gasping for air the morning we was having a terrible blizzard, with thunderblasts and winds that cut through a person like steel knives. Your poor, sad ma washed that tiny cold, blue-white body in the basin and dressed him in a long white dress. We burned all the other clothes he wore. Your grandma Rachel came, and before I or your ma knew what possessed her, she was kneeling on the floor in front of the chair where I rocked Will. Now, we know she was overcome with grief. That bad day she pressed her hands together, like this, and bowed her head and prayed like she was a Holy Roller, promising the Lord that Will would be raised in a manner not to shame Him. She said she knew Granville's soul floated toward Heaven as surely as dogs have little puppies."

"Grandma Rachel said that?"

"That's what she meant. Next day Old Charles transformed one of the babies' cradles into an aromatic cedar box with a lid. Your ma lined it with cattail down and covered that with a soft, sunbleached, muslin cradle blanket. Your pa used a pickax to dig out the frozen ground so that the cedar cradle coffin could be buried. Come spring he made a cross from cedar heartwood. Your ma planted them hollyhocks by the shed and started being overindulgent with Will. I'm going to tie a little bag of asafetida around my neck to calm my nerves. You want one?"

"Don't give me one of those little bitsy sacks of weeds. It'll make my nose run," said Charlie. He swirled the tea leaves in the remaining drops of liquid in the bottom of his cup and slouched down in the chair.

"Oh, give that here and I'll see about your fortune," remembered Malinda.

"Is there more to see besides me being handsome?" Charlie laughed, knowing she'd said that earlier only to please him. He felt a deep love for his grandmother.

She studied the inside of the cup, turning it this way and that way. "Don't get too set on staying in Missouri. Life will be what you make it, wherever you are. You'll see—I'm right." Her chin sunk to her bosom.

Charlie straightened up. "Is that in there? I ain't leaving! It's Ell that wanted to go. But, jeems! She's over that stupid stage."

"Wouldn't surprise me if all of you went somewheres."

"And leave you?" Charlie was shocked.

"Don't worry about me," she said. She got up, went to her bedroom, took her old maroon, handknit sweater off the hook, and put it on.

"Are you all right?" asked Charlie, wiping perspiration from his forehead.

"I'm just a little chilly. I can remember when the wind howled around the corner of this house and we kept the firewood inside to feed the stove."

"I'm going, but I'll be back tomorrow," said Charlie, baffled by his grandmother's unusually strange actions.

"We ought to have Grandma Malinda stay at our house until she feels better," said Charlie that night at supper. "She's acting addled. The heat from her cookstove has baked her think box."

Mary gasped. "Charlie! Where do you hear such awful things?"

"It's true. You should go there yourself and see. I hear stuff at the smithery, at school, you know, all over." Charlie reached for the butter. "Ma, she's cold when it's hot enough to go without a shirt. She called me *Joe*."

For the next few days Mary and Ell went to see Malinda each afternoon. Ell asked questions about lucky charms, scent-makers, or recipes for dyeing cloth. Malinda seemed fine when giving Ell this information, but when she tried to talk about present-day activities, her words sounded as if she'd stirred her thoughts in a butter churn and spread them in a heap on the table.

"Stay with us awhile," Mary begged her mother-in-law. "Let me cook for you."

Malinda smiled, trying to correlate a couple thoughts, but she didn't pick up the correct pieces. "Have you seen how big the woods violets are this year?" she said, making a circle with her thumb and forefinger to show the enormous size. Then she looked at Ell in a mysterious way and said in a whisper, "You'll teach school in a God-forsaken place, child. Don't be discouraged. In the end you'll be a healer of men."

"Oh, pooh, Grandma. I'll teach right here in Livingston County and prescribe herbs here. You can bet on that."

Malinda shook her head and whispered, "I wouldn't."

*   *   *

"Your mother is spooky," Mary said to Joe on Friday. "I do think we'd better have her stay with us. She's getting forgetful. Yesterday Ell and I found her cellar door left wide open."

Joe slapped his hand against his thigh. "After church, Sunday, you bring her here. Fix the bed on the screen porch. That's settled."

Saturday after lunch Charlie ran to visit his Grandma Malinda before going to the smithery. He liked to walk through her old shingle yard that still had piles of wedged cedar. He imagined the time his grandpa, Old Charles, had made those neat stacks. Charlie went to the back door of the little gray, one-story house. "I'm here! Grandma! It's Charlie!" He went inside. The kitchen was empty. The oak-planked floors were scrubbed white. Thin, lacy white curtains hung at the windows of the front room, and a flowered cotton material was strung across the two alcoves at the side to shut off the bedroom and bathroom. The material was drawn back so that Charlie could look right into the bedroom. He saw his grandma standing next to her massive, handmade oak bed. She was reading her Bible. Her lips moved and her finger traced the words. She cleared her throat and closed the book and snapped the silver clasp. She shuffled to the trunk at the foot of the bed, bent to pull the lid open. Charlie smelled camphor and saw the stenciled star lining. He watched her take out a yellow hair bracelet and hold it in the sunlight a moment, then she ran her hands over a pair of high boots with spool heels and laces on the inward sides.

Malinda closed the trunk, put her hand in the middle of her back as she straightened. She shuffled toward the flowered curtain and started to pull it closed. She saw Charlie and nodded fondly. Charlie moved slowly and eased his hand into the bony one of his grandma. They stood together several minutes. Charlie heard the soft stirring of the flames and hot air rushing up the chimney of the wood range. "Are you cold again?"

Malinda released her hand. Charlie looked up and saw the old, tanned, lined face washed over with tears. He heard a faint rush of air in his grandma's throat that was almost inaudible with the noisy blast of hot air going up the kitchen stovepipe.

"Cold for a day in May," she said. She added water to the teakettle and put it back on the top of the range. "The wind used to be so strong in these here parts that it blew the ducks' feathers onto the chickens, and the chickens' feathers onto the ducks."

Charlie laughed and sat on the leather couch. "Do you know more of those silly stories?"

Malinda sat in the rocking chair. "Not so silly. You know how the wind can blow. Well, once it scooped the cellar from under a house, but left the house alone." She chuckled. "And we had a dog called Shep. That dog dared to bark at a twister moving in on him and the wind came and left so fast it turned the dog plumb inside out." Her eyes began to sparkle.

Charlie had slid sideways on the couch and was laughing hard.

"In the hot dry summer I've seen grasshoppers so large they picked their teeth after eating the last ear of corn in a field. They picked their teeth on the barbs of the barbed-wire fence."

Charlie looked like he was having a spasm. He held his sides and laughed. "I have to get a drink," he said, catching his breath. "Even the guys at the smithery can't tell such good stories as you."

"Here, we'll both have some good, hot tea." She lit the kerosene lamp on the kitchen table. "I like it better than the electric."

Charlie looked up at the bare bulb above the table.

"It's more like home. The light is better, not so bright that it hurts your eyes."

"It's not dark, yet," said Charlie.

They drank steeped tea with milk and plenty of sugar.

Malinda hummed softly, enjoying Charlie's company.

"Pa said you could come and stay with us," said Charlie. He put his cup and spoon in the sink. "Oh, not so we could take care of you, but so we could see you more often. I could board up the screened porch so you wouldn't feel the breeze. It would be your room. Will could move in with Frank and me like he does every winter."

Malinda sipped her tea and did not answer for a moment, then said, "Thanks, Charlie. I hope you're as generous with food and board to all down-and-outers. I'm down for sure. I have to work this out my own way. I was looking for my leghorn bonnet with the pink roses framing the underside of the straw brim. I want to wear it. There's this thing going through my head. It's so loud, I'm surprised you don't say something about it."

Charlie was surprised. "I don't hear nothing, only the wood fire crackling in your stove. That thing is roaring!"

"In my heart lays a cold stone. I aim to thaw it. Listen now. I hear a whole choir singing, 'O, My Poor Nelly Gray.'"

"Will it ever stop?"

"In time, I suppose." She shuddered and hummed a while. "The days are flat, Charlie."

"Grandma Rachel says, 'In time everything heals.' You want to know what I say?" She nodded and Charlie went on, "Time makes some things worse."

She smiled. "Rachel can't think deep. You're right. You want the Henry rifle now?" She pointed to the rifle on the wall rack. "No one has used it for years. You ought to learn to hunt, even if it's for varmints, like gophers."

"Oh," breathed Charlie excitedly. "You really meant I could have it?"

"Of course. I told you Old Charles wants you to have it. Lookee here. The firing pin has a divided head. It strikes both sides of the cartridge rim at the same time. I learned a lot from Old Charles." Her laugh was cracky. "I'll find a couple boxes of cartridges for you in a moment. Old Charles always said, 'There's no chance of a misfire with this here baby 'cause there's no dead spot on the priming ring.' Holds fifteen rounds. But a sixteenth can be loaded in the chamber. Your pa, who's my boy, told me that the soldiers with Sherman carried these rifles clear to Georgia, and the opposition complained, 'That damned Yankee rifle is loaded on Sunday and fires all week.'"

Charlie looked at his grandma. He'd never heard her swear before, even telling what others said. He was brought up to believe that women never cussed and that men never cussed in front of women. Charlie turned the rifle over in his hands feeling the smooth, blue-black frame. He examined the metal plate on the butt, being careful the muzzle was pointed away from his grandma. A strange melancholy took hold of him. He thought of the grandpa he'd never known, Old Charles, stalking a buck deer in crisp autumn air. Charlie's fingers roamed back and forth over the side plate, and the sad gloom was suddenly replaced by an explosion of excitement.

"Here's two full boxes of forty-four cartridges and another half-full. That ought to last a while. You get more at Hoppe's Hardware," said Malinda.

"Thanks, Grandma—I've never felt so—so big," said Charlie, wanting to convey his deepest gratitude. He pushed the cartridge boxes into the front pockets of his shotguns. Then it dawned on him that Hoppe's Hardware had been out of business for five or six years. He looked at his grandma with his eyes closed partway so he could see clearly. She looked happy and her face had a rosy color. Her eyes shone.

"I know how you feel," said Malinda.

"Maybe Will felt this way when he got his pony, Scratch," said Charlie.

"It's not the same with Will. He's a taker, same as Frank. You're not. You're a giver. You can't see now. But your friends will know. Say! You want to spend your life in that there gloomy smithery?"

"Well, Grandma . . . I like horses and people—"

"Well, Hell's bells, excuse me, but times is changing. Ain't they? Know what I think will be next for a smithery?" Malinda pointed her teaspoon at Charlie. "Shoeing racehorses. Racing's in the East and it's moving West. You'll see. Might kind of keep that in your mind. I read the papers!"

"Will has cattle ranching in the back of his mind. He told me."

"The day will come when he'll ask you to stake him for a ranch. It had better be land you want also. And some more advice that won't harm none: Be beholden to no one. That goes for relatives, too."

"Grandma—you coming home with me, maybe just for a few days? You can watch me target practice." He held up the rifle.

"You go to the edge of town and shoot away from houses, shacks, cows, and stuff. A rifle is not like a rope."

"Yes, ma'am. I know. You coming?" Charlie asked again. "For supper?" He was marching around the room with the rifle held over his shoulder.

"Nope. I'm staying. This here is my home." Malinda laid the pewter spoon solidly on the table.

"Come by in time for church tomorrow. Ma's expecting you."

Malinda's voice was soft and sad. "Between the dish and my mouth all food turns to fodder; even my blackberry wine has lost its pleasure."

Charlie picked up his rope from the chair and shoved it high on his shoulder. Satisfied that it was comfortable, he held the rifle in the other hand. He gave his grandma a hug and kissed her thin, cold lips. She pulled out a paper bag from her large apron pocket.

"Take this to Ell. It's only a few rare herbs and things that are hard to find these days."

"Grandma, I only have two hands! My front pockets are filled with shells! I have the rifle and my rope!"

"I'll stuff it in your back pocket. It's not so heavy, nor bulky. Just don't lose it."

He picked up the rifle and went out the back door. Malinda followed him into the yard. She stopped at the pump and filled a bucket of water to take into the house. She hesitated as if forgetting what she wanted water for, then she offered Charlie a drink from the dipper. "Better than piped water, eh?"

"Yes, ma'am. Thanks." Charlie walked on through the shingle yard, passing rows of neatly stacked thin cedar shakes. Charlie had one hand on the rifle barrel and the other on the butt. He had to stop to hitch up his shotguns. The cartridges pulled them down over his small hips.

Malinda stood at the back fence. When Charlie turned, it was hard to see in the evening light, but he felt certain his grandmother waved. He waved and then grabbed hold of the rifle barrel. He'd spent the whole day with his grandma Malinda, not once thinking about going to the smithery.

Charlie did not go inside the house right away. He knew his father and Will were back from the smithery because he heard them talking. He sat in the old swing by the shed. The leather seat was cracked. Gingerly he tested the strength of the rusty chain links fastened to the wood beam nailed across two oaks. The swing creaked. He held the rifle on his knees. He thought of Grandma Malinda saying, "In a swing, waiting for the cat to die—watch one's life go by." He sat there a long time. He wanted to feel the rifle in his hands without anyone asking him questions or taking it from him. His father might say he was too young for a lever-action rifle and put it on two nails high on the front-room wall. Frank or Will would want to hold it and feel it.

The air was damp and cool. He had to hitch up his shotguns when he left the swing. He was hungry. The excitement in his belly had died down some. He went to the shed, fumbled with the wooden latch. The door squeaked. He was careful not to kick the weather vane. He stood the rifle against the wall and put the boxes of cartridges on the floor next to it. The dog brushed against his legs. He went outside, called the dog out, and latched the shed. He went inside the house.

Joe looked up from the paper. "It's late, son. Your mother worried about you. We missed you at the smithery."

"Ma knew I was visiting Grandma Malinda. She gave me some roots and things for Ell." He took the brown paper sack out of his back pocket. He hung up his rope. "Do you think she's really going to come here?"

"Really. We are going to tell her tomorrow. Did you eat supper with your grandma?" asked Mary.

"Nope, only tea with sugar," said Charlie.

"There's milk in the pitcher, greens and bacon on the back of the stove. When you finish, clean up the dishes and go to bed."

"Thanks, Ma." Then he added, "Pa, I'll work at the smithery all day Monday."

In the middle of the night Charlie thought about the rifle. Next to his rope it was the most important thing he'd ever owned. He heard the rumble of thunder and moved his legs stiffly and opened one eye. He listened and heard the thunder again, but this time it was a pounding on the front door. He climbed out of bed and heard voices. His father and mother were talking, but he couldn't understand what they were excited about. He put on his shotguns. Frank sniffed in his sleep. Then he heard a sharp, ear-piercing scream. He knew it was Ell. Charlie's breath came in short gasps. He ran to the living room.

Orin Gale was there with another man Charlie didn't recognize. They smelled like a bonfire. Orin was saying, ". . . so sorry, it was over when we got there. Nothing we could do. It must have gone up in blazes like a tinderbox."

Will came from the kitchen with a coal-oil lamp, which he set on the top of the cold potbellied heater. Frank got up and came into the living room, rubbing his eyes, and stood close to Mary. Ell was in a heap on the floor. Joe wiped her face with a wet cloth.

"What's the matter with her?" asked Charlie. He could feel his heart thumping.

"She burned to death," said Will. His voice seemed to come from a long way off.

"What?" Charlie thought his mind was befuddled with sleep.

Will's voice broke when he explained. "Grandma Malinda—her house. All the shingles—all burned. It was a catastrophe!"

Charlie felt like a hot wind hit him in the face and a hard-clenched fist hit his belly. His mouth was dry. All the air went out of his lungs and he sat on the floor, feeling like he was going to be sick.

Orin Gale said, "If there's anything we can do, tell us. I'll be at home or the livery all day. It's a pity. She was one of the best-liked old souls around here."

Joe shook hands with both men, hardly hearing what they said. When they were gone he sat next to Mary on the davenport. Will sat on the opposite end with his head in his hands. Ell was up sitting in the rocker. Her head was back and her eyes closed. She moaned softly. Frank stood with his back to the door, sucking on the corner of a small blanket.

Charlie was dizzy. He went to the back door. Outside everything was a gray haze. The morning light was beginning to lighten the eastern edge of the sky. He took a deep breath to clear his head and went to the shed to get the rifle.

Will heard the slam of the screen door when Charlie came back. "Where'd you get that?" he asked.

Charlie stammered, "She—she ga—gave it to me."

"Yesterday?" asked Will.

"Ya."

Slowly Joe leaned forward to examine the rifle. "This was my pa's—Old Charles's."

"Old Charles wanted me to have it," said Charlie.

"Did Grandma say that?" asked Joe.

"Ya."

"What else? What other things did she say?"

"She told me some funny stories and gave me some advice. She was cold. She had singing in her head. She said she was staying home, not coming to stay here."

"What do you mean—staying?" asked Joe. His voice was high-pitched.

Charlie swallowed to moisten his throat so he could talk. "I told her we'd like to see her more often. Like you and Ma said. I said she could sleep on the screened porch. She didn't want to come." Charlie licked his lips. "She wanted to wear a straw bonnet—one with roses. She said nothing tasted good." Charlie stopped. He felt a lump like dry, mashed potatoes in his throat, shutting off his wind.

"Did she say she *wouldn't* come?" Joe persisted.

Charlie's eyes burned. It was like using binding twine. Each question pulled and twisted and cut into his heart. "Ya."

Joe put his hands to his face.

Charlie said in a whisper, "Pa, I think she knew it was going to happen. She tried to tell me—in a way."

"Knew what, son?" Joe's voice was soft, matching Charlie's.

"That the kitchen stove was too hot. That she had a sickness."

Mary wiped her eyes. "I thought she was getting better. Her memory was more clear."

Charlie felt hot tears on his face. "Her old memory maybe, but for everyday things, no. She couldn't even remember who I was. She had something that time made worse!" Charlie choked.

Ell sat straight up. "She knew all the medicines!" she cried. "Why didn't she use them?"

Charlie went to the kitchen and brought back the sack Malinda had tucked firmly into his back pocket. "She sent this to you."

"Oh, joy!" sobbed Ell. "It's little packets of leaves and things all labeled. And lookit! A roll of bills!" She began to count. "One hundred and four dollars! This was for me to go to Kirksville! But I'm not going—and she knew that." Ell held the roll of bills to her breast and cried, "Oh, Grandma!"

Frank knelt before Ell. "She should have sent for Doc Reed. He would have fixed her."

Charlie moved his foot so that it touched Frank's. "Her sickness was different. It was a sadness. Like lonely."

"But she had all of us." Ell wiped her eyes with the back of one hand.

"She wanted her bonnet—and high-button shoes—and Old Charles!" cried Charlie. "Can't you see she wanted to live in her time, not ours?" His eyes went to Joe beseechingly. "Oh, Pa! She told me. I knew she was going to—to die, for a long time. I just didn't think about it enough to say anything. I knew, but I didn't believe." Charlie gasped and ran into the kitchen. He sat at the table with his head in his hands. He could not control his sobs.

The next morning Charlie put two nails in the front-room wall and hung the Henry rifle. He stepped back and let the look of it soak into his mind. He squinted to read the barrel mark: HENRY'S PATENT OCT. 16, 1860.

Joe came out of the bedroom, put his arms around Charlie, and held him like he was a little kid no older than Frank. "After the war in 1865 my pa put this rifle up on a shelf. It was his symbol that no one would use it for killing. It was a sign that killing of people was over."

Will came in from the porch. "I could get some good shots off with that."

Frank stood in his bedroom doorway. "Can I use it for shooting gophers?"

"It's up to Charlie," answered Joe.

Charlie could not answer. The mashed potato lump in his throat was back and much bigger. Hot, salty tears blinded him. He ran out into the yard, up the street to the stables behind the smithery. There Joe left horses that he would shoe that day or the next. Charlie sat on the stable floor with his head covered by his arms and cried. Finally he blew his nose in a clean rag he found poked on a nail on a feed stall. He got out the brushes and brushed down each horse, and when he was through his hand was steady and his eyes dry. It made the horses feel refreshed and took the edge off Charlie's grief.

Two days later Charlie was nauseated by the overpowering, sweet-spicy scent of yard flowers. There were white and lavender lilacs, late tulips, spirea with satin ribbons, and white cards with black names. The shades were pulled, making the house dark. No one spoke above a whisper and everyone walked on tiptoes.

Mary and Joe shook hands with neighborhood men and women. Rachel and Riley came all dressed up. Mary put her head on Rachel's shoulder. "Oh, Ma, you can't imagine how much I'll miss Malinda."

Rachel gave Mary a fresh handkerchief to dab at her eyes. "You know, the last time I saw Malinda she said to me, 'Do something foolish!' I thought she was insane. But she explained. 'Old age is creeping in and you ought to get around to doing what you want.' You know, she was right! You think she knew her time was short and she became sort of—careless?"

Mary's eyes were puffy and red-rimmed. "We all know Malinda had unusual perceptions."

Riley shook hands with Joe. Riley looked strikingly well dressed in his black suit, in place of his farmer's bib overalls. "Your ma was the beginning and the end of an era. She and me had disagreements. But I liked her." Riley shut his eyes and when he opened them the tears spilled into his beard.

"Thanks," said Joe, taking his father-in-law's hand.

Will sneezed and blew his nose loudly, causing people to stare. "The flowers make my nose and throat itch."

Someone said, "Malinda always had flowers in her yard."

Another said, "And she gave them away. She was always giving something. She gave love with all of it."

Charlie felt hollow inside and his head seemed to be filled with wool. He felt woozy and thought it was from the different smells coming from the covered dishes, cakes, and pies on the kitchen table that people brought. The disease burned her, not carelessness. Grandma Malinda would enjoy being with all these people who loved her. She was never naggy. Not like Grandma

Rachel. Right away Charlie was ashamed that he even thought to compare his two grandmothers.

There was no casket. There was a plain, square cedar box, which had been put together in the back of Spence Stone's furniture store. There was no body. In the box were ashes that Joe and Orin Gale, the plump, red-whiskered, livery owner, thought must have been Malinda—if she died in bed. That was where they found her platinum wedding band in a heap of black charcoal and gray ashes—where the heavy, hand-carved oak bed always stood.

Reverend Talbott came up the porch and into the house. He was out of breath. He shook hands with Mary and Joe. Then, standing by the purple lilacs, he spoke in a deep, somber voice that went from a crescendo to a diminuendo and back in full force. He praised Malinda Irwin as if he'd known her all his life, not just over a year. Then he left, saying he had another appointment.

Joe and Orin Gale went to the cemetery. They buried the square, cedar box beside Old Charles. "I'll have something written on a large shale stone," said Joe.

"I'll help you find a good-sized stone in the grass and weeds by them new railroad tracks, just outside the town," offered Orin Gale, brushing back the pompadour of red hair.

"I'll chisel out something on the stone. Make it nice and neat, with four straight lines around it, like a box," said Joe.

Later Will and Charlie took the flowers to the cemetery. Charlie thought loving someone was like going fishing. You caught the fish and were excited, beyond reason, brought the fish home, and were pleased above good sense to have them in your house. You talked about them and looked at them. You enjoyed them, then finally they were consumed, used up, and gone forever. You could talk about them, but you could never again enjoy their sight, nor feel nor smell. He wiped his mouth on his sleeve.

Will's eyes watered and he sneezed. When it was over he turned his back on the blanket of flowers, raised his face to the clean, fresh sky, and let loose a string of epitaphs and blue curses that would have embarrassed any farmer at the smithery.

Joe sat at the kitchen table. He took off his suit coat and rolled up his shirt sleeves. He put his head in his big burly hands. The windows were open and a breeze made the dimity curtains billow back and forth against the screen, like pressing air rhythmically into the hot forge. Joe got up and went to the cupboard. He reached to the highest shelf and pulled down a cigar box. On the outside were large letters printed in indelible pencil: IMPORTANT IRWIN PAPERS.

He put the box on the table and poured himself a cup of cold coffee. Inside the box the first paper was his clear title for a quarter section between the Middle Fork and the South Fork of the Sappa Creek in the state of Kansas.

I'd like to go back and try the irrigation, he thought.

The paper underneath was older, yellowed and brittle with the words: DEED OF TRUST—CHARLES B. IRWIN—CHILLICOTHE, LIVINGSTON COUNTY, MISSOURI. Underneath that title was a penned addition: GIVEN TO JOSEPH MARVIN IRWIN, AUGUST 24, 1865 by CHARLES BURTON IRWIN. Joe stared at the paper several minutes, thinking about the time Old Charles had written those words. Then he decided that tomorrow he and Will would go to the burned ruins and take all the scrap to the town dump. We'll hitch old Flame to the plow and turn the rest under. The lot won't look too bad. It's flat and already has an iron gate that can be built on to. I'll sell it to someone who wants to build a house in town. He folded the brittle paper carefully and brushed the small, dry, yellowed paper flakes onto the scrubbed wood kitchen floor.

FOUR

Splitlogs

Two years of too little moisture had piled the yellow dust of the Missouri hardpan against fences and farm buildings. Farmers feared another scourge of grasshoppers, which would strip the land bare of any green thing, as it did during the seventies. Some farmers pulled up stakes, rode away from their dried fields to seek work in towns. The grain-hauling flatboats from Chillicothe Landing on the Grand River forks to St. Louis were few by the autumn of 1887.

Transients, tramps, panhandlers, and bums, lean men with sunken cheeks, without work, walked Chillicothe streets singly or in pairs seeking handouts for menial labor. They swung down from empty box cars on the Hannibal–St. Joseph Railroad empty-handed. The woolen pants, shirts, and heavy work boots they wore were their only possessions.

Housewives believed these men marked the board or concrete walks next to their homes if they were especially generous with a free meal or a job of chopping wood for the jingle of pocket money.

The men congregated before Gale's saloon and Pool Hall and around the beer parlor of the Grand River Hotel, or on the U.S.

Post Office corner. They waited for the settlers and farmers coming into town for supplies and then pestered them with questions like "Need a hired hand?" or "Need an extra worker for harvesting?" or "Need a thrasher?" "I'm a dandy handyman—could you hire me for a month, or couple weeks, maybe a few days?" Less than half were lucky and found something for a dollar a day, working from sunup to sundown.

After fighting his way through eighth grade, always big for his age, Will could see no use for more school. For the last five years he had worked full-time with his father in the smithery. Ell at sixteen, with long, topaz-colored hair, taught in a one-room country school, getting there each morning on the back of Will's pony, Scratch. She dispensed herbs and roots to the children and their parents when they were feeling poorly.

Frank was physically small for his ten years and thought his schoolteacher was dead-set against him. He complained of her making him stand in the corner, staying inside during recess, and rapping his knuckles smartly with a ruler. "For what?" he complained. "Nothing. Well—once I threw a spitball and it stuck in her hair."

Charlie day-dreamed of being as tall and strong as a stretched-out grizzly bear. He still carried his lariat, but he used it for emergencies, such as getting a kitten out of a tree or catching the possum that got into the school's trash. Charlie was good in sums and take-aways and naming state capitals. Charlie completed fifth grade. It was his last formal education.

From that time on he had to learn by his own ingenuity and intelligence, because in mid-April 1888 his father announced that the Irwins were moving to Kansas. "We're going to be well-fed farmers. I'm sick and tired of being poor and skinny as a bed slat."

Joe said, "Crops here are so poor they bring only thirty-five cents a bushel, and that's ten cents less than it cost farmers to grow. Farmers are leaving this area like flies. The smithery customers have certainly slacked off, so I have almost nothing to do. The only income is from the cordwood I'll bring to town this fall."

"What makes you think it's better in Kansas?" Charlie was skeptical.

"I've been reading this here pamphlet. Lots of folks going West. I've been there and I know it's possible to use downhill irrigation and not have to wait for rain. Look, right here in black and white it says, 'A wheat field will ripen like golden waves in the sunshine,' and 'Fields of barley like crushed velvet, silvery, then green in the breeze.' Can't you just see it?" Joe was enthusiastic.

"Why can't farmers here use downhill irrigation?" asked Charlie. "Grandpa Riley never did."

Joe scratched his head. "That's just it. Riley's land is table flat and too far from the river. Your ma and me remember Kansas around the Sappa area; swales and swells. We'll make a go of it this time. So—we're going to sell this house and the smithery." Joe slapped his thigh to indicate the finality.

The next couple of days were spent sorting, throwing out, and packing.

"I hope there's country schools in Kansas," moped Ell.

Mary reassured her. "The most important thing is that we'll be together. Pa'll build a decent house, from lumber. We'll have chickens. There'll be a schoolhouse for you. Frank needs work on arithmetic and Charlie more reading. There's two pupils. We'll tell Pa to trade some blacksmithing tools for books."

"Ma! I want to teach real pupils, not brothers!" Ell moaned.

"It's funny," Mary said. "The things we want most are vague unknowns. The things we'll miss are commonplace, like the hollyhocks in the backyard. I'll miss the afternoon walks carrying fresh zinnias, cosmos, or marigolds to the cemetery for the graves of baby Granville, Malinda and Old Charles." She sighed and looked up at Ell's unhappy face. "My thoughts seem to be with those who have passed away."

"Ma, look forward to new things and stop thinking of the past. Kansas is a breadbasket," said Ell. She brightened, her eyes seemed to go from olive to clear emerald as she talked. "This move may be the best thing for all of us. I used to think I'd never find a school here, but I did. I'll find a place to teach in Kansas. There must be settlers' children who are eager to learn. Working with brothers will be practice until I can find a real schoolhouse." Suddenly her problem was resolved and she smiled.

Mary felt better seeing Ell smile. She brushed her hair and changed her dress. She took the old cocker spaniel, Squirt, to her mother, Rachel. For years Rachel and Riley Brassfield lived in nothing but log houses on their farmland. Now for the first time Rachel and Riley let their sons do the farming and they lived in town in a white two-story that had a porch on three sides.

Rachel was never happier. She called the house and everything in it hers.

"I'll be glad to have something of you and your family to take care of," said Rachel, taking hold of the leash and tying it to her clothesline. "See how the old dog runs. He likes it here."

Mary knew leaving the dog would break the children's hearts, but it was better than having it die on the way to Kansas. She was trying to be sensible.

While his mother was gone, Charlie took down his Henry rifle, cleaned it with a strip of cloth on the end of a rod. He oiled the barrel and admired the shine of its blue-black metal. He wrapped it in one of his shirts and laid it gently under his bed. He heaved himself on the bed and sobbed with his face buried in the soft, goose-down pillow. He'd grown up with the dog. He couldn't imagine the family without it. Utter sadness created a lump in his throat. Charlie had no ambition to do anything, only stay curled in a ball on his soft, comfortable bed. Silent tears wet his pillow. Taking the dog to Kansas could surely mean its death. Finally he reasoned that it was best to leave Squirt behind. His sorrow lessened and the lump in his throat subsided. He was ready to go West.

Two weeks later Joe was in Clem's Groceries to buy sugar, flour, dried beans, cornmeal, and salt pork. Then he took the wagon to his father-in-law's place in town. For a few minutes Joe and Riley talked about crop yield and soil conservation. Most of Riley's land had been timbered, and when it was cleared and grubbed it was as mellow as an ash heap. Riley planted corn easily with nothing but a hoe, then prayed for life-giving rain. Some years he was lucky and the rains came. Other years he was unlucky and the skies remained cloudless during the growth period, from June through August.

Joe bought a pair of workhorses and a milk cow, named Clover, from Riley. Riley scalped his son-in-law. Joe knew he'd paid too much, but would rather avoid the fuss of accusation. Riley was known to be tightfisted and cagey. Joe could bargain, but not with relatives.

Joe thought of the time Rachel wanted the electric lights put in her house in town. Joe was stringing the electrical wires, and Riley squinted his oval, faded blue eyes and said, "If the Lord wanted a light at night, he'd a'made the sun shine twenty-four hours a day. When it's dark I go to bed the way the Lord intended. Don't expect me to pay for this fool incandescent light.

It'll more'n likely make us all blind. If I charge around breaking furniture I can't see, you'll have to pay for it."

After pocketing Joe's wad of paper money for the horses and milk cow, Riley said to Joe, "You'll be planting late, I 'spect."

Joe said he'd probably not plant anything except winter wheat, and maybe he'd just begin some farrier rounds and plant nothing at first. "I saved some of my most useful farrier's tools, and I gotta get the lay of the land in Kansas, so's to make a go of it."

"Can't get no money from a farrier's business if Kansas runs into a blasted drought. That'd make it no different from here," said Riley.

Joe said that he'd heard there were fewer droughts. "And there are men traveling around the state of Kansas who make it rain."

That took Riley by surprise and he looked suspiciously at Joe. "Hell's bells, that's tampering with the Lord's business. A feller can't do that!"

Joe scratched his head and said, "I should think if he had the know-how and was paid, he could."

Joe went to Riley's back porch and said good-bye to the old dog, Squirt. He had to close the door fast before the dog came out to rub up against his leg for more scratching between the ears. It was enough to bring a pang to his chest.

Riley had more to say to Joe, so he caught his attention by jabbing him in the midsection with his thumb. "You're taking my girl, Mary Margaret, and all her young ones. Rachel and me'll miss 'em. Who knows when we'll see Mary and the kids again. You going to put her in a damn soddy like before?"

Joe's feelings were hurt. He couldn't take those words any longer, so he strung the workhorses and cow behind his wagon and pulled out.

Riley came running and yelling, "Cripes, I'd like to go! But I'm too old to start. Besides, Rachel wouldn't take the prairie heat, and the damn wind and cold. You take care!" He waved both hands above his head.

Joe leaned over and waved one hand, keeping the reins taut in the other. He couldn't remember when he'd heard Riley use so many *damns*. "I'm going to cut me a rusty!" he called, meaning he was going to make good come hell or high water.

The next day Will's pony, Scratch, and the cow, Clover, were tied to the back of the wagon. Joe and Mary sat on the wagon's seat looking toward the future. Frank, Ell, and Charlie sat at the end of the covered wagon looking back on the sights they passed.

Will rode the stallion, Flame.

Charlie could not remember when his father did not have old Flame. He could barely remember the drought of 1878, when Joe hitched Flame to a wagon and went from one farm to another as farrier.

Charlie tried to remember eight, nine years ago when he'd first ridden to Kansas in a covered wagon with his brothers and sister. He closed his eyes and could see his mother carrying baby Frank, Ell running through tall grass, his father and twelve-year-old Will stacking hunks of grass and dirt to build a one-room house that had no windows and a stiff cowhide door. Charlie had heard stories about his father paying ten dollars to file for a land patent in a town called Oberlin. Then six months later he spent his entire savings of two hundred dollars at the Oberlin Patent Office in exchange for a paper showing clear title for one hundred sixty acres. This paper had meant a lot to his father because it showed that his quarter of a section was exempt from attachment for debt.

At the end of two years of near backbreaking work, in the spring of 1880, Charlie's father reluctantly put his family and goods back into the covered wagon and returned East to Chillicothe. Joe's hopes were unfulfilled. He never had a chance to try his idea of irrigating from one of the creeks or diverting a stream into a series of ditches between his rows of grain.

Charlie's memory of going back to Chillicothe was more clear. He envied Will, who was tall and strong. He was solid with wide shoulders, thick arms, and thighs. His hair was golden and his large oval eyes were as brown as richly tanned leather.

Charlie's reminiscence was spoiled by a sharp voice near his right ear.

"By the time I was Charlie's age, I worked hard. Charlie ought to stop being an annoyance, stop playing with that rope, grow up, and learn a trade," said Will, riding by the back of the wagon and pointing to the rope Charlie was thoughtlessly tossing out to pop the heads off the tall, wild timothy.

"Who sez?" snapped Charlie, winding the rope over his elbow and shoulder. "The last time you suggested I do something I got so bee stung that I couldn't sit and it was torture standing."

"I told you to go at that hive careful to see if there was honey. I didn't tell you to poke a stick into the fool thing." Will laughed. He knew he'd told Charlie to put a stick into the center to see if honey clung to it.

"You're the one that gave me the stick!" cried Charlie. "I ought to tell Pa what you did!"

"Why, you wouldn't snitch! I ought—"

"Will! Charlie! Hush!" It made Joe mad as a wet cat to hear the boys raise their voices and bicker. "Or I'll see that you both get the razor strap. Now—neither of you open your mouth until suppertime!"

Joe followed the Quincy, Missouri, and Pacific tracks. By the afternoon of the second day they passed through St. Joseph, a border town.

Riding up alongside the wagon Will asked, "Pa, where do you suppose Jesse James lived? I heard he married and took the name Howard so's no one knew who he was, then he got hisself killed. Killed in his own house by his own brother for a ten-thousand-dollar reward."

"That's a lot of money for anybody's dim-witted brother," squealed Frank.

"We're not going by that place," their mother said.

"With that kind of money I'd go West and buy me a cattle ranch," said Will, dropping back to keep an eye on the cow and pony as they approached the ferry to cross over the Missouri River, which was an opaque, brown color. The river's banks were high cliffs on both sides that had been cut to make a sloping wagon road to the ferry docks. Charlie counted five floating logs going down river as they crossed the rushing water.

Joe leaned over and whispered to Mary, "The brother, Charles James, was pardoned for that murder."

Mary turned her head and faced her husband. "Joe, that's perfectly terrible!"

"Well, it's not a woman's place to worry about such. I just told you the facts," said Joe, looking out the corner of his eye at Mary.

The weather held fair and dry. Joe forded the wagon across the Delaware and Big Soldier rivers, ignoring the difficult and dangerous railroad bridges. The Kansas and Pacific train puffed across the prairie twice a day, one westbound, one eastbound.

Charlie waved at the trains. Engineers waved back. The powerful chugging sound was exciting to Charlie. He thought the tracks looked like there was no beginning and no end.

Going through Topeka, Joe told about Fort Folly, a roofless log structure that had been erected more than twenty years before as protection against Confederate raiders. Joe was only fifteen when he joined the Missouri Militia. Joe told how the Civil War brought Federal soldiers to Chillicothe, which was a base for supplies and operations for the militia commanders. Joe fought at Wilson's Creek and Pea Ridge. When he came back to Chillicothe, he said he was surprised to find the Confederates had burned Graham's covered bridge. There was no other way to cross the Grand River, so he went along with the Grahams and hauled oak timbers by oxen and hand-hewed a new bridge. "Then I got work with Earl and Foreman Sloan in their livery stable. That's where I learned blacksmithing and how to buy and sell horses. But it wasn't long before them Sloan brothers gave up the livery business and moved to Ohio, where they bottled and sold their famous liniment. It's good for sprains and bruises in horses as well as humans."

Charlie said, "You know how to make it, Pa?"

"Not the exact formula, son, but I know what's in it for the most part. Stuff farriers been using for years before the Sloans began making it for everybody and his horse."

The wagon road took the Irwins beside the Kansas River. When it was time to ford the Blue, Joe was thankful for the dry weather. They crossed the Republican on a ferry, not much more than a log raft. Near Junction City, Mary suggested she buy greens, such as string beans and cabbage. She found only potatoes and turnips for sale.

During the preparation of the evening meal Mary confessed to Ell, "We are about shut of meat. I should'a had your pa lay in another barrel of salt pork back there where I got these potatoes."

Joe overheard. "Don't fret. Salt pork gives me the trots anyways. Me and Will might find some fresh game."

During supper Charlie complained, "These potatoes taste like spoilt buffalo chips."

"That's turnip," said his mother. "It's good food. If you can't eat them, give them to your pa."

"They give me gas," said Joe, picking out the turnips that were mixed with the potatoes.

Mary looked exasperated with both Joe and Charlie. "Then leave them on your plates and say nothing."

Charlie broke into a broad grin, looked at his father, and shoved his plate to the center of the quilt that was their table on the flat ground. "Nothing."

Mary laughed until tears came to her eyes.

Joe couldn't see the humor. He felt his wife was far too tolerant, even on the borderline of indulgent, with the children. Joe tried to think of something to say and finally noticed some low, rocky bluffs in the distance. "It's hard to imagine what it was like on this plain when Injuns were riding over them flinty hills." He pointed and everyone looked and he could see they agreed. "Then came the traders and trappers, the army on horseback, and next the pioneer settlers, then miners, cattlemen, sheep herders, ranchers, and farmers. By jing! This country is so vast nothing can stop a man with big ideas. There's opportunity for everyone. The Irwins are getting their opportunity and high time, too!" Joe slapped his thigh.

Mary said mostly to herself, "The greater the risk, the greater the reward or—complete loss. I guess we know that." But still she felt the excitement of the wide rolling hills.

Now they passed fewer and fewer settlements and the sky was an immense blue dome overhead. Charlie anticipated the trains passing twice a day.

One morning Ell said, "I wish there was a little cloud of dust on the horizon, like a dust devil. I'd watch it until it grew larger and all of a sudden turned into another wagon."

"What if it was a band of Injuns?" said Frank, pulling his mouth down at the corners to frighten his sister. "You'd jump and hightail it over that bluestem grass like it was a boardwalk."

"Naw!" she said. "No Injuns can scare me. I'd give them the evil eye." She squinted and opened one eye halfway.

"Wanna know what I'd do?" Charlie eased himself between Ell and Frank so that he could still see the wide expanse of land and the bare rim of horizon where thunderheads formed.

"Naw!" repeated Ell.

"Aw, cripes! You're no fun!"

"Charlie! Watch your tongue!" Their mother turned on the front seat so that she could look inside the wagon.

Charlie decided his mother could hear cussing and secrets no matter how much noise the wagon wheels made nor how far away she was. He stuck his tongue out as far as possible and curved it upward and half closed his lids so he could easily look down.

"I did what you told me, Ma!" he called, smirking.

Mary shook her finger in Charlie's direction and tried not to smile.

Joe gripped the reins tighter and thought soon Charlie would go too far and get the thrashing he deserved.

"Tell me what you'd do if you saw Injuns," whispered Frank.

"Not now," said Charlie.

"Aw, why not?" Frank whined.

"All right," Charlie said, "but you have to stop whimpering like a lost pup. I'd use my Henry rifle. I'd watch and just before they nocked their arrows—Bam! Bam! I'd make some bite the dust before the rest left so scared they'd wet their pants."

"Injuns don't wear pants," whispered Ell, "just a skirt in front and back."

"And sides?" questioned Frank.

"Bare naked," said Ell sensuously.

Joe stopped to make camp early. This gave Mary and Ell a chance to wash clothes while Joe and Will went out with Joe's rifle to hunt for a deer coming to the river for the late afternoon drink. Will carried the fish trap made with willow switches so that it looked like a kind of basket. He'd used the trap often on the Grand River to catch catfish. To make the basket he'd wrapped young willow sticks around a small barrel, then wove more willow sticks up and down the sides. The barrel was removed, the open end closed, and a kind of door put in. This trap was weighted in water with rocks and left in a deep hole, but tied to the bank with grapevines. Usually Will threw a handful of corn in the trap—not ordinary shelled corn, but fermented about a week until it was sour. He had only some spoiled, old potato peelings tied in a bandanna he hoped would attract the fish. He could just see the basket full of fat, white-bellied cats eating on those peelings. He'd grab that vine and haul up the trap before the fish could get out. Then he wondered if he'd find any vine down by the riverbank. If his father and he didn't scout up a deer, he'd be sure to get a mess of fresh catfish.

"The sun bleaches good," said Mary, spreading dishtowels on the bluestem grass to dry.

"I hope Charlie's going to shoot away from the wagon," said Ell, looking at Charlie and Frank with their heads together. Charlie had talked his mother into letting him practice shooting the Henry at buffalo chips.

"Charlie's twelve," said Mary, as though age had everything to do with safety.

Frank was begging Charlie to let him try just one shot. "Only one?" A tear clung to Frank's long, dark eyelashes.

"I'm using three shells," snapped Charlie. "That leaves me only two." He looked at the colors of the spectrum on that teardrop and Frank's sorrowful face. "So, do what I tell you and don't waste your shot. Hold steady. Aim at the chip up there in the notch of that rock. Here, lay down on your belly and put the barrel on my leg. Is that high enough?"

"Huh, I see the chip in the sight! Charlie, I can see it! Can I squeeze the trigger?"

Charlie felt perspiration run down his back. "If you are aiming low the lead could bounce off the rock and hit Ma's Dutch oven. Then we'd both get a whipping. So, be sure what you see before you shoot."

Frank pulled the trigger. There was a sharp ping, like a hard object striking a rock at an angle. Then without meaning to Frank pulled the trigger again, only this time the gun was pointed half-way up the sky line.

Charlie pulled his leg up and grabbed the gun. "I told you not to! Jeems!" shouted Charlie.

Their mother had come halfway toward them. "Charlie! Charles Burton Irwin! Bring that gun here this minute!"

Charlie sighed and moved toward his mother, but not before he looked into Frank's brimming eyes.

"Were you trying to kill us? Look at the hole in the wagon cover!" She moved to look at it from the other side. "Two holes —Mercy! It went clean through!"

"Holy mackinaw!" said Charlie, feeling queasy.

Ell grabbed him by the shoulders. "You could have hit me—or Ma! You want us buzzard bait?"

Charlie understood their being upset, but he couldn't see why they thought he did anything on purpose. He glared at Frank, who was wailing in fright.

Their mother snatched the rifle from Charlie and hurriedly pushed it in the back of the wagon. Bam! She jumped back and looked around. The three children were staring. She was looking at Charlie. "Now see what you've done!" She was shaking.

Charlie pushed his sunbleached hair from his eyes. He could see his mother's face was pale underneath her suntan. "Ma, the safety wasn't on. You grabbed so fast! I'm sorry."

"Don't say sorry to me, young man!" She grabbed Charlie's arm and pushed him against the back of the wagon. "Don't move an inch!" She looked around and picked up the best thing she could find to whip Charlie with, the spatula. Charlie saw red spots in her cheeks and a mean look in her eyes that he thought would make an icicle feel feverish. He felt the blows, gritted his teeth, and dug his fingers into the wood of the wagon. Once he raised up on his toes so that the blows would not all fall on the same stinging spot.

When Mary calmed down, she said, "Get into the wagon and put the safety on that gun. Then don't shoot it again until you are sixteen."

He knew there was no use being logical and telling her that he hadn't shot it yet.

"Then you and Frank take the bucket to the creek for water. When your pa comes he'll see those holes in that canvas first thing."

"Yes, ma'am." Charlie moved fast with Frank sobbing at his heels. They went to the edge of the cutbank and saw the creek ten, twelve yards below.

"You let me shoot your gun! So it was all your fault!" cried Frank. "Get rid of it! It's nothing but trouble!"

Both boys grabbed at the slippery, dried grasses and eased themselves down the cutbank to a little gravelly beach. Charlie reached way out to fill the bucket. He watched the water edge up inside and listened as Frank scrambled around on the rocks looking for a flat one to skip in the water.

Suddenly Charlie felt Frank grab his arm and saw him point a jerky thumb over his shoulder. Charlie turned and nearly skidded off the tiny gravel bar. Behind Frank an unfamiliar brown face was smiling.

The stranger wore no shirt and looked as though he'd lost his pants. His underwear was short and split at the thighs, and made of a soft leather. Charlie's heart thumped. His mouth was bone dry. His legs were frozen, and he watched two other smiling brown strangers come alongside as silent as wildcats in the moonlight. All three were dressed alike and wore their hair in braids, except one who had his braids stuck to the top of his head with daubs of mud. Their eyes were deep brown, like the middle of a black-eyed Susan blossom. Charlie could see cheekbones beneath the skin because there was no excess fat anywhere on their bodies.

The first stranger looked from Frank to Charlie, then to the steep bank. He had a blue jay's wing feather in his hair. There were tiny laugh lines at the corners of his mouth.

"I'll help," he said as friendly and plain as morning light.

The words startled Charlie into action. He grabbed Frank and began to push him up the cutbank.

The man held the water bucket by the bail and wedged moccasined feet into chinks and crannies as if they were steps. Near the top the three strangers laughed out loud, and Charlie and Frank scratched and clawed at grass, rocks, and roots to pull themselves up. Charlie's bare feet stepped on loose rocks, causing tiny slides. Finally, at the top, Charlie paused to catch his breath.

Frank was breathing down his back and whispering real loud, "Injuns! Real Injuns! We'd better run!"

Charlie said, "Thanks for the help" and reached for the bucket in preparation to run right back to camp as fast as possible.

The man carrying a carved walking stick stepped in front of the bucket of water. "Have you food?" he asked. "Biscuits, corn bread?"

Charlie straightened and looked up. "Sure."

The man with the feather in his hair stepped forward. "We lost our gear. Cattle rustlers dipped into our small herd. We tried to scare 'em off, but we were caught in our own loop last night. They got away with our horses, clothing, grub, and cattle. We tracked 'em, but lost the tracks in the river over yonder. We were looking when we heard your three shots. That's a sign there's trouble."

Charlie was astonished. "You don't talk like Injuns. Injuns don't get stole from."

The man with the feather then spoke something that was gibberish to Charlie and Frank and the three men laughed. "That was Wyandot. If we spoke in our language, you wouldn't understand us. If Indians have something another person wants, they get stole from. It's the same anywhere. Those that don't have grab from those that do have."

Charlie nodded.

"We're from Kansas City and don't usually dress like this. How do you think our people are going to look at us when we walk into town?" He held out his arms from his sides.

Charlie could see it could be a funny situation. "You live in a house, not in a tepee?"

"A house in town."

Again Charlie was astonished. "What will Ma and my sister think when we walk into camp with you?" His eyes moved across the three near-naked men.

"We'll follow behind you," said the leader. "Tell your mama that we are friends."

Charlie and Frank ran excitedly. Once Charlie turned his neck backward to see how fast the three Indians were walking. The leader carried the water bucket real steady.

"Ma! Oh, Ma!" Charlie cried. "Give us biscuits! I need biscuits for my friends."

"Whoa," said his mother, catching Charlie and Frank in her arms. She had not seen the strangers. "You can't be hungry al—"

Ell screamed, "Lord 'a mercy!" She scrambled under the wagon and cowered behind one of the wheels. Her face was white as a bleached buffalo bone. Mary's mouth stayed open, but she could not speak.

Frank grabbed his mother's skirt. He tried to explain fast. "Wyandots. From Kansas City. Lost gear. Rustlers. Injuns. Friendly."

"Ma, these men are friendly. They brought the water without spilling a drop," said Charlie, breathing hard.

The lead man put the bucket beside the campfire that was mostly ashes and a few red coals. He hesitated only a moment to see if Mary was going to speak first, then said, "Ma'am, we mean no harm. We are sorry if we frightened you and your girl child."

Mary was amazed. To her knowledge Indians were not supposed to speak so well. She heard Ell sobbing and thought, these men look exactly the way we all imagined. But, God in Heaven, they act like real people! No wonder Ell is so frightened.

The man with the feather in his hair continued. "I am Matt Splitlog and these are my brothers, John and Mark." John had the wooden cane. Mark had dried mud holding his braids on top of his head.

"We're Irwins," said Charlie, feeling he was reminded that he was the man of the family as long as his pa and Will were out hunting and fishing and that he should be doing the introductions. "This is Ma and under the wagon is Ell and here's Frank and me, Charlie."

The Splitlogs nodded. Matt shook hands with Mary, then Charlie, and Frank, then nodded toward Ell. She was not crying, but hugging her knees and rocking back and forth.

Charlie wanted to show that he was courteous same as his pa would be to friendly strangers. "We're going to the Middle Fork of Sappa Creek. Pa has got a homestead and he's going to farm."

Matt hunkered down on his haunches and the other two men

sat in the grass, eyeing the lumps and bumps under the dishtowels near the cookfire.

Charlie rummaged around in the kitchen utensils and brought out three tin plates and three spoons and gave them to his ma. "Those men are awful hungry," he said.

Mary was caught off guard. She quickly took the plates and added lightly browned biscuits, which were still warm under the dishtowel. "I'll make some mush to go with these. Oh, you can have some boiled turnips, too."

"Never mind the turnips," said Matt.

Charlie was certain now that he liked these men. He sat beside Matt, who ate three biscuits before saying another word. Matt brushed the crumbs from his fingers and spoke loud enough for Mary to hear as she stirred the cornmeal in the hot water, over the fire's bed of coals. "I know the area you will travel going to Sappa's Middle Fork. When you get to Salina, past Abilene, take the wagon road north along the Saline River for a spell, then follow the road across country northwest. It's a shortcut and avoids a couple river crossings."

Mary tried to remember what he said. He went on. "You'll pass through some small towns and the only big ford is on the south fork of the Solomon near Nicodemus." His eyes lighted up and he smiled a moment. "Colorful place. Nice folks there. You can get fresh provisions. Then it's only a few days' travel before you'll be on your Sappa Creek—Middle Fork."

Mary spooned out the mush into each man's plate. She got the canister of sugar from the back of the wagon. "Tastes better with sugar." Then she passed Matt the dipper so that he and his brothers could drink from the bucket of fresh water. Mary repeated the directions for the shortcut to Sappa Creek's Middle Fork, and felt pleased with herself when she got them correct.

When the three men were finished eating, they used the dipper to rinse out the cooking kettle, plates, and spoons. They wiped everything dry with handfuls of grass. Matt put the kettle and eating utensils next to Mary's kitchenware in the back of the wagon. Then he walked around the wagon. He could hear Ell moving from one side to the other. Finally he asked, "Are you folks traveling alone?"

Mary hesitated. Charlie could tell that his mother didn't want to say that he and Frank were the only men in camp this afternoon. "Pa and my brother Will are hunting close by. They more than likely have a deer or some fish and are on their way back.

That's why Ma had fresh biscuits ready," said Charlie.

"I've not heard a shot for game. Did you?" he asked his brothers.

Mark kept a straight face. "I only heard those three—uh—misfires."

"Jeems! And you thought we were in trouble!" Charlie said, laughing.

"You were!" countered Mary. "Your target practice backfired into the wagon canvas. That's trouble." Her eyes sparkled and Charlie could tell that she was not so angry now. She was telling the story more as an incident that deserved a good chuckle.

"Pine tar ought to cover those holes," said Matt. He was sitting on his haunches again, chewing on a grass stem. Frank was sitting between the other two brothers, motioning for Ell to come out from under the wagon. "I suppose you'd never guess I went to Training School in Lawrence, Kansas?" said Matt.

Mary was again astonished. "Training School?"

"Yes, ma'am. I trained in United States history. In winter I teach our children. Some of our womenfolk also went to the Training School and teach the children. We have a good school." Matt's eyes had a way of sparkling so that the listener knew he had some kind of secret joke. "I'm like a schoolmarm."

Ell sucked in her breath, causing Matt to look out the corner of his eyes as she came out from under the wagon.

"Ell's a schoolmarm herself," explained Charlie. "She hopes to teach at our new place, if she can find pupils."

"Pshaw, you'll find kids anywhere that want to learn," said Matt, squinting at Ell. "Especially if you use those McGuffey's *Eclectic Readers.*"

"That's just what I use," said Ell, sitting beside her mother.

"I saw them in the wagon close to the dishes. I guess you use them every day," said Matt.

"I work with Frank and sometimes Charlie after supper," said Ell.

Mary was rather enjoying the company. She had decided the three men were really friendly and harmless. She was glad that Ell had come out of her frights and was feeling easier around the strangers. Ell could not keep her eyes off the copper-colored men. She was fascinated by the smooth rippling of their muscles whenever they moved.

Charlie was wondering how the three men would get their next meal. "Do you ever make stone arrowheads?" he asked.

Matt laughed. "My pa can make a half dozen in just a couple of minutes if he finds a good flint bed. But none of us had to learn in order to keep meat on the table, so it's becoming a lost art."

"Isn't it cold at night, without—uh—shirts and—uh—trousers?" asked Ell.

"We can keep walking and it won't seem cold," said Matt. "But Lord help us, I'm hoping we can track down those buzzards and by nightfall have our gear back along with those six fat cows."

"What if you don't?" asked Frank.

"We'll just have to dog after them until we catch up," said Matt. "Don't you worry. We'll do what we can."

"If Pa were here he'd give you part of the deer he's bringing in or some of the catfish," said Charlie.

"If he gets a deer; I haven't heard the shot yet," said Matt, standing up. The other two brothers stood right away.

Mary wrapped the remaining biscuits in a dishtowel. "For your supper," she said, handing Matt the package. Then she gave them a lard bucket filled with fresh milk.

"Thank you kindly," said Matt.

Now Charlie's mind was racing. He was going over what had happened just before the Splitlogs had come to the water hole. Frank had yelled about the Henry rifle as if it were a red-hot piece of iron, "Get rid of it!" Next Charlie thought what Grandma Malinda had said about the rifle being used for peace. Today his mother told him he couldn't shoot it again for years. He climbed into the wagon and brought out the Henry rifle. It seemed the right thing to do. He handed it to Matt, saying, "It's mine. Take it. Maybe we'll meet somewheres and by then you'll have your own rifles. It needs cleaning."

Matt was so surprised his mouth fell open. His brothers' eyes grew big and they said together, "Kindness is its own reward."

Matt held the rifle out toward Charlie. "Nobody loans a valuable weapon, especially not to strangers."

Charlie shook his head and pushed the rifle back. "I'm not a nobody. I'm loaning it to friends. It's meant to be used to keep men alive." He reached into his pocket. "Here's a box half full of shells."

The three Splitlogs smiled. Matt said, "We'll see you in Abilene or Nicodemus. This will keep us in grub until we get our own gear. It may be a lifesaver."

Charlie felt good. He held out his hand and said, "Thanks for bringing the water up the cutbank."

Matt sighted with the rifle along the prairie's skyline, made the cutoff sign, walked past Mary, and put the rifle over his shoulder. He turned. "Your boy's certainly not an Injun-giver—is he? We honor him."

Mary's hand flew to her mouth and she nodded.

Matt waved John and Mark on. "The rifle will be preserved and returned. Don't stay out in the prairie sun long without your bonnets. If you get too dark you'll be taken for Exodusters. Not that there's a thing against Exodusters. But until you acquire some wisdom, you might find them a problem." Matt chuckled and moved behind his brothers through the dropseed and beard-grass.

Ell was quiet. She watched the muscles flex in Matt's jaw and neck as he talked.

Charlie did not move for a long time. He noticed the sun seemed brightest when a cloud just began to cover it and then again when it first came out from behind another cloud. A meadowlark flitted behind the wagon. Frank and Mary gathered dry clothing off the grass. Ell had her eyes closed as if she were sleeping against the back wagon wheel. She thought of the pleasing copper color of the Splitlogs' lean muscular arms and legs, chest and back. She found the graceful movements of their near-naked bodies strangely exciting. She wondered if that was what frightened her.

Charlie still felt good about letting the Splitlogs take his rifle. He felt his right thigh. It still stung where his mother had whipped him good.

Before dark Joe and Will came back with a small buck deer thrown behind the saddle of old Flame. Will rode his pony, Scratch, and behind its saddle was the willow trap, half full of fat, white-bellied catfish. "Nothing better than cats rolled in flour and fried in lard with a few onions. Fish are all gutted and clean for you to cook, Ma." He and Joe dragged the buck deer to the creek to skin. When they came back, supper was ready. No one said much during the meal. Charlie noticed that Will wolfed down his food. The Splitlogs must have been hungrier, yet they were more mannerly.

After supper Mary and Ell cut up the venison and put the strips over a wire Joe rigged on top of a long trough dug in the ground that held a grass-fed, smoky fire. The wire with the drying meat looked like a short clothesline to Charlie. He sat hunched over the back of the wagon reading one of Ell's McGuffey's books when he heard his mother telling his father about the stray bullets and the Splitlogs. Next he heard the tramp of his father's boots on the hard-packed ground as he walked to the back of the wagon.

"Charlie, you can kiss that rifle good-bye. For every privilege there is a responsibility. It was a privilege for you to have that old Henry and your responsibility to take care of it to the best of your ability. Do you understand?"

"Ya, I understand. I did that, Pa," said Charlie as steadily as he could muster.

FIVE

Abilene, Kansas

Approaching Abilene at the confluence of Turkey Creek and Smoky Hill River, Joe told his children about the numerous cattle trails that came in from the south.

One of the shortest but most traveled routes was the Chisholm Trail, which started south of San Antonio and went nearly due north to end in Abilene, Kansas. The Shawnee Trail also began in San Antonio and ran through Indian Territory, crossing the southeastern corner of Kansas. Before reaching Kansas this trail split into two; one branch went to Junction City.

The Western Trail began near San Antonio and crossed Kansas into Nebraska. A branch of this trail followed along the eastern boundary of Colorado and Wyoming. Cattle on this route were placed on the open range, not in stockyards. Longer than any of these was the Long Trail that began in Brownsville, Texas, went west along the Platte River into Wyoming and Montana after passing through Kansas and Nebraska, then ended in Canada.

"Will we see a cattle drive?" asked Charlie.

"The cattle leave Texas in May or June, and there may be as many as seven thousand head in a herd of young animals," said Joe. "But if the herd is of older and larger cattle, that are more nervous and the fighting type, there may be only one to three thousand in the herd. Yes, you'll see plenty cattle and soon."

"I think I can almost smell them," said Ell, holding her nose.

Abilene grew from a one saloon, one trading post, wide place in the road, to a rough town with a dozen soddies, to a booming town of three hundred people in a few years. The cattlemen were never known to hoard their money, so dancing, horse racing, and gambling became a thriving business. At one time Abilene had forty saloons with a dance hall or gambling room between every two saloons.

Joe said, "I've heard tell Abilene was one of the roughest towns in the West in the sixties. More than three million head of cattle were driven here in the sixties and seventies."

"What's the roughest?" said Will.

"The wildest place was Dodge City. It was headquarters for bandits and outlaws who come from the gold fields of Colorado and California thinking to make even more money robbing cattle-men and cowboys instead of miners and merchants. You can imagine the fights and shootings and robberies. The graveyard near Dodge City is called Boot Hill because so many men were shot in some quarrel while protecting themselves or others and they 'died with their boots on,' " explained Joe.

"I heard that more than five thousand cowboys were paid off at the same time once in Abilene," said Will.

Joe nodded. "If eight men are with every thousand head of cattle and each man has five to ten horses, in case one becomes weak and dies, or is stolen by Indians, you can see the number of people and animals that can come into Abilene."

"Pa, where did all those people stay?" asked Ell.

"Are there hotels for such an army of men?" asked Mary, suddenly interested.

"Cowboys sleep on the prairie and eat at their own outfit's chuck wagon," said Joe. But he didn't tell all he knew. For exam-ple, the only accommodations the cowboys really wanted were saloons, gambling houses, and brothels that were open all night. From the desire of these cowboys came the custom of rolling the chuck wagons of the various outfits downtown at night and park-ing them in front of the saloons to feed their carousing members.

It was near suppertime when the Irwins rode through "Texas Abilene" on the south side of the railroad tracks, where the longhorns were driven into stock pens to wait for sorting and shipping. Their Texas cowpunchers camped nearby. Both Will and Joe waved to the men meandering around their chuck wagons. The air was pungent with smells from the stock in the yards and the spicy foods simmering over cookfires. The air was dusty and flies buzzed everywhere. Some cowboys swaggered in and out of the Old Trail's End House facing the railroad tracks. This was a flat-roofed, two-story limestone building that had other saloons and gambling halls on the west side.

A cowboy standing on the boardwalk waved at the Irwin wagon.

"How do I get out of town, cowboy?" asked Joe, his lips pulled thin.

"Just keep going straight ahead past McCoy's Addition and you'll be out of town!"

"Good! Thanks a million!" Joe felt some better. He had read about Joseph McCoy. He was the man who originated the idea of driving cattle from Texas to the railroad in Kansas. The wagon lurched forward. Joe crossed his fingers and hoped that Mary and the children paid small attention to the ladies he saw who were talking and laughing farther along. He was so bent on moving quickly and finding a place to camp all night that he drove into the street along McCoy's Addition without seeing that it was completely blocked with household goods from the gray frame houses standing between saloons and dance halls. He had to pull to a halt fast. "What's this?" he yelled.

The answer came right away from a man who was obviously not a cattleman. The man had on a black suit and his thumbs were hooked inside his black suspenders, which lay against a starched, white shirt.

"This is McCoy's Addition, or better called the Devil's Half Acre! Pull up over there on the other side of the tracks and wait."

"I can't stay here!" Joe was offended and upset with this awkward delay. His wife and family were hanging out the wagon gawking at every passerby they could ogle.

The man in the black suit smiled and waved Joe on toward the tracks. "Stay overnight. It's safe here. Outside of town there are road agents, thieves, and robbers who scout for travelers the likes of you."

"See, Charlie! We could use that rifle you so gallantly gave away. You birdbrain!" Ell poked Charlie in the ribs.

"Yah, some thief will come after our stuff. We only have one gun to hold this gang of robbers off," added Frank, looking for a place to hide.

"Only a dumb jackass'd give their rifle to some Injuns," said Will, giving Charlie a dirty look.

Charlie hung his head, but he thought, they're a bunch of scaredy-cats. What could happen here to hurt us? There's cowboys everywhere for protection. It's a well-known fact that cattle drivers fight for fair play and justice.

Joe waved his arms and his face turned red. "Look, man, I have a wife and children—"

The man stepped off the boardwalk and came closer to the wagon. "Mayor Avery's my name. Carl Avery. Go on over the tracks. You can see the crossing from here. Keep your missus and little ones inside for the night."

"I'm not happy with this situation," said Joe, pounding his fist on the wagon's wooden seat to show his displeasure. "Someone should have told me to steer clear of this town—this, this Addition. Now I'm forced to camp in the middle of—wickedness." He sputtered with anger.

"I have explained why you are better off here tonight," said the man who called himself mayor. "By morning you can move on safely, as the bandits will be moving on to easier pickin's. We are fortunate to have plenty of cattlemen here during this year's purge. Oh, yes, there could be petty thieves taking furniture and clothing, or even the girls taking each other's clothing or satin sheets. You might hear gunshots, but it's safe over there, I guarantee. Have a good evening."

"Damn it!" Joe swore. He could not control his resentment even though he looked down on men who cussed in front of women and children. He could see no way out. He certainly didn't want to camp outside of town to be exposed to road agents and their ilk. Besides, it was getting late to look for a campsite.

"Water's fifty cents a gallon for as much as you want!" called the mayor. "Get it at the Abilene Oasis!"

"That's robbery!" yelled Joe.

Mary leaned out the wagon and said sweetly, "Thank you, Mr. Mayor. We'll camp right here and make the best of things. There'll be something to tell our grandchildren about the town of Abilene. And we can add that we met the mayor personally."

Mayor Avery waved. Joe drove to the crossing. When he finally stopped, he turned to Mary. "I swear I don't know what came over you. You spoke out and made yourself bold with little cause. Mayor Avery said for you and the children to stay inside."

"But we've already seen," she said, biting her lip.

The Irwin wagon was just north of Abilene proper. Here there were a couple dozen one-story frame houses, each with ten to twenty rooms. Between the houses were saloons, dance halls, and gambling rooms.

They ate a cold supper inside the wagon of salty smoked venison, milk that Will brought in from the cow, and some leftover biscuits. The children went to the end of the wagon to investigate a commotion across the road.

A couple men, not cowboys, carried furniture and bedding to a wagon beside the tracks. "Are they stealing?" asked Frank. No one answered, because without warning several shots rang out. Then pandemonium began. Frank ducked behind Mary's trunk. Cowboys and cattlemen ran down the road after the two men. One thief stumbled and fell, a clock rolled from his arms. Will hooted. Another shot, then two more. Frank was shaking.

"Aw, those shots are in the air," said Charlie, kneeling at the back of the wagon where he could see.

"That one man is still down," whispered Ell. "Is he dead?" She looked panicky, like she wanted to hide with Frank.

The crowd of cowboys converged and mingled and sent out shouts from the low buzz of voices. Then the cowboys moved away, leaving the street empty.

"Don't lean out. Keep your heads inside!" ordered Joe. He wondered what fate had led him here. He wished his wife and children would not stare so boldly at these women who seemed to be moving in and out of the saloons and dance halls, resigned to the ruination of their goods. The sprawling gray houses were dark beside the well-lighted saloons. The houses had never seen a whitewash. But Joe saw in the late afternoon light that they all had white lace curtains and the windows sparkled shiny clean.

Mary thought how much better were these houses than the soddy she was going to be calling home. Surely these places never had bedbugs nor fleas. She'd heard of the sheets with lace and the fine silks and fur pieces and brand-new high-button shoes. It took a roll of money to buy expensive furnishings and clothes. She pulled Ell back because she was leaning out of the tail of the wagon calling to girls as they passed.

"Where are you going?" Ell had called to a wiry, black-haired girl, who looked more Mexican than anything else.

"My friend," said the lean, dark girl, "in this place you go down like scummy water."

"Don't call those floozies over here," warned Joe. He saw that most of the girls stayed on the other side of the tracks, where the saloons and gambling houses were.

Frank crow-hopped his way from behind the trunk. "Some of the girls look about like Ell. Is this their home? Don't they have a ma or pa?"

Joe cleared his throat. He thought it was going to be hard to explain to a ten-year-old about the boardinghouse girls of Abilene, especially with Mary and Ell listening. "Son, these girls haven't the kind of home Ell has. These girls don't generally stay here permanent. They are looking for something better. But while waiting and looking they take a man's cash. Everyone has some hard-luck story and they expect trinkets of lace, or gold and silver, just for listening to their story."

"I know some stories," said Ell. Will glared at her for interrupting.

"These girls don't get attached to any one man, like Ell might one day," Joe said, hoping he was making some sense. "You see—they ain't looking to be married right off." The words were hard for Joe to put together. He wished the words would roll from his mouth like a full river in the spring. He saw Mary and the children with their faces toward him, their ears full of hearing.

"I'm not looking to be married either," said Ell, glaring at Will.

Joe scowled at his two oldest children and tried to go on explaining the best he could. "They don't use real names. They call themselves something fanciful, like 'Sweets' or 'Peaches.' They usually have some talent and can sing and dance and make their partner feel happy and waste a lot of a man's time."

Now Will, who sat cross-legged in the back of the wagon, put his chin in his hand, elbow on his leg, and listened attentively to see just how much his father would tell.

"It's said some take opium—they call it laudanum—to make the time go by, or spirits to make the time more pleasant, but I suspect most later on get married and settle down like everyone else. They probably try to keep their past a secret."

"Why would a girl do that?" asked Charlie. "If a girl can sing and dance, I'd think she'd be pleased to talk about it."

"Well, these—uh—dance hall girls are different," said Joe, taking a deep breath. He could feel the perspiration on his back and under his arms.

Mary thought he'd done very well and was about to tell him so, when he added a sentence. "The girls are what some call hussy, a jade, a dirty dove." Joe stood up and stretched. His explanation was over. He was not going to say more. He expected that if he went on, he'd say too much. Even so, he was prepared for Mary to ask him later how he knew this much. He wasn't going to discuss more of the seamy side of life with his family. He was a gentleman and showed them respect.

Joe had made the girls seem like performers to Charlie. He

listened to the fiddle music and singing and watched the lights that came across the tracks. It was like a circus and was as exciting as a medicine show. Charlie wanted to walk along the boardwalk and peek into each open door to see what caused the laughter and shouting he heard. "Ma, I could go across there and get water in the bucket."

"Oh, no, you can't! Neither can anyone else go across those tracks!" Mary was quick to say. "We have plenty of water in the barrel."

"If I go, you'll never know," smirked Will, teasing his mother.

"You do, I'll know," Mary said, slapping the comforters down so that Will and Joe and Charlie could sleep under the wagon. She moved boxes around so that she and Ell and Frank could sleep inside the wagon. "I'll unmend those two little holes in the wagon cover, so's to keep an eye on you," she said to Will. He laughed and winked.

For prudence's sake Joe divided the money he carried, giving Mary half. "God forbid either of us is robbed. But part of a loaf is better than none. You can divide yours with Frank and Ell. Sleep with it pinned on your undergarments. I'll divide some of mine between Will and Charlie."

Mary nodded and agreed. "Put your money in the inside watch pocket of your trousers. Then you and the boys sleep in your trousers."

Everything was quiet around the wagon, but Charlie could not sleep on account of the music coming from across the tracks. He sat up. The girls were in front of the saloons, or inside. The lights there were bright, mostly from coal-oil or kerosene lanterns. Joe snored. Will stirred.

Charlie whispered, "Let's go for a walk."

"If Ma found out, she'd kill me for letting you go over there," said Will, yawning.

"You said she'd never know," said Charlie.

The two boys sneaked across the track and stood around watching the cattle drivers go in and out of the saloon called Abilene Oasis. Charlie recognized Mayor Avery, the portly man in the black suit. "Good evening, sir," said Charlie. "Say, do you know the Splitlogs, three Injun brothers who brought a big herd of cattle here?"

The mayor looked quizzical. Then he brightened and his face shone as he moved under a lamp. "I never heard of that outfit." He brushed the flying moths away from his face. "But I heard something that'll put a couple of cartwheels in your pocket, right here at the Oasis in a couple of hours. So don't wander far."

"A couple of cartwheels!" repeated Will.

"A couple of hours? Much obliged," said Charlie, reaching out to shake the mayor's hand. The mayor turned and went inside the saloon. He was whistling.

Charlie stood on his toes trying to get a good look and at the same time listen to the piano music inside. He didn't recognize the tune but he found it catchy enough to hum.

Two girls, walking backward making eyes at the cowboys walking toward them, ran into Charlie and Will. "Pardon me," said the girl with long reddish hair and a brown wool cape around her shoulders.

"Excuse us," said Will, getting a sweet flowery smell of their perfume, which was more pleasant than the tangy odor of the stockyards.

"You cowboys need a drink?" She was blond with short curls and wore a man's black suit coat. Both girls had on rather short dresses of a flimsy flowered cotton. Like nightgowns, thought Charlie.

The blond opened her eyes wide and gave the two Irwin boys the once-over. "Red, you're as dizzy as a witch. Didn't you notice one of these cowboys is a baby. A kid, wet behind the ears!" She put her finger on Charlie's chest, making him blush.

"I'm not as young as you think," Charlie said. "I'm Charles Burton Irwin and this here is my big brother, William."

"Glad to meetcha. I'm Wild Honey and my friend is Red Stockings." She nodded but did not take the hand Charlie offered, so he pulled it back to his side. He thought the customs of Abilene were probably different from those he was used to.

Honey brought out a small, wooden box of thin cigars from her beaded reticule. She lighted one, striking the match on her fingernail.

"I'll buy some whiskey," said Will, feeling in his watch pocket for his father's money. He smiled and talked about shoeing horses and sawing hardwood as the four of them walked into the Oasis.

Charlie felt light-headed. Inside the saloon his bare feet seemed to barely skim the sawdust floor. The place was filled with noisy cowboys and cattlemen. Charlie wondered if anyone ever slept around here. Coal-oil lanterns were strung across the ceiling and over the bar. However, the corners of the huge room were in the dark. They edged their way through the crowd. Some bearded guy made a grab for Red, but she sidestepped.

Will looked confused. "Say, do I have to tip—pay anything under the table, so to speak?" he whispered, and wrinkled his forehead.

"Don't be a hick," sniffed Honey. "Get the bottle and let's get out of this stuffy place."

"I'm not a hick," said Will. "I feel like a nighttime hooty owl." He took the roll of greenbacks from his watch pocket and counted off two. The man at the bar took both. Honey's eyes were wide open the whole time Will had his father's money roll out.

"Come on, I'll show you where to put your tip, Cowboy," Honey murmured in his ear as she put her arm around his waist, her hand on his pocket. Will took a swig from the bottle and gave it to Honey. Charlie noticed that her teeth were yellow-brown. She cooed, "Sweet William, try a cigar. It's imported. A man looks sexy with one of these in his mouth. What do you think?"

Charlie was sure Will would roar laughing at that kind of simpy talk. But Will put one hand around Honey's waist and took the cigar with the other, giving it several puffs. His smile turned crooked and his face turned red and he coughed. Charlie thought it served him right. Will hunkered down like he was moving uphill. "You're a bear-cat!" he said. "My hands are sweaty and my heart's apounding."

"Oh yeah?" giggled Honey, her pink tongue traveling around her red lips.

"You have many cowboys as friends?" Red asked Charlie. She combed her long reddish hair. Playfully she ran the comb through Charlie's hair a couple of times. The stroke of the comb turned his brain to mush, his stomach to aching, his legs to noodles.

"Hey, stop that!" said Charlie, pulling himself together. "I can comb my own hair when it needs it."

"Yes, I'd say I've known a lot of cowboys. If you know what I mean." Red answered her own question.

"Like that one back there in the saloon? Is he someone special?" said Will, teasing.

"That's no cowboy. He was just funnin'. When times is slow he gets us business. He's an—an agent. Like when the hog drivers come in the fall. They don't have so much money, being paid less than a dollar a day, and they don't have much comfort, sleeping on the ground rain or dry. Hog drivers want to drink, shoot out windows, and race. They have to be told what we're here for."

Charlie asked, "What are you here for?" The minute he asked he wished he hadn't. All eyes turned on him. He felt like a clock whose time had run out.

Red's mouth turned down and her face looked flinty hard. "That guy in there is hired by Mattie Silks to see we serve the customers."

That information was meaningless. Charlie shut up. He wanted to know who this Mattie Silks was, but he didn't want Red to think of him as an ignoramus kid. He began to hum with the music coming from the dance hall two doors away, "Sweet Adeline," and fight off the black flies.

"You sing all right," said Red, her mouth lifting at the corners.

"I was born in 1875. My birthday is August fourteenth."

She gasped and grabbed for the whiskey bottle.

Charlie felt a delicious, undefinable longing somewhere in his midsection. He found that he didn't have to drink when he raised the bottle to his lips and no one knew the difference. Will and Honey whispered and giggled and nuzzled close to each other.

"Let's go to the train depot and lay on the benches," said Honey, nipping at Will's earlobe. Little gusts of wind blew the flies away.

"I wouldn't mind sitting on one," piped Charlie.

"Let's go round to the other side," purred Honey meaningfully.

"Charlie, you wait here," said Will. "Don't follow or I'll punch your teeth out. And don't get any ideas."

"How long you gonna be?" asked Charlie. A film of perspiration broke out on the palms of his hands. He felt dizzy. He wanted to go back to the wagon, but also he wanted to stay a little longer. Will didn't answer his question.

Honey patted Charlie's arm. "Don't do anything racy, Chuck." She winked at Red, who was pouting, then put her arm around Will's waist and pulled him into the shadows.

A prestorm stillness was in the air. Charlie looked around. "I wonder when Will's coming back?" There was a sudden splatter of raindrops on the boards. Red got up and moved with Charlie close to the side of the depot under the overhang. In one jagged flash of bright, white lightning he saw that her face was pale, thin, and pimply. He thought, she doesn't get enough to eat. She shivered and he moved close and put his arm around her shoulders.

"Hey!" called Will.

Charlie leaped away from Red as if he'd felt a spark from a bonfire. Red laughed.

Will's shirttail hung out and Honey's hair was wet and blowing. "We'd better get back," said Will. He cuffed Charlie under the chin. Will looked at Honey and said, "I'll stop by again when I get the cattle going on my ranch."

Charlie shook Red's hand and said, "So long."

The rain had stopped and Charlie heard the dance hall music, felt the dampness of the boards on his bare feet, and smelled the overpowering odor from the stockyards. Will tucked his shirt into his pants. They were halfway across the railroad tracks before Charlie broke the silence. "How was it?"

"What?" said Will.

"You know—with Honey?"

Will grinned and hit Charlie under the chin again.

Charlie felt a pulling spasm inside. He looked ahead at the wagon. Everything there was quiet. The moon came out from behind a cloud and made the wagon's canvas top glisten snow white.

"Wasn't so much. No better'n riding a horse full tilt across the prairie and coming back, out of breath and spent."

Charlie thought of that feeling, pure exhilaration, and it made him excited.

Will laughed softly and put his hand on Charlie's shoulder. Suddenly he stopped and put his hands in his pockets. He cried, "I've been robbed!"

"Sshh! You want to wake everyone?" said Charlie.

"I don't have the money Pa gave me. He'll tan my hide!"

Charlie grabbed Will and made him hunker down in the wet weeds. "I saw Honey eyeing your roll of money in the Oasis. I thought you noticed."

"Oh, geez, I feel terrible," moaned Will.

Charlie took out his roll of money. "Keep this in case I don't get back until daylight. Think of something to tell Pa."

"What are you going to do?" asked Will.

"I'm not sure. You crawl under the wagon and into your blankets. I'll get Pa's money." Charlie got up and walked through the weeds back to the tracks. He stopped halfway and looked back. Will was out of sight. He sighed and hitched up his damp shotguns. He had no idea what he was going to do. When he got to the saloons he looked for the mayor and found him in the Oasis.

"A girl called Wild Honey took my brother's roll of dollar bills. Ten of 'em. They belong to my pa."

Avery could see Charlie was just a barefoot kid. "Remember I said there was money to be made. Come with me, cowboy." They went into the Oasis. Avery said, "Your money's here!"

Charlie saw no money. He blinked so his eyes would water and he could see better in the smoky lantern light.

A ring was drawn in the sawdust about ten feet in diameter. There were four or five men standing at the circumference of the ring. "Get over there with those other cowboys and wait for my instructions," said Avery.

Charlie didn't know what this was all about. He stood on the edge of the circle and looked at some others who were doing the same. They looked like ordinary cowboys to Charlie. He rubbed his sweaty hands off on his shirt. Then he saw a man coming from the back of the saloon with a big, black, cast-iron frying pan filled with silver dollars. The man held the skillet with his two hands wrapped in dishcloths.

"Get down on one knee!" called Avery, "and when I give the word, reach for the cartwheels. Keep feet behind the ring!"

Charlie saw that the pan of cartwheels was going to be dumped into the circle. He dug his toes into the sawdust. He was sure he could grab ten. That was all he needed. He let his pent-up air go out just as the man spilled the dollars in the sawdust. The room was quiet. Charlie knew there was a wide band of men behind him waiting and watching to see who could grab the most coins.

"Make your bets!" Avery yelled. "Each contestant has a number."

Charlie felt someone pin a cardboard on his back and whisper in his ear, "Four."

Avery hollered, "One, two, three! On your mark! It's yours, cowboys! Go to it! Now!"

Charlie could feel his heart pounding and smell the sawdust in front of his nose. The sawdust smelled scorched, like it came fresh from a burn pile at a mill. He pushed for the pile of several coins lying together. His hand closed, then he let go with a startled cry. The others were hollering and yelling. One cowboy was holding his hands close against his chest and whimpering. Charlie looked at his own hands, one had the outline of a dollar in white and it stung as if he'd been hit with a dozen rattlers. The silver was hot, as though it had been in a forge.

"Go after it!" someone yelled. "Shovel up those there cart-wheels!" "Grab in there, number three!" "I'm bettin' on ya', number one!"

Charlie tried again, using his left hand, thinking that the metal would be cooled some. He let out an awful yowl. The coins hadn't cooled much. He could never hold one coin long enough to claim it as his own. He tried scooting one, but that was not in the rules and Avery thumped him on the back with a fist. Avery's face was against his. "Be a sport!" Avery yelled. "The money's yours for the taking!" Charlie smelled whiskey on the mayor's breath and saw the bottle in his hand.

The tips of Charlie's fingers were sore. He spit on one hand and then the other. This helped some. Avery's face was against his again. Charlie saw the whiskey bottle. He heard laughter above him. Never in his life had he heard of this kind of enter-tainment. The excitement he'd first felt had gone sour. He felt bitter anger. He wanted to double his fists and punch in the face of Mayor Avery. Charlie got to his feet and lurched forward mak-ing certain his toes never went beyond the drawn ring in the sawdust. He grabbed for Avery's bottle, brought it over the ring with one hand and poured the contents on a dozen coins nearest him. They sizzled and steam formed down close around them, smelling like alcohol. A couple cowboys rolled into the ring over top of Charlie trying to scrabble their aching hands toward the cooler, wet coins. The wet sawdust was pressed against Charlie's shirt and face. His back felt as though it would break with the press of bodies. He could not turn his neck because someone had a leg clamped over it. He tried not to breath wood chips into his lungs. He prayed this game would end. Then he heard a shot from a pistol nearby.

"It's over, cowboys!" cried the Mayor. "We've had our fun! What's directly under you is yours if you can handle it! Get up!"

Charlie mustered all his strength, rolled over and with aching hands scooped eight coins into his pocket and grabbed for two more, but lost them to someone else. A man with a rake pulled the remaining coins to one side, shoveled them into a coal bucket.

"Here's your extra money! Don't ever say Mayor Avery ain't fair!" Avery gave each player two cartwheels from his own pocket. Charlie was declared the all-time winner. "Number four is top man! No one has ever had the guts to cool off his pile of cartwheels with my whiskey! This man is a thinker!" Then aside to Charlie he said, "Man, you look like a pup. They're taking cowboys young these days. You lose your boots playing cards?"

The men close by hooted and hollered and pointed to Charlie's bare feet.

Charlie didn't reply. He was sucking his fingers to take some of the heat out. He heard the comments and laughter before he found an opportunity to move out to the boardwalk for some air. He spread cool, damp, rain-laid dust on his burning hands. That eased the pain some. He drew in a lungful of clean, fresh air. He was going to have a hard time keeping his pants up where they belonged with ten silver dollars in his front pockets. The cook from a nearby chuck wagon had his head back chuckling to the sky as Charlie walked by. "Hey, you the kid what snookered Avery out of a handful of cartwheels?"

Charlie nodded.

"Hey, better let me give you some rope to tie up your pants. You got some weight in them there pockets." He cut two pieces of clothesline rope and attached them to the loops around Charlie's waist and made him a quick pair of suspenders.

"Much obliged," said Charlie, stepping down from the boardwalk and hurrying across the tracks, thinking how friendly some people were.

Back at the wagon he rolled under the blankets next to Will, who smelled like sour mash. Joe sleepily opened one eye and told Charlie to keep covered so he wouldn't catch cold in the damp, rainy air.

Charlie turned on his stomach and put his hands out in front into the cooling mud just outside the wagon wheel. Sleep came fast.

SIX

Nicodemus

The cookpot and dishes were washed and packed into the wagon. Charlie rummaged around in the pewter spoons trying to look busy until he found the can of venison grease. He rubbed some on the palms of his hands to keep the hardened, burnt flesh soft while new skin formed underneath.

Will milked the cow and put the fresh can of whole milk inside the wagon out of the sun. "We ought to cool it in the creek awhile," he mumbled. But no one was interested in waiting longer to be on the road.

Mary and Joe studied the black and white map printed in the back of one of Joe's pamphlets extolling the virtues of Kansas farmland. Joe said, "If we continue along this way, due west, we'll hit Fort Hays. That place is like Abilene, with cattlemen coming in daily with herds to be railroaded to the East."

"Well, then, do like I say," said Mary. "Follow the Solomon River northwest and when it splits stay with the southern fork."

Joe rubbed his eyes and folded the pamphlet. "We go as far as Salina today. So we cross the Solomon by bridge. Tomorrow we move northwest through farms and prairie and I pray there are wagon roads between the small settlements." He pulled his wife close to himself and looked at her contentedly, then gave her a quick kiss on the forehead. Joe did not believe in demonstrations of fondness in front of children. "This will be new land to me."

Charlie clenched his fists for courage and interrupted. "Pa, Ma, promise to hold your tempers until Will tells about the money he had for safekeeping?"

Joe made a growling sound in his throat.

Mary quickly spoke. "Don't say anything until you hear him out." She put a hand on Charlie's rope suspenders and nodded approval.

Joe closed his mouth.

Will looked at Charlie and scowled. He swallowed and said, "Did you feel the wind last night? It came just before the rain."

Joe's mouth was pulled taut into a fine line. He shook his head, indicating he didn't feel any wind last night. Mary kept a hand over her mouth.

"Well, it woke me and I began to worry about all that money Charlie and I were responsible for. I got up to make sure Charlie and I still had it. I felt in Charlie's pocket and sure enough there was his roll. I felt in mine and I had a roll the same size. I thought to be on the safe side I should count the money. And you wouldn't believe how strong the wind was. It blew all ten of my one-dollar bills all over the prairie before I could get them rolled up and into my pocket. Jeez, I knew you'd thrash me alive if I didn't figure out something before morning. So I figured I was in deep trouble." He looked at his feet and swallowed again.

Mary's mouth fell open. Charlie rolled his eyes skyward and he crossed his second finger over his index finger on his right hand.

"Well, when I was a little kid I had a trick for getting money out of the cracks between the boards in a walk. I put gum on the end of a stick. I scraped some wax off the top of one of Ma's jam jars, put it on the end of a stick, and here's what I brought back for you." Will looked out toward the wooden boardwalk across the tracks, then dumped ten cartwheels from his pockets at Joe's feet.

Charlie bit his lip and kept the backs of his hands toward his parents.

Joe was dumbfounded. "If you hadn't been so careless you'd still have those greenbacks. I never heard of anyone using wax to pick up money." Joe bent to look at the coins.

Charlie prayed his father would not pick up the coins. His prayer was answered when Ell scooped them into her apron and squealed with delight. "Will! Could I try? Could we look for more? Oh, Pa, please!"

Charlie put his aching hands inside his pockets. Joe shook his head. Mary shook her head and said, "Heavens, no! It's time to move on. There's no time to be greedy. Will retrieved his father's money and more. I for one am proud of him." Her face shone as she smiled at Will.

Charlie felt his aching fists relax. His breathing was easier. He heard Will sigh.

Mary rested her head on Joe's shoulder, feeling the roughness of his river-washed, unironed muslin shirt. "I feel like a true pioneer this day," she said. Charlie and Will climbed to the wagon's seat. Will held the reins, ready to move. Will called, "Pa, you want to ride Flame or hitch him to the wagon and give one of the workers a change of pace?"

Joe shook his head. "Will, you know better. You don't break up a good pair of workhorses. Suzie and Jed work best as a team. Split 'em and we'll have nothing but trouble. I'll ride Flame until noon anyways. Your ma and I talked of going to Salina, then heading off northwest. New country and it might be interesting. We'll see how other settlers do with cattle and crops."

"I'm ready," said Will.

"Giddap!" he called to the team.

The Irwins left Abilene. The wagon scattered half a dozen dogs that had come around to sniff and survey and Charlie was reminded of Old Squirt. Will began telling Charlie about the Kansas land and cattle raising.

Mary, sitting inside the wagon, watched her eldest talking serious, using his hands to make a point. She was struck with the notion that Will was no longer a child. He was nearly as large as Joe, although his coloring was sallow and pale. She stared at his face and was surprised to see a shifting in the eyes from her angle of view, not the same concern Joe possessed, not the deep interest in the big picture of a subject. Will would never be a thinker. She thought, he is destined to be a doer, and a great one for talking with no concern for consequences.

The wagon rattled on the rackety wooden bridge over the Solomon River, which was a shallow tannish stream flowing between banks fringed with willows ranging from small shrubs to moderately large trees. The willows were like green silhouettes, standing out against the sere prairie, making the curved pattern of the river visible for miles.

At noon Will stopped the wagon west of Salina against a wind-sheltered bluff. Ell found the cream-white rock rich in fossils of snails and tiny, prehistoric fishes.

Joe and Will were interested in staring at the rich wheat fields, still yellow-green and laid low by wind, then altogether moving upright, then pushed down, then straight up, then down.

Charlie felt a sense of awe and wonder, especially when they forded the Saline River. He thought, maybe no one has ever forded this water in this particular place since the world began.

Two days later near Sylvan Grove, Ell told Joe, who was driving, to stop the wagon. She pointed to a strange-looking bird she'd watched fly from cottonwood to cottonwood tree. It was big and black, about the size of a wild turkey. Charlie laughed because it looked like a carnival clown with wide stripes of red and white on its face. Its bill was yellow and its neck was longer than it seemed right for the size of its head. While Ell was pointing, the bird began tapping on a dead cottonwood trunk. Its head hammered the beak so that the sound was like an iron mallet on an anvil. When it flew off it appeared awkward and not sure of itself. The huge wings *whooshed* and beat the air. Charlie was amazed at the amount of sawdust and wood chips the bird left at the base of the rotten tree. His hands still hurt.

Joe said, "I imagine we'll see more unusual sights as we go West. Maybe that bird doesn't even have a name yet. There's probably some plants that haven't been named either."

They passed settlers' farms. Some were fenced with posts that were columns of split rock. They were the same off-white color as the limestone bluffs. Some posts had a brown streak running down through the stone, which was the color of rust. Barbed wire was fastened in tiny wedges in the stone. "If wood is scarce, man makes something else to take its place," said Joe. "I guess quarrying them rock posts ain't easy. Looks like a six-foot post'd weight near 400 pounds."

"How'd you suppose men come by them?" asked Charlie, holding his hands in his pockets.

"I suppose they use iron bits and wedges. Looks like the stone breaks clean. That first farmer to think of stone fence posts was mighty enterprising," said Joe.

"Look there! See the stone hill? Looks like someone has chopped it out pretty good," said Charlie.

"Well, I'll be!" exclaimed Will. "I'd'a gone right past and never seen that."

They forded the Saline River again and found some of the places they passed were more than wagon roads crossing; they were clusters of farms and a small general store next to the road. These infant towns had names liké Lucas, Waldo, Paradise, Natoma, and Plainville. Often now Charlie pointed out skulls and bones of long-dead buffalo in the bluestem grass.

Joe explained to his children, "I should guess there were hundreds of men on these here plains after the Civil War. Some of the buffalo hunting was for sport, but there were others who took to trading for buffalo hides. Hides were better'n money. These men went in groups of a dozen or more with wagons and horses. They only camped where a big herd would pass. The ones that were good marksmen did the killing and the others took off the hides. Hides were made into bundles and cured back in camp, like we cured that deer hide. Once I heard that Bill Cody was hired by the Kansas and Pacific Railroad to hunt buffalo to feed the men who were laying them tracks."

Will let Charlie ride Flame and sat on the wagon seat beside his pa. "Remember that there buffalo skinner came to the smithery a couple'a years back?" asked Will. "He made out that skinning those beasts wasn't easy."

"I don't remember that," said Charlie, riding close to the wagon so he wouldn't miss anything. His hands were still pink on the palms, but they no longer were crusty and throbbing. He held the reins lightly.

"Punks like you were in school," said Will. "That buffalo skinner said sometimes he'd have to finish killing an animal with his knife 'cause it only had a broken leg from a stray bullet. Geez, that man's clothes were stiff with dried blood and guts!"

"Will, that's awful!" cried Ell, pretending she was offended by her brother's description.

"He ate only buffalo meat and hardtack and drank coffee laced with plenty of grounds. He slept in the same clothes and never shaved nor cut his hair. He looked like he'd been pushed out of jail 'cause he wasn't worth the keep," said Will.

"I gave him some of that leftover Sloan's Liniment on account of the bad bite, probably a blowfly, on his lip. Just getting close to him was a chore. He stunk something fierce," said Joe.

Mary put her hand to her nose.

"Don't worry, Ma," said Frank. "I'm not going to be a buffalo hunter."

They crossed the muddy Solomon River again, but it was

much more shallow here and there was no bridge. After the crossing Charlie lay on the floor of the wagon and stared at the swaying white canvas top. He listened to the wind and churning of the wagon wheels. His hands had healed. But when he was not doing anything, he kept in his fists a pad of raw wool he'd found in Ell's medicine box.

At night the family camped close to the rails. Charlie was lulled to sleep by the persistent song of the scalloping telegraph wires that followed the rails.

The wagon rolled along the slick mud ruts during thunderstorms and gentle rains and dried and dusty grooves when the days turned to scorchers in the treeless prairie.

Between Ell and her three brothers there existed a loose relationship. Will was for the most part condescending to Ell and his brothers. Frank looked up to the others, but never in a worshipful manner. Charlie had a fondness for all, which turned once in a while to unexpected sentiment. He was unalterably loyal to his sister and brothers and to his mother and father.

The day after the second crossing of the Solomon the Irwin wagon moved over low bluffs and dunes, keeping in sight of wagon tracks and telegraph lines. A mile ahead were a group of low buildings that looked like a small farming town. Joe drove the wagon through the town slowly so not to stir up dust. Mary waved to several women who sat in homemade-looking wooden chairs in front yards. A bandanna was tied around one woman's head. They all wore wide aprons that covered the entire front of their cotton dresses. Some were barefoot, others wore leather moccasins or sandals with the front cut open so toes were exposed.

Charlie watched from the back of the wagon. He pointed, "Ma, lookee there, darkies. See, Pa? What is this place?"

A youngster dressed in a pair of faded and patched overalls looked out from the doorway of a squat, stone hut. "This here is Nicodemus! Our church has a pumper organ!" The boy ran behind the wagon.

"I know what an organ is!" yelled Charlie, waving his hands.

The boy was about ten, Frank's age. "If you all want to picnic, the schoolyard is south a ways. Turn here; see the shade trees ahead?"

"Thanks!" called Charlie. "Ma! Should we stop? It's Nicodemus! The colorful town!"

"Why, this is an Exoduster place!" said Joe. He pulled the

wagon beside the creek close to the one-room, gray-white lime-stone schoolhouse. He let the horses and cow nibble the sweet grass laced with dandelions and drink creek water.

"That's the second time I've heard that word. What is an Exoduster?" asked Mary.

Joe said, "As I recall, a group of ex-slaves came into western Kansas. They built three towns. Hill City was one. Nicodemus the other. I can't recall the third—something biblical. These people from the South were so excited about a place of their own that they spent life savings on railroad fares and land patent fees. In the end they had nothing left to spend on home-building materials. They made dugouts or burrows, some used blocks of lime-stone from their fields. They burn sunflower stalks for heat. They're mainly farmers, but I heard there was some preachers and lawyers."

"Must be pretty smart to build three towns," said Charlie. "This is where the Splitlogs were to visit."

"I'd like to see those Injuns for myself," said Will.

Ell's hands were sweaty and she felt a tingling in the pit of her stomach. "Let's have our noon meal here," she said. "Maybe the Injuns are waiting for us. Something exciting might happen. I can feel it."

"Are there any Injuns in town?" Charlie asked the boy.

"Not that I know about this day," he said. "But I know Injuns, yes, sir."

Ell spread the quilt. In a few moments Mary found dry twigs and had water boiling over a stone fire pit. She put dried venison and sliced potatoes in the boiling water.

The boy stood at the back of the wagon sniffing the delicious cooking smell. "Hey!" he called softly, but clearly. "I could race you two." He looked at Frank and Charlie. "I'm Zach."

Charlie introduced himself and Frank, then drew a line in the dust with his bare toe. "This is the start. We'll go around the schoolhouse three times. The loser eats last."

Zach's face brightened; he wanted to ask if the winner ate first, but he'd already surprised himself with a flash of boldness. After the second time around Zach slowed and panted, "My side aches."

"Bend over and bite your knees," Ell suggested.

Zach bent double and the pain subsided. The three boys dropped to the warm grass. Mary and Ell brought them plates of meat and potatoes and each a spoon. Zach smiled and bowed his head quietly.

When no one spoke, he said, "We all give our thanks to You, Lord, for this here 'licious slumgullion." Then his head popped up and he said, "My ma says it's growin' pains." He pointed to his side.

"She's probably right," said Ell. "You go to school here?"

"Yes, ma'am, and to picnics." He turned to Charlie and Frank. "Man, you should see the watermelons and barbecues. Your ma and pa square dance?"

"Of course," said Frank.

"We all do if there's some fiddle music," added Charlie. "You, too?"

Zach laughed. "Fiddle music and square dancing makes us happy as a horse in spring pasture." He liked these white folks. "If you ever go up to Tindall Hill, you can get enough gooseberries for a pie."

"I like pie," said Frank.

"I can pick berries. We had wild blackberries back in Missouri," said Charlie. "You got a horse?"

"You see many horses on these streets, mister?" asked Zach.

"None, 'cept ours," said Charlie.

"Well, everyone has a horse, but it's out in the fields." Then he hung his head and rolled his eyes up to see if anyone was still looking for him. " 'Cept ours. It's standing in the shed waiting for my pa."

"Where's he?" asked Frank.

"Want to come to my place?" asked Zach, standing up. "You can see him and my ma."

"Huh-uh," said Frank. "I'll come if Charlie does."

"Not much else to do," said Charlie. Will and Joe were discussing where they were going to spend the night, and their mother was on the quilt, resting with closed eyes.

Charlie told Ell where they'd decided to go. She looked around and thought of reading for a while, then on impulse said, "Mind if I come, too?"

"Oh, no," said Zach. "Ma likes company. I'm Zach Fletcher."

"I'm Ell Irwin. I guess you know my little brothers."

"We're friends," Zach said, grinning broadly, so his teeth seemed like bright stars against a black night sky.

Inside the stone hut was one room containing a couple of wooden chairs, a table and stove, and a large iron bed. Charlie wrinkled his nose against the strong musty odor. Mrs. Fletcher was pressing prairie flowers in a wooden frame lined with blotting paper.

"I said to Zach this morning that this day, with white lamb clouds against the bright blue, was for adventure," she said. "You are friends of Zach's and welcome in our home." She saw Ell staring at the bed. "Yes, daughter, we all sleep in that there bed. That's Mr. Fletcher. Ever since he's worked on the town's church, he's been too tired to get out of the bed."

"How long does he need to get rested?" asked Charlie.

"Child, only the Lord knows. Mr. Fletcher had so much energy and enthusiasm, but since the town isn't growing and doesn't need a carpenter, or stone mason, Mr. Fletcher just laid down for a rest." Tears were in her eyes. "The Reverend Roundtree, he preaches at our church, has been here persuading Mr. Fletcher to get up out of that bed. But he hasn't budged."

"Do you feed him proper?" asked Charlie.

The man was curled in the middle of the bed. He was a bag of bones on the snow-white, flannel sheets. His brown eyes sunk deep into his head and his mouth looked shriveled like a plum hung on the tree too long in scorching sun.

It's become small from nothing to eat, thought Charlie.

Mrs. Fletcher looked at Charlie with large, sad eyes. She patted her glossy, kinky black hair and sighed. "Son, there has not been anything in the minds of the good people of this town that has not been tried. The Reverend comes once a week and reads my man passages from the Good Book. These same words my man once read by hisself."

"Maybe he read too much. Sometimes when I read, my head aches," said Frank with a sigh. Ell hit Frank in the side with her elbow to keep him quiet.

"Don't hit me!" cried Frank. "I'll tell Ma you hurt me."

Ell tiptoed closer to the bed.

Frank was breathing hard and making loud whimpering sounds.

Charlie tried to shush Frank.

"I'll tell on Ell if I want," sniffled Frank. "And I'll tell about you and Will going across them tracks at Abilene."

Charlie's mouth flew open.

"I saw you leaving but I couldn't stay awake to see you come back."

Charlie spoke between his teeth, barely moving his lips. "Don't be a tattletale. Mind your own business and someday you'll grow up in one piece."

Mrs. Fletcher got up and stood between the boys. "Do you

know how lucky you are to have a brother, each of you? The Lord sent you here and you're goin' make the most of it."

Ell looked away from Mr. Fletcher, who was staring at the whitewashed stone wall. "You sound just like our ma."

"God bless her, then," said Mrs. Fletcher. "She'll raise you right."

"The Reverend?" asked Zach. "Do you know him?"

"No," said Ell.

"He has a brand on one side of his face. When you look at him, it's the first thing you see. He got it because his master was mad. The master's son taught the Reverend to read and write. The master didn't want no *nigger* of his to know what he knew."

"Did he run away?" asked Charlie.

"Must have to get here," said Zach. "He teaches us at the school. Even the granmommies and granpoppies go to learn to read 'n' write."

"I taught first graders," said Ell. "During spelling bees I helped older folks with their writing."

Both Zach and Mrs. Fletcher looked up at Ell with respect.

"Land sakes, you're but a child yourself. Some of our folks would light up to see someone as pretty as yourself teaching 'em. Landsakes alive!"

Ell smiled, enjoyed the flattery, then went back to look at Mr. Fletcher curled in a tight fetal ball.

Mrs. Fletcher showed Charlie and Frank the kinds of flowers she put in the flower press. "I make pictures with flowers. Put them between waxed paper and iron over with a warm flatiron." She pointed to some of her pictures on the wall behind the kitchen table. There were wild daisy, goldenrod, columbine, prairie phlox, clover, primrose, morning glory, and verbena.

"He's not sick, just tired. His nerves are worn out," Mrs. Fletcher said again, nodding to Ell, who had her hand on Mr. Fletcher's forehead.

Ell came back beside Mrs. Fletcher. "Ma'am, my grandma knew about healing with herbs and all kinds of magic. She taught me some."

"She's a teacher?" asked Zach.

"Yes, in a way. She was known as the lady doctor."

"Daughter, if it's witchcraft and conjur medicine, it's been tried, besides both Baptist and Methodist praying and laying on o' hands."

"But," insisted Ell, "a growed man staying in bed when it's

daylight, that's not right. Something's wrong."

Zach started punching Frank in a friendly manner. "My pa used to show me how boxers punch."

Frank crossed his arms across his chest for protection and said, "He ain't doing that now."

Mr. Fletcher had not made a move since the three Irwin children came into the one room hut.

"Naw, you heard Ma. His brain stopped working when his nerves broke down, so all the rest of him quit." Zach's eyes fell to the floor and his bottom lip quivered. "He's a good pa. He jus' worked too hard on our church."

One look at Zach caused Charlie to feel sad. "Maybe I could sing for him," Charlie said. "My singing makes my pa laugh."

Charlie hesitated a second or two and when no one said "don't," he sang several songs and danced a little jig.

Mrs. Fletcher smiled, but Mr. Fletcher didn't move, not even to swat the fly crawling on his scrawny neck.

"I ate with these here folks," said Zach. "They had the best slumgullion." He began to describe what he had to eat and his ma's eyes grew round.

"You askéd my boy to sit with you and eat?" She patted Ell's hand. "I'll show you how to make a flower press for yourself."

"I'd like—I'd want to try," said Ell, thinking hard what Grandma Malinda would do or say in this same situation. Then she decided she'd move straight forward. "Let's try to get Mr. Fletcher up on his feet. He has no fever and his heartbeat is strong. He needs nourishment and something to jolt his mind into action."

"Oh, daughter, if we only could. I'd do anything. You talk like a healing woman, but you look so young. Like you'd faint at the sight of blood and the smell of sickness."

"I don't, honest." Ell did not say that she'd gone on many house calls with Grandma Malinda and held torn flesh so that the stitches would hold the sides together without a pucker and leave little scarring. She did not say that she had seen birthing and broken bones pierce through the flesh and heard the screams of pain. She didn't say that she had made conjur tea and poultices and salves and had wrapped bandages tightly on sprained ankles. "I could make sassafras tea, but it needs strength, so if you have dried hollyhock roots and horseradish roots to add, I can say some words, and if the boys go outside to gather sticks and trash for the fire, you and me could concentrate."

Mrs. Fletcher looked skeptical, but she said, "Shoo, now boys, you heard this here daughter. We're goin' work something out. Shoo!"

The front door screen slammed three times as the boys went out one by one.

"I'll get my dried roots out here and you can pick what you want. I'll try anything, like I said, even from the medicine of sodbusters." Mrs. Fletcher rolled her eyes toward the ceiling and smiled to herself. "Your folks are sodbusters, ain't they?" she asked apologetically.

"Huh-uh," said Ell, now more interested in stirring the mixture in the black iron kettle on the top of the wood stove.

Mrs. Fletcher piled in kindling, getting a good blaze.

Ell mumbled words she'd learned from Grandma Malinda. She tried hard to think of each conjur line, wanting it just right.

"Oh, Lord, stay with us," murmured Mrs. Fletcher, "this daughter is so young in body, but old in mind. She knows life is not easy. Put Your hand on her arm. Guide her. Hear? You guide her. Keep Your Brother Satan out. This here is no Black Magic. Lord stay with us."

Ell heard and the corner of her mouth creased into a pleased smile. She sang her words softly, bending close to the supine form of Mr. Fletcher, looking for any movement. "Oh, body find the mind! Bring out the thoughts, share your voice! Come together! Closer! Closer!"

The boys came back inside the house with some flat limestone plates and smooth sticks. "Ma, you could use these thin rocks for a flower press, maybe frame them with these sticks if they was split just right," said Zach excitedly.

"Shhh!" said Mrs. Fletcher, then in a whisper she told the three boys to sit on the floor against the wall opposite the bed and be still as a hole in the ground. Charlie recognized the smell of sassafras and thyme and the head-clearing horseradish. Still whispering, Mrs. Fletcher said, "One whiff of that delicious aroma and Mr. Fletcher'll sit up by hisself. Watch, watch, watch."

Ell decanted clear hot brown liquid into a tin cup and brought it close so that Mr. Fletcher could smell. His eyes rolled under the opaque lids. Ell held her breath. His head moved. It moved slowly. Ell thought her eyes were seeing things not true. She looked at Mrs. Fletcher, who had stopped chanting with her arms held in midair over her head. Mr. Fletcher's head moved back and forth. Ell dipped her finger in the deep brown tea and dabbed it on his thin purple lips. A noise barely audible came from Mr. Fletcher's gaunt chest. Ell dabbed more strong tea on his lips so that some ran down the corner of his mouth and made a brown stain under his ear.

"Drink," Ell urged. "Try, please. Drink. You will feel refreshed as a bear coming out of hibernation."

"No, no," Mr. Fletcher's voice called from the center of his chest cavity.

"It could make you feel good."

"No, no."

Mrs. Fletcher let her aching arms down to her sides, tears streamed down her face. "Sassafras tea was once your favorite. Come back to us. Get out of the bed. We gather around you. Life is just so long. Don't throw it out. Find yourself and come back."

"No, no." Mr. Fletcher's voice sounded like a clock with a broken spring.

Mrs. Fletcher pulled back the quilt, then the soft flannel sheet, and held her man's head up. Something dropped with the quilt, which made Charlie look up. It sounded like a piece of stovewood. Charlie couldn't understand stovewood in the bed with an ailing man. He looked beside Mr. Fletcher on the white flannel. His eyes widened. He blinked, looked again. For certain, there on the bed, close beside Mr. Fletcher, was the Henry rifle he'd lent to Matt Splitlog. Charlie's Henry rifle!

Ell was on the other side holding the tin cup to Mr. Fletcher's lips. He seemed to be drinking, but his eyes were closed, not seeing what was happening in the hut.

"No one can expect miracles," said Mrs. Fletcher, wiping the tears with the back of her hand. Her black face had a sheen. The temperature in the stone hut was now ten degrees higher than outside. The fire in the stove flickered strongly.

Frank and Zach were sitting limply against the wall rolling an aggie marble back and forth to each other.

Charlie felt a shiver move up his spine. He was surprised that in this heat his hands seemed cold and stiff. He willed them to move. He forced his feet to walk close to the bed and reach ever so slowly for the rifle. It was his rifle!

All the while Mrs. Fletcher was singing revival songs and Ell was singsonging magic words, the healing medicine words she'd learned from Grandma Malinda. Ell's eyes were closed. Her hands were on Mr. Fletcher's arms, rubbing them back to life.

The blue-black barrel was in Charlie's hands; he felt the plate on the butt and his heart beat in his throat.

"This is mine," he said clearly.

Mr. Fletcher moved out of Ell's grasp and out of bed so fast that Charlie bumped and stumbled toward the door, then ran against the screen door. Outside Charlie tripped on the pile of sunflower stems the boys had gathered for the stove. The safety was pushed and Charlie blundered into the side of the stone hut. The gun went off.

Mr. Fletcher yelled louder than any Indian *kiyi*ing on the warpath. "You're shot dead!"

Charlie wondered how a man could sleep with a loaded gun in his bed! He grabbed the gun tighter and ran to the back of the hut. Mr. Fletcher was right behind him wobbling and stumbling.

Mrs. Fletcher was in the doorway. "Glory hallelujah! Glory hallelujah!" she hollered. "My man's on his feet! Mr. Fletcher's running! Praise the Lord!"

Frank and Zach squeezed out around Mrs. Fletcher and went out the screen door. They chased after Charlie, who was running headlong toward the back shed. Inside was an old workhorse. Charlie stood panting against the wall, trying to pull the door shut behind him. He heard the footsteps coming toward the shed. He held the gun so the barrel pointed toward the ceiling and pulled the trigger. The shot was loud and the kick knocked Charlie flat on the floor. The horse whinnied and shied away to the other side. Charlie was afraid the horse would be so frightened it would kick if he got near. Charlie hoped the shot would make Mr. Fletcher stop running after him.

It made someone yell and cry and holler for him to stop. He recognized Frank's voice yelling loudest. Charlie hid behind a large gray stone grinder. His heart pounded in his throat and he could not calm it, nor push it down in his chest where it belonged.

Mr. Fletcher's thin, charcoal face looked in the doorway. The door's hinges creaked in the breeze. His eyes were open because Charlie could see the clear whites around the deep brown centers. However, Mr. Fletcher evidently couldn't see so well. He left, leaving the door swinging and groaning.

Charlie could hear feet running hither, thither, and yon and he heard the calls for him. Then he heard great wrenching sobs. The running and calling stopped. Charlie put his rifle to his shoulder after making sure the safety was on and walked out of the shed.

Mrs. Fletcher was wiping tears from her face. Her shoulders jerked with her sobbing. Mr. Fletcher was beating some bushes saying, "He's shot dead. Shot dead. Dead."

Zach was standing close to his ma. Ell stood with her hand on Frank's shoulder scowling fiercely as Charlie came out of the shed.

Ell yelled, "Why'd you do that?" She shook her finger at Charlie. "Now look what you've done! You've spoiled the conjur words and the herb tea is spilled! And you stole his gun! I can't believe all the trouble you've caused, Charlie!"

Mr. Fletcher turned and said as clear as spots on a yearling deer, "Shame on you, son, causing so much commotion."

Charlie felt the shiver along his back as the breeze evaporated the wetness from his shirt. "But—but this is the Henry rifle Old Charles gave to me. It's mine! Can't you all see that!" Now Charlie was doing some shouting himself.

"It *is* his!" yelled Frank, running to examine the stock. "Geez! How'd it get here?"

Mrs. Fletcher seemed dazed, looking from her man to Charlie.

"Lord a'mighty!" Mr. Fletcher said, pointing a stick-thin finger. "You're only a puny paleface. You give that there rifle back to me straightaway. I promised by my life to keep it for *a man.*"

"It's mine!" insisted Charlie, feeling his hands ball up.

"A man—you are not a man! You danged whites are all alike," said Mr. Fletcher, shaking his bony shoulders. "You see someone has something, you say it's yourn. This was given to me while I lay worn out inside that house, on the bed. I promised I'd keep it for the rightful owner, who is *a man.*"

"I'm the owner." Charlie started to back away, thinking that a crazy, sick man, a woman, and a boy couldn't do much to him, and besides, he had the rifle. "Let's go to the wagon," he said, and motioned to Ell and Frank.

"Mr. Splitlog say I should keep the rifle!" called Mr. Fletcher in a thin watery-sounding voice. His hands shook like aspen leaves in the breeze. "He say the owner is *a big man*. This man, he will come here, and then I will let him have the Henry rifle. If you take something belonging to this big man, all the Wyandots in Kansas will be down on you. You hear of scalping? This will be not hair removal, but head removal!" The speech was long and tiring. Mr. Fletcher leaned against Mrs. Fletcher, who was still bewildered.

Charlie's mouth gaped open. Frank and Ell's mouth gaped open. Charlie grunted, then the words formed in his head and he licked his lips so that he could speak. "Matt Splitlog? The three Indian brothers? They came to our camp."

"You know Matt, John, and Mark?" Zach asked.

"Sure. Ma gave them biscuits and mush."

"Wait here!" Zach ran into the stone hut. When he came out he was waving a white cloth, like a surrender banner.

Ell's hands flew to her mouth. She took her hands away and cried out, "That's Ma's dishtowel, the one she wrapped around the biscuits! See—it has blue forget-me-nots embroidered in the corners."

Zach smiled. "She's right. It has blue flowers sewn in the corners. My ma thought it was so pretty she used it for a tablecloth."

Mrs. Fletcher stood with her hands to her mouth.

Mr. Fletcher stood on weak, bony legs, stock still, staring at the three Irwin children.

By this time several neighbors were standing around whispering among themselves.

Mr. Fletcher stretched out a long skeletal leg from under his white nightshirt. Charlie moved back a step. Mr. Fletcher moved one step forward and held out his trembling polelike arm. Charlie backed off, hugging the rifle. "This rifle is mine and I aim to keep it."

"No—I ain't goin' take that gol-durned gun. I believe it's yourn. I want to shake your hand and say thank you. I haven't felt so good in a long time."

"A miracle!" called Mrs. Fletcher. "Praise the Lord! We have witnessed the unbelievable. Thank You, Lord. Many thanks!"

"Hosanna!" shouted one of the neighbors. "Amen!" cried another. Soon the neighbors were down on their knees with their arms in the air shouting praises to the Lord.

Charlie moved closer to Mr. Fletcher. Ell put up her arm so he wouldn't move too close. "What made you see the truth?" asked Charlie, puzzled by all this emotional ruckus.

Mrs. Fletcher pulled out a rickety wooden box from a patch of wild currant brambles and pulled Mr. Fletcher over to sit there. He sighed and slumped over as if sitting were a chore. He explained that the Exodusters gave the three Splitlogs flour, ham, and dried grapes for the town's well they'd helped dig a while ago. The Splitlogs dug rock for posts around gardens to keep the deer out of the grain and vegetables. Matt left a rifle with Mr. Fletcher to shoot the fox that was raiding chicken coops. Mr. Fletcher shot the thieving fox and went back to bed to wait for the owner of the gun to come and claim it.

"What if we'd not come home with Zach?" asked Ell.

"But, daughter, you did, and you brought life back to Mr. Fletcher," said Mrs. Fletcher, full of faith.

"Who's that *big man?*" asked Frank.

Mr. Fletcher folded his hands in his lap and closed his eyes, as though resting so that he could say what he had on his mind. Everyone hushed to hear. "A child will be a big man, my son. Your brother fed the Splitlogs by loaning them his rifle. That sounds *big* to me."

"Amen," said the neighbors in unison.

"Mr. Fletcher, don't forget the power of this sister," reminded Mrs. Fletcher. "She has a power most has forgot to use. She has a soft heart when it comes to the ailing. She'll help many a destitute folk."

"Glory to the Lord!" cried the neighbors.

Ell smiled and wiped tears from her eyes. She could not speak. She put her arms around Mrs. Fletcher.

Charlie shook hands with Mr. Fletcher and was surprised at the strength in the grip. There were tears in his eyes.

Mrs. Fletcher invited the neighbors in for tea. They stood or sat where they could, some on the empty bed. They sang praise hymns and sipped the hot herb tea. "What is this?" the neighbors asked.

"Mostly sassyfras," Mrs. Fletcher whispered.

Mr. Fletcher drank as though he'd had a pile of rock salt for breakfast. His eyes were wide in his cavernous face. He did a couple skips and a hop to show how well he was.

Everyone smiled and clapped for his dance. Charlie thought his arms and legs looked like burnt willow sticks poking from the white nightshirt.

Ell gave Mrs. Fletcher another hug and whispered some conjur words of safekeeping in her ear. "We are going now," said Ell. "Keep the—tablecloth."

Charlie invited Mr. Fletcher to come to the Sappa country to go fishing if he ever got the urge.

"Maybe I'll bring the Splitlogs," said Mr. Fletcher with a grin. "Those boys get restless and have to get away from their own place once in a while. It's the Injun blood in them."

Frank fingered an aggie in his pocket, debating whether to leave it with Zach. Charlie noticed the debate Frank was having with himself.

"Give it to your friend," said Charlie. "It won't hurt."

Frank grinned and rolled the marble toward Zach. Zach said in a playful way, "Put up your dukes," and feigned a couple friendly little jabs toward Frank's jaw.

Mrs. Fletcher ran after them. "Here, take this." She gave Ell her flower press, explaining that her man could make another first thing tomorrow morning. "Praise the Lord for today's adventure," she said.

"Sassafras 'n' hollyhocks, thyme 'n' horseradish makes a powerful cure," said Ell with a smile. She ran ahead. She could hardly wait to tell her mother and father about the herb tea and Mr. Fletcher, all arms and legs, chasing after Charlie, who found his Henry rifle.

Mary had the stewpot, plates, and spoons packed inside the grub box and the quilt folded and put on the wagon seat. The three children talked at the same time, spilling over with the story of Charlie retrieving the Henry rifle.

"It's hard to believe," said Will. "How do we know Charlie didn't make all this up?"

"He couldn't," said his father. "The story is too fantastic."

"I kind of hate to leave this colorful place. The schoolyard has been restful for me," said Mary.

"That's the trouble with some folks. They is never satisfied. And just look at all the foofaroo tucked inside that there wagon. Oooo-weee! Mercy, it will take a huge hut to hold all them goods!" The words came from Mrs. Fletcher, dressed in a clean white apron and long, full gingham skirt and blouse made from a flour sack. She was all smiles. "I had to come to thank the folks that raised those chilluns. Why, they put Mr. Fletcher on his feet again. I thank the Lord that the sun rose on this day and put the notion in your head to come to Nicodemus!" She embraced Ell.

Mary climbed off the wagon seat and shook Mrs. Fletcher's hand. "I'm Mary Irwin. That's my husband, Joe, and our oldest, Will. There was a lot of goings-on at your place? I hope my children didn't upset you. If they did I'm sorry."

"Don't say sorry. I praise the Lord for this upset! You might say it was them Splitlogs that caused this hallelujah day. Them boys are good at judging the mind-set of folks." She patted the tiny black dog held tightly in the crook of one arm.

Joe came forward and held out his hand. "I am glad to meet you, ma'am, and hope your husband recovers. Say—I'd like to buy some vegetables if you have some for sale."

"Oh, the Reverend Roundtree will give you plenty of greens. Too bad his pole beans ain't ready." She was looking from Joe to

Charlie. Charlie was edging up to pet the dog.

Joe said, "Point me in the right direction to this Reverend's place and I'd be mighty obliged."

"Straight up the dirt road. He has all his produce growing in the front yard. Say, you folks ain't got a dog tied up in there?" She pointed toward the wagon.

"No," said Joe. "We ain't had a dog lately. But we used to have one. Stayed outdoors mostly. The kids liked it."

"Somehow I knew," she said. "Sodbusters need a good dog. This one's mother's smart, runs from every cat in town. The male that stood up to her is the one chases racoons out of the town's garbage. Zach picked this here puppy, so it ain't the litter's runt either." She held the pup around the middle with her right hand and shoved it into Charlie's hands. It was black as a lump of coal, and not much larger than a good baking potato. "Hang on, son, it's lively."

Charlie held the pup close to his chest and put his hand on the soft, warm fur. He could feel the fast thumping of the pup's heart against the slower thumping of his own heart. It was a wonderful feeling. "Thank you!" said Charlie, and a tingling went up and down his back.

Joe cleared his throat. "A pup might not ride too well."

"If you feed it and let it get your smell, it'll get used to you soon enough," said Mrs. Fletcher, watching Charlie put his face down against the pup's dark fur. "Chilluns needs a dog. And you can train it to keep deer outen your cornfield, or hunt according to your preference. You can see it's a good mix, some Irish setter, some sheepdog, some racin' greyhound."

"Maybe you ought not give this dog away. I don't have a thing to give you in trade," said Joe, sadly rubbing his hands together.

"It's a present. Mister, I don't trade for no present."

"What if one of the children let it go? You can see it'd come running right back here," said Mary, but half wishing Joe would accept the present.

"That's no problem." Mrs. Fletcher took out a thick braided-cloth leash from her wide apron pocket and tied it around the pup's neck.

Charlie looked up and saw that Ell wanted to hold the little furry pup and that Will wouldn't be opposed to holding the end of that multicolored leash. Frank looked as if he thought the pup belonged to the family already.

Joe chuckled. "Mrs. Fletcher, to oppose you is like blowing against the wind."

Mary let out her breath and petted the tiny pup.

"Yes, so take it and keep your breath," said Mrs. Fletcher. Her dark eyes shone, then dimmed, and her body stiffened. "I want to ask you something. I need advice."

"Well, now," said Joe. "I don't know if—"

"Hear me out first," she said. "It was a heart-tearing sight to watch my man sicken and grow thin. But something happened before that. Maybe it was worse. This whole town died while we watched. Nicodemus was full of life and hope and good folk. Then the southwest winds came and seared the crops and gardens. Then the town turned sick and some of the folk moved out. The church was hardly filled come worship time." Mrs. Fletcher took a deep breath. "You think Mr. Fletcher's sickness was loneliness for a town filled with happy folks? Seven years ago we had five hundred souls and now there are less than two hundred. Mr. Fletcher helped to build this town for all those bright folks." She hesitated and looked from Mary to Joe, hoping that they understood what she was trying to ask. "Today is different. Today Mr. Fletcher got his head shook and an idea broke loose. Listen, he wants to welcome all folks that come through this here town. He wants to give them a restful place to stop, to eat, and to choose a souvenir to take away. He wants the settlers going West to come through here." She looked hopefully from Joe to Mary, who did not fully understand. "Folks might like my pressed prairie flowers, or the Reverend's collard greens, or something Mr. Fletcher carves from the post rock. What do you think? It was your chilluns that started this idea." She paused and saw for sure that Mary and Joe now understood.

Mary nodded and smiled. Joe said he thought it was a dandy idea. "Oh, ladies like flowers—all kinds. The settlers will need vegetables, they'd probably like blackberries and wild currants if you have them ready-picked. The word'll get around and you'll have wagons clattering here so thick you'll be bellyaching about the dust."

Mary said, "Women might look for quilts and dresses for their newborn babies." Mrs. Fletcher's eyes shone and she hugged Mary.

"Thank you, folks. That's my answer. I have to leave now—vespers." Everything was still for a moment like a silent prayer.

Mary suddenly had an idea of her own. "Could we—uh—we'd like to worship with you. If you think the puppy would stay quiet tied here in the wagon and if you wouldn't mind having us."

Mrs. Fletcher's face lighted up in the afternoon sunshine. She took Mary's arm and started walking toward town. Charlie tied the leash and Ell brought a pan of water for the pup, then all the other Irwins followed after the two women. They stopped in front of the exiguous Methodist church, built of Kansas limestone. Mrs. Fletcher pointed to the bell in the yard. Zach stood beside it with a rope, ready to pull the clapper. "It came from a steam locomotive," she said with no other explanation, because the bell began to clang loudly.

Inside they were seated on backless, wooden benches. The preacher noticed the newcomers and nodded. Charlie noticed the preacher's right cheek had a deep red scar in the form of an X. Charlie noticed the ugly scar before he saw that the man wore a white muslin shirt with shirring at its yoke and buckskin trousers and leather sandals. Charlie knew it was the Reverend Roundtree that Zach had talked about.

The inside walls of the church were whitewashed sod and post rock and shook with the hymns "lined" by Reverend Roundtree. The singing of all those rich voices reminded Charlie of honey pouring from delicate china pitchers into a fine milk-glass bowl.

During the sermon, impassioned amens rose again and again. The words rolled from Reverend Roundtree's mouth like the river pouring out of the hills in the spring, Charlie thought.

The sunflowers, goldenrod, and spiky yellow sage near the altar looked so bright that it could have been Easter Sunday.

There were candles everywhere. There was a large candle above the pulpit. There were no stained-glass windows, but there was a melodeon behind the pulpit. The organist, in a black coat and leather breeches, was skilled in pumping out soul-stirring tones by pushing air through the metal reed by the bellows, operated by his nimble bare feet.

Afterward the Irwin family shook hands with about everyone in town. Frank turned his hands over to see if any of the black had come off after shaking so many black hands. Zach teased him.

"Bless you," the Reverend told them.

"Much obliged," said Joe, who still wanted to purchase some fresh vegetables.

The Reverend hung on to Joe's hand as if reading his mind. "Mrs. Fletcher told me about your need for greens. Follow Zach to the end of the street. He'll get you a gunnysack full of collards, spinach, and lettuce." He saw Joe reach into his pocket as if to pull out a couple of bills to pay for the greens. "No, my friends, this is the Sabbath, we don't take money on the Sabbath. We give in joy and the joy comes back to us. Believe, my friend. You are always welcome in Nicodemus. Lord, go with this man and his family."

That warm summer evening the Irwins rolled across the prairie in the moonlight. They sang all the familiar gospel hymns together. After a couple of hours they stopped on a gravel bank of the Solomon River. Charlie said, "Is it some kind of miracle that the people of Nicodemus sing the same songs we sing? Maybe they thought we learned their songs real fast."

"No—I think they knew we worshiped the same," said Mary.

"Lookee at little Nicodemus, sound asleep on my lap," said Charlie, pointing to the curled-up black pup.

SEVEN

Homesteaders Union Association

For the next couple of days the Irwins made good time riding on the stage road. They forded Prairie Dog Creek and drove on through Colby until they came to the end of the railroad track. Then all there was for the eye to see was undulating plain covered with rich buffalo grass. A creek flowed through the middle of the bottom land and there were hardwoods growing beside the willows. Joe looked around and suddenly announced with a whoop, "This is it!"

Sparrows flittered and chickadees chirped. Squirrels ran across the trees.

Joe looked hard at this land where the weather could bring heavy winds, sleet or rain, or dust and drought. This land was the lure which meant poverty or prosperity, apathy or adventure, and repression or the freedom to develop one's own future. Joe found the three flat stones buried at the northwest corner of his section. "We're home!" he cried.

Charlie could see there were no forests to clear, no swampy places to drain, and the grassy vegetation would make easy plowing. The rocks and boulders could be piled at the edge of a field for a fence. There was a constant movement of air, the humidity was low.

First thing Mary looked for was the old soddy she remembered. It was dark all year long, with dirt from the walls and roof sifting, always sifting into everything. When there was rain there was mud on the floor. The beetles, roaches, spiders, and mites came out of the dirt. It was an ongoing battle to prove who were the inhabitants of the soddy. Mary could not find a sign of the old place. It seemed to have melted back into the land.

"That is no concern," consoled Joe. "We'll have a home better than the first. It will be cool in summer and snug in winter."

"A dirt house?" asked Ell, sulking in a corner of the wagon like a cat that's had its tail stepped on.

The pup jumped out and sniffed all around, then waited for Charlie to climb out of the wagon.

The next few days Joe went over what he remembered was his quarter section. He couldn't understand why the old soddy was missing or destroyed. "Ought to be something left to show where she stood," he said to himself.

"Pa, lookee here," said Charlie. "These stones might have been piled at the corner of the parcel—but they seem kicked loose and scattered. Could snow or water do that?"

"I don't think so," said Joe, examining the assortment of limestone. Some of the rock contained fossils of small worms, crinoids, and mollusks, showing that water had covered this land thousands of years ago. Some of the rock was a mass of tiny concretions, built up layer by layer around some small nucleus, looking like it was made of tiny round granules. Each granule grew as it was rolled by waves or currents. There was some marl, or stones rich in clay, and some containing silica in the form of chert. "These stones were collected by man, because there are several varieties here. They could be the stones I used on the old soddy. I can mark off our section from the corner with the three stones buried. We'll plant vinegar bottles upside down over stakes with the corner plot measurements inside each one. There'll be no question of property lines, nor ownership."

While Joe and Will worked on sighting the property corners and putting in marking stakes, Frank and Charlie scrounged the prairie for buffalo chips, sunflower stalks, and dried sticks from the willows and oaks along the creek bank. This was fuel for their mother's cooking fire.

The season was late for planting much of anything. Joe decided a barn should be built first. The family lived in the wagon. Some days Charlie went with his father and Will to use the breaking plow, which threw up the sod in parallel strips three to five inches thick.

One afternoon toward the end of July, Charlie was by the creek with his father building a slicker, a sled with pole runners. Joe wanted to use it to haul the fifty-pound chunks of sod up to the place he'd selected for a barn. A slicker could be pulled across the slippery prairie grasses. Nick was with Charlie for company. The pup grumbled low in its throat and became tense and its hair bristled. Charlie looked around to see if another animal were close by and he wished he'd brought his rope. He waved the pup back and moved to a clump of grass where his rifle lay. He stood still to listen. Someone called, "Hullo there, neighbor!"

Charlie called back and Nick began barking and jumping like a crazy animal. Charlie said, "Nick, hush! Down, boy!"

The pup stopped barking but stood, sniffing the air in front of its nose.

Charlie called to his father, who was chopping a slim oak for a pole, and a man came over the small rise. The stranger wiped his face with a strip of faded blue cloth. He was short, with a barrel chest, thick arms, and a bushy white mustache and beard. He carried a Winchester, wore a wide-brimmed felt hat over gray hair, a flannel shirt, blue denim pants, and heavy work boots.

"Jack Collins," he said, coming down off the rise.

Charlie thought Mr. Collins was probably out hunting. But a man who wandered around the prairie in the hot sun hoping to find game looked as crazy as the frantic pup. Charlie wanted to say something, but he only held out his hand and said, "Charlie Irwin, and here comes my pa, Joseph Irwin. Are we neighbors?"

"I would guess so. I have a homestead over near Shermanville. It was Barney Bronson told me you folks was here."

"I don't know a Bronson," said Joe frowning.

"Barney's a homesteader, like the rest of us. Knows everyone around for about four counties. Someone new comes in and he knows all about the family. He's our newspaper."

Nick sniffed the man and then lay down under a clump of tall grass. Charlie brought out the lard bucket packed with corn pone and hunks of roast rabbit. He took another bucket to the creek and dipped it full of water.

Mr. Collins drank the bucket half-empty and ate quickly everything Charlie passed him. He picked his teeth with a piece of dried grass stem.

Joe was eating and asked Collins if he were farming.

"Yup, same's everybody," Collins answered.

"What about this Bronson," asked Joe, digging the last piece of meat from the bucket.

"He was one of the first homesteaders to file a claim in these here parts," said Collins. "Everybody knows him. You will, too. Say, did ya know about them gol-durned land hunters jumping claims just to get the big fee? I call that plain unprincipled! We settlers were here first. We don't want to be robbed by those Johnny-come-latelies. Why, they was scared to come here when the land was vacant, 'cept for the buffalo and a few Injuns. I say we got to get ourselves organized."

It occurred to Joe to ask about what might have happened to his old soddy, but he said, "Did the cold weather drive a number of range cattle into the towns last winter?"

"Yup, some," Collins said. "There was a couple weeks when someone's cows huddled in the shelter of the general store and livery stable in Goodland last winter."

"If I get me a herd I'll have to get me some barbed wire or set posts at the corners of my barn and house so's the cattle won't rub hollows there."

Collins's head jerked up. "Say, that's what I come to say. I'll give you a hand with your building if you plan to start right away."

Charlie saw his father look pleased and shake Collins's hand. Collins stayed and helped Joe with the slicker. Charlie could see that he was cooperative and full of chatter. In addition to his farming, Collins and his three sons were bone gatherers. They had a crew of men and five teams that were hitched to wagons, and when the wagons were full of old buffalo bones they went to the Kansas–Pacific railhead about sixty miles east of their camp near Shermanville. The bones went to plants in the East, where they were pulverized into fertilizer for Pennsylvania and Ohio farmers. Collins was in northwest Kansas a couple of summers, not going farther south than five, six miles from Beaver Creek. He seemed to know everyone who homesteaded the area.

"I betcha' I've collected more than a thousand tons of bones, including buffalo, antelope, horse, but none them wild cows, their bones is too light to be worth the effort," said Collins. Slowly he added, "What do ya think? Want to join up?"

"Sure, I'd like to," Charlie said right away. "And maybe Frank could help out some, too. He's my younger brother."

Collins looked at Joe.

"What? Do I want to join your bone-hunting crew? No, thanks," said Joe.

"Look, Joseph, I was referring to protection. You join our organization and you can get help with problems of the claim contesters and them free-roaming herds you mentioned."

"I've not heard of such a group," said Joe suspiciously.

"That's another reason I'm here," said Collins. "Most of the cattlemen are organized and are offering five hundred dollars for evidence to convict a man of killing range cattle. You can see, with proper incentive, a man might turn in his neighbor. When drought hits him hard and his children cry for food, temptation is fierce. A man could butcher one of his own yearling for veal, sell some to friends, and suddenly find hisself accused."

Joe said something about personal freedom and not getting nosy with any neighbor's private business. "Every man has a responsibility to his neighbors as well as to himself," said Joe.

"Just my sentiments," said Collins. "Have you been notified by the Oberlin Land Office that someone's contesting this here claim of yours?"

"No!" Joe said immediately. "I've paid full price for my quarter section. I paid in seventy-nine. It's on the books. The Oberlin Land Office has got the record."

Charlie felt the muscles in the back of his neck go tense.

"Then you're safe—I suppose."

"Yes—what's to suppose?" asked Joe sharply.

"Well, you know Barney Bronson? He was county assessor in eighty-five."

Joe made no comment.

Charlie was trying to put things together, but there were pieces missing.

Finally Collins said mournfully, "Barney Bronson says he has proof that he was the first homesteader and lived in this here county five years. He came to Sherman County in eighty-one."

"Well, a man likes to draw attention to himself at times," said Joe, holding his temper. "I see no harm in that."

"If Bronson took a page out from that record book, leaving his record on the first page, it would seem that you have not paid up your claim, Joseph."

Charlie saw now how the pieces fit snug.

"You mean he would ask me for a fee to take off his contest?" Joe was showing annoyance. "Whole thing don't sound real neighborly."

Charlie watched Collins roll a cigarette.

"That's where the Homesteaders Union Association can be of service. We're having a meeting over to Art Stahm's dugout the fifteenth of August, starting eight o'clock. I'll show you where to find his place."

Collins found a sunflower stem and drew a crude map in the dirt. "You'll meet Bronson like I said. He's been invited to this same secret meeting."

The following day Collins sent his oldest son, Rob, to help Joe.

Joe staked off a plot of level land for the barn. Rob and Will cleared all of the growing material from the plot. Then Rob showed Will how to dry wild grape leaves and then crush and roll them in thin paper for a smoke. Charlie and Frank smoothed and pounded the cleared surface with a spade to form a hard earthen floor. By noon Collins brought his grasshopper plow to slice strips of sod from the earth easier and faster than Joe's breaking plow. The plow was harnessed to the workhorses, Suzie and Jed. Will and Rob chopped the strips into bricks. These were loaded on the slicker so that Flame, led by Charlie, pulled the sod bricks to the barn site, where Joe and Collins worked.

On the fifteenth of August, Joe asked Will to ride horseback with him to Art Stahm's dugout. Will begged off, saying that he'd promised Rob he'd go into Goodland to see what was happening in town. Charlie saw the disappointment on their father's face. "Pa, I'd like to go with you," said Charlie.

"Well, thanks, son, I think you are too young to join that association, but you can ride with me. I'm glad the moon's bright so we can watch for trail signs and talk at the same time."

Several men were there already when Joe and Charlie arrived. Collins introduced the Irwins to Art Stahm, a short man with piercing black eyes. His black hair was straight, below his ears, and he had a high forehead. He wore small steel-rimmed glasses. Stahm consulted his gold watch on a heavy chain every few minutes. Stahm introduced Joe to Barney Bronson.

He was not as Charlie had imagined. He was a big man, about the size of Charlie's father. He wore a buckskin shirt and buckskin breeches with moccasins on his feet. He was blond and blue-eyed. Bronson seemed surprised, almost startled, to meet Joe and Charlie Irwin, and his squinty blue eyes searched the one room, as though looking for a back door, though his head did not seem to move.

Charlie thought Bronson's face was much too pale for a farmer, more like the sickly look on the underbelly of a catfish. His feet in those thin-soled moccasins would be mighty sore walking over broken sod and clods of dirt and stones.

He was forced to sit in the only chair available between Joe and Charlie. He ignored Charlie, cleared his throat, and said to Joe, "Lived six years on the southwest four-fifteen, six-thirty-eight. Made my settlement the twentieth day of June, eighteen eighty-one." His watery blue eyes squinted at Joe's face.

Joe lowered his head, feeling embarrassed with such close scrutiny. "Made mine in seventy-nine," Joe said. "And I've got the carbon copy to prove it."

Now Joe watched and saw Bronson blanch like that same catfish overlong out of water.

Charlie wanted to shout "Hooray and hallelujah!" for his father.

The new candidates for the Homesteaders Union Association were led outside to wait for the preparations for their initiation. There were only six new members invited to join. Charlie was taken out of the dugout with the candidates and told he was to wait there until the initiation was all over. He had expected that, but he would have liked to see what went on in that secret part of the meeting. Joe winked at him, and he thought his father knew how he felt and on the way home might tell something. He sat by himself on the grass and stared at the moon glistening in the sky, which was salted with sparkling stars. He was close enough to hear the conversation of the men waiting to be initiated. He pondered why the conceited Bronson was invited to be in the HUA. Charlie had the feeling that his pa felt Bronson had something to do with the destruction of the old sod house and removal of the plot stakes. He wondered how his pa could feel comfortable around the deceitful man.

As a matter of fact, Joe was talking himself out of joining the Homesteaders Union Association when Collins came out and called Bronson back into the dugout as the first initiate. Bronson went inside and the door closed behind him.

"Hey," Joe said to Collins, who was still outside looking over the men. "I'm not feeling too good. Think I'll just get my horse and boy and we'll go on home. Sorry."

"Joseph," said Collins, coming to his side quickly and touching his hand lightly.

"It's Joe," said Joe irritably.

"Don't go, Joe," said Collins. "You don't seem to have a fever. Maybe just a little fright at this secrecy and oath business. It won't take long, not for you and these others anyway. For Bronson, yes—it might be longer." His voice was lowered.

Charlie could not help himself. He blurted out loud, "What's so special about a dude like that?"

"I thought you had it figured—you are quick with other things," Collins snapped. He was irritated that the kid spoke up.

"Figured what?" Joe answered. "That you settlers want a claim contester and cattle informant in your midst? What is this organization, a bunch of thieves and informants? I want no part of this!" Joe had let his anger show and started to leave, motioning for Charlie to follow. The other initiates were staring at them.

Collins grabbed Joe's arm. "Listen, we're in business to protect ourselves against men like that! If we take in a man that informs on his neighbors, we can scare him into secrecy. He'll know that we all know about his past deeds and we'd be the first to correct the situation if it happens again. This is a way of keeping him in line—on our side. Don't you see that?"

Charlie was dumbfounded. He could see the logic, but doubted if he could have figured it out for himself.

Joe looked at Collins, then at the other four men. They nodded in approval. Joe was not certain. He wanted to think. Collins shook his hand and left.

"There's no law enforcement to protect us," said one of the men.

"We settlers are defenseless alone," said another.

"I had to pay fifty dollars because I was five days late beginning improvements on my land. During those five days we had a blizzard, wind and snow. My God! No one could walk a straight path across the frozen ground, the wind came acrost so hard. It was Bronson turned me in for half my fee. We're not fond of him either," said a man with heavy shoulders, thick arms. He was short and stocky like Collins, and his broad face was bristled.

The fourth man, his brown eyes barely visible because of the way he squinted after years of farming against sun and wind and dust, said, "Stick with us, Joe. We need thoughtful men like you. And your kid's all right, too."

Collins came out of the dugout letting the light from inside make a broad fanlike pattern outside on the dirt and clumps of yellowed grass. Collins said, "Joseph—Joe Irwin, next." He stood next to the door trying hard to appear official.

Joe cleared his throat, touched the wide brim of his hat, looked at Charlie, and nodded that it was all right, and walked in behind Collins.

Charlie could see that the center of the room had been cleared except for a couple wooden crates stacked on top of one another so as to be waist high. They were covered with bleached, pure white flour sacks. Collins closed the wooden door.

Now Charlie saw why the other four men stayed huddled together; they were looking in the only window of the dugout where the heavy oiled paper had torn and left a good-sized hole. There was a trumpet vine growing over the side of the dugout and in front of the window, so that no one from inside could see those faces outside looking in. Charlie could hear Stahm read several oaths that his father was asked to repeat. The first being not to contest a neighbor's claim during his absence. Next not to tear down the house of a neighbor while he was away.

"Goddamnit!" said Joe. "Any man that knows me even the faintest knows I wouldn't do those things! Why do I have to swear to these things that are my nature anyway?"

The men outside murmured to one another. One came over and said to Charlie, "Your pa's a scrapper and stubborn to boot. You wanna see?"

Charlie pulled himself up from the grass and followed the man to the window. The men moved a little as Charlie climbed up on a stone. Then the heads behind Charlie adjusted so that they could all see what was going on. Charlie could hear them breathing close around him.

Stahm was looking at the dirt floor. His breath was coming in quick gasps. He said, "Damnit, just repeat after me, neighbor."

Joe's eyes fell to the homemade altar and he put his hands around the sides for support.

"Go on," Collins said to Stahm.

Other oaths were repeated that were strong reasons for settlers supporting the protective association. When Joe spoke, his voice thundered in the room. Charlie thought it was because his father had decided if the organization was good, he'd enter it wholeheartedly.

Joe was kneeling and putting his right hand on the open Bible that was on the white altar.

"Repeat after me," said Stahm, regarding Joe cautiously. "I do solemnly swear not to tell anything that may in any way lead owners of cattle, which may be running at large, contrary to law, and destroying the settlers' crops, to discover who has killed or crippled or in any way injured these same cattle, when driving them away from the crops or at any other time. If I do, then I shall expect this Homesteaders Union Association to use me thus."

At this crucial point a straw dummy in a red shirt and blue denim trousers, with a rope around its neck, was floated past Joe.

The straw dummy so startled Charlie that his knees buckled and he felt himself hit the side of the rock he stood on. His arm was scraped. One of the men behind him had an arm around his middle and stood him back on the rock. "Hanging's part of life. Better get used to it." Charlie felt squeamish and didn't want to look through the window. The stocky man with his face full of bristles put a steadying hand on Charlie's back. Charlie could hear the four men around him snickering. He looked up and saw that his father's face was white and he had his tongue clamped between his teeth. Charlie felt better seeing his father had been frightened by the hanging dummy also.

Bronson must have been frightened into secrecy that night, because Charlie never heard his father say to anyone that Bronson sold information for money after his initiation into the HUA. Charlie never asked, but he was certain the Irwins' paid-up claim was never contested.

EIGHT

House-raising

It took close to a month of slow, tedious work until, near the end of August, the Irwin barn was complete. One corner of the barn was kept clear as living quarters until the sod house was finished. Pieces of sod more than a foot thick, stacked on top of one another, made the barn sides. The roof was reinforced with split oak logs tied together with willow. Layers of sod went on top of the logs. There were no windows. For light Joe used a coal-oil lantern, or left the door open. The door was a wooden frame hung with thick deer hide. The four horses and cow were kept in crude stalls on one side along with a place for hay. Hay was the fresh-cut prairie grass. On the other side was a bin made of split logs for the oats Joe bought from Jack Collins.

The weather became rainy and Joe moved the horses and cow into the barn. Mary moved herself and Ell inside the barn at night. They spread comforters over the oats, wiggled down to make a bowl-shaped bed for themselves. The three boys and Joe slept in the wagon.

One day Mary told Joe that the thing she wanted most of all was a kitchen stove. She did not like to cook in a fireplace, nor over an open fire outdoors. Joe counted his money and one clear morning announced that he and the three boys were going into town, Goodland, for supplies. He went directly to the General Mercantile and bought the only Majestic cast-iron cookstove in the store. The clerk told Joe that stoves were brought by wagon from the town of Wallace. "Wallace gets 'em from the East by rail. Don't sell more'n two or three a year."

It took the clerk along with Joe and his sons to load the heavy iron range onto the wagon.

The clerk said, "Grease her well. Heat cures the grease into the metal, then she don't rust." Then he cautioned, "Ride easy. Cast iron's brittle and can crack if youse take to bouncing from rut to gulley."

Joe braced the blue-black pieces of flue pipe in front of the stove and drove as carefully as he knew how back over the prairie.

Mary's delight astonished everyone. As soon as the stove was set on the ground she put twigs inside the firebox and burned them to see how the stove heated up. She made biscuits in her griddle on top of the stove. She cooked them on one side, then on the other side. She heated a bucket of hot water for a bath and sent the boys to the creek to hunt wild plums or persimmons for a pie. That night she asked Joe to put the stove in the barn so she could bake and cook in any kind of weather.

Joe said, "I can't."

"Sure you can. Will and Charlie can help," she said. Her sunbonnet brim hid her disappointed face.

"But I ain't about to. There's dry grass in the barn. You don't want it to go up in a blaze from a spark out of the firebox?" asked Joe.

She said, "I'll cook outside in the clearing until the house is built. Charlie can fix the wagon-cover tarp over it for shade and to keep off the rain."

"I'll build the house next," said Joe, and he pulled Mary close against his chest. "It'll have real windows, not paper soaked in grease, and curtains at the windows and those fancy little vases to hold flowers for the sills."

Mary felt better knowing Joe understood she wanted to begin her domestic duties in a cheerful place.

Joe saw the smile flicker at the corner of Mary's mouth and her eyes light when she turned her face toward him.

"Can we have three bedrooms and a big kitchen?" she asked.

"Yep, if that's what you want."

Mary put her arms around Joe. "Don't let me get carried

away. It wouldn't do any good for you to get rich. I'd have you furnish my house with an inside well and fancy fixin's for furniture. Then I'd insist you get the latest plows and maybe another horse."

"And not an extra piece of meat hanging in the kitchen rafters?" cried Joe.

"Don't bellow! I'm just telling the truth, that we both know. Money seems to burn a hole in my pocket and in your pocket," Mary said with a sigh.

"You can't fault me for wanting to buy everything for you. You deserve the best I can give. I know coming out here was not an easy decision for you."

Mary tightened her arms around Joe. She put her face up for his tender kiss.

However, Joe did not build the house next. He and the boys built a sod chicken house. Joe said it was for Ell. Ell pouted the whole day it was going up. "Am I going to feed those stupid chickens and gather eggs?" she whined. "It's just another chore. I swear! The only thing those stupid chickens are good for is to use their flesh to draw poison from a snake bite!"

"Ell!" chided Charlie. "Nothing wrong with that! Think of all the chicken and dumplings and egg pie chickens are good for. I'll feed those chickens for you."

Ell's face changed. Her downturned mouth turned up. Her green eyes sparkled. She was jubilant. "Oh, Charlie, will you? I knew I could count on you. You always know how to make me happy. Oh, joy!"

"I'll fatten your chickens and sell 'em. I'll buy you books, so you can be the best teacher in the Sappa area," teased Charlie.

Ell admitted that Charlie had a way of taking the burden out of ordinary chores. "Charlie, I love you most," cooed Ell, "egg pie second."

Her words of flattery gave Charlie a warm glow. "It's just a way to get through the muddle of every day," he said and began singing "Nobody Knows the Trouble I've Seen" in a deep voice to make Ell laugh.

She sobered and looked demure. "I've been wondering if Pa's friend, Jack Collins, would send his children here if I started reading and writing lessons."

"Ask him," said Charlie. "But his boy Rob is too old for lessons."

"Charlie! If he wants to come for lessons, you can't stop him because of age. Besides, I kind of like the way he looks. He makes me feel good. He gives me tingles with his eyes."

"He gives me goose bumps," said Charlie.

"There you go—teasing me because I told you how I felt."

Ell did not have to wait long to talk with Jack Collins. He came on the first of September to collect the bones Charlie and Frank collected and paid them a few cents for their effort. He also brought a half carcass of deer. Behind him came Rob carrying a hammer, wedges, and squares. Then came a large, strapping woman carrying a pick and shovel. Behind her was a passel of younger children. Charlie counted two towheaded boys and three towheaded little girls.

"Time you started your house or you'll be in the dark barn all winter!" called Collins.

"Well, I've marked the space and cleared the ground of grass and roots," said Joe. "I was about to cut the sod. You don't think I'd let my family live in a barn in winter? Why, there ain't no windows!"

"Windows you gots to have. That's why we come in one of the bone wagons. It can haul more'n yours. I figure we go to Wallace for lumber for the frames and window glass while the others get started on the posts for the corners and roof supports and cutting plenty of sod," said Collins. "You can count on the HUAers coming for your house-raising."

"How far is this here Wallace?" asked Joe, remembering the Mercantile clerk mentioning the town.

"Maybe thirty, forty miles south. We ford the North Fork of the Smoky Hill River and get a view of the highest point in Kansas. Wallace's the only place I know where there's window glass. Your woman has her heart set on letting daylight shine in her place, just the same's my Cora here." Collins pointed to the large, coarse, yellow-haired woman.

Mary was helping Mrs. Collins put the pick and shovel against the chicken house and asking her to sit at the table under the canvas lean-to Charlie had built. Mary put a kettle of water on the stove for coffee and called Ell to stir up some cornmeal mush for the five little children. Rob spoke right up and said he'd like mush himself.

Ell looked at Rob. He was close to Will's age, twenty or twenty-one. He was built like his father and mother, broad-shouldered and short. His face was tanned and his hair almost cottony-white from sun bleaching. He never took his eyes off Ell.

Charlie thought Cora Collins looked robust enough to simmer down those young ones, but she paid no heed to them. They banged cups on the table and stood on the wooden benches Will had made. Charlie herded the five boisterous children out beside the barn to show them some rope tricks so that his mother and Cora Collins could talk. "You kids stop your racket or I'll tie you all together with this here rope," Charlie threatened. "Don't you have manners?" He swung his rope in a loop above their heads. They had never seen anything like that before. They watched in silence, their eyes wide, their mouths open.

Charlie was thinking that Cora Collins did not look like the kind of a woman most men would stare at more than once. She was so homely that even a horsefly wouldn't look at her twice. Charlie saw his father and Mr. Collins leave in the bone wagon and wished he'd asked to go along. He knew they'd be gone overnight because Cora Collins had quilts for her brood to stay here all night. "Guess I'm stuck with you chickens like some old mother hen," Charlie exploded out loud. The children thought he was funny and laughed. The children thought Charlie was wonderful when he found a short rope and showed each one how to spin it.

Ell called that the mush was ready. The children clustered around Charlie. He noticed that Rob followed Ell. Charlie thought it would serve Rob well if Ell spilled hot mush down his front when she turned too quickly. Then he'd run fast as a scalded cat.

Mary pulled the youngest Collins child on her lap. The little towheaded girl was not bashful. She sat contentedly. Mary fed her mush from a cup and a small wooden spoon. Charlie gave his mother a grateful look. He thought, if she'd take a couple more of these rowdy kids he wouldn't feel like he was being mauled by bear cubs. Charlie noticed that Cora Collins's eyes were orange-brown. His mother's were deep green in the morning light. Cora had freckles across her nose and under her eyes so that Charlie knew she neglected to wear her sunbonnet. Her forehead and cheeks were lightly tanned. She smiled at her boy Rob and opened her mouth.

"Mrs. Irwin—Mary—that was my own ma's name. Bless her soul. She'd shake a finger at me if she could see the offspring I've got and the dirt house I live in. But she's gone, so's I don't have to explain to her. I'm glad I have another woman to prattle on with. You know, I sometimes talk to Rob like I would with another woman. I get so lonely for company my age. We'll talk all day." Her eyes twinkled and her hands moved when she talked. "Say, I do envy you that kitchen range out here." She winked. "Your Charlie seems good with children. Your Will and Frank can get the tools lined up and maybe start some sod cutting while Rob and Ell take a couple horses to ride out and tell some of the HUAers about your house-raising. By tomorrow this place will be buzzing louder'n any hive pawed at by some brown bear."

Charlie frowned. So that was it. Cora Collins could sit and talk with his mother all day while he took care of the children and Ell went on horseback over the countryside with that bobcat, Rob. Well, he'd do something about that there notion. Charlie untangled himself from the tiny arms and legs of the children and went to Ell with a big smile on his face. "Sis, these kids want you to tell them a story and then they'd like to learn to write their names. You musta talked to Mr. Collins."

"Yes, I did. He was happy as a colt in an apple orchard."

"See, I told you he'd like the idea. So you show the kids what kind of schoolmarm you are. Rob and I will invite the settlers to the house-raising."

Rob was leaning against the wagon. He made one step forward and took Charlie's arm. "You've got it wrong, pal. School starts tomorrow. Today Ell and I ride out. We talk to the settlers. Didn't you hear Ma?"

Charlie growled. He didn't know what to say. He looked from Ell to his ma, and by that time a couple of the towheaded children were pulling at his trousers. He knew he'd lost the argument. Thus, he had to herd five little kids for the rest of the day. By afternoon Charlie tied all five children together in his rope and told them to see if anyone could get loose before Injuns came over the hills. He flopped down in the tall grass, closed his eyes for a short rest. Next thing he heard the hooves of horses clattering into the yard. The two horses, Suzie and Jed, were lathered as though they'd been run hard. Rob climbed down and went to the water bucket for a drink.

Ell said, "Charlie, if you cool out the horses, I'll untangle those kids for you." Her face shone with perspiration and pleasure. There was a smudge of dirt under one eye. The buttons on her dress were fastened wrong; there was an extra loop at the neck.

"What happened?" asked Charlie.

"Not much." Ell's eyes crinkled with joy. "Rob rode like a

gust of wind. I had to keep up. It was wonderful! I feel vibrant
—full of life! Rob's different, like you said."

"Fix your dress before Ma sees it," said Charlie sharply.

"Oh—I undid it to feel the wind all over my body. You ought
to try it. Oh, joy!" Ell sighed.

"Did he touch you?" asked Charlie, squinting against the sun,
feeling a tightness in his belly.

"Charlie! That's evil! He didn't. But what if he did? Would
you want to know how it felt?" She shivered and straightened her
dress.

"Wash—wash your face," stuttered Charlie, feeling sweaty on
the palms of his hands. "I'll take care of the horses. You untie
those giggly kids. Be careful—you'll think an avalanche hit."

Charlie unsaddled the horses, brushed them with handfuls of
wild grass, and turned them loose behind the barn in the little
meadow.

After the supper dishes were washed and put away, Mary said
to Charlie, "I've enjoyed this day. Did you and Ell enjoy the
Collinses' young'uns?"

Charlie looked where Ell was holding Nick while Frank
printed DOG with a stick in the dust so the children could imitate
the letters. The youngest child had a minute-long attention span
and left drawing in the dirt to pet the pup.

His mother went on. "I see Frank is interested in those
young'uns. And look there, Will's found a friend in Rob. That's
real nice."

Charlie knew that Rob and Will had their heads together talking about women and at the same time rolling cigarettes made of
Rob's dried grape leaves.

Charlie nodded. He was not going to spoil his mother's good
time with some foolish telltale stories or fleeting bad feelings he
had about Rob Collins. The children had worn him down and he
was glad when it was bedtime.

The four older boys slept in comforters in the wagon. The
women and little children slept in the barn. Mary fixed a place in
the oats for herself and Cora, then she lay comforters on the
sweet, dry grass for Ell and the five little children.

Before daybreak Ell started a fire in the stove. Charlie got up
and splashed cold water on his face and neck. He rinsed out his
mouth with water two or three times and said, "My turn to milk
Clover. But why'd you get up so early?"

"I want to wash my hair before all the settlers come," said Ell.

"Are many of them HUAers?" asked Charlie.

Ell said, "Most, I think." She carried the bucket of hot water into the barn, protecting her hands from the hot bail with a wad of rags.

Charlie sat on the wooden bench beside the stove a moment to warm himself and was startled when Rob sat beside him.

"She's something to look at." Rob was looking at the barn.

"You like our sod barn?" said Charlie, rubbing his eyes.

"Your sister, you dunce! Ever notice how she presses her lips together, but still there's a curve at the corners? Her braids caress her white shoulders when she dips rainwater from the barrel. Her eyes looked dark as India ink, but her skin is creamy as moonlight."

"You're cracked!" cried Charlie. "No one ever talked about Ell like that. She's only a girl! Besides, she was shivering under a heavy shawl while she poked sunflower stalks into the range. You couldn't see no skin. Jeems, you're daft."

Rob stood by the warm stove and stretched lazily. "I imagined, my friend." He smiled and looked at Charlie through pale cyanic-colored eyes.

Charlie snorted and said, "You've time for another hour's sleep. Better get it before the others wake up." He clanged the milk pail on the edge of the range for emphasis and went off to the barn. He left the deer-hide door hooked by a thong to a nail so he had some light inside as he milked the cow.

Charlie's mother and Cora were already dressed and babbling with Ell, who was sponging herself. Cora looked at the tiny stitching in Ell's white muslin drawers and camisole. This made Ell pleased because she'd done the sewing herself. Ell gave Cora a splash of her good-smelling rosewater, then she bent over a kettle of warm water with a cup of vinegar added. The kettle was on the milking stool.

"Ma, I need the stool if I'm to do the milking," said Charlie, feeling bored and silly standing around waiting for women, who could talk a donkey's hind leg off, to stop so that he could do his chores.

"Give your brother the stool. You can bend on your knees for that rinsing." Mary left to make biscuits in the first morning light.

Ell flipped her hair so that Charlie's shirt was splashed. "Hey," he said, "I don't want to smell like pickles!"

Ell laughed when Charlie ran his hands over the wetness on

his shirt. She gave him the stool and threatened to splash again. Charlie ran to the other side of the barn and was glad to sit himself under the cow. He had dipped a rag in the soapy water bucket to clean off Clover's udders. Ell called, "If the milk tastes like lye soap, it'll be your fault!"

Charlie rolled his eyes and made a funny face.

One of the little Collins girls climbed out of her warm comforter. "Can you do that to my hair?" she asked Ell.

"Mine, too?" came several other wide-awake children's shrill voices.

Ell was surprised at their eagerness. "Of course, as soon as I get the soap out of mine. How about baby Carrie?" The youngest nodded her towhead and picked straw from her long cotton dress, which she'd slept in.

Cora left to admire the cooking stove again and to help Mary.

Charlie concentrated on the squeeze and pull of milking when his eye caught a shadow by the door. It was Rob standing inside against the wall so that his face was clear in the bluish light of dawn. Charlie saw Rob's eyes move up and down. He watched Ell in her drawers and camisole. Charlie did not stop milking, but he worked in slow motion. He watched the expression on Rob's face and could tell when his eyes stopped along the edge of Ell's neckline, where the cleavage of her breasts was apparent under the camisole when she bent to wash the baby's hair. Charlie's breathing was shallow. The pull and squeeze rhythm of his hand became stronger. The cow switched her tail and stepped forward. Charlie hitched the stool forward and held the pail between his knees tighter.

Ell looked up with a start. She seemed to realize that Rob had watched her for some minutes. Speechless, she let her eyes fall from the top of his sun-bleached hair, over his tanned face with those sulky eyes and lips, over the gray cotton shirt to the gray denim trousers with threadbare knees, to the dusty boots that were laced over muscular legs.

"So? Do you like what you see?" Rob asked in a husky voice.

"Why are you here?" Ell asked, pulling the drying sheet around her shoulders and picking up the little girl to cover the front of her undergarments. Her eyes snapped with the reflection of the first hint of sunlight.

"Your ma sent me to say you should cut the primpin' and get out to see the crowd that's already here to help build your new house."

"She didn't!"

"Here, let me help you dry Carrie's hair. Shoo, outside, let the sunshine dry your hair," he called to the other children, and motioned with his hands as they went out the door. "Looks like your hair needs rubbing with the sheet." Rob reached to catch the end of the bath sheet and pull it away in his strong hands.

Charlie saw Ell's eyes widen, and instead of moving away she moved closer. She set Carrie on the floor. "Go outside with your brothers and sisters. The sun will dry your hair and make it shine," she said. Her voice was low in her chest. Outside the sun was beginning to rise, making the prairie awash in pale yellow light.

Ell stood still. Rob rubbed her hair and let his thigh touch Ell's thigh. Rob moved one hand down the sheet to Ell's shoulder, where it rested a moment, then began to creep downward until it rested full on her small breast. Charlie saw Rob's fingers curl. He heard Ell's breath draw in, but she did not move. Her eyes were closed and her face showed a sensuality Charlie'd never noticed. Rob's face had the same lustful quality around his full mouth. His body swayed and the hand cupping Ell's breast slipped inside her camisole.

Charlie could not take his eyes away. He saw Ell push herself against Rob. She moaned and pushed his hand tight up against her breast once again. His hand holding the bath sheet slipped to her shoulders, then around her waist.

Charlie's hands stopped pulling and squeezing; they were held tight between his knees. The milk pail was on the floor at his feet. He tried to pull his feet back and put his weight on them. His legs were soft as boiled macaroni. Charlie stood up. The stool scraped the floor.

Rob dropped the sheet. His heavy lids opened and the pale-blue circles stared coldly at Charlie. "Where the hell'd you come from?"

At first Charlie's mouth felt numb and he could not clear his befuddled mind to speak.

Rob said, "Get out of here. You're no better'n a sow bug." He lunged for Charlie, who ducked behind the cow.

Rob was determined that he was not going to let Charlie stand in the way of his desires. He'd see Ell later. He thought, let her stew awhile. Rob stalked out of the barn.

Charlie waited for Ell to pull her dress over her head, then went outside with her. She began to brush the children's fine hair, keeping her eyes down. Charlie was sure Ell was waiting for her heart to stop thumping. He knew he was waiting for his heart to slow down. He did not understand his flustered feeling. He wanted to strike out, to do something physical, hit Rob in the solar plexus, shake Ell until her eyes popped out. His breathing was deeper now and his hands shook. He took the pail of milk to the creek for cooling. He broke off a bunch of willow branches that were full-leaved to put over the top of the pail to keep insects and rodents out. When he got back to the wagon and the shade he'd rigged over the table with the wagon's canvas, he saw that Rob had been right. People were arriving for the house-raising. He poured himself a cup of scalding coffee.

Ell was fighting off the steam of passion by washing all the buckets and kettles she could find. She looked at Charlie and became flushed. She began to help Cora heft the half deer onto an oak spit held by a tripod over a fire pit. Cora said, "My dear, the little ones look pert with their hairs fresh-washed."

Some of the settlers brought puddings and casseroles. The men sought out Will and went out to cut bricks of sod. Charlie nudged Frank, who was sitting at the table. "Time for you and me to get to work."

Frank said he'd not finished all the biscuits he planned to eat, and he was not a slave waiting for orders from a master. Charlie left the table in a huff. Actually, he was not ready to face Rob while cutting sod. The thought of him reminded Charlie of a scruffy tomcat chasing a she cat in heat. Charlie decided he'd talk to Ell as soon as he could. He began to greet the newcomers. His mother admired and thanked the women for the food that was brought.

Sarah Melstrom explained her covered dish. "Mrs. Irwin, it's not my usual good quality. It's stewed rabbit and I had only a few scrawny onions and scraggly carrots to flesh it out."

Mary knew she meant it was her best-made dish of stewed rabbit. The food was each woman's finest. It was their way to show off their creative talents. It was their escape to color and variation from the drab, hard farm life. There was gooseberry pie, navy beans and noodles, custard pudding, clabbered milk, potato dumplings, and rhubarb cobbler.

Charlie shook hands with the bachelors and pointed them in the direction of the sod cutters. Jess Tracey, Wes Holmes, Frank Leslie Miner, and Art Wells came because of the anticipation of lots of good food.

Some families came in wagons, such as Wilt Clayton and his wife, Clara, and their three children, John and Kate Bray and their boy, Goy; Al and Sarah Melstrom and their little girl, Artie.

Mr. Bill Hill, a small, shy man, came by himself in a wagon. He brought a crock of persimmon beer and told Charlie that he was originally from Indiana, but had been in western Kansas for some time now.

Charlie was glad to take the crock to the creek to keep cool. He told Mr. Hill, "You sit down and have a cup of coffee or some creek water." When Charlie came back he said, "The day's turning hot. I doused my head in the creek." He slicked back his sandy hair, letting the water run down his neck. Hill was on his second cup of water.

Mr. Hill unbuttoned his shirt collar and rolled his sleeves. "I want to say something before I go to work."

"Maybe you should talk to Ma, or wait until Pa comes back from Wallace," said Charlie, who looked at Mr. Hill's dusty black shoes and dusty black suit. The jacket lying on the table was covered with hundreds of tiny seeds called sticktights. "I hope you're not a claim contester."

"Oh, no!" Mr. Hill ran his hand though his gray hair. "Some folks criticize my work, though. I brought the darkies to Kansas."

Charlie looked at Mr. Hill. "But you're not—not—"

"No, I'm not a darkie. But I'm human. I found a lawyer in Topeka, took him to Nicodemus, and together we set that town up on a lawful basis and let the citizens run it themselves. It's in a slump, but it will snap out of it when more southern darkies decide they can do well farming in Kansas."

"You founded that colorful town?" Charlie was astonished.

"I found those people were being soaked with fees for assistance in obtaining land and filing homestead papers. My lawyer friend and I cleared out the trouble in the Oberlin Land Office. We tar-and-feathered a young man named Bronson who was collecting those high fees."

Charlie's mouth fell open. "I met a Barney Bronson once. Dressed in buckskin pants."

"Same man. He's out of this country now. Went East to tell of his adventures in the Wild West. I heard he was mortally afraid of being lynched and hung not by citizens of Nicodemus but by white folks."

Charlie was stunned. He hardly felt the hot sun on his back drying his shirt and hair.

"How's your black dog?" asked Mr. Hill. "Mrs. Fletcher wants to know."

Charlie's breath exploded. "You know her—Zach—and his

pa? You know about Nick?"

Mr. Hill exploded with laughter. "Yes—it was the best story I'd heard in a long time. Unbelievable! But truth is stranger than fiction."

Charlie reached out to shake Mr. Hill's hand. "My pa says that, but I never knew what it meant until just now. Imagine that old man sleeping with my Henry rifle. Imagine me finding it in that place!" Charlie called the pup. "See. Nick's hardly a pup now. Doing fine. We couldn't do without that dog."

"I'll tell Mrs. Fletcher. Would your pa object if Matt Splitlog and Reverend Roundtree dug you folks a well?"

"Why would he do that?"

"Because Roundtree is a darky and Splitlog is a redskin."

"My pa went to Reverend Roundtree's church. Matt Splitlog is my friend. Jeems, who's to object? Are the other Splitlogs coming?" Charlie was already anticipating his welcoming of the three brothers.

"No, Mark and John are staying in Nicodemus to weave baskets or string beads for the settlers coming through. The town has a new industry—selling local crafts and homegrown edibles to settlers going West. Maybe it'll be a good-sized trading post in a couple of years."

"Pa and Ma will be pleased to see Reverend Roundtree again, and I want Pa to meet Matt. But I don't understand why they'd come all the way to Sappa country to dig a well."

"Son, it's a way of doing a kindness. Look at these people here today. Likely you've never met most."

Charlie nodded.

"Well, the next time you'll want to do some kindness, like help a new family build a house or barn, dig a well, pull a dumb cow out of a marsh," said Mr. Hill. "Some of this began with a kind-hearted young man and a rifle, you know."

"I didn't know it then," said Charlie.

"That's most commendable," said Mr. Hill. Then he looked shy again, as if he'd talked far too long. "I need to find a shovel or a pick."

"Mr. Hill," started Charlie. "You—you shouldn't work in Sunday trousers and those shoes, sir. Maybe we could talk with Ma and she'd find something of Pa's you could wear. My brother Will might have a pair of boots for you."

Mr. Hill winked. "See what I mean about kindness? I've already done most of my job. I'll make a couple of cuts with the shovel, then be on my way to tell my two friends to come dig your well."

Charlie opened his mouth, but Mr. Hill interrupted. "Don't fret, I'll see your mama before I go."

Mr. Hill carried the shovel when he went to talk to Mary. Charlie could see he was shy and had a hard time getting started, but once he got a conversation going he was all right. Charlie was sure his mother would tell Mr. Hill about what a hard worker Will was, that Frank was the baby, and that Ell was like Grandma Malinda and wanted to be a teacher and healer. Charlie went off to find Ell.

Going from the wagon to the barn, Charlie met two new arrivals, Otto Hurst and Marietta Roberts. Some of the women were cutting sod. The men loaded it on wagons and the slicker and hauled it to the area marked off for the house. Some of the boys spread fresh green cow manure on the hardened dirt floor. "Hey, what's that for?" asked Charlie, holding his nose.

"It's vile! It doesn't belong in a house. Who told you to do this?" shouted Ell, waving her arms and making a face.

One of the boys explained that when dried, cow dung would make a shiny, hard surface on the packed dirt and the smell would be gone in a few days.

"You'd better be right, or in a few days I'll find you and take you apart!" shouted Ell.

Some of the women were preparing more food over small fires or sitting on blankets in the shade of their wagons, tending young children or napping babies.

Charlie nodded to the women and called to Ell, "Hey, now you're talking like my sister!"

"Charlie, can you imagine a floor of cow pies?" She began to giggle.

"Listen, can you imagine Reverend Roundtree and Matt Split-log coming to dig a well for Pa?"

"They are? Reverend Roundtree and one of those Injuns? Oh, my goodness! Gosh! What's going to happen next?" She sat with her back against a boulder.

Charlie sat on the bare ground, careful to avoid a prickly pear. He sifted the dust through his fingers, letting the wind carry it three, four yards away. "I'm not a fortune-teller, but if you don't stop leading on—being friendly with Rob Collins, you'll fix things so that you'll never be a teacher. How many kids does Mrs. Collins have?"

"Five," said Ell, wondering what Charlie was talking about.

"Six, counting Rob," corrected Charlie, "and the little ones in a chain, each year."

"Ya—poor Mrs. Collins, maybe she doesn't know what caused all them kids. She's not too smart, you know. But she's not Rob's ma. His ma came from some mail order Mr. Collins answered. She died of fright when a plague of grasshoppers caught her out in a field and started eating her clothes. The story actually frightened me—it must have been awful. Rob was four or five and saw it."

Charlie said, "Ell, you're not good for him. He's not good for you. Why, any girl that is nice to him will be"—Charlie bit his tongue, then decided to say it out loud—"with child before he even talks about marriage."

"Charlie! I'm not that kind!" Ell cried. "Why are you talking like this? Just because you saw Rob give me a hug and kiss me. I'm old enough for that!"

"Rob would have taken more if I had not stood up in the barn, and you know it. I think that's what makes you so angry."

Ell began to cry. "Charlie, he gives me shivers. I like the feel of them. I think of him near naked like those Injuns. It gives me a strange feeling and it frightens me, but I keep thinking anyway."

Charlie suggested, "Why don't you talk to Ma about your feeling."

"No! She wouldn't know anything about my feeling! I couldn't," sobbed Ell.

"Then promise me something. Will you?"

"I don't know."

"Promise me you'll not let Rob think of you as a girl who is easy, you know. And you won't let him touch you—put his hand where he wants, the rest of the time he's here."

"Oh, why not? Then after that?"

"Before that, you'll notice other boys and you'll compare them to creepy Rob. There's something not right with him. I swear!" said Charlie.

"I don't believe that!" said Ell.

"Because you won't let yourself believe. Just watch for a while and keep yourself busy, not in a lather so your eyes are clouded."

"Humph! You sure have some notions!" Ell got up and went to help their mother with the noon meal.

Some of the families came because they could remember when Joe and Mary Irwin were here before and no more than poor dirt farmers like themselves, but driven out by the dust and drought. And here they were back again! The women wanted to see what kind of furniture Mary brought this time, if she had embroidery on her nightdresses. They wanted to see with their own eyes what changes had taken place with the Irwins. When neighbors came to a house-raising, not many secrets were kept.

The men were interested in the mechanics of the house building. The back wall of the Irwins' house was cut out of a hill.

After the midday meal the men did not stand around but went right to work again. Mary asked Charlie to dig a trench in the ground to keep leftover food cool. Charlie dug a square hole about four by four feet. Mary lined it with clean, damp dishtowels. "This'll keep the food fresh for tomorrow," she said.

The evening meal was mostly navy beans, corn bread, and coffee. The men sat out on the wild grass and talked about trenching below the surface of the floor. That is cutting a narrow ditch all around the perimeter of the house so that they could start the walls from the trench with chunks of evenly cut prairie marble. The children were rolled into blankets under the wagons. Mary saw it was getting dark. She went to each family and to the bachelors, saying, "You better lay here for the night." She brought out her extra comforters and fixed places in the hay for some of the women and small children who were not already asleep or did not want to sleep out under the stars.

Charlie could see no moon, but the stars forming the constellations winked like cold firelight: Cassiopeia, the Big and Little Dipper, Sagittarius, and Scorpio. The stars looked as if they could be touched. The falling stars whooshed through the dark heavens with a sparkling trail and no sound. Charlie put out his hand and the next falling star seemed to fall through his fingers like water. When his hand grasped around it, nothing was there. The star vanished like so much smoke in the wind.

By noon the next day Joe and Collins were back with the dimension stuff, two by eight boards for rafters, window frames, and sills, a door frame, and three glass windows, a couple hundred pounds of hard coal for Joe's forge, and three painted china vases for Mary, one for each windowsill.

Reverend Roundtree and Matt Splitlog came in about the same time and helped unload the wagon. Charlie was glad to see his pa shake hands with Matt and hand him a forked branch. Matt walked over the area in front of and beside the house. Under the lea of the hill on the east side the stick he held in his two hands dropped, pointing to the very spot Matt said a well should be dug. He promised Joe water at about twenty or thirty feet. "If I'd been back of the house on the hill, might be forty feet."

Andy Melstrom, Al's brother, built a pulley, or windlass, using small poles and oak logs. His pony pulled the end of a rope just far enough to raise a bucket out of the well hole to be emptied. Then the pony backed up to lower the bucket again.

Charlie yelled down the well hole, "Can you men get to the top for your noon meal?"

"Oh, for certain," called Reverend Roundtree. "Bill Hill told us he left persimmon beer. I can climb out of anything for that!"

Ell poured milk for the small children and coffee for the women. Mary poured the beer for the men, who smacked their lips. Will and Rob pretended they were full-grown men and drank their share before going back to work on the well digging. Others put undressed V-notched logs at the corners of the house and laced the two-by-eight oak rafters with willow sticks to hold the sod. The cow dung was dry to Hurd Horton's touch. He was ready for the floor's final treatment. He went to his wagon and brought up a couple five-gallon cans of fresh cow's blood. He'd saved it after butchering for the Errington and Rich grocery store in Goodland. He called in a couple of the bachelors to grab a broom. Several brooms lay in the bed of his wagon, stained brown from previous floor paintings. The men swept off the excess cow dung. Les Miner called out, "How thick should this blood be spread!"

"Until it's all used up. Then wash the cans in the creek and pop 'em in my wagon over there. It'll be a nice floor!"

Miner was not sure about that. He'd never heard of putting blood on top of the dried cow dung. Art Wells, also working the floor, explained, "Blood on top of dried dung makes a packed dirt floor nearly impervious to water, besides giving it a rich dark color."

Ell brought a dipper and a pail of creek water to the men sweeping the coagulated blood over the entire floor. "I hate this place! This soddy'll smell like a barn or slaughterhouse! It's vile!"

"I have to agree, it smells like a wolf den now, but the best opinion here, this'll be one of the finest floors in Sappa Meadows." Miner smiled. He was a rangy young man in his mid-twenties. His hair was tawny, nearly the same color as Ell's. "I thought I was going to be putting on a roof, but here I am sweeping a floor. Might as well be wearing an apron."

This made Ell laugh. She poured water over Wells's hands

before she'd let him hold the dipper. He had a shock of unruly dark hair that covered his ears. "I feel like a bloody savage," he said.

Ell held a hand to her lips. "Sshh! There's a true Wyandot digging the well, and he becomes furious if you call him savage."

"Is that right?" asked Miner. His brown eyes looked her square in the face. He looked like someone who would treat everyone fair. Ell could see that he didn't look like he'd cut a man down with words just because he knew something about him. "The Wyandot a friend of yours?"

"Oh, yes. We met on the trail coming to Sappa Meadows." Her eyes twinkled merrily. "I think you've named our place! Sappa Meadows! I like it. What's your name?"

"Frank Leslie Miner."

"I'm Art Wells. We're pleased to meet such a pretty girl out in farming country."

Ell blinked her long eyelashes.

"Say, will you have supper with me?" asked Miner, surprising himself with his boldness.

"Why, sure, if you wash real good first." Ell pinched her nose and went off to take the water pail to other workers.

Miner and Wells double-scrubbed before sitting in the grass a little ways from the other men, waiting for Ell to bring her plate of boiled squash and cabbage and salt pork. "The boiled cabbage smell mixes right in with the odor of that floor," she said, tucking her long skirt underneath her black-stockinged legs.

"Believe me, in a couple of weeks the smell's gone and the floor's hard and shines pretty as a new penny." Wells had his tin plate nearly clean.

"I just hope." Ell sighed, picked at her cabbage. "I should have gone to the creek for some sourgrass for greens."

"Don't fret, this is good grub." Miner went back for seconds. Wells drank the juice from his plate. Miner came back and said, "Your folks have one of the best soddies I've seen. And look how good the grass grows out here in your meadow! Oats and wheat'll grow as well. You crochet or knit?"

"No," said Ell. "Is that important?"

"It is to me. So, you cook and read. What else?" Miner's eyes looked directly at her, so she blushed.

"That's the only reason you boys came here—to eat. How'd you know I read?"

"We seen you with the younguns, reading, writing, and making them sit still with stories. We worked quiet and heard them stories." Wells picked his teeth with a dried grass stem.

"Art! Don't tell our secrets! You know we didn't make any mistake coming for the food," said Miner.

"Want me to teach you to read and write?" Ell teased.

"Maybe I'm foolish to say this—but I already know," said Wells.

"I taught first graders in Chillicothe."

"Ya? Well, guess what I do," said Miner.

"I know you don't own a restaurant, because you'd eat all your profits."

"I'm a farmer, but I've worked in the silver mines in Colorado, Cripple Creek, and I've done books for the mining company. We had a Chinese cook, always made chop suey, stew with rice."

"I've never met a miner before," Ell said.

"So, now you've met Les Miner. I brought your pa a gift."

"For the housewarming?" Ell was surprised that a bachelor would think of such a thing. It was usually the women who brought gifts of food and small things for the new house.

"I brought some seed corn. It's special. It's named after the old man that first grew it in Kansas. Sherrod's White Dent. Wells gave me a couple handfuls of seed first. I've grown it two years," said Miner.

"I knew a man who grew it," said Wells, motioning for Charlie to bring his plate over and sit with the three of them. "Listen, this man had corn that was resistant to those gol-darned, pesky borers and grew three ears to each stalk."

"Maybe your pa and I can start something new in Kansas if we get good yields," said Miner.

"This is the second time Pa's been here. The drought of seventy-eight was too much and the winters were hard on Ma," said Ell.

Charlie set his plate on the grass. He was worn out from lifting huge sod blocks, but didn't want to admit that in front of anyone. "Was last winter as bad as some guys said?" he asked.

Wells was half-asleep with his arms around and his head on his knees. Rob Collins walked by and came back to sit down. Charlie picked up the empty tin plates and told Rob to take them to the women for washing. Rob scowled and looked at Ell. She was looking at Miner, who was saying, "I'll tell you something. It was called the Killer Blizzard and came the first of the year. There was wind, rain, and then it was twenty below and there was wind and snow. Until the end of January the temperature averaged between fifteen to thirty below. Lots of people froze to death and nearly all livestock died of cold or scarcity of feed. I found birds and jackrabbits frozen to death on my place."

Rob muttered, "Damn cold winter," and left with the dirty plates.

Charlie thought the account was fascinating. Ell thought maybe it was exaggerated, mostly she was interested with the rich timbre of Miner's voice.

Charlie said, "Jeems, that was cold! I hope our house keeps the wind out."

"That house is tight as a woodtick in a dog's tail," said Wells, stretching his legs out and rubbing his eyes. "Soddies are better than board houses out here. They'll hold up under a pile of snow, high winds, gully washer rains, and the moisture-eating hot suns."

"I'd have a puncheon floor if it were mine," said Ell. "Then I'd use a splint broom. Can't use nothing but a feather duster on a dirt floor—if you can stop holding your nose long enough."

"Aw, don't complain so danged much. Remember what I said. It will be fine, just give it time. I'm gonna leave that sack of seed with your pa. Thanks for the food," said Miner.

"You're welcome, Mr. Miner," said Ell.

"You ought to just call me Les," said Miner, pulling Wells to his feet. The boys waved and ambled off to work.

When the boys were out of hearing distance, Ell said to Charlie, "They're all right. But that one with tawny hair sure can talk."

Charlie inspected the progress at the well first thing after eating rhubarb pie for breakfast. He was surprised how much was done. Sand was reached at the floor of the deep hole. Split logs shored up the sides. His father had a rag tied around his head to keep perspiration from dripping into his eyes. The ugly scar in the form of an X on the side of the Reverend's face was crimson. Matt saw Charlie at the top of the hole. "Heave-ho! Here comes a bucket of sand." Andy Melstrom's pony pulled the rope and Melstrom emptied it on the pile of clay and sand. The pony backed up and the bucket was lowered. "We ought to strike water before noon," predicted Matt. "Charlie, get us more logs. Right away!"

Charlie found Art Wells and the two of them rolled half a dozen logs that were in a pile by the creek onto the slicker and pulled them up beside the house. "Hey!" yelled Charlie. "Pa and the guys in the well needs these split right away!"

"Keep your shirt on!" called Les Miner, climbing down from a window frame. Miner and Collins placed iron wedges at the right intervals and hit them with heavy sledgehammers until all six logs were split in less than twenty minutes. Charlie and Wells dragged the logs into place and one by one put them down the deep hole. Then Charlie lay on his belly for a moment to get a better look inside. He could see that the three men in the well had to move fast because one side was caving. Charlie motioned for Melstrom and Wells to have a look. Matt was wedging a log in place and oozing sand popped it flat on the floor.

"Gotta get this wet sand out of here," said the Reverend, who had taken his shirt off and hung it over the handle of a shovel not in use. "Clear the way! Coming up topside with a full bucket!"

Melstrom nearly tripped over Charlie as he got back to his pony to pull up the bucket. Two, three bucketfuls and the new log wedged into place. The three men on the bottom of the hole sighed with relief and began to wedge in more logs. Then they dug the sand from the bottom. Charlie moved out of the way, then decided to take one last look. The bucket was brimful and slowly coming up. He heard the rope snap, then saw the bucket tumble back into the hole. "Yowee!" he yelled when he heard the snap.

The strange cry was enough to cause Matt to look up and see the sun glint off the bucket's side, then nothing but the falling shadow. He darted to the middle of the hole and pushed the Reverend, who was doggedly digging with his head down, to the side where Joe was holding a log in place. Joe was smashed against the log and the jolt caused more sand to gush out from behind the barricade. The falling bucket missed the Reverend's head by inches.

"Hey, you up there! You all aiming to scare or score?" Reverend Roundtree hollered.

Charlie was holding his breath. "Jeems! It was an accident!"

"It was your yelling that alerted me—so thanks, my friend!" called Matt. He secured the bucket, refilled it, and sent it to the top while Joe and the Reverend pushed the logs upright and into place against the hydrostatic pressure of the wet, oozing sand.

Charlie stayed at the top with Melstrom and checked the rope at periodic intervals. It wouldn't do to have any more mishaps.

About noon the men at the bottom of the well had decided to abandon the wedging of the split wood. Water had begun to flow in from the bottom for good. The three men tried to get all the lumber away from the sides and let it rise to the top with the water. Melstrom and Charlie sent the bucket down for the small sticks and pieces of dimension Joe had used. Suddenly Joe called, "Matt, grab the rope! Let the damn wood float up! Tread water! Watch the wood!"

The water crept up fast. It was like bubbling brown porridge. Matt grabbed the rope, cut the bucket off, and heaved it with all his strength to the top of the hole. If Charlie had not caught the bucket in midair near the edge, it would have fallen back and sunk out of sight in that oozing thick brown water.

Matt slipped the rope loop he'd made over the Reverend's head and down under his arms. The Reverend moved up the side of the hole. The pony strained with the rope. Melstrom urged it on and dived to the edge of the hole when he saw the Reverend's hands clawing and pulling at the mud and rocks. The minute Reverend Roundtree was standing up, caked with mud and sticks and sand, a cheer came from the gathering crowd of women and children. "Hooray! Hooray!"

The rope disappeared again. Matt secured it around Joe, who clung to a log caught against the side. Before being pulled upward, Joe tugged and heaved to loosen the log. Wood left to rot in his well would contaminate his good water. When he was safe the cheers greeted him. Joe waved back, but did not keep his eyes on the group. He kneeled and put his face over the well to make certain that Matt had his head above water and the rope under his arms, ready to be lifted out. There were more cheers when Matt came over the edge.

Mary and Cora brought out the crock of leftover persimmon beer. Mary'd wrapped it in layers of newspaper to keep it cool for this momentous occasion. The night before she'd found the recipe printed on fine vellum paper waxed to the side of the crock so that it appeared at first to be a decoration.

Mash and add 1 cup cornmeal to 1 full gal. washed ripe persimmons. Add 5 gals. water and 4 cups sugar. Let set until fruit rises (3 to 4 days). Strain and drink. Or bottle and seal. Liquid is fizzy and light-colored. Fill bottles only 2/3 full as it may be explosive if opened on a hot summer day.*

*Reprinted with permission of Ferne Shulton, from *Pioneer Comforts and Kitchen Remedies.*

Charlie helped take the logs and boards from the well by snaring them in a lasso loop. There was all of fifteen feet of water—more than Joe had hoped for. Joe had privately figured it would take him, with his three boys, all next spring to get the well dug. Now it was done and the remaining beer was the right touch to celebrate with.

When the beer was gone the well diggers went to the creek to wash off the mud. Charlie tied a tin cup to his rope and brought up a sample of the heavily sedimented well water. He knew it would be clear in a day or two. He found Ell and told her to try his sample.

"Charlie! It's full of gravel! I don't have a gizzard. I think you are trying to poison me!" Ell tossed the muddy water out and threw the cup at Charlie. "That water is so thick a snake could have been hiding in it!"

"Poisonous snakes float on water!" called Charlie.

NINE

Housewarming

Joe wanted to give these men something for their valuable labor and time. He looked at his house. The windows were already in the frames. The soddy was large, like he'd marked off, with enough space to divide into three bedrooms. The kitchen range was already against the wall, making that part look like a kitchen. Joe began to talk with Matt, the Reverend Roundtree, and Jack Collins. "I'd like to pay for this labor and time."

Collins said, "You couldn't hire any one of us to do this work. Not even for you. People here are proud. You have our friendship. You owe us your friendship. One day we'll call on you or your woman for something."

"That's no more than fair," said Joe. "But still I'd like to do something now."

Reverend Roundtree eyed the pile of hard coal Joe had brought in from Wallace. "You're a smith. Why don't you make something?"

Matt eyed the portable forge and the tools that lay in a heap on the ground near the chicken house. "A steel-bladed knife that holds its sharpness. Any man'd find that useful."

By afternoon Joe had the forge together and fired up. He selected a bar of steel and turned it over in his hands to make certain it was perfect for what he had in mind: a bowie knife, with the blade and hand guard all from the same metal piece. Joe agreed with Matt. A man in this country had use for a good bowie knife. Joe heated the metal a red-orange and hit the end lick after lick, shaping it just right with his hammer. Joe concentrated on making the blade. He wanted it to be his best work.

Not wanting to be outdone, Mary asked Charlie if he could help her make a splint broom from an old hickory pole she found in the wagon. "Ma, it'll take me until next week, if I find out how to make one. I've never seen it done in my life!" said Charlie, wondering why his mother had asked him to do this chore.

"Well, start now and use a sharp jackknife to hurry it," said his mother, pouring water from a pitcher into Nick's empty pan. "Seek out Reverend Roundtree."

"Does he have a jackknife?" asked Charlie.

"He has understanding and creativity," said Mary.

Charlie and Reverend Roundtree sat near Joe's portable forge and took turns shaving fine splits from the bottom of the pole up ten inches, removing the very heartwood, then shaving from ten inches above, down close to those at the bottom, turning the top splints down and tying them with wire.

"That'll make a woman's floor look bright and grateful. The splints are thin and soft enough to be used on a treated dirt floor, I believe," said the Reverend. "Where did this sharp, two-handled shaver come from?"

Charlie explained that it was from the cordwainer's set of tools that had once belonged to a grandfather he'd never known. "But some say I resemble him."

"That tells me he was a fine man," said the Reverend.

Joe was finished making the bowie knife. He was pleased. It was one of the finest he'd ever seen. The hand guard was smooth and straight. He made a handle out of a piece of cedar heartwood he found among a box of gear. He gouged his initials in the handle, then cleaned it out with a hot fine blade. He liked the balance and feel of the knife. He could see any one of the men around his place cutting the tops off a field of beets or turnips or harvesting corn or skinning out a deer or cleaning fish.

Will was working with some of the bachelors putting the stovepipe and chimney in place. Mary warned them not to scratch her floor.

Everything was completed before supper. The women decided everyone would eat outside even though the range was all ready to burn stove wood. They planned how they would use the remaining food. When that was over the women went to their wagons or reached into their pockets for a small remembrance to leave with Mary. This was customary. The men sat around on the gravel bar on the creek to wash and refresh themselves, and to wait for the women to put supper out.

Charlie sat around with Ell while she and Frank played school with the Collinses' young ones. He could not help but hear the chatter of the women and the good-time voice his mother had as she laughed and talked.

Effa Belless was sitting at the table under the canvas directly across from Mary. "You should have my recipe for good haying water," she said. "My ma made it all the time and took it to my pa's haying crew. Heat like today made their throats feel like they'd swallered slaked lime. This is it: You mix two cups of wild honey with a cup of cider vinegar, stir, and keep in a glass jar. Then add four teaspoons of that mix to every glass of water you put in the water tub for the field. You can crush in cinnamon or clove if you have any."

An old woman smiled broadly because she'd brought a tiny poke of cinnamon, and she hurriedly pulled it out of her apron pocket.

A couple of the women brought candles, one a tatting spool, another spice sachets and a piece of muslin home-dyed with bluebottle blooms and alum.

Mrs. Russel gave Mary something new, wrapped in fancy blue and white paper. It was store-bought soap that was so light it floated on water and was labeled boldly: IVORY.

Kate Bray brought a cough syrup bottle filled with rosewater and glycerin. Clara Clayton brought a white hen, which was put into the chicken house and given a plate of water and a handful of potato peelings.

Cora Collins gave Mary a cotton pound sugar sack full of tiny pearllike chive bulbs. "The leaves are the best thing for salads and you'll have lilac-colored flowers from them."

Mary said thank you over and over. "Thank you, chives will be in a garden close to the house early next spring."

Marietta Roberts told folklore stories. "A horseshoe hung in your chimney flue will protect that white hen from hawks."

Ell heard that and rummaged through Joe's boxes until she found an old horseshoe.

"Were any of your boys born on January first?" Sarah Melstrom asked.

"No," said Mary. "Will is closest, February 27th."

"Maybe—that's close enough. He should be lucky in raising cattle."

"He'll be glad to hear that," said Mary, giving Sarah a quick hug. "Charlie, go fetch the men. Let's eat before sundown so there'll be more time for dancing. Joe's going to play his fiddle tonight."

The women chattered like magpies as they brought out the food from the cooling trench and arranged it on the table. Some with small children fed them first so the babies would not be whiny when the men came to sit with them.

Charlie heard the men laugh, splash water, and run around snapping shirts or belts at one another. For three days they'd worked hard; now it was time for fun and relaxation. "Why did the farmer take his nose apart," asked Jess Tracey. "To see it run!" he whooped. "Here's another: Why did the farmer put a chair in the coffin? Do you give up? For rigor mortis to set in!" The men whooped.

After supper, while the women were doing the dishes and the men were tramping down the grass to make a smooth, slick place for dancing, Cora and the old woman who'd brought the poke of cinnamon put up horse blankets as temporary curtains between the rooms in the new soddy.

"It'll be nice for them to have a private place," said Cora.

"Nice," the old woman said with a laugh. "I guess we know what you think is nice with all them children you have. We've all had it. When winter comes, there'll be more of it."

Cora looked properly shocked, but she could not wait to tell Mary what the old woman had said so they could have a good laugh.

The sun moved quietly down below the horizon. Instantly there was a different light. It was a mix of cloud-reflected sunlight and early starlight. The golden glow reflected off each object it touched so that everything stood out as if giving off an inner luminescence. Each stem, blade of grass, stone, crack or abrasion, bird, beak, and feather was more defined than with the energy of pure daylight. The radiance that separated each thing from the whole object also seemed to fan out and unite everything with the eerie glow. The gray shadows darkened, people talked in hushed voices.

The mood was right for Mary and Joe to go over the threshold of the finished house first. After they were inside a few moments according to custom, the others went in quickly, bringing some piece of household goods, such as the cedar chest, rocking chair, a bundle of clothing. Some were disappointed about the meagerness of the furniture, but others nodded in quiet approval. Several men brought armloads of sweet, wild grass to put under the bedding until wooden bed frames could be made. By now the light was faded to dark gray and the twinkling stars were clearly visible. People's voices became bright and gay. They chattered like a flock of sparrows.

Joe beat a tin cup on the Majestic range for quiet. "My family and I thank every one of you, and to show our appreciation we'd like to give a gift to each of you." A murmur went through the crowd that sounded like a babbling brook right after a thunderstorm. Joe beat the cup on the range. "You and I know that's impossible, so I'd like to give each man a chance to have this brand-new bowie knife." He held the knife above his head so all could see. "Then some lucky lady will have a chance to own this splint broom." Mary held the broom high.

The murmur grew to a loud buzz like the wind in the tops of trees, and then there was a clapping of hands.

"I saw both of them there prizes being made this afternoon," someone said. "Joe's a right smart smith," said another. "My old lady'd like that swell broom."

Ell had paper slips with everyone's name. Charlie put the slips in his father's broad-brimmed hat. He took the hat to the middle of the crowd, stirred them a moment, then held the hat on the top of his head so he could not see inside. All the time he was talking to keep the crowd quiet and amused. "I'll tell you what I'm going to do! I'll get these papers mixed real good! The first name that is pulled out will be the proud owner of Pa's dandy present to you all—the all-purpose bowie knife, if he be a man!"

Someone joked, "And if *he* be a woman?"

Charlie answered, "Then that woman is the happy owner of the splint broom Ma made." Charlie looked over the crowd as he held the hat on the top of his head, adding to the anticipation. An idea popped into his head. "We have a genuine preacher here with us. Reverend Roundtree from Nicodemus! He will lead us in prayer, so everybody, bow your heads." Charlie nodded his head, nearly spilling the papers from the hat he held on top, toward the Reverend who was as astonished as the others. But Charlie saw the first look on the Reverend's face and knew everything was all right. The Reverend was pleased as a cat with cream. Some of the people had not noticed the Reverend's dark skin and now stood back as if awed or afraid of someone different.

Reverend Roundtree was used to public speaking. He picked up a wooden kitchen chair and stood on it so everyone could have a good look. People moved around from the back so that he faced everyone. The only noise was the scuffling of feet; people, for the most part, kept their mouths closed, waiting to see what would happen. They saw the Reverend's shirt was spotless, where it was caked with mud a few hours before. His trousers were clean and dry, but stiff from being dried by first being beaten on a large stone, then lying out in the hot sun. His boots were shiny from being polished with handfuls of cottonwood leaves. He smiled and the wide X-shaped scar on his cheek looked more like a cross. His hands raised and spread out, encompassing everyone in the room. He bowed his head. The people's nervous stirring quieted. "Oh, Lord, our Father in Heaven, we, Your chilluns, thank You for this here powerful feeling of friendship. We praise You! Oh, Lord, remember us the year round. Bless this house and all who enter it. We praise You! Hallelujah!" He raised his head and the people responded.

"Hallelujah!"

The room beams seemed to vibrate and dirt sift from the walls to the shiny dark floor. The Reverend put his arms down. "This is the best house-raisin' I've been to in my entire life. The fellowship is strong and the food is excellent. What we needs now is music. Mr. Irwin can play his fiddle and we'll sing 'The Old Rugged Cross.'"

Charlie took the hatful of little papers from his head. He saw that no one was standing back with awe or fear. In fact, when the Reverend had them sing "I'm Gwine to Alabamy," many were toe-tapping and hand-clapping. Charlie wondered if he could get back and have the drawing. It seemed people had now put that behind and were more eager to sing. It dawned on him this was what Colonel Johnson was saying when he told Charlie not to upstage him. Charlie motioned for the Reverend to step off the chair a moment. The people kept singing, "For to see my mammy—Ah."

Charlie said, "Don't upstage my drawing for the prize too long, cuz at midnight this house turns to a punkin."

The Reverend chuckled and winked at Charlie, then climbed back on the chair and sang with the people. Charlie sang so loud he could not hear the others. It felt good. When the song was over, Charlie moved in front of Reverend Roundtree. "I'll tell you what I'm going to do right now!" Charlie's voice boomed out around all the people. "The Reverend will reach into this hat I'm holding on the top of my head. He will give it one more good stirring. Then he will take out one slip of paper and open it." Charlie could feel the Reverend stirring the papers, and the room was still as snow falling into a moonlit river. Charlie moved to one side and looked up. The Reverend held a slip in his hand and his eyes were shut tight. "Open your eyes and read the name of the lucky winner!"

The Reverend looked at the paper and his black eyes grew wide, then they squinted down, as if he couldn't read the writing. His mouth formed a circle, then flattened out as he licked his lips. "The Lord, he is playing tricks on my eyesight!"

"What does the paper say?" someone shouted. "Let Charlie read it!" called another.

The Reverend handed the slip to Charlie, who nearly doubled over with laughter. "Folks, you saw that this here drawing was fair and square. Isn't that right?"

Everyone answered, "Yes!"

"Well, the name Reverend Roundtree pulled from my pa's hat is his own! The bowie knife goes to Reverend Roundtree!" Charlie turned and reached up and shook the Reverend's hand. The Reverend was all smiles. The crowd was all smiles and applause. Charlie felt a great relief, because he saw what the Reverend had at first imagined, that the crowd could have as easily turned and made wrongful accusations. Joe presented the knife in a leather case to the Reverend. Charlie felt the need to keep the momentum going. He climbed up on the chair.

"I need a lady volunteer to stir the papers and pull out another winner!" he called.

Cora Collins came forward and stirred with her whole fist. The people held their breath to see what would happen this time. Charlie held the hat up and bent so that Cora could just reach in. "Now, on this bit of paper is the name of a lady—"

"What if it's a man?" came a voice from the back.

"We'll draw again!" Charlie smiled. "On this paper may be the name of the lady who will have her floors shining with gratitude. She'll have a new splint broom!"

Cora held the slip of paper between her thumb and forefinger as her eyes moved over the crowd. "Cass Minney, Grandma Minney!" There was a buzzing in the crowd and a movement on the left side. Finally some of the people moved away so that Charlie could see the old grandmother who had brought the tiny poke of cinnamon. She was sound asleep in his ma's rocking chair.

Mary was beside the old woman, patting her hands and whispering in her ear. Her eyes flew open and her toothless gums parted.

"For me? Thank you! Mine? Why I've never won anything before!" Mary gave her a hug and laid the broom across her lap. Both women had watery eyes.

Cora whispered, "Praise the Lord! It couldn't have gone to a better lady!"

Charlie was back on the chair waving his arms. "There's dancing out on the prairie, and I know for a fact that my pa is playing the fiddle and Reverend Roundtree is calling the square dances!"

Charlie gave back his pa's hat and saw Matt smiling and talking with Jack Collins. They were both as happy as Charlie that the Reverend had won the bowie knife. Charlie was going to say something to the two men, until he saw Rob Collins sidle close to Ell, who carried a saltcellar.

"What's the salt for?" Rob asked. "You fixing some grub for your other men friends?" His eyes ran over the length of her.

Ell's green eyes locked with Rob's blue ones. "Some of us women that felt the need to make a wish sprinkled salt over our left shoulder," she said and turned her head away.

"Take a walk with me. You wished for me, didn't you?" Rob had a pleading in his voice. He leaned purposefully closer. Ell felt the goose pimples rise, but it was not all excitement. She felt anger. He'd looked at her like some prize filly he'd found and intended to break in. Such conceit! she thought.

Charlie wanted to step in and tell Rob to get lost, but he decided he ought to see if Ell was right first. She'd said she could take care of herself.

"Hell's fire, who'd miss us?" he insisted. "We could get to be real good friends."

Ell was not only angry, she was afraid Rob could make a scene and spoil this wonderful time for everyone. She decided to walk with him, staying near the square dance area.

Les Miner put his hand on Charlie's shoulder. "I've been looking for your sister. I'd like to dance with her. You seen where she went?"

"Sure," said Charlie. He had a feeling of relief. "She went outside, probably wanted to dance."

Miner hurried outside. He caught up to Ell. He saw that Rob walked with her, but chose to ignore him because he was known as a troublemaker in the area, used to making everything go his way.

"I'm glad the Reverend got your pa's knife. Course, I would have liked it," Miner said.

"Actually, the Reverend worked harder. He's still working, listen . . ." said Ell.

They could hear the Reverend calling, "Hunt your partners, and a do-si-do we'll go!"

"You be my partner?" said Miner

"I love to dance," said Ell. She looked at Rob.

"Go on—I can't dance. I'll wait," Rob said. "Then I'll take you for that walk."

"Thanks," said Ell. She turned away from Rob, but heard him cuss under his breath.

"Damnit, I'll have my way with you yet!"

"Nice the old woman got the broom. I like her, even when she's sleeping, better'n that pest, Rob. He's not likable in my book. Your folks are sure well liked. Nice thing to do. You know, the drawing. Makes folks feel appreciated."

Miner was talking close to Ell's ear. She enjoyed the tickling sensation his breath caused and she giggled.

"What if you'd won the broom?" she said.

"Well, I can't clean house any more'n I can sew lace on a collar. Anyway, that's woman's work. Don't you think so?"

"I think that's what most men would say. I'd say a person ought to do what he does best. For instance, if I can set a broken bone better'n you, then I ought to do that. If you can make lye soap better'n me, then you ought to do that."

Miner's brown eyes were flecked with yellow and reminded Ell of a friendly pup. "A little girl like you can set broken bones?"

"I can," she said matter-of-factly.

"Then your logic makes sense. Let's dance."

Everyone was dancing. Frank was hopping up and down with one of the Collinses' little girls. Charlie twirled baby Carrie around several times. She became dizzy and staggered around him giggling. He munched on a pocketful of dried apples. The smaller children held their hands out for pieces of apple. Once in a while Charlie danced around with a child sitting on his shoulder.

Rob was with Will when they heard of some of the men

cracking a couple of jugs of hard cider that were in the back of the Brays' wagon. The two of them joined the drinking until Rob noticed Ell sitting in the grass talking to Art Wells, while Miner went for eats.

"I've got some unfinished business," he said to Will, and ambled over to Ell. "You avoiding me?" he asked, smiling so that the lantern light near Joe and the Reverend glinted off a soft gold barely traceable mustache above his lip. "What have I done to deserve such treatment?" He was trying to be charming.

Ell knew she'd promised to walk with him and now wished she hadn't. "I'm not avoiding you," she said, but turning her head so as not to meet his gaze. "I have to be a good hostess and dance and talk with everybody. It's expected of a good neighbor."

"Be a good neighbor and take a short walk with me, then," he said.

There was no way out. She rolled her eyes skyward as if to say, I'd prefer not, but I must, after all, he worked on the soddy.

"I'll probably eat that corn pone Les is bringing for you!" called Wells.

"See, I said you bachelor boys eat everything in sight!" Ell called back teasingly.

"I'm not letting you go this time," said Rob. He took one of Ell's hands. "We'll go down by the creek and sit on the gravel bar. I'll show you my favorite constellation."

Twilight was long gone and the sky glittered with millions of silver stars. The air was still, bone-dry, and cool. An owl somewhere in a tree by the creek called. A whippoorwill called back. Ell did not take her hand back. She felt relaxed and fancied she could make the walk something enjoyable.

"See there in the western sky is Venus, a planet of love and beauty," he said.

She saw it bright and clear, low on the horizon.

They walked without speaking. Then Rob had his left arm around Ell's waist, and he moved in front of her and put his right arm across her shoulders and held her hard against himself, his left hand slipping down past the small of her back, resting on her buttock.

Ell gasped and she became alert. She pushed herself free and ran to the gravel bar. "Now show me your stars."

Rob was displeased he'd let her go so easily. "You'll like what I show you," he said dreamily.

Ell felt a curious warming in her midsection. She was inquisitive of what he'd show, but also, since the experience in the barn and talk with Charlie, she was fearful not knowing what liberties he might try.

"You can't be afraid of me?" he said roughly.

"You? What's there to be afraid of? Your parents are friends with mine," she said. "Thus, you must be honorable. What do you want me to see?"

"Honorable—right," he said. He felt suddenly off balance. No one had called him honorable before. "Why don't we just sit here and watch for falling stars? They look so close you can catch one. See the five stars in the shape of a chair? Know who sits there?" he asked. He lay back on the gravel to look up.

"That's the old Greek Goddess—my grandma told me," said Ell.

Rob turned and pulled on her arm. "I'm supposed to tell the answers." He laughed arrogantly.

She lost her balance as he pulled and she fell off the stone she sat on. Her legs flew out and her skirt billowed upward. She began to laugh and get up. It was an opportunity Rob would not let pass. He rolled to her, took her head between his large hands, and pressed his mouth to hers.

Ell felt his lips warm and hard as they moved against hers. His hands held her shoulders and one leg came across her thighs so that she could not move. She felt his tongue move against her lips, along with a tingling sensation that spread downward to her chest and to that strange place in her belly where the fire grew and spread wherever he touched her. She opened her mouth and his tongue darted between her lips. Ell pressed her tongue against his and her heart seemed to swell and beat faster. The wet kiss was a wonderful new sensation. Her hands grasped at his shoulders and curled around his neck.

Time was suspended. Rob's breathing was fast and he fumbled at the hooks and eyes on the front of her dress. His hands brushed against her breasts.

"Don't! Don't do this!" she whispered.

"One look! Ell, please!" he pleaded.

His words gave Ell a delicious shiver that roared down her back to that center fire. His hands worked on her camisole. Suddenly one hand slid under the garment and cupped her breast. Her whole chest was on fire. It was an eternity before her hands covered his and pushed them aside with astounding strength. She heard a twig snap. Her mind awakened and became alert. She heard shouts and footsteps, or was it her imagination?

Rob knew he could overpower her, and he desperately wanted to. But something in the back of his mind held him, either the look on her face, or the compliment she'd given when she said he was honorable. "Jesus Christ!" he whispered. "I just want to look. I won't hurt you. You'd feel good just showing me, I promise. Give me my way!"

"I can't!" she whispered. "Don't spoil this night. There's someone coming!" She twisted away and her fingers were clumsy as she put her clothing in order.

Rob swore again and moaned as he pulled himself away from her and stood up.

"I hear noises!" Ell felt ill at ease. She gave a stifled laugh and started back toward the dancers.

A rustle in the grass and a drunken roar of surprise caused both Ell and Rob to jump back. It was Will toting Charlie's Henry rifle. "I'm looking for a pal to do a little target practicing with me!" he shouted. "Hey—I've found him! Come on, Robby. I'll prove I can shoot better'n you." Will staggered out on the gravel bar. "I've three tomato cans for targets and a handful of shells."

Ell knew she'd run into trouble. Will was so shaky he couldn't hit the side of a barn.

Rob took one look at the rifle and his eyes gleamed. "Let me sight through once. You think we can see in this light? There's only half a moon up there."

"I'll put the cans on that big white rock. We'll see it. Who was that with you? You and one of the boys came out to skip flat stones in the creek or tell dirty jokes?" asked Will. "Or you scouting Injuns?"

Rob chuckled.

Ell was running so fast she had a stitch in her side. She stopped and bent over to ease the pain.

Charlie was coming down the path with his rope over his shoulder.

"Hey, Ell! I thought you were dancing. You see Will? He swiped my rifle and ran around bragging about what a good shot he is. I aim to rope him and bring him in before Pa finds out he's been in the hard cider. Jeems, I hope he doesn't fire that rifle."

Charlie didn't wait for an answer but ran on toward the creek.

He found Will and Rob setting up the empty tomato cans and swung the rope around his head a couple of times. Will must have heard the whir of the loop in the air, because he turned his head to look across the gravel bar just as the loop settled around his shoulders. The rifle clattered to the stones and Will yelled as though he'd been caught in a bobcat trap. Rob hid behind the big white rock, thinking they'd for sure been attacked by Injuns.

Charlie tied his end of the rope to an oak tree and went out to pick up his rifle. He kept beyond the distance of the rope length. He heard Will moaning and Rob breathing fast little shallow breaths. He picked up the rifle, wiped it off on his sleeve. Then he went to Will, who was lying on his face.

"Don't shoot!" cried Will. "You can have the gun!"

"Damn tootin', I can!" yelled Charlie. "And why'd you think I'd shoot you? I'm Charlie—your kid brother."

Will groaned again.

Charlie put a foot in the middle of Will's back. "Give me the shells you swiped, or I'll stomp on your back."

"Take the shells out of my right front pocket. Don't stomp on my back—I'll throw up. Oh, I'm not feeling so good."

Charlie took the shells and put them in his own pocket. He waited for Will to heave. Then they went back to the dancing and sat on the sidelines to watch. The little children were all asleep in wagons, or under wagons.

Ell was dancing with Miner. She spotted Charlie. "Let's tell my brother Charlie to get some water or coffee for Pa and Reverend Roundtree. They've been playing and hollering out dances for quite a while."

"Now, that's good thinking!" said Miner. "I'll go with Charlie and get me some salt pork wrapped in corn pone. Dancing gives me an appetite. You want some?"

"I can't eat anything more. I just want to dance. So hurry or I'll find your friend Art Wells to dance with," teased Ell.

They took both cold water and hot coffee to Joe and the Reverend. Joe asked Charlie to stay and sing a while so that the Reverend could rest his voice. Charlie not only sang, but also did a few rope tricks to entertain the crowd and give his pa a rest from fiddling.

Back with Ell, Miner said, "You know this is the most fun I've had since some of the boys gave a Welshman some likker and took his carbide lamp so's he thought he'd been poisoned and had gone blind."

"You didn't?" Ell giggled.

"No—but some other sport did. That Welshman came near

putting his teeth down the sport's throat when he found it was a joke."

Ell and Miner danced until the pearl-gray dawn appeared. Then Miner remembered he'd left a few chores at his place. He smiled, patted her hand, and hurried off to locate his horse. He turned and called, "See you sometime soon."

Ell waved and smiled. She realized she was tired and for the first time noticed most of the people had already left. Her mother and Cora Collins washed dishes inside the new sod house. Charlie dried and stacked them.

They could hear the last stragglers call out good-byes and the wagon wheels grind over gravel. There was singing in the distance as the wagons rolled down the two ruts called a road.

Jack Collins came in the house to say that he had all the little children rolled up in blankets and in the back of the wagon. It was now sunup and time to go on home. Cora wiped her hands, gave Mary a hug, and waited for Jack to shake Joe's hand. Then they were gone.

"That's everyone," said Joe with a sigh. "It's just us, the Irwins, and this land now."

"Someone ought to see if Rob Collins is still at the creek!" said Charlie.

"He's in the back of the wagon, dead to the world. As sound asleep as Will and Frank are on the hay back there in their room," said Joe.

Charlie went to the boys' bedroom and fell into his blankets, not bothering to remove more than his coiled rope. He was asleep instantly.

Ell took a candle to see where her blankets were in her bedroom and blew it out after curling up in a down quilt. She knew she'd sleep through the next day.

Mary arranged the comforters over the clean hay in her and Joe's bedroom. She pushed extra hay under Joe's place.

Joe's voice was quiet. "It is going to be a good home. The people are the best. My dear, look at that sun coming up through the window. You'll have to get some curtains up. Won't bother me now, though. I'll sleep all day."

"Me, too," Mary said with a sigh. "Those women are wonderful. I'm kind of looking forward to new settlers coming in. We'll have more parties."

"This was not only a party—it was work. Don't you know what a party can be like?"

She murmured, "I guess I do."

"I'll tell you what. I'll wake up at noon and if the younguns are still asleep and I feel more strength, I'll show you a party in the hay, Mrs. Irwin."

"I'm looking forward to it," she said with a smile curling her lips. She closed her eyes and was asleep.

TEN

Goodland, Kansas

Goodland grew from one soddy, which housed the Sherman County Development Company, to several hundred soddies from June to November 1887. The business buildings were lined side by side along both sides of a wide dirt road called Main Street. Several of the buildings were fronted with clapboard so they looked modern and permanent. The expensive, eight-thousand-dollar wooden courthouse was at the eastern end of the street. There were rumors that a future Rock Island Railroad line would run parallel with Main Street.

That fall a Grand Rally was planned by A. B. Montgomery, the secretary of the Sherman County Development Company, to show off Goodland as a rapid-growing, booming agricultural center. Montgomery had no idea that later he would be called the Father of Goodland. The Homesteaders Union Association put on a drive to name Goodland the Sherman county seat. It was opposed by a few businessmen who preferred the county seat to be Eustis, a town boasting of a sheriff and a jail, which Goodland lacked. Eustis was a mile northeast from Goodland.

On Friday, November 2, the Irwins attended the Grand Rally. Two brass bands played and A. B. Montgomery gave a speech about the humming town of Goodland. He had a gold watch in his vest pocket that was attached to one of the vest buttons by a gold chain. He looked at the watch frequently as he talked.

"I'd like a pocket watch," said Charlie.

"You have to be somebody big first," said Frank.

Joe looked at the boys, meaning that they should hush so that he could hear the speech.

Montgomery was saying that there might be as many as thirty-five hundred people in Goodland this day for the Grand Rally. When he sat down, there was a speech by a man who represented the opposing town, Eustis, for county seat. This man was Jesse Tait, editor of the Eustis paper, the *Dark Horse*.

"Let's go. I've heard enough," said Joe. "Eustis hasn't a snowball's chance in mid-July. By summer she'll move her main buildings over to Goodland. Eustis is as good as dead as a town even before the election."

They walked to the edge of town to see the horse-racing event.

"I've always wanted to race. Always," Frank said in a high-pitched voice.

Charlie knew that Frank could stick to any of the horses. "Pa, he's so small the horse won't feel a thing. If Frank digs his heels in the horse's sides and talks into its ear, he could have a winner."

Joe scowled, but told the horse owner, who wore a sheepskin jacket and a wide-brimmed hat, that Frank wanted to try out as a jockey.

Charlie saw Frank's eyes light up. Frank broke away to rub the legs of the black horse he'd chosen to ride in the first of the races.

Later the racehorse owner in the sheepskin jacket spoke to Joe, who'd come to see the finish of the races. "On horseback your kid is beautiful, agile, smooth as royal blood. He's like a little prince and we ought to pay him to ride for us." The man reached into his pocket and said to Frank, "Here's two bucks. You can ride for us anytime." The man put his hand on Joe's shoulder. "Your kid came in first on anything he rode. It must be a natural-born instinct. When he rode I saw him shift weight ever so slightly, had me worried, but as I watched I saw the horse slow down or speed up as the weight shift seemed to direct."

Frank smiled, blinked, and wrinkled his nose so that the freckles ran together like overfilled mud puddles, but Charlie felt the man overdid the flattery with Frank. Joe got close so that

Frank could hear him over the string band. "It's time to leave. I'm proud of you, son."

Still grinning, Frank raised his eyes toward his racehorse friend.

The morning of November 19, 1887, Les came after Charlie and Ell to go to the rally in Eustis.

After sampling the food at the K. P. Hall the three young people decided it was time to leave. The wind had come up and the clouds were the kind that can dump bushels of snow in an hour or two. Charlie was excited because he was sure he'd spotted Rob Collins's cotton-white head in the center of a bunch of boys. "Where there's Rob, there's trouble," he whispered to Miner.

Ell wanted to stay for the dance, but she didn't want to run into Rob, and she knew it would snow before they hit Sappa Meadows. Reluctantly she climbed into the wagon and pulled a quilt tight around her lap and saved some to wrap around Miner.

Charlie climbed into the back and wrapped himself in another quilt. He kept his face out of the wind and felt warm, contented, and sleepy. He was not sure he really cared whether Eustis or Goodland became the county seat. What did it matter? He didn't have to decide.

Miner looked ahead but he thought how beautiful Ell looked in the white shirtwaist with tiny tucks around the neckline and on top of the puffed sleeves. Her deep-green flannel skirt matched the color of her eyes and was tight-fitting at the waist, but had a wide ruffle at the bottom that swept the tops of her patent-leather shoes. Now her hands were resting in her brown cloth muff. Her brown coat fit snugly over her skirt. Mary's silver filigreed cameo brooch showed at her neck. The wispy, wild fringes of hair poked out around the edge of her wool cap and were blown tight against her face. Miner thought about touching one of those soft, quince-colored wisps. He looked back and saw that Charlie's eyes were closed. "Tired?" he whispered to Ell.

"A little," she said. "It's the constant wind."

"Either hot or cold," he said, putting his arm around her and holding the reins in the other hand.

The wind blew down Charlie's back. He pulled the quilt tighter. He looked up and was surprised to find his sister and his friend sitting close together. "Jeems!" he yelled. "Have you two chucked your senses or is it getting that cold out here?"

Miner's face turned crimson. He turned to look at Charlie.

"That's right. It must be way below freezing. And the wind's blowing so hard we couldn't hear each other unless we sat close."

"I didn't know you liked to talk!" Charlie yelled against the wind.

"Well—there's times, like when lots of people are around, I can't talk at all. But when I'm with good friends, like you, it's easier to say things. You know, some people make all the difference." Miner turned back and drew Ell even closer.

"I know. With some people I feel as out of place as a cow in the front room!" hollered Charlie. He adjusted the quilt up around his ears and again closed his eyes.

Ell whispered to Miner, "What do you see when you close your eyes?"

Miner was amused. He felt a warm glow in the pit of his stomach. "I see green eyes and shining, fawn-colored hair, a little pink nose."

Charlie's eyes flew open. He hooted. The wind carried Miner's words to the back of the wagon. "Sounds like you see the tabby cat in the barn! Want to know what I see with my eyes closed? I see a rope in a perfect loop floating above the clouds."

Ell turned so that she could see Charlie. She smiled and stuck out the tip of her tongue. "A rope is all you ever think about. If you went to a wedding, you'd have your rope over your shoulder."

Miner pulled back his arm and held the reins loosely in his hands. The horse plodded along the road, unheeding of the light snowflakes that dusted its back.

"Close your eyes, Ell, and tell us what you see," said Miner.

A deep sigh arose from the middle of Ell's chest. "I see firm, warm lips, a strong chin, rough as sandpaper." She ignored Charlie's laugh and looked toward Miner, her eyes crinkled half-closed.

Miner felt a warmth spread through his loins. This girl with the flashing green eyes could arouse a man with words as well as with the way she caused her eyes to glisten, her head to tilt, or her graceful body to move.

"Watch out," warned Charlie. "I heard Will say that half the men in Goodland are in love with Ell. I think she encourages them. You remember how that brain-sick Rob Collins acted when he saw the girl he thinks he's mad about hanging on to the arm of someone else?"

"Charlie, hush!" cautioned Ell.

Miner let the horse have more slack and hoped Charlie could

not see how he felt. He vowed that he'd never let Rob Collins, nor his ilk, have Ell. He was drawn to those flashing green eyes like a nail to a magnet. She was his girl. He could take care of her. The snowflakes were larger and coming in eddies with the wind gusts.

Suddenly Charlie knew that Miner was gathering courage to court his sister.

Ell spoke and her words were so unexpected that Charlie felt like he was hit with a sheet of ice. "I've thought of going back to Missouri because I miss teaching."

Charlie sucked in his breath and hoped no one heard the faint hiss of air going to his lungs over the howling wind. A dull ache throbbed in his chest. He knew his ma and pa would make a fuss. He'd miss Ell even if she was a girl. He didn't want her to leave. A family ought to stay together, he reasoned.

The snow made noiseless white swirls under the horse's hooves.

Miner was so startled he could not speak right away. Finally he said, "Have you thought of teaching around here?"

Charlie held his breath, knowing she'd taught the Collinses' little ones off and on.

"Yes," she said. "The Mennonites have a school for their own kind and Reverend Wallace and his wife have the settlers' school near Gandy. Frank goes there with mostly kids from the Gandy family. Then there's a Mr. Koon with a school in Shermanville. That's north eight or ten miles. There's no schoolhouse for me."

Charlie felt cold air creep across his shoulders and thought, so that's what she wants—her own schoolhouse. He hitched the quilt up some.

Miner had a momentary emptiness in his belly and his chest squeezed tight with a stabbing pain. It wasn't shyness, but some real physical infirmity now that made it an effort for him to talk. Miner was frightened. He'd never been weak or frail in his life. He thought a good belt of corn whiskey would loosen the cords in his neck. "Are you some kind of quitter?" he sputtered.

Ell pulled herself up so her back was straight. The snowflakes blowing against her long lashes made her blink. "I hate it! This wind and cold and then the wind and heat." Her eyes watered and spilled over so her cheeks were shiny wet. She found a handkerchief in her reticule and wiped her eyes.

Charlie's mind was numb and he could not think. He let the quilt slip so that he could hear better.

"You don't look too happy with the idea of leaving," said

Miner, breathing deep into the cold air, then saying quickly, "Try thinking of the wind that ripples and flashes the tall grasses or pushes the snow in swirls that look like froth on an ocean wave. Think of heat and drought causing the prairie grasses to grow roots as deep as a two-story house. That root-tangled soil is unfazed by most plows. That's why it makes such good sod brick. Have you ever thought of this country as beautiful with wine-colored grasses and a rainbow of wildflowers blooming like a granny's patchwork quilt? The groves of trees around creeks and springs are like cool, green islands of shade in summer. People here are like solid, country rock. They endure days of isolation, snowed in. They survive weeks of dehydration while under the summer glare. Their hearts are big. They'd do anything for a neighbor in trouble, and they always look for some excuse to have a party. There's never a locked door. Even the thieving land grabbers honor a man's home if it's being lived in. These folks find peace of mind on this prairie that they won't get from a mountain or forest. Mountains and forests make these folks suffocate. Sure, sometimes they get feisty, but it fades and everyone's friends. Stay and you'll see I'm right. Try to like this prairie a little. It grows on a person, I swear."

Charlie wanted to stand up and clap his hands and cheer. It was the best Kansas speech he'd heard. He turned to say so, but Miner was not paying Charlie any heed. His head was close to Ell's and she was saying something in a low whisper, which sounded like "I've had a sign."

"A sign?" repeated Miner.

"I found a stone with a hole in the center. The small end pointed to the east, like an arrowhead, in the direction of Missouri."

"Superstition? You run your life by meaningless signs?"

"Don't be sarcastic!" Ell pulled the quilt tighter around her throat. She brushed at her eyes with the back of her hand. "My grandmother taught me signs. She was wonderful. She could have read medicine if she'd had the chance. And she'd have been a famous medical doctor. Actually she was a well-known herb doctor."

Miner hardly thought before speaking. He was not playing a game, but he was fighting for something he desperately wanted. "Ell, you're the wonderful teacher here. You can be famous. Honest. You're smart with letters and numbers and wonderful working with little children." His throat ached. "And you learn fast. Your ma told me you learned to crochet and did some of them rugs at your place. They sure add a glory of color to the floor. I wish I had one for my place."

Ell's emerald eyes lighted with the praise. She relaxed. "I could make you one before I go."

Miner squinted down the nearly invisible road. He hoped the horse was on the road to the Irwin farm as he turned and looked at Ell. "Look, if you really wanted to leave—it seems to me that you'd be acting happy."

Ell's hand came out of her muff and went to her mouth and tears welled again in her eyes. She wiped her eyes and blew her nose, then sat perfectly still. She brushed Miner's arm when she put a hand back inside her muff. "Once I start crying or feeling sad, it's hard to stop."

Miner felt a tingling all the way through his coat and sweater sleeve. She looked at him and smiled and he saw the snowflakes melt off her rosy cheeks. Miner thought he was going to black out. It was a moment before he could breathe normal again.

"You're right," she said. "Honestly, I find the buffalo grass with patches of wildflowers a lovely sight. I care about prairie people like you." She took out her handkerchief and wiped her eyes with finality. "Truly, I like you."

Miner wanted to hug Ell. He wanted to hold her delicate pink face close to his, to feel her warm hand over his wind-chilled hand. He wanted to hear her soft voice rise and fall as the wind undulated in the yellow, dried grasses that were now covered with fluffy, white snow. He felt vibrant with joy. She cared about him. She really liked him.

Charlie couldn't take the silence. "Going around the coffeepot trying to find the handle will about cover the extent of Ell's travels to Missouri, I'd reckon." No one disagreed with him so he continued. "How come you live alone?"

"I guess you mean me," said Miner, stretching out his legs as if he had a cramp in each one. "Well, mainly, I ain't found anyone I want to live with." Now he paused. He wanted to say more. He was not sure the time was right. He squeezed his chin thinking that the longer he waited the more uncertain he was.

Charlie and Ell sat quiet, neither dared to breathe.

"Oh, you mean my folks," said Miner, hedging. "Pa was a Colorado miner and was shot over the Independence claim. Ma died of pneumonia the next winter."

Ell's hands went to her mouth. "I had no idea," she whispered.

"I never told you before."

She put her hand on his arm and left it there.

His heart pounded so hard he thought everyone could hear it. Then miraculously his mind cleared and he had a sudden idea about Ell's teaching. "The Wallaces teach mostly older kids and let them go in the fall and spring for harvesting and planting. Well, listen to this idea. You teach the young'uns and keep 'em in school all fall, winter, and spring until the weather gets hot and dry. You could really learn 'em with all that time. Forget Missouri. It's behind. Your life is here—with these little schoolkids and me."

Charlie let out his breath before he exploded. He wanted to climb up to the seat and shake Miner's hand.

Ell cried out in a funny, high-pitched voice, "My life with you?"

"Yes. You and me." Miner almost choked. He did not intend to say this. He'd wanted to think about it longer. He'd never really thought about having a wife. Why, early this morning a wife was the farthest thing from his mind. And there was a burr to his happiness. He was certain that Ell was the sort who needed more than a sod hut to decorate and keep clean from bedbugs, cockroaches, and rats. She was strong-minded and would have a say in what her man did and how his work would affect her. She needed challenge.

Ell was quiet as the wagon pulled up into the yard beside the Irwin soddy. She did not make a move to get out of the wagon. Miner's chest was tight with anxiousness and his heart beat with hope. He hoped Ell's hand still on his arm was a good sign.

Charlie was up folding his quilt. He nudged Miner. "We're home, old-timer." Charlie stamped his feet on the ground to shake out the stiffness and shake off the numbness. "Say, you want to stay at our place till this snow blows itself out?"

Miner was tempted. "Thanks." He was out of the wagon now, helping Ell climb down. "I'd best get back and feed my stock and get the wood inside before everything's hidden from sight. Look at those flakes coming down!"

Charlie folded the other blanket and left it on the seat of the wagon. Then he walked backward toward the soddy's front door. He grinned because he was sure neither Ell nor Miner saw him as they stood there holding hands, looking at each other as if they were statues. Ell moved first by putting her hands up to Miner's face. She kissed him full on the mouth, then broke away, and fled inside with Charlie.

Then and there Miner promised himself he'd talk to families

with small children ready for school around Goodland. And he'd build a one-room soddy for Ell to use as a school wherever she wanted it. He thought, by God, it's a good feeling doing something for another person. I'll get on this project right away. He climbed into the wagon, picked up the reins, and started his horse on a slow turn and then back down the lane to the main road. He whistled into the wind, enjoying the snappy bite of the blowing snow. There were swirling white sheets moving this way and that, depending on the wind gusts.

Ell hung her coat and muff on the wall peg and then stood in front of the wood-framed, oval mirror above the pie table. She smiled and put her fingers to her lips. She looked at one side of her face, then the other. She took off her bonnet and fluffed her hair around her face. Then she pulled out the silver combs and let it fall down her back. She held it up in a golden ponytail. Not yet satisfied, she let go so that it hung like a shawl. She tossed her head to shake the hair down her back like a long sheaf of wheat.

Joe was stirring some horse liniment he'd made. "What's the excitement in Eustis?"

Charlie was warming his feet by the kitchen range. "Not much. About the same as Goodland's." He inhaled the head-clearing camphor in the brown liniment mixture.

"The election's in three days. Then we'll know which place is *big*," said Joe.

"Pa, we didn't stay for the dance because Charlie thought he saw Rob Collins," said Ell.

"Maybe he did." Joe looked at Charlie. "You scared of that Collins kid?"

"I don't know. He acts before he thinks—remember?"

"Rob's nothing but an immature rascal," said Joe. "If he's smart he'll grow up and forget about being a rascal."

"I'm glad we don't have rascal problems," called Mary from the bedroom, where she was putting a mustard plaster on Frank's congested chest. He had one of his winter colds again. "My heart aches for Cora Collins, raising all those children."

"What about us?" asked Charlie. "Do we make your heart ache?"

"You're not the same kind of rascals!" snapped Joe. Then he stepped over and put his hand on Charlie's shoulder. "Rely on your good sense. It'll get you through most situations." He poured liniment through a funnel into a brown glass gallon jug. Joe was a prodigiously huge man. Over six feet tall and weighing close to three hundred pounds. He gave confidence to anyone who was around him and assurance that nothing dire could happen if he were in charge.

Will had come into the soddy from the barn. He'd cut off a ham roast from the dressed deer hanging frozen from the rafters. "What if Goodland wins the election and is legally the county seat? Eustis will have to give up its files of county records to Goodland."

"Miner and me heard that Eustis has some people who will get a junction to forbid removal of those records. I thought *junction* was 'to join together,'" said Charlie. He pushed his hair from his eyes.

Will chuckled and Joe held up his hand. "Son, that's *in*junction. It means those people forbid anyone from Goodland taking those papers from Eustis."

"That doesn't sound right to me," said Mary, washing off the venison ham.

"'Tisn't. And I 'spect the HUAers will do something about it, even if we have to fight this gol-durned blizzard," said Joe.

"I wish I could go with you to vote," said Charlie.

"Les'll vote," said Ell.

"Sure, he'll vote for Goodland so that when it's the county seat, there has to be a school for little kids. Les knows a wonderful schoolmarm who'd love to teach them kids," said Charlie, dancing a little jig in front of Ell.

Ell's face went fiery red. "Charlie! You didn't have to listen to everything, then blab. That's sneaky!"

Joe held his hand up so she would stop yelling.

"The wind was pretty loud, maybe I didn't hear everything. But I saw everything. You kissed Les while I was trying to get the front latch unfastened."

Ell's mouth was open but no words were coming out.

Charlie halfway wished he hadn't spilled the beans about Ell's impetuous kiss. He tried to smooth it over. "Boy, I really liked what Les said about the prairie. He's smart, you know. I could love this land like he does." His eyes twinkled and he felt better.

Mary looked up from the range. "I'm glad Ell likes Les."

"Does that mean he's your sweetheart?" asked Will.

"Ma! Will! Charlie!" Ell was furious. "It's none of your concern—my likes and my friends!"

Joe wiped the liniment off his hands on a dishtowel. "But it's my business! I'm head of this here family! I'd like quiet! Ell is too young for sweethearts!"

The rest of the evening Joe watched his daughter from the corner of his eye. He could see that she was not a girl, but nearly a young woman and good-looking. She had a teasing quality about her that he'd never noticed before. He could see she was not too young for a sweetheart.

When they were all in bed, Mary snuggled close to Joe. She felt a great comfort being encircled by the enormous frame of her husband. She whispered, "Ell's been ready for courting ever since we came to Kansas. She is, what some say, ripe."

"My daughter called ripe?"

"I'm surprised you've not noticed how she attracts boys like honey attracts flies."

It was several minutes before Mary heard the soothing sounds of Joe's snoring.

For the next couple of days the Irwins watched the blizzard from their soddy's front windows. On the third day the low hills were visible against the pale blue sky. Joe, Will, and Charlie shoveled a path to the barn, taking turns. The cow was milked and Mary took warm water out to the stock for drinking right away before it froze. She added leftover pork bones to the hot mush she took to the dog, Nick. Joe had wild hay piled high in the barn. The cow and horses had their own stalls. Joe laid by staples, such as sugar, salt, flour, corn meal, salt pork, beans, vinegar, and yeast, on sod shelves in the barn to see them through the winter. The barn was good protection from snow and fierce winds.

Frank was getting over his chest cold and ready to go back to school. Mary suggested Will take Frank to school and go after him while the rest went to Goodland to vote for the county seat.

Will said he might just go to Eustis and vote. Joe nodded his head to let Will know it was a good idea.

Before the cold weather had come, Joe plowed a couple acres for his winter wheat. Going to Goodland on voting day, he stopped the horse and told Charlie to scrape through the snow to the frozen ground. To Joe's delight Charlie found delicate green blades piercing the soil. Charlie covered the hole to keep the tiny shoots warm and jumped into the wagon.

"I'm certain I can grow potatoes and vegetables to keep in a root cellar next winter and a half dozen acres more of winter wheat," said Joe, smiling at Mary.

"That will be nice to go with the bread, beans, and salt pork we have now," agreed Mary.

Joe drove directly to the courthouse. Joe went in to vote, leaving Mary, Ell, and Charlie in the wagon. Ell kept looking at the people going into the courthouse. Charlie knew she was looking for Miner.

Afterward the Irwins went to Marietta Roberts's Restaurant. Charlie and his father drank hot soup from two-handled cups. Mary asked advice about piecing together her quilt squares. Ell asked Marietta if she would help her sew a suitable schoolmarm's dress.

Marietta thought. She wiped her hands on her apron and sucked in her cheeks. She was a good-looking, middle-aged widow with brown hair braided and wound on her head coronet fashion. She was respected by everyone for her ambition, managing a restaurant and sewing. "I can order a soft brown wool for a jacket and skirt. Who's the schoolteacher?" Her eyes went from Ell to Mary.

"I am," said Ell proudly. "I'm going to be the first schoolteacher in Goodland when it's the official county seat."

"I admire your confidence and your politics," said Marietta. "Are you absolutely positive that Goodland will be Sherman County's seat?"

"Yes. I saw the sign. During the last blizzard, the snow blew toward Goodland and left Eustis bare," said Ell.

"Oh, land sakes! That always happens!" Marietta's dark eyes shone. "In winter the wind always blows that way."

Ell did not crack a smile. "The sign means people will move in the same direction, leaving Eustis."

Marietta's face creased with smile lines. She nodded her head. "Yes, we'll see. In the meantime I'll check on the price of the brown wool."

By midnight the votes were counted, and as Ell predicted, Goodland won. In the town guns and revolvers were shot, anvils pounded, as people celebrated All that was needed now was for the county commissioners to canvass the vote and declare Goodland the permanent county seat. But next day, besides a thick snowfall to put a damper on more celebrations, an injunction was served on the county commissioners by the town of Eustis that enjoined them from canvassing the vote. The allegations were that no election notices were posted and that the ballots had been mixed together. Therefore everything was over, but the results were not official.

For the next several weeks Joe watched the newspapers carefully to find how the difficulties of the county seat would be resolved. There was no immediate resolution. The roads became icy and frozen.

Joe took Charlie on farrier rounds. One day, after Christmas, the axle on the wagon broke and had to be repaired on the spot in a sleet storm. Joe and Charlie sawed down a cottonwood. Charlie held the tree trunk steady while Joe used an ax and knife to whittle it down into the shape of an axle.

Joe read in the paper that Goodland would open its official post office on New Year's Day, 1888. Jim Warrington, one of Joe's HUA friends, was postmaster in the one-room soddy on Main Street. A stage would take the mail, once a week, to Wallace for sorting and bagging for the mail train.

On January second, posters appeared on barns and town buildings stating that Goodland was indeed the seat of Sherman County. Mary wrote a long letter to her folks in Chillicothe, but when it was finished no one could take it to the post office. Snow was falling and drifting deep against the soddy and barn. Roads were hidden for a week. Then the snow stopped and the wind seemed to increase and the temperature dropped to $-30°$ F.

Ten days later, when the weather moderated, Jack Collins came on horseback to announce a meeting of the HUAers in the Goodland Courthouse. To everyone's surprise, Goodland was not yet legally the county seat, because the town of Eustis had not officially registered its votes.

That same day Les came to the Irwin soddy to ask Will and Charlie to ride to Eustis with him. He explained that John Navert was the self-appointed sheriff for Goodland and he wanted someone to go to Eustis for those unregistered ballots. "Martin Tomblin, lawyer and president of the Goodland Town Company, believes Eustis is foot dragging, so he's offering two town lots and a couple hundred dollars in cash for those records. Rumor says George Benson has the records in a trunk in his basement."

Will was ready to go as soon as he heard there was money for the job. He said, "I heard Jack Collins tell Pa that Tomblin has rags soaked with turpentine wrapped around straw. Those turpentine balls can be torched and thrown on Benson's porch. That'll make Benson give us those records!"

Mary gasped and put her hand to her mouth.

Les said, "We're not taking any fire balls. We're taking Charlie with his gift of gab. He'll talk Benson or his wife into giving us the records."

Mary's hand came away from her mouth, but she clicked her tongue against her teeth to show her disapproval. She said, "If you have to go, dress warm, it's still freezing out there."

The boys wore woolen stockings inside their boots, two flannel shirts under sheepskin-lined coats, two pairs of woolen pants, and gloves inside woolen mittens. Charlie thought one flannel shirt was enough for him. Two were cumbersome when he put his lasso over his shoulder. He offered the flannel shirt to Les, who gladly put it on. They pulled their caps over their ears and told Mary they'd be back by noon.

She clamped her top teeth over her bottom lip so she wouldn't say anything. She knew she'd see the boys nearer suppertime.

Charlie held his scarf over his nose and bent over his horse for warmth. Les waved, saying they'd bring Joe back from the courthouse if the HUAers meeting was over.

They rode straight for Eustis, down the main street toward the Benson house. The house was clapboard with a wide wooden porch. The back part was the original old soddy. The boys hitched their horses to the gate post and went on the porch. Will took off his mitten and knocked with his glove on.

Mrs. Benson looked from the window and motioned them inside. "Don't stand out in that Arctic air. Come right on in," she said and closed the door quickly. "Are you boys on some errand?" Her blond hair was tucked under a cotton kerchief.

"Yes, we are," said Charlie. He looked around the room. "Is Mr. Benson home?"

"No, George is with Eustis's Mayor Dayton at the Sherman County Bank. I'll get you lads some hot tea. Put your feet next to the wood stove. Get warm before you go outside again. They say the weather's moderated, but it can't be more'n ten, fifteen degrees warmer. You can still freeze your toes. Did you want to see George?"

"That's all right. We really came for something," said Charlie. He sipped the hot tea, wondering how he was going to ask her for the voting records.

"I suspect George sent you. He mentioned that he wanted to store the voting records in a safe place at the bank." Mrs. Benson winked. "I'm glad to get shut of them myself."

"I can understand that," said Charlie.

She lighted a candle and the boys followed her to the basement. There was a lock on the trunk. Mrs. Benson said she didn't know where George kept the key. Les said that the trunk had to be opened right away. She nodded and went upstairs. The boys were in the dark. Charlie's teeth chattered and he was afraid to move. Mrs. Benson came back with the light and a hammer. Les hit the lock several hard blows and the clasp broke. Mrs. Benson took an armload of papers out. She divided it into two piles and shoved each pile in the front of Will's and Les's sheepskin coats. "You're too young to be carrying such valuable papers," she told Charlie.

He was exasperated and wanted to tell her he could take some of the papers.

"Here, I want you to take George's pipe to him. He forgot it this morning. Here's his tobacco pouch." She handed them to Charlie and patted the top of his head. Charlie nodded. He wanted to run out the front door.

Les put the teacups in the kitchen sink, then shook Mrs. Benson's hand and told her thank you. Will shook her hand and smiled.

Once the boys were out the door, they hurried to mount their horses. Charlie stopped to put the pipe and tobacco in one hand and pull his soggy scarf over his nose. Will and Les trotted down the street. As Charlie mounted he heard boots squeak the cold snow. A man turned in at the gate and looked up at Charlie.

"Say! That's my pipe!" he cried. "Why you little thief!" He grabbed Charlie's leg, pulled him off the horse, and tipped him over his shoulder.

"I'm not a thief!" yelled Charlie, waving his hands and kicking his feet.

"Sonny, I'm George Benson and that's my pipe in your fist!" Benson grabbed at the pipe and tobacco pouch and managed to shove them in the pocket of his coat and still hold on to Charlie, who thrashed about. "Stop fighting me!" yelled Benson.

Charlie was taken to the Eustis jail several blocks away. The deputy put him behind bars, then talked with Benson. Charlie hollered, "What about my horse! It's too cold to leave him standing out there!"

Benson said he'd bring the horse to the stable behind the jail. He added that he wasn't inhumane.

"I'm innocent," said Charlie. His bottom lip stuck out. "Do I get a trial?"

"Wait to see what the sheriff says," said the deputy, who was clean-shaven in contrast to George Benson, who had a full, coffee-colored beard.

Charlie was certain Benson did not know that Will and Les

were on their way to Goodland with the Eustis voting records, and he'd never tell.

"What were you doing with my pipe?" asked Benson, combing his fingers through his beard.

"I was bringing it to you," sniffed Charlie.

"Won't hurt to cool your heels awhile." Benson shook hands with the deputy and left.

"My heels are pretty near froze," said Charlie, pulling off his mittens and rubbing his gloved hands together. The jail was not heated. The only stove Charlie could see was a round potbelly in the office. The deputy closed the door to the office. Charlie was alone with a canvas cot, no mattress, no blanket, and a china pot with a top. He pounded on the vertical iron bars. "Hey, deputy! Don't I get lunch and a blanket? I'm freezing, you know!" He wished he had the second flannel shirt. He threw his rope under the cot.

The deputy opened the door. Charlie felt the warm air. "I got no orders 'cept stay in this here office and fill out my report," said the deputy, whose eyes were like raisins poked into a plump dough-face. "What's your name, occupation, and where you from?"

Charlie held on to the bars with gloved hands and said, "I'm John Brown, ask me again and I'll knock you down!"

"Don't give me that arkymalarky. Your name, I already know anyways. You look like one of Joe Irwin's boys."

"Charles Burton Irwin. I'm a rancher. I'm from out West."

"Are you guilty or not guilty?"

"What else have you?"

"That's all. Did you steal Benson's pipe and fight with him?"

"I'm mute."

"Kid, you got more guts than you could hang on a fence rail," said the deputy, scratching one pudgy cheek. "I'm writing on this report that you are to be hanged in the morning. I hope it will be a lesson to you ever after." The door slammed shut.

Charlie lost his appetite for lunch. He thought of hanging and his neck ached. There was no window. He lay down and thought of home and the cheerfulness of his mother and father. He knew his father was gruff, but it was because he cared for him. His mother would cry if he were hanged. His eyes watered and he rubbed them with his scarf, which was stiff with frost. He wondered when Will and Les discovered he wasn't following them. He sat up and hugged his knees to keep them from shaking.

He imagined Benson going home. He could almost hear him shouting at his wife. She'd cry. Hot tears slid down Charlie's face. He sniffed and ran his sleeve across his face. He remembered something his father once said: "Rely on good sense to get you through."

He heard a door slam and no more noises in the office. He had no idea how long he'd felt sorry for himself. His stomach growled. His heels kicked against his rope under the cot. He bent and picked up the rope and wound it around his fist and left elbow. He pushed his fist and rope through the cold bars. He sucked in his breath and his mouth turned up into a tiny smile. He twirled one end of the rope with his right hand. His hand was cold. He grunted and drew his hand close to a space between the bars and blew his warm breath toward it. His eyes were accustomed to the dark and he could make out the door to the office. He could not really see the doorknob, but he knew where it should be. He twirled the rope faster and let it fly out farther and farther until it hit the door with a *bonk* and the floor with a *swak*. The two sounds were as loud as a close clap of thunder.

Charlie pulled in the rope, coiled it, and twirled and tossed again and again and again. He was not shivering. He could feel the perspiration under his arms. Once the rope hung up on something, then slipped off. "Okay, catch this time!" he cried. The rope was caught! He gave it a tug and the loop cinched and held tight. "Here goes nuthin'," he said, and jerked hard. He knew he couldn't turn the knob, but if the latch didn't fit tight, he was sure it would spring open. He gave it another tug, pulling the rope taut against an iron bar. "A miracle!" he shouted as the door flew open and he felt the rush of warm air.

He saw the red twinkle of the banked fire in the potbellied stove. He tied his end of the rope to one of the horizontal bars. His hands ached and he could see his breath vapor in the air. He lay on the cot. After a while he was sure the air was warmer. His eyelids grew heavy.

He woke to find his neck had a kink and his feet were cold. He stood and stretched and wondered if it was morning. He pulled off his gloves, loosened his scarf, and pushed up his cap. He used the china pot. Minutes later there was ice on the chamberpot sides. His mouth tasted like he'd eaten something rotten. The fire was out in the potbellied stove. He heard noises.

Charlie half hoped it was not morning. He remembered the threat of hanging. The door opened and a man with brown hair slicked back with grease tossed a gray wool cap on the coat rack, then took off his sheepskin. The man whistled and poked inside the stove's fire box, put in kindling, and struck a match on the bottom of the top drawer of the desk. The man went out and came back with several hunks of cordwood. He dropped one in the fire box and the rest on the floor. He adjusted the damper. He turned and looked at Charlie. "Say, what are you doing here?" He looked startled.

Charlie could see light from a gray sky through the outer door. "Slowly freezing to death," he said.

"I wasn't informed of a prisoner. I'm Sheriff Albright." He picked up a paper from the desktop. "Aha, you're one of the Irwin boys—a rancher, this says. What are you doing here?" he repeated.

Charlie decided not to answer any more questions.

The sheriff examined the door and the rope attached to the knob. "This your work?"

Charlie's teeth chattered.

The sheriff pulled the rope off the knob and Charlie snaked it back between the bars. He drew in a deep breath and asked his own question. "Does that paper say anything about a hanging?"

"Nope. Not that I can make out." The sheriff's mouth turned up at the corners and his blue eyes twinkled. "I bet you Deputy Benn put you behind those bars! He gets a bang out of scaring kids. You're not old enough to be my prisoner."

Charlie did not mind being called young this time. He grinned.

"That must be your horse in the stable. Leave the blanket that's on its back and hightail it home, son. Whatever it was you did, don't do it again."

"Does that paper tell what I did?" Charlie put his bare hand on one of the iron bars. The skin stuck to the freezing metal. He pulled and some of the skin came off. Tears welled in his eyes. He sat to cradle his hands in his lap. He thought frozen skin hurt as much as burned skin.

"Someone wrote: Fighting and Stealing. But both are crossed out. I can't keep you here. Your conviction sheet is unsigned and invalid."

Charlie couldn't say a word. He let the tears fall in his cupped hands.

Suddenly there was a loud pounding at the outer door and there stood Will, Les, Jack Collins, and Joe grinning as big as mountain cats. "You had us worried. But you look all right!" shouted Joe.

"This kid a relative of yours?" The sheriff pointed to Les.

"Yes, in a way, a young brother," said Les.

"Young brothers are always in the way!" said the sheriff with a loud laugh.

"I'm his pa!" cried Joe. "He's done nuthin' to be in jail for!"

"I know that!" said the sheriff, getting up from his chair. He put cotton gloves on and unlocked the cell. "Say, you gents hear the news this afternoon? The city officials of this one-horse town wouldn't count the ballots, so their votes don't count. George Benson is breathing fire and fury because he kept those records at his place where no one could get 'em. Three little bitty kids took the ballots from his wife, hauled them to Goodland, and counted 'em. But it didn't count for much. Those ballots are worthless."

"Yup! We heard," said Jack Collins.

When they were outside Will told Charlie they didn't get a cent from Tomblin.

Money didn't seem important to Charlie. "What time is it?" he asked.

"Suppertime!" cried Les.

"I wasn't in jail overnight?" Charlie was dumbfounded. "I sure hope the new jail in Goodland has more than one wood stove. Honest, I might've froze if I didn't have my rope to open the office door."

Joe helped Charlie on his horse. He tossed the blanket on a pile of hay, then held his hand up. "Honest, anyone that tells Mary that Charlie spent the day in jail will get his tongue pulled through his nose!"

Les Miner later told the story of riding to Eustis, getting the voting records, and taking them to Goodland. "When me and Will got to Goodland, we counted the yeas and neas in the courthouse. Eustis voted 256 for Goodland and 106 for itself for county seat. The votes aren't worth anything and don't mean much, because even before they were counted, Goodland was finally made the official county seat."

The first election for Goodland's city officers was held on April 24, 1888. An HUAer, E. F. Murphy, was elected mayor for a salary of one hundred dollars per annum to be paid quarterly. Five new councilmen were elected. John McCune was the first police judge and J. W. Navert was elected sheriff.

Among the first ordinances for Goodland, as the county seat, was a poll tax. Businesses were required to have licenses. Activities that were prohibited included prostitution, games, gambling, fast riding and driving on the streets, riding wagons on side-walks, and running of cattle or other domestic animals at large.

By spring Tait had his newspaper building and his loyalties moved to Goodland. On the seventeenth of May he wrote, "Goodland holds the prize."

Many businesses from Eustis were moved to Goodland. The small frame buildings were loaded on several wagon beds and moved by teams of horses. The sod buildings were taken down "brick by brick" and carried by wagons to Goodland, where they were quickly put back together. Tait wrote, "The buildings are moving so fast that our reporter has been unable to keep up with the exits."

On the last day of May, Tait wrote, "Our building made the trip from Eustis to Goodland without cracking the plastering or disturbing a brick on the chimney."

The county seat fight had occupied the news so long that now the editors had to find something new for readers of newspapers. The *Goodland News* stated, "Since the cruel county seat war is over, it is no picnic to fill a paper full of local news for the reader, and if we publish a chapter of the Bible now and then, you need not growl. It might be news to some of you anyway."*

Charlie thought of all the activities that had taken place during the last six months. His father called the events the "politics of growth." Charlie thought the events were more like growing pains. He decided that if he were ever a mayor or sheriff—and he had the certainty of youth that he could do anything he put his mind to—he'd be clear-headed in his thinking. He'd never falter in his duty. He'd make plans and see the job was carried out posthaste. He'd learned that decisions mattered. He'd never waste time with name calling, gun fighting, liquor drinking, or tobacco spitting.

He'd learned something about politics. If a person's viewpoint was defeated by a majority vote, it was unseemly to lick your wounds in public for all to see. If he were in a public office, he'd lick the wounds of defeat in private and at the same time figure out a way to see the situation for something good. Charlie told himself he'd never shilly-shally from one side to the other nor would he be wishy-washy and take the middle road. A man that straddles the fence could end up with a mighty sore crotch.

*Reprinted with permission of Betty Walker, from the Sherman County His-torical Society, Goodland, Kansas.

ELEVEN

Wild Horses

At the onset of 1888 there was no railroad within Sherman County, Kansas. By spring of the same year people in the county had seen railroad survey teams with tripods and transits on pack horses or in wagons. The men carried measuring chains and left wooden stakes for the proposed railroad beds. A branch of the Rock Island, the Chicago, Kansas and Nebraska Railroad, ran a survey from Jansen, Nebraska, to Colorado Springs. Their proposed roadbed was staked out a half-mile south of Goodland's courthouse.

The federal government gave land grants to early railroad companies, who in turn sold their land grant to have money to build their rail line. As soon as Jesse Tait located his newspaper in Goodland, Joe went to see him. "I've talked to the HUAers, and they suggest that the county hold a special election to vote on selling a given amount of railroad bonds. If the election carries, then the railroad whose bonds are voted can issue and sell their bonds. The money from the sale of those bonds could be used to build us a railroad."

By the time the last spring snow melted, a special election to obtain permission to sell the CK and N bonds was over and had carried. The mud thawed and dried on the dirt roads. The fields were right for plowing. Will did not mind getting his hands dirty

nor his shirts sweaty in the course of farming. He made no deliberate decisions for himself. His blocky shoulders were right for
his short neck and large head. His dark eyes were full of fun,
with no serious depth of an intellectual. Yet he was nobody's
fool. He kept a written account of all that was spent and all that
was earned on the farm. He was at times boisterous and animated, and once when asked if he'd work for the railroad construction gang, he nodded his head, saying, "I don't know where
I'm going, but I'm on my way for sure." Thus events happened
for Will with no before nor after thought.

Then one day Will gave the farm and farrier bookkeeping
notes to Charlie and went to work for the railroad construction
gang grading the ground west of Norton so that it was flat or
banked at the correct angle. He made the railbed ready for the
next workers with the black, creosoted ties and steel rails.

With his first paycheck Will bought Charlie a nickel-plated
stem-winder and stem-setter watch. Charlie was overjoyed. However, he would not say yes to Will again concerning the use of his
Henry rifle.

Next Will bought a couple bars of quality cast iron so that his
father could forge new front-door hinges for the Irwin soddy.
Then he bought himself a pair of mules to use pulling the road
scraper used in construction of the railroad bed. Each of his
mules cost him three times as much as the railroad company paid
for those heavy gauge, steel scrapers, which were $7.25 up to
·$10.50, depending on whether they held three and a half, or five,
or seven cubic feet of dirt.

The scraper's bit was controlled by the team driver, like Will.
When the scraper was filled, it was flipped over to unload. Will
fit right in with the other noisy workers, who continually yelled
to their animals, "Gee, haw, whoa and giddyap!" and sang ribald
songs. Some of the gang were foreigners, such as the frugal
Mennonites from Russia, the hardworking Bohemians, called
Bohunks, Irishmen, smelling of whiskey and tobacco and as anxious to spend their money as Will, and a few Welsh slate miners,
whose voices rose and fell like singing birds. The pay was good,
two dollars for a twelve-hour day. Thus, many homesteaders
worked with their own teams of horses or mules. The workers
stayed in tents in camps near the construction. Temporary stables
were built for the work animals. As the work progressed the
camps were moved.

On Friday, the 30th of March, 1888, fifty teams, with wagons
filled with three sizes of scrapers, tents, bedding, cooking uten-

sils, and gear belonging to the construction gang went down Goodland's Main Street like a holiday parade. The gang was going to make camp forty miles west of Goodland and work their way back east, moving tons of dirt along the survey until they met the remainder of the gang coming west from Norton. The two gangs planned to meet in Goodland by summer to join the two tracks into a single line. Goodlanders and homesteaders came out to watch the construction gang and its teams go through town. The *Goodland News* said, "It was the most substantial evidence of a railroad for this part of the country we have had, and gave the people both in town and country lots of encouragement."

The businessmen gave out cigars to the railroad workers. Tait's *Dark Horse* reported, "Every man in the outfit left town smoking and promising to be back by summer."

Goodland's Main Street was renamed the Boulevard. Before June was half over hitch racks were put up along both sides of the Boulevard.

While Will worked on building the railroad, Charlie helped his father on farrier rounds, traveling from farm to farm, repairing horseshoes, plows, or applying a little medical knowledge to the ailments of horses and other livestock or farm animals. Charlie often listened for the whistle of faraway trains and once in a while could see smoke against the eastern horizon on those rounds.

Charlie was now nearly six feet tall. Beside other boys his age he looked like a giant. His bright, brown eyes took in everything and his mind recorded every item. His mouth seemed small until he smiled, and then it stretched across the bottom of his face. He no longer dreamed of being as tall and strong as his brother Will; that goal was in plain sight.

Charlie was looking for a new goal. He was quick to learn from observation and experience. He knew the best goals were hard to attain. He'd seen his Grandmother Malinda fight for a goal of happiness, only to have loneliness consume and destroy her. He was aware of the backbreaking hours his folks spent just to keep food in their bellies and the dirt soddy halfway bearable. He saw his folks were serious about conforming to their values in life. They were so serious that Charlie could never let loose his true feelings in their presence. At times he'd like to yell and stamp his feet or call Frank a dumb crybaby. Other times he wanted to put his arms around Frank and tell him not to whine, things would get better. But Joe was gargantuan and gruff and formidable to Charlie. He felt uneasy doing anything outside of a narrow band of parental-acceptable behavior. Thus, he was never overly happy nor overly sad in front of his folks.

This was not to say Charlie did not let himself go on occasions. Most everyone knew he had a quick temper followed by quick contriteness. He could make sour-faced Frank laugh with his high exuberance. By the time he was thirteen or fourteen he'd concluded life was not to be scrimped and saved nor was it to be wasted. Life was to be used fully and enjoyed. Charlie surprised his father with the thoroughness of the accounts he kept in Will's farm and farrier notes. And he began keeping records of household bills, weather, including rainfall and hours of sunlight, and the amount of feed bought and used by the livestock. His mother said, "Don't you want to add to your notes how much water I use for cooking and washing?"

For pure joy Charlie liked racing on foot or riding fast on horseback. He outraced every boy his own age. Some said it was because his legs were so long, others said it was the length of his arms that propelled him like a windmill. He seemed to have charm and good manners so that people liked him. He seemed to enjoy carrying out his chores and never grumbled about cleaning out the barn, adding sweet-smelling hay to the stalls, brushing down the horses, or milking the cow. Next to people he liked horses. He liked their looks and their smell and to watch their gracefulness. When he was with people, he liked to exchange thoughts and was amazed at how much he learned or how differently others thought about some of the most common things.

Unbeknownst to Charlie his next goal was already in place. He was slowly confronting the conflicts that would fall in his way as he took over the leadership of the Irwin family. Already he'd decided he wanted the Irwin name to be important—mean something more than a sodbuster or dirt farmer. He seemed to realize that if he wanted something done, he had to get it started and nurse it along himself.

One day Charlie pointed out a little flat place, protected by hillocks on two sides. He and his father were returning home from doing some horseshoeing. "Pa, that would be just right for Ell's schoolhouse. The place is halfway between our place and Goodland."

A few days later Joe and Les Miner put up the one-room school soddy. Charlie told his father how the children would enjoy seeing sunshine or rain or wind clouds, so Joe bought two glass windows. Then Miner surprised everyone by putting in a cast-iron stove and three rows of poplar wood benches. Charlie gently reminded his father that the children would need an outhouse because they would spend the entire day at the school. He built a two-hole sod outhouse. At the same time Miner made Ell a desk, more like a rough-hewn table, and a chair, like a tall milking stool.

Youngsters, five to twelve, came to Miss Ell's School. Ell loved teaching and the children loved her. She understood their fantasies and readily entered into their make-believe play world. Ell was consistent when dealing with the children's lessons. The children's folks paid what they could for the schooling, from twenty-five cents to as much as a dollar a week. With the first month's money Ell bought a dozen slates. With the following month's salary she bought a set of seven volumes of the popular McGuffey's *Eclectic Readers*. She did not mention going to Missouri again.

At seventeen Ell was a beauty. Her skin was a clear rose-pink. She had slim legs, slender hips, and a shapely bosom. Her long lucent hair, once amber, was now more like a flaming sunset. Her bottle-green eyes shone with a come-hither look that promised unknown pleasures. Her nose was a perfect triangle and her mouth a wide, pleasant, upturned arc. Her voice was quiet, but she spoke with conviction, because she was well versed in the classics and newsprint of the times. She never hesitated to ask if there were some point she did not understand in any conversation. Her consistency fell apart when she dealt with men. Then she relied on her instinct.

Young and old men flocked around Ell. She spoke with cool politeness, but her eyes shone like liquid hot greenglass. She always smelled of fresh roses, even in winter. Intuitively she knew how to wear her homemade clothes so that with the slightest movement her figure showed off to perfection. However, she habitually laid her clothes on her bed or the floor or a chair rather than on the hooks her father had fastened into a board on the dirt wall.

Most of the men, including Les Miner, were in a constant state of excitement when near her. Rumor said she was Miner's girl. Still that did not detour the ogling and hopeful dreams of the other men. Another rumor said because Ell had spurned him, Rob Collins went to work in the Colorado coal mines so depressed that he no longer took an interest in the opposite sex.

Little Frank still used the cart he and Charlie rigged up to scrounge the prairie for old bones for Rob and Mr. Collins. Frank now took his collection to the Goodland Livery, where he was paid the rate of six dollars for a thousand pounds. The bones were stacked and held until the train would run through town and take them east to be crushed into fertilizer.

On one of the first warm afternoons of early spring, Charlie was beside the barn practicing rope spinning over his leg when Frank came up on the old, plodding Flame with the little cart full of bleached buffalo bones.

Frank's face was flushed and he was puffing for breath. "Charlie! Hundreds of horses! Wild! Down in the meadow. Maybe you could rope one. Wanna try?" He slid off the horse.

Charlie helped his young brother unhook the cart and put Flame in the barn, rub him down, and give the horse some oats. Then the two boys ran to the small meadow next to the creek.

They sat behind a clump of willows and looked in awe at the statuesque, magnificent horses silhouetted against the prairie sun quietly nibbling the grass between the sagebrush. At first scent of the unfamiliar humans the horses were skittish and ran from the low meadow, up the creek to a low rise, then out into the prairie. Charlie could not get close enough to put a loop around any of them. He and Frank marveled at their shaggy, thick coats and strong, straight legs. Charlie remembered he read somewhere that wild horses were not native. He told Frank they were from the Spanish Barb and Andalusian horses that were brought over by Spanish explorers in the early 1500s. "Some of those horses escaped or were left by the explorers and they began to live like wild animals, forming bands. The ones that survive are the strongest."

For the next two, three mornings Charlie came early. He sat alone against the clump of willows to watch the horses. There were plenty of stallions, but some mares stood around under the few trees by the creek. He noticed places where the grass was mashed close to the ground, as though the mares had come back to the meadow to sleep. Several mares looked as though they were ready to foal any time. He marveled how the mares, heavy with foal, could run and how graceful they seemed. Looking at them, he had a sense of freedom and toughness. He wanted to move closer, and as he crawled in the grass one of the stallions stopped grazing. Charlie felt the horse look right at him.

He meticulously examined and recorded times when the horses moved from one place to another. He never forgot his nickel-plated pocket watch, pencil, and notebook. Usually he brought leftover breakfast biscuits and bacon to munch on. Once he forgot. He stretched out on his stomach and nibbled the grass like a horse. He thought it was not unlike young dandelion greens his sister picked for spring salad. He found the horses grazed an hour after their first morning fill of water. Then they grouped together as though talking over their plans for the rest of the day. For two hours they grazed again. About midday they rested. At two o'clock they grazed again.

Before the sun went down, always about six o'clock, the herd went to the creek again to drink before finding their places for the night. The mares with foals preferred the tall grass against small rises in the earth where they could lay down and be sheltered from the wind. The stallions bunched together in a clearing or sought protection from a willow or alder clump. They did not lie down. He noticed half a dozen young stallions were pushed out of the main bunch. Each time they were ejected the young stallions moved closer to the mares as though looking them over for a possible mate.

Charlie learned that the wild horses generally drank most heavily early in the morning, at first sign of light. Then for about thirty or forty minutes the horses could not run fast. He found if he got up before sunup he could lasso one stallion. But the animal reared and pawed the air so that Charlie could not hold on to the rope. The next day he came back hoping to get the rope. He rode one of the workhorses and came up behind a group drinking their morning water. He edged them away and toward the small corral his father had made at the edge of the meadow. Often Joe kept the workhorses in this corral when he was using them in the fields. The workhorse whinnied and the stallions darted in all directions. Charlie was able to get one into the corral. He could not take the workhorse close to the wild one, which reared up and would bite.

Charlie had no idea how he was going to tame the horse. He had never talked to anyone about bronco-busting. He reasoned he had to tire the stallion, so he ran it around and around the corral by keeping the workhorse behind it. He was astonished at the stamina the wild horse had. After a week of running around and around each morning Charlie was about to ride close enough to throw a gunnysack full of heavy dirt onto the horse's back. He went wild. The sack of dirt was thrown off. Next day Charlie got the sack of dirt back on the horse. He wanted to strap it on. Only after another week could he do that. Charlie was lucky one morning and herded the stallion wearing his rope into the corral. The end of the rope was badly frayed, but he knew that could be mended. It was ten days before he could touch the rope. Slowly he loosened it and flung it off the animal's head. The rope touched the ears and the stallion reared back and darted against the side of the corral. Charlie ran to the opposite side and climbed over the fence. He wondered if he had enough patience to break these wild horses.

Joe had seen the wild bunch and after finding the first strange horse in the corral knew what Charlie was doing. He decided not to interfere and not to tell Mary, who would worry about her son's safety. Joe believed a person should depend on no one but himself; then he had no others to blame if things went wrong, and he learned to do the best job. Joe also believed in letting his children be free to make their own decisions. He knew children could stub their toes, but it was better to do that and end up with scraped knees during childhood than mollycoddling them so when it was time to leave home the adult children could not take care of themselves.

It never entered Charlie's mind that one of these wild horses might rear up, knock him over, step on him, or kick him. After days the horse with the bag of dirt on his back was glad to have Charlie undo the strap and put a saddle in its place. He thought he'd never get a bit in their mouths. Charlie cinched the saddle one morning, climbed on, and rode one of the horses around the barnyard. The horse was nervous, but it did not buck.

Charlie asked Frank to sit on the corral fence and time one lap around the barnyard. Frank was eager to hold Charlie's watch. He climbed the fence and held out his hand as Charlie rode by. The watch slipped as Frank grabbed. It fell to the ground. The horse stepped on it, breaking the glass and mutilating the face. Charlie was afraid to yell at Frank for fear the horse would become frightened. He pointed in the direction of the house. Frank climbed down, hung his head, and walked slowly. Charlie followed him halfway to the house. He talked in a normal tone as he patted the horse's neck. "You dumb cluck. Will bought me that watch because he used my Henry rifle. Now you broke it."

Charlie's mother saw him and called, "Where on earth did you get that big horse?"

"Out in the meadow. Ain't he a beauty? Want to see another I got?"

"Charlie Burton Irwin, come here this minute!" she called. She was dumbfounded. It was hard to believe Charlie had corralled and tamed two horses and no one knew until now.

Joe pretended to be astounded. He asked Charlie how many

horses he could break before summer.

"Maybe two, three more. That's all. It's nearly a full-time occupation. I have to get up early to work with them so I can do my regular chores during the day."

"How about if I work with you? Then you could have time to brush them and make them look good. I could sell each one for at least fifty bucks. We'd be rich," said Joe.

Together they brought in six more biting, fighting horses before the herd moved on to safer ground. Two of the horses were mares, one yellow, the other pure black, that had not yet foaled. Charlie was not sure how to tame the mares. His father scratched his head and decided a bag of dirt on their backs could not hurt. "But I'm half afraid to put the girth strap on."

"We could wait until they foal; maybe that'll make them gentle."

"Or scared to death," said Joe, scratching his head. "What do you think?"

"I'll put the strap on and not pull it tight," said Charlie. He talked to the horses and let them watch him with their wild, shy eyes.

Without saying anything to Charlie, Joe sold two of the stallions to the livery man. Charlie asked for the money. "I got the horses and broke them; the money is mine."

"I sold them for the best price I could get. This is a family. Everything goes to the head of the family to be used as I see best."

"But what do I get out of it?" Charlie was heartbroken. He'd worked hard with those horses and grown fond of them.

"You get a roof over your head. You get food in your belly. You get the finest education in the land on how to be self-sufficient," answered Joe.

In the middle of the night Charlie thought he heard horses whinnying. He grabbed for his pants and a candle and headed for the barn. On the way he called out to his father, "Pa, I'm going to check the mares." Charlie was still put out and thought his father might ignore him.

Joe was right behind him. He grabbed some bottles of antiseptic and rags and dipped a bucket of hot water from the laundry tub on the stove.

The yellow mare's ears were back and she was sweaty. She lay in the middle of a pile of hay. Charlie took off the girth strap. The colt came easily, feet first, then head and shoulders. Charlie went to the next stall to see the black mare. He took away the girth strap and her foal came just as easy. It was a black filly.

"That running free sure makes a horse strong," said Joe. "Take a look at those foals, up on wobbly legs already. See how straight the legs are."

Charlie thought they looked turned in at all angles. The yellow and white colt fell, then awkwardly stood up and nudged the mare to stand so he could nurse.

"No one has to tell him what to do."

"Just like the calves, or dogs or cats," said Joe matter-of-factly.

"Colts seem smarter. Can we keep these foals?"

"As long as they don't eat us to the gate of the poorhouse."

"Thanks, Pa." Charlie, still under the influence of the miracle of birth, wanted to put his arms around his father.

"Don't thank me, son. You did it. You brought them mares into the corral. I told you stallions would be best."

"Those mares will make good workhorses. Frank and me'll train the colt and filly. Maybe we'll make racers out of them. You can take 'em to the fair. Frank'll ride 'em. I'll pick up the bets." Charlie smiled just thinking about it.

"The sky's the limit with you," said Joe. "I guess your thinking can't bounce any higher than the sky. Let me tell you something. When your thinking does come down to hit the dust, keep it there. Don't get those highfalutin ideas stuck in your head. We're just common sodbusters. You'll have more than scraped knees. You'll have a nosebleed one of these days if you don't tone down your thinking. Did I say I wouldn't ever sell them foals?"

Charlie's heart hit the ground. He blew out the candle after making certain the mares and their foals were fine. He could not sleep. When the sky began to lighten to a dull gray, he fell asleep thinking how he could keep the colt and filly so he and Frank could train them.

In the morning his mother said, "I'm glad the wild stallions are gone. Your father has strung them out behind the farrier's wagon and taken them to the farmers along his route. He was sure he'd sell all of them. I thank God only the mares and their foals are left."

Charlie did not say anything. He went out to look at the foals and bring oats and water to the mares.

All spring Joe grumbled about the trouble the mares caused him. However, in the quiet night hours he whispered to Mary that he was so proud of Charlie and actually glad to have the extra mares. They would be strong horses to hitch to his plow next spring, if they weren't in foal again by that time.

Mary agreed. "You were able to buy seed potatoes and another plow because of the extra money Charlie's horses brought in."

Joe put his arm around her waist and pulled her close. "You think I'm too hard on him?"

"Charlie uses his head. He thinks before acting. You like that in a person. Why don't you tell him that? Giving advice is fine, but praise can go a long way," said Mary.

"I would give a brass-studded bridle if the others were like him. Will's so forgetful at times I wouldn't be surprised to hear he put his candle to bed and blew himself out. I hope to Saint Peter he remembers to feed his own mules a bite of oats once in a while," said Joe. "Let Charlie be, he's learning to get for himself."

Several days later Joe saw an advertisement in the *Sherman County News*. For forty cents in postage he could send for a nickel-plated stem-winder and stem-setter watch. He wrote for the watch. He put Charlie's name on the return address.

The weather warmed so that on Saturdays, Mary and Ell brought the chicken supper outdoors. The Irwins sat on quilts and ate with their hands, not letting plates and forks spoil the good flavor. Each talked about their week's adventures.

One suppertime near the end of May, Frank was not hungry. He was quiet and kept his hand against his left jaw. Ell noticed the jaw was swollen and guessed he had a sore tooth. She suggested oil of cloves to ease the pain. Frank shook his head. "Then chew on a piece of bull nettle root," she said. Frank would not open his mouth.

Joe rummaged through his farrier's tools for a pair of pliers, but Frank moaned and groaned so loud the tools were put out of sight.

Mary tried a warm, flannel rag on his jaw.

Charlie remembered reading an ad in the *Dark Horse* about a tooth extractor and rummaged through the old papers. "Listen to this," he said. "Dr. L. L. Shively, the magnetic tooth extractor and dentist, will be in Goodland May twenty-sixth through twenty-ninth. Fifty cents to have a tooth pulled, one dollar for difficult extractions, but watching is free. Prof. E. P. Lgarnger, the celebrated solo violinist, will give a Grand Concert during the work on the street; he is also business manager for Dr. Shively."

Joe got the wagon out early Saturday morning and gave Charlie a half dollar to pay the dentist. Mary fussed over a place in the back of the wagon where Frank could lie comfortably on a couple of quilts.

Prairie puccoons, with single white flowers and lobed leaves, stood out beside the roadway. Charlie knew that if he broke off a piece of the puccoon's root it would ooze red juice as if bleeding.

In Goodland Charlie found an empty hitch rack along the Boulevard and patted Frank's shoulder. "Come on. You gotta stand in that yonder line." Both boys noticed the violinist played louder whenever a patient yelled. When it was Frank's turn he hung back.

"Charlie, sit in the little canvas folding chair and see how it feels."

"I don't have a toothache."

"Go on. I want to know it's safe." Frank shoved Charlie so that he backed into the camp chair.

Dr. Shively was about thirty, with a pox-marked face, shaggy, oily hair, low forehead, and beaklike nose. He grabbed Charlie, pulled his chin down and looked inside his mouth. The dentist had to hold Charlie's face to one side because his beak nose was so long he could not move up for a close look. He spoke sparingly, took pliers from a bucket of rinse water, and began tapping the upper row of teeth. "Hurt?" he said after he'd tapped the lower teeth.

"It's—I'm not—"

"Tell him it's the last double tooth on the left, top row," Frank whispered.

"Uumm," said the dentist, leaving his hand in Charlie's mouth.

Charlie reached out for Frank. Frank pretended he could not see Charlie's hand waving. Charlie made a noise in his throat. The dentist took this as a sign that he had put the pliers over the aching tooth. His right knee lay across Charlie's lap. His left hand rested on Charlie's sweating forehead. Charlie's hands shot up and grabbed Shively's right arm.

"Hold tight, sonny!" yelled Shively.

There was a slight grating noise as the tooth pulled away from bone and flesh. Shively's knuckles were white. His muscles bulged in his upper arm with the pulling. Charlie's eyes watered and he salivated. Then everything came free and the healthy bicuspid was held up as a trophy with its long, triple root dripping red. It looked like the broken root of the white puccoon.

Shively handed Charlie a tin cup to dip into a bucket of clear cistern water. "Wrench," he said. "Fine specimen." He waved the tooth around for all nearby to see, then he cleaned the cavity with a swab of cotton dipped into tincture of opium. "Numbs the hurt."

Charlie's jaw hurt and his tongue continued to probe a hole large enough to hide a gold piece. He was angry. He let out a yell that would scare a tired work-bull off his bed ground. He grabbed for the bloody molar from the end of the pliers, let it roll to the center of his fist, and jabbed Shively with a fast upper cut to the chin.

"I had no hurt until you caused one!" he said. His eyes were squinted down against the glare of the sun off the rinse water. His eyes seemed to shoot sparks.

Shively stepped backward. He shook his head and grabbed for Charlie. "I don't want to fight. Just a dollar for that there tooth."

"A buck for a perfectly good tooth?" Charlie sputtered. His arms were pinned tight against his back by Shively so he couldn't move.

"Not an easy extraction," explained Shively, letting one of his big hands free to pick up the pliers. He brought the pliers close to his nose, which was close to Charlie's face.

Charlie heard violin music and someone singing "Darling Clementine."

Frank said, "Pay the man."

Charlie glared and began backing away. Shively put his hand close to Charlie's chest. Charlie could see the man's nostrils move in and out. He reached into his pocket, let go of the tooth, and felt the nickel-plated, stem-winder, stem-setter. The dentist's warm breath was on his face and his hand took hold of Charlie's shirt. Charlie's hand came from his pocket holding the precious watch. Shively held on to Charlie and tapped the watch with his pliers. "That old ticker work?"

"It's not old," said Charlie.

"I'll take it," said Shively, letting go the shirt and grabbing up the nickel-plated watch. He put it to his ear and smiled when he heard its loud ticking. He looked at the sun, then at the time. "About right." He motioned to his next customer to sit in the chair. Frank sat.

Charlie's jaw throbbed. He felt himself pushed to one side. He saw no one with sympathetic eyes. People stared ahead watching Shively pocket the shiny watch and open a black box that seemed to hold a thousand different teeth and a flat bottle. Shively nodded toward Frank, smiled, uncorked the bottle to let at least a three-finger measure trickle down his throat. He put the bottle back into the box, then picked up the bloody pliers, rinsed them, and wiped them on a piece of rag that might have been a lady's skirt at one time.

Frank pointed to his abcessed tooth. Before he could pull his finger away the tooth was out and Shively held it out for all to see. The violinist hadn't pulled the bow across the strings. Frank rinsed his mouth with water from the tin cup. The extraction site was dabbed with cotton and numbed.

"Four bits," said Shively.

Frank motioned for Charlie to pay. "Hardly hurt," he said, smiling. "Thanks."

"Thanks for nuthin'," mumbled Charlie, giving Frank the fifty-cent piece.

Frank stepped off the walk and took hold of Charlie's arm. "I'm glad you had yours done first. I wasn't scared. I didn't yell."

Charlie felt sick. He knew he ought to have known better than let Frank push him around. "That was a rotten trick. I won't let you forget that you owe me a new stem-winder."

"Let's go home," said Frank. His tongue probed the hole where his aching tooth had been.

On the third of July the first train of the Colorado, Kansas, and Nebraska, a branch of the Rock Island route, came whistling and clanging into Goodland. Frank and Charlie cleaned out the horse stalls, made sure there was plenty of water in the trough and oats in the feed bins. They could not hear the train, nor see its coal smoke.

The two boys went to the meadow where the horses grazed with the cow. Charlie ran to the creek and back several times as he had every day since the colt and filly had been born. He paced himself slow at first, then on the last run he pushed to go as fast as he could.

"What if the wild horses come back? Will the mares go with them?" asked Frank while Charlie stood bent over, breathing hard.

"Pa says they won't. He says the wild ones won't be back this year." Charlie panted. "I wish I had my watch to time my runs."

"Will you get more horses for Pa to sell next spring?" asked Frank.

"How do I know? Maybe they won't come back. We ought to start walking the colt and filly. Say, tomorrow you could find out how to train a horse for racing. Ask your racehorse friend. He'll be in town for the celebration."

Frank nodded, nuzzled the side of the filly's head, and went to the house with Charlie, saying, "We could name them Sunny and Tar Baby. I heard Pa call the mares Golden and Midnight."

The train that had come as far as the western outskirts of Goodland was a work train carrying wooden ties and rails necessary to complete the track. Will was there, and at the end of the day he and the other railroaders collected a free cigar with their pay.

The next day, the Fourth of July, Goodland was packed with people from all over who wanted to see the final piece of track put in, connecting Goodland with the East and the West.

Charlie kept looking for the black engine to come puffing down the tracks from the east. He saw only the cloudless sky. He heard the Coronet Band practicing behind the courthouse all morning. By noon the saloons became overcrowded, and the crowd grew on the wooden platform in front of the small depot.

Frank nudged Charlie and said excitedly, "I hear the whistle! Honest, I do!" He pointed toward Colby. "It's the Iron Horse coming!"

Charlie squinted. He could not be sure he saw smoke or clouds low on the rim of the blue sky. Then suddenly there were church bells clanging, men whistling, and rifles and pistols going off in the air. People were crowding the platform and spilling over close to the tracks. The train was coming. Charlie heard the wheels clinking and saw the gray puffs of smoke. He felt a tingling sensation crawl down his back and his heart beat faster.

People shouted and clapped and threw their arms around each other. Dogs barked and horses snorted and reared back as if they were going to break their tethers. Some men yelled at the group of boys close to the tracks. The boys paid no attention and ran to meet the engine as it came in slowly. The engineer waved. The boys scrambled over the cowcatcher and up inside the cab and out on the diamond-shaped smokestack. The engine puffed steam and the engineer blew the whistle and rang the bell for some minutes as the boys jumped down to the ground.

Railroad and city dignitaries along with the newspaper editors crowded around as Marcus A. Low, president of the CK and N Railroad, dressed in a dark suit and bow tie, his blond hair slicked back, shiny with perfumed mineral oil, pounded in the last spike to hold the final shining rail.

Mr. Low invited everyone to look inside the chair car to see the comfortable maroon-colored plush seats and sample ice water from tiny, folded paper cups.

Next Charlie wandered to the edge of town to watch the baseball game. Will was catcher because he was big and had long arms that could reach out for the ball, high or low. The railroaders lost to the Goodland team, and the Goodland team lost to the little town of Ruleton, ten miles west on the rail line.

Frank entered the horse races with the boy riders. He won his first race and from then on did not even place. His father took him aside when he saw the disappointment in the boy's eyes. He told him if he'd done his best, there was nothing to be ashamed of. But as he saw it, Frank kept his head too high and kicked the horse far too soon. "Don't get haughty, keep your head down, and pace your horse. Do some practicing at home."

They watched Charlie in the boys' footraces. Charlie hunkered his big shoulders down and bent his knees. He lost the first race and decided it was his boots that held him back. For the next race he wore only his wool socks and his pants. He made his long legs stretch way out. He won easily. Sweating happily, he pocketed his two-dollar prize money.

Ell and Les Miner asked Charlie to watch the parade led by the Coronet Band. So much dust was kicked up by the parade on that hot day, Mary and Joe took to one of the side streets to drink their fresh-bought lemonade. There was a display of a threshing machine. Joe looked the machine over carefully. He wanted one.

Frank asked his father for a nickel to ride the merry-go-round swing. There was a violinist who encouraged the passersby to try the thrilling ride. The advertisement said it "takes you once around the world and back to Goodland." One patient mule was its motive power.

In the evening there was a display of fireworks that caused the people to say "Ooooooo" and "Aaahhh!" In Goodland's opera house was a dance with music by the Coronet Band.

Charlie wasn't much interested in dancing with girls. Just shy of fourteen he felt a girl was about as insipid as oyster stew without oysters. He saw Frank talk to some racehorse owners and thought it best not to interrupt, so he wandered up and down the Boulevard and several side streets looking for his older brother, Will. The ice cream shop was busy and the saloons were well-lighted and busy. He found Will bending his elbow with some Chinese and Irish railroaders. Will saw Charlie and came out on the boardwalk.

"Nice night?" asked Will.

"Yep," agreed Charlie.

"Want to go looking for some female companionship?"

"Nope," said Charlie. "But I've heard if you go past the courthouse and down to the last soddy, it gets pretty interestin'. There's some Mexican girls and an Indian lady that board there with Miss Rose."

"Charlie, you son of a gun! You been there?" Will's eyes were round.

"Nope, but I heard some guys talkin'."

"If I had more money I'd buy another drink and maybe go there. You got any money I could borrow?"

"I got two dollars from the footrace. I'm saving it to buy another pocket watch."

"Another? Where's the one Pa got you?"

Charlie instantly wished he'd kept his mouth shut. "Well, I sort of lost it. Now, don't go telling Pa."

"Lend me your two bucks and I'll be quiet as an oyster about your watch when I'm with Pa."

Charlie wondered how he could get out of this trap he'd put himself into. He hadn't been too smart. He put his head in the air and tried to act like he couldn't be pushed around. "I reckon you've smelt out the wrong hound's butt this time."

Will put his arm around Charlie and his other hand in Charlie's pocket, taking out the two silver dollars. Will dropped his arm and gave a long, low chuckle. "You know, with me, you have about as much chance as a rabbit in a hound's mouth." Will walked slow and easy back into the saloon.

"Have a fine evening," Charlie said, and worked his tongue around in his mouth, then spit alongside the boardwalk. Why was it that he was so angry when his own brothers outsmarted him? he wondered. He took long, fat steps back to the opera house.

The *Dark Horse* published an article on Thursday, July 5, 1888, which stated, "Early on the morning of the Fourth, crowds began to assemble from all directions, and by eleven o'clock it was estimated that there were no less than five thousand people in and around the city. Many had been watching the progress in the building of the railroad and the approach of the Iron Horse, and today they would get to see the first passenger coach run into the city of Goodland."

On July 6 the *Sherman County Republican* printed a large cartoon of a rooster crowing with the headlines "HURRAH! HUR-

RAH!! HURRAH!!! COCK-A-DOODLE-DOO. Goodland connected to the outside world by Railroad and Telegraphic Lines. The first train arrived in Goodland on Tuesday July third. Following this grand achievement there was a mammoth Fourth of July celebration."

That fall Mary entered her currant jelly in the Sherman County Agricultural Association Fair and won a blue ribbon.

With six or seven other young ladies Ell entered the Lady Equestrians. Their horses were brushed and combed so the coats shone. Ell rode sidesaddle, so her green skirt showed off beautifully against the silky, red-chestnut coat of the horse she rode to teach school each day. As she approached the judges in the grandstand, she drew her green satin ribbons apart and took off her bonnet. Her long golden-red hair flew out along with the horse's mane and fine, brushed tail. The reddish colors meshed as one long streamer as she paraded by. Her green eyes crinkled, her mouth curled into a smile. The judges were on their feet applauding. One of them announced loudly, "Miss Ell wins first premium!"

Jim Gandy took first place in the boy riders' horse race and Frank took second. Charlie came in first in the footraces and also in the mule race, but he had to forfeit each award because it had been decided that only one member of a family could be a winner in the races. Frank had raced first. Fred Warren's long-eared mule was awarded first money and Art Wells was given first in the footraces.

Charlie was crushed. He could not figure how the judging could be more unfair. "Next year I'll enter under a different name, by jeems," he said to himself, but he knew he wouldn't. He wanted the Irwin name to be important, but also honorable.

On the way home from the fair Ell waved her bonnet in the air and announced to her family and the wide prairie, "In two years I'll be Mrs. Frank Leslie Miner. You can bet your last dollar on that."

Mary was all hugs and kisses with Ell.

Frank said, "It's time. Les is at our place so much, I already think of him as part of the family."

Joe said, "I like Miner all right, but two years is a long restraint on any man."

"Hush," said Mary. "Young people understand self-control these days."

Momentarily Charlie forgot about the unfairness of the county fair racing judges and thought about Miner as a member of the Irwin family. It sounded swell to him. He always liked Miner.

Two years later, in September 1890, the Irwin soddy was filled with activity in preparation for the forthcoming wedding, set for the eleventh. Charlie whitewashed the inside dirt walls, making the cockroaches scurry out of the sod to find new homes as he filled in holes and crevices. He was surprised by a three-foot bull snake that came through the ceiling over Will's bed. After a scramble with a spade he managed to chop the snake in half and throw the remains out onto the scrap heap at the side of the house. Serve Will right if I'd left the snake in his bed and pulled the comforter up over it, thought Charlie.

"Ma! Do you want the ceilings whitewashed?" he called.

"This place looks so clean and bright, I wonder why we never thought of doing this before," she said. "The light seems to come in from all over. Yes, do the ceilings. Oh, my, how bright and beautiful it is in here!"

Charlie had whitewash running down his arms and spattering on his face and down the wooden handle of the mop he used. When the job was complete, he pulled up the old newspapers that had protected the braided rugs, kitchen table, beds, and chairs from being covered with calcium hydroxide. He dumped the left-over solution out the front door, then seeing it stay in a puddle on the stone walk, he took a broom and tried to sweep the flat stepping stones clean.

"You've made the walkway white as if it were snow. I like it. Thanks," said Ell, shaking scraps of material and threads off her apron. She was making her wedding dress from muslin bleached white as a christening dress, with tucks and stitches so dainty they were nearly invisible. The front yoke was scalloped and had cutout designs embroidered on it and on the leg-o-mutton sleeves. Mary had splurged and purchased from Marietta Roberts a long piece of blue, changeable silk for the sash. Joe took Ell to town and bought her the finest pair of soft kid, high-button black shoes.

Will no longer worked on the railroad, but had bought himself a dozen head of white-faced, red Hereford cows and several hogs. He promised Ell he'd butcher a hog and roast it for her wedding-day feast.

Ell talked to the folks of her schoolchildren about delaying the beginning of school a few days after the wedding so that she and

Miner might have a short honeymoon. Everyone was pleased that she was going to continue teaching. "We'll start school on the fifteenth of September," she promised, and invited all the folks and children to her wedding. Many were the same good people who had come to the Irwin house-raising several years before.

Reverend J. C. Dana, from the Goodland Methodist Episcopal Church, was going to conduct the wedding ceremony. It was a time all would remember for many years. The sun shone and it seemed the everlasting wind had stopped just for this day.

Ell stayed in her bedroom with the flowered curtain pulled across the front until the ceremony began. It was bad luck to be seen by the groom until the wedding time. Her mother stayed with her, giving her last-minute advice and pushes and pulls to the wedding dress.

Miner was waiting in the boys' bedroom with Will to keep him company. Will was the best man. Charlie felt a tinge of disappointment and jealousy because he thought he was the best friend of Miner. Hadn't he been witness to their first kiss?

The smell of freshly ground and roasted mocha coffee was strong and delicious in the soddy. The soddy was decorated with wild asters and Queen Anne's lace in wide-mouth canning jars. Outside, Will's hog roasted on a thick, green sapling.

Reverend Dana brought out a mouth organ and blew a note. The guests hummed "Here Comes the Bride." Miner and Will hurried to the area near the front door where the airy white Queen Anne's lace was poked in little bunches all around the wooden frame. Joe, dressed in his best wool pants and dark wool jacket, mopped his face with his handkerchief and went back to the curtain to escort Ell to the doorway. Mary came out to stand with the women guests, her nose shining and her eyes brimming with tears.

"It's always this way at weddings, especially the first child's," consoled Cora Collins, who had tears spilling over her red cheeks. "This is the most beautiful part of a woman's life. See how she glows with heavenly light. I hope Mr. Miner knows what he's getting."

"A woman is the most precious thing in any man's life," agreed Granny Harris.

"Her light shines as pure as these white walls," said Nora Lewis.

"Ssshhh," said Mary.

The ceremony was short. Afterward the kitchen table was moved out into the yard along with quilts and blankets to serve as places for the guests to sit, visit, eat, and drink. The table held a large bowl of steaming boiled potatoes covered with thick sour cream, and a platter piled high with the roasted pork. The wedding cake was yellow, because the egg yolks had to be used, and filled with chewy raisins, and covered with icing that was syrup beat up with egg whites. The pot of coffee was emptied and more was made. The guests danced to the music of Bill Gandy's fiddle and Reverend Dana's mouth organ. Whiskey for the men was passed around in a jug after each dancc. Each man who danced with the bride pinned a greenback onto her long, full white skirt.

Without warning the music and laughter stopped. Rob Collins stood in front of Ell. His shrill, drunken voice rang out, "If you're too good for me, you're too good for him. No one will have you when I'm done!" He pointed a revolver at Ell. His hand shook so that the end of the gun went from her face to the blue silk sash and back to her face.

"You're crazy!" shouted Miner, who was held back by several men.

Old Nick and the other dogs barked. Rob eyed the dogs for an instant, then his eyes flashed back to Miner. "No, I ain't. I know what I'm doing."

Jack Collins cried out, "You damned fool! I told you to stay away for good!"

Rob's pale blue eyes grew cold. "Nobody gives me orders. Don't move or I'll shoot. I mean it!" All the time his eyes were frozen on Ell. She stood rigid. The greenbacks on her skirt fluttered like leaves on a quaking aspen.

"I want some singing," ordered Rob. "Good singing at this here wedding and this here killing. This is a beginning and an ending. It starts shiny white and finishes dull black. Sing, damn you!"

No one moved. There was complete silence except for the buzz of the bees in Mary's hollyhocks. At the far side of the crowd, a hunched-over figure on a blue and green quilt gave a moan that grew into a kind of wail.

Charlie recognized his mother's cry and his mind worked fast. He saw everyone frozen as in a painting. Only Rob seemed alive as he jerked his body to spread his feet apart and thus brace himself, then his body swayed back and forth. Charlie started humming in time with the swaying. At first the sound was faint as though caught in his throat. The moaning from his mother was louder. His hands bunched. He didn't have his rope, but his fingers reached for it. No one else had a weapon. Weapons were left in wagons, saddlebags, or against the wall inside the soddy. Charlie visualized his rope on top of the bedroom bureau. Next to the bureau was his pole bed with the Henry rifle on two nails above it. He hummed louder and looked at the people. Frank's face was gray as smoke, Miner's face was ashen. His mother's wailing rose and fell. Charlie prayed and kept humming, hoping others would pick up the song. They sat numb as in the grip of some helpless spell.

Charlie saw Rob's look of contempt as he shifted his gaze from Ell to Miner for a short moment. Then he heard Reverend Dana humming and he nodded and moved his head ever so slightly trying to make others understand and join in. Several little children cried. Charlie looked at them and nodded. One watched him and began to hum, then others joined so that slowly, one by one, everyone was humming the old hymn "I Would Be True." Not a word was sung, nor said. Charlie was on his hands and knees. He inched backward slowly, keeping his eyes on Rob, who continued to rock back and forth. Rob had a smile on his face, as though enjoying the humming, but his eyes never blinked and his chest seemed to heave in and out with the swaying.

Charlie edged behind a couple of men, sat on his haunches, then rose behind the men and stood next to Will who was next to the soddy door. He passed Will as though he were invisible, pressed against the door frame and inched across the front of the open door, then took one step backward and was in the shadow inside the soddy. He did not feel perspiration trickle down his back. His throat was constricted and his humming came in pieces, similar to his breathing. He had to think fast. He found his rope and gripped the hard cords. Then he boosted himself to the bed and reached up to the wall for his Henry rifle. Nervously he fumbled in the bureau drawers for cartridges. When he came out the door into the sunlight he could not see Rob at all. He had to move so the sun was not in his eyes. Suddenly Rob yelled, "You're going to pay for everything!" Charlie froze, but the humming went on.

It seemed to Charlie that the crowd had inched away, leaving Rob more ground. Charlie held the rifle vertically against his back, out of Rob's sight. He moved past Will to the back of Rob. Beyond that thick, cotton-white head of hair he could see Ell's face, her mouth drawn tight, her eyes wide with fear.

Rob's shirt and trousers were buff-colored like a young buck. The thought passed through Charlie's head that to shoot him would be like shooting an animal. Charlie moved slow. He wanted a clear path between himself and Rob. When he was certain Rob could not see, he held the rifle up to his eye. Close by a woman gasped and scuttled sideways like a crab. That made several women look up and draw in their breath or shuffle their feet. Rob was alerted. He turned and was facing Charlie's rifle. "Oh, no, you don't!" Rob shouted. "You can't stop me!"

Charlie saw Miner move up behind Rob and pull Ell back into the crowd that was getting to its feet and moving away.

"You're out of your head," said Charlie. "This isn't really you, Rob."

"Shut your face, you overgrowed fly-roost."

"If you go through with your plan, you'll hang."

"Back away!" Rob's breathing was labored and sounded like the steam engine coming into Goodland.

"Listen to me." Charlie tried to keep the Henry on Rob. His mouth went dry as a parched field.

"You never learn, do you, Irwin? You're the same kind of crap as the rest of your tribe. I could blow your head off easy as a gopher's." Rob's short spurt of laughter held no mirth.

"Drop your gun," pleaded Charlie, moving closer. "You could kill someone."

"You son of a bitch, I could blow your brains out!" Rob moved from side to side as though the humming had not stopped. His shirt was stained with perspiration, his eyes were red-rimmed and his mouth twitched.

Charlie raised his right foot and stretched it out slowly in a long stride and pulled his arms out full length so that he pushed the muzzle of the rifle against Rob's left side.

Rob's face flushed, his cheeks grew full as the exhaled air rushed out. His arms flung up and outward as the shot rang out. His eyes bulged and he fell to the ground, holding his bleeding shoulder.

Charlie had not fired the Henry. He was shaking and thinking Rob shot himself. But Rob's weapon was leveled on Charlie, always. Holding on to the rifle, Charlie bent to pick up the discarded revolver. It was not warm and smelled of oil, not powder. He slipped on the safety and heard Rob moan.

Jack Collins peeled out of the crowd. "Son! I shot you! Forgive me!"

The crowd was surging forward and Collins looked at Charlie. "By Jesus, Charlie, you stood in my line of fire so long I thought I'd have to fire to get you to move." His voice cracked. He was down on hands and knees examining Rob's wound. "Better get you into town." To Charlie he said, "I don't know where he got that revolver, but get it out of sight."

Charlie had the revolver under his belt and felt inundated by the gaggle of voices. A passage opened so that Collins and Reverend Dana could carry Rob to the Collinses' wagon. Charlie felt his knees buckle, so he sat on the ground and put his head between his knees.

"That was a purty thing you did there, son." Charlie felt his father's hand on his shoulder and the swell of the words in his head. He looked up. "But why didn't you use your rope? You had us petrified with that rifle."

Charlie didn't feel like talking. He wanted to lean against his father's broad chest and feel the solidness of it as he had when he was small.

Miner took Charlie's hands and squeezed them hard. "I owe you, brother." Ell edged in and, with no concern for her wedding dress, sat on the ground beside Charlie and put her arms around him. He felt nearly smothered and had to push her away so he could get some air in his lungs. Then Will crowded down against him, saying in his ear, "You stupid bastard. You could have nailed him right there and no one would have blamed you."

Charlie didn't reply, but he gave Will a look that would have peeled bark off a tree.

The Collinses' wagon scraped gravel and drove off.

Mary had a damp flannel rag in her hand. She wiped Charlie's face and hands as if he were a small boy. "Come, son. Put the rifle away and have something to eat." She moved back to help the guests, who were again flocking around the table. The past tension gone, they talked and laughed in loud voices.

Frank brought Charlie a piece of wedding cake. Charlie smiled but pushed it aside. Someone passed the brown whiskey jug to him. Will coaxed, "Take a swallow, Charlie. It'll stiffen your legs and set your head on your shoulders."

"I do feel wobbly," admitted Charlie, and he took a drink, hoping his older brother was right. Then he took another and he did feel better. He got to his feet and walked easier. He gave the rifle to his father to put away. "Thanks, Pa. Put it above my bed. It ain't been fired, so no need to swab it out. And put this out of sight." He handed his father the revolver. It's the first time I ever gave Pa orders, he thought. He took the jug from Will and had a third drink and now felt much stronger after the liquid got past the place where it burned in his throat.

"Have more," teased Will. "Can't hurt. Hey, don't cry in the jug, it makes your drink weak."

Charlie forced a weak smile, wiped his eyes on his sleeve, and took another drink.

Charlie was not sure when all the guests left.

Ell and Miner fixed a place to stay overnight in the barn before they moved into Miner's place the next morning.

Some of the young people, railroad section crew, farmers, and cowboys from the county, came to the Irwin homestead about midnight, when they figured most everyone was asleep. They shivareed the newly married couple by banging on iron frying pans and kettles and blowing tin horns. The racket was so much, Mary got up and invited everyone inside for coffee and more wedding cake. That's what they wanted anyway.

It was not long before Ell and Miner came into the soddy fully dressed.

"Not in bed yet!" yelled one of the boys.

"We got dressed," said Miner sheepishly, his arm around Ell and his face beet-red, "as soon as we heard the horses come up the road."

"I bet it took longer to put your clothes on than take them off," another joked.

Charlie lay in bed and swore to himself. The room spun and he'd been up several times feeling like he was going to die, if not this night, tomorrow for sure. Once Will came to see if he wanted some coffee and made fun of him and his pale face in the candlelight. Frank slipped out of bed and came back in his underwear, munching cake. He'd picked out the raisins and offered those to Charlie.

"Go away," said Charlie. "Don't jump on the bed. Can't you see I'm not well?"

"Will says you have buck fever. Pa says you had too much whiskey. Which is it?"

"Frank, if you ever grow up and think about something besides eating and horses, you'll know." Charlie put his hands on his head to keep it from flying around the room like a balloon about to burst. His insides were tangled and tight. He vowed he'd never try whiskey again as long as he lived, at least not more than one or two swallows.

TWELVE

McGuckins

Charlie and Frank exercised the two foals, Sunny and Tar Baby, each morning. The foals pulled against their lead shank, eager to run.

Charlie said, "Frank, act like Pa! Let 'em know who's boss. Don't let 'em get away with nuthin'. Their life has to be in a narrow track." He seemed to know that with horses it did no good to lose one's temper nor to be rough. Consistent tough, but gentle, training was best.

The mares were strong, but the strain of pulling a plow or grubbing out roots and stones showed on each of them. They slowed down, tired easily, by the time they had heavier and slightly darker winter coats.

By spring the young horses' baby hair had shed. Sunny's lighter spots were gone and she was golden like her mother. Tar Baby stayed black as tar.

Charlie and Frank found training the young horses took all the patience they had along with a bucket of oats or a couple of carrots. During the morning hours the boys led Sunny and Tar Baby around and around the meadow by a lead rope attached to biteless head stalls. This walking helped the animals lose their nervousness at being restricted and held back.

"Keep 'em in a narrow track, like I said. Don't force them, or they'll get mean and ornery. But make sure they know you're in charge," repeated Charlie. He knew neither he nor Frank could make the horses do something they didn't want to do. Horses could be stubborn as mules. Charlie adjusted their halters so they would be used to having their heads handled, and he rubbed their ears so they wouldn't be balky when it came time to put on a bridle. Sunny and Tar Baby were walked or run until both boys were tuckered. Neither thought that was too much strain for the horses.

Charlie took one horse at a time and put an old bridle over its head. "You kinda' fool 'em into thinking it's a halter," he explained. "If the headpiece accidently touches their ears, they'll be ornerier than a rat-tailed horse in flytime." Charlie talked all the while Frank slipped the bit into each horse's mouth. "It's only a hunk of rubber. Won't hurt you none."

There were more weeks of patience to get the horses used to something on their backs, such as saddle and rider. Then months more of running. By the time Sunny and Tar Baby were two-year-olds they were well molded into racers. Crowds of yelling people didn't faze them. When Frank was in the saddle, sweeping his hand down over either horse's neck, it was running, body stretched out, ears cocked back flat against its head.

Nothing Frank could think of compared with sitting on a racing horse. Tar Baby's strides lengthened to a fast gallop and the rail whizzed by. Sunny pulled out so she looked almost long of body as she turned on the speed that thrilled Frank. "She's a flier," he said. "She can keep up with Tar Baby easy. You can bet your bottom dollar on either and be a winner. I'm sure."

Frank no longer rode other trainers' horses in the county fair races. He rode his own and showed others how to ride, to control a horse by getting a tight hold on its mouth, digging in with his heels, whispering soothingly in its ear, and always his hand and seat firm. His reputation as a first-class jockey and trainer had begun.

Charlie pulled in three, four more mustangs, gentled them, and sold them himself. He was not sure what he'd do with his money yet. Sometimes he thought of owning a horse ranch. Other times he thought of buying land. He was a consistent winner of the foot racing and rope spinning during the local fairs. He still loved the deliciously exciting feeling that applause from a crowd gave him. He was a keeper of the Irwin account books and he kept the notes on the two racehorses.

Again when winter came, Charlie insisted that the racers be

taken for daily gallops, even through mud and snow. He checked their legs. He had Will file the sharp edges on their teeth and look over their hooves for bruises or cracks. When there were signs of wear, Will shod the front feet. Will said with hind feet bare the racers were not apt to kick their front feet and cut the coronary band.

Will knew nearly as much as his father about veterinary medicine, so he now did most of the farrier's work. He planned to build a new soddy barn for his stock. He dreamed of being a dairy farmer. That way he wouldn't be constantly depending on weather for a decent growing season and good harvest as his father did.

Joe wanted a thresher to make harvesting easier and faster. Threshing machines weren't new, but their popularity was increasing. Finally, in the fall of 1892, Joe rented a McCormick Harvester. The machines were called binders and were pulled by four horses. The binder cut grain, gathered the stems into bundles, tied the bundles with twine, and left them on the field.

Joe left so many bundles that he had to ask Will, Charlie, and Frank to gather them up. The boys stood a dozen bundles on end to form a kind of tepee. The tepee was called a shock. Shocking the bundles kept the heads of grain off the ground. When the field was partly covered with the spread-out shocks, Mary came out to help with the harvest. She laid two bundles across the top of the shock to shed the rain and snow.

Mary sold her eggs and friers in town and added roasting ears for five cents a dozen.

Mary especially missed Ell. She would think of things to tell her about one of the farm animals or how fast the baby chicks were growing. Ell and Miner visited on Sundays and stayed for dinner. Then Mary was so happy to have them around, she forgot what she had saved to tell. "Oh, never mind," she'd say, smiling uncomfortably.

A Texas-born Farmers' Alliance movement took the place of the old Homesteaders Union Association. Joe wanted the alliance to back a movement for grain elevators and mills along the railroad tracks. "If we modernize, Goodland could be a permanent settlement," he said at one of the meetings.

A. B. Montgomery, secretary of the Sherman County Development Company, stood up, ran his finger between his collar and throat, smoothed his graying mustache, then said, "This summer's heat's about to suffocate me. Creeks and ponds are dry. Pastures will soon be scorched. With no crops, who needs a grain elevator? Half the wells in the county will go dry by midsummer. What Sherman County needs is a rainmaker!"

A finance committee was named, and before the meeting was over a fair amount of money was collected. Montgomery was elated. He decided the rainmaker would be in Goodland during the County Fair.

Joe was chairman of the committee to erect a temporary building according to the rainmaker's specifications. The building would house the rainmaking apparatus. Joe and his committee put together a twelve-by-fourteen foot, two-story, unpainted structure in a week. The ground floor had a single door, facing east, away from the prairie winds. The second story could be reached by a ladder and had a small window on all four sides. These windows were covered with black oilcloth. The plans called for a good-sized hole in the roof so that the mysterious gases that were supposed to produce the rain could rise and form clouds.

Charlie put waist-high stakes into the ground in a circle around the raw, wooden building. The stakes had metal eyes on top so that a rope could be threaded through. The rope was to keep curious people from harm when the rainmaking apparatus was revved up and to keep anyone from disrupting the operation. As compensation for putting up the stake and rope fence, Joe let Charlie walk around the fairgrounds.

He went to the paddock where Frank was going to race Tar Baby. On the way he watched a couple prizefighters, their bodies shining from sweat. He saw a man in a dirty white apron selling hunks of chocolate candy. Standing close to the fence he saw Frank hunkered close to the neck of Tar Baby, riding a length behind his opponent. "Keep an even pull on the bit!" he yelled.

An unfamiliar voice at Charlie's elbow said, "Look at them go! You like horses?"

Charlie looked down and saw a girl with brown hair, soft like good tanned suede, and clear, deep blue eyes. She was small-boned, less than five feet tall, and couldn't weigh a hundred pounds. Her pixielike quality distracted him and now the race was over. He hadn't seen Frank win and he was annoyed. "Yes. I aim to have a ranch full of horses one day."

Lightfooted, the girl ran along the fence, disappearing into the crowd that yelled "Atta boy! Frank Irwin! Champion Jockey of Sherman County!"

Frank came down the track leading Tar Baby. When he saw Charlie he said, "I won five dollars!"

Charlie was all smiles. "That's great! I get half, remember I helped train the horse and you owe me a stem-winder pocket watch." He climbed under the fence and helped Frank walk the horse to the paddock. He was cleaning Tar Baby's quivering nostrils when he heard the voice again.

"Is that your horse?" The voice was like wind sighing in the treetops, soft and melodious. It broke into Charlie's thoughts of rubbing the horse dry with the old rag Frank held out.

"Hey, what do you want?" Charlie looked down into wide, ink-blue, intelligent eyes. The girl must have ducked under the fence when he wasn't looking.

"Nothing. Just talk."

"You made me miss seeing my brother come over the finish line." He tried to sound put-out. His voice cracked.

The girl laughed, a lighthearted trilling sound, then she said, "It was a lovely sight. I'm sorry you didn't see it." Her eyes turned dark purple, like woods violets growing in the shade. "You going to the depot to see the rainmaker come in?"

"Nope. I'll see him when he gets to the fair."

"I'll see you." Her feet hardly touched the ground, she was that light.

An unusual warmth ran up Charlie's backbone to his neck and face. He felt a kind of elation. He was sure it was not because Frank was Champion Jockey of the county. He enjoyed the feeling but was puzzled by it. He looked at Frank, who was smiling and rubbing down the horse. "Winning the race makes you feel good, huh?" said Charlie.

"People are waving at me from the fence. Men tip their hats and women dip their parasols. I'm a celebrity!" said Frank.

Charlie looked at the flannel-gray clouds overhead. "Enjoy it because tomorrow this rainmaker's going to be a winner."

The next day the gray clouds were gone. The sun moved alone in the blue sky. Charlie thought about the rainmaker and wondered what he looked like. The Irwin family headed for the fairgrounds early. They didn't want to miss a thing.

There was already a crowd around the rainmaker's building. Joe told Mary about the hole in the ceiling of the second floor. Will and Frank went to check on the racehorses. Charlie moved close to the rope. He was curious how rain could be made. He looked around and thought most of the town had come to see also.

Staring at the rainmaker's building was a serious-looking couple with a dozen children huddled around their legs. The mother's face was smooth as porcelain, as though if she dared smile it would crack in a thousand pieces. Her gray dress buttoned high under her chin matched the gray poke bonnet where her brown hair was pushed nearly out of sight. The father was forbidding, with dark-brown hair and sideburns that met a broad beard and steely blue eyes.

Without meaning to, Charlie's eyes met the inquisitive blue eyes of one of the children. She stood on the outer edge of the family circumference. It was the pixielike girl who talked to Charlie at the fair yesterday. Her fine brown hair was blown around the impish set of her mouth and upturned nose. Her face glowed and her arms waved as she explained something to the younger brothers and sisters. She was the only one of this family wearing some color. The long blue flowered skirt swung around her ankles. Her black button shoes were scuffed on the toes. The other children were dressed in all black or gray to match their solemn folks. I wonder who they are? thought Charlie.

"Oh, look, that must be the McGuckins," said a woman to her husband, who was standing next to Charlie. "I heard they came from New York State, then Missouri's Livingston County, before coming here."

Charlie raised his head in their direction. He found that information startling and hard to believe. Then he wondered if the girl knew his Grandma and Grandpa Brassfield.

Mrs. McGuckin directed her eyes toward Charlie. He felt his toes curl. Then birdlike, she cocked her head and said, "This is the Lord's day, son. You are going to observe one of His miracles performed right here."

The rainmaker came out of the building wearing a black cape with a red satin lining and carrying a black cane. He had a black top hat and white duck breeches tucked into black alligator-skin boots. But this rainmaker resembled the medicine man, Colonel Johnson, of years back. He no longer wore ten-dollar gold pieces as buttons, and he had no mustache. But he still had that high belly up under his vest from which thundered a slow, deep voice. Charlie pushed on the rope to see if he could get a closer look.

"Colonel Johnson!" called Charlie. "Remember me and the Irwin Smithery?"

The rainmaker colored slightly pink and said, "The name's Dr. Melbourne, son." He moved closer to Charlie and Will. Both were more than six feet tall and together weighed more than three hundred and fifty pounds. Surprised, Dr. Melbourne took Charlie's hand. "Hell's brimstone!" he whispered.

"I'm the kid," said Charlie, grinning, pushing his hair out of his eyes.

"I don't recall a body as big as yours. But now I see the same alert brown eyes and mop of sandy hair. Jehoshaphat! You came to see my splendid performance. So, the show continues. I'll see you later."

Dr. Melbourne strutted about showing off his knowledge about rain. He told the people about the wind bringing in clouds. "It's a scientific fact that water is made from two colorless, tasteless, and odorless gases. They are called oxy-gin and hydry-gin. If lightning strikes a mixture of these gases—*wham! bam!* Water is formed. Therefore, if I can generate hydry-gin and let it get up into the atmosphere to mix with the oxy-gin there, and a wee spark or bit of lightning hits—zap! That's rain!"

A couple of men in work boots and overalls carried a ten-gallon, glass carboy filled with a clear, oily-looking liquid from a wagon on the street to the door facing east. Next they brought in a couple of long, foot-wide strips of corregated sheet metal. Melbourne opened the door so the things could be carried inside. He closed the door before Charlie had a good look inside. Then he came close to the rope and grasped the hands that were outstretched. "Folks, welcome, all of you. I'm grateful to be invited to your beautiful town. You know who I am, Dr. Melbourne, the well-known rainmaker from Australia."

People buzzed like bees in a meadow of alfalfa. Charlie saw his auburn hair was flecked with gray. He wore a huge gold ring with a diamond setting. "Are there alligators in Australia?" asked Charlie.

"Don't push on the rope. I'm not parading out here to answer questions."

"I had no idea you were in the business of making rain," said Charlie, following him around the rope fence.

He moved close to Charlie and whispered. "I'm in the business of making money. Are you interested, Your Honor? Then bend way down, Corporal, and come through the barricade. I could use some help." He looked up at the clear blue sky.

Charlie was on the other side of the rope in a second. He took a deep breath and stepped to one side of Melbourne, who shook his hand and turned to the crowd. "Folks, you wonder what a tall man can sense that the rest of us ordinary people cannot? Well, my friends, this young man, one of your very own citizens, is going to tell you when to expect rain. He's going to smell the clouds forming."

"What?" Charlie heard himself say.

"You know—test the crowd. Work their fancies, entertain."

"But I've never smelled clouds!"

"Don't matter. Sing that new song, 'Home on the Range.' You'll knock 'em over."

Charlie swallowed. "Tell me how you use the metal sheets?"

Melbourne took off his cape and flung it around Charlie's shoulders and pretended he was fastening the neck piece as he briefly described rainmaking. "I'm going inside," he nodded toward the temporary building, "and do my experiment. Pray for rain clouds! Talk to the folks. Sell my famous anodyne, used by the social set in Australia. Use your spiel!" He patted Charlie on the back. "My Lord, you sure grew big!" He disappeared inside the building.

Charlie gulped and turned his face up to the sky. "Ladies and gentlemen!" He wondered where Melbourne kept the anodyne. "You have seen the famous Dr. Melbourne from the home of kangaroos. At this very moment he's preparing the final stage of his experiment." Charlie moved from one foot to the other, not quite certain what to say next.

One of the men in work boots and overalls placed a wooden box full of little brown bottles beside him. The man went into the building without saying a word. Charlie held up a bottle and felt his heart flutter like a butterfly. "This tiny bottle contains Australian painkiller made from secret ingredients." Charlie waved his hands. He felt the air swish the cape around his ankles and billow it out around his sides. People were quiet. Their eyes were on him. He walked slowly along the inside of the rope as he'd seen Melbourne do. Then he saw her, the tiny, pert Miss McGuckin. He pretended he was talking only to her. He used some of Melbourne's exact words. "This medicine is used by the social set in Australia." He read from the label. "One bottle, two bits. Only twenty-five cents. This pain reliever acts in harmony with the laws of life so perfectly it cleanses the blood of all disease." He paused, giving Miss McGuckin a chance to think on his words. "Who'll be first to have this rare curative? Yes, ma'am, two bottles. You won't regret your purchase. Yes, sir, one. And one here!"

Charlie sold until the case was empty, and miraculously another full case appeared at his feet along with a cigar box for the loose change. He began to sing the first verse of "Home on the Range."

He looked skyward. No clouds except for a few beginning to form low on the northern horizon. He wondered what Melbourne was doing. He filled his hands with more brown bottles. He saw Ed Murphy, the railroad ticket agent, run through the crowd and stand in front of him. Murphy waved his green, celluloid eyeshade. "I've got to see the rainmaker quick!"

"He's doing his secret experiment. No one can see him," said Charlie.

"Son, we've been gettin' wires from towns all along the northern line into Nebraska! People are drowning!" He sputtered the words.

Charlie gasped. The crowd buzzed and rumors flew. Charlie held up his hands. "The depot's deluged with telegrams telling of thunderstorms and flash flooding, bridges washed out. I'm going to tell Dr. Melbourne to shut off his rain machine for today."

The crowd *aahh*ed in one breath, then began to talk in a buzz. "He created rain! He actually did! Rain to the north! Rain's needed here!"

Murphy was knocking on the door of the unpainted building. Melbourne came out and stood beside Charlie. He eased the cape off Charlie's back and winked. He called out, "I'm telling you what I'm going to do! I'm going to set up my secret apparatus tomorrow morning and bring rain here. I won't fail you! Glorious, quenching rain! Think about it! Pray about it."

Charlie was exhilarated. He shook Melbourne's hand and promised to see him in the morning.

When Charlie caught up with his folks, his father spoke first. "Back there you reminded me of the time you sold liniment for the medicine man. You were only a boy then—but now? It doesn't seem decent for a local boy to act like a sideshow barker, talking about manmade rain, singing and selling."

"Pa! Dr. Melbourne *is* Colonel Johnson. Didn't you see?"

"Blasphemy! Settlers and people of Goodland paid good money for Dr. Melbourne. They set hopes in him. What do you think they're sayin' right now about you selling Australian tonic? It don't set right!"

"I promised Dr. Melbourne I'd be back tomorrow."

There were certain rules in the Irwin family. One was never to break a promise.

Mary's voice was steady. "Chores, then if there's daylight, you can come to town. That's that."

Next morning Charlie was up at the first hint of light. He planned to work steady and be done by noon. There was not a cloud in the sky when Charlie saddled his horse and left for town without lunch.

"I expected you this morning," said Melbourne, his face dark.

"Well, yes—there were chores," said Charlie.

"Don't blot out your transgressions. Just sounds like your saddle slipped to me," said Melbourne. His two assistants looked at each other and laughed quietly. He told Charlie to follow him up the rickety stairs.

"My pa worked on this building," said Charlie.

"Slapped up this building, you mean. Now, pay attention, Your Highness, because if you know how this works you can talk to the folks with some intelligence. Made more anodyne last night. Couldn't get the right-sized bottles, so charge thirty cents for these."

"The labels say 'twenty-five cents.'"

"Costs to import from Australia. Tell folks what a bargain they're getting, Admiral. I'm speaking honest with you. Wouldn't unless I was offering you a position on my staff. You want to come with me? We'll make a fortune off this rain business. When it fizzles out, there's always another scheme or fad waiting for us. What do you say, partner?"

Charlie, in his wildest dreams, had not expected such an offer. he hesitated to give himself time to think.

"Speak up. You're full grown. Think of the advantages. You'll get out of this godforsaken town, see the country, meet important people. You'll be important. Your picture will be in newspapers."

This was persuasive stuff for an eighteen-year-old, son of a farmer and farrier. Charlie wanted to shake Melbourne's hand and tell him yes right there, but he continued looking at the bottles of painkiller that didn't come from Australia at all. Finally he reached out, took the rainmaker's hand, and said, "Thank you, Colonel Johnson." That was an unintentional slip. He was embarrassed. "I mean Dr. Melbourne."

"Well, you'll have to keep your wits about you. Names used

correctly are important. A name can change with an occupation. People relate your name to your occupation and residence. I'm Dr. Melbourne from Australia."

"Yes sir, I'm sorry."

"That's another thing. Don't apologize. Whatever you do, act as if that is the way you intended. Make it the other man's problem. He's the one that should be sorry."

"I'll learn," said Charlie.

"That's the right attitude, Mate!" He clapped Charlie on the back. He showed Charlie how acid was poured slowly from the carboy into a large granite pitcher that was already more than half full of water. It took the two assistants to do the pouring of the clear syruplike acid. Charlie heard rumblings as if the mixture were boiling in the pitcher. A mist rose from the surface. When the pitcher was full, Melbourne turned with a flourish and stood beside the metal sheet. "The dilute acid is poured over the zinc, which stands in a granite tub. All precaution is taken not to spill. See the black spots on the floor? Even dilute oil of vitriol burns wood, clothing, and skin."

Charlie moved back, spellbound. There was a great effervescence when the diluted acid came into contact with the zinc. The bubbles hissed and popped.

Melbourne pushed the oilcloth curtains aside. The crowd was growing outside. "The hydry-gin gas is bubbling and rising heavenward. Go tell the folks, Partisan. Make them believe in miracles."

Charlie backed down the rickety steps and opened the door. He wore a cream-colored coat with large pearl buttons and a wide-brimmed felt hat to match. Melbourne said he was a knockout in the outfit. Underneath he wore his muslin shirt, black wool pants, and black boots.

Charlie raised his hands as he'd seen preachers do when giving the benediction at the end of Sunday service. The crowd quieted. He moved slowly, looking at the people as he talked. He felt a bond with his audience, as if a thin string tied them together as he talked. He could feel the string tighten when the audience was attentive and slacken when restive.

He pointed to the steam rising from the opening in the upper story. "Similar to fog." The folks understood and nodded. "See clouds moving in from the north?" They were! A whole bank of light, fluffy, white clouds was blowing in. "I smell the rain coming. Get your umbrellas ready."

*   *   *

Two days into Dr. Melbourne's experiments, a breeze, softer than the others, brought the first splatters of rain. People moved together in little groups and watched the rolling thunderheads. The breeze multiplied into a driving wind. Lightning cracked and thunder roared and the rain poured. Folks held papers and scarves over their heads if they had no umbrella. Some moved for shelter in buggies and under blankets in wagons.

Charlie was left standing alone, soaked. The cream-colored coat and hat showed their shabbiness and stains. He backed against the building, waiting for someone to open the door. The wind gusted into driving rushes of cold air. A couple of running men stopped and waved to him as if giving thanks for the downpour. Charlie thought his father would be pleased. He wanted rain. He thought his mother might fix something special for him for supper. Then another thought struck him. He wouldn't be home for supper. The mental image of his mother's sad, gray-green eyes pulled on his heart. Then he thought, why can't I leave to make my own life? Ma and Pa can make out without me.

Finally one of the assistants opened the door and helped Charlie bring in the empty wooden cases. The assistant smiled when he saw how bedraggled Charlie looked. The rainmaking apparatus was downstairs against the wall. The granite tub caught the rain that pelted through the hole in the roof. Melbourne sat on an overturned case eating bread and cheese. Charlie sat beside him. He was honored and overwhelmed to be in the presence of a man who could control the forces of nature. "You did it! You deserve more than praise!"

"Money is all I ask for." Melbourne smiled and offered Charlie a piece of bread. Charlie took off the wet coat.

The rain stopped as quickly as it started.

Melbourne opened the door and said to Charlie. "Help load this gear into that wagon over there. Kiss the girls good-bye, Duke, we're on our way to Lincoln, Nebraska. Hitch your horse to the back of the wagon. We'll take it along so you won't get homesick."

Charlie thought he saw the pixielike McGuckin girl standing against the rope, watching him haul gear to the wagon. When he stopped to look again she was gone. He packed boxes, glass spoons, stirring rods, and beakers into a straw-filled barrel. The black stallions tied to the front of the wagon snorted as though eager to be moving on. Melbourne piled some lumber from the building into his wagon. The assistants pulled up the stakes holding the rope Charlie had strung. They rolled the rope and tucked it into the wagon beside the wooden stakes.

"My pa bought that rope," said Charlie.

"A good man. You're living proof, huh?" said Melbourne, then in a loud voice he said, "Come here! Hang your jacket up to dry properly. Pay attention to your costume. Your hat needs to be rounded out over a pot so it'll dry without streaking or shrinking." He handed Charlie a white, granite saucepan. "If your hat shrinks, we'd believe it was your head that swelled. Tee-hee!"

Charlie nodded and pulled the hat around the bottom of the saucepan and put it on top of the lumber. He laid the damp coat nearby. Melbourne had spoken to him the same way his mother spoke when he was forgetful. His folks had every right to speak up if he didn't please them. But if he were old enough to do a job, he was old enough to see for himself what had to be done. Maybe if he couldn't see what was considered important, the job wasn't for him. Drying an already scruffy coat and hat wasn't much to get riled about. He went back to the building to see if there were something else to go into the wagon. He went to find his horse. The girl was there beside the hitching post.

"I wiped off your horse and saddle. I didn't think you'd mind. Ma had a pile of rags in our wagon, so after I wiped our horses I just did yours. You look better without that dirty, cream-colored coat."

Charlie bit his lip. He knew he should tell her he was leaving. He felt horrid, like he was getting a stomachache. The words would not come out. He told her thanks and walked back to the wagon without his horse.

A. B. Montgomery shook hands with Dr. Melbourne and handed him a brown envelope. "Your expenses plus fee for bringing that lovely rainstorm. This morning there was not a cloud in the sky. I didn't think you could pull it off. But I'm a total believer now."

Dr. Melbourne grinned so his white teeth gleamed in the late sun. He pocketed the envelope, then shook hands with Montgomery.

"You might get more rain tomorrow, a kind of aftereffect. I sent waves of hydry-gin into the atmosphere, and some of it may not be used up."

"How'd you do that?" asked Charlie as Dr. Melbourne turned to leave.

"I use my head. Listen here. I watch the clouds and I follow the rivers and creeks and valleys and I move where it's most likely to rain."

Charlie was aghast. "But that's fraud!"

"Quiet there, don't get flooded with holy enthusiasm. I use my head and I read all the latest scientific books and papers I can get my hands on.

"If you're coming, tie your horse to the wagon, Your Highness."

Ed Murphy from the depot came to shake Melbourne's hand. "Watch this, my good man," Melbourne said out of the side of his mouth to Charlie. He extended his hand to shake Murphy's. "Say, Mr.—ah—"

"Murphy," whispered Charlie.

"Mr. Murphy, I thank you for warning me yesterday about the strength of my rainmaking." He clapped Murphy on the shoulder. "Here's something for you. Take this buckeye. I brought it all the way from Ohio. Carry it in your vest pocket, all your enemies become kind to you." He saw Murphy wore no vest. "Now, if you were to carry it in your lower pocket or a purse—" Melbourne hesitated just a moment.

"I don't carry no purse," Murphy said, and laughed. He pushed his eyeshade higher on his forehead.

"Oh, I know that, but if you were to give this to a friend that does, or just leave it in one of your lower pockets, you or she would expect prosperity," Melbourne said and winked.

The ticket agent's eyes lit up and he said, "Why, thank you a heap, my friend," and he hurried back to the depot.

Charlie almost doubled over with a spasm of laughter. "Say, how can you give someone almost nothing and make him so grateful for it?"

"Son, it's a funny thing about people. They like little surprise presents. Then they remember the times I make right moves. To the point, the times I made it rain. So, I build a decent reputation. This work depends primarily on reputation. It pays better than hawking salves and alteratives, but it don't hurt none to push that, too, if the folks have money to spend."

Charlie blinked. "You gave Mr. Murphy a worthless seed and he'll remember you for it?"

Melbourne sniffed and wiped the back of his hand across his nose. "Master Irwin, are you listening to me?"

"Oh, yes, sir, every word."

"Well, then, I must be speaking in Hindustani."

"Oh, no, sir, I understand your words. But I don't see—" Charlie was afraid he did see and he wanted to be certain.

"Let's see now. For helping me with this little experiment I want you to have this cork from the alkyhall bottle. Bottle's empty. I used the alkyhall in the last batch of anodyne you sold. Wait a minute, I'll carve your initials in it. Then, also, you may have one of these Australian anodynes. It cures anything from corns to laryngitis. Come now, get your horse and then hike yourself up in the back of the wagon, right next to that carboy. You'll have to tuck your legs in."

Charlie put the bottle of tonic in his front pocket and the cork in his other pocket and dug in the mud with his boot. He cleared his throat and wiped his hand across his eyes so he could see without squinting. "I'm not going. I've decided to be a famous rancher and raise horses. If you ever come by my place, stop in. I'll always be CBI like the initials on the cork." He reached out to shake hands with Melbourne.

Maybe Melbourne had kind of figured Charlie had other plans because he said, "Horses? You ever think about racehorses? Don't forget me, Senator. I could work the odds for you."

Charlie walked past the empty rainmaking building to his horse. He saw the girl standing by the wagonload of kids. She came toward him.

"Boy, that Doc Melbourne can chew the fat," he said.

"You seemed to be chewing some yourself."

"Well, I really owe him. I learned a lot about clouds and stuff."

She seemed kind of quiet and Charlie didn't know if he'd said something that hurt her feelings. Her eyes looked sad and far-away.

He reached in his pocket and took out a cork with his initials. "Here's a souvenir. It's the top to one of those big bottles Dr. Melbourne has for mixing his anodyne ingredients."

She rolled it around in her hand, smelled it, and looked at the neatly carved CBI.

"That's my initials," said Charlie. "Stands for Charles Burton Irwin."

Her blue eyes looked like spring violets. "Thank you. I'll keep it. My name's Etta Mae McGuckin."

"Say, one day maybe you could come to our place."

The violet eyes glittered and her mouth turned up into an

impish smile. "It is better manners if the boy goes to the girl's place."

"Well, I—I could come tomorrow. Does you pa need a plow sharpened or a horse shoed?"

"My pa asked yours yesterday to look at our dog. When he comes, come with him. I make good gooseberry pie." She looked toward her wagon. "Uh-oh, Pa is fixing to leave. Bye!"

"Pie! Good-bye!" The musical rhyme rang in his ears. He decided to give the bottle of anodyne to his pa and a handful of long, slim cattails he'd find in the slough to his ma. Supper would taste good.

In the weeks that followed, the pixielike girl stayed in Charlie's thoughts. He hauled wood from the creek banks, harvested wheat, stacked hay during good fall weather, and before the warm stove at night he repaired a harness or read from books Ell had left behind: Virgil, Thomas Gray, Hesiod, John Dryden. Frequently he looked in the fire box to the flickering flames and indulged in dreamy contemplations. He thought about Etta's brown hair, sky-blue eyes.

Charlie rode eagerly with his father on farrier rounds, hoping to stop at the McGuckin place. He watched young girls in town, seeking a certain toss of the head, a manner of skipping to cause the skirt to swing jauntily. When he could stand it no longer, he asked, "Pa, those new settlers—McGuckins—weren't you to do something at their place?"

"McGuckins? Oh, that was a hound dog with worms. A son-in-law sent word the dog died."

"What a shame. Shouldn't we look at their other animals?"

Joe looked up from polishing his fiddle. "Whatever for? I wasn't asked."

"To say we're sorry—about the dog?"

Amused, Joe said, "A dead dog?"

"We could go to church—see the McGuckins there." Charlie's heart thumped. He waited for the answer.

"If you feel the need to give condolence for a dog or to hear one of Reverend Dana's sermons on Hell's fire and damnation, go. You don't need me nor your ma. We've other things to do. Irwins and church don't seem to mix well. Stay here. Read the Bible. Take a walk by the creek, you'll feel the presence of the Lord. Think on it."

The next Sunday, Charlie sat in the back pew so he could see who came into church. The McGuckins came and took one complete pew for their brood. Charlie moved up. Etta smiled. She did not turn to look at Charlie, but he felt she knew he was there. Her cheeks were tanned and taut over the facial bones.

Mr. McGuckin surveyed his row of children. He said so Charlie could hear, "It's against the commandments to sing poplar songs like that 'Home on the Range.' But it's a mark in your favor to sing church hymns." His head turned farther, his eyes lingering on Charlie, uncertain and fiery.

For a moment Charlie held his breath. When it was time to sing, Charlie did his best. The sound came from deep inside his chest and resonated from his diaphragm to his palate.

The boy in front of him stopped swinging his legs, turned, and whispered, "What's your name?"

Charlie hummed the *amen.* "Charlie. What's yours?"

"Curly." The boy turned quickly and looked straight ahead. His father was inspecting the row of children from the corner of his eye.

Charlie studied the head of brown, curly hair, then bent forward and said quietly, "Tell your sister, Etta, I'd like to take her home."

Curly's back stiffened, but he did not turn.

Charlie's mind was elsewhere for the remainder of the service. The moment the benediction was over, he was on his feet. The McGuckins took their time getting out of the pew. The parents pressed their lips together as a sign they disapproved of the children's lingering. Each child took a long look at Charlie as though knowing by osmosis that he'd whispered to Curly. "I'm Walt," whispered the last child, who was barely in his teens. "Do you like Etta?"

"Maybe," whispered Charlie, feeling embarrassed.

"You can't take her home," Walt said, hardly moving his lips.

When Charlie was out the sanctuary door, the McGuckins were piling pellmell into their wagon. His heart beat fast. Momentarily he wished he'd said nothing to Curly or Walt. It wasn't any of their business. He then saw Etta. She smiled and waved. He pulled himself up straight and walked purposefully to the McGuckin wagon.

Mr. McGuckin's face was weathered, lined coarse by the action of wind, sun, and rain. He stood beside the wagon as his wife climbed, unaided, to the seat. His hands remained at his sides. He did not reach to take the hand Charlie proffered.

"Good day," said Charlie heartily.

"What is it you want?" said Mr. McGuckin tartly.

Charlie kept a friendly look on his face. "I came to ask permission to take Etta home in my wagon." He could feel perspiration on his palms evaporating, making his hands cold.

Mr. McGuckin's acerbity caused Charlie's shoulders to slump. He looked for Etta. She was helping the smaller children find places to sit comfortably. Mr. McGuckin was talking.

"It's the smart alecks like you, you know, that give young people a bad name these days. Singing popular songs. I haven't forgotten."

Charlie thought he heard some stifled giggles, then wasn't sure. Maybe it was the wind in the treetop. His heart sank. "I beg your pardon, sir. I will stay directly behind your wagon and let Etta out when we are at your gate." He could feel the clammy fingers of wind at the back of his neck.

"Don't beg my pardon. I don't allow Etta, nor any of my offspring, to ride in a whippersnapper's wagon." Mr. McGuckin climbed into his wagon, clicked his tongue, and at the same time picked up the reins. His two horses moved together in step, *clip-clop, clip-clop*.

Dumbfounded, Charlie stood rebuffed. Etta waved. He imagined tears in her violet eyes. Her gray bonnet hung down her back and the fine, brown silk threads of her hair shone in the sunlight.

"Be gone. You younker!" Mr. McGuckin called.

Charlie's head snapped up. He wanted to wave, but his hand wouldn't move. When the wagon was out of sight, except for the rolling ball of dust behind, he thought, why in blue blazes am I standing here? I'm a fool. Women! They are a nuisance, inconsistent, vexatious, an annoyance, a plague, sour gall, an effrontery to man's intelligence. He was thankful his brothers, Will and Frank, weren't around to tease him. He vowed he'd face this and all misfortunes with fortitude. He'd show those who knew him that he had integrity, high standards, and an appreciation of his fellow men.

Reverend Dana came across the churchyard to Charlie's side. "Doesn't take the congregation long to clear out these days."

"Is it against the Lord's commandments to sing popular songs?" asked Charlie.

"Not that I heard directly. So long's the singing's not accompanied by swearing and spirits." He looked at Charlie firmly. "You have a run-in with McGuckin?"

"No, sir!" Charlie was adamant. Then he added, "Not of my making."

"I suppose it's none of my business, but I'm going to warn

you that McGuckin is a stern, unyielding man. He's against and intolerant of any temptation, gambling, even laughing, it seems. In some ways he's been made sour because of the heap of acid in his life." He waited, then added, "Opposite side of the coin is your ma. She's soft-hearted, forgiving, tries to please. She sees a healing power in fun and laughter."

Charlie did not find the contrast pleasant, but felt forced to comment. "Life doesn't have to be a bitter pill. Does it?" Charlie walked toward his wagon. "I want mine to be an exciting adventure."

"Most get what they want. It's a matter of attitude. Keep the Lord's commandments, and do the best you can each day. See you next Sunday?"

"I can't say next Sunday for sure," said Charlie. "But I'll see you again for sure."

The ride home was pleasant. Charlie's mind was occupied with what he might have said to Mr. McGuckin. Jeems! He could have told him he'd outgrown the smart-aleck stage and never was a whippersnapper. He combed his brain for wise phrases he might have used. Mr. McGuckin was a fool, a shallow-brained, insensate eccentric.

Charlie was so deep in his exasperation that he hardly noticed and did not question the dark, quivering cloud coming straight for him, low on the road. When the strange cloud was nearer, his eyes widened. It appeared to be a brightly colored, shimmering swarm. It appeared to be thousands upon thousands of teeny-tiny orange, white, and black birds, all fluttering together. He stopped. When the fluttering creatures were closer, he recognized them. Butterflies! Then he was inundated with butterflies. Some lighted on his head, shoulders, and hands, on the horse's head and nose. The horse shivered and switched its tail. To Charlie this was a beautiful, wondrous sight, exciting. The insects fluttered their wings, then let the breeze carry them along before they flew again. Some rested on the alternate, lance-shaped leaves of the milkweeds. Some plants were covered with butterflies so that they looked like exotic, tropical flowers. The butterflies moved south and he wondered if they followed the call of the Canada geese. He estimated that the butterfly cloud was a mile long and half a mile wide; how deep he was not sure, maybe a few hundred feet.

There were stragglers long behind the main cloud. He got off the horse and examined a few on a milkweed. Their wings were ragged and torn. Poor creatures must have come a long way, he mused. Why? Where were they going? Why? Some Pied Piper calls in butterfly language. He climbed into the wagon, held up on the reins, staying dead still. He listened. He could hear nothing unusual, only the constant whooshing of the wind across the flat land.

Confidence in Melbourne's rainmaking ability was expressed the following spring when he was asked to produce crop rains in forty western counties at ten cents a cultivated acre. After his departure from Goodland, the Inter-State Artificial Rain Company was formed. The president was Ed Murphy. Martin Tomblin and A. B. Montgomery were directors. Montgomery went to Topeka for a charter and to visit with the attorney general about the irrigation laws applying to rainmaking. This company made a deal in Temple Texas to sell one of their rainmaking machines for fifty thousand dollars. In 1892 a man from Tulare, California, came to Ed Murphy to contract for rain.

That same year Dr. W. B. Swisher of Goodland chartered the Swisher Rain Company, which went to Texas and Mexico to operate. A third company was the Goodland Artificial Rain Company chartered with J. H. Stewart as president. That summer Dr. Melbourne returned to Kansas to produce half an inch of rain over six thousand square miles near Belleville for five hundred dollars.

A reporter for a Dodge City paper wrote: "If Kansans are gullible enough, and Providence helps the wizard out with one or two coincident wet spells, this is liable to prove a good thing for Melbourne, who, of course, is not in the business for his health."*

Winter came and summer, then winter again. The drought was broken.

During a conference on rainfall and irrigation held in Wichita, Kansas, during the summer of 1893, Mr. A. B. Montgomery gave a talk stating that he'd operated the Inter-State's rain machine three times during the spring growing season in Sherman County and as a result of sufficient rain there were one hundred thousand bushels of wheat produced. He ended his speech by pointing out that there was little wheat produced in any of the surrounding dry counties.

*Courtesy of the *Sherman County Historical Society Bulletin*, Goodland, Kansas, Vol. 5, No. 3, Jan. 1980, "The Rain Makers."

From March to August, Goodland's rain companies operated at various locations in Kansas and Nebraska. Each claimed credit for any rain that fell. However, by the first of September the rainmaking experiments slacked off and by the end of the month most experiments were canceled by the growing number of skeptics.

In Minden, Nebraska, a president of one of the Goodland rain companies was tied to a pole and treated to the fire hose by active doubters to show that president how a spray of water can easily be made with no prescribed mumbo jumbo and secret operations.

One warm afternoon in the summer of 1894, Les Miner ran into Rob Collins in the Mercantile in Goodland. Rob allowed as how he was back for good, looking for a job as hired hand. He asked Les if he were hiring. Les said his spread was not large enough.

Les noticed Rob's speech was slurred and his words slow. He supposed Rob had been drinking. Rob turned ugly and threatened Les for scorning him and not giving him a job. Rob said he'd kill Les the next time they met and it was a promise. He crossed his heart to show he was sincere.

Les tried to think of something to say, but couldn't. He noticed Rob was nervous and kept looking around at people who passed. No one looked at them. Les walked away, his knees watery.

Les didn't tell Ell. He didn't want to frighten her. He loved her so much he didn't want to do anything to hurt her. But he dreamed about running, running faster and faster so his chest was on fire and his legs ached. Rob was always a few steps behind him. Rob's feet went *bam, bam* on the wooden boardwalk. The dreams were worse than the real thing. In reality Rob never chased Les. Soon he was afraid to sleep for fear of dreaming that Rob caught him. He avoided Ell, he couldn't talk with her. One day he decided he had to hold on to his sanity. He had to talk to someone. "Let's go visit your folks. I want to talk with Charlie," he said.

"I hope you say more to him than you say to me," Ell said. "I know something's bothering you, but if you don't say, how can anyone help?" Tears ran down her cheeks. "You don't see me anymore. I could be dead," she sobbed. "What can Charlie do? We'll be squandering his time. He doesn't understand being married."

Les shifted uneasily at the kitchen table. "You wouldn't have said that if you knew as much as I."

"What makes you think I know nothing?" Ell sounded angry and sobbed harder.

"I hate fusses. Let's go see how your folks are making it." Les was stern. He got up and went out, saddled two horses, and waited for Ell. Her eyes were red. He rode ahead and said nothing.

Mary and Joe were delighted. "You don't come often enough to suit either of us," said Joe, taking Les aside to talk crops and land irrigation. He wanted to lay pipes from the Middle Fork of Sappa Creek to the small meadow.

Mary saw immediately that Ell had been weeping. She asked no questions, biding her time for the explanation. She busied herself making the meal. When the table was set and the platter of meatloaf, bowl of boiled potatoes, boiled green beans, jams, and biscuits were in place, she called, "Come, while it's hot!"

"Eat, we'll talk later," said Joe, munching steadily on meat and potatoes.

Will and Frank eyed Les, wondering exactly why he'd come this particular day. Charlie looked at Ell, who watched Les like a hawk, and knew there was more to this visit than farm talk.

"Why can't we talk while we eat?" asked Frank.

"Hush," said Mary. "Isn't it enough just to have these two at our table again?" She shook her head and fixed her eye on Frank for being so insensitive. "Leave things be."

"If leaving things be by ignoring them is so valuable, we ought to admire the ostrich with his head in the sand," said Will, pouring coffee into a saucer to cool it.

Mary cleared the plates away. Ell got up and took the serving bowls from the table. Les caught Charlie's eye. "Show me the latest wild bronco you've tamed."

Out in the meadow Les watched a black-maned red stallion munch the grass. He put his hand on Charlie's shoulder. "I have something to tell you. If I don't tell someone, I could blow wide open like a puffball in the hot sun. Rob Collins is around Goodland again." They sat on the grass, each chewing on a wild-rye stem. Les told Charlie about his meeting with Rob and the subsequent disquieting dreams. "I don't know why his threat bothers me, except I believe he would not hesitate to shoot me, or club me, or choke me to death. I married the girl he wanted. Truly, I don't believe he knows what love is. Not in the way most people feel."

Charlie was quiet for a long time. He stared at a fat bumblebee gathering yellow pollen on its legs from jimmyweed flowers.

"Well," said Les, "what can I do? I can't tell the sheriff. He'd think I was a cracked brain. Maybe I am. What do you think?" He bit the wild-rye in two.

"I think there's something else. You've kept the whole thing from Ell. She's your wife. If you can't tell her, you have no business telling someone else."

Les stood up.

Charlie's throat grew tight. "You say you love Ell. Then share everything." His words sounded brittle, unlike he intended.

"It would frighten her."

"Haven't you noticed? She's already frightened of something."

"It's because I've been such a bear to live with," Les flashed.

"There's something else. Something's got her bleary-eyed."

"I grind my teeth at night like I could eat the sights off my six-gun. She hates the sound."

Charlie looked up as something flashed at the top of the rise. "Sit down. She's coming over here."

"Why is she doing that?" Les said in a strangling voice.

"Maybe she'll tell us," said Charlie.

The wind blew Ell's hair like an amber-orange fan around her face. She was crying. She'd picked a bunch of milkweed flowers.

The flowers reminded Charlie of the time a couple years back when he'd found himself in the center of a cloud of butterflies.

"This is men's talk," said Charlie, "so dry your eyes and you can join us. I'll tell you about the time I saw a bunch of butterflies light on those pink and white flowers, completely covering them."

Ell smiled and dabbed at her face with a wadded handkerchief.

"Monarchs lay eggs on the milkweed. Grandma Malinda told me," she said, sounding like she had a head cold. She sat beside Les, facing Charlie. "I got the flowers for Ma's window vases. I came to talk."

"It's running in the family. Shoot. What's on your mind?" Charlie pretended to button his lips shut.

She took Les's hand in hers. "Don't tease. I'm scared to death. I didn't want to worry you about something that happened in town. But the more I thought about it, the more frightened I am. Remember when I went after the dress Marietta's making for me?"

"Is Miss Roberts ill?" asked Les.

"No, far worse. Rob Collins is back." She said it with finality, as if that event heralded a new era.

Charlie pushed the hair out of his eyes. "Jeems! Incredible! One guy with rats in the balcony affects two normal people so that they act addled. Did he chase you?"

Her eyes had a faraway look, misty. "Chase? He rushed at me headlong."

Les put his arms protectively around her and drew her against his chest.

"Don't squeeze so tight," she gasped. "I can't talk if I can't breathe."

"I could skin that snot-nose alive!" Les waved his hands and stood up. "I'll pull his picket pin!"

"Sit down. Hear Ell out. Blast it! I swear, when I'm married I'll listen to my wife before I jump up and go off half-cocked."

Les was indignant. "What do you know about marriage?"

"Nothing. Except I've noticed my folks. Their spats don't seem to mean much. More like funning each other. They respect each other. They like talking things out. I used to listen to them murmur after I should have been asleep, when I was little."

"I want to talk," Ell said quietly. "If I hold in any longer, I'll explode." Her voice rose. "I don't want to seem amiss. I'm frightened. My appetite's gone. I can't sleep!" She ended on a high crescendo.

"Start at the beginning. There'll be no interruptions. I promise." Charlie glared at Les.

Les sat down and took Ell's hand in his and said, "So, you went after your dress, then what?"

"Yes, then I go to the Mercantile for chalk for school. When I come out someone comes up behind me so quiet I never suspect. A voice says, 'Afternoon, Miss Ell. Permit me to sit in your wagon a few minutes. We'll talk old times.' My legs turn to tapioca. My mouth dries like parchment. I know without turning my head it's Rob. I get into the wagon and tell the horse 'Giddyap!' Rob moves in front of my horse. Honest. I can't believe my eyes. I pull the reins in to avoid him. He's quick and swerves this way and that, but always stays in front of my horse. I have to stop or run him down."

"You should have run the son-of-a-gun down!" snorted Les.

"Hush! We promised," reiterated Charlie.

"He jumps to the seat beside me. He's grinning and puffing.

He leans toward me and says in a loud voice, 'You're the feistiest but prettiest woman in the whole state of Kansas. Every man that looks at you is mad with desire. Me most of all.' I can tell his passion is up." Ell looks sideways at Les. "He's ready for—"

"My God! That reprobate!"

Charlie reached out a sweaty palm and touched Les. "Sshh!"

"Marietta and I played beauty parlor. Tinted talc is on my cheeks and berry juice on my lips. I do look fixed up. Rob leans near and I can tell he's had spirits. He's hesitant—gropes for words."

Les brightened and he nodded.

Charlie fixed him with his eyes. Then he sighed, relieved when Les was silent. Charlie breathed faster, waiting for Ell to continue.

"I accuse him of drinking and he says it is me that makes him dizzy with cravings. Then he says real quiet, in a monotone like this"—she makes her lips tight across her teeth—"'If I can't have my way with you, I'll fix you so that no other man can.' Oh, Lord, his eyes are fearful. They dart back and forth like blue steel buttons—cold and cruel."

Les shivered, but Ell went on.

"There's a bunch of settlers across from the Mercantile. I waved to them when I went into the store. I'm friendly. They wave back. Now out of the corner of my eye I can see those men gabbing and laughing. Rob inches closer. All of a sudden he's pressing his lips against mine. Right out in front of everyone, in broad daylight. His hand is on my—bosom. I feel it, tight." Ell stopped to catch her breath and look at Les and Charlie.

Les's mouth was open and his eyes were wide. His hands were clutched around his knees.

Charlie seemed to be studying his sister. He was mesmerized by her voice modulations. He sensed her words were more than a simple confession. The words were something tangibly intimate between a married couple. The words were bold and exciting to Charlie.

Ell went on. "I jerk the reins and my horse starts off. I scream and my horse trots. I slap the reins and break away from that— that maniac. The horse runs like a cat with its tail on fire, down the Boulevard, past the settlers, leaving a cloud of dust. Rob clutches the seat instead of me. He cusses. At the end of the Boulevard I turn the wagon around and drive into that dust cloud. Rob coughs. I pull up my foot and, honest to goodness, kick him in the side—hard. He loses his balance and falls into the street. I haul up the reins, stop. The settlers make a circle around Rob's body. Some laugh, from nervousness, because Rob doesn't move. One man asks if I gave him the bloody nose. Someone suggests they put him in my wagon and I take him to his place. I say no. I feel kind of faint. I don't want that man in my wagon under any circumstances. I lose my head and shout, 'Keep him away from me!' My head clears and I'm not going to faint even though my hands tremble."

Les took a deep breath and flexed his hands. He waited silently for his wife to continue.

Charlie was aware that some of the settlers hung around downtown to watch the ladies. He knew that one lady they watched was his sister because her features were good to look at, like fine-cut pink and white cameo. She was the respected schoolmarm of Sappa Valley. The men looked, but anyone who made an indecent advance was as welcome as a rattler in a chinchilla farm.

"My shout brings Rob around and he sits up, looking like he doesn't know what's happened. When he gets to his feet, those six settlers are after him, punching, pummeling, kicking, tripping. He gets more than a nosebleed. His face is so swollen his ma wouldn't know him. He sure can't see much when he limps off to the north part of town. He's a real pitiful sight."

Charlie detected a curious, savage joy in his sister's face. She'd enjoyed the fight for her honor. With a mere kick and a shout she'd rallied half a dozen men to defend her reputation. Justice was in her hands. She'd enjoyed that feeling of power.

Les was boiling. "If I see that man, I'll shoot him where he looks biggest! I swear it!"

Charlie rocked on his haunches and said softly, "Nobody's going to kill Rob. He'll destroy himself."

For a moment the three sat motionless. No one spoke. No one dared be first to break the spell those last words cast.

Les was the first to speak. He told his own latest experience with Rob, then hung his head. "I'm so ashamed I acted like a bear. Worrying about myself, I pretended to be protecting your peace of mind." He put his arms around Ell. "My God! You're shaking! We were both so scared we couldn't talk." He held her close.

She closed her eyes and held her face to Les. The kiss was sensual, born of the overwhelming relief flooding through them.

Charlie felt as though he were privy to the deepest emotion between a man and woman. He had a throbbing sensation in his abdomen where it joined his thighs. His legs would not move. His breathing was shallow and fast. He felt trapped in a swamp, not able to pick up his feet. He was able to choke down on himself and take a deep breath.

Ell and Les had broken apart, each visibly affected by the highly charged emotion. Ell looked at Charlie with eyes that shone. "What are we going to do?"

Charlie gulped. "Jeems, you know better than I."

Her eyes opened. "Think on it, Charlie. You brought us together. You listened to us. Now what?"

"Well, I'm thinking on it." He bunched his legs under his bottom and boosted himself upright. His legs tingled as though they'd been asleep. He walked around, clearing his head. "Have you some goal? What do you honestly think of farming?" He looked at Les.

Les's face colored as red as the setting sun. "All I know is farming and mining. But I've always wanted to work with ciphers. I keep my books so they balance from top to bottom, bottom to top, and sideways. I enjoy that and would like to do it full-time. But I figure it's too enjoyable to be my everyday job. Now, what has that got to do with this—this other stuff with Rob Collins?"

"I'm working on it." Charlie grinned, feeling now he was in control of his emotions. His breathing was easier.

Then Ell began to talk. "You know how scared I am? Some days I go away from my school soddy with this surge of fear that Rob is outside waiting. I carry a broken vinegar bottle. It's a weapon. I'm prepared to get him first. I daydream that my last living act is writing my name in blood on a slate. I write his name in my blood, so people know." Her voice cracked. "My heart pounds when I go to school and when I leave, when I go to town now, which is only once since the episode, because I forget what I am there for, and I have palpitations and have to come home."

"I haven't been for supplies." admitted Les.

"I know one thing." Her green eyes brightened. "Those men, the settlers, will fight for me. I can count on them."

"Sure, they're loyal to you. You represent their ideal. A decent woman is on a high pedestal. But if someday"—Charlie looked down at his hands—"Rob gets you to his place? Will the men think you are something out of their reach? So the question isn't, what can you do. It's, where do you go."

"Go? What are you thinking?" asked Ell.

Les got to his feet stiffly. "How about Colorado Springs? I've mined thereabouts. I could do it again."

Ell was quiet. Charlie knew she was thinking about her school. She thought of miners with bent rheumatic backs and sickly babies and women with cataracts. She pictured herself clearing, like magic, the cataracts with herbs, straightening the stiff backs with salves, and making the babies fat and healthy with teas. She could start another school. Her mind filled with fantastic expectations. Now her heart beat with this new anticipation and thankfulness. This suggestion gave both her and Les an honorable escape. "Yes," she said, "we'll move. I'd not let a maniac shame my family." Ell was not in the least ashamed of seizing this opportunity.

They ran back to the soddy. Before going inside Charlie caught up with Les and asked, "You ever hear of a homesteader called McGuckin?"

"Nope," said Les, "never did. Why? Is there someone in that family like this cotton-headed, cotton-mouthed character that has given Ell and me fits?"

"You're a goon. But I gotta thank you. You got me to thinking that no one, even a person's family, has the right to take happiness from another. For a couple years I've been knocking around like a blind dog in a meatmarket. No more. I'm going to call on that pixie, if she's not spoken for."

Ell giggled. "Pixie? A little person? Charlie, you're demented. You suppose it's from listening to your sister and brother-in-law?"

"I'll tell you one thing for sure," said Charlie, his eyes flashing. "I wouldn't marry a schoolteacher. I'll tell you the reason why. She makes a soup of polliwog tails and says it's raisin pie."

"That's vulgar and horrid!" yelled Ell, but she was laughing and some of her anxiousness was forgotten.

That evening Les explained to his father-in-law that he was about fed up with sporadic rains, crops dying in drought, dying with rust or rot, and he was seriously thinking of going back to Colorado and mining. He explained that he and Ell'd talked it over and she was eager to start a school for miners' kids and use her knowledge of herbs on those who were interested.

Ell told the news to Mary. "If mining turns out to be worse than farming, Les and I will be back to farm with you and Pa," she promised her mother. Mary was aware of the pine scent from incense in Ell's clothing and hair. The aromatic essence triggered a feeling of melancholy. "You two won't be back," predicted Mary with a catch in her voice. "Your husband is intelligent. He wants control over his life. Farming won't permit a man to control. Farming directs a man's actions." Her brown face was drawn. Her fingers drummed on the side of her rocker. She was a sparse woman, not well padded, as were so many settlers' wives. She wore her shawl even in summer to keep the constant wind off her parchmentlike skin. Her steps and hand movements had become jerky. At the end of busy days standing on her feet, she complained of swollen ankles. "I wish we'd divided the land among the boys. Maybe bought twice as much. Keep everyone together." Her voice sounded harsh. "Your pa thinks about it, but he never does anything. He leaves the doing to Will—who only does as he pleases."

Ell fell to her knees, put her head in her mother's lap. Mary continued her rocking back and forth in the chair. She patted Ell's hair. "You smell like a summer day, my dear. Send us letters."

"Yes, I will," said Ell quietly. A mist covered her eyes so that she could not see. She blinked and tears dropped to her mother's lap. "Oh, Ma, I will miss seeing all of you."

Mary's hands pressed down on her daughter's shoulders. Tears ran down her cheeks.

That night in bed Charlie tried to recount the day's emotional upheavals. He felt drained and empty. His mind could not hold one thought in front of another. He was asleep before he could recall his uncertainty about being drawn into Les's problems and his role in the solution.

The first few weeks after Ell and Les sold their land and were gone, Mary had to work to find strength to get out of bed mornings. A letter in Ell's handwriting and smelling like pine told her that Les had a job in a coal mine. They rented a one-room house and Ell tramped the foothills for herbs to treat lung disease. "I want not only to cure those men with the cough, but to prevent the others, mainly my dear Les, from getting sick. This is my mission. I'm fascinated with herbs that cure disease." Ell's letter was passed to each member of the family.

Men are fascinated with Ell as moths are fascinated by a flame, thought Charlie. Out loud he said, "We ought to send Ell a big bouquet of turnips for settling our minds about her welfare."

Frank snickered. "Do that and she'll carve your statue in butter."

The letter made Joe feel magnanimous. "Let's pack some grub and all go on rounds with me early tomorrow morning." Hopefully he looked toward his frail wife. "I'll stop wherever you want. You can pick sulfur flowers or anything to fill your window vases."

"I declare I'd have gone stir-crazy if I'd stayed home another day."

Next morning she hummed as she put bread, roast beef, and a jar of red-currant jelly in a basket. The air was cool, the sun bright, promising a warm summer day. "I'll fill a couple of jars with well water and I'm set."

Charlie added water to slick the front lock of his hair back into a pompadour. He teased, "Ma, I bet you'll talk the hide off the first cow you see." He was six feet four inches tall and weighed one hundred seventy pounds, so that he looked rangy at eighteen.

Mary gave him the cutoff sign and gave the picnic basket to Will to put in the back of the wagon. Will was near six feet and as dark as his father. His shoulders were broad and his hands large enough to pick up a watermelon in one. He weighed close to one hundred ninety pounds.

"Ma, you'll talk so fast we'll smell sulfur burning," teased Frank, helping his mother up to the wagon's seat beside his father. He was small for sixteen, not weighing more than a hundred pounds.

"You just wish you could listen to my intelligent newsworthy palavering instead of holding up the leg of some balky horse," said Mary, reaching up and pinching the back of Frank's thin arm.

"Hey, that hurts!" Frank cried. "What'd I do?"

"That's just 'cuz I love you," said Mary, giggling. They rode in silence, enjoying the sunshine.

Frank clapped his hand over his mouth and pointed. A young girl ran across the front of a soddy. The girl seemed familiar, yet different. She was like the girl who had pestered Charlie at the county fair two summers back. He took his hand away and whistled low. "Cripes, we heading there?"

Joe chuckled, agreeing with his youngest son's taste in female pulchritude. "Yup. Name's Lewis." Joe brought the wagon up into the soddy's yard, helped Mary down, then rolled out the portable forge.

"Let the boys help you with that," scolded Mary under her breath.

"When I get so old that I can't lift my tools out of the wagon, then I'd better quit blacksmithing," snapped Joe.

Frank was out standing before the lissome girl, who had short brown hair, curly at the ends. The bangs were lifted off her forehead by the breeze. Her eyes were a startling violet-blue.

"Howdy. This the Lewis place?" asked Frank

Charlie was taking the anvil from the back of the wagon and looking around for the stand to set it on when he heard her answer. It wasn't her words that made his knees turn to pudding, it was her melodious voice, like a bird singing for the joy of sunshine.

"Yes, did you folks come to see Ray? He said he had a couple horses needed new shoes."

"This is the friendly farrier's wagon," said Frank.

"I'll tell Ray the blacksmith's here." She ran lickety-split to the back of the soddy, then to the barn.

Charlie watched her skirt fly around her legs, like a big blue butterfly fluttering against the wind. His hand felt clammy as he ran a finger around his collar. She was like the pixie-girl who had now become a figment of his imagination and daydreams. He was reminded of his conversation with Ell and Les when he vowed to call at the farm of the McGuckins.

The lithe girl came back and showed Joe where to set up his forge and pointed to the man coming from the barn. He wore faded blue overalls, and his shirt was unbuttoned and on the outside. He pushed his blond hair back with a tanned hand. He shook hands with Joe, saying he'd been expecting him. Mr. Lewis did not seem much older than the rosy-cheeked girl.

Mary smiled and stepped forward. "I'm Mary Irwin."

Charlie thought he saw the girl catch her breath. "It's nice you came," she said. "We don't get much company."

"I came because the day was too beautiful to stay in a dark soddy. I'm going to spread a blanket under the poplar tree and do a little mending. I'd be pleased to have you sit with me."

"All right." The girl looked in the back of the wagon at the other blacksmithing apparatus. Charlie set the anvil down and came for the bag of coal. The girl put her hand over her mouth. "You lifted that anvil by yourself? I don't think I ever saw anyone that strong."

Charlie was catching his breath, letting his hands rest on the coal bag. He thought her voice sounded like fast, white rapids in a creek that was knee-deep with clear, cool water.

Suddenly she said, "Look there!" She pointed to a black and white, plump, big-headed, slim-tailed bird that deliberately impaled a field mouse on a hawthorn bush at the corner of the soddy.

Charlie looked closer and saw other dead mice wedged into a crotch of the same branch. The bird sensed someone near and flew close to the ground. With rapid wingbeats it sailed over the soddy and out of sight.

"What kind of bird hangs its food out like a man would hang a deer carcass?" Her eyes were near purple in the shade.

"That's a shrike. He generally comes in fall, tells us winter is near."

"That's silly, it's summer," said the girl.

"Birds can get mixed up. Like some people. Maybe it's a crazy bird." Charlie laughed, then his heart made a sudden leap. She had stepped closer and was looking up into his face.

"You are like Charlie. Charlie Irwin!"

"I know—I am! You're Etta. Etta Mae McGuckin!" Then he stopped suddenly and his heart fell to the ground. "Is that man your—your—" He couldn't say the word.

"You're crazy! Ray isn't my father. You don't remember much. Ray is my brother-in-law."

"Oh, jeems, I'm glad." Charlie held his hand out.

Her small hand was lost in his huge one. It was a few moments before she withdrew her hand and Charlie thought he was going to black out. His heart beat so hard he was certain everyone could hear. His whole hand tingled as if singed with a hot flame.

"I can tell you are all related, one family, because there is a resemblance that is common. You have your ma's hair and your pa's build and eyes." She was skipping beside Charlie to keep up.

"Ma, this is Etta Mae. I met her—two, three years ago, in Goodland."

"Well, what a coincidence. Sit on the blanket," said Mary, making room. "It's hot enough to sunburn a darky." She took off her sunbonnet, ran her fingers through her thin, damp hair. She noticed how pretty Etta was.

"I'll get you a dipper of water from the well," offered Etta.

"Nothing like sweet water to slake your thirst—we have a couple of jars of water in the wagon, but I'd rather have the cooler well water," said Mary, pulling darning cotton through the heel of a stocking.

Etta returned with the dipper full of water and a boy about five, dressed in overalls, barefoot, and hanging on to her skirt. "This is Jimmy. He's my sister's boy. I look after him so that

Kate can put up the corn and green beans without him underfoot; you know how it is with young'uns."

"What a handsome boy. I like yellow hair and blue eyes. I bet he'd like a handful of raisins." Mary got up and rummaged in the wagon and deep into the picnic basket and came out with a fist of dark raisins and dried prunes. "See the size of my little boys," joked Mary, pointing to Charlie firing up the forge. "I can't hold them on my lap at all."

"Do you want a little boy?" Jimmy asked.

"I'd like to hold one," she said.

Jimmy plunked down contentedly in Mary's lap and munched on the raisins and prunes.

Charlie came back, hardly able to take his eyes off Etta. He untied the horses that were munching at the thin, yellow grass. He pulled tools, liniment bottles from the wagon and carried them to the barn. He looked back and saw his mother and Etta both sewing and chatting. Jimmy had his head down on Mary's lap, asleep. The day was warm, but the breeze from the west kept the air comfortable.

About noon Charlie came back to the shade tree. "Sure is nice to sit in the shade where the air is cool for a while. Been working the forge all morning."

"You shoeing Ray's horses?" asked Etta.

"That's nearly done," said Charlie, stretching his muscular arms upward to relieve the cramped feeling. Then he was on his feet again and bringing the picnic basket to the blanket. He whistled. "Going to make a meat sandwich for Pa, Frank, and Will. I guess Ray'd like one, too. How about you?" He looked from Etta to Mary.

Etta spoke right up. "You wash up before you get food out."

"Of course," said Charlie, his face turning pink under the tan. "Where's the soap?"

"By the basin on the bench over there next to the front door."

Charlie poured well water in the basin and made a show of washing his hands as far as his elbows and then his face. He wet his hair and combed it back with his fingers, throwing the wash water out on the stubbled grass.

"Pass inspection?" He held his hands up.

Etta smiled and nodded. "Excuse me. I am so used to telling brothers and sisters and Jimmy what to do, I just talk that way without thinking."

"Oh, I understand how that is. I have a big brother that'd like to tell me what to do."

Mary said, "Make the sandwiches and don't talk so loud, you'll wake the baby."

"I'll take him to the house," said Etta apologetically.

"No, leave him be. He'll wake up if you move him. Anyway, it's cooler in this breeze." Mary leaned her back against the tree's trunk and ate the sandwich Charlie handed to her. She closed her eyes and rested.

Charlie whistled softly and put the bread away after he'd made himself a second jelly sandwich. "Say, we could dance before I go back to work." He whistled a little louder.

"I don't know how to dance."

"Come on, then, I'll show you. It'll come in handy when someone asks you to one of those Farmers' Alliance dances." He took her hand and put his arm around her waist. And he was not disappointed. His heart thumped. "You put your left hand on my shoulder and we'll be off on the right foot."

"No one'll ask me to a dance," she said sadly.

"Oh, yes. A girl as light on her feet as you." Her head hardly came to his shoulder. He picked her up, hands around her waist and danced around with her toes just skimming the dusty ground. She giggled. A soft bubbling sound. She didn't say anything. She listened carefully to Charlie's instructions and caught on quickly and was soon dancing the two-step as if she'd been doing it since first grade. Charlie lost all track of time. He could hold her all day.

She broke in on his whistling. "You don't think I'm clumsy?"

"Oh, no."

"You once thought I was a pest."

"Oh, I forgot about that. I don't seem to mind it now."

She laughed. "I told you I'm bossy. I guess you'd mind if I'd go overboard with telling you what to do. Kate and Ray sometimes poke fun at me and say I'm loutish."

"I'd never say that." Charlie dared hold her a little closer. He could hardly breathe, so he let up some.

The sun was three quarters across the sky when Kate came out of the soddy. She was taller than Etta, but she had the same kind of small-boned look and light-brown hair, which hung in two braids down her back. Her complexion was fair and clear and her eyes dark blue.

"Kate! Come meet the Irwins!" cried Etta.

Kate's mouth turned down at the sight of her sister dancing in the front yard. "You should be in the house. Look at you! Hair flying around and your sleeves pushed up, the neck of your dress unbuttoned. What is this?" She had not noticed Mary, who was awake and bouncing Jimmy on her knee in time to Charlie's whistling. "Oh, my!"

"Come and rest a spell. Etta says you were canning. Hard job but nice to have the vegetables when the snow is deep. I'm Mary Irwin and this is my middle son, Charlie." She patted the blanket again. "Sit, Mrs. Lewis. We're having a little fun. Helps forget the heat. You've been in that soddy cooking all day. Time to rest."

Kate started to take off her apron, then thought better of it. "First nap Jimmy's had in a week. How'd you do it?" Her eyes were suspicious.

Mary took it as a compliment and smiled. "After raising four of my own I just did what was natural. He ate some raisins, drank a little water, and listened to Charlie whistling tunes. I do believe I had a little nap myself and feel much refreshed for it."

"There's never been an afternoon party here. We don't sit on this stubble much. We stay in the house unless we're working in the fields or garden. I never thought of coming out here for the noon meal." Kate eyed the picnic basket and the jelly bread Mary was fixing for Jimmy. Mary made another quickly and handed it to Kate.

"You could invite them inside to wait for the men to be finished," said Etta. She looked at Charlie and blushed.

"Our pa would have a cat fit and step in it if he knew I left folks out in the yard," said Kate. "You should have told me." She spoke angrily to Etta.

"I left you so you could do the canning the way you like. Pa's not here to say what we do. Charlie will show you how easy it is to dance." Etta's eyes brightened.

Charlie took the hint and danced around with Jimmy, all the time whistling. Then he gingerly took Kate's hand and danced on the dusty ground, avoiding the dried grass because she, too, had bare feet. Kate was not as graceful as Etta, but Charlie was sure if she'd been moving around with her own husband, she'd be more relaxed and would soon forget herself and smile. He hummed a slow polka and took steps around the blanket. Kate got her feet mixed at first, then found the pattern and grinned with delight.

Mary hummed with Charlie and clapped her hands, and soon Jimmy and Etta were clapping in time.

Now Kate wished she'd come out of the house sooner. She drained the dipper of water that Charlie brought to her. She fanned her face. She said, "I'm sorry I was rude. I guess I was tired."

"Forget it," said Charlie. "Excuse me, I have to go back and see if Pa needs me."

Kate told Mary her family came all the way from Rochester, New York, by train to first live in Missouri, then western Kansas. "Pa told us to be sedate and never laugh overmuch or it'd make as many lines in the face as frowns. I've never liked it here much until today. You don't have as many lines as our ma. Maybe laughing isn't so bad." Kate was uncertain. "Pa does a lot of reading, but only from the Bible. I don't think he's read another book," said Kate.

"When I was in school he'd take books away from me, saying they weren't fit to read. I had to hide most everything I read," said Etta. "I keep my books here at Kate's now."

"How is one to know what goes on in the world if one doesn't read?" asked Mary, astonished.

Kate colored. "Pa's old-fashioned. And Ma goes along with him to keep peace." She looked at Jimmy, who sat quietly in Mary's lap. "For a long time I've known Pa's ways weren't all right." She looked at Etta. She'd said more than she intended and was confused. "It's disloyal for me to be talking this way. I'd better stop."

Joe and the three boys came to the front and began loading up the wagon.

Charlie said, "I hate to just dump out these hot coals in the forge. You want them for your cookstove?"

Kate brought out an iron skillet for the coals. Then Charlie loaded the forge and anvil into the wagon beside the other gear.

They washed in the basin by the front door. Joe shook hands with Ray Lewis and said, "I'll send one of the boys back for those chickens and potatoes next week. You can settle up the rest with him. It'll come to five dollars and thirty cents counting the treatment we gave your house cat for worms. Keep using the medicine once a day for two weeks. Cat'll be all right. Keep it away from the vegetable garden."

"Mighty obliged to all of you," said Lewis.

Charlie said, "I'll come next week. Maybe we'll dance again." He grinned at Kate and Etta.

Lewis shook his head and began to laugh. "I'm not exactly laughing at you, but I can't help it. A tall muscular fellow like you, with calluses and broken fingernails, work hands, showing girls how to dance. That beats all! You're not only tall, but smart." He wiped his watering eyes and shook hands with Charlie. "I'll look forward to seeing you."

Jimmy pulled on Mary's skirt. "I wish you could come, too."

"Sometimes wishes come true," said Mary, giving the youngster a hug.

Charlie climbed into the wagon and nodded to Etta. She looked exactly the way he'd imagined in his mind's eye for the past couple of years.

The following week Charlie eagerly hitched one of the mares to the empty spring wagon and drove to the Lewis farm to collect half a dozen laying hens and a sack of potatoes for part payment for farrier's work. Joe told him to collect the money if he could, and if not, sign an I.O.U. for more farm produce. "One of his yearling hogs comes to mind," suggested Joe.

As Charlie tied the mare to the Lewises' poplar tree his breathing came faster. It kept time with his beating heart. Kate opened the door to his knock and gave him a sly smile. Charlie felt something was amiss. His pulse quickened and he dismissed altogether the speech he'd prepared riding out to say to Etta. "Good morning. I'm here to collect on the farrier's work that was done last week."

"Ray has everything," said Kate.

She was pushed aside as Jimmy came roaring out the door, grabbing at Charlie's legs. "I knew you'd come!"

Charlie picked the child up and swung him to his shoulder and danced around in front of the house. "I can see the top of the barn!" Jimmy squealed.

"Where's your Aunt Etta?" asked Charlie, putting Jimmy down.

"She went home. Grandpa needed her to pick corn."

Charlie felt a lump in his throat.

Kate was back at the door. "Mr. Irwin, Ray is getting a crate for the hens and hog. Potatoes are out back in a gunnysack."

"I'll get it," said Charlie sharply.

"Wait a minute," said Kate. "Would it be an imposition to ask you to drive three miles up the road to Pa's place? We have a butter churn that belongs to Ma." Kate's voice was kind of trembly and her eyes looked at Charlie, uncertain.

"Yes! I mean, no! I'll take that churn up the road. Would you let Jimmy ride up and back? It's no trouble for me. Honest."

* * *

Jimmy pointed to a neat, rather large, but spare soddy. As Charlie pulled the wagon to the front he noticed a pile of bundled sunflower stalks and cattails, dried and tied. He guessed they were used as fuel or in an old rush light like his Grandma Malinda used to own.

Charlie whistled loudly as he lifted Jimmy from the wagon, hoping Etta was inside and would come out. His hands felt sweaty. He knocked. Mr. McGuckin opened the door. A frown spread across his lined face. He pushed his silver-rimmed eyeglasses back up his nose and looked Charlie over.

"I'm here, Grandpa!" called Jimmy.

McGuckin stepped aside to let Jimmy in, then stepped back as if blocking the entrance until he'd finished checking over Charlie.

Charlie could hear a gaggle of voices inside talking with Jimmy.

"I brought your butter churn from your son-in-law, Ray Lewis."

"Put the churn by the door. I don't intend to buy any of the foofaraw you're peddling, so keep right on moving. I never buy anything I don't need." McGuckin's gaze was fiery.

"Yes, sir," said Charlie. He thought, in two, three years the man hadn't changed. He wondered what was biting him. Charlie felt a tug of pity for someone who treated life with so much anger. "You're not obligated to pay me for bringing the churn to you." Charlie tried to be amicable. He set the churn by the front door and caught a glimpse of a lace curtain move through the one window in the front of the soddy. Then in another instant Etta was outside beside her father.

"Oh, it's you! Pa, this is Mr. Charlie Irwin. I told you about the good job he and his pa and brothers did at Kate and Ray's. Shoed the horses, remember? Maybe you'd like him to look at your horses?"

McGuckin didn't answer, he was running his hands over the butter churn, making certain it was not cracked or in any way mistreated.

"Come in. Ma will be glad to see you. We wondered who brought Jimmy—actually we thought Ray and Kate had come."

Charlie stepped inside and she closed the screen. "Pa's well meaning, you know. He doesn't like strangers. He says he has enough people to look after with all of us around." She pointed to the flock of children hovered around the kitchen table, watching. Two older boys were dishing up rice pudding for the younger children. "That's Curly and Walt," said Etta.

Charlie remembered Curly. The boy was now near five feet ten and filled out. His hair was still in dark ringlets, like a mop on his round head. The young man looked up with brown eyes and nodded to Charlie. He winked at Etta, which caused her to be flustered for a few seconds. The other young man called Walt had ordinary brown hair that hung below his ears. His eyes were deep, rich blue, like Etta's. "Have a seat. There's still plenty of pudding to go around."

"Thanks." Charlie slid into a space at the end of the near bench. He was next to Mrs. McGuckin at the foot of the table. The empty chair at the head he assumed belonged to Mr. McGuckin.

Mrs. McGuckin passed a clean bowl and spoon to Charlie. "Etta made us pudding," she said, tucking a stray, limp strand of brownish hair under her gray bonnet.

"How are you, Mrs. McGuckin?" said Charlie, holding out his hand.

She took a sip of tea.

Charlie brought his hand back. "My ma would send her greeting if she'd realized that I was going to come here. I brought the churn from Mr. and Mrs. Lewis. Jimmy rode up with me."

Mrs. McGuckin looked up. "Don't go yet. We thank you." She dipped her teaspoon into the tea and noisily sucked the spoon dry. This made Charlie once again think of his Grandma Malinda.

Charlie ate his pudding. He especially liked the raisins and cinnamon that Etta had added and told her so.

Mr. McGuckin came back to the table. The children sat still and fell silent. Mr. McGuckin said, "I had me a tannery business back in Rochester. Left it to get into farming. Had a revelation one morning, you know. The Lord said to me in a voice just as clear as your own, 'Brian McGuckin, you are appointed food supplier, henceforth.'"

The children's eyes were on Charlie.

"There's no disputing the call of the Lord. Sold my tannery and sought the place He wanted me to plow. Hit Missouri first. That wasn't it—nary a drop of rain the whole summer we was there."

"We *were* there," corrected Etta.

"We weren't there long," continued Mr. McGuckin. "We took

the train's daycoach and looked at all the places in Kansas. When the train stopped at Goodland, I knew this was where I'd been headed. It's just about the last town in Kansas of any account. The land was flat, needed no clearing. I found this place for a homestead, and just as I was moved in and got the roots grubbed out of the soil and the wheat coming along pretty good, this here rainmaker came and sent water. From that time forward there's been enough rain and my wheat's pure gold. The Lord smiled on me."

Charlie excused himself and said he had to get Jimmy home before sundown.

McGuckin put his gnarled hand on Charlie's arm. "The Lord has spoke to me a second time. You want to know what he said?"

"Has *spoken*," corrected Etta again.

"Yes, sir. I was spoken to. He said I was to look up to Him as a lighthouse of salvation in the stormy sea."

Mrs. McGuckin put her spoon noisily into the teacup and gathered her skirt around her thighs. "It was the wind a-blowing in your head, Mr. McGuckin." She moved tight-lipped into a bedroom behind a flowered curtain.

Charlie was amused and turned to Etta, who had covered her face with her hand. She said she'd walk him to his wagon.

In the living room Charlie saw how white the curtain was against the window. Everything looked neat and clean. Then he saw the rush light in the corner. "My grandma had one of these in Missouri," he said. "She had a stand made out of cast iron. I guess my grandpa made it—maybe my pa, I don't know. She stripped rushes bare of the skin and left only the ridge at the back to keep the tender pith from spilling out. She tied a bunch of them together, about enough to make a bundle the size of my arm. The bunch was dipped in grease."

"Like this?" Etta showed him a bundle of oily rushes clamped to the holder in the black stand. Underneath was a pan to catch the drippings and ash. "Pa had a blacksmith make this in Missouri."

"Yes. When my pa hears about this, he'll have to come himself to see. He always teased my grandma, saying it was a lamp for the meaner sort, meaning the poor. My grandma was a notorious herbalist, so a rush light suited her."

Etta said in a confidential tone, leaning close to Charlie, "Ma doesn't like to hear Pa tell of his salvation or his callings by the Lord. She thinks he's a might tetched about that subject and leaves the room. She wasn't being rude to you."

"I didn't think much of it, except funny, humorous like," said Charlie. He looked down at Etta's soft, warm brown hair, which was pulled behind her ears and tied with a blue satin ribbon. She wore a flowered gingham dress. Charlie thought she was lovely.

Curly and Walt clattered away from the table bringing Jimmy with them. "This kid eats too much. You can take him home," teased Walt.

"If you ever need someone to help with the blacksmithing, remember me. I'd like to learn," said Curly.

"I'll tell Pa. If I decide to go west, you can take my place."

Suddenly Etta looked down-in-the-mouth. Charlie noticed and wondered if it was something he'd said.

"Etta, he's not going away tomorrow!" rumbled Curly. "Holy smoke, women take everything seriously."

"Ya," said Walt, "Etta ought to get married. She's tired of taking care of Ma's kids. That itinerant preacher's been getting up nerve to ask Pa if he can court her." Walt's eyes were bright and he looked over to Curly. "Isn't that right?"

"Yep," said Curly.

"What itinerant preacher?" asked Charlie.

"Brother Morton," said Walt. "He sets up a tent in the lot next to the courthouse. You ever gone?"

"Nope. Never heard of 'im," said Charlie.

Etta twisted her hands together and looked uncomfortable.

Suddenly Jimmy darted out the front door and climbed into the wagon.

Charlie wasn't far behind. He didn't want to look at Etta. His heart ached. He looked at the wagon's wheels and said more to himself, "I'm going to have to set this wagon wheel in the watering trough."

Jimmy looked over the side at the wheel.

Charlie explained. "Lookee there how the iron hoop is kind of loose."

Etta hunched down for a look. "Couldn't you take a piece of iron out and strap it back on? Then, if the wood swells, the iron is harder and holds the wood in."

"Hmmmm, never thought of that. That's a swell idea."

A breeze riffled Etta's hair. She turned her head and ran back into the soddy. Charlie jumped into the wagon's seat and squeezed his eyes down. Jimmy climbed to the seat beside him. "Etta likes you," he said.

"I hope so." Charlie was smiling. Then he opened his eyes and carefully threaded the reins through his fingers. His big, square hands with the long limber fingers were fastened to strong wrists. He thought about the day he'd have a team of his own and Etta'd sit up on the seat beside him. It would be hard to see any finger move as he threaded and climbed the reins. He began to whistle "Onward Christian Soldiers." Jimmy swung his feet in time. They passed a place where the bear smell was so strong Jimmy put his nose down against Charlie's chest. Charlie didn't bother to look around to see if the bear was near the road. He would take Jimmy home, then head on to his own home.

The hens flared at one another and cackled. The porker snuffled loudly and oinked at the flighty chickens. Charlie yelled, "Shut up! What do any of you know about real feelings, anyway?"

THIRTEEN

Etta Mae

On Sunday morning the weather was clear and warm. The wheat swayed in the breeze. The corn was ripe on the stalk. Charlie washed and shaved, and put on a clean shirt, his Sunday trousers, and black, ankle-high shoes. "Ma," he said, "I'm going to hear that tent preacher."

"What for?" asked Mary, starting morning biscuits.

"No reason. I just never heard one of those wandering, Bible-carrying men. You suppose I could take some of them biscuits, some cold beef, and a raisin pie in the picnic basket? If the service is overly long, I'll be hungry on the way home."

The tent was up when Charlie tied the reins to the tavern railing. He slowly ambled across the street to the vacant lot next to the courthouse. It felt warm inside the big tent, out of the wind. He thought it would feel warmer if all those wooden benches and folding chairs were filled with people. At the front was a wooden podium, scarred and scratched, as though it had seen a lot of Sunday services.

Charlie took a seat by himself toward the back so that he could see both front and back entrances and not miss Etta when she came in, but he'd told himself it was to see the preacher better when he came in.

He saw Etta, standing near the front with a black satin bonnet and a dress of dove-gray. Her eyes went over the congregation and stopped when she spotted Charlie. She turned and all Charlie could see was her back.

Brother Morton preached about the easy road to hell and damnation. He was a man in his fifties, bald except for a fringe of white hair over each ear. When he talked his white eyebrows moved like fuzzy caterpillars chasing one another. Surely Etta was not attracted to this man, thought Charlie. The more he watched, the funnier Brother Morton became. Charlie moved beside Ray, who stood and flexed his knees and moved up on his toes to keep from being drowsy.

"You believe I could bring Etta to your place after this show? I brought one of Ma's raisin pies," Charlie whispered, letting Jimmy climb on his lap.

"Depends."

"On what?"

"On her pa. He's been trying to get Brother Morton to court Etta."

Charlie felt his knees might buckle. Then what Walt and Curly said was true. He was astonished. "McGuckin couldn't do that! Just look how bizarre that man looks," Charlie said loudly.

People nearby said, "Sshushh."

"I'd say he was ridiculous for looks. Kate says he's a scaramouch. I don't know what that is, but it sounds good," Ray whispered.

Charlie didn't know what a scaramouch was either, but he was going to find out. "Why would McGuckin pick this man?"

"His nature, I suppose."

"I pray a man's nature's not all inherited," Charlie said, leaning close to Ray.

"Naw—Kate's not like her pa. Neither's Etta. If I hadn't married Kate, I'd probably have waited for Etta." He winked at a woman in a straw leghorn bonnet who shushed him.

Charlie bowed his head for the prayer and joined in the loud *amen*. When it was over he moved to the front with Ray, carrying Jimmy, who was sleeping. Etta and Kate were moving toward an exit, so Charlie put Jimmy in Ray's arms and followed after them.

Outside he could not find Etta and Kate. He looked up and down the hitching rails and saw McGuckin alone beside his wagon. Charlie walked toward him. He saw McGuckin lower a newspaper-covered jug, cork it, wipe his mouth on his sleeve, and push the jug under a gray blanket in the corner of the wagon.

"Good to see you again, Mr. McGuckin," said Charlie, holding out his hand.

"You spying on me?" McGuckin asked suspiciously.

"Oh, no, sir. I came to wish you a good morning and ask what an itinerant preacher has that Reverend Dana don't satisfy."

"I have no time for you. People who belittle Brother Morton are heathens. I have no use for you. I wish you a good riddance."

Charlie took a step back. He hadn't come to retreat. He stepped forward. "I ask a question and you answer like I was some kind of rubbish? Maybe it's not you answering, but the spirits from that jug." Charlie put his hands in his pockets to keep them from shaking.

"Oh—now it comes out. You came for a sip of my medicine, eh?" McGuckin leaned on his wagon box and reached under the gray blanket. Suddenly he stopped and looked up and down the street, then he uncorked the jug and took a long swig. "This here cost me a whole cartwheel. It's the best cough remedy a man can buy. The best I buy leastways. About cured my cough."

"Does Brother Morton brew spirits?" asked Charlie confidentially.

"It's a sideline. Only he once told me he made more on the spirits than he did on the collection plate." McGuckin laughed and offered Charlie a sip from the bottle. "Just try a little on your tongue. It'll make you appreciate Brother Morton's talents."

Charlie had the jug to his lips. He decided if this was the way to be friendly with McGuckin, he'd better go along this once anyway.

"Don't pour down too much, heathen. I need it. You ain't ailing like me. That medicine calms my nerves. Give it here."

Charlie swallowed and felt fire like a double-blade sword go down his throat. He sputtered and his eyes watered. He coughed and handed the jug back. He was reminded of being drunk as a fiddler's clerk at Ell's wedding and the sickening consequences. He'd made a vow never to feel that way again.

McGuckin took a long pull and chortled, "Say, heathen, you like my medicine?"

"Not overly much," said Charlie, thinking his breath was fiery.

"One more taste and the cough'll disappear. One more."

Charlie didn't want another taste. He wanted to talk with McGuckin about that Brother Morton. He looked around, wondering where the rest of the McGuckins were.

"They all went to get something to eat," said McGuckin, noticing Charlie look up and down the street. "Won't be back for a few minutes. Told 'em I weren't hungry, go without me."

"Say, is Brother Morton married?" Charlie tried to sound casual.

McGuckin flushed. "Told me he had a woman in Dodge, but ditched her. Wants someone to travel with him."

"Does he have anyone in mind?" Charlie felt like he was sawing off the branch he was sitting on.

"Never said. But I'm fixing to offer him a deal. He'd be like a personal physician to me. He'd be one of the family."

Charlie didn't want to hear any more. Those words depressed him so much that he drank a couple more rounds with McGuckin. He was not able to pull himself away.

McGuckin on the other hand was more friendly and put a hand on Charlie's shoulder. He began singing hymns. After three or four he looked up into Charlie's face and said, "My wife and children respect and obey me. I see to that. I'll never let them be touched by a heathen. Never, by cracky!"

Charlie was befuddled, but he knew he preferred singing better than hearing McGuckin's irksome rules, so he belted out a couple songs. Soon there was a crowd around the two men as they sang. Charlie grinned gloriously at the crowd. Then he saw Etta with her bonnet off and her hair shining in the sunlight. He wavered on his feet, pulled himself up straight, and sang something of his own, "Beautiful Etta Mae, on this lovely day, ride off with me, without delay!"

Charlie heard McGuckin growl and felt him touch his elbow. When he turned to look, McGuckin punched him square in the nose. Charlie caught his breath, lost sight of Etta, and balled up his fist to swing back at McGuckin.

McGuckin moved to the hitching rail to untie his team. Charlie's swing landed on the wagon box, making a loud retort as the board split. His right hand hurt something terrible. Skin was scraped off the knuckles. His nose bled. The crowd was quiet. Charlie stood out like a tall man at a funeral. Then Ray Lewis was beside him. "Better ride on home and forget the whole thing," he advised.

He felt lightheaded and dizzy sick. He didn't open his mouth. He heard the buzz of voices and the snickering and stifled laughter all around. He was the joke. He stumbled to his horse, grabbed the reins, and managed to get through the blur of faces and out onto the dusty road.

He was not far before that dizzy sickness climbed up from his stomach to his throat. He stopped and hung over the side of his horse. He was sick. His stomach squeezed and he gagged. Charlie shivered and wiped his mouth with a clean bandanna. When he got to a pond, he got off his horse and wet his bandanna so he could clean up. The cold water felt good on his face. He dabbed at his shirt and trousers. "Darn that cussed man," Charlie said out loud. But inside Charlie knew the whole stupid episode was his fault. He supposed Etta had seen what a fool he was. Ray Lewis was right. Forget it. For a second time in his life he vowed to leave strong spirits alone. He opened the picnic basket. The food that should have been so attractive sickened him. He heaved the raisin pie as far as he could into the tall weeds and followed with the biscuits and beef. The raucous crows cawed thanks. Charlie welcomed the cold bite of the wind.

In November, Joe asked Charlie to accompany him on farrier's rounds. "Before we get snow, better get the sleighs repaired." Gradually, over the last few years, Joe's hair had turned gray. Charlie was suddenly struck by the change. He was startled to see his father's huge calloused hands were not evenly tanned, but had a spattering of dark pigmented spots.

"Pa, you should let Will, Frank, and me do more of this work. We can, you know. Some afternoons, you stay in the house and keep Ma company. She'd like that."

Joe snapped, "If I sat in the house afternoons, your ma'd go around me like I was a swamp. The day I don't work is the day I can't justify my existence."

The last place on the rounds was Lewis's. Charlie and his father checked the livestock. Joe picked up the hind foot of the plow horse. He tapped the cracked hoof with his fist. "Better use tips on these brittle hooves. I'll work on this next round, in a week, ten days." He slapped the horse on the quarters and shook hands with Ray. "You owe me nothing for today, everything else looks good."

Before Joe had the wagon turned around and headed down the road, Jimmy ran out to greet Charlie. Joe was patient while Charlie danced around the wagon with Jimmy, then told him to let the boy go back inside or he'd catch his death in the icy wind.

"Etta's here," said Jimmy.

"Aw, well—she don't want to see me," said Charlie sadly. What more was there to say? Etta had other fish to fry.

"Afternoon," said Etta, pulling a thick woolen shawl tightly about her slim shoulders. "She *does* want to see you."

Charlie's jaw dropped.

She waited for him to collect himself.

"Afternoon to you," Charlie managed.

"My pa, Mr. McGuckin, has a cow that is ready to give birth, but it doesn't look right. He'd like to have you look at it, Mr. Irwin. Ray was to go check on it later if you didn't show up. Lucky you came."

She wasn't talking to Charlie, she was talking to his father.

"Hop in, son. We'll scoot right on to McGuckin's," said Joe.

Charlie nodded to Etta and started for the wagon.

"Uh—is it all right—uh, could Charlie stay here and maybe teach Jimmy some songs? On your way back you could stop for him."

"For the little tyke, Jimmy?" asked Joe, teasing. "Sure, I'll do that." He flicked the reins and called "Giddyap," leaving Charlie surprised.

"Let's go in. I'm cold," said Jimmy, taking Charlie's hand.

Kate greeted Charlie warmly and began to set cups for tea on the kitchen table. "Haven't seen you in town on Sunday lately," she said.

"That's right," said Charlie, stirring another teaspoonful of sugar in his tea and feeling his nose.

They laughed and Charlie knew he was out of the doghouse with Etta. He relaxed and enjoyed the tea. "Say, you wouldn't have a biscuit to go with this?"

Etta jumped up and brought a dishtowel full of biscuits to the table.

"Would you have some jelly?" asked Jimmy, his eyes gleaming as he looked toward Charlie.

When Kate picked up the teacups, Charlie said, "I know there's a reason for me being here. What is it?"

"It's about Pa," said Etta. "He's festering inside. He blames you for his mortification."

Charlie looked away. "He's right."

"But you don't understand. You had no way of knowing." Her face was sober, her eyes were inky-blue. "Pa's had this thing about drinking for a long time—maybe before I was born. Ma never said a word to us kids, but we knew he had spells. People talked about him and he left one job after another. He tried to run away from the problem. He got the tannery thinking he'd be so busy he'd not be tempted. But he couldn't handle it. The problems made him drink, and the more he drank the more problems. In Missouri he didn't have his own farm. He was a hired man and he was fired. That rubs salt into a wound for any man.

"Then he came here and took to religion. Ma was so pleased she even thanked Brother Morton once. All the time he was selling Pa spirits. Reverend Dana knew, but Ma ignored his hints. It was you that opened it up so we could see." Etta paused.

"That's not a high honor," said Charlie.

"Well, Pa agrees with that," said Kate. "There's some people that call him names, like *souse* and *pickle*. Some call out things like 'Where'd you find your nose paint now that Brother Morton's gone?'"

"Brother Morton's gone?" Charlie brightened.

"Oh, yes, right away. Three weeks ago. And good riddance. He gave me the creeps," said Etta.

"Listen, Pa sees you the cause of people laughing at him. He said if he lives to be a hundred, he'll remember it was you that humiliated him," said Kate.

"What do you want me to do? I could talk to him. Tell him people forget. They really do." Charlie could feel the wetness forming on his palms.

"He has a gun. You saw it in the house, over the mantel, a shotgun," said Etta. "Next time you see it, maybe it won't be over the mantel."

"No, he's not that foolish," said Charlie.

"We're not sure," said Ray. "We don't want you to take any chances. Keep clear of him. Let your pa or brothers go out to his place, but don't you go."

Tears ran down Etta's cheeks.

Kate took over. "What do you intend—what are your intentions?"

"With respect to what?" asked Charlie dumbly.

"My God," said Ray. "Etta's crying her heart out over you and you don't know. I thought you were smarter."

"Why I—I thought—I reckon I didn't think at all! Walt and Curly, they said—and Etta said that old knave of a preacher was so polite—and Mr. McGuckin said he was fixing to take him into the family—so naturally I thought—I'm a fool!" Charlie cried. "I made a stupid mess of everything!"

Etta's head was up and she was watching Charlie for some sign. Her small fists were clenched, her bosom moved up and down at the same time Charlie heard her breathe in and out. She wiped the tears away and more came.

Charlie felt numb, his mouth was dry. "I'm sorry," he mumbled.

She wanted him to say more, but her anger rose to shut off her patience. She slid off the bench and went blindly out of the soddy and up the road. Her shawl flapped madly in the breeze at her back.

Charlie went to the door, watched. She had her hands up to her face because she was crying.

"Go after her," said Ray quietly. "I'll talk with your pa when he comes back."

Charlie trailed after her. He knew Jimmy and the others were watching from the front window. He had a lump in his throat about as big as a crab apple, and he could not swallow it. He saw Etta stumble. She was such a little thing, stumbling up ahead and crying her heart out. She didn't deserve it. He should have told her how he felt. Now it was too late. Now she hated him. He tried running, then slackened his pace and just lumbered along.

She felt helpless. She'd not intended to let him see her cry. She was almost blind because of the tears. She had no idea he was behind her. She pulled her shawl up around her throat. She felt the day broken and lost. She was alone, her dreams were gone.

She kicked at the ruts in the dirt that was the road. She kicked a stone and it hurt, she stumbled. She tried to ignore the pain but it was great. She hobbled a few yards off the road and squatted in the tall weeds. A swarm of gnats flew above her. She'd upset their quiet. She put her face in her hands and cried. She sobbed. No one could see her—what did it matter?

Charlie stood over her. He did not know what to do. For a short moment he felt waves of cold and hot shame. His mind could think of only one thing. He bent and put his wide hand on her shoulder. Then he reached down gently with two hands and straightened her head so that she looked at him. She was tiny and delicate as a pale-pink spring beauty. He'd really never thought of her like this before. It gave him the tingly feeling. He felt exhilarated. He felt strong and sure and he slipped one arm around her.

Etta tried to break away and she might have slipped and fallen if he'd not held her. "Hold on, there," he said.

"Don't!" She pulled away and would not look at him again.

"You're not really hurt," he said. "Stand up and dry your eyes."

Etta stood, not looking at him. She dried her eyes on the edge of her soft blue skirt. She felt his strong hand and arms and knew she'd not try to pull away.

"That's better," he said. "You tripped on that big stone in the road back there, that's all."

He stepped away from her and she looked up.

Charlie was beyond thinking one way or another. He knew only that she was here and there was nothing that was important beyond that. "Etta, I love you." The words were uttered as something fresh from him, something not pondered over, or thought out. He reached to draw her in tenderly to the protective circle of his arms.

Her arms went around his waist as he pulled her close. As his lips touched hers he felt lifted right off his feet, in a way a man fording a stream hits the middle and unexpectedly runs into an undertow that lifts his feet right off the bottom, then sets him down gently before he has time to catch his breath.

Charlie straightened up. "If we do this often you'll need a stepping stool."

She giggled and put her arms around his waist and buried her face in his abdomen. Charlie didn't move. He looked at this slip of a girl that could cause such a powerful feeling in him. He felt good, a joyful all over feeling, and she knew how he felt, he was certain.

Her hair was fluffed out around her face. She smiled at Charlie. No matter what, she thought, it will always be like this. He'll smooth things out and mend the breaks. "We'd better go back," she said softly. "Your pa will be looking for you."

Then a shadow came across her face, a sadness. "What shall we do about my pa? Oh, Charlie!"

"Stop," he said. "Don't spoil this. We'll tell my pa and go one step at a time."

Joe's wagon was outside the barn. The forge was fired up and he was replacing the shoes and putting on tips on the brittle hooves of the old plow horse. They watched as he burnt the shoe in place, cooled it in the slack bucket, and nailed it on. Then he pushed a new pair of horseshoes into the center of the red-hot forge, and with his left arm over the bellows pole, he worked as though he had all the time in the world. The pumping came as naturally as his easy breathing. As his arm kind of floated up and down slowly with the pole Charlie thought of trout moving their fins to keep perfect balance when they seem to be resting on the bottom of a creek bed.

"You better let me talk to him," whispered Charlie.

"Well?" questioned Joe when he heard the whispering.

"Pa—we, Etta and I, are going to get married," blurted Charlie.

Joe's smile was broad and welcome. "Well, now, that's fine with me." He looked at Etta kind of dancing around Charlie. He liked her. She was pretty—no, lovely. Her kind of beauty was the lasting kind. She had a lot of spunk for a young thing. He liked that, too. "I think your mother would like to know about this, so be sure to tell her as soon as we get home." He went back to the horseshoes.

Etta could not hold her words a minute longer. "Look here, Charles Irwin, you never once asked me if I wanted to marry you. You assumed I'd want to. What makes you think—" Her eyes were flecked with reflections of sparks from the forge.

Charlie pulled her close to him, so that she stood under the crook of his outstretched arm and put his hand over her mouth.

"I'm as surprised as you, Pa. This morning I never thought about being married. This afternoon I think marriage is—is the natural thing to do," said Charlie.

"I'm not surprised," said his father laconically.

"Sunday, when you're not using the wagon, I'll go out and see Etta's pa. He'll give his blessing—he'll have to."

Etta was jumping up and down and waving her hands.

"If the young lady's not suffocated by then," said his father. "Let her say something, son."

Charlie took his hand from Etta's face. She took a deep breath.

"I thank you, Mr. Irwin. Between you and me I'd be pleased to be Charlie's wife—if he'd ask me." Etta was convulsed with giggles.

Charlie's heart leaped with joy. The words were like sweet birdsong on a warm spring morning. He tried to calm his emotions so that he was composed. "I just realized that I'd be far better off if I had you around. In fact, from now on I can't think of being without you. I can't see that being with me would be too hard on you. You'd probably get used to it. Will you be my wife, Etta?" Charlie stood as straight as he could, all six feet four inches.

She reached out her hands. "Oh, yes," she whispered.

Joe chuckled over the joy the two were having just play-talking. Then he interrupted. "I have to ask something. You are such a mite of a girl, how old are you?"

"I'll be nineteen on the twenty-third."

"Fine. Charlie's eighteen." Joe turned his back and pumped the forge.

"I'll always be older." Etta smiled smugly and put her arms around Charlie's waist.

That evening Joe said to Mary, "Horses and a good woman sure make a man go whistling, when he's young enough to pucker. Listen to Charlie a-humming and a-whistling even in his sleep."

"Pa, he's not asleep. Charlie's burning a candle. He's figuring how much of this place is his, or can be his, if he either pays or works for it. He's going to bring that darling Etta here to live. I'll have to fix the place up." Mary turned on her side and put her arms around Joe. "Those two'll make each other happy. I liked Etta the first I saw her."

"She's a gal that knows her own mind," said Joe, holding Mary close and thinking of all the joys and sadness a couple can have together.

When the McGuckins' wagon pulled up into their yard on Sunday, Charlie was standing beside his horse waiting. Mrs. McGuckin nodded. Curly and Walt said, "Good to see you." Etta took her bonnet off and let her hair hang loose as she helped the younger children from the wagon. Mr. McGuckin frowned and motioned for Walt and Curly to unhitch the team of horses.

Charlie started off gingerly. "Sir, I'd like to apologize for the way I behaved to you in town. I pray there'll be no permanent injury to you in this area. I've already told a number of folks it was my fault." He looked at the split board in the wagon. "It'll blow over. By spring people'll be gossiping about something else. I think you know I'm right." He was racking his brains for the right words to lead him to his purpose for being there.

"Who told you to think for me?" McGuckin said, brushing off his black wool trousers, smoothing the collar of his matching coat, and pulling his bowler hat to the middle of his forehead. He turned to Etta and said, "You look like the wrath of God. Put your bonnet on. What has come over you?"

"Oh, Pa! And Ma!" she cried twisting the bonnet's ribbons. "I'm—Charlie and I are getting married."

Charlie felt the breath go out of his lungs. He heard the tittering of the kids standing around gawking, their eyes wide and mouths open.

McGuckin looked as if he'd been hit by a bolt of lightning.

His voice was a monotone. "That's something. That's it. That's the worst piece of news I've ever heard in my life. That's not the end of this story. That's —" he began to sputter.

"Mr. McGuckin, I'm here to ask your permission to court Etta. I'd like Mrs. McGuckin's permission also." Charlie was sweating.

Mrs. McGuckin nodded her head the least bit and, keeping her gaze on her husband, said, "Come inside the soddy." Then to the staring kids she said, "Go on! Shoo!" She flapped her skirt as if she were scattering a bunch of chickens.

Charlie stood nervously with his wide-brimmed hat in his hand until Mrs. McGuckin indicated that he should sit on the bench next to the table. "I'll get a board and replace the one that's split on your wagon," he said.

"You're a blamed liar," said McGuckin between clenched teeth.

"I don't want to offend you, nor fight with you," said Charlie, looking directly at McGuckin.

"Looks like you have and you might," said McGuckin.

"I apologize."

"Damn that Brother Morton," said McGuckin under his breath. "He's pulled up his tent stakes and left. I can't settle this thing without my cough medicine."

"I haven't heard you cough once," said Mrs. McGuckin. "Don't pretend. We all know about that medicine. It's the devil's brew."

Charlie felt like he was in the middle of a hornet's nest. "Next week I'll bring Etta home from Sunday service in my wagon, or to her sister Kate's place. That'll give us a chance to talk."

Charlie looked at Mrs. McGuckin and thought he imagined a slight flicker of a smile. He kept his eyes on her. She took off her gray bonnet and fluffed out her thin, graying hair, in a way that reminded Charlie of Etta. To win this day meant everything to Charlie. He felt clumsy and unsure, but he had to continue. He moved one hand toward Mrs. McGuckin's hand that lay on the table, but he did not touch her. He lowered his voice so that everyone had to sit quiet to hear. "There's so much peacefulness in this valley. You notice it's dark green in summer where the clouds shade it and bright green where the sunshine strikes. That long, narrow road I came up is like two lines drawn through the gold side of a quilt my ma made once. The other side of that quilt was the same color as your rye field, green with rich brown patches of prairie soil.

"There's an excitement that comes sometimes so sudden you have no time to think about it. The thunder and lightning, the wind and snowdrifts as high as my head, the time the grasshoppers came in shimmering clouds that sounded like wind rushing through treetops and ate every green leaf and blade of grass in the meadow, the lone wild horse that wandered in and grazed with the regular bunch . . . these are little miracles." He pulled his hand back and folded it with the other on top of the table.

Mrs. McGuckin brushed her hand across her eyes. "Oh, my. That's beautiful. Let's have some tea." She got up and put several pinches of tea leaves from a tin can into the teakettle on the stove. Etta and some of the younger girls put cups on the table. Walt brought out an empty tomato can filled with spoons. He set it next to the sugar bowl.

McGuckin hit the side of his cup with his spoon for attention. "Shucks, that was only talk. Didn't mean a thing. How in Hades you expect to take care of my daughter? Is your old man going to give you his homestead or the farrier circuit? Oh, no! Wait, you sing—hell's bells, I almost forgot. You expect to sing in some tavern to collect enough money to keep a wife?" He was getting worked up. "I think you're tetched in the head. Maybe I should go after the sheriff or have you sent to that hospital in Denver that has only crazies." McGuckin was standing. "Your pa ought to have something to say about all this, I bet."

Charlie thought he was getting nowhere, except more and more exasperated. "My pa is not marrying your daughter. I am. Good day to you all." He was up and heading for the door, not looking back.

"Sit down, Mr. Irwin. Don't say it's a good day until I tell you it is a good day. We ain't finished."

"Brian, do be careful. Your face is red!" said Mrs. McGuckin.

Charlie wished he were out the door, on his way home. He'd had about all of this talk he wanted. "All right, what is it?"

"In my opinion you are shiftless, dirty, and ignorant. Look at the mud and dust on your shoes." McGuckin seemed pleased. As his anger came he felt he was outshining Charlie and he would soon have the boy completely cowed.

Charlie looked at his boots. He'd wiped them off with a damp rag only this morning, rubbed in grease, and polished with a wad of sheep's wool. "Like you said, that's just talk. Words with no backing don't mean a thing. Etta and I invite all of you to our wedding."

It became as noisy as an empty wagon on a hard-frozen road.

Everyone was talking at once. Etta got up and poured tea. She set the kettle down in front of her pa. "Listen, I have something to say! The wedding will be on the first day of January. Charlie and I are going to start at the beginning together. He's going to ask Reverend Dana to marry us."

"Amen," said Mrs. McGuckin. There were tears in her eyes.

"Don't tell me what you are going to do, Etta Mae McGuckin." McGuckin's face was purple with rage. "Irwins are heathens!"

Charlie hardly heard him; he wondered how this could end and his liking for McGuckin was wearing thin. His words came out slow. "I'm proud to be an Irwin. We are not held back by our pa, or our ma. If we make a mistake, they don't pretend like it wasn't ever done. They give advice if we ask, but they let us take the responsibility." The words astounded him. McGuckin was huddled against his wife. He had a hangdog droop to his shoulders. Slower yet, Charlie said, "Etta, get your things, I'll take you to your sister's place." He held out his hand.

"I'm ready." She put her hand in his and held on like a frightened child. Curly handed her the heavy wool shawl. "So long," he said.

Etta pulled one hand away from Charlie's waist and wiped the tears from her eyes. She was in the saddle behind Charlie. "You did fine," she said.

He didn't look back but his mouth turned up into a smile. "Look here, Miss McGuckin, you never once consulted with me about our wedding date nor the preacher. So what makes you think I want to be married in the Methodist Episcopal Church on New Year's Day?" His eyes sparkled.

"Would you rather wait until June?" Etta asked, giggled, and put her head against his broad back.

Charlie and Etta were married January 1, 1894, in the Methodist Episcopal Church of Goodland. Most everybody was there: Sheriff Navert and his wife, Martin Tomblin, Jesse Tait, Marietta Roberts, A. B. Montgomery, George Benson and his wife, several members of the Farmers' Alliance, Ell and Les, Curly and Walt McGuckin, Kate and Ray Lewis. Mr. and Mrs. McGuckin did not come.

Mary spent hours cleaning, straightening. She made the windows of the soddy shine by rubbing them with wadded newspapers. She baked three white cakes and put them together with white frosting. Ell made jars of mulled cider.

Etta and her sister Kate made the white wedding dress with mosquito-netting veil. Charlie gave Etta a bouquet of fresh violets that matched her eyes. He managed to get them by train from someplace. The place was his secret.

Etta was given away by her brothers Curly and Walt who made it to the church at the last moment. Etta was breathtaking in the layers of thin, meshlike marquisette of her wedding dress. She wore Ell's pearl necklace and borrowed Mary's silver, filigreed brooch and Kate's silver bracelet and blue petticoat. The blue petticoat she wore underneath her white muslin one.

During the ceremony Reverend Dana asked Charlie quietly if he had a ring. Charlie put a wide platinum circle on Etta's finger.

The weather was fair, but cold. The sun was covered by high clouds so that it looked like a white china plate. There was three, four inches of fresh snow on top of the foot of packed old snow. The roads were cleared, sleighs had packed the snow hard. After the ceremony people piled into sleighs and pulled fur robes high under their chins, ready for the ride to the Irwins' soddy for refreshments.

Ell asked Etta how she knew Charlie was the right man. Etta was quick to answer that she had heard if a girl counted the stars each night for nine nights, she'd dream of her future husband on the ninth night. "I dreamed of Charlie all nine nights!" Etta said. "And I tried something else. I wrote my full name on a paper, Etta Mae McGuckin. Under my name I wrote Charles Burton Irwin. I canceled out the matching letters in our names and said 'true' and 'false' to each uncanceled letter. My name ended true and Charlie's name ended true. That's proof enough!"

Ell was delighted with this petite girl who was Charlie's wife.

Frank and Will and Les threw rice, the fertility symbol, into the sleigh Joe drove that carried Etta and Charlie. Joe grumbled about all the good rice pudding going to waste. He paid for a room in the hotel in Goodland so that Etta and Charlie could be alone for a couple of days before they went to Colorado Springs for three days with Ell and Les.

FOURTEEN

Floyd Leslie

By 1895 Goodland was eight years old. Most every house in town was frame, but in the rural areas nearly every house was sod. Outhouses were behind all frame houses, soddies, and business houses. The streets in town were wide so that a horse-drawn wagon could easily turn around. The streets were dirt, dusty in the dry season, muddy in the wet season. Only the larger businesses had sidewalks, which were board planks.

Crops were good that year. Joe had a magnificent potato crop. Fall wheat averaged sixteen bushels to the acre and went for fifty cents a bushel. There was good competition for the grain among the three buying firms. Looking ahead in a practical way at the growing market for wheat, oats, rye, and corn, Editor Tait wrote in the *Dark Horse*: "It is ascertained that the chinch bug is subject to cholera and the disease is killing them out. We don't suppose this will make the least bit of difference, as next year we will have a cousin or uncle of the chinch bug come along and ruin more wheat than the first bug."

Etta and Charlie celebrated their first wedding anniversary by staying in bed until the sun was fully up. Etta was five months pregnant. "Remember the first time I bedded you?" whispered Charlie.

"My brothers and your brothers banged on pots they'd

270

sneaked from your ma's cupboard." Etta snuggled close to Charlie, putting a small foot across his muscular, hairy legs.

"Ya, they banged so loud we had to invite them in before the hotel threw us out. The more noise they made the more aroused you became. Oh, my dear, who could have guessed this tiny body of yours held all that wildfire. You were as eager as I." Charlie put his hand underneath her flannel nightgown and felt the turgid tips of her breasts. "You have everything I want." He could feel the tingling sensation start in his loins and grow into the warm urgent throbbing. "Come on, let's see if we can finish together. Oh, Etta, I'm ready. I'm big as a horse and need to be loved." His hand had moved between her legs.

"Charlie, I love you, I'm ready, easy, easy." She found it hard to say anything. His warm, hairy chest was against her face. What he was doing between her legs was marvelous. The sensation was so overwhelming and so pleasurable that she closed her eyes to all sight and her ears to all sound. She was lost as in a fog and she moved deeper and deeper into the mist. Her body took over and moved rhythmically on its own.

Charlie held himself back, letting the excitement build slowly. He held himself on his elbows, not letting all his weight rest on Etta. Making love to her gratified all his senses. He thought of her as a pixie that enchanted him. She brought him to this state of euphoria and at the pinnacle he exploded.

After breakfast Etta caught Will before he went out to check on his red-bodied, white-faced Herefords he'd bought with money from selling several of the mustangs. "I have to wash clothes today. I can't hang them outside, they'll be stiff in seconds. Please, could you string up a clothesline in the kitchen, near the stove?"

"What a bossy sister-in-law," joked Will. "You kissed Charlie and now he thinks he's the prince instead of the frog. Why doesn't he string up your clothesline and wet wash?"

"'Cause I think he went to meet your pa. Your ma keeps opening the door to look for him. He's gone half an hour and she worries."

Will nodded. He understood. The day was bone cold and the wind cut like a butcher knife.

"Frank, please go out and hang some gunnysacks on the chicken house for warmth. Wrap my shawl around your head and neck before you put your sheepskin on. Your ears could freeze white today," said Etta.

Frank took the shawl. "Where'd Pa go on a day like this?"

"Town, to get a couple sacks of oats and a barrel of salt pork. If you'd talked Will into butchering one of his beefs we wouldn't need the salt pork."

"Ah, geez, Etta. How'd I know Pa would get it in his head to go out today? I hope to God he wore two pairs of wool pants."

"I don't know, he left before I was up."

"Ya, you and Charlie stayed in the bed a long time this morning. What for?"

"Don't think about it. It's none of your business." She flushed and went to check on the clothesline.

"Does it hurt to do it, when you're—you're with child?" Frank had Etta's shawl around his head and shoulders.

"Frank R. Irwin, didn't your ma tell you anything?" snapped Etta. "Is it up to me to tell you about everything?" With a broom handle she stirred the boiling white clothes, which were in the tub on top of the stove.

"Pa says the more one knows, the more joy there is in life," answered Frank with a smirk on his face.

Mary parted the curtains that separated her and Joe's bedroom. "What's that? You want me for some explaining here?" Her long white hair was neatly twisted in a circle at the back of her neck and held with tortoiseshell combs and hairpins. Her hazel eyes were dull even after sleeping all night.

"You feeling all right today, Mary?" asked Etta. "We're getting the wash hung and keeping the wind out of the chicken house."

"I'm fine. Only I wish the swelling in my ankles would go down. Used to be after a night's rest they was fine, but look there, they look like two sticks of firewood instead of ankles." She held her skirts up for Etta to look.

"Stay off your feet and I'll rub them for you in a bit." Etta put the boiling white clothes in a tub of cold rinse water, then wrung out as much water as her small hands could manage.

"I could help you with that," said Mary.

"No. If they drip I'll get the mop."

"Smells like laundry soap in here," said Frank, going out the door with an armload of gunnysacks.

Charlie burst in the door. "Pa's coming up the road. He's with someone!"

Mary was looking out the window. "Who can that be? There's a horse tied behind our springboard."

Joe opened the front door. "I have a man, a woman, and a passel of kids. I'm sending them in where it's warm."

Charlie went out and put blankets on the Irwin horse and the strange, big-chested brown. He gave them a couple fistfuls of oats and some hay and cracked the surface of the well for a bucket of water. He rolled the barrel of pork to the woodshed next to the barn and put the sacks of oats inside the barn door as fast as he could manage. He was curious about the people his pa had brought home.

In the house Mary and Etta were feeding a boy, about four, and a girl, about five years old. "Where's the other kids," asked Etta.

"This is all, far's I know," said the strange woman. She was not much older than Etta, but she was taller. Her hair was yellow as sunflower petals and her eyes watery blue. "The mister probably called 'em a passel 'cause them two sound like a dozen kids when they take out after each other."

"They scrap, huh?" asked Charlie. He saw the boy kick the girl under the table when they ate.

The man was big-boned, tall, like Charlie, but weighed maybe thirty pounds more and was about fifteen years older. He had brown hair, a receding hairline, and a small mustache above his upper lip resembling the tip of a horse's tail. He held out his hand to Charlie and smiled so that the corners of the steely gray eyes crinkled. "Horn's the name, Tom Horn. I'm grateful for the shelter." Etta brought him and the yellow-haired woman a plate of potatoes and butter beans and bacon. "And the grub looks good. I'm hungry enough to eat a saddle blanket."

"Pa'd do that for anyone out in this cold. You looking for a homestead for your family?"

"Not my family. I ran into 'em down the road a piece. They were walking, but not sure where they was heading. She hasn't mentioned her old man once since we been moving north. Didn't know where we were until we met your pa. Too cold to be lost." Horn stopped to concentrate on eating.

Later, after supper, Charlie saw that Horn was a gentleman around women and that he instinctively knew to talk politics with Joe, horses with Frank, cattle with Will, and roping with Charlie. Horn noticed the Henry rifle Charlie had finally laid on two pegs in the wall beside the door. "You ever been to Mexico?" Horn asked Charlie, looking over the rifle.

"Nope, not yet," said Charlie.

"This here piece reminds me when I was living with Apaches and all I had was a short forty-four rimfire Henry and a bowie knife. You want to know what happened to my Henry? I'll tell you in a word: lost. Yes, sir, I lost it. You ever hear of the earthquake of eighty-seven? Well, sir, we were headed for the town of Bavispe, which was shaken down to its foundation. I was leading about fifty Apache scouts for Captain Emmet Crawford of the Third Cavalry. We had half a dozen pack trains. We bivouacked amidst the earthquake rubble of Bavispe. The pack mules and horses and rifles were stolen by smugglers who'd sell everything in the States. I chased two smugglers with my bowie knife, slashed them both so that more than likely they bled to death. When I got everything back together I couldn't find my Henry rifle. To this day I don't know if one of those smugglers took it or one of my Apache scouts. There was some rumor that Geronimo came into possession of a rimfire Henry. We passed Tupper's Battleground on the Sierra Madre when a storm made everything so dark we could hardly see from one cutbank to the next. Then the hail came. It was so cold I can feel it now. Waugh! It was over in a few minutes, leaving a regular torrent running in the bottom of the ravine. We were looking for Geronimo and his renegades. I wanted to get Geronimo back to San Carlos so bad I could taste it. I'd do anything."

Charlie had never heard anyone talk about the adventures of being a scout before. He was spellbound. Horn was a talker who knew how to use his voice and face to attract an audience. Charlie watched how he used his hands, then how his face changed expression as he talked. The man is good-looking, even though he is getting bald and has a nose so large he could store a small dog in it, Charlie thought.

"You've had some experiences," said Will. "So what are you doing in the prairie country?"

"I'm getting away from all the killing. I saw Captain Crawford and some of my closest friends killed and scalped by hostiles. I even saw a man half et by a bear." He looked up to see if the ladies were listening, but they were all in the bedroom getting the children to sleep. "He was the worst used-up man I ever saw. The cavalry surgeon couldn't do anything. He was crushed in every bone and bitten in every muscle. The man was a sheepherder. Some of the men in the sheep camp allowed as how the bear had been eating their sheep and got tired of mutton and when it came on a hog it decided to have a mess of that. Ha Ha." Horn laughed, holding his sides.

None of the Irwins laughed. Charlie looked pale and had cold chills. Frank held his stomach and looked ill.

"Well, I've been deputy sheriff of Yavapair, and Gila County. I won a prize on the Fourth of July at Globe, near the San Carlos Reservation, for tying down a steer. There was a county rivalry among cowboys from all over the territory as to who was the quickest man at that business. I won the prize at the Territorial Fair in Phoenix a couple of weeks later," Horn said with a swagger. "I won it in forty-nine and one half seconds. The Pinkerton National Detective Agency at Denver wrote to me stating that they wanted me to work for them. Well, I never did really like the work with Pinkertons, so I'm headed for Wyoming and work with the Swan Land and Cattle Company as a range detective."

Charlie noticed how Horn started a story and became sidetracked and told several things before getting back to the intended story. He decided maybe that was because the man had seen and done so many things. He longed for the cold weather to break so that he could ask this Horn fellow to demonstrate his roping ability.

Will and Frank gave up their beds for the yellow-haired woman, Plucky, and her two children and slept with Horn under piles of quilts on the hay in the barn.

Horn liked to talk after supper each evening. Charlie wondered if the talking wasn't too braggy. The stories didn't always tie together well. Will and Frank enjoyed the stories immensely. Charlie noticed that Horn's piercing gray eyes sometimes seemed to look past his listeners and into some distant land where he lived in his imaginings or rambling.

Mary and Etta seemed to revel in taking care of Plucky and her two children. Etta was thankful that she no longer suffered from the incapacitating sickness and the overwhelming desire to run outdoors to get away from the smell of cooking, which had been nauseating. The day after the big January thaw Horn announced that he would be leaving the next day if the warm weather held. He offered Will twelve dollars for old Flame, who was now a swaybacked nag and a beloved family pet. Will was loath to part with the horse, even though he knew he'd never be offered more.

"I was told by Apaches there are Sioux up north and they'll take half of everything I have. Figured if I have two horses, I could give them your old nag. A man is crippled as a bird without wings if he's without his own horse. Twelve bucks is more'n the horse's worth. Taking it off your hands now saves you a lot of extra oats and hay," said Horn.

"It's yours." There were tears in Will's eyes. "You taking Plucky?"

"You can see there's only two things I'm afraid of—a decent woman and being left without a horse."

Plucky told Etta that she'd just as soon stay around Goodland, if there was a place she and her two young'uns could stay. Etta said Plucky might live with Marietta Roberts.

The temperature fell during the night; snow fell also. The wind made drifts like small sand dunes against the west side of the soddy and barn, against cottonwoods and hillocks.

Charlie couldn't sleep. He heard noises, probably the wind blowing, but they kept him awake. As soon as it was light he was up. He tucked the quilts around Etta so she could sleep longer.

Then Charlie had a crazy idea. He thought he'd take Sunny for a short ride on the thin patches of snow, skirting around the drifts before everyone was up. He knew he could get a tongue lashing. Then he decided he was master of his own destiny, old enough to make his own decisions. Let Frank be angry when I get back. He'll get over it. Then he saw the picture of Will and Plucky cuddled up in the barn and chuckled, sighed, and felt real good.

Quietly he took the saddle and horse out of the barn, letting the dog, Nick, out at the same time. The dog began to jump and yip around in the snow. "Sshh!" warned Charlie. "You'll have everyone awake asking questions before I leave." He shut Nick back in the barn. The dog squealed and whined and scratched at the door a few seconds, then was quiet.

Now Charlie noticed in the brighter morning light that snow was trampled around the barn door. He didn't dwell on it, thinking it was himself and Nick and Sunny that had trampled most of it. He snugged up the saddle so it wouldn't slip and rode toward the creek and out onto the settlers' road in the direction of Ruleton, a little town not more than ten miles from Goodland. The air was sharp and his sheepskin and wool cap hardly enough. The thin early morning clouds were gone and the fading stars hung so low it seemed he could touch them. Charlie tucked his nose deep into the front of his coat and pulled the horse around the drifts. He let his mind wander and thought of expanding the farm, maybe building a soddy for him and Etta and the baby, somewhere creekside of the Sappa. There was the place in front of his eyes, the little meadow with its two protecting hills on the northwestern side. The cottonwood skeletons swayed in the wind.

Charlie turned for home, ready to do the morning chores. He stopped and gazed one last moment at a wisp of haze against the sky, trailing out more like smoke than clouds. Must be fog rising from the Sappa, he thought.

Then his thoughts crystallized. The Sappa is mostly frozen. The air is sharp and dry. He bent his head to think better and saw prints around his pony's hooves. On closer inspection he found the front left foot of the prints turned in exactly like old Flame's! Charlie did not wait to ponder if Sunny could go through the drifts. He pulled the collar up on his coat to keep his ears warmer. Ice cracked as Sunny walked across the frozen marshland when he was nearer the creek. He pushed his mittened hands under his armpits a few moments. When he came around the hills he could easily follow the tracks of two horses. Flame was following a man on horseback.

It had to be Horn. Charlie saw the pinprick of firelight at the base of the west hill. And he thought he saw someone move against the snow-covered hill. "Hello! Hello, over there!" he called, and waited for an answer, watching his steamy breath flow away and disappear. He only heard the snuffling of Sunny. The horse was not used to carrying a load in such cold weather.

Charlie and the horse continued to move across the meadow. Charlie couldn't figure Horn. It was too cold for anyone to be traveling far. He was welcome at the Irwin soddy. Why hadn't he stayed? The land seemed still except for the fire. Charlie wondered where Horn had found the wood so far from the creek. Then he saw the bundles of dried sunflower stalks tied with familiar twine. "Pa," he called, "is that you?" His legs were so cold they felt like numb chair legs. He slid out of the saddle and awkwardly jumped up and down. When he broke through the snow crust he sank to his knees. His feet began to tingle and ache. "Jeems!" he said under his breath. "What's going on?" Around the fire were large dark patches that faded out to a blood red, then a pink in the snow. Charlie's stomach tightened.

The horse lay in the snow. Charlie looked away and smelled the hunk of thigh meat sizzling on a tripod over the flames. The man stirred and jumped up. His eyes rolled and the bloody comforter slipped to the hard-packed snow. The horse's belly was slit where all the entrails were removed and the blood drained out. The entrails were in a frozen heap behind the horse. Charlie could not speak. He breathed deeply to quiet the wave of nausea that swept over him.

"Go back!" Horn yelled. "This is my business!"

Charlie was immobile. Old Flame was like a large empty pouch. It was impossible.

"Why?" he whispered.

"The horse was old. Couldn't take the bitter cold. I left you good money for it." Horn went back to the protective carcass and sat on the blood-stained comforter. He hugged his knees. "Soon's this nag died I knew what I had to do. Pack the meat in the hide and use that to trade the Sioux. It was too cold to skin the animal out, so I did enough to keep me warm for the night with the thought of completing the job in the morning. Had to build me a fire or the damn wolves'd be here by the time I closed my eyes."

Charlie looked at Horn and felt anger and disgust, but it was mixed with sadness for the old beloved horse. His hands clenched and he could not feel the ache in his feet anymore. He swallowed, trying to push aside the lump of ice. "Mr. Horn, you were sheltered and fed at our place. This was no time to set out anywhere."

Horn fingered the leather binocular case that hung across his chest. The case was open and be brought out a roll of paper money from it. He counted out eight bucks and handed them to Charlie. "Horse worth twenty bucks to you? I left your brother twelve. Here's the difference."

Horn had shoved his wide-brimmed hat back on his head and Charlie could see his hard glasslike gray eyes in the firelight. Those eyes were as cold as the ice under his boots.

Charlie took the eight dollars and put them in his sheepskin's pocket. "Wyoming's a big place. Don't get lost," said Charlie.

Horn nodded and glanced ever so slightly toward his big-chested hunter tethered to a small scrub oak.

"We're friends now, huh? I'll run across your trail again. We'll trade roping tricks. Give my thanks to your ma and that sweet wife of yours. Someday you can tell me how you managed to lasso such a wonderful little lady. And a word about that Plucky; she's one of them widows whose greatest need's to have her weeds plowed under."

Charlie held the reins and led Sunny across the meadow and out to the settlers' road not looking back. His mind whirled. The sky was cold gray by the time he brought Sunny to the barn. The minute he opened the door, Nick began barking again. "You knew Horn had left and tried to tell me," said Charlie with a sigh. "I saw the signs and ignored them. Darn!"

Frank sat up and rubbed his eyes. Will sat up and brushed the sunflower-yellow hair from his chest. He smiled at Charlie and shrugged his shoulders. "She came in last night to get something from Horn that belonged to her. I thought it was the binoculars. But Horn grabbed them from her like they were some heirloom of his. Cuffed her on the face, knocked her down. Geez, I had to put her in a pile of quilts to keep him off of her."

Plucky was awake, pulling a quilt up around her bare shoulders. She smiled at Will and said in a husky voice, "Don't worry about me. Don't think unkindly about Tom Horn. He brought me and my kids here alive. I give him credit. He can survive most anywhere."

Frank was watching Will and Plucky. He crawled out of his blankets and brushed the straw from his pants and shirt, which he'd left on for warmth. "Geez, it's too cold to sleep in the wherewithall," he murmured. "You two must be out of your tree!" His eyes stayed on Will and Plucky. "Where's Mr. Horn?"

"He's gone. He needed to get over into Wyoming for that job," said Charlie.

Around Saint Valentine's Day, Etta told Charlie that she could feel the baby inside her move. "Now I know he's in there," she said happily. "He's more active in the evenings, when I first go to bed. That's when he wants to play."

"Just like his pa, huh?" chuckled Charlie. "What'll we name him? How about Joe Marvin after Pa?"

"Or Brian, after my pa?" Etta giggled. Then she was serious. "I really like the name Leslie. You know, after Les Miner," said Etta, snuggling against Charlie, letting him put his wide hand over her belly to feel the baby move a tiny arm or leg.

The ground stayed snow-covered during all of February and March. Then the chinook winds came and melted the snow almost overnight. The ground was wet and soggy, hard to plow. Joe was afraid the hot weather would come suddenly and burn out all the corn and wheat seed. He said, "Farming is as unpredictable as weather." He spent hours checking the tiny green shoots of wheat. By mid-April the stems began to elongate fast.

The day he discovered the rosettelike leaves developing near the ground he sang all the way home. When he found two or three nodes, the thickened swellings on the stems, he danced around the table and played his fiddle after supper. "The crops will be good this year! It's no crime to celebrate good fortune!"

Mary stayed calm. The only time for true celebration was at

harvest time. But she did enjoy seeing Joe in such fine spirits and told Charlie that if her ankles weren't so swelled up she'd get right up and dance with him. Her arthritis had flared up again during the spring, causing her legs to ache, and her hands had deep burning sensations when she clenched them.

Charlie and Frank spaded the kitchen garden for their mother. The turned-over earth dried out faster. Mary and Etta put in seeds of pole beans, squash, peas, beets, turnips, lettuce, and watermelon.

Etta held her hands under her distended abdomen and said, "I think my watermelon is about to drop any moment. It gets heavier every day."

"You have a couple more weeks," said Mary. "I'll write to Ell today. She'll be the best help you ever saw."

"My own ma could come," said Etta.

"Child, we'd both like that. But she's all those young'uns of her own to care for. Besides, you think your pa would let her come?"

Etta's face fell. "I guess not. Pa thinks I married into irreligious heathens." She added, "I'm sorry."

"Land sakes, after meeting the Splitlogs, I don't know what heathens are," said Mary hastily.

"You don't know what heathens are—?" whispered Etta.

"That's right. Those 'uncivilized' men practiced the Golden Rule like it was meant to be practiced. Someday I would like to shake their mother's hand. It's the mother that teaches values. Motherhood is a responsibility. I'm telling you, Indians are not all heathens," said Mary, "and no Irwin is a heathen either!"

One afternoon Mary and Etta weeded the kitchen garden, then brought the kitchen chairs outside so they could rest and enjoy the warm sunshine. The willows along the creek were lush with soft, green leaves. The few oaks had long, caterpillarlike, greenish-yellow blossoms that fell at the base of the tree in thick carpets. The Indian grass out on the prairie was knee-high; by midsummer it would be eight feet. The prairie was rich with wildflowers, yellow sawthistles, purple phlox, and white starlike flowers. A marsh hawk skimmed silently over the waving green grass toward the meadow and creek beyond. The land seemed an extension of the soddy and the people who lived there. Etta wiped the yellow pollen from her black high-button shoes with the hem of her long skirt. "I have to take these phlox inside. Flowers bring beauty to the darkest of corners," she said.

"The air smells like rain," said Mary, and she looked at the sky. "I thought so. See that dark cloud coming in from the south-west? There's lightning in it." The cloud was tinged with purple, the outer edges a bilious yellow.

Charlie herded the cows into the meadow and helped Will and Frank bring the horses up to the barn. "Boy, that's going to be some storm," he said. The new green blades undulated as a churning green sea.

"Hear those chickens squawking," said Frank, coming into the yard.

"Yup. Reminds me of Plucky's kids," said Will.

"How's she doing?" asked Charlie, carrying Etta's chair into the soddy.

Will took his mother's chair. "She's fine. Got her own soddy off the Boulevard. She's working for Len Ching. You know, that Celestial across from Marietta's. She waits tables and does a good job serving up Chinese noodles with sweet and sour pork."

"I hoped she'd stay with Marietta," said Mary with a sigh. "Would have been good for those children. Given them something solid to hang on to. Oh, well."

Charlie put his arm around his mother and led her into the soddy. Outside the gathering clouds were rumbling. Charlie and his mother went to the door. The chickens were quiet and the buzzing of the flies stopped. The air was heavy with moisture, but dead still. Off to the west the sulfurous-edged clouds moved toward the center of the sky, over the soddy. Suddenly the wind rushed in as if to fill a vacuum. The rushing sounded like a great fall of water. Mary clung to Charlie.

Etta was bewildered and grabbed out to hang on to something. She clung to Will. Frank moved against Etta and she slipped a protective arm around his waist.

Charlie felt the wind against his eyes and had to half-close them. The chicken house floated upward to push against the hill-side. The barn's roof lifted up and slid down seemingly in slow motion, to the very spot the chicken house was. Charlie felt a tingling on his arms, but was unaware it was dust and dirt blown against his skin.

The Irwins huddled together, under the door frame, hardly breathing, until rain pelted the ground and the outside light changed from an eerie saffron to the familiar gray of a rainy day. With the first rain came marble-sized hail.

"Thank God, the house is still here!" cried Mary.

Etta put kettles and pots under the leaking roof on the kitchen side of the soddy. "Wind must of pulled a lot of sod off the top.

But that can be fixed." Her breathing was labored.

"I gotta sit down, my legs are wobbly," sobbed Mary. "Oh, my God! Where's Pa?" Color drained from her face. Her now moss-green eyes were wide. "Lord-a-mercy!" she cried. "Where is Joseph?"

"He's here!" Joe's voice yelled back. He climbed from behind the kitchen range. "Looks like a tornado hit us!" He was dripping wet, grinning.

Everyone began to talk. Joe never saw the chicken house and barn blowing away. The wind was not so bad in the wheatfield if he bent low to the ground. It was the rain and hail that sent him to hightail it for home, where he found the kitchen side peeled off like someone took hold of the top and tore downward.

In the midst of noise and confusion no one standing in the door frame had seen the gaping hole behind the Majestic range. Joe came into the soddy through that hole and ducked behind the stove for protection.

Joe and Charlie tried to close off the huge gaping hole by pinning up a couple of horse blankets and some gunnysacks.

Not until the next morning did the rain let up enough so anyone could go out to see the damage. Joe's voice quivered. "Looks like this family has to shore up a lot. All the wheat and corn's gone. Garden's a worse mess than if a herd of deer had spent the night there. Hail beat it to death. Killed everything!" He held his hands out. "Hell's bells! There's plenty of time to repair the house and build a new roof for the barn."

Mary looked around. Tears streamed down her face. "The chicken house!"

"I'll fix that, too," said Joe, putting his arm around his wife. For a few moments they clung to each other.

"We'll all get started right away. Won't be like we have to cut out a bunch of sod blocks. We just have to find out where they fit and put them back," said Charlie. He tried to keep his mother from seeing that some of the chickens were crushed to death under the heavy blocks of sod. There were no live chickens in sight. "When the chicken house is done, we'll get you a broody hen or two and you can hatch some chicks. We'll start your garden right away. Seeds'll sprout fast in warmer weather."

Will found one of the workhorses with a wooden plank in its neck. It was dead. The mustangs were all right. Their hay was soaked. Etta tried to bend over and carry the damp hay out where it could dry.

Charlie spoke sharply, "Don't do that! I hear you puff with the least little exertion. Jeems, if my belly were that big, I'd set and give orders. You write a letter to Ell. Someone's bound to go into town in the next few days. Ell ought to be getting here or else the baby will come and she'll miss using her mumbo jumbo."

Etta put her hand in the middle of her back and smiled gratefully. "I'll sit."

Will and Charlie went to town the next day. They found the Goodland Post Office damaged but open for business. The barber shop next door was blown down. The Mercantile had no roof and was damaged by rain and the rough handling of the goods. They stared unbelievingly at Len Ching's. The Chinese restaurant was boarded up—closed.

"Let's see if Plucky and those kids are all right!" cried Will. They hurried the team to the little soddy off the Boulevard. The land was as bare as if it had never existed. No one seemed to know where Plucky and the Celestial had gone, until they met Martin Tomblin. He said, "You'll never believe this. That Len Ching got Reverend Dana out of bed to marry 'em. Ching took his new bride to Ruleton to open a restaurant. Can you beat that story? A blond woman with two white-haired brats marrying a noodle-eating man?"

Will was tight-lipped, staring off into space.

The two Irwins bought dimension wood and nails from John Foster's lumber yard, then drove out to Swarts's Ice House. Mary wanted one hundred pounds of ice to keep the milk and some of her cooked things fresh for a few days.

"I know it's an extravagance," Mary had told Will. "But it'll be nice also to have for Etta. Her time's any day and chipped ice in a glass of water would go down easy with her."

Joe never wanted to be called stingy. He had called out, "Get two hundred pounds for good measure!"

There were others who were wiped out of their money crop that spring. However, Joe had his portable forge. Right away he began the farrier rounds. He bartered his work for last year's potatoes, scantlings, gunnysacks, or anything he thought useful. That year the settlers had little money and even less material goods to barter, yet their horses needed treatment and their farm equipment needed repairs. The Irwin family was certain to get along.

Next to the last day in April 1895, Etta could not sleep early in the morning. She got up and put a couple sticks of wood into the range to heat water for a cup of tea.

Ell, who had arrived a few days before, stirred on her cot near the stove. "You all right?"

"My back aches and I can't sleep. I was thinking of my own ma biting on a peeled sassafras stick and pulling on rags tied to the bed so her knuckles were white. Will I be like that when my time comes?"

Ell got out of bed and pulled a quilt around her flannel nightgown. She put her hand gently on Etta's bulging belly. "Dropped a lot in the two days I've been here."

"Maybe it's just colic. I have a kind of pushing up here." She used her hands to show a tightness in her belly. "It comes and goes."

"Tell me when it comes," said Ell, leaving her hand on Etta's belly.

Etta gritted her teeth and waved her hand.

"Contractions," said Ell. "Maybe today we'll have a new Irwin."

"Today?" asked Etta, her pixie face pink from the heat of the range. "I'm not ready. It's way too early to wake the menfolk. They'll be cranky."

"If this is the day, you can't put it off. Ready or not, the baby comes." Ell went to one of the curtained bedroom areas and called out, "Men! This is the day you have been waiting for. The moon is in the fourth quarter and right for second planting. Get that seed corn that's in the barn and the wheat Les sent. Get it in the ground. You might have a crop or two yet."

Mary was up before the men, her hair combed and a fresh apron over her dress. Black stockings were pulled to her knees, rolled, and knotted so they'd stay up. She wore her black high-button shoes, but did not have them buttoned over the ankles. "Ankles swelled even in the morning now," she complained. Then her face brightened and she hugged her daughter. "Ell, you married a good man. One that would send seed to Pa is all right. Your pa's been brokenhearted about losing his crops. This'll get him busy and he'll forget the troubles. Thank you. Thank you."

"Ma, when Etta wrote about that wind and hail, I knew what we had to do. Pa always said the family should stick together. So Les and I are doing our part."

Mary's eyes misted. "You sound like your grandma Malinda."

"Maybe I really am her. She loved life. She might have come back and taken over my soul. Go sit with Etta at the table. She's got some pains this morning." Ell half-believed she might be a reincarnation of Malinda Irwin.

"You're as daft as I remembered," said Charlie, pulling Ell's apron strings. "What do you think of my wife? She just pretending she's going to have a baby so she won't have to weed the garden?"

"Are we going to plow those fields again to put in more seed?" asked Frank, coming out of his bedroom to pull on his boots.

"You're as whiny as I remember," said Ell.

"If I'm going out for all day, I'm taking some bacon and biscuits," said Will. "Otherwise I'll starve."

"Me, too," agreed Charlie.

"I'll put together enough for all of you, including your pa," said Etta, bending over to ease a contraction.

When Ell saw the biscuits and bacon Etta had put in a dishtowel, she yelled, "Don't you men touch that! You'll get cramps from eating food handled by a birthin' woman. Throw it out! Here, Ma, you wrap up this bread and give them some pork rinds."

"Throw away good food! Come on, sis," said Charlie, rolling his eyes upward. "Is Les prepared for all this waste you conjur up?" He took the biscuits and bacon out the door, all the time surreptitiously munching on a good thick piece of fried bacon. He called to the old black dog. "Here, Nick, better than stewed squirrel this morning."

The dog got up slowly, almost blind now, and smelled the salty meat. Its head lifted so that Charlie scratched behind the ears. "You can have it all if you don't drool on me," he said, putting the food on the dirt between the dog's front paws. He wiped his hands on his denim pants and found the sack of dried corn and sack of wheat Ell had brought. He put one on each shoulder, met his father in the front yard. "Get the team and the plow," he said. Then, thinking suddenly why he was going out at daybreak, he put the grain sacks on the ground and ran back inside. "I just want to say something to my wife," he said to Ell. Etta sat on the edge of the cot Ell had slept in. "I wanted to tell you—uh—have a good birth day."

Ell and Mary put their hands over their mouths to suppress their giggles and turned their backs on the couple.

"I love you," whispered Etta.

"When it's over you can have Marietta Roberts make you any kind of new dress you want. Have it all silk if you want. The meadowlarks are singing outside. I'll leave the door open so's you can hear when I'm gone." He kissed Etta lightly on the forehead and tasted the salt from her dampness.

"How do you like the name Floyd Leslie?" she called as he left. Charlie gave no indication he'd heard.

He picked up the sacks of seed and headed out toward the field. Not seeing the others ahead of him, he looked back and saw them standing around the door of the barn. "Come on! Shake a leg!" he called.

"In a minute!" yelled Will. "We have a piece of work to do here first."

Charlie stalked over to the barn. "Frank get caught in a bear trap that was lying around?" He smirked.

"Old Nick is dead," said Joe sadly. "You feed him them rations Ell said to throw out?"

"I did."

"See, here on the floor, Nick throwed up most of what was et. Then looks like he just laid down and died." Joe's eyes watered.

"How could you be so stupid!" cried Frank. "You heard Ell say throw them things out. For chrissake!"

"That's a bunch of superstitious hogwash," said Charlie.

"It happened though," said Will, shaking his head.

"Ya," admitted Charlie, "the dog was awful slow coming to get breakfast. I think Nick was ailing then, but I was so wrapped up in having a baby I didn't notice anything else much."

"Charlie, take Nick in a gunnysack and bury the remains on top of the little hogback next to the first field Frank and Will are going to plow. I'll take your sacks of seed," said Joe.

"Pa, why me?" Charlie's heart was on the ground.

"You saw Nick last. Nick counted on you and you let him down. You ignored the signs." Joe's lip trembled.

Charlie grabbed the shovel and gunnysack. His eyes clouded with water. He was consumed with rage and grief. He dropped on his knees in the dirt and shoveled the dog's bodily remains into the coarse bag.

All the time he dug the grave he felt strong pains in his belly. His insides pulled together. He plunged the gunnysack into the hole and filled dirt in over the top. He stopped to wipe perspiration and tears from his face. The perspiration stung his eyes. His belly ached and he hunkered over the fresh-dug earth. He pulled out his bandanna from his back pocket and a three-inch hunk of withered root fell out. "Son of a gun," he said, picking up the twisted root. He thought, that sister of mine beats all. Who else would do such a thing. He waved the root in the air and detected a faint sweet odor of sweet flag, or calamus. How'd she suppose

I could make tea from this out in the field? Maybe she thought I'd just take a nip out of it. He put the root in his mouth and sucked on it, then took a small bite and chewed it. All the time he was hunched down to ease the pain in his gut. He straightened to put his bandanna back in his pocket. He felt better. "That's the fastest thing in the world for a bellyache," he said aloud. "I guess Ell knew I'd munch on that spoiled bacon." Then he laughed, thinking he was getting as superstitious as Ell.

Joe and his three boys worked all day plowing and reworking the fields and planting. On the way back to the barn in the twilight Joe said, "Tomorrow we'll go out with the farrier's wagon."

"Not me," said Frank. "I'm bushed."

When they were in sight of the soddy, Charlie ran, not thinking of being tired. The door was closed, but he rushed in and stood a moment, feeling a blast of heat from the range. "It's hot enough in here to bake a batch of cinnamon rolls!"

"Sshh!" said Ell. "Can't you see your wife has had a busy day and is asleep? She drank a quart of stinkweed tea."

"When will she wake up?" asked Charlie. "I want to ask her something."

"Maybe tomorrow morning. What do you want to ask her?"

"A baby? Do we have a baby?"

Ell could not hold back her mirth. "Look at Ma sitting in the rocker. She's holding her first grandson."

"Jeems! A boy. Let me see him." Charlie bent over the blanketed bundle in his mother's lap. The little red-faced thing waved its fists in the air nervously and opened its mouth and howled. "That's Floyd Leslie!" he cried, so excited he could hardly stand still. "Oh, Pa ought to see him. The newest Irwin cub."

"Go wash your hands and you can hold him," said Mary. "He's yours, you know." There were tears in her eyes.

That reminded Charlie of the real sadness, and he said, "Old Nick died this morning. I buried him on the knoll in front of the first cornfield."

"Birth and death are a pair," whispered Ell.

FIFTEEN

Summer Days

The railroad roundhouse at Goodland originally had ten stalls for engine repairs and was now adding more. This stone-and-brick structure was located three hundred yards north of the tracks and a little west of the Boulevard, not far from the frame depot, which was at the foot of Broadway and the Boulevard. Inside the depot was a beanery, or dining room specializing in baked beans and bean soup, that was constantly busy with road-house workers.

Mr. Henry H. Auer built a small, frame restaurant near the depot, hoping to take in some of the roundhouse business. He specialized in sandwiches and fast service. When his business did not flourish as he had anticipated, he decided to sell. The June 21 issue of the *Goodland News* stated, "The buyers took immediate possession, and while the invoice was going on, they 'set up' cider, lemonade, and cigars free to everybody that came in. After the invoice was completed they found that they did not have enough to settle and the trade was declared off, leaving Auer to foot the bill for the free entertainment."

Before June was over, screen doors were put up by most everyone in town to avoid the flies.

Joe put a screen door on the front of his soddy so that Mary could leave the front door open for air and keep out flies and other bugs.

Before she left, Ell suggested that the bedroom walls and ceilings be covered with gunnysacks, then with colored voile. "It would keep dirt and dust and bugs from sifting into beds and clothing."

"What'd happen when there's another tornado and the roof blew off?" asked Mary. "The voile would be ruined. On the other hand, if I had a beautifully decorated soddy it'd look like I was acting uppity. I can't do that. Flowers in my windowsill vases is decoration enough. And I can change that color with each season."

Etta was amazed at the fuss made over baby Floyd even after Ell went back to Colorado Springs. The baby was treated like a prince. The moment he cried, Mary picked him up. "I love having a baby in my house again," she said. She rocked the baby and let Etta do the baking and canning. After supper she sat in the same rocker and sewed a comforter or flannel gown for the baby. Etta's mother had had a baby almost every year and no one thought much about making a fuss.

Etta had not seen her folks since before she was married. A couple of times Mary suggested she and Charlie take the baby to the McGuckins. Etta made excuses.

During the Fourth of July celebration in Goodland, Charlie talked with Ray Lewis. McGuckin had a dog that ran afoul of a porcupine. "He needs a salve of permanganate of potash and lard to keep infection down," said Charlie.

"You and Etta take a jar out to him. I'll pay for it," said Ray.

Etta was nervous. She would have backed out in a second if Charlie had hinted at an excuse. She bathed the baby and dressed him in a flannel diaper, belly band, and flannel shirt. The day was warm. "At least all the kids will be glad to see us," said Etta with a sigh.

Mr. McGuckin said little the whole time. Mrs. McGuckin brought out gooseberry pie and coffee. She held Floyd so that Etta could eat. Etta said the coffee must have boiled all morning, it was that strong.

Mr. McGuckin said, "There ain't no strong coffee, there's only weak people." He looked at Charlie.

Charlie thought he was going to clout him about not having the baby baptized yet. He didn't.

Etta's brothers Curly and Walt sat next to Charlie. The flies came through holes in the screen door. The smaller children ran around with open hands or folded newspapers swatting and grabbing and yelling.

"Horses hate the flies, too," said Curly.

"Mix a concoction of equal parts pine tar and lard and smear it on the horses," said Charlie. "It's messy and smelly, so it keeps the horseflies, deerflies, mosquitoes, and gnats away."

"I'd put it on myself," said Walt, slapping at the flies settling on his bare arms.

Etta looked at the broken screen. "You have an old rag or some cotton lint?"

One of her little sisters brought out a pillowcase full of cotton scraps. Etta showed her how to make little wads and fill the holes in the screen. "Walt'll put pine tar on those little balls and no more pesky flies," said Etta.

"Do the Irwins do that?" asked the child, called Hannah.

"No, their screen is not broken," said Etta. Etta put her arms around the little girl and kissed her. "See if you can talk Ma and Pa into bringing you and the other kids for a visit. You'd like the Irwins."

"They're heathens and eat worms."

"That's not true! Who told you that?" Etta was steamed.

"Pa," whispered Hannah. "Don't get mad. I didn't believe him. I like Charlie. Your baby smells good."

Etta couldn't think of anything to say. She thought, one can count on Pa to plant an untrue idea. Despite herself, however, she was stirred by the feeling of her own mother's arms around her. Mrs. McGuckin said, under her breath, "Come back again."

Charlie held his breath, then bent and kissed Mrs. McGuckin's sallow cheek. "We'd be mighty pleased if you, Mr. McGuckin, and the kids would come to Sunday dinner—after service."

Etta was surprised, but pleased. "We could have a picnic in the meadow."

The children sang out, "Oh, let's go!"

Etta and Charlie looked at Mr. McGuckin, sitting at the kitchen table.

McGuckin looked with surprise at Charlie. "Me and my missus and the brood will think about coming to your place on Sunday. It'll be a chance to talk with your pa about your boldness, impudence, and how your manhood's distended your hide. If he's as wise as you say, he'll see that I judge from the strength of truth, even though I'm a weak man without my tonic."

Charlie sighed and stood, holding out his hand to shake

McGuckin's. He did not feel lighthearted, but he did not feel downcast. He thought, I'll tell Ma to fix thunder and lightning stewed down to a fine poison for McGuckin on Sunday.

Out in the yard Curly said, "Don't let Pa fool you. He's not weak from no tonic, he spent all yesterday putting his M brand on his yearling calves. He's worn out from that. Ma watches him with an eagle's eye so he can't touch spirits. It chafes him. Don't count on him and Ma coming to your place. Walt and me will be there. Count on it."

Etta relaxed when they stopped at Ray and Kate's place to let Jimmy hold baby Floyd. On the way home they stopped in town to get a newspaper for Joe and pick up mail from the post office. There was only a single letter to Mary from Joe's oldest sister, Elizabeth.

On the high-centered, twin-rutted road toward Sappa Meadows, Charlie pulled up on the reins and stopped the horse. "Look at all the columbines. Let's get some for Ma's window vases."

"That's why I love you," said Etta. "You're always thinking what others would like." She spread a blanket in the shade of the wagon box and carefully laid the sleeping baby on it. She took off her shoes and stockings and ran barefoot through the prairie grass colored with scarlet columbines, pink and white clover, and tall purple gentian.

Charlie tied the reins to the wagon's seat, dropped to the ground, and felt all the earlier tension drain away. He chased a scared rabbit and called to Etta, who was nearly hidden in the tall grass, "We're cavorting like fat ponies in high oats."

"Your running's a mighty miration, I mean gyration," teased Etta. "Look, here's a game trail by this little creek." She pointed to the shiny, fresh deer droppings and the many dry gray-green ones that had wintered under the snow.

Charlie put his arm around his wife and smelled the fresh soaplike odor of her hair and clothes. He held his breath and listened. A male grouse was drumming. It started slow and rapidly increased the tattoo, announcing that it had staked its claim to a piece of land. Charlie pointed so that Etta, too, saw it standing on a chalky stone, beating its powerful wings to cause the air to rush into a vacuum created by this beating. "Put, put, put, put-put-put-ut-ut-urrrr." The grouse vanished and Charlie sat on the chalk stone, took his boots off, and stretched his legs. He felt the warmth rise through his feet. The stone was in an area of white rock that was crisscrossed with ancient marine coral. It reflected the sun. Ahead was a dip in the terrain with a large bare place that would hold a quantity of rainwater, but was now flat and dry with a lacework of cracks. A redwinged blackbird balanced on the tip of a scrub willow growing in the middle of the tiny creek. It flashed scarlet and yellow epaulets and with a clear flutelike sound sang a short song.

Charlie took a deep breath and felt the tingling sensation flow from the pit of his stomach to all parts of his body. He half-closed his eyes in order to sharpen his view of the gentle rolling hills of deep green, blue, and wine surrounding him, and above, the clear blue of the sky. The sun seemed to focus on this spot, on him. It was his place. This earth was a part of him. He again squinted his eyes. He could see the line of trees that grew along the Middle Fork of Sappa Creek. To the left he saw the Irwin soddy tucked up against another rise of land. He looked in the direction of Goodland and only imagined he could see its buildings lined along a wide road. To the right, which was southwest, the land seemed completely flat, only the grass waving under the push of the wind and the patient horse munching the rich grass at its feet and the baby content to sleep in the wagon's shade after being bounced from one relative to another. To the west there was a gathering haze between the blue and green. This grayness seemed to mesh both sky and land so that neither was distinguishable. It made Charlie wonder what was beyond.

Without a clear break in his musings he was aware of the wind whipping Etta's blue cotton skirt and lifting her hair in little peaks. She, too, was looking, her hand on her forehead, shading her eyes. Again he was acutely aware of the smell of fresh laundry soap still minutely entangled in her clothes, and like hearing the various instruments in full orchestra, he also smelled the sweet coumarin from the bruised wild dropseed grass as he crushed it with bare feet, the bitter scent of daisies, and the sweet nectar of the clover. These blended in a huge satisfying fullness. He sat down, pulling Etta with him, and watched a bee moving from one flower to another. He moved his hands over the grasses, uncovering little bugs, grasshoppers, ants, and mites, busy with daily chores, living there next to his earth. Charlie was filled with gladness that he was here at this moment on this dynamic land. "My dear, I love you," said Charlie, lying back with Etta across his chest.

"I shall always love you," Etta said, kissing him full on the mouth. She thought, when there is love, one puts all else aside—

parents, brothers and sisters, children. After that one doesn't think at all, but uses the senses. One feels, smells, listens, tastes, and looks. Love is a banquet. Love is rapture, ecstasy, intoxication, an orgy. She felt Charlie's hands on her, heating her flesh with fire. She smelled his smoky perspiration, the dry alkaline chalk rock and spicy crushed grass. She heard his quick breathing and the beating of his powerful heart. She tasted the saltiness of his skin. She saw his beautiful brown shoulders and chest with the curling brown hairs. Her eyes closed. Love is a gorge with steep heights blocking out everything but the narrow pass. She was as eager as he. She forgot everything except the complete enjoyment of the shared sensual pleasure.

When she opened her eyes, the tall grasses and the red and yellow columbines swayed against the deep-blue sky.

Charlie buttoned his trousers and helped Etta straighten her clothes. His eyes sparkled. "What would your pa say to that!"

Etta giggled and it sounded like water gurgling over a rock wall.

"I think he would be envious. Oh, oh, I hear what our baby is saying." Etta flew back to the quilt. Floyd waved arms and legs and cried with sucking sounds. "He's hungry." She curled her feet under her and sat with a straight back to nurse her child. Her breasts were swollen and already sticky with milk as a result of the lovemaking.

Charlie had nearly forgotten about the letter posted from Atchison, Kansas, for his mother. He went out to the empty wagon for it. When he came back, Etta whispered, "Where's the columbine?" They both laughed at the private joke.

When Charlie handed the letter to his mother, he sobered. The handwriting was small and pinched. He had a feeling this day was suddenly coming to an end.

Mary went to the coal-oil lamp to see better. "Wonder why your sister wrote to me?" she asked Joe. "You suppose she's coming for a visit?"

"Why now?" said Joe, putting down his newspaper.

Mary finished reading the letter and came back to her rocking chair. Her voice was flat with no emotion. "My ma and pa are gone. Ma last year and Pa this."

Joe moved his chair next to her.

"Your sister, Elizabeth, she's the one wrote this letter to me. The boys buried Ma in the yard under that big old shagbark hickory—not in the town cemetery like Old Charles and Malinda. She went to a church supper and ate some homemade sausage."

"What about Riley?" asked Joe.

"He was chopping wood in the heat and just sat down to rest, and when he keeled over no one could get him going again. I can't believe they're gone."

"Was he put in beside Rachel?"

"Yes, under the shagbark." Mary wiped her eyes with her handkerchief.

"I can see it now," said Joe. "That was the place Rachel and Riley liked to sit in summer and sip cold tea. Remember that?"

"Yes," said Mary. "Laura, my oldest sister, and her husband are going to move back there. My two brothers are still on the farm with their families. That's a big place. Always has been. There's at least three hundred acres, maybe more now, if the boys have started homesteading the adjacent land. They ought to."

"I suppose your brothers have a pretty big herd of cattle by now—they were always good at luring in strays and fixing their brand on 'em. A man hears stories about his in-laws."

"Joe, they're your in-laws," she said sharply.

"Out-laws," he corrected. "Your brothers, leastways."

Mary sat back, thinking of the farm and of Chillicothe, the fields, the cattle, the dusty roads, the heat of summer, the ice-cold of winter. Her ma and her pa were gone. She could see the barns, henhouse, haycocks, meadowlarks, sleds on the snow-slick hills.

Charlie, Will, and Frank were quiet with their own memories of their grandmother and grandfather Brassfield. It would be summer in Chillicothe. The bittersweet would be twining up the trees, the sunny places would be brilliant with orange trumpet weed, and there'd be nettles and beggar's-lice. Charlie could hear his grandmother Rachel's voice calling for him to wipe the dust off his feet and to put his rope away before he caught one of her setting hens with it. He thought, soon's Floyd is old enough I'll show him how to use a rope. He went outside to the barn, found his old rope, and began to twirl it. He was pleased at what he could still do. Ought to do more of this every day, he thought. Then he heard his mother and father talking outside. His father said, "Would you like to go back again?"

"Yes," said his mother quickly, then, "No—Joe, I'm not sure."

Charlie went to the barn door and saw them sitting up on the wagon's seat. His mother had her hands in her lap and her shoulders drooped.

His father was looking out over the prairie. "You could go to visit your sisters and two brothers," he said. "You could take the stage to the Kansas Pacific Railroad Station at Oakley. With what I got from blacksmithing, there'd be nothing to stop you."

What he got blacksmithing was chickens and hogs, potatoes and canned goods, thought Charlie.

"Do you think they'd be glad to see me? Maybe I could take Etta and Floyd with me. I could show off my grandson."

Charlie's father pulled his arm off the back of the seat and turned slightly so that he could see Mary's face. "Truthfully, I'd like to see you right here. Mary, dear, it wasn't either of your brothers nor any of your sisters who wrote to you. Any one of them could have, last year and this year."

The sun was low in the sky. Charlie shivered. His mother did not look at his father. She said, "Maybe they didn't know where to send a letter. Maybe they were too busy getting everything straightened out—afterward."

"And maybe they was too busy arguing about who was to get what and if they didn't have to figure you in—well, there'd be more for them. I like it here, without no one asking me to lend them money they never intend to pay back. Without no one to know about my horsethieving and cattle rustling brothers-in-law, and laughing behind my back when I pretend I don't know what they're talking about. But if it would ease your mind and make you feel better, I ain't the one to tell you to stay here. I'll take you and Etta and Floyd to the train in town tomorrow."

Charlie took a deep breath. He never knew all this. When he was smaller, life was much simpler. He began to appreciate what his mother and father were feeling. Then he thought, I'd never really appreciate this if I weren't married. Etta makes all the difference. Etta going to Chillicothe? Is this true?

"Well, yes," said his mother, "that's right. I'll think on it."

They went back into the house. Charlie hung up his rope and went in to take care of Floyd while Etta and his mother prepared supper. No one said a word about Chillicothe.

Joe stayed far over on his side of the bed and Mary was far over on her side. She could not sleep. She knew that as a child she'd loved her parents. As she grew older her ma's shrill voice and her pa's sticky fingers when it came to cattle always irritated her. Riley's attitude had always been, easy come, easy go, and his sons lived just this side of the law. Their rule was, never get caught red-handed. Well, they'd never had any big scrapes with the law. So maybe they were all right now. They'd certainly be glad to see her and baby Floyd. They'd be surprised, too. She'd like to see a proper kind of town with boardwalks up and down all the streets for a change and real frame houses. "I could visit my old friends and talk to women who have wallpaper on their walls, instead of newspaper or gunny material covering dirt. I could talk about furniture and curtains and they wouldn't think I was trying to be snobbish."

Joe said, "Is that really so important, my dear?"

"Yes, sometimes it is."

Joe got up and pushed aside the bedroom curtain and went out the front door.

Mary could feel the west wind coming inside the soddy and hoped that Joe would close the door when he came back. Her head ached, her legs ached, her ankles were puffy, and she felt miserable.

He shut the door when he came in. "Think I'll dig potatoes tomorrow. Charlie and the boys can begin to pick the corn. You know, I'm thinking of letting Charlie run the farm and divide up proceeds between the Irwin men." In the back of his mind he was thinking Charlie might add another quarter section or two until eventually they had a whole section of land. This pleased Joe. "Charlie's a married man now and he can take the added responsibility."

"Charlie's always taken on more responsibility," said Mary.

"Yup, with only five years of real school, he knows more than most grown men I've met. He's good at figures and at sizing up a good horse as well as men." Then a burr caught in Joe's throat. Will might be furious with Charlie in charge. Then maybe not. Will had never shown any inclination to being tied to a farm. It wasn't that he was scared of work; he'd do his share if motivated; if not he'd lie down beside the biggest kind of job and go to sleep. Frank was not good with figures. He knew horses and that was about all. Frank did not understand men and business, he was too easily swayed. He had no convictions that were his own. He believed what anyone told him. "I'm sure glad Charlie's bride is that slip of a girl called Etta. She brings a lot of cheer and good sense to this place."

Mary rolled over and smoothed out the quilts. "Etta and I are going to can the beans from the garden tomorrow. We should have done it day before yesterday. We'll snip some marigolds for the window vases."

Joe sat up on the edge of the bed hardly breathing, afraid to move or to speak.

"You see, if you don't stand in the way of my going back," said Mary, looking down the quilts to where her feet made tiny mounds, "I'd rather stay here more than anything."

Etta's brothers, Curly and Walt, came in time for the Sunday dinner. Their hair was coated with fine dust the wagon wheels had kicked up. Walt coaxed a dog out of the wagon. The dog's legs were thin as telegraph wire.

Charlie was out in the yard in a moment, shaking hands with the McGuckin boys, a pleased smile across his face. "Come in. We're all at the table."

"First," said Walt, "we'd like to give you and Ettie a late wedding present, this here greyhound dog."

Charlie stared. He could not believe that they'd bring him such a gift. "Is it good for herding cows or for chasing deer out of the corn?" He patted the greyhound on the small head and scratched behind its ears, then persuaded it to lie in the shade of a currant bush.

"We thought we owed you something," said Curly. "You know we never stayed around to give you and Ettie a shivaree, and before we could think of anything you up and had a baby."

"What he's saying is that we went to Abilene to buy cattle for Pa," said Walt.

Charlie grinned. "You bought a dog in Abilene?" His grin grew wider.

"It's a racing dog!" whooped Curly. "It's the latest sport! We made some money in Abilene betting on dog races. We remembered the rumor that Goodland's going to sponsor a coursing club!"

"This lean-looking hound has such a small face it looks like a dime's worth of dog meat," Charlie scoffed.

Etta came out and examined the funny-looking dog. "You boys have the dumbest idea of what wedding presents are all about. I swan!"

"This is serious," said Curly. "Tait's going to print something in the paper about Goodland being host for dog races. Charlie, you train your dog and we'll take bets on him!"

"I never heard any rumors, but I'll read the papers more

closely. Thanks for the doggonest present I ever got," Charlie said, and held his sides laughing. "You boys going to help the critter?"

"Dog's yours now," said Curly, brushing the dust out of his hair.

Everybody went inside to eat. The greyhound sniffed at the tether Charlie had put around its neck and tied to the base of the prickery currant bush. The dog was white with black ears and huge black spots on its back, which looked as if somebody had spilled pine tar on it. After dinner Mary went out to see the new dog. "Let Joe see it. He knows something that'll help its legs." She picked up a front paw and the dog pulled it back. When she pulled the hind legs out the legs twitched and the dog growled.

"Get a bucket of hot water and some washing soda. Make a solution to dip the legs in," said Joe, sitting beside the dog. He estimated it weighed about seventy pounds. He said it wasn't skinny, it was built that way, slim, streamlined. He pointed out that its head was narrow and its ears thrown back and folded, its chest was deep. The hind thighs were wide and muscular.

"You can call it Lightning," suggested Walt.

The dog was quiet. Its head was between its paws. Its eyes were closed, but its ears twitched once in a while.

Walt explained. "You should have seen us coming out of Abilene. We were riding horseback ahead of it and it chased us. Of course, way back, there was some rubes chasing it and hollering, 'Come back Alex!' That *was* its name, Alexander. But that dog had no intention of going back. It wanted to be with us."

Etta gasped and said, "Sounds suspicious. You swipe that dog?"

"Aw, Ettie," said Curly, his eyes twinkling and his voice syrupy, "you don't have to say that. Every man looks out for hisself. If an opportunity arises he steps in and makes the best of the situation."

"Amen!" said Will, looking over the dog.

"We all have standards," said Frank, hunkering down to pet the dog.

"Honestly, how'd you get this dog?" Etta made her voice stern.

Walt pursed his lips and looked heavenward. "We already said. Haven't you heard, never look a gift dog in the mouth?" He held his finger up so Etta wouldn't butt in. "We're glad you married Charlie. He isn't asking a lot of questions about your gift. This breed of dog is royalty. Curly and me heard that the ancient Egyptians were partial to this breed. Henry the Eighth had all his noblemen rear and train greyhounds."

"Doesn't look gray to me," said Charlie.

Walt smiled and continued, "To get a greyhound to run you have to get it to chase a rabbit or something that moves. The eyes are sharp but the nose is dead. It can't smell."

"It's skinny as a lightning bolt," said Charlie.

"Has good muscles. Notice how its hocks are well back? Gives it leverage for running," said Joe.

"I know that," said Curly. "Never feed it raw catfish. There's flukes in fish."

"I can feed this here dog. You watch." Joe went back inside, slamming the screen.

Charlie nudged Lightning to its feet and dipped each leg into a bucket of warm washing-soda solution. "Guess I do this three, four times a day for a while. Then I'll start walking it around the yard. If it does all right I'll start some runs."

"Like I said, rabbit chases are best," said Walt.

Joe brought out a tin plate with several beef marrow bones and a liberal spooning of gravy from the dinner biscuits. Lightning's tail came up and moved in a semicircle. Its dark eyes were bright and expectant. The women went inside to wash the dishes. Charlie chewed on a timothy stem and watched Lightning eye the dish for several seconds before licking one of the bones. Then it took a bone in its mouth and slowly moved it to the shade of the house. When it finished cracking the bone, it rested its head between its front paws, licked its lips, yawned, and closed its eyes.

"Honestly, Lightning doesn't look like much of a racer to me," said Charlie.

At the end of two weeks' care Lightning's legs were healed. Each morning, at dawn, Charlie and Etta ran the dog. Then it was given a mix of boiled squirrel and gravy. One morning Charlie suggested taking Lightning out to the meadow, where rabbits burrowed under grass. With much keener vision than smell, Lightning flushed out a rabbit within minutes. It ran until the rabbit was far ahead, then it cut across to intercept it. Etta was so astonished and pleased at this showing of great intellect. She skinned the rabbit the dog brought back, stewed it, and served it to the dog that afternoon.

* * *

Early in August, 1895, Tait had a two-column article in the *Dark Horse* about the Goodland Coursing Club, which was following the rules and constitution of the American Coursing Club. So far there were ten local members.

Charlie went to town and had a talk with the club's president, Bill Walker, who owned a black greyhound named Amorita. Charlie joined the club and was told that Goodland was to be the national meeting place of the famous Kenmore Coursing Club. "People from several states will be here in mid-October," said Walker, scratching his blunt nose. "Rules will be printed in all the papers. The race will be held eight miles southeast of town. The sheriff and two deputies will control the crowds."

News of the large amount of winnings to be given away was in all the local papers and even in Denver and St. Louis papers. Many out-of-towners came to Goodland that fall to see or participate in the dog races. The first race began on the seventeenth of October. The crowd formed the shape of a crescent and moved ahead when signaled by a racing marshal. At the center of the crescent a man on foot, called the slipper, led the two dogs that raced first. Rhea, the white greyhound, belonged to Frank Robinson, and Sherman was John Jordan's dog.

Rhea and Sherman were fastened together with a spring collar. Charlie stood to one side, with Lightning on a leash, with the other men who had dogs that would race this first day. A man let a rabbit out of a wire cage. The rabbit jumped into the track where the short grass made it easy to run. The crowd stood still. Not a word was spoken. No one wanted to frighten the rabbit off the track into the weeds. As soon as the rabbit was eighty to a hundred yards away, in a straight line with the dogs, the leashes were slipped from the spring collar. The dogs were free to run.

Charlie held tight to Lightning until it was his turn. No one but the judge and the dogs' owners were allowed to follow the pair of racing dogs up the track. At the end of the course was a finish line drawn deep in the dirt. The rabbit was then forced to run into the tall grass where the dogs could not see its movement. Then the dogs slowed and stopped. Rhea had won. The next pair of dogs were put in the slip and the crowd moved forward again watching for a rabbit to be let loose, run the course then hop into the trampled tall grass.

Once in a while a dog caught a rabbit. A good race dog would not bite the quarry, but would hold it gently and on command from its owner let the rabbit go. The next day the winners of the previous day's races were put on the program and run off in the same manner. By doing this the card was reduced until only two dogs remained. They raced to decide the first- and second-place winners. When Lightning won the first day Charlie felt on top of the world. "We need posters on the telegraph poles about dog racing," he said to Etta. "Our dog has as much chance to be a final winner as any. I want everyone to come to see Lightning."

But the second day Charlie was concerned about Lightning. The dog's legs were holding up, but its muscles twitched. It was getting tired. Rabbits were getting scarce. The ones that did hop onto the course were fast. Excitement ran high making the dogs nervous.

Some men with racing hounds had come in from Denver by train. These men were friends of a man who brought some fresh rabbits in wire cages from Colorado Springs. The men from Denver had four dogs that they wanted to enter in the races.

Judge Mulcaster had to make a quick decision. He didn't want a fight to break out, so he told the Denver men that the first race would be between two of their dogs, followed by a second race between their other two dogs. The two winners would be allowed to run against the winners of the previous day's race.

Before the fourth race Van Hummell, a doctor from Kansas City, told Charlie he was going to check on his dogs and the men handling them. Charlie nodded, but was so interested in the race he didn't see him leave. Van Hummell's dogs were tied with others to a poplar tree waiting their turn. Van Hummell petted his dogs. They all lay quietly, almost asleep, at the base of the tree.

One of the Denver men carried a paper bag smelling like decaying melon rinds. Van Hummell wrinkled his nose and thought it was trash from some picnic. But when the Denver man came back in front of the tree the bag appeared empty. He nodded to Van Hummell and went back into the crowd.

Van Hummell stepped around the tree and saw scattered garbage and an empty trash can overturned. In the middle of the damp, moldy mess were melon rinds mixed with scraps of bacon. The dogs were gorging themselves. Van Hummell called to his handlers. "None of this mess, not even the trash can, was here ten minutes ago. I swear it," said one of the handlers.

Van Hummell was so indignant he told both his handlers to find their own rail fare home. With his dogs on leashes trotting behind him, he looked for owners of the remaining dogs.

Charlie untied Lightning, who licked at the bacon rinds. The dog's eyes were half closed as if it wanted to sleep in the shade. Van Hummell told Charlie what he suspected. "It's not proof, but it's mighty suspicious. Those Denver men want our dogs out of the race." Then he went to the judges with his complaint. Charlie followed, pulling Lightning after him. "Those men ought to be disbarred. They came late anyway," he said.

"Only if you can prove conclusively they fed garbage to your dog," said Mulcaster. "It's possible you didn't notice the trash can by the tree when you tied your dog."

"Darn tootin' I didn't!" exploded Charlie. "It was brought in about fifteen minutes ago!"

"Did you see it brought in?" asked Mulcaster with raised eyebrows.

All day the decisions of the judges were a disappointment to Charlie. A fast St. Louis dog, called Chloe, was out of the races early because it remained standing a few seconds before directly pursuing the rabbit. It was given no points. In the third race Walker's dog, Amorita, was defeated by a dog from Cripple Creek because of poor slips by Ralph Taylor of Denver. Likewise, Lightning failed to win because of poor slips, despite the fact that the hound held the rabbit in its teeth and bent it in a right angle for the kill, which was worth at least two points in anybody's book. Two cowdogs from Colorado Springs won over local greyhounds of championship form.

Van Hummell suggested Goodland not invite the Kenmore Club for a national meeting again. Lightning seemed to hold his head down and it limped. Deep down Charlie knew the dog's legs were weak. Lightning never would be a winner.

Charlie noticed a group of men talking. He recognized one of the Denver men. He meandered over beside the group. Lightning stayed close to his side. "You Denver boys put on a mighty fine race," he said. "I congratulate you."

"Thanks," said the man he'd recognized. "Looks like Colorado's cowdogs won over some of your locals." He pointed a sharp fingernail at Lightning. "It looks like a champion—but fate had her way, so it's a loser." The man smiled a sickly grin.

"You boys sure know how to make winners. Thanks for coming to Goodland," said Charlie.

"Maybe the race will be in Denver next year. We'll tie your dog's ears together again," he said, and laughed. "We'll outrun any dog from this rainmaking burgh."

The innuendo about Goodland's rainmaking efforts several years ago was not lost on Charlie. The man was bad-mouthing Goodland. Charlie gritted his teeth and tried to keep his mind on what he'd come to do. "You boys can understand my predicament. I've lost some money. That is, Lightning, my hound and I, are flat broke after entering a few of these races. Entrance fees, you know."

Someone said snidely, "You don't look like you're starving."

Charlie felt like lashing out. He bit his tongue. "I have a young wife. She doesn't understand gambling and racing."

"Let her grow up," said another with a snicker.

"You're right, my friend," said Charlie. "Look at that hound. She loves that dog. She used to get up before daylight and bathe its feet. Then bathe them two, three times during the day. She still walks it regularly. When it had ticks she put hot wax on them and pulled them off. She fed it balls of butter and bicarb of soda for a sour stomach. Can you believe this? She thought it was constipated and gave it an enema of soap and water."

"After that it ran good?" asked the Denver man with a wink.

"It's a winner!" said Charlie with a straight face. "My wife calls it a treasure. It was a wedding gift from her brothers. Those fellows paid a lot for it. It was a thoroughbred and a champion in the East."

Someone slapped Charlie on the back as if to say, the dog must be worth something. "You got papers on your hound?"

"Not me," said Charlie. "But maybe my brothers-in-law do. Who knows? They were secretive to me about how valuable that dog is—I think they told my wife everything. You boys married? Well, you know how it is with in-laws—no trust."

The man nodded, understanding perfectly.

"Have a drink, pal. Make you feel better." One of the men took a half-full flask from his hip pocket.

Charlie turned it down and passed it along to the man next to him. The sky clouded over and the day darkened. Lightning lay at Charlie's feet. "Thrashers ask a high price nowadays," complained Charlie, keeping his voice low and mournful. "A dollar a day and you have to watch them all the time."

"You a farmer?" one of the men asked.

"You're right, again. But it's not all sunshine and roses. I can tell you. There are crooks. Like those thrashers," said Charlie. "Oh, I should hold my tongue among friends."

"Oh—well, we all understand." The bottle was emptied and another came from somewhere and made the rounds. Charlie simply passed it on to the man next to him. By now the line of dark clouds was almost overheard. He moved his feet and acted as if he were getting ready to leave. He bent to pet Lightning.

"Don't go, not just yet. Say, how would you like to sell me your dog?" This was the man from Denver. He was called Jack and his black hair was oily, as if he'd put grease on it that morning.

"Well—I never thought of selling," said Charlie, acting surprised. "It would be hard to go home without the hound. The wife, you know." He laughed nervously.

"But if you're broke, you could use some money. I'm thinking of offering you fifty dollars for that sleepy-looking hound." The man rubbed Lightning's ears.

Lightning stiffened, laid its ears back, and growled low in its throat. "Hush!" Charlie's voice was deep and curt. The dog became quiet and relaxed. Charlie noted that the man saw how well it obeyed. "I would never give it away for that! I'm sure it cost more, much more when it was purchased with papers and all."

The sky looked like rain. A strong breeze came up. Lightning had its nose in the direction of the wind.

Jack balanced on his toes, then back down on his heels for a few minutes as if in deep thought. "If I offer something like seventy-five dollars, would you respond to that?"

Charlie stood a moment, rubbing his upper lip with forefinger and thumb. He could feel the stubble of his whiskers beginning. His voice was unhurried, "Nope. I couldn't. Not at that price. This here is a genuine thoroughbred. It's worth twice as much, if not more. Guess I'd better be going before I get caught in a downpour."

Jack pulled the brim of his felt hat low over his face as the first few drops of rain hit the dust. "I'll give you a hundred and fifty smackers for that hound and not a cent more, thoroughbred or no."

Charlie got a tingling feeling in his chest and the top of his mouth started to go dry. "There were two days of entry fees that were taken from my pocket. Twenty dollars each day."

"Yes, I can understand how you'd feel losing that." Annoyed, Jack reached deep into his pants' pocket. "Twenty and another twenty—" Then he counted out one hundred and fifty dollars and held them out toward Charlie's face. The money smelled like tobacco.

Charlie blinked once, slowly raised his hand, and at the same time held out Lightning's lead rope. "You've got yourself the best greyhound in Sherman County, Jack. Good luck in Denver." Charlie scratched Lightning behind the ears and patted its head. "So long."

Jack smiled and looked pleased.

Charlie felt like he was going to burst. He kept his face forward and his head up. He felt the splatters of rain. It was about ten minutes before he got into the wagon.

"I think you'd better get this old buckboard home before we are all wet as frogs in swamp water," said Charlie.

Frank asked, "Where's Lightning? What's the matter, Charlie? Are you crying or is it the rain?"

"I don't know if I'm laughing or crying," admitted Charlie, "but I sold that hound to one of those Denver fellows. I hope it was the fellow who dumped garbage and threw the race. I cleaned him for a hundred and ninety dollars!"

The wagon moved. Charlie sat back, closed his eyes. His whole face relaxed.

"Wow! One hundred and ninety bucks! I heard that Denver crowd was tough as whang leather," said Will, handling the horses. "How'd you do it?"

"I don't really know. Kept my temper. Let the guy talk. I pretended I was Colonel Johnson, then Dr. Melbourne. Honest!"

"You can buy an honest-to-God thoroughbred greyhound," said Frank.

"Not on your life!" said Charlie. "I'm finished with dogs. I'm going to get Ma a new oilcloth for the kitchen table and Pa some of those new rust-resistant corn seeds. The rest I'm saving."

"You could divide the rest with your brothers. We could have a whale of a good time," said Will.

"The rest is for Etta." Charlie watched the jagged streaks of lightning. "Let's move! Someone up there's fixin' to pull the cork!"

SIXTEEN

Colorado Springs, Colorado

Will was restless that fall. He made several trips to the little farming town of Ruleton, west of Goodland. Twice he took Frank on the pretext of checking out some Herefords that were for sale. They came home with hangovers instead of Herefords.

It was a cold, pale October morning when Will and Charlie went out to clean the barn. The lush prairie grass lay dry and yellow underfoot. Above, the weak, icy-white sun displayed a white ring. Charlie took the shovel and scooped a black pile of manure out the door. Will scraped manure and hay from the floor into a pile with a hoe.

A gloomy day for a lowly chore, thought Charlie. The barn and soddy seemed pitifully shabby. The wind gusts blew little spirals of dust around the barn door and rattled the faded weed stalks on the roof of sod.

"Wouldn't you be smart to look somewhere besides Ruleton for those Herefords you have your heart set on?" asked Charlie.

Will looked up from his mucking hoe. His eyes, fixed on something outside the barn door, were quiescent.

"What's the matter?" scowled Charlie. "You run out of money?"

Will closed his eyes, drew a weary breath, then opened them.

"No, it's not money, nor cows that's on my mind. It's a girl."

Charlie's leather glove slipped on the shovel handle. "Jeems! What's so unusual about that? You've had girls on your mind for years, lots of girls."

"That's just it, lots of them. Remember that dance Frank and I went to in Ruleton? I wasn't in Ruleton for a dance. I wanted to find Plucky. She's gone—moved—disappeared."

Charlie shifted first one foot then the other. "You want to tell me about the dance?"

Will settled on an old wooden crate. The hoe rested against his knee. He pulled off his gloves and rolled a cigarette, put it in his mouth, struck a match on his thumbnail, and inhaled deeply. He picked a speck of tobacco off his tongue. "Charlie, I'm going to tell you something. I want you to keep it under your hat."

The blue smoke hit Charlie's face. He liked the aroma, but his eyes watered, so he moved to see Will better. "You in some kind of trouble?" He felt his stomach tighten and anger rise in his throat.

"Not yet."

Charlie saw red. "Not yet? Sounds like trouble around the corner! There's enough trouble keeping this farm solvent without you bringing more problems. You know how Ma and Pa have their heart and soul tied up in this seedy place. They believed it would make them free. But look at them! They're slaves to this land! You bring in your problems and you tie them tighter to the land."

Will stared straight ahead through the gray daylight. "I thought you loved this land."

"I do. But I know what capricious weather does. I'm thinking of keeping a record on rainfall, frost, snow, sun, temperature. Maybe that will give us some reason for planting certain crops at certain times. It's irony that Pa was the one who told me knowledge is freedom."

Will looked exasperated. "What I have to say is not related to irony or to some figures you want to keep in a ledger. Maybe I won't tell you. I'll work it out myself."

Charlie leaned forward. "Start at the beginning."

"I will, but don't interrupt with some fool remark that has no bearing on the subject." He stepped on his cigarette and pushed it with his boot against a pile of manure. Charlie nodded, wishing Will would get on with his story. Will was old enough to take his own responsibility, to be master of his own actions.

"I always wondered if I'd ever get involved with a female. I only took Sam Oldum's sister to the dance because Frank had set it up."

Charlie squatted down on his haunches and leaned against the door frame. He closed his eyes and hoped Will wouldn't take too long to tell about his female problems. Charlie thanked the Almighty God he was married.

"Sam Oldum's sister was pretty and nice enough, but there was this other girl, Arnold Rick's sister, who attracted me. I admit I had a couple drinks before the dance, but only to bolster my depressed state. This Margaret Rick is like Etta. She's blond and easily riled. Small, agile, blue eyes, and giggly."

Charlie was thinking of Etta's sweet smile and her gay chatter that was like the tinkling of a silver bell.

"After the dance I persuaded Arnold Rick to take Sam Oldum's sister home and I took his sister home. Her folks are plain homesteaders like ours. The drought and cold winter nearly wiped them out, same as us. I got to talking with her pa and one thing led to another. Remember the first time Frank and I went to Colorado Springs to see Ell and Les? Margaret went with us to have her earache cured." He rolled another cigarette.

"This girl, Margaret? She went where?" Charlie asked.

"To Ell's place. She was wide-eyed, like a kid, when she saw the mountains and the pines."

"Frank was with you?"

"Yes."

"What did he think about taking some girl to Ell's?"

"Well, he knew we were taking her so that Ell could cure the earache, so he didn't say much."

"And Ell, what did she think?"

"She liked Margaret right away," he lied. "It was her idea that we get married."

"Married!" Charlie jumped and the shovel clattered to his feet.

"Ell said I could be in a lot of trouble. Margaret is fifteen." Will gave him a look so full of meaning that he froze.

"Ell signed the marriage certificate. Margaret's Ma can sign underneath if she wants."

Charlie's knees thawed to water. "Her folks don't know? You've been married since July? Why didn't you bring her here? Earache? What about an earache?" Charlie became so wound up that his questions ran faster than a nickel-plated wristwatch.

"Margaret had an earache. Nothing cured it. So I told her pa about this famous herb doctor I knew in Colorado." Will smiled wanly.

"Why would her pa let you and Frank take her anywhere? He didn't know you that well."

Will looked embarrassed. "Mr. Rick thought Frank and I were rich ranchers. That man is too dumb to roll rocks down a steep hill. I doubt he can write his name. He and his wife were honored to have Frank and me take their ailing daughter on the train, at our own expense, to have a noted herb woman treat her."

Charlie was livid. This was his older brother; eight years older. "I can't believe you!" Charlie raised his hands and let them drop at his sides.

Will was contrite. "We took care of that girl. When we brought her home her earache was cured."

"If she's pregnant, the secret won't be kept long."

"Oh, you think you know everything." Will got up and stood opposite Charlie against the door frame. "That's the sour note." Then he brightened. "Ell's tea cured her earache. I could take her to Colorado on the pretext of a further examination. Ell certainly has something for pregnancy. Hasn't she?" He glowed, believing he'd solved the problem. "I'll use coitus interruptus until Ell fixes Margaret up with something, just in case. It will work out. There's no big problem. Thanks, Charlie, talking to you helped a lot. See, I know some things Pa never told me."

"Don't thank me yet. Your problem is still there, multiplying. You have a wife and I am led to believe you've *known* her more than once."

"Charlie, say it! I've fucked her. And it was good every time."

Wind roared between the barn and the soddy, and dirty gray clouds rolled across the halfhearted sun. Snow swirled through the open door like confetti.

Charlie put his big hand on Will's arm. His voice was grave. "Don't make this worse by being an ignoramus. You go after her now! You talk to her ma and pa. Tell them how much you care for their lovely daughter and what a good husband you'll be. Stay near the truth."

"I can't. They think I'm a rich rancher. How can I tell them I live with my folks? I'll be the laughingstock of the whole Rick family."

Charlie saw defeat in Will's stare.

"When Margaret is here with us, Ma, Pa, Etta, baby Floyd,

Frank, and you, she'll know you're all right. She'll forget about money rich and feel love rich."

"I don't know."

"You won't know until you try—run the experiment. Go get Margaret and bring her home. You want me to go with you?"

Will shook his head and began to finish the mucking job. "I've thought of something else. There's not one smithery that Frank and I could find in Colorado Springs. You know how Ma wants the family together? Well, I could open up a blacksmith shop in Colorado Springs, and if it's a success you could bring everyone there." Will smiled at Charlie's stern face.

"Let's work out one thing at a time. First on the list is this barn," said Charlie. "Second on the list is your wife."

The raw wind pushed leaden clouds across the stale October sky. The ground was white. The cottonwood trees at the creek's bank were bare. Their leaves were buried under the snow. Their sap was cut off at the roots.

Charlie stood at the window breathing the warm stagnant air of the soddy, wishing he could fling open the door and find the prairie green and fertile and the air sweet with the aromatic smell of blossoms. To see Will bring his wife home on horseback, bundled in a blanket so that only her eyes and nose showed, was a shame. He felt hot tears in his eyes for the girl his brother had so scurrilously taken in and wedded. At the far end of the road, where it met the sky, he saw the riders thump heels against the horse's ribs and the horse trot faster. Charlie grabbed the door and ducked outside. He waved both arms and whistled between his teeth. Will gave one long, shrill whistle back. Charlie hurried inside.

"Etta! Ma and Pa! They're here! Will and his bride!"

Etta was first to greet them. Will jumped off the horse and pulled the willowy girl off as though she were as light as a cornhusk doll in a blanket. He pushed back his hat and said, "This used to be Margaret Rick, but now she's Mrs. William Irwin."

Margaret's face turned red as she folded the blanket and handed it to Etta. Her deep-blue eyes were veiled in apprehension and her hands trembled. Long blond hair flowed around her shoulders.

Etta put her arms around Margaret. "Welcome to the Irwin clan. We are glad Will brought you home."

"I thought this was a big cattle spread," said Margaret. "I had no idea it was only a soddy." There were tears of disappointment in her eyes.

"Well, one day we'll have an Irwin ranch," said Etta brightly. "Come, I'll show you around. You want to wash?"

She was introduced and Etta took her to the bedroom.

Mary looked at Will. "Son, she's a baby. You brought home a baby bride. Be gentle. It's a wonder her ma let her go. What's happening to boys and girls these days? They're grown before their time."

"Ma, her folks know you'll take care of her. I told them how you fuss over us."

Mary glowed with his flattery, but she wasn't fooled. "I only fuss over babies. Didn't Frank come home with you?"

"Yes, but when we got to the branch in the road, he didn't turn toward the soddy. I bet my last dollar he went to tell some of the boys to hold a shivaree tonight," said Will.

She got to her feet unsteadily and shuffled to the kitchen shelves. "I'll be making coffee cakes."

Margaret came out with her long ecru-colored hair in pigtails and a comforter wrapped around the long nightdress Etta had put on her to keep her warm. She sat in Will's lap like a sleepy child.

"You like sugar in hot tea, honeybun?"

She snuggled against Will's chest and nodded yes to his question. Her dark eyes had blue shadows around them so they looked even larger.

Etta put water in the teakettle and wood in the fire box. She got raisins off the shelf for Mary.

Charlie thought, Margaret looks like she's going to suck her thumb. Baby Floyd cried. He excused himself and went to change the baby and bring him out for Margaret to see. "Guess you want supper, huh?" He fed Floyd bits of biscuit left over from the noon meal. The boy reached his chubby hand for more, at the same time Margaret took a whole biscuit for herself.

Charlie and Etta put Will and Margaret in their room. They piled quilts on the kitchen floor near the range for themselves.

"How many nights'll we sleep here?" groused Charlie.

"Sshh! In the spring you'll help Will build an addition. Make it big. If Frank gets married he'll want a room of his own."

The boys came on horseback and someone brought a buggy. They beat on kettles with wooden spoons and whistled. Etta tried to hush them when they came inside, but it was no use. They were bound to give Will and his bride a memorable shivaree.

Frank and Curley took Margaret out to the buggy on the pretense of showing her something new. Will ran after them with his shirt-tail flapping, but it was too late. They were back in thirty minutes. Frank called out, "Will, your missus is all right! Walt spun around on the ice down in the meadow a couple of times! Scared her half to death! Ha! Ha!"

"I'd be petrified!" Etta said to Charlie.

The remainder of the winter was mild. Charlie went with his father to the Farmers' Alliance meetings and heard men discuss the possibility of an overabundance of destructive insects in the spring. One settler suggested bringing in harmless insects that would destroy the harmful ones. "Ladybugs eat aphids. That's a scientific fact."

During March 1896 the weather became surprisingly warm. Joe and his boys planted wheat, corn, and oats before the dry weather began. Charlie plowed a kitchen garden at the side of the soddy. Mary's ankles ached so that Etta planted the garden.

By May it was obvious Joe's wheat crop was infected with the red spores of leaf rust. He discussed the disease with the three boys and finally, with a sinking heart, torched his wheat fields so that they were black smudges on the dry earth. Other farmers were forced to do the same. Some even went so far as to hunt out patches of the meadow rue, which was the alternative host for the rust. They burned the patches of rue, hoping to control the rust.

Another scourge hit the farmers during the summer. The fishy smell of stinking smut was carried by the wind from some fields where the kernels of grain were replaced with the black spores the farmers called smut balls. The Turkey Red wheat brought to Kansas by the Mennonites in 1874 was wonderfully drought-resistant and hardy, but was not immune to the rust and smut that flourished during a time of high humidity and thick morning dew.

"I don't know which smells worse," said Joe, "the blackened fields of stubble or the mildew in the damp earth of the soddies."

When Charlie went to town he heard talk about jointworms, chinch bugs, aphids, grasshoppers, and corn borers.

"Looks like the worst year yet," he told his father. "I hear many settlers are selling for any price or leaving everything to go West and start over or to go to relatives in the East." He felt a deep fatigue and lassitude come over him.

His father said, "Son, we could always get by in years past doing farrier work. But this time no folks have anything to pay for my work." He turned his face away from Charlie.

Charlie reached out to his father. "Pa, I'm going to send Will and Frank to Colorado Springs to look for a building to house the new Irwin Smithery. We can read the signs of poverty as well as anyone. We're not going to pray for something that won't happen. We're going to start over in another place." Inside his chest he felt his heart nearly stop, waiting for his father to say something.

The shoulders slumped as his father pulled out a faded bandanna and blew his nose. "It's hard to believe," he whispered, "but you're right." His head bowed. "Your ma will cry when she hears. Be prepared for that. But it won't all be sadness for leaving. She'll have some joy seeing her children in one place. The family will be together." Again, he blew his nose.

Charlie felt anger rise to his throat because life was so formidable.

A week later, night was fading away and Charlie was aware the crickets' chirp had begun. He knew the temperature was rising, because the chirp was increasing. He lay quietly marking off fifteen seconds on his pocket watch held in a ray of light coming through the curtains across the front window. He counted the number of chirps in fifteen seconds and added the number thirty-eight. Three times he checked the number. He put his hand on Etta's shoulder, "Etta, it's eighty outside right now, six in the morning. Think what the temperature'll be by noon."

"Did you get up and look at the thermometer, Charlie Irwin?" mumbled Etta, still groggy from sleeping in the summer heat.

"No, but I'm right. I've been working this out for a couple of weeks. Go check for me and you'll see I'm right." He was up, pulling on his trousers. "One thing I'll like about moving— maybe we'll get our own bedroom. It's not decent for a man to sleep on the floor in front of the open door in summer and in front of the kitchen range in winter."

Etta rolled out the other side of the quilts, slipped into her gingham dress, and ran to the kitchen wall, where the mercury thermometer hung beside the calendar from the Farmers and Merchants Bank.

"This reads eighty-two." She folded up a quilt and threw it at Charlie. "What you going to do with all those figures and measurements you keep in your ledger when we move?"

"Well, Miss Smarty, I'll do a couple of things. First I'll tell Mr. Tait down at the *Dark Horse* how to measure the temperature if he can count the chirps of the cricket fast enough, and he can print it in his paper. Then those folks without thermometers will know exactly how hot it is."

"Or cold," put in Etta.

"Then I'll keep my record and make some kind of graph for the rainfall and temperature and give it to the Farmers' Alliance before we leave, or mail it to them. Maybe I'll keep some records somewhere else, too. You see, I can do things with figures besides—"

"Charlie! You wouldn't, not now! Sshh! The others will be getting up! Stop teasing!"

"Once you said you'd do anything for me," said Charlie, putting his boots on.

"I meant it. I will, but I get to choose the time and place." Etta's face shone with perspiration.

Charlie bent and kissed her cheek. "Salty."

"Mum, mum," gurgled baby Floyd.

"This little boy made a lake out of his crib." Etta fussed over the baby. "Here, hold him. I'm going to take the sheet to the line to dry." She went outside.

Charlie let his boy hold on to a chair. He could walk if there was something to hold on to. Charlie folded the quilts, put yesterday's biscuits on the table, along with tin cups and plates, and built a small fire in the range to boil coffee.

Etta flew inside, letting the screen bang. "They're coming! They're bringing a herd of something—mustangs!"

Charlie could hear the hoofbeats echoing against the low hills. He looked out the screen. "Not mustangs. Those are scrub cattle! No! Yearling calves!"

"How many?"

"Jeems! Looks like a couple dozen! What if those boys spent money on cows instead of a smithery? Gol-durn! I'll skin them both so's Ma won't know them from fresh rawhide. Excuse me!"

The others got up to see what was going on.

"It's Frank and Will!" cried Mary, clapping her hands. "Why, they've a whole herd of calves. We're not in the beef or dairy business. Are we?"

Margaret ran out barefoot to meet Will, not bothering to put a wrapper over her nightdress.

The men on horseback waved their hats and called in duet, "Yahoo! Look what we brought for you!"

Will was first to jump from his horse. The yearling calves milled around the yard, bawling.

"Those are some sweet dogies," said Will. "We found them

out in the bluestem west of Ruleton. Nobody was around. So we figured someone was working ahead of a roundup. But we hadn't seen anyone behind. We figured someone ditched them, and if no one claimed them on the way home they were ours. None carry a brand." He was breathless.

"Soon's I get something to eat, we'll take them to the meadow and under half crop their ears so's they'll match Will's Herefords." Frank pulled his gear from the back of his horse.

Charlie took the horses to the barn. When he came back everyone was at the kitchen table. Charlie poured himself a cup of coffee, moved away from the hot stove. He felt uneasy. He was glad to see his brothers, but all those calves made him nervous.

Joe stood, one gnarled hand on Frank's shoulder. He looked across the table at Will, who had Margaret on his lap. His right hand raised and shook. No one spoke. Then with the ferocity of an angry bull Joe roared. "Get those calves off my land! They ain't legit! Someone'll spread the word if they ain't done it already. I suspect we'll see Goodland's new sheriff before sundown." He lowered his hand and sat down slowly. His mouth was set in a straight line.

"Oh, no!" cried Margaret. "Say it ain't so. Tell us those cows weren't rustled."

Will's face was white. He dropped his head against Margaret's shoulder.

Joe released his hand from Frank's shoulder. Frank sprang up. "I'm taking those calves to the meadow."

"Eat your biscuits," said Charlie. "Pa and me have something to talk over." He motioned for his father to step outside.

"Pa and I," murmured Etta, nursing Floyd. Suddenly she clapped a hand over her mouth, put the baby in Mary's lap, and went out to the well, where Charlie and Joe were talking.

Charlie and Joe on horseback herded the noisy calves away from the house, across the field of lespedeza blooms, to the settlers' road. Neither man said a word. Charlie saw the droop to his father's shoulders and felt a constriction around his heart.

When one calf bawled for its mother, the others started. When one calf farted, the others followed.

They rode past Ray Lewis's place, staying several hundred yards on the far side of the road. When they reached McGuckin's place, their clothes were wet with perspiration, and dust streaked their faces. Charlie reined in his horse and put his hand out for his father to stop. The calves continued. "Let them get over in the pasture, off the road some, into the little dip of land," said Charlie. "I'll go along now and see they all stay together."

"I don't know about Etta's idea," said Joe, uneasylike. "That girl's got spunk, but her pa's got a temper." Charlie waved. Joe sat woodenly and watched his son edge the calves into the gully. When Charlie came back he pushed his hat back on his head and looked surreptitiously toward the McGuckin yard. Everything was quiet.

Charlie fanned himself with his hat. "Glad that's done," he whispered.

"You think McGuckin'll keep those strays? Or will he report them to the sheriff?" asked his father.

"I guess we'll see," said Charlie. "Let's head home before the folks are up and about."

When they were passing Lewis's again far out in the field, away from the road, his father said, "Thanks, Charlie. You and Etta got us out of a tough spot."

Charlie smiled. "I hope the boys learned something."

"Darn tootin', they did. I had a mind to let Will and Margaret stay in the soddy, so's he could raise his cows, while the rest of us went to Colorado. But I've changed my mind. We'll stay together and keep an eye on everybody."

"I'd rather be the watcher than watched," said Charlie.

Midmorning the next day the newly elected sheriff, John McCune, rode into the Irwins' yard.

Will was telling about the building next to the Antlers Hotel that he and Frank had signed for in Colorado Springs. "I have the deed in my other shirt pocket. Jeez, I hope Margaret hasn't washed it yet." He went to the bedroom and brought out the deed.

"Etta's done all that child's washing," said Mary, not unkindly but bluntly.

Margaret was staring dreamily out the screen door and saw the glint of the sheriff's silver star. She flung her arms around Will and cried, "Will! Oh, Will! He's come for you!"

"What do you suppose McCune wants?" Will looked as innocent as possible and motioned for Etta to take Margaret to the bedroom.

"He's going to ask about Will's sticky rope!" sobbed Margaret. "He'll take Will away. I'll have to go home and admit I married a rustler. Boo-hoo!"

"Hush!" glowered Etta, dropping a diaper in Margaret's lap.

Margaret wiped her face and looked sulky.

Sheriff McCune must have heard Margaret's wailing because the first thing he said through the screen to Joe was, "Everything all right here, Mr. Irwin?"

Charlie stood by his father and studied McCune's face through the screen. He was clean-shaven, with a large, straight nose. His thick red hair was drawn back behind his ears and held in place with petroleum jelly. His mouth was large, not indicating a great deal of sensitivity. His chin was round with a cleft, leading Charlie to believe that he was unwavering, and this was confirmed by his wide-set brown eyes which looked out with patience.

"Yes, sir. Just fine. Will got himself a new bride and she's not used to seeing roaches and mice come out of the walls of the soddy like the rest of us. Sometimes fusses a lot about it." His upper lip trembled slightly as if agitated by some inner ferment.

"I know the type, high-strung and easily overwrought. My own wife was that way for the first year we were married"— McCune looked at Will shyly—"until we had our first baby." Then he added, "Children settle a woman."

Charlie knew he'd seen Etta take baby Floyd and follow Margaret into the bedroom. He wondered when McCune was going to state his reason for being out in Sappa Meadows. Charlie was cautious, but not discourteous. "Come in. Coffee's on the stove."

"Heard you folks were selling your place and heading West." McCune sipped the coffee carefully so he wouldn't burn his tongue. "It's a shame to lose good folks like you."

Charlie was certain he meant what he said, so he pointed to the envelope on the kitchen windowsill. "That's the deed to a building in Colorado Springs that's the future Irwin Smithery."

McCune's eyes roamed around the soddy and finally settled on Charlie. "Some Farmers' Alliance men found McGuckin with two dozen calves that don't suck his cows. McGuckin says they ain't his, but he's going to keep them because he knows where they come from."

Frank backed away against the wall.

Will opened his mouth and started, "Why, that dirty damn—"

"Hey! Remember McGuckin is my father-in-law," said Charlie, feeling like he was in a house of cards that would suddenly collapse about his shoulders.

"Sure, but he don't come over here," said Joe. "That man has a notion that the Irwins ain't religious enough. He hasn't even been to see his daughter since the wedding a year and a half ago.

Can you imagine not wanting to see your grandson? Don't you think this eats on him?" Joe's face was red except for two small white spots in the middle of each cheek. His white beard twitched against his chest. "It'd please him to see a son of mine have his good character sullied. It's a mean thing to do when we was fixing to move because the land don't provide enough."

McCune wiped his face with his handkerchief. "This hot spell ought to break soon. It's got us all on edge." He turned and looked at Frank, who sat in the darkest corner of the room. "Where were you yesterday morning?"

Frank was startled and let out a loud burst of air. "Why, early yesterday morning Will and I left the town of Kanorado. Charlie told you we'd bought a building in Colorado Springs."

"Oh, yes." McCune's hands balled and then relaxed. "You were expecting your boys home yesterday?" he asked Joe.

"Well," Joe cleared his throat. "Charlie and Etta, his wife, were looking out the window for them."

Charlie heard his mother's rocking chair. *Crick-crack, crick-crack*. She was sewing, holding the cloth close to her face when she pushed the needle through. He thought of the crickets and what he was going to tell Mr. Tait about how to determine the temperature.

"It was warm yesterday, I figured about eighty near dawn. Pa and I went out on the farrier's route before the noon heat could sap our strength. We saw some calves on McGuckin's place. I think they're truly his. The talk from him is just from jealousy and should be ignored." Charlie stared at McCune's sweat-stained boots.

McCune stretched out his hand cordially to Joe. "I think you're right. I'll tell McGuckin to quit bellyaching and get those calves branded in the morning. Thanks for the coffee." He got up and went out to his horse, which was switching its tail to keep the flies off. "Heartbreaking to see so many fields burned black on account of the rust. You have a buyer for the place?"

Joe nodded. "Yup, some dude from Topeka talked with Tomblin at the bank and Tomblin sent him out here. Wants possession next week, when his wife and kids come out by railroad."

"You've a lot of packing to do. Don't envy your missus. You know women usually have to make all the decisions about what and how to crate things." He paused. "Say, I'm sorry I troubled you. My hunch was right. You folks have no use for a couple dozen young cows. Well, good luck." He rode off in a cloud of dust.

Joe came inside, sat down. Charlie could see he didn't want to speak, but felt he must. His eyes looked misted. He ran his hand through his white hair and motioned for Frank to get up out of the corner and sit at the table beside Will. "I don't believe you boys are stupid. But you knew those were rustled calves. The Alliance men could have hanged you for bringing them here. Now, get this straight. Irwins pay for what they get one way or another. If we ever start a ranch, it'll be with cattle that are paid for!"

The two wagons were packed tight with goods the Irwins had accumulated. Mary's eyes were red. She had so many memories. The old soddy seemed a part of her. Somehow it seemed strange that, with such a momentous change taking place in her life, the summer should continue hot, the prairie grass should blow dry and yellow, and the willows along the edge of the creek should be bright green as she always remembered.

Joe drew a blue bandanna from his hip pocket and dabbed at his mustache. "I could use some of that winter wind, cold as blazes, right now."

"Well, we're on our way!" exclaimed Charlie. "To a town of eleven thousand souls. That's bigger than Goodland."

"It'll be twice the size in another five years," said Will. "Coal mining and gold mining make use of horses. We'll have plenty of shoeing jobs."

Joe nodded. He'd made a fair deal on this Kansas homestead, sold the steel plow and workhorses for twice as much as they'd cost him. He'd made good money on the mustangs, too. Joe clicked his tongue and the four-horse team started slow at first. The women rode in the wagon. The three boys were on horseback, and one milk cow was tied to the back of the wagon.

Joe followed the Colorado, Rock Island, and Pacific Railroad tracks. The rounded contours of prairie land leveled off toward the horizon. Every gully and blowout was hollowed out by the wind and faced the same direction, south. Once they stopped for a midday meal beside a tiny stream whose thick Indian grass crossed over the clear band of water.

They forded creeks and shallow rivers, camped outside such towns as Burlington, Bovine, Limon. Then the land began to swell upward and there were dark evergreen forests. They no longer rode through patches of purple tasseled Scotch thistle and the annoying devil's claw, with seeds that clung to everything that moved and touched them. Joe moved the wagon fast through patches of locoweed before the fresh cow would have a chance to put its head down to try the succulent-looking green plants with violet, cream, or white flowers.

Etta found the pink wild rose blossoms and wanted to take a couple "stalks" to plant beside their new house. Margaret brought in a pale lavender columbine she found by a stream. Will had to send her back for the water bucket she was to fill. "Are you so slow-witted you forgot to bring up water for the supper?"

Her eyes filled with tears. Mary called her to spread the quilt for the table. "Child, dry your eyes. Find a sugar sack and each noon stop, hunt the sunflower stalks that rattle in the breeze. Put the seeds in your sack. We'll have a flower garden."

At night the full moon brought howls from coyotes and wolves. There were fireflies winking in the sage and bats swooping out of the trees over the campfire.

One day four wagons retreating eastward passed. Charlie saw that the strangers looked tired and defeated. Joe stopped to tell them "hello." The man driving one of the wagons called, "Man, you go too far west and the rock mountains have a wind so fierce it pushes trees to one side so they are stunted. Nary a grass is able to take root in the rock. I'm warning ya, turn back."

Another called out, "Howdy to you all. The West is country better left to Injuns and mountain goats."

One of the women looked at Etta holding baby Floyd and shook her head to and fro. "Buried our Laddie two days ago. If you want to see your boy growd, turn back."

"We're not going through no rock mountains!" snapped Joe. "And if we did, we'd use an Injun for a guide." He banged the front of the wagon box.

Toward evening the team pulled the wagon over a rolling ridge that was so gentle it was hardly noticeable, yet at the summit there was a panoramic view of a spruce forest and blue mountains. The dark green looked cool and inviting. The wagon wheels screeched as they rolled along the brown sandy loam past the sagebrush and juniper and into the shadowy lane with its canopy of dark branches covered with lacy patterns of thin green splinters against a gray-blue sky. The aroma of resin was strong as a breeze whispered through the tufted spindles. Daylight dimmed and a few log houses passed with lance-leafed cottonwoods growing by the back-door creek.

"Shouldn't we make camp before night?" asked Mary.

The horses plodded on the road made soft with layers of brown needles. Ahead were yellow lights, more wooden houses, and amazing gaslights along the main street.

"We're here!" shouted Will. "Now to find a little place numbered five-thirty on a street named South Nevada."

The plank house did not look little with a newly built porch on three sides. Les came out, the light behind making him look dark and muscular. "Yo! Who's there?" he called.

The wagon rocked to a halt and Joe shouted, "It's the Irwin clan here to camp on your new veranda!"

Ell was out in a second, grasping first one then the other, a smile at her mouth, tears streaming down her cheeks.

Charlie and Joe were more than pleased with the building Will and Frank had found next to the Antlers Hotel. It was sturdy wood, rainproof, and could easily be converted to a blacksmith shop.

During the warm days of August, Joe and his three boys fitted out the smithery and advertised for business. The women looked at frame houses the family might buy or rent. There were not many. The town was booming.

A week passed. At the end of August they looked at a house on West Huerfano Street, number 116. "It's too small," said Margaret with a pout.

"I wish it weren't locked, so we could go inside," said Etta. "I think it's bigger than it looks." She held her hands against the side of her face and looked inside. "It's not far from the smithery."

"Maybe the men could add a couple rooms to the back," suggested Mary, sitting on the steps to rest her legs. "It looks clean."

"It's a doll's house," said Margaret, refusing to look inside.

That night Charlie said, "We'll stretch the house to fit all of us. Tomorrow I'll go to the register of deeds and see if we can buy it."

"The Irwin hibernacle!" said Ell, clapping her hands. "I'll help you buy furniture."

Joe cautiously conserved the money he had from the sale of the Kansas homestead and livestock, but Ell told him he could buy furnishings cheap from the part of town called Little Lunnon.

Many Englishmen came to this part of Colorado Springs to work in the mines. When a mine closed they moved to another mining town in Colorado. Because money was necessary to move, the Englishmen sold family heirlooms for a song. "You have to buy fast, because when the English decide to slip out, there are others from that country who slip in to buy the house and snatch up the extra household goods. At his job, Les hears about who is moving because of a mine closure. He will tell us when the next Englishman is moving," explained Ell.

"Sounds like this place is built on slippery waxed paper," commented Charlie.

Etta and Mary divided the two large bedrooms with yellow chintz curtains and put matching curtains at the windows. Margaret had been a great help putting on wallpaper with a yellow rose pattern to go with the chintz. Etta and Margaret calcimined the other rooms in the house. Mary sat in her rocker and held baby Floyd. With Ell's help they bought mahogany dressers, brass candlesticks, and canopy beds. However, Margaret chose an Empire bed, solid head and footboard, with an eagle's head carving. Mary found a large mirror with beveled edges for her own bedroom and a low four-post bed for Frank. Etta liked the banister-backed chairs with rush seats to go with an elegant Hepplewhite plain wood table.

When the family was settled, Etta told Charlie that she had a secret which couldn't be kept much longer. "We are going to have another child, a playmate for little Floyd."

"When?" he asked, wide-eyed.

"Before Christmas."

"I've been so busy at the smithery I never thought—I never noticed—I—" he stuttered.

"You never noticed the morning sickness before we left Sappa Meadows."

He held her close, cradling her face in his huge hands. "That's wonderful news. Are you sure you've not worked too hard?" He kissed her upturned face, eyes, nose, and mouth.

"No, what I couldn't do, I had Margaret to help."

"But she's incompetent. Jeems, she can't do anything!" he cried.

"She's learning. It's that she never did anything at home. She'll grow up. Be patient. She thinks Will is the king."

Charlie said he'd wait and see. "In the meantime Pa can make a new trundle bed for Floyd so the newest member can have the crib."

"You think of the perfect things. Floyd will have new furniture same as us. Thank you, Charlie."

"Honestly, it's you who does the right thing, dear. A new business, a new house, a new baby."

Pikes Peak attracted eastern tourists. The railroad brought them to the heart of the city. The same railroad ran behind the smithery. It stopped at the Antlers Hotel for the convenience of invalids who came for the clear mountain air and pure mineral springwater and grand mountain views for a few weeks. The Chicago, Rock Island, and Pacific Railway had its western terminal and roundhouse at Colorado Springs. The CRI & P publicized the area as a "Scenic Wonderland and Health Resort." Physicians praised the dry air and bright sunshine, and established several tubercular sanitariums.

From the beginning Etta felt at home, as if this were the kind of place she'd dreamed about. Cottonwood trees were planted twenty years before along the streets and in the parks. The trees were irrigated by ditches along the streets. In summer petunias, marigolds, moss roses, and even vegetables grew in profusion along the borders. Anyone could use the ditch water for washing, just for the taking, but clear, cold drinking water was sold in the streets by the barrel for twenty-five cents.

The city had recently recovered from the silver panic followed by the gold strikes at Cripple Creek to the west, over the mountains. The gold strikes caused the city to become a lively industrial center with several ore-reduction mills, railroad shops, millworkers, and miners, who came to town on horseback and eventually needed a blacksmith's services. The Irwin Blacksmith Shop thrived.

Etta and Margaret joined the fashionable afternoon promenade to the post office, hoping to hear from relatives in Kansas. They learned to play croquet on the hard ground behind the house. Baby Floyd was walking alone and had cut his first teeth.

The Irwin family had a Thanksgiving dinner without the usual roast hens from Mary's flock. Charlie brought home a goose and Les brought several wild ducks. After supper they sang hymns and the songs they remembered from childhood. Joe brought in the trundle bed for Floyd, and Charlie gave Etta a joint stool. This was a stool to sit on and rock the crib. The stool's legs could be removed so that it could be suspended on a frame with heavy steel springs to rock back and forth.

On the eighth of December Ell was called in. Etta was in labor for twelve hours. Charlie stayed by her bedside, held her hands, and kept a cool cloth on her head.

"It shouldn't take this long," she repeated over and over.

"Boys are obstinate," Charlie said to reassure her.

Their second child was a girl, healthy and pink, with a fringe of light fuzz on her head.

Charlie had decided on the name Joe for the new baby.

"You'll have to use Pa's name another time," said Ell.

Etta's face was moist with perspiration and her eyes half-closed when she answered. "It's best to use things when you have them. The baby will be named Joella."

Mary was rocking outside the bedroom and had heard the name through the curtain. She smiled to herself, well pleased with the choice. "I always liked the name Mildred," she called out.

"That's the baby's name, Joella Mildred," said Etta. Her eyes were deep violet and in another minute closed with sleep.

After Etta's second baby was born, Charlie always came home from the blacksmith shop for supper. On the other hand, Will occasionally worked late or stopped at the corner saloon after closing up the shop. It blazed with tin lamp reflectors hung on the walls and smelled of unbathed bodies. Some evenings he walked to the south side of Colorado Avenue to visit the bars and dance halls and came home long after supper, smelling of murky smoke and sweet cloying spirits.

Margaret never scolded her husband, but at night when he lay beside her she searched his face for an answer that never seemed to come.

To Will his time was something personal and needed no explanation nor discussion. He felt it was not gentlemanly to take his wife to the places he enjoyed going to. It would be wrong in his thinking to take Margaret to the Spiritual Wheel, which was a speakeasy equipped with a revolving disk on which a customer left twenty-five cents and was given a glass of liquor from the barkeeper, who was hidden out of sight behind a gaudily painted partition. Will had the notion that his wife needed the protection of home, like a child. He knew she'd be cared for by Etta and his folks. She'd remained innocent and pure, requiring only his love and approbation from time to time when he found it convenient.

Margaret had changed from the sweet, clinging child Will had married in Ruleton. There she was gullible enough to believe he was a big cattle rancher running a huge spread near Goodland. Now she'd learned people were not always what they pretended. She was an apt pupil for Etta's lessons in home canning, milking the cow and making cheese, cooking, and keeping a house and babies neat and clean, with time left for marketing, shopping, or playing cards or croquet.

During the winter Mary seldom went outside. The cold air caused her joints to stiffen and her ears to ache. She sat around the living room potbellied wood stove on Etta's joint stool and rocked the baby.

One morning during a February snow Margaret and Etta were washing clothes and pinned them up to dry on a line strung in the kitchen. Floyd was playing with wooden blocks, Mary and Joella were dozing. Etta noticed a slight thickening around Margaret's slim waist and asked, without malice, but with a sister's curiosity, "So, when can we expect another addition to the Irwin family?"

Margaret seemed surprised and did not immediately answer. When she found her tongue, she seemed confused. "Addition? What do you mean? Am I adding additional pounds? It's the cream and mashed potatoes. I enjoy cooking and eating. I never ate as well home with my ma and pa. How about you?"

"Margaret, I meant you might be in a family way. You and Will want children, don't you?"

"Will hasn't said. He doesn't say much. He goes to work, comes home mostly when I'm sleeping. He works hard at the blacksmith shop."

"Of course he does. He works as hard as Grandpa Joe, Frank, or Charlie."

"Harder!" said Margaret, stamping her foot.

"Well, maybe. Joe's not so young and it's difficult for him to get around, so he depends more on his boys. He's put Charlie in charge of the bookkeeping. Charlie kept track of all that at the Sappa Meadows place. I was wondering if we couldn't do some of the bookwork at home. Help the men out. What do you think?"

Margaret had paid no attention to the last few words. She pulled a clothespin out of her mouth and flung a wet petticoat on the line. "Will's the oldest, so it makes sense for him to be in charge. Tell me this: Why does your frigging Charlie take over like he's the big cheese?"

Etta was astounded. Her mouth gaped open. She could not believe her ears.

"And what's more," Margaret went on, cursing fluently, her face red with anger, "you boss me. You tell me to do this and don't do that, pick up this, put down that, feed the babies, feed the milk cow, fetch ditch water, take a bath. I don't like someone telling me when to take a bath or wash my hair. I don't want someone telling me how to stir the strawberry jam and pour it into scalded jars."

Etta gasped and shouted, "Hooray! You're standing up for yourself. Now, I like that!"

Margaret puffed, "I'm no fool. I want to know why Will is being pushed out of the blacksmith shop."

"Pushed out? Who told you that?" Etta was perplexed.

"Will told me. Said he was told to leave a few times, so he went out to talk with some friends. That's why he was home late."

"Oh, my!" Etta felt her face burn. She wondered what she was to say to this young girl who was in the process of becoming a wife fighting for not only her rights but those of her husband. She felt guilty because she understood what was taking place. Etta saw from the corner of her eye that Margaret was moving close. "I'm going to tell you because you'll find out anyway. Your husband spends more time in the speakeasy than he spends at the blacksmith shop. At times he's come to work at noon staggering and shaking from bottle fever. He couldn't shoe a horse all fuzzled like that. Charlie tried to hide Will from his pa by sending him home early. But Joe's not a fool. He told Will to leave the spirits alone or he'd be looking for a job on his own," Etta said. Her heart thumped and her face burned.

Margaret began to cry. "Damn you," she said. "I half-suspected." The rest of the morning she shuffled from one chore to the next, sniffling.

"I don't think gloominess is so good for your growing baby," said Etta, glancing at Margaret's thickening waist again.

"I'm not in a family way!" snapped Margaret. "Don't you go spreading such rumors." Her smile was mildly triumphant. She dried her eyes and sat in a chair with a pan of potatoes to peel in her lap.

"Margaret, it's no crime. It's bound to happen. Just caught you off guard, that's all. It won't be bad. You can grow up with your young one. Will likes children."

Margaret relapsed into silence.

"Will's sister will do the midwifery. You like her."

"She's called to the wealthy stone homes, sometimes to Little Lunnon?" said Margaret.

"Yes, and she goes to the tin huts and canvas tents of the miners. She's a medicine woman and treats each patient with the same compassion."

"Could she tell me if I am or if I'm not in a family way?" She was disconsolate.

"I'm certain Ell could do that." Etta's face brightened. "Let's get the lunch, and while the babies are napping with Mary to watch them, we'll go for a walk in the snow and call on Mrs. Les Miner."

Margaret's reddened eyes widened, then crinkled at the corners. "A baby could explain why I've been feeling kind of poorly and never wanting to get out of bed in the mornings."

From several pertinent questions about Margaret's monthly periods and the onset of the squeamish feelings, Ell judiciously announced that Margaret was two months along in her first pregnancy and she could expect a baby by mid-October. She served warm blackberry wine with sassafras sticks in translucent porcelain cups with saucers to match.

Then Ell showed them where she'd placed the antique mirror in her bedroom. Margaret gasped at the floor-length lace curtains framed by curtains of wine velvet that were held back by twisted silk cords. "I let the daylight in or close it out so that it is like night in here." She demonstrated by loosening the cords.

That same evening in their bedroom, Margaret told Will she was in a family way and that because of his inclination toward spirits, Charlie was in charge of the blacksmith books.

A Pandora's box was opened.

"Etta ought to mind her own business!" stormed Will. "And you have no business discussing me with her!" He faced Margaret and lurched forward with clenched fists.

Margaret climbed across the Empire bed. "Don't lay a hand on me when your mind is muzzy."

Will swung across the bed. Margaret slid away.

"Please," she said, "calm down. You're acting like a bully."

Will came across the end of the bed. Margaret crouched in the corner a minute, then scooted across the bed again.

"Don't hit me!" she cried. "I don't want the baby hurt! Stop!"

Will was infuriated and lashed out at Margaret's hands that protected her face. He struck her chin and her head hit the headboard.

"Please don't hurt me," she whispered through a fat purple lip.

Will's gorge was up and he saw only the ugly purple lip—the swollen lower lip. Everything else was a shadowy gray scrim.

When his eyes and head cleared his mother was pulling at his shirt, crying for him to halt. He was hanging on to Margaret's long hair and beating her head against the eagle's-head carving.

Margaret's face was ashen, her lip was twice its normal size, and her jaw was red and shiny. Her eyes were closed.

Mary pushed Will, who was shaking, aside and put a cold damp cloth on Margaret's head. She murmured, "Poor child, poor child" as Margaret came around.

"Why did you hit me?" Margaret asked Will, who had tears running down his face.

"I'm sorry," he said mechanically.

"You dirty devil!" Margaret climbed off the bed and went to the living room with Mary.

Two nights later Will came home carrying a pint bottle of whiskey. He lurched for the leather chair, ignoring those seated at the supper table. He was near six feet tall and his legs stretched far out in the room. His eyes sparkled in the light from the kerosene lamp.

"I don't give a damn what you think. This is my life," he said, tipping the bottle to his lips. "I go out each morning to earn a living for a wife, who does what all women do, gossips. But you know what she wants to do? She wants to walk along the street pushing a baby buggy with the town's society women, showing off her stylish clothes. My wife has class."

Joe said, "Put the bottle down, son. That's nothing but rotgut that'll ruin your liver."

"Ho! I'm no one's fool. I know you favor my teetotaler brother. I'm sick and tired of getting my pay from my own pa. I aim to do something on my own. I'm hightailing it out of this outfit."

Mary had her head buried in her hands. Margaret was staring past Will, as though she saw something on the opposite wall. Frank's face was white as milk glass. Etta slipped her hand in Charlie's.

Joe said, "Son—no one is asking you to leave. Think of your responsibilities to your wife and to your regular customers at the smithery and then to yourself. I'd say you have only one or two outstanding faults. First, you are not overzealous in any work, second you imbibe, as we have recently witnessed, to the point of belligerence. Your chief virtue is amiability. The decision of what to do in the future is yours." Joe's whiskers trembled against his chest as he settled his back against the slats of his chair.

To Will, who was used to making his own decisions, but not taking into account the consideration of others, this viewpoint brought obligations. To accuse him of being at fault was unfair. A man's life was his own to live his own way. If someone, even his father, blamed him for something that didn't follow expectations, well, that wasn't his problem—it was his father's for interfering with his life. His eyes lifted to his father's face, an immobile mask with piercing dark eye slits. Those eyes cut to the quick. He knew he'd leave.

"I won't be working for the Irwin Blacksmith Shop!"

The following morning, with great composure, Will asked for his back pay. Despite the ankle-deep snow and galelike wind he moved Margaret into a rented tin hovel at the coal mining Timberline Camp.

In the afternoon Mary had a "spell" while ironing on the board placed over the backs of two chairs. She put the flatiron back on the stove and clutched at her chest.

"Everyone's upset," excused Etta, getting a cup of hot tea for Mary. "Relax. The ironing will keep."

Mary talked in a monotone. "Remember when you used to run and then complain of a side ache? I feel like that. Only the pain's in my chest. It's like a wet leather thong drying and getting tighter under my arms. It must be this cold weather. This house is drafty."

Suddenly the teacup and saucer fell to the floor and Mary looked straight ahead. She didn't say another word. It was as if she never felt the hot tea that spilled across her lap. Etta put her to bed, then cleaned up the tea and broken china. Mary slept all day and part of the next. When she got up she seemed good as new.

"I just had a spell. It was nothing, forget it," she said.

Because she seemed perfectly well, everyone took her advice and forgot the incident.

The wind growled outside and the windows rattled. The windows were beautifully decorated with frost scenes of some primitive forest with tall, lacy ferns. A braided rug was put across the bottom of the two doors leading outside to keep the icy fingers of cold air from seeping in. The rug also kept the powdery snow from sifting in.

"If we were at Sappa Meadows I'd have this kitchen floor packed with a couple of bushels of cattail down and a braided rug over top," said Mary. "These days my legs ache to the very marrow." Her pinched face looked at Charlie, dressed with two pairs of wool socks and two pairs of wool pants, ready for the walk to the blacksmith shop.

"Ma, if you were as tall as me, you'd find all the heat up near the ceiling. Keeps my head warm, while my knees and feet freeze."

He kissed his wife and patted his mother's graying head. He left for the smithery, saying, "Either Frank or I will be back at noon for our lunch. No time this morning. Have it ready, all right?"

Etta, nursing Joella, nodded.

"Of course, she will," said Mary.

The day was March 4, 1897. Etta baked bread while the baby slept. Mary was good at keeping Floyd out of mischief. She taught him finger games and nursery rhymes. The two-year-old was the light of her life.

Etta, seeing everything was under control inside, put on her black overshoes, coat, scarf, wool cap, and mittens. She went out the back to the little shed to feed the milk cow and see that it had water. It was warm in the shed because of the animal's body heat. She gave the cow more hay and cracked the ice on the water trough. Coming back she noticed how the air pierced, then numbed her skin. The snow under her feet squeaked as she walked. There were drifts of snow against the west side of the house and shed.

Back inside she blew on her fingers before taking off the overshoes. She heard Joella crying and looked up. Mary was lying in a heap on the floor and Floyd was beside her with the flour sifter she'd left on the kitchen table. Flour was everywhere. Floyd was grinning up at her, turning the handle with his chubby fingers. "Mama. Sleep." He sifted flour over his grandmother.

Etta threw off her wraps and knelt on the floor, pulling Floyd to her lap. "Mary! Grandma Mary! What is it?" Etta's eyes were wide and she gently patted the cool cheeks of her mother-in-law, Mary. "She—she doesn't hear me." Suddenly she realized that Mary might not hear ever again. She was holding Floyd so tight he was crying. Etta put him in his bed and went back to Mary. She did not hear the babies crying. She put her arms around Mary and shook her. "Wake up! Wake up!" Mary stared back at her with open eyes, her jaw slack.

Charlie opened the back door and saw Etta's wraps thrown in a heap on the floor and in the next moment saw her crouched down beside his mother.

Tears streamed down Etta's face and dropped into the flour, making tiny puffs like dust. "She's only fifty-two," Etta whispered. "I was outside. I wasn't with her. Why then?"

Charlie's breath came quick and sharp. "Help me put her on

the bed and get this damn flour off her face and arms. It makes her look so—so dead white." He sobbed.

The next days blurred together for Charlie and Etta. Charlie remembered the wooden coffin his pa made at the shop. He wouldn't let anyone help. He closed the shop.

Ell and Etta washed Mary's body and put her best dress on over her good corset and petticoats. Who took care of the babies, Charlie could not recall. But he remembered the frozen clods of earth as they hit the lid of the pine coffin with the single rose carved in the top. Joe and his children stood huddled under the cold blue sky, bound together for strength, comfort, and warmth. Ell asked the Baptist minister, whose two babies she'd delivered, to give the final service at the cemetery. There were no comforting friends. The Irwins had not been in Colorado Springs long enough to have close friends. Mary Irwin's death was barely noted in the local newspapers. However, her death left a hole too large to mend easily in the hearts of her husband and children.

For months afterward Joe could not talk about Mary without his voice cracking or tears filling his eyes. Charlie often was wakened at night to the soft sobs of Etta. He held her close and was himself comforted. Then, quiet themselves, they'd hear the still softer rhythmical sounds from Joe's room. It was a sighing —as quiet as a summer breeze whispering in the treetops, or a cat walking through the tall prairie grass. "Poor, poor Pa," Charlie'd whisper, "he loved Ma more than his right arm. We have to help him mend his broken heart."

Etta answered by pulling Charlie's arm tighter around herself and murmuring, "Will doesn't help by staying away and ignoring his father. He and Margaret didn't even come to the cemetery."

"We all know that," said Charlie with a tightness in his voice, "but we know in our hearts that Will needs us, maybe more than we need him. Wait, have patience, he'll come around. Ma used to say patience is a virtue seldom found in woman and never found in man. We'll have patience, even though it's a virtue few people are willing to wait to develop."

SEVENTEEN

Cheyenne, Wyoming

As soon as the weather warmed, Charlie took the family to the summit of Pikes Peak on the cog railroad. He was enchanted with the scenery. There were grotesque rock masses of red sandstone, huge upthrusts of gypsum, a cave where winds howled constantly, crannies where doves and swallows nested, sentinel timberline pines with rough, gray, weathered bark, dwarfed, gnarled limbs, snow-bent and grotesque.

Charlie was more and more convinced that he was not going to spend his entire career in a dark smithery. He dreamed of prairie land edged with scallops of blue mountains and fringed with green pines. He imagined herds of graceful horses in meadows feeding upon acres of nutritious wild hay.

In the evenings Joe read the newspapers from front to back. Once he commented to Charlie about all the newcomers moving into Colorado Springs. "I never know what language a man's going to use when I greet him at the shop. With all this riffraff coming in to work, there'll be more miners than anything. A paintbox mix of people, those miners are: black, white, red, and yellow."

Etta laughed and reminded Joe that not so long ago they were newcomers.

Charlie reminded him that the smithery business was making

more now than it ever had just because of that paintbox of people.

"We have a good business. The Irwin name is well known. I don't want to go back to starve-to-death farming, a sod house, and past hardships. I don't mind saying good morning to anyone, as long as I can work on his horse and see the color of his money," said Charlie.

Joe folded the newspaper. "Son, just once before I die, I'd like to grow me a good crop of rust-free wheat." Then with a gleam in his eye he said, "Speaking of different people, there's a certain bohunk widow woman who brings her horses to the shop. I thought I understood her meaning, but she was way ahead of me. You know the one. She uses Pozzoni's powder on her face to make it white. Well, by jimminy, she asked me to her place for dinner."

Charlie's eyes widened. "Pa, she probably liked the way you talk. She's probably lonely. You don't have to ask my permission to go out and enjoy yourself."

The next couple of evenings Joe was quiet, saying nothing about his widow friend. Finally Charlie asked, "Did you have a good time Sunday afternoon at that widow woman's house? She cook good?"

Joe cleared his throat. "Well, I told you she's way ahead of me. She knows each move before I make it. I was touched by her kindness to have me to dinner. She's as good a cook as Etta. So, I leaned over—wagh! At my age I should have known better!"

Charlie's eyes lit up and his mouth curved into a smile. "Yes?"

"Pshaw, I reached out to pat her hand. She held on like a calf with lockjaw. I told her she was a passable cook. She told me that I not only warmed her hand, but her heart."

Charlie put his hand over his mouth to suppress a chuckle.

"So then I lost my head and kissed her cheek."

"What did she do?"

"She gave me a peck on the lips and said that I was certainly not cold yet."

"And you said?" urged Charlie.

"And I said that both me and my little daughter-in-law were looking for someone like her to cook, keep my socks clean, and if she wanted to come over twice a week, it'd be fine with us. We'd pay her fair and square."

Charlie burst into laughter.

"It's not so funny when you think it over," snapped Joe. "That's not what she wanted me to say. I insulted a good customer." He paused, looked up at Charlie, and began to laugh. "Oh, well, what the hell, there's others where that one came from." Joe took out his clean, faded bandanna and wiped his eyes. "Customers I need. I don't need, nor want, another woman to call my own. One was enough to last me a lifetime."

Charlie understood his father. He meant that Mary was the only woman in his life and there could never be a replacement as long as he lived.

In August, Charlie took his father and Frank to the thoroughbred and quarter horse racing at Pikes Peak Meadows. After that Frank could hardly be kept at the smithery. The excitement of the track, the horses expending all their energy in a graceful run, pulled at his imagination.

The first of October brought snow to whiten the mountaintops. Two, three days later snowflakes, large as goose feathers, fell on the valley, settled, and melted. A week later Margaret came down the damp hillside by horseback, eleven miles from the Timberline Camp to Ell's place on South Nevada Street. Inside Ell's place, out of the frosty wind, Margaret caught her breath at the sight of the sunlight that came through the parlor window and reflected from dozens of little glass prisms hanging from the ceiling.

"It's the latest thing," said Ell. "It's like having bits of sunshine in the house." She wore a dark-green cashmere basque that looked like it came from Paris. Margaret felt like a yokel in her heavy cotton shirtwaist and long pleated pant-skirt she'd worn for horseback riding. "I've become fascinated with collecting antiques," said Ell. "Come see a most unusual thing in my bedroom."

On a Sheraton candlestand was a glass globe filled with water, which concentrated the light of candles behind it, then threw the light out on a spot of roses in the patterned rug.

"Oh my! I could look at the light from the globe all day," said Margaret, holding her hands on the top of her skirt where it protruded out like a round boulder on a hillside. "It's a hundred times more beautiful than the view from my kitchen window, which is nothing but a lot of black coal dust." She sat on the feather mattress of the four-poster bed and sank to her hips. "I'm big as a house!" she cried. "That's why I'm here. It's past the fifteenth of October with no sign the baby is ready to sample the Colorado air."

"Lay back so I can see if the baby has dropped," said Ell, gently pushing and probing. "You haven't long to wait. Stay here. I'll send word to Will."

On the nineteenth of October 1897, Margaret had the most beautiful baby girl Ell had ever seen. Margaret named the child Gladys Laye. For two weeks Ell kept a bag of asafetida tied around mother's and baby's necks to keep germs away. Ell gave Margaret teas and infusions laced with castor oil and condensed milk.

The day Ell was certain Margaret could care for her baby girl herself, she put on a feathered toque that matched the green cashmere bodice of her dress. She helped Margaret into a rented Wood Bros. buggy. Les came out of the house wearing corduroy trousers tucked into high-laced boots and a corduroy coat at the same time. Margaret asked how her horse was going to get back to the Timberline Camp. Les answered, "I'm riding your horse. You don't think I'd let two women and a baby ride alone up to that mining camp, do you?"

Margaret had to laugh. "I rode down from that camp alone."

Before returning the Wood Bros. buggy the next day Ell and Les went to see the Irwins.

"Margaret's baby is like a play doll, she's so perfect," said Ell.

"Will held the baby like it was fine Wedgwood. A baby will be good for them," said Les, giving Ell a secret, longing look.

Ell gave him an arch smile, which he translated to mean that she was not ready for such responsibility, especially not while diphtheria was sweeping the mining camps.

The first real winter storm came in November, leaving several inches of snow. From then until spring, storm succeeded storm, freezing, thawing on rooftops, drifting against fences and into coulees. There were glorious, short intervals of sun, which melted and compacted the snow. The house was always warm, with kitchen range and parlor stove going full blast.

Etta bought fresh meat from Antelope Jim's Market. Jim called his meat beef, but customers knew it was usually deer, elk, or antelope. Etta enjoyed living in town. She joined the Fortnightly Club and heard the latest literature discussed. The club ladies met in the Antlers Hotel next to the Irwin Blacksmith Shop. In the hotel lobby modern electric bulbs replaced candles in the tin lamp reflectors, which were shoulder high on the walls. Electric lamps were on the tables where coffee and cakes were served.

In the spring the children gathered wild strawberries on the stony hillsides. In summer the family spent weekends on the side of Cheyenne Mountain with gallon pails tied around their waists so they could use two hands to pick wild currants, chokecherries, and wild plums.

Before noon on the twenty-fifth of September, Etta had her third child. Ell again helped with the delivery at home. Charlie named the infant Pauline Lorraine and gave out cigars to customers at the blacksmith shop. He grinned and asked one of his customers if he liked music. The customer was a little surprised by Charlie's question, but told him, yes, he liked music. Charlie grinned more, handed the man a cigar, and said, "Here's a band."

Charlie didn't smoke, but the baby's easy birth was an occasion for celebration. He put a cigar in his mouth, bit off one end, and lit the other end. He began shoeing a big Percheron, a draft horse, belonging to the city's fire department. Charlie moved the cigar from one side of his mouth to the other. He took the horse's back left foot in his large hands, braced the hoof against his aproned hip so he could file a rough spot. He inhaled slowly to make the tip of the cigar glow. He blew out the smoke, feeling its warmth and a bitter burning sensation in his throat and mouth. All of a sudden the horse jerked.

Charlie grabbed on to the hoof. At the same time he shifted the cigar so that some of the hot ash fell on the horse's leg. Again the big horse jerked. This time the hoof flew out of Charlie's grasp. The horse turned sideways. The movement was so fast Charlie didn't have time to think about stepping back. The horse raised its leg and kicked. The edge of the hoof hit Charlie squarely between the eyes.

Everything went black and quiet for a moment. Charlie lay flat on his back. When he came to he was bewildered for a moment. He put his hand to his forehead and he could feel no pain, but his fingers traced a deep crescent or half-moon indentation between his eyes. As his fingers continued to move over the impression, the numbness faded and was replaced by a deep throbbing ache. The wound now stung like he'd been hit with a white-hot poker. Without warning the wound began to bleed profusely.

Charlie sat up and bent his head. He was stunned at the sight of blood dripping and felt faint. He heard the swish of the horse's tail and felt a surge of rage that brought him to his feet. The lightheadedness was replaced with the rush of anger for the horse that knocked him to the floor and caused his head to throb unmercifully. His hands were balled into tight fists. He knew what a swift kick from a horse could do to a man. He'd seen men who were never the same after being kicked by a spooked horse. Those men suffered from blindness, paralysis, slurred speech, absentmindedness, or worse, he'd seen one man die from a hard blow by a horse's hoof in his father's smithery in Missouri.

Charlie gingerly felt his forehead again. His head throbbed and felt like he'd been beaten with a giant sledgehammer. His hand was covered with sticky, bright-red blood. Slowly, because each step jarred his head, he walked unsteadily around to the front of the big Percheron. The horse now seemed to be waiting patiently for Charlie to finish the shoeing job. Charlie looked at the black head of the horse, took a deep breath, stepped back an arm's length, squeezed his right fist down as much as possible, let out one booming, rafter-rattling cry, and hit the horse between the eyes with all the strength he could muster.

The horse's legs folded like an overused camp cot's. The jughead horse lay on its side at Charlie's unsteady feet.

Frank and Joe heard the bloodcurdling cry and felt the building tremble when the horse fell. They ran to see what was happening to Charlie.

Charlie held his bandanna to his pulsating forehead. He saw his brother and father from the corner of his eye, which he could not take off the stunned horse. "I killed him!" he cried.

"That's unbelievable!" said Joe. He stared at the prone horse in astonishment.

Frank's face was pale. "Why?" he squeaked.

"Because that blasted gol-durned beast gave me a huge headache!"

"The horse is really out cold, unconscious!" said Joe, hardly able to believe what his eyes told him. He could not believe his middle son possessed enough strength to knock out a big draft horse. "Oh, my God! Let me look at your head! There's a chunk of skin hanging down like an open door."

"It flaps when you move!" cried Frank, looking pale green.

"Hold still!" said Joe. "I'll get that skin in place and wrap a clean rag around your head. That'll hold it in place." Joe rummaged around on one of the shelves and came back with part of an old pillowcase, which he ripped into strips. "It'll heal together in a couple of days. Bend over a little more. I'll dab a little turpentine—Hold your head up!"

The pain was excruciating. Charlie barely heard his father speak. His knees sagged. Blackness closed out everything once again. He lay sprawled on the plank floor. He heard his father call from somewhere far off. The inside of his head seemed to twirl. He opened his eyes and saw Joe and Frank peering down at him anxiously.

"Come on, sit up!" called Joe. Joe's strong arms were under Charlie's arms, lifting him forward. The gray mist melted away and his father's voice was clear. "Drink! Frank'll get you more water. Do you feel all right? Is your eyesight clear? Answer me, son!"

He did feel better. The dizziness disappeared, but the enormous throbbing in his head was there. Cautiously he felt the bands of torn pillowcase that were pulled tight and smooth around his head. Joe could heal a wound as well as most men who called themselves doctors. What worried Charlie was the comatose horse lying on the floor with myriad flies buzzing and crawling over it.

"Will I owe the fire department for one horse?" moaned Charlie, looking at the limp form on the floor.

"I'll get the damned knothead back on its feet before someone from the fire department comes. Don't worry about that horse. It's not hurting as much as you," said Joe. His hands massaged behind the horse's ears and back of its head. The ears twitched. Joe moved away fast. He called for Charlie to move away. "When the horse raises its head and gets up, no telling what it'll do! I hope it doesn't go crazy!"

Charlie stood with his father and Frank outside the door. The horse whinnied, shook its great head, and got to its feet. It shook its head once again and then seemed to wait for someone to lead it to one of the stalls in back. Cautiously Joe led the horse. It seemed gentle enough and not the least crazy. He gave it water and fresh hay and came back to tell his boys that the horse seemed better off than Charlie.

"I'm heading home. Enough has happened today," said Charlie.

Frank said, "Remind me never to start a fight with you. You have power! A man that can knock out a horse with one blow— that's really something!"

"Aw, don't worry. I'll never hit a man like that," said Charlie, holding his head. "What man would kick me as hard as that blamed horse!"

From mid-August until the end of October 1898, most everyone was talking about the dense meteor showers that were visible each night. Some said the earth was passing through the tail of a comet. Others claimed that the falling stars were a warning of some disaster to hit the earth, such as floods, storms, earth-quakes, or volcanic eruptions. Charlie heard some men at the blacksmith shop say the meteors were the result of so much gun-powder burned in the atmosphere during the Spanish-American War.

Several evenings Charlie and Etta stood in back of their house in the pitch dark to see the hundreds of meteor trails, like silver streaks in the night. "I'd like to see the full sky, out on the prairie, where it's not hidden by mountains," said Charlie. "I bet it's a spectacle."

Etta understood what he meant, but she'd been observant her-self. "Charlie, you wouldn't see more shooting stars. Just notice how they all seem to come from a well-defined band."

Her astute remark pleased Charlie. "If I were to find a ranch that was in a remote area, far from a town, you'd be a wonderful teacher for our children."

It was high praise, but Etta did not reply. She really liked living in the city. She'd dreamed of sending her children to the school in Colorado Springs. While they were in school learning, she'd read, join a women's club, sew, and learn to play the piano —when she talked Charlie into buying a piano.

Joe would not let Charlie go back to work until all the swell-ing was down and the discoloration on his forehead faded. Char-lie enjoyed being nursed back to his former robust health for a few days, then he became bored with so much idleness. He read newspapers and farm journals. Toward the end of his recupera-tion he took several short trips by horseback to look over the grazing land in eastern Colorado. He was restless to get back to an active life, but he knew he did not look forward to the dark smithery.

His dream for a horse ranch drove him to look over the dry farmlands, the outcroppings of sandstone, shale, and limestone. The Colorado prairie grass seemed good, and he imagined sev-eral hundred head of cattle grazing along the flat high plains and broad rolling prairies that met the foothills of the magnificent Rocky Mountains. The only thing that held him back was the profitability of having the sole smithery in the city of Colorado Springs. It was impossible and foolish to pull up stakes and leave a money-making concern.

Etta listened but she did not share his enthusiasm for this desolate, open prairie land. She loved the security of the blue mountains.

Charlie was back in the blacksmith shop, doing nothing but

handling the money and bartered transactions for the first few weeks. He took notice of the amount of money each week that went into the First National Bank. He was marking some of the money in his mind for down payment on the dream ranch. He even went without new leather boots and a new wide-brimmed felt hat. Frank and Joe could not understand Charlie's self-inflicted parsimony and thought it a residue left in his mind due to the kick in the head.

When the bandages were removed, the head wound was healing well. But it was still a noticeable red crescent between his eyes. Charlie would carry this crescent-shaped scar for the rest of his life.

In the spring of 1899 there was a minor boom in the gold- and silver-mining business. The railroad brought carload after carload of black powder through Colorado Springs to be used in blasting the mines. Many times these boxcars were left on a siding behind the Antlers Hotel and the Irwin Blacksmith Shop until the mining companies sent a wagon out to collect their share of the powder.

Four-year-old Floyd played in the cinder piles near the tracks. Etta watched him constantly so that he'd not wander onto the tracks nor around the boxcars in demurrage on the siding.

Ell and Les came often to visit. Les sat at the kitchen table with Charlie, Joe, and Frank and talked about his accounting business at the mine, then listened to the Irwin men tell how Joe wanted to build on to the blacksmith shop, make it twice as big, and take on two more men. "I sure wish Will would come back," said Joe with a sigh. "There's a place waiting for him right here. A family should stay together."

Ell and Etta went to the parlor to talk women talk. Ell said that Will was working hard, staying sober, and doing well at the coal mine. Margaret was again wearing clothes as big as a circus tent, which was proof of her impending motherhood and also proof that Will spent time at home in the evenings.

Etta showed Ell the new dress she was making to wear to the Fortnightly Club meeting. It was brown pongee with a lighter brown taffeta petticoat.

In August, Ell came to visit in a carriage. She wore a changeable taffeta dress with a full-brimmed, royal-blue hat with matching willow plume on the top of her reddish pompadour. "It was too warm to walk," she explained. "I came to tell you that Margaret stayed only ten days at my place after she had her baby boy."

Etta was pleased Margaret had a boy. "What did she name him?"

"Will did the naming. The baby is called Charles Marvin."

When Joe was told about the new baby, he was most pleased. His middle name was Marvin and his father's name was Charles. "Will's still a member of the family. He let us know where his feelings really are when he named my new grandson. My God, I'd like to see those babies."

Before summer's end Charlie showed his father the smithery's account books and how much money he was giving Frank. "I believe we should raise Frank's salary. Maybe yours and mine. We can afford it."

Joe drew himself up and squinted his farsighted eyes into slits to see better. He studied the pages of the ledger intently. Then he waved his quaking hand through the air. "Hell's fire! I knew we were well off—but this much frightens me. Rich men come to an unhappy end. This can't last! Certainly raise everyone's salary by ten percent and hire someone to build a couple bedrooms on the back of the house. The way you and Etta are adding to the population, it's become a regular nursery."

The next morning Charlie woke with a strange premonition that something was about to happen. He climbed out of bed and checked on his three sleeping children. The house was quiet and his footfalls sounded as loud as the clang on the anvil in the shop. He added kindling to the kitchen range, restarted the fire, boiled a pot of water, and made coffee. Still he was uneasy. He stirred condensed milk and honey into his coffee and complained because there would be no fresh milk until the cow was milked that evening. He decided he was unsettled because of more rumors of another miners' strike.

Miners were a rough breed of men. Even when working they were never satisfied. They always wanted higher wages. Several times they threatened the mine managers with pickaxes. Some of the miners came to town armed.

Charlie finished his coffee and wondered if he weren't borrowing trouble. He went out the back door, holding the screen so it would not slam and waken the others. The first hint of dawn was coming into the eastern sky, reddening the mountain peaks.

It was a wondrous sight and thrilled Charlie. He took several breaths of crisp morning air. Then he went inside, dressed, and walked to the blacksmith shop.

He rubbed some of the smudge off the shop's back window

and opened the back door to give more light inside. He stood looking at the rows on rows of boxcars loaded with black powder waiting to be sent up to Canon City or Coaldale or Cripple Creek. If there's a strike, they'll be here indefinitely, he thought. He stepped outside. The door slammed. Charlie looked at the door. No, it was open. His eyes raised toward the line of boxcars and saw them silhouetted against the sunlight that was moving ever downward from the top of the mountain to the floor of the valleys. Maybe someone shot a pistol, he thought.

With no warning there was another loud, sharp crack. Then a bright, yellow-white light flashed, followed by a thundering boom. Charlie was out in the field behind the blacksmith shop trying to locate the origin of the light that was followed by orange sparks and more deep booms. Rocks and sticks of wood flew through the air and hit gardens and roofs. Charlie felt the earth under his feet vibrate, giving a rocking sensation like a powerful rock slippage during an earthquake. The next shock seemed to roll through his chest. From the corner of his eye he saw the back half of the hotel next door sway back and forth, then split wide open. He turned and fell to his knees with his hands over his head to avoid being hit with flying splinters. When he looked up, the back door of the shop was off the sheet-iron hinges he'd made. It lay in a pile of cinders Floyd played in. Over on the tracks he saw long branches of yellow flames engulfing several boxcars, more explosions, and sparks filling the sky like red shooting stars. "Fire! Fire!" he yelled.

He never recalled running home. But he found himself in the backyard holding Floyd and Joella. Etta held baby Pauline, comforting her cries, "Hush-a-bye-baby-hush. Sshhush."

Frank ran to the yard in time to see billows of heavy smoke roll from the railroad yards. The rising sun was red through the black pall that spread over the sky. He was speechless, his legs leaden.

Joe came from the house waving his pants and boots. His white hair and beard were awry and his legs pathetically scrawny beneath his flannel nightshirt. "What in Sam Hill's going on?" he shouted. "Where are those blasted cannons? We're being attacked! This here is a siege! Take cover!"

Charlie put Floyd in Frank's arms and grabbed his father's arm. "There's no war, Pa! It's the black powder on the railroad siding! The shop is flat. The Antlers is unrecognizable." Tears streamed down his face. He saw the sagging roofs, blown-out windows, and collapsed eastern walls of houses next to his.

"Looks like a ninety-mile-an-hour gale hit!" blubbered Frank, finding his tongue. "Look at my bedroom, you can see everything. The wall is completely gone!"

There were several more explosions, then more sparks and flames and black smoke. The three children were screaming.

Joe ran to the front of the house; his pants were on, but he was still waving his boots. "Get the shotgun! We'll hold 'em off!"

"Please don't say that," called Charlie. "It's not a war." He wiped his eyes and saw that Frank and Etta were also crying.

"We're not alone. Look at the places across the street," said Charlie in a hushed tone. "Jeems, people are going to need help."

The city's fire engine drawn by two big Percherons raced down the street and around the corner to the freight yard. Bells clanged and wheels screeched. Mothers called their children, dogs barked, chickens cackled, horses snorted, people ran along the street carrying blankets, books, kettles, lamps. One man carried an ax. There were half a dozen men with buckets of water from the irrigation ditches along the street. They splashed the water over the outside walls of their houses to keep the sparks that the wind carried out over the city from starting a conflagration. The ditches soon became mud holes.

Charlie told his father to get dressed and go with him to the area of the shop. He grabbed Frank's arm. "Let Etta take care of the children. They'll be all right here. People are trapped in the hotel. We gotta help!" Frank ran whimpering toward the hotel.

Joe was the last to leave. He gathered his wits and realized what had happened. He went through the house and made certain it was structurally sound for Etta to stay there with the children. "Honey, just don't go back in the two back bedrooms, mine and Frank's. We'll have to shim them up tight later. If it looks bad, keep the kids outside. Lots of broken window glass. Maybe move some of the furniture out. Oh, hell, forget that!" he shouted. "Come see for yourself what's happened to the side of your room. We're damn lucky you took them babies outside."

Etta left Joella with Floyd and carried Pauline in her arms back inside to see what Joe was talking about. There were splinters and plaster over everything. In the back the roof was half-gone and the outside wall all gone. The beds and dressers were crushed under the weight of two-by-fours and ceiling plaster. Then Etta looked in her room, which was crowded with the big double bed and Joella's crib and the old wicker bassinet.

The crib was smashed against the large bed. When she saw the bassinet in shreds, the little wooden pieces, small as matchsticks, scattered all over the room, her heart shattered. She sobbed into the baby's blanket she was holding around Pauline. Joe tried to comfort her. "There, there, Ettie. Don't take it so hard. It was just a basket. Other stuff, costing a lot more, is busted. The main thing is we're all right. Ettie, don't cry." He put his big arms around her quivering shoulders.

It wasn't the cost. That baby bassinet was a kind of link to Etta's family, to her past. Her sister Kate had given it to her when Floyd was born. Etta'd slept in the little basket herself, as had her brothers and sisters and Kate's Jimmy and her own Floyd and Joella. Now it was in smithereens. She could not stop crying. Her whole world seemed shattered. Then suddenly she remembered that all of Joe's possessions were under sticks of wood, bits of tar paper, crushed, broken, maybe torn to shreds. She looked up and said, "Yes, the Lord has power to destroy, but He's compassionate. Look, we're all safe."

"You'd best check on Floyd before you say any more, Honey," said Joe with a crooked grin. "That boy can get into more trouble in five minutes than an orphan girl in a poker game, if you know what I mean."

He was right. Floyd had left Joella alone, without shoes. He'd filled the baby shoes with dust, threw them in the air, yelling, "Boom!" and watched the dust slip out like long puffs of smoke. To Floyd, the dust bombs were like the billows of smoke coming over the treetops from the railroad tracks. He laughed, ran back and forth throwing the dust bombs. Joella crawled in the dirt, coughing as she breathed the dust in the air.

Etta grabbed Floyd, dusted his clothes, hung on to him as she shook out the baby shoes, and let the stream of salty, stinging tears run down her cheeks. When the tears ran dry she sat on the ground with her arms around her three children. She rocked herself from side to side.

Joe came out to the back carrying the Henry rifle. The sight of the gun frightened Etta. "You're not taking that gun to the shop?"

"No! I found it under a battered bureau drawer when I was hunting a clean shirt in all the mess. I'm giving it to you to keep handy. This rifle'll stop any of them miners that get an idea they can loot our place and—who knows what else they'll think of." He closed his mouth. He handed the rifle to Etta.

She took it and was surprised at the smooth coolness of the barrel. When she looked up Joe was gone.

She thought, I don't know how to use a gun. I can't shoot. I can't go around carrying a gun and a baby. She took the rifle inside. "Floyd, you look after the girls. Don't let them crawl out of your sight."

His little face was tear-streaked and sober. "Yes, Mama."

Etta moved clothing and bedding from the broken side of the house to the untouched side. She looked out the back several times to check on the children. They sat still and watched the sky.

The orange streamers of fire were being contained in the freight yards, but there were sparks that rose and were blown toward the city like tiny red meteors that turned to cold ash before landing.

Etta propped up the broken crib with chunks of stove wood. She brought Pauline inside and put her in the crib. A neighbor woman startled Etta. She'd come to ask how things were. She told Etta that closer to town the houses were nearly all destroyed by the blasts. "In town the Antlers Hotel and your man's blacksmith shop were flattened. I come to say I'm sorry, Missus Irwin."

Etta nodded. She'd guessed as much about the blacksmith shop.

Etta and the neighbor woman made hot coffee and biscuits for their less fortunate neighbors whose homes were splintered to the ground. She sent the men to town to work with Charlie, clearing away debris to find those crying for help. Charlie sent them back to Etta when he felt they needed a rest. After feeding a dozen people supper of sow belly, more coffee, and biscuits, Etta brought the crib inside and set it up in the parlor. She put Floyd and Joella to sleep bundled in comforters on the floor. She invited homeless women, strangers with their children, to come rest in her home.

One man came to the back door about midnight. "Missus Irwin, I came because your man sent me. I'd go home, but I have no home. I'm looking for my wife and little girl." The man held his cloth cap between his hands.

"Come with me," said Etta. He stood in the doorway to the parlor and tears spilled over his chin when he saw that his wife and child were sound asleep wrapped in a quilt on the floor. Etta gave a dishtowel filled with fresh biscuits for Charlie, Frank, and Joe to the man after he'd rested an hour.

"Your man is quite a leader," he said. He put his fingers to his lips. "Listen, hear those explosions? I'm warning you, Missus, they'll be coming here before daylight. The sheriff deputized men to dynamite those buildings and houses that are unsafe. It's said some of the dynamiters enjoy their work overmuch and destroy more than necessary."

Other men came for a short rest, then went back to take orders from Charlie, who had taken charge of the rescue squad at the Antlers Hotel. One told Etta, "Charlie Irwin is some organizer. He has a brigade set up to clear sticks and slabs off every place he hears the slightest noise. He's even set up overturned wagons and caught a runaway team of horses."

Another said, "It's a pleasure to work with your man. He's saved half a dozen lives this night, ma'am."

"Ja," agreed a big Swede, warming his hands around a hot tin cup of coffee. "He's a powerful son of a gun. He lifts the wood beam off a man's back. That beam held up the second story of a house. That's some man!"

Etta could hear the dynamiters coming closer. She guessed they were miners with blasting caps and sticks of dynamite. She decided to rest a moment herself and sat in the low sewing rocker she'd pulled to the kitchen. She laid the Henry rifle across her lap before closing her eyes. She told herself she'd never use it, nor need it, but she felt safer in case a dynamiter strayed into the neighborhood.

It was still dark when Charlie came to the back steps and into the back door. He had only his pants and boots on. He'd given away his hat and corduroy coat and flannel shirt. His face and chest were streaked with dust, soot, and sweat.

Etta's eyes snapped open. It was pitch dark. She imagined she saw two half-naked hairy men standing over her. She smelled their sweaty bodies. She pointed the nozzle of the rifle barrel at chest level. "Get out!" she screamed. "Get out! I'll blast you to pieces! We're off limits to dynamiters."

Charlie's voice came from the dark, calm as a barrel of rainwater: "Dear, put the gun down. I'm your Charlie. I'm tired. I doubt I could swallow a rifle's iron pellet. Don't shoot—please."

Etta put the rifle back on her lap. Tears ran down her cheeks.

Charlie moved the rifle to the corner and smiled. "Two things you did wrong. You left the safety on and the dang thing isn't loaded. One thing you did right. You scared the pea soup outa' me. If I'd been any other man, I'd have hightailed it out of here faster than it takes a snake to lick up a fly."

Frank and Joe came home about the time the women and children left by twos and threes, thinking more clearly with the morning light, now able to collect their valuables from the scattered debris that was once a home.

A two-block area in the center of downtown Colorado Springs was demolished and on either side of that area other buildings and homes were badly damaged.

The Irwin horses kept in the stalls behind the shop were gone. The stalls had vanished and the shop was in scantlings. The heart of Colorado Springs was on the ground. But Charlie Irwin made the people pick up their spirit and start over. He gave them hope. Each day Charlie, his brother Frank, and his father, Joe, went out to help people clean up and begin rebuilding. Charlie talked to W. S. Stratton, the mining district's famous millionaire, who lived in a modest home on North Weber Street. "The citizens need money to rebuild. If they stay they'll be the backbone of the city. Loan the folks money, and in six months the women will be hanging up blankets on the line to air, beating carpets, and washing windows. In a year you'll have every one of the loans paid in full, earned some interest, and the everlasting regard of those citizens."

Stratton, suffering from a kidney ailment, was not sure it was wise for him to do such a thing as lend money like a bank.

"Then set up a trust fund that people can borrow from," suggested Charlie.

"You are one heck of a salesman for a cause you believe in," said Stratton. "I'll set up a fund at the First National, and anyone in need can go there for an interest-free loan. But the loan will have to be repaid within three years."

"Fair enough!" shouted Charlie, shaking the white-haired man's hand.

The city of Colorado Springs was twice the size it was when Charlie and his family moved there a few years ago, going from twelve thousand to twenty-three thousand people. His father often complained that all the people moving into the city stifled him. Frank went to the racetrack at Pikes Peak Meadows and longed for racehorses, or a trotter that pulled one of those little carts, or sulkies. There was no place in town where he could raise horses. It was against the city's health inspector's rules now to have chickens in the backyard. The Irwin family was forced to get rid of their cow. Charlie decided to put the family quarrels to rest and took the cow to Timberline for Will and Margaret and their two small children. He did not stay long because the children had a colicky influenza that was sweeping the Timberline community.

Six weeks after the powder blast Charlie announced at the supper table that he'd decided not to rebuild the blacksmith shop. He said he had a plan to move to the eastern part of the state where Joe could grow rust-resistant wheat and Frank could raise horses. "If there is a strike at the coal mines, I think Will might come with us. He was so glad to get our milk cow. He even talked about having a dairy herd of his own and selling milk to the city. He could sell milk to any number of little towns no matter where we went, if that's what he wants."

Etta stood up, stopped nursing Pauline, fastened her shirt-waist, put the baby over her shoulder, and patted the tiny back. "Charlie, we all know what everyone wants to do, but what is it you want to do? Are you moving to a place where you can do what you want? It's good to think of others, Charlie, but what of yourself?"

Charlie's mouth hung open. He looked around and saw that his father and Frank were smiling. "Well, what's the matter with you? Don't you want to go to see someplace new?"

"What do you think of eastern Colorado's prairie?" asked Joe.

"Well, it's like Kansas. It's all dryland farming," said Charlie.

"We know what that's like," said Frank. "So what about Nebraska or Wyoming? Yeah, Wyoming, that's where that fellow Tom Horn was headed."

"Ell told me most all of Colorado's homesteaded," said Etta. "Couldn't we find somewhere near a city that has lots of space? Space for a ranch."

"Etta, you willing to take the kids and move to a ranch?" asked Joe.

"If it's close to a city or town where there's a school. Everyone knows I like it here. But here there's mining and no room for a ranch."

"How much do we have in the bank?" asked Frank.

"Well," said Charlie, hesitating, "not as much as we had. Seems the black powder wiped some of the money out. We have three thousand dollars."

"What do you mean!" cried Frank. "We had a hell of a lot of money saved!" He glared at Charlie.

"I gave a couple hundred to Tom Henry's widow and another hundred to Jeb Stahl's son to buy more sheepdogs. He had a lot killed by the blast. There were some who were too proud to take a loan from W. S. Stratton. They needed something to get them started, so I gave them a little, sort of anonymous."

"You spent—you gave away our money without asking?" cried Frank.

"There wasn't time to ask. I'll take it from my pay. I keep good books," said Charlie. "Listen, the Lord gave me a nudge at the right time for those folks who were dead broke with no way to rebuild. I was so gol-durned thankful that none of my family was hurt. I wanted to help those unlucky bums." The palms of his hands were perspiring.

"As I see it, we were saved for some reason. You going to fault Charlie on his kindness?" Joe stared at Frank until he put his head down. Then he looked at Charlie. "The Irwins have strong backs. We can do anything we put our minds and hearts to." His eyes were liquid, soft, and gentle. He dug his fists in both eyes and sniffed once.

Etta was amazed. She knew nothing about this charitable giveaway her man conducted. At first she was like Frank and even opened her mouth to give Charlie a good scolding. The more she thought about it, the more she bit her tongue. She saw Charlie in a different light. He seemed pleased. The whole affair seemed to greatly please him. He really enjoyed telling how some of the people reacted to finding an envelope with money under their front door.

Charlie was a big man, six feet four inches tall. He weighed close to two hundred pounds. He ducked his head to go into an ordinary door frame. His heart is as big as all outdoors, Etta thought. How small I'd be to try to change him. Smaller than I am already.

She was still tiny like a pixie, just barely five feet high and weighing one hundred pounds. "Let's go north to Wyoming. Someplace we've not been. If there's not enough money to buy a ranch, we'll homestead. You men can be cowboys. Learn how others run their ranches." She felt exaltation in her heart. She was ready to start over.

"I could do odd jobs, like blacksmithing, until we get our feet on the ground," said Joe. "I'd look over the land and get me a quarter of a section to homestead and grow me some rust-resistant wheat." His eyes crinkled. "I remember Horn. He was going to work for a Swan Land and Cattle Company somewheres near Laramie or Cheyenne. I always thought that was a peculiar name. Let's go find out if there's such a place as Swan Land. By cracky, let's go before there's a big row between employers and miners —started by labor leaders. Look at it this way: With more people using the railroads, the individual mines getting their own black-smith for the mules, where is our business going to be?"

"You're saying it's a good time for some bohunk to buy the land where our shop was? Maybe he'll put in a grocery store. We'll shore up this house good and tight and get her sold," said Frank. "We gonna take a vote on where to head, before someone reneges? Charlie wants a ranch, Pa wants wheat, Etta wants a school, and I want racehorses."

"Keep Will in mind with cattle," reminded Charlie.

The vote was unanimous for Wyoming. The state was un-known and new and therefore held mystery and excitement. Joe's face was flushed. "I feel like I did when we first set out for Kansas. That was unknown territory to me and your ma." His eyes were watery.

Etta went over and kissed his cheek. Then she kissed Frank on the cheek and Charlie on the mouth. "I reckon we'd better plan, because once we get there, there's no turning back."

The last morning meal in the repaired, repainted frame house was not a real pleasure for anyone. The three children were fussy. Etta wished they'd left without eating. She kept going over lists in her mind, making certain she packed all the necessities for the children.

Charlie felt perhaps he'd forgotten something. Some last-min-ute signature on the land or house deed. Joe was weary and short-tempered. The night before he'd visited Mary's grave with a handful of blue harebells and columbine. Before that he'd gone early in the morning to tell Ell and Les good-bye and then for the first time found his way on horseback to Will and Margaret's place. Will was not home. Margaret was overjoyed and woke both her recuperating children to see their grandfather. Before he left, Margaret cried with her arms tight around his neck. "I hope Will and me can follow soon," she sobbed.

Frank was depressed and getting cold feet. He said he was not certain about going to a place he knew nothing about.

With a wagon and newly bought team of two horses, the Irwin family headed north along the railroad tracks. The atmosphere was so clear that hills and mountains that were far away seemed near. At night the stars shone so brilliantly they looked within reach. The Irwins met section gangs along the Denver and Rio Grande Western Railway replacing ties. The shining rails ran in silver ribbons for miles; block signals raised or lowered their wooden arms. Etta and the children put Indian paintbrush, fire-weed, and columbine in a jar of water to decorate the supper table, which was a quilt on the ground.

Charlie whistled at the picketpin gophers that sat motionless on the black ties. Floyd pointed to huge hawks that feasted on dead rabbits or sat watchful on the peaked roofs of the deserted tarpaper shacks that dotted the prairie alongside dry creek banks. They saw the Castle Rock and Denver with clusters of boxcar houses with the smell of boiling cabbage. They passed frame houses squatting near tall water tanks along the tracks. They passed sand-washed flats, deeply-gouged arroyos, belts of pine and birch, small creeks in meadows outlined by willows, red-dish-orange with sap, sunflowers, rabbitbrush, red and yellow wild currants. In the distance they saw snow-covered peaks. During the day they saw shy deer and curious antelope. By twilight they saw coyotes shaded with gray, black, and tan.

The Irwins traveled through the fertile valleys of the Cache la Poudre and South Platte rivers after leaving the northern Colorado coal fields and experienced a sudden electrical storm. Everyone huddled inside the wagon and feared washing away when the rain came in a deluge of water, wind, thunder, and lightning. The horses stood with their heads down, water washing over their hooves and lapping at their knees.

Joe explained to Floyd why the railroad tracks were built high on a levee in the flat country. "A cloudburst can't wash the tracks out. Look at us—water up to the wagon hubs. The track is clear of water."

"What if we get in trouble, Grandpa Joe? There's no one to help." The youngster peeked out the front of the wagon and saw nothing but sagebrush flats peppered by huge waterdrops coming so fast that they ran together in long, thin streams of water.

"Why, we'd wait for the next train or use the standard distress signal of three shots," explained Joe, putting a hand on Charlie's Henry rifle. It was wrapped in a canvas case Etta had made.

"Could I pull the trigger?" asked Floyd. His eyes were wide and shining.

"We don't need help. Not unless it gets wet enough to bog a snipe," said Joe.

By evening the rain stopped, leaving the pungent odor of greasewood. The next day they came into dry range country, where the wind set tumbleweeds bounding along beside the wagon for miles. The wagon passed a string of settlements with shoddy stores, more like trading posts, but no saloons nor gambling halls that had filled the speculative townsites in the coalfield district.

The wagon went by thousands of Herefords and Shorthorns grazing on the open range. Crossing the Colorado border into Wyoming they passed more white-faced cattle grazing freely. They were passing through ranchlands belonging to Francis E. Warren, a senator from Wyoming. Charlie was unaware that this grazing land belonged to anyone, let alone a U. S. Senator.

The brown rolling hills were broken once in a while by weathered rocky outcroppings. One gray sandstone outcrop was carved by the constant wind and fierce cloudbursts into a high-walled corral. Joe pulled back on the reins so that he could look at this naturally formed fort. The eastern slope was protected by the rocky terrain; the west slope had thick growths of underbrush along a creek.

Charlie said, "I bet my boots that this was the sight of many Indian battles, and maybe even bandits holed up here, out of sight of lawmen."

Floyd asked to explore the eighty- by thirty-foot fort. Etta, fascinated by the looks of the natural fortress, said this was the place to have the noon meal, "out of the wind."

As Charlie ate a lunch of biscuits washed down with creek water, he imagined the battles that might have been fought, staining the gray rock walls blood red. He said he was ready to look over the town of Cheyenne before going over the broad plain that gently sloped to meet the Laramie Mountains to the west. Cheyenne was laid out parallel with the Union Pacific Railroad and the streets diagonal to the four directions.

Joe left Etta, the children, and Frank on Crow Creek to make camp while he and Charlie set out on foot for town. They located the newspaper office of the *Wyoming State Tribune-Leader*, asked about land for sale in the area. The Irwin men were advised to move out twenty, thirty miles from town and homestead.

Charlie knew Etta would like Cheyenne with its ten thousand people, cement sidewalks, and electric lights. Joe found that Cheyenne was really the capital of a vast cattle-ranching area. Many of the ranches were owned by Europeans, many deals made "by the book," and range detectives were hired to safeguard the stockmen's interests. Cheyenne was made state capital nine years before, and its gold-domed capitol building cost the enormous sum of one hundred and fifty thousand dollars.

They turned to leave the newspaper office, and a young reporter got up from his desk and waved a piece of paper. "I forgot to mention there's a quarter section on Horse Creek that has a couple of buildings. Frank Sinon's place. He wants to sell— move back East. I think you could get it reasonable. Land around there is available for homesteading. It's maybe forty-five miles out."

Charlie shook his head. "We want something not too far from town."

"You don't want anything close to town—too expensive. Lots that were a hundred and fifty dollars ten, fifteen years ago are now twenty-five hundred dollars. Go on out and look this place over. Go to Horse Creek, then a little way east to Meriden, and you're there. Look for a bunkhouse made from railroad ties. You can't miss it!"

Joe drove the wagon north on a dirt road until they came to the creek that fit the description of Horse Creek. He turned up the two-rut road to the east and passed a couple log buildings, close together. He and Charlie decided that could be Meriden. They saw the house made of ties and knew they were on the right road. The place was deserted except for flocks of crows. A ridge of bare hills rose far away in front of the broad acres of rolling grassland. Behind was a ridge of pine.

Etta and the children looked in the windows of the cabin and explored the outbuildings. There was no stone fireplace in the cabin, which was rectangular, about twelve by fifteen feet, built by notching the ties and fitting them one above the other at the corners. The joints between the ties were battened with wood chips over which a chinking of mud or clay mixed with dried hay was daubed. There was no foundation. Earth was banked around the base to keep out the cold and wind.

The roof was made of rough slabs covered by rough wooden shingles. The front of the cabin had a door in the center and a small window on one side, of the barn-sash type; that is, a single sash with four small panes, hung on hinges to open out. There were no windows or doors on the north, which was common practice in the windswept open country and also in places where snowfall was heavy and slow to melt, but there was a door off to one side with a window opposite on the south.

The stovepipe rising from the back of the black, potbellied iron stove was collared by a piece of sheet iron and projected above the roof. There was an attic or loft in the bunkhouse with a window on the south side. Frank, Joe, and Floyd could easily sleep in the loft. There were four beds against the walls built of rough lumber and fitted with springs made of rawhide. Etta saw only two chairs at the crude table. The cowhide on the seats was cracked, but could be easily replaced. On the wall near the stove she saw two Happy Jack lanterns, made from tin syrup cans and lit by candles.

The men tramped through the tall grass to see how many rabbits they could scare, while they daydreamed about the heads of cattle or horses they could raise on such a fine place. Portions of the land were overgrazed stubble, as though the previous owner had many more cattle than the land was able to sustain.

Charlie knew this was the place he'd dreamed about. The Irwins camped three days by the cabin. Frank spent most of the daylight sitting on the edge of the corral fence looking over at the creek. He hoped to see mustangs come in for water. Joe went through the makeshift barn and knew what he'd do to repair and enlarge the building. He knew where he'd put an icehouse, blacksmith shed, toolshed, and chicken coop.

Going past Cheyenne, Etta had seen the old brick and stone homes, many with stables and chicken coops in their back yards. There were cottonwoods and poplars giving shade to the houses. Her heart was set on one of those houses in town. However, for now she saw that the ranch land had great possibilities for the Irwin men, so she kept her mouth shut.

On the third day Joe went to town on horseback with a checkbook in his pocket. No one expected him back until the next day.

"As soon as Pa has everything in order I'm going to homestead some parcels of land," said Charlie. "Here's my idea. All of us are going to sign homestead papers, me, Frank, Pa, and you, Etta, for quarter sections. That'll make a whole additional section. That'll make us ranchers!" Charlie was excited.

"If Will and Margaret were to move here, there'd be six of us homesteading," said Etta, caught up in Charlie's excitement.

Charlie was thinking of the layout and what could be done with all the land. "Too bad Floyd and the babies aren't old enough to homestead," he joked.

"We'll need an official brand for our stock to show our ownership," said Frank. "Can we do that? How about an *I* in a circle or an *I* in a diamond shape? Pa can make the branding iron when he gets some tools. And you can do the branding, Charlie."

"You'll learn too, Frank," said Charlie.

Joe was back before midnight, tired but triumphant. "I got the whole one hundred and sixty acres for about two dollars an acre.

There's money left to buy a thrasher, fix up the barn, get some stock, and build a blacksmith shed."

"What about a house and extra food and clothing?" asked Etta. "Maybe if we'd first build a small place on one of the other quarter sections we could talk Will and Margaret into coming."

Joe munched on some warmed-over fried potatoes and hot coffee. "Listen, there are some real big ranches around here, run by real cattle barons, mostly Englishmen and Scotchmen—eight to ten sections. You want to compete with them? You thinking that big?" Joe was laughing. "What's this about other quarter sections?"

"We're going to homestead as much as we can," said Charlie. "If Will and Margaret come out, why, we'd have six extra quarters."

Etta sat up in her blankets. "That's it! That's the symbol for the ranch. That's our stock brand. Can't you see? Why six! Y6! Have the Y's tail make the 6!"

"I'll go to the courthouse and register our brand. No one else can use it. We'll officially be ranchers!" cried Charlie.

That fall before the first snow the Irwin men refurbished the barn and bought several dozen head of broad-shouldered Texas Shorthorns, and Joe planted several acres of winter wheat. Etta scrubbed and scoured the bunkhouse with lye, and scraped and polished the stove. She made curtains from bleached flour sacks: As soon as they could get back to town, the four adult Irwins signed for homesteading rights on four quarter sections northeast of the main ranch. Etta began writing a series of letters to Margaret, hoping to entice her and Will to Wyoming.

While the newspapers are filled with stories of the Spanish-American War and Battle for Manila Bay, it will surprise you to know that a gentleman named Elmer Lovejoy, living nearby in Laramie, owns a bicycle shop and made a horseless carriage. Honest. Charlie is going to take us all to see the machine as soon as the snow melts. If you were here you could come with us. I'm convinced we'll be seeing these machines on our roads. They travel at twelve miles an hour.

In another letter to Margaret, Etta wrote glowing words about the city of Cheyenne.

This city has a three-story train depot with a tower that is a landmark for anyone coming into town. There is a fountain, with a series of levels of water, for horses or dogs.

Fort Russell is a permanent military post here, with about twenty-seven buildings. It's quite a sight to see the infantry parading, knowing some of the troops are going to Cuba.

We have a two-story city hall and jail and a state capitol building, whose dome is covered with gold leaf and patterned after our national Capitol in Washington. There are seven churches. Three of them on opposite corners, which is called Church Corner. We have a hospital, whose first building was constructed by a Dr. Graham and a *Dr. Irwin*. No relation, Joe says. The first high school in this territory was built in Cheyenne.

A month later she sent another letter.

Margaret, you would love the celebration that takes place in late September called Frontier Days. At noon cannons are fired at the fort and all the churches ring their bells and the engines in the railroad yards blow their whistles. Citizens fire shotguns, rifles, and pistols in the air. The streets are decorated with red, white, and blue paper ribbons. The fair is officially opened. The ladies who sit close to the open arena raise and point parasols toward steers or broncos that come too close to the fence, so the animals always turn in another direction. This is a wonderful sight. Before this festival there is a fair where ladies exhibit baked goods and needlework, even babies are judged for most beautiful and cutest. Your little Gladys could easily win the first, and I believe your Charles would win the second category.

Margaret sent a reply.

Will has added a dozen more dairy cows to the one you folks gave us. We sell milk and butter to miners around here. It's a good living. The children are growing up fast and have not taken the diphtheria nor whooping cough.

W. S. Stratton, Charlie's wealthy friend, is rumored to be ill, some kidney trouble, and going to Carlsbad for the mineral-water treatments. He went to London, taking his private physician, to sell the Independence silver mine to some outfit there. They say he got eleven million dollars. I can't count that high!

Etta continued to entice Margaret and Will away from Colorado Springs, with the hope they'd soon come to live in Wyoming on homestead land adjacent to the main Y6 Ranch.

The sport for men here is horseback riding and horse-racing. There are shooting matches and picnics in public parks. Noted performers stop here on their way to San Francisco. You and I could go to the theater.

Andrew Carnegie offered Cheyenne $50,000 toward a free public library. Besides telegraphs there are telephones in the newspaper buildings. Water and electricity are in the city's houses. It's all real modern. Charlie says you can have a telephone when you come out to homestead, if wires are strung out this way. He's sure they will be.

In order to buy all of the lumber and other equipment the ranch needed, Charlie and Frank had to hire out as cowboys on the nearby ranches. Thus they began asking about jobs. Joe, Etta, and the children were to be left on the ranch. Joe built a new outhouse. Etta closed up the chinks with mud reinforced with straw inside and outside the house. Joe put up plank, one-room shacks on the homestead land.

Charlie heard at the Stock Growers National Bank in Cheyenne that the Union Stock Yards National Bank in Omaha was looking for a man to herd beef cattle from Omaha to the Pine Ridge Indian Reservation in southwestern South Dakota. Charlie knew this was something he could do, the job paid well, and he could quit at any time.

What he did not know was that the United States Government had promised the Sioux in 1882 twenty-five thousand cows and a thousand bulls if the adult, male Sioux would sign a paper giving away fourteen thousand square miles of land. The government sent a man as interpreter, who had once been a missionary, to the Sioux in order to get as many signatures as possible. This man not only told those in the Pine Ridge Reservation, but all in the Great Sioux Reservation, that if the men failed to sign the agreement, the Sioux would lose rations and annuities. He had boys as young as seven years old mark an X beside their name to obtain the necessary three-fourths of the adult male signatures. It was not until the summer of 1889 that a final agreement was signed that took lands from the Great Sioux Reservation and in turn promised payment in cash and cattle to the individual reservations: Park Ridge, Rosebud, Red Cloud, Lower Brulé, Crow Creek, Cheyenne River, and Standing Rock. Then the government began delivering the cattle in large herds in 1899.

Charlie needed a letter of recommendation for the job of foreman of the cattle outfit. He thought of the men he knew in Colorado, General William Palmer, promoter of the Denver and Rio Grande Western Railroad, and W. S. Stratton. These two men knew Charlie as a fine blacksmith, but not as a man who could ride horseback all day herding cattle. Then he remembered he already had a letter given him by his Farmers' Alliance friend, Marty Robinson, who had been a dryland farmer and was now a real estate broker. Robinson gave Charlie the letter the day the Irwins left Goodland. Charlie dug through the *Irwin Important Papers* and finally found what he wanted.

July 18, 1896

To whom it may concern:

I take pleasure in recommending Chas. Irwin Esq., a young gentleman whom I have known for a number of years, as a horseman in way of driving and taking care of horses. He is considered an expert in this locality. Sober, honest, industrious, and willing to work, he enjoys the confidence and good will of all with whom he had been associated with here. Anyone in need of such a man would do well by employing him.

Yours, etc.,*
M. Robinson

Charlie took the Union Pacific train from Cheyenne to Omaha as soon as the spring thaw began. From the Union Stock Yards National Bank, he was sent to the C. J. Hysham & Co., Beef Contractors. Suddenly he found himself in charge of twenty-five hundred second-grade scrub cows and one hundred scrub bulls bound for the Pine Ridge Sioux Indian Reservation. He was foreman for nine cowboys and a cook with a chuck wagon.

Day after day the eleven men ate dust and tried to prevent

*Original letter from the Charles M. Bennett Collection, Scottsdale, Arizona.

stampedes as they rounded up straying animals. Each night they ate beans, bacon, and biscuits and drank boiling-hot coffee that was strong enough to float a boiled egg. In the twilight one of the cowboys plucked the strings of his banjo and another played his mouth organ while the rest, led by Charlie, sang sad songs, mostly about lost love or the cruel cowboy life. The men used their own language: calling biscuits "hot rocks"; tobacco, "makings"; a skunk, "a nice kitty"; a saddle, "a rig"; cooties, "seam squirrels"; stealing, "yamping."

Often when the evening air was still and sultry, jagged lightning blinked back and forth between rolls of dark clouds that built up in the southwest. When the clouds disappeared, the dark sky was full of star-bright twinkles that looked to be as small as pinpricks or as large as a balled fist. Other times the entire night sky was blacked out and there was no light except from the reddish glow of the campfire. When the fire went dead, there was pitch blackness and night sounds of the high, fast chirps of crickets and cicadas in the grass and sage.

Charlie noted the temperature in his record book by counting the short, shrill sounds of the crickets. The nights it rained the men sought cover in ponchos and ducked under the chuck wagon. Next morning they ate cold biscuits and beans under deafening wind and rain, mounted up, herded their cattle through muck and swollen creeks. Usually by afternoon the sun beat down from the cloudless sky. Then the air was hot and humid.

At Pine Ridge, Charlie was shocked. He could not believe the appalling conditions the Sioux were expected to live in and call home. Three rows of a couple dozen one-room, unpainted frame houses looked like they'd come from the poorest section of some shantytown. On the roofs, shingles were askew and missing.

A breeze brought a swirl of dust past Charlie, who was on foot, having picketed his horse in front of the sutler's store. The dust devil sailed between two sagging, gray houses to a skin tepee, where it broke up. The dust blew against the tepee flap just as it was raised. Charlie saw an old man hunched down, come out, straighten up stiffly, and walk across the bare earth toward him. The man's dark skin was tough and wrinkled. His clothing was shabby, a rolled red cloth held his stringy gray hair back from his face, which was shrunken so that his nose seemed much too large. His eyes were deep-seated, dark, and bright.

Charlie lowered his head and wandered a little ways away pretending not to see the old man. He didn't have the heart to face a fellow human that was forced to live in such squalor. He walked silently past women with loose-fitting cotton dresses and children in faded flannel shirts and patched Levi's, barefoot. He could not bring himself to look directly at any of these people. For some reason he could not explain he didn't want the people to think him a nosy white man, trying to ease his conscience by being a do-gooder and bringing them this large herd of cattle. Here he was a businessman, and he'd brought these people scrub cattle for their meat and hides. It was the scrub cattle that really bothered him. These people saw what he brought them. They knew. It made Charlie feel second-class. He vowed to talk with his boss in Omaha and ask for a decent herd next time.

Finally his natural friendliness won out and he began to talk with some men and boys. When the old man came into the group, he shook his hand, sensing that he was venerated by the others because of age and experience. "I have never been here before," explained Charlie. "I was hired to leave that big herd of cattle for your people. Some are poor and need to be slaughtered right away, cut up for making stew. Others you might want to use for breeding."

The old man nodded; his facial expression showed little. "You are welcome." He held his hand out again.

Charlie seemed to know instinctively that it was not mannerly to strike up a conversation with the women or girls without first being introduced or having had a long friendship.

The loose skin on the old man's cheeks moved up and down. "I have not told you my name. You have not told me yours."

"Oh, I'm sorry about that. I'm Charlie Irwin, C. B. Irwin from Cheyenne, Wyoming."

"I'm Red Cloud," said the old man simply.

For a moment Charlie was stunned. He knew full well that a Red Cloud had fought against General Custer. That in 1876 Red Cloud had advised his Oglalas not to go anywhere with the Sioux that followed Crazy Horse. The other men were smiling. Charlie knew this old man could certainly be Red Cloud. He estimated the old man's age to be between seventy-five and eighty. He'd learned somewhere in his early schooling that in the fall of 1822, there was an unusually large, blazing star illuminating the western sky with a red glow in the black of the night. Or had he heard that story recently when discussing the unusually dense showing of meteorites last summer? "I heard that seventy-seven years ago a great warrior gave his name to a newly born son. On the night of the birth there was a red, glowing ball of fire in the sky. The name of the father and son was Red Cloud."

The old man looked up at Charlie. "A red cloud at night impresses all who see it. My own son is called Jack Red Cloud." He was pleased that this white man had heard how he got his name.

One of the men whispered something to the old man. The others continued smiling, saying nothing, but waiting for the old one to take the lead, as was their custom. Red Cloud said, "Years back there was an agent here called Dr. James Irwin. Is he your father?"

It was Charlie's turn to laugh. "No, sir. I never heard of your agent, Dr. James Irwin. My father is Joe Irwin and he's the best blacksmith I know."

Red Cloud looked pleased. He told Charlie that he had a quarrel with Dr. Irwin about sending too many of their own supplies to Chief Crazy Horse. For questioning the rights of Crazy Horse, Red Cloud was ousted as chief of the Oglala Sioux. "But what is there to life if a man cannot state his feeling as freely as the whippoorwill or argue with another like the frogs around a pond at night? You are understanding, not like the other Irwin."

Later Charlie learned from the present agent that Dr. Irwin's wife, Sarah, wrote the life history of that old Shoshone woman, Sacajawea, who accompanied Lewis and Clark to the West Coast. Before the Irwins were transferred from the Wind River Reservation to Pine Ridge, fate intervened. There was a fire in their office and the handwritten papers and other important documents went up in smoke.

Charlie turned down the invitation to spend the night at the agent's frame house. He stayed with his men and slept next to the creek, in sight of skin tents of the Sioux. This way he showed preference for neither the government men nor the Sioux. The Sioux were quick to note that these white men stayed "on the fence," or halfway between the white and red man. Red Cloud said, "Our friend prefers the sighs of the wind drifting over the creek, for he knows all things share the same breath, the beasts, trees, men."

Charlie saw that the Sioux were crowded in the single-room houses, as several families were assigned to each house. He estimated there were approximately six thousand Oglalas living on the Pine Ridge Reservation, though not in the village of Pine Ridge itself. There were about twenty-five hundred grown men. A crier was sent out to bring the men in to claim his cow or bull. This one animal per adult man was to be the beginning of a larger herd for each man according to the government order. No account was given to how many adult men were in each family, or whether the family had access to water, grazing land, or hay.

In the morning Charlie was appalled to see women scrape green mold off a slab of bacon and drop it into a boiling pot of water. No one had taught them how to slice and fry bacon, nor to cut the rind away with the mold. The men preferred the lightweight, comfortable moccasins their women made to the thick-soled, heavy, ill-fitting black boots they were forced to wear. These boots were the same footwear given to the U.S. infantry-men. They were made at the military prison at Fort Leavenworth, Kansas, from coarse leather. The uppers were fastened to the sole by brass screws. Rights and lefts were indistinguishable, they were usually oversized, and the square toes did not conform to the foot's shape. Some of the children had coughing sickness, tuberculosis, because they were forced by the agent to live in close quarters and not allowed to move on horseback across the land. While Charlie was there, a young woman died in childbirth because of lack of sanitation on the part of the reservation doctor, who came late. This lack of heartfelt caring seemed bitterly cruel and tragic. But it was a hopeless situation forced on people who had little authority to do anything for themselves and who had centuries of tradition of doing everything for themselves.

Charlie talked to his nine cowboys and the cook, Salty, about staying over an extra day to meet with the Indians who came in for their single cow or bull. "We'll talk to them about winter care for the animals. They're not used to looking out for stock. We'll teach them the use of the bulls and cows to add young ones to the herd. Maybe I'll have time to tell them how to breed horses to use on roundups, separating cattle from the main herd, or bring-ing in a bunch-quitter."

"The Injuns'll be sick and tired of sitting on their cans listen-ing to all that palavering!" yelled one of the cowboys. "They barely tolerate taking words from the agent now."

"You're right," agreed Charlie. "Salty, you think you can fix enough coffee, with lots of sugar, for—oh—maybe two thou-sand Indians? They'll listen if there's eats afterward—same as the rest of us."

Salty's head shook from side to side. His round face looked sad with his mouth turned down. His hands were thrown out in front of his chest. "I can't boil water fast enough to keep up with that kind of crowd for one thing, and there's not enough tin cups in the chuck wagon for another."

"No problem," said Charlie, full of confidence. He pushed his hair off his forehead and put his big brimmed hat on to hold the hair in place. "I'll talk to the old gentleman, Red Cloud, so he'll spread the word for the Sioux to bring their own cups. The agency'll loan you a couple washtubs to boil water in and give you extra coffee and sugar."

"Swell," said Salty. "I can manage, then."

Charlie pushed his hat up a little on his forehead. "The rest of us are showing those men how to let their cattle graze and how to round up and cut one or two for butchering—can we do that?"

The cowboys nodded their approval. "Hell, yes."

Charlie went off toward the agency office singing to himself, knowing he could convince the government men to let him borrow a couple washtubs. The coffee and sugar would naturally come next.

"I'll bet you boys a good lariat them Injuns make a feast of roast beef out of the cow we butcher for demonstration. Kiyi! This'll be a regular party," yelped Salty, dancing around.

When it was time to demonstrate cutting out a couple of the cows from the herd grazing in the wide pasture in front of the little shacks, Charlie had Red Cloud appoint a dozen men to come in on horseback. They would follow Charlie and his men on horseback. Suddenly one of the Indians came close, touched Charlie's arm, nodded for him and his men to keep their horses quiet. The man, dressed in wool pants and flannel shirt, but barefoot, held a butcher knife between his teeth. The men mounted behind him had bows and arrows in their hands. The man with the butcher knife made his horse spurt out ahead, and he ran neck and neck with a frightened cow. Suddenly he hung low in the saddle. In the next instant several more of the Sioux followed, their long hair flying. Twelve men on horseback went pell-mell into the herd of milling cattle. Twelve cows lay dead on the dusty pasture. Before anyone could blink, twelve more men climbed on the horses and were out hunting a cow or bull to bring down. There was so much *kiyi*ing and jumping up and down, no one paid any attention to Charlie, who ran around like a chicken with its head cut off, trying to get the killing stopped. Then before Charlie could get to one of the cows to bring back for a butchering demonstration, women of all sizes and shapes swarmed around the dead animals in the field, sang a high-pitched tremolo, flashed wooden-handled butcher knives in the sun, cut the hides down the back, exposed the red meat.

In three quarters of an hour several dozen cows were skinned, cut up into pieces, and brought to drying racks beside the tepees for more slicing. Old women built fires in pits they dug quickly on the parade ground. Stewpots appeared with boiling water ready for the hunks of red meat. Other women hung strips of thin meat for jerky or pemmican on the spindly-looking racks of willow sticks. Nothing was wasted. The fat was put aside to render down when the fires were low. Bones and hooves were kept for marrow and gelatin, and then ground into a flourlike meal.

Charlie knew the Sioux had bested him and he was impressed. The agent was stymied. "The Sioux did more, faster, better than I've ever seen. Why? Because a bunch of dumb cowboys put ants in their pants—gave them enthusiasm? Mark my words, it won't last. Next time you're here, those people'll be the same, indifferent, indolent primitives you first saw," he said.

"So, then we'll have more festivities and your Indians'll perk up. They need motivation—something they can relate to their old ways—not oppression. Did you see those fellows ride their ponies? Jeems, it was wonderful," Charlie said.

"I'll admit it was a beautiful sight, seeing those men hang low so only their feet show. They haven't done that before that I've seen," said the agent.

"Why not have some horse races for the men—sewing bees for the women? They'll like that. They'll like you."

The agent shook hands with Charlie and said, "I'll have to do it on my own. Washington sends us no orders like that!"

Charlie laughed. "Rules, huh? Man makes them. Man breaks them."

"Hell, you could work with these people better than I," the agent said with a smile, wiping the sweat from his face with a bandanna.

Charlie went to say good-bye to old Red Cloud. The old man thought his men had played a good joke on Charlie and his cowboys by beating them to the slaughter and showing how fast the Oglala women could butcher a few dozen cows. "Easier than buffalo." Red Cloud laughed and assured Charlie that the women knew how to use every bit of the hide for moccasins, leather boxes, or bags. "What they don't need, they sell to the whites for a dollar and a half a hide and convince them it's genuine buffalo skin."

Charlie grinned all the way back to Omaha, thinking about how he thought he was so smart, wanting to show the Sioux how to butcher a cow.

Later he told Etta about his first trip to the reservation, ending with, "Those people have butchered animals long before you and

I were gleams in our fathers' eyes. Was I stupid for thinking I could show them a thing or two? You bet! They worked over those cows so fast it'd make your head spin. My dear, you could learn something from those women," he said with a chuckle. "I sure learned from those men riding horseback."

EIGHTEEN

Francis E. Warren

Before the year was over, Charlie was sent to the Pine Ridge Reservation twice more. Then C. J. Hysham sent him to Fort Yates, North Dakota, and the Standing Rock Reservation. Charlie was foreman of the outfit taking beef cattle to these Hunkpapa Sioux. He brought lemon drops for the children and packets of needles for the women, who used them for sewing the tiny colored seed beads they used for decoration on leather goods. He brought the men tobacco and cigarette papers.

Charlie became friendly with George H. Bingucheimer, Indian agent at Standing Rock. This agent was fiercely individualistic, honest, and forthright. He was short compared to Charlie and had a black brush-type mustache across his upper lip. His office and sleeping quarters were a one-room log cabin, similar to the houses built for the Indians by the government. Charlie enjoyed sitting with the agent in one of the several wooden chairs under a poplar tree in front of the office.

Bingucheimer said that twenty years before, Sitting Bull had advised his people at Standing Rock not to sign white men's papers. Sitting Bull'd seen the Sioux's land shrink each time "white chiefs let Sioux chiefs touch the pen." Because none of the Indians could read, they had no idea what they were asked to sign. It was the old story about the Sioux cajoled out of fourteen thousand square miles of land in the Black Hills. After Sitting Bull's death the Hunkpapas left Standing Rock. Some went south to Pine Ridge for Red Cloud's protection, but most were forced by U.S. soldiers to move to the Wounded Knee camp, where horses, guns, land, and lives were taken. Finally, Bingucheimer explained, the Hunkpapas left Red Cloud's Sioux and were re-admitted to the Standing Rock Reservation.

"There must have been a lot of Indians moving around Horse Creek, where my father has his ranch," said Charlie, "because I've found several arrowheads on high ground, above Horse Creek."

"Horse Creek!" said Bingucheimer excitedly. "Horse Creek, close to the Nebraska border?"

"Yes, that's it. Why do you ask?"

Bingucheimer could not wait to tell Charlie about the Horse Creek Treaty that took place fifty years before.

"Colonel David D. Mitchell, a Virginia fur trader who fought in the Mexican War, was superintendent of all the western Indian country in 1851."

"That's a little before my time, but my father was born in 1846 and he remembers people that were fur traders," said Charlie, leaning back so he had his chair resting on two back legs.

"Well, Mitchell, along with the first western Indian agent, Tom Fitzpatrick, supported a general peace treaty between the U.S. Government and all the Plains Indians. Mitchell and Fitzpatrick promised the Indians gifts if they'd come to Fort Laramie on the North Platte to discuss peace and justice."

"As the crow flies, Fort Laramie's not more than thirty miles from our ranch," said Charlie.

"Ten thousand Indians came," said Bingucheimer, using his hands as he spoke. "The gathering was so large it had to be moved to the meadow at the mouth of Horse Creek, thirty-five miles downstream from Fort Laramie."

"I know right where that is," said Charlie. His brown eyes were wide with surprise and interest.

"This was the largest assembly of American Indians ever held before or since," said Bingucheimer.

The next time Charlie took beef cattle to the Hunkpapa at Standing Rock, he went to some trouble to bring better than scrub animals. Bingucheimer was impressed with Charlie's compassion for the Indians.

"Say, how did the treaty work out?" Charlie asked. "Did the

government keep its word and give the Indians fifty thousand dollars' worth of goods every year for fifty years?"

"No. Peace prevailed and all went well until 1854, when some hungry Sioux butchered a poor immigrant's cow. Two officers at Fort Laramie sent an army detachment to arrest the Sioux, instead of the usual punishment, withholding goods of equal value at the next Sioux annuity distribution and paying the immigrant for his loss. The Sioux was scared to death."

"Agitated as a June bug," said Charlie.

"Ya. He resisted arrest and the historical Grattan Massacre was the result."

"Next time I come around you can tell me about that massacre," said Charlie.

"I'll tell you now that there was no more fifty thousand spent on goods for the Indians. From then on there were other bloody confrontations between Indians and whites, Indians and Indians. Now, half a century later, the Indians are on reservations and wards of the government. They depend on people like you, C.B., to bring them decent cattle for meat and hides."

Before the big November snowfall Charlie learned that all the cattle owed to the Sioux reservations by the U.S. Government had been delivered. Charlie was out of a job. He was disappointed there would be no more history lessons from the Indian agent at Standing Rock.

Another disappointment waited for him at the Y6 ranch. His father had built a substantial shed for his blacksmith shop. He spent a lot of money for new tools. Frank continually complained about the new shed. He said that the space could have been put to better use if the shop were built onto the barn. Also, he resented the money his father spent, saying it could have been better spent on a couple of new saddles which Frank wanted.

Instead of helping his father in the blacksmith shop or working in the barn, Frank spent whole days at Frank Meanea's Saddle Shop in Cheyenne. The two-story, brick building on West Seventeenth Street had a huge salesroom in front and a well-equipped workshop in the back with more than twenty leather workers. Frank looked over saddles priced from twenty-five dollars to fifty-five dollars, pack saddles at eight dollars. Twelve-foot long bullwhips sold for three dollars and fifty cents, quirts for seventy-five cents to two dollars. Frank looked longingly at the leather collars and cuffs from fifty cents to three dollars. He itched to spend money. When he found his father would not pay him for the days he spent away from the ranch, he was really angry.

"Geez, Pa! I need gear for my horse. I need to get other horses and saddles for them."

"Frank, keeping horses, buying saddles, brings no income, unless you actually sell them for more than·you paid for them. Also, you get income for gear and more horses if you spend your time working," Joe said.

"I don't like to work in the blacksmith shop. I like to work with horses and I don't have much to work with," wailed Frank.

Joe exploded. "Dadburn it, son! You are the whiniest person I ever heard. I thought when you were growd you'd stop crying and bellyaching. But for once't I was wrong. You go out and work with the horses, rub 'em down, brush 'em, feed 'em, anything, but don't complain about me spending my money. If you want money to spend, get your own. Another thing, stop complaining about the weather, the way Etta makes gravy, the location of the smithery, the bitter taste of my coffee."

Frank was stunned. "I only thought you could put a pinch of salt in the coffeepot, Pa, that's all."

"See, that's what I'm talking about! If you want something done, do it!" shouted Joe.

Frank went into the house, rolled up a couple of his flannel shirts, some wool pants, Levi's, boots, bandannas, and underwear in two, three blankets and left without saying good-bye or when he'd be back.

Joe found out Frank was working for a dollar a day and a place in the bunkhouse as a ranch hand for an aristocratic fellow from the East named John Coble. "It's west of here at the Iron Mountain Ranch."

"I'm heartsick that you two quarreled," said Charlie. "That kind of thing pushes the family apart." He waved his hands.

"You know I believe in keeping the family together," said Joe, "but truthfully, it's been quiet since Frank's been gone. Now that I know he's not far away and earning an honest dollar, I don't fret about him. So leave him be. Don't go bringing him back in a hurry."

That evening Charlie heard more disquieting words from Etta while she mended. "I'm tired of being isolated, not seeing another woman for weeks. I miss the city. I miss being close to town. What's to become of our children? Floyd will grow up knowing nothing but cows, horses, and blacksmithing. I want him to read and write. While you were gone I read him Edwin

Markham's poem 'The Man With the Hoe,' and he can repeat the first four lines by heart. Our son is smart. The little girls need a place to wear nice dresses, and they should live in a modern house with indoor plumbing." Etta rubbed her eyes and looked at Charlie.

Now even Etta was against him. She might have stopped to think how he felt with no job, Frank gone, and Pa glad of it. A gray mist covered Charlie's eyes, his bottom lip trembled, and he held back his rage and disappointment. He sat down next to the potbellied, sheet-metal heater. "Are our young ones angry with me also?" His words were sarcastic.

"They missed you. We all did. In a way I'm glad your job taking cattle to the Indians is over. Now, don't get some lame-brained idea about rushing off to Bonanza Creek or to Alaska because gold's been discovered there. We want you to settle down and work here."

Charlie was bone-weary and at a loss for poetical words befitting this delicate crisis. Jeems, women had a way of making a man feel like the worst ogre in the world. "I wrote to you. Didn't you get my letters?" He was afraid she'd ask about the many letters he thought about, but didn't write.

"Only two. I wore them out with rereading." She drew herself up.

"I'll find something to do close by. I'm going to look around as soon as I get caught up on my sleep. You can count on that."

He saw her hands reach out as she pushed her chair closer to him. Her lithe figure moved beneath the full-skirted cotton dress. Her eyes were icy-blue. Her fingers were cold and pressed hard into his palms. He was always a little startled at the strength she possessed.

"I am counting! Actions count more than words." She pulled her hands back and raised her shoulders in a shrug. Her mouth was a straight line.

Charlie rubbed his palms together and began to tell her of his own longings on the trail between Omaha and Pine Ridge and Standing Rock. He told of his fatigue, being in the saddle all day, eating dust or hunkering down in a rain slicker. With pathos he told the terrible difficulty the Sioux were going through, converting thousands of years of living close to the earth to being clothed and force-fed by the whites' customs.

Etta listened intently, and he saw her mouth grow sad, her eyes grow soft violet and liquid. "My heart goes out to those people. In a roundabout way I know how they feel, uprooted from their homeland and dependent on strangers. I came from a family that had more rules than yours. Really, I didn't know how to think for myself when I was first married. I expected you to tell me when to wash my hair. At least I speak your language."

Charlie was astounded. He'd thought Etta was the black sheep of her family—the one who spoke out of turn, who acted and thought for herself.

"It wasn't so much that I was trying to be different than the others or embarrass my folks. I have always been curious and need to have that curiosity satisfied." Color flowed together in her cheeks until just under her wide eyes two small, bright-red spots blazed.

"You are the most curiously intelligent woman I know." He smiled as though to keep the talk from going sour. He stood up and held his arms out. Without hesitation she put her mending on the floor and was out of her sewing chair, standing close against him. Charlie thought that women need a lot of assurance and a lot of love. He bent down and kissed her forehead, then her lips. "Oh, dear, I missed you so much. You are my best friend."

Tears streamed down her face. "Charlie," she whispered, "I have an idea I'd like to be a friend to those Indian women."

The idea surprised him. "Well, that's possible—who knows the future? Would you relish living on a reservation with the Sioux? One of the agents said I could do his job better than he."

"Charlie Irwin!" Etta pulled away and stood on her toes so that she'd seem taller. "I've been telling you I would like to live in town, not on a reservation in South Dakota. I've been telling you our children should go to real school in a real town." She dropped to her normal height, but kept her head high. Her eyes sparked like sapphires. "You could blacksmith in town and occasionally come out to the ranch to check on everything."

Charlie now felt giddy from lack of sleep and the complexities of all this emotional upheaval. "I'm sorry, Etta! We can't do anything until we get the ranch paid for and homesteaded. Besides, none of the young ones are ready for school yet. If you want to teach Floyd poetry, go ahead. But in the meantime this is our home. This is where you and the kids stay."

"I suppose you think I can live anywhere, just so that you have a job that brings in money to save for a new barn and horses."

Jeems! How did I get back into this? thought Charlie.

"Dear, I'll start a ranch house right after the barn is finished. Maybe I'll get you indoor plumbing. I'll find a ranch job close by—better yet, I'll look for one where a man's wife can cook for the hands." He waited for the blow. He expected Etta to lambaste him severely for such a thought.

To his surprise she sank into the sewing chair and burst into tears. "Oh, Charlie!" she cried. "That would work out just right. Will and Margaret are coming. They'll need the ranch house. You understood after all!"

Charlie was on one knee beside her. "Certainly I understand." He looked at her tenderly, wondering if he understood anything at all.

She put her arms around his waist. His hand went around her neck. They seemed to float together in a pocket of weightlessness.

Joe coughed and they sprang apart. Charlie saw her face turn red to mask the fiery spots in her cheeks, and her breasts rose and fell unevenly. He felt his face turn hot and a vein in his neck throb.

"We're just going to bed," he said. "I'm not waiting for supper."

"That's what I came to say. With the little tykes asleep there's no need to make a hot supper. I'll just find myself some cold meat and biscuits, maybe an apple. We'll talk more in the morning." Joe laughed heartily and fanned himself with the newspaper.

Charlie felt like he, too, needed fanning. It was a grand feeling. He glanced at Etta, who was busy rolling darning floss on a spool, her eyes averted. He was so glad he'd married her. She could make him hot and flustered even after three children. Well, he knew what to do when she acted like that, moving close, and pressing herself against him. He said, "Come, Mrs. Irwin," in a hearty voice.

"Yes, sir," she whispered, her hand slipping into his, "I'm ready."

The next morning he left early to look for work on several of the nearest ranches. In his pocket were two letters of recommendation. One was from his friend, the Indian agent, George Bingucheimer, and the other was from the Hysham & Co., Beef Contractors. Everyone was cordial, but no one had need of an extra hired hand.

Charlie told himself he could not go back to Etta without some kind of a job. He rode his horse all the way into Cheyenne. He stopped to look at the bulletin board in Frank Meanea's Saddle

Shop. Often a rancher pinned a slip of paper to the board, stating he was looking for a hired hand or that he had cattle or hogs to sell reasonably.

"Looking for something, mister?" The man who spoke was almost as tall as Charlie. His rich dark hair, parted in the middle, grew over his collar in the back. He had large ears that stood away from his head and deep brown eyes and an oblong face that looked distinguished. His mustache turned up at the corners above his mouth and was much lighter than his hair.

"A job," said Charlie simply.

"Ever do any anvil clanging? Blacksmithing?" asked the man.

"Yes, sir, I've done my share," Charlie said with a shrug.

"Come work for me." The man smiled and his face brightened.

"I'm Charles Burton Irwin and new here." From the first clutch of hands Charlie felt this man knew more and could do more than he.

"You'll double as my blacksmith and horse wrangler."

"But you know nothing about me," protested Charlie. "How do you know I can tell a horseshoe from a crowbar? I have a couple letters of introduction here in my pocket." Charlie took out his letters and handed them to the man.

"Do you know who I am?" The man had a fresh, bright look. He read Charlie's letters quickly.

"No, sir." Charlie shook his head and took his letters back, refolding them so they would fit in his pocket.

"You're probably the only one in this town that can say that! I'm Francis E. Warren, ex-governor of the Territory of Wyoming and presently senator of Wyoming." He made a wry face as if making fun of the titles. "My spread is called the Lodgepole Ranch and it's south of Cheyenne."

"Do you need a cook and dishwasher?" asked Charlie anxiously.

"Nope. Have one called Bobcat, who also doubles as horse wrangler."

Charlie could not turn the job down. He would just have to make Etta understand that until there was enough money, he'd have to work away from the Y6.

That winter Charlie was able to get to the Y6 once or twice a month. Whenever the weather permitted, he helped Joe put up one-room pine-slab shacks on the homestead property. The inside was finished with tar paper held down by laths fastened by shingle nails in tin disks. Since the shacks would be used only in the warm months, they were also covered on the outside with tar paper and laths. The slabs on the roof were covered with tar paper, with one-third to one-fourth pitch to shed snow in winter. Since these shacks were not accredited toward improvements on a homestead, a barn was usually the next substantial structure that was built. Charlie also began to long to have Will and Margaret come to Wyoming to help build barns and homestead the Irwin land.

Charlie's first job for Senator Warren, whose livestock company was one of the largest outfits in Wyoming, was to make proper iron hinges for all the corral gates. He had no idea that more than eighty years later, some of those same hand-forged hinges would still be in use. Warren was impressed with the work of his latest, young hired hand. He liked the way Charlie handled horses and the men he worked with. Often Warren worked in the blacksmith shop with Charlie, so they became good friends. Charlie began to learn the ranching business. From Warren he learned that a lot of the beef from Cheyenne was not sent out in boxcars to the east on the hoof, but butchered into quarters and shipped in refrigerator cars.

"That meat arrives in good shape," assured Warren. "Charlie, you're years behind the times. Some buyer sent beef quarters as far as France for their army during the Franco-Prussian War. Ranchers out here are modern. That's why I have a telephone in the ranch house. Saves me going to town to check if my supplies are in. I can stay here and talk to a shopkeeper, the freight agent at the Union Pacific, or someone in the capitol building."

Another time Warren told Charlie that business in Cheyenne had been rocky during the 1880 to 1890 decade. "Morton Post's bank closed its doors in 1888; the same year, because of overexpanded cattle business, the Union Cattle Company went bankrupt. The year before that one of the largest ranches in the area went bankrupt, the Swan Land and Cattle Company."

Charlie drew in his breath. And didn't say anything for a few minutes. Warren believed that Charlie wanted to know more about what was taking place in the state.

"I was governor from 1885 until 1886, after Thomas Moonlight served in that office. He was a Kansas Democrat appointed by President Cleveland. Not one of the stockmen in Cheyenne liked Moonlight, because he was out to break up the big ranches. So when President Harrison appointed me to take Governor Moonlight's place, I couldn't refuse. Wyoming became a state and I resigned when I thought things were back on an even keel and the Republicans could run things for a while. I went back to ranching."

In a matter of a few weeks Charlie was made top cowhand. Warren had told him about the Johnson County War. "The cattlemen imported gunmen from Texas to kill cattle rustlers. But the rustlers became so bold, they were only stopped by federal troops."

Charlie was surprised. He'd never heard of all this going on while he was growing up.

"The whole thing is summed up in a recent copy of the *Denver Times*," said Warren. "I'll get it so you can read it. It will help you understand how the cattlemen around here feel about rustlers and about local lawmen."

The article was written by Frank Benton, a Colorado-Wyoming cattleman who began his career as a cowboy, then as a settler with a little bunch of cattle in Johnson County, Wyoming. Charlie lay on his bunk bed and read by the light of a flickering kerosene lantern. He was appalled at that.

> . . . Well, these cattle rustlers kept getting worse and more powerful, till they finally elected a rustler sheriff, and it became impossible to convict a cow thief, no matter if he was caught red-handed in the act. . . .*

By the time winter was over Charlie was Warren's assistant foreman over a dozen cowhands. Charlie's job was to go to Texas to pick up five hundred head of Shorthorns at a ranch between the New Mexico border and Amarillo. This was the first time he'd been down in the semiarid rangeland. The hot scythelike, southern winds that tore through a man were similar to the winds he'd felt across the prairie in the Kansas summers. At the Texas ranch Charlie asked if he and his crew could sleep in the bunkhouse out of the constant wind once before starting back north. The ranch hands were glad for a few extra dollars and made the arrangements. Charlie and his cowboys were to sleep during the day so that the regular hands had their usual use of the bunkhouse at night. This worked out until the ranch hands complained that Charlie and his cowboys sang all through the night waiting for daylight.

"It's worse than the coyotes!" one man cried.

"Aw, shucks," said Charlie, who could see the humorous side

*Courtesy Charles M. Bennett Collection, Scottsdale, Arizona.

to most things. "That there was the coyotes who came to sere-nade us. Everytime Bobcat here plays his Jew's harp, the coyotes pick up on the chorus and yodel."

Charlie and his men found themselves heading back for Wyoming in the dark, right after supper. They hurried the Shorthorns through the desert, swam rivers, and pushed on to a dry camp. By morning's first light they followed a windswept trail to a stream twenty-five or thirty miles away. The lead steer always instinctively moved out ahead, away from the billowing dust kicked up by the rest of the herd. On each flank rode a cowboy.

The leaders moved faster when they smelled water. Then came the other cowboys on horseback with the pack horses stringing behind. The mess wagon had a shabby canvas tarp over the top and was drawn by four mules. The wagon driver swung the wagon upstream and unhitched the team, which went to the water to drink their fill. The cattle and horses also stood in the water to drink. Dinner was prepared. The fording was done in the morning at sunup. Whenever Charlie came upon a lush green meadow, he was as eager as the cattle to mill around on the grass. The cows, steers, and heifers were fat. This was a quality herd.

Dodge was one main business street running parallel to the Sante Fe Railroad tracks. The most active business was done in the saloons. The city reminded Charlie of Abilene, Kansas. There was a hotel at the end of the street, Cox's Hotel, but the cowboys would rather sleep in their blankets under the stars than inside on a lousy mattress. The cook loaded his mess wagon at York, Parker, and Draper's store, which was in the center of the beer parlors and gambling houses. Charlie's outfit moved on to Denver, then on to Cheyenne.

About mid-September, Warren came out to the bunkhouse one evening and asked Charlie to come into the ranch house. The two men sat at the kitchen table sipping hot coffee with thick cream and sugar. Warren finally said what was on his mind. "Charlie, I want you to go to the upcoming celebration in town, the Frontier Days. Dress in your best red shirt and Levi's and polish your boots. This is some kind of annual exhibition our town is becoming well known for, and I want you to see it. So, you and I are taking the day off. Two of my friends, Warren Richardson, from the Union Pacific Railroad, and Colonel Slack, ink-slinger on the Cheyenne *Sun Leader*, came up with this idea for the celebration. The first Frontier Days was in 1897, three years ago. Richardson had the Union Pacific put on excursion trains with special rates.

Red, white, and blue bunting and the Stars and Stripes decorate all business buildings. People wear Frontier badges. The excitement is highest at the fairgrounds."

"Yes, I've read about the upcoming happening in the papers. Seems to be a big event," said Charlie. "Last year my wife and father took our children. I was out of town. They especially enjoyed the sham battle by troops from Fort Russell."

"That's why I'm asking you," said Warren, not waiting for Charlie to say more, "you're no imitation. Actually, you're a politician—oh, not in a derogatory sense, but meaning you are a statesman who seizes opportunities. You have aspirations and an underlying set of decent principles. You're enthusiastic. Would you believe I used to think my hired hands, from foreman on down, were muttonheads? You've changed those men or opened my eyes. C.B., you get the best from people, because you expect it, you dwell on their good qualities. The dust and barnyard manure that is in everyday life does not cling to you. I specifically remember you saying, 'The country is so beautiful,' after you brought in the Shorthorns. 'The mesquite is in bloom so that the desert is patched with scrambled-egg yellow, against the rain-fed green.' You also said, 'The oleanders grow as trees in Amarillo, perfuming the air with pink, white, and purple flowers.' I know what Amarillo looks like—dirty, dusty, squally brats, yapping dogs, conniving Mexicans. Not once did you complain about the wind nor rain, the thickheaded cows nor the cantankerous men."

Charlie swallowed all the coffee in his cup. He didn't know how to react. He wondered why Senator Warren was telling him this, but he didn't have to wonder long.

"I'm taking you with me because you don't drink."

"I don't condemn a man if he does," said Charlie.

"Befuddles the brain."

"Sometimes a man needs something to help him unwind."

"Get on a horse and ride a piece."

Charlie nodded. It wouldn't do to argue that a man was not always where he could get on a horse.

"I have another, more important reason for your company tomorrow," said Warren. "I want you to meet some friends. Actually, I'd like them to meet you. Ever think about entering politics? You're on the ranchers' side as much as I. You could start off small at first, get your feet wet, run for mayor of Cheyenne." Warren had a terse, direct manner of speaking, always to the point.

Charlie twirled his spoon on the table. He was flattered and surprised. This was a field he'd never thought about. He hadn't yet learned the ranching business. He couldn't leave one field unfinished and jump to another. Even Etta would frown. "As mayor of Cheyenne I'd stress justice and decency. But there's a big drawback having me as mayor. I'm not a native of Wyoming. I've just begun to learn ranching. I'm not prepared to fight publicly. That doesn't mean I'm indecent nor unmanly. I'm truthful and showing respect for your idea. When I'm better prepared, I'll consider your offer."

"All right—think about it. But what do you mean 'prepared to fight'?"

"Oh, that's one of those secrets of life. It's a rule. You know, some men feel it's a sign of weakness to be courteous, to show kindness, to protect the weak, respect women, be gentle with animals. We know that's just and decent. A man can uphold just and decent ideas so long as he's prepared to fight for them. When he fights hard enough, he earns the respect of his opponents."

It was Senator Warren's turn to be surprised.

"You are even more of a statesman than I'd suspected. Meet me here after breakfast tomorrow," he said. After that he described the half-mile race staged for the previous year's Frontier Days celebration. "It was a delight. The contestants rode a quarter of a mile on horseback, dismounted, turned their coats inside out, remounted, rode an eighth of a mile, dismounted, lighted cigars and put up their umbrellas, mounted, and rode in carrying umbrellas and smoking cigars." He told about the reenactment of the first election in Wyoming, an imitation lynching, a pioneer wedding, a fake Indian attack on an immigrant train, and stagecoach holdups, that the audience enjoyed.

That evening Charlie washed a yard-square, solid-red neckerchief in soapy water, then soaked it in salt water and vinegar for half the night so that the color would never run. In the morning he waited in the kitchen of the ranch house. He wore a clean red shirt and blue Levi's. His boots were fresh-polished and his neckerchief was knotted in the back of his neck.

Warren came down the back stairs whistling. The horse had been hitched to the buggy. Warren stepped up, brushed off the seat board with his tan calfskin gloves that matched his trousers and jacket. He sat and picked up the reins, waiting for Charlie to get in. "Let's go! Giddyap!"

All the way into town they did not talk much. Charlie began to sing. Senator Warren looked sideways at him, then his eyes twinkled and he sang with Charlie, "Barbara Allen," "Git Along,

Little Dogies," "The Red River Valley," "The Old Chisholm Trail." The two men went back through the same songs until they spotted the dome of the capitol far ahead above the center of the road.

"So, you sing to unwind," said Warren.

"I spin a rope to relax. It is physical and leaves my mind free to wander if I'm not trying out a new loop," said Charlie.

"Exactly," said Warren.

The town was overflowing with people in a festive mood. There were long streamers hung to hitching posts and the lamp poles. Warren stopped in front of the Cheyenne Club. This huge two-story brick building had a wide veranda around two sides facing Seventeenth and Warren. It had a mansard roof and out front nineteen hitching posts.

"We'll freshen up here," said Warren.

They went inside to use the rest room. Charlie instantly thought of Etta and knew she'd have taken great delight in the huge porcelain bathtub. He washed his hands at the porcelain bowl and dried them on a rough, snow-white linen towel. He rolled his sleeves down, buttoned them, straightened his neckerchief, slicked down his hair with his hands, using his long fingers for a comb. He surveyed his looks in the wall mirror and added water to his hands and combed his hair again. He noticed that his forehead, which was always shaded by a hat, was pale compared to his clean-shaved cheeks and chin.

Warren took him to the lounge on the main floor. First he showed him a picture of two bulls which had two six-shooter holes near the bottom. One bull was lying down next to twin trees, a bullet hole in its front left tibia. The other bull was standing and the second hole was in the ground, below the left front hoof. "This was painted by a man by name of Nesker about fifteen years ago. He called it 'Paul Potter's Bulls.' Those holes bored by a six-shooter were made by the hand of John C. Coble."

"He isn't a very good shot with a forty-five. At least if an oil painting is his target," remarked Charlie.

"Well, John thought the painting was a travesty on Wyoming livestock. In an inebriated state he pulled out his gun and defaced this beautiful painting."

"I kind of agree with the man—the bulls are scrawny and look malnourished," said Charlie.

"Well, he was suspended from the club and later resigned. One day you'll meet him. Actually, he's a fine, dignified, honorable man."

Charlie knew he'd heard of Mr. Coble from somewhere, but at that moment he could not remember where. He was looking at pictures of horses, and Bierstadt's engraving titled "In the Heart of the Bighorns" when Warren broke in on his thought.

"Phil Dater was one of the first presidents of the club, then came Charles Campbell. He's a splendid Scotch-Canadian, solid and conservative. A dozen years ago he had trouble because of the terrible winter of eighty-seven. In his more prosperous days he ranched with Johnnie Gordon, whom we call the Wyoming poet; he's an irrigation expert. Worked on a land project on Horse Creek not far from your ranch."

Warren took Charlie on a quick tour, showing him the billiard room, card room, reading room with *Harper's Weekly* and *Monthly*, the *New York World*, the *Spirit of the Times*, the *Boston Sunday Herald*, and the *New York Daily Graphic*. The kitchen and wine cellar, stocked with Geisler champagne, St. Cruz rum, Zinfandel claret, Old Tom gin and Red Dog whiskey, were in the basement. Charlie's head was still reeling from the beauty of the washroom. On the stairway they passed a large, broad-shouldered man, who was slightly bald, but his bushy straw-colored eyebrows seemed to make up for the loss of hair on his head.

"John, I want you to meet my friend and foreman, C. B. Irwin—John Clay." Then, turning to Charlie, Warren said, "Clay is going to put the Swan Land back on her feet." Then back at Clay he said, "We're on our way to the festivities. Come with us."

"All right, come on up to my room. I'd like to put on a more suitable shirt. More like yours," he pointed to Charlie. He was dressed in a black suit with a vest and tie and white shirt. His accent was Scotch. He was well educated, self-confident, and pleasant.

The room on the second floor was furnished with a hand-carved walnut bed, marble-topped dresser and commode, and a ceiling-high walnut wardrobe. The fireplace was topped with a marble mantel inscribed with Shakespearean quotations. The wine-red carpet was thick, rich wool, matching the brocaded satin and velvet drapes. Charlie could not believe anything could be so luxurious. Later he learned that membership was limited to fifty men, initiation fee was fifty dollars, and dues were thirty dollars a year. The rules were strict, no profanity, no drunkenness, no fighting, no cheating at cards, no smoking of pipes, no betting, and no games on Sunday. Many of the members were cattle barons, who spent summers in Cheyenne and winters in

Europe. The club was in bad financial shape, mostly because of the 1887 losses sustained by the members, so that bond holders on the building had to accept twenty cents on the dollar. The building had been taken over by the Club of Cheyenne and in a few years more would be known as the Cheyenne Industrial Club.

John Clay joined the two men. He wore a red flannel shirt and stiff, new Levi's. "We'll walk," said Clay. "Pioneer Park is not far."

No admission was charged to the fairgrounds, but the uncovered bleacher seats were fifteen cents and grandstand seats were thirty-five cents. They took seats in the grandstand after some pushing and jostling through the crowd. They were four rows up from the judges' stand. Here Charlie was introduced to E. A. Slack, the editor of the *Sun Leader*. He was six feet one and weighed two hundred and thirty pounds. Warren told Charlie that the man used a sledgehammer when he wrote an editorial. "That man reminds me of you with his tremendous willpower, indomitable energy, and high personal character."

Charlie learned that John Clay had been president of the Wyoming Stock Growers Association from 1890 to 1895, when he was introduced to W. C. Irvine, the present president. Irvine was a big man with large penetrating brown eyes, a big nose, and a cigar constantly in his left hand.

Warren leaned over and told the men to hush and watch the show. "Charlie here could be a contestant if I'd given him more than a day off. Charlie can do anything he sets his mind to. He could be mayor."

"Only if there is trick roping and the others are really poor," said Charlie with a laugh, "and the mayor thing is a little far-fetched for now."

The rodeo seemed to attract the most shouts and applause from the audience. Suddenly Charlie thought how much Frank would enjoy this event. Then came the steer roping, which caught Charlie's interest. The steer was given a one-hundred-foot start on the roper. Five-year-old steers were used. The first man's rope snapped when he made the "trip and bust." Hugh McPhee of Cheyenne made a record time of forty seconds to rope, bust, tie his steer, and remount his horse. Charlie's hands were sweaty. He could feel his own rope slide, tighten, slide again as he imagined himself roping a five-year-old steer.

After the roping contest Warren waved to a man in a dark-brown shirt and light-tan trousers and a round face under a wide-brimmed hat. "Governor Richards, I want you to meet a friend of mine."

Richards excused himself and came up the plank seats. He shook hands with Warren as if they were old friends. "This is the best Frontier Days so far. I can't wait until the bucking horses come out. I've got my money on Thad Sowder, the cowboy who won the championship this year in Denver."

Warren put his hand on Richards's shoulder. "This is C. B. Irwin. One day we'll be hearing more of his name—mark my words. He's a good Republican already and just the kind of man we need in the office of mayor or House of Representatives." Charlie shook hands with DeForest Richards, noting that he seemed short of breath and his face was flushed. He wondered if the man was nervous or embarrassed around Senator Warren or ill.

The bucking-horse contest was announced and the men sat down.

"People really go for this event," said Warren.

"Why's that?" asked Charlie.

"Violence, son. People are not so far down from the trees that they don't enjoy blood-and-guts violence."

"I've heard a lot about Buffalo Bill Cody. He puts on a similar show? Mostly entertainment."

"Certainly, that's what this is. Buffalo Bill found what people would pay for. That's an entertainer. Our boys from the West entertain by doing what they do on ranches every day." Warren winked. "Most every day, anyway. The townspeople eat it up and cheer for the fellows they know. The easterners never saw anything like it, plus they get a chance to see some of the most beautiful country in the world."

"I feel the same way about the western prairie and mountains. It's hard for me to stay in the blacksmith shed all day," said Charlie.

"I have a daughter, Franny, in an eastern school. She writes that those folks think we still fight red men and eat buffalo and tame rattlesnakes. It's her first time with easterners and females at Wellesley."

"Was she raised on the ranch, sir?"

"Of course. She's an excellent horsewoman. She likes any kind of outdoor thing, hiking, camping. You and your wife must meet her."

"If she's a girl with her own mind, Etta will take to her right off." Charlie had to talk above the applause of the crowd because the bronc riders were lining up and the broncs were being pushed forward. Suddenly he drew in his breath. He recognized Frank among the bronc riders. He felt anger rise in his throat. He took a deep breath and saw that his reaction was foolish. Frank was on his own. He could do anything he pleased. He remembered that earlier he'd thought how much Frank would enjoy this horse show. Soon he felt some kind of pride that Frank had found out what was going on in town and had joined in the affairs. He concentrated on the event and nearly forgot the man he'd come with. Charlie stomped and clapped and yelled encouragement to all the contestants and especially to Frank, who tried desperately to stay on the saddle, but was thrown to the dust. Frank was game. He scrambled to his feet and took the option of remounting his animal for a second attempt.

The horses were saddled in the arena for everyone to watch as the rider and his assistants handled the animal. The assistants quickly pulled off the saddle as Frank held his horse by a rope attached to its halter. One of the assistants tied a blind over the horse's eyes. Another fellow grabbed the horse's ears, twisting them to cause enough discomfort to distract the nervous horse's attention from the feel of a new saddle that was being carefully placed on its back. Frank gave the rope to one of his assistants and tightened the cinch to his liking. Then he climbed in the saddle and nodded for the blindfold to be removed and the rope dropped. The bucking began. Frank raked the sides of the animal once with his spurs and the horse reared its head high, then lowered its head and reared its back. Frank could not ride this bucking horse to a standstill. He was once again thrown in the dirt. The crowd yelled and applauded and called for him to try again. He walked slowly to the side of the arena. Charlie thought he detected a limp in the right leg. He sighed with relief. At least his brother was still in one piece and able to walk away. He'd not placed in the event, but he was not hurt.

The next rider, Thad Sowder, had the crowd standing. He remained several minutes on his outlaw, or bucking horse. Then for a moment it seemed the man threw both hands down in front to grab onto the saddle.

Warren yelled, "Did you see that! Sowder grabbed leather!"

Sowder was still on his wildly thrashing horse, hanging on to the saddle horn with one hand now. He continued to ride until the horse came to a standstill, wheezing loudly.

The crowd was yelling.

Warren said, "A decision in favor of that young man is unfair to the other contestants."

Charlie was learning. He had not known that this balancing act was to be done with one hand only; using two hands at any time was enough to disqualify a rider.

"There may be some truth to the rumor that a decision was made in advance of this contest." Warren stamped his foot.

"Can the townfolk disqualify dishonest judges?" asked Charlie.

"Maybe. What this town needs is a good manager of the whole fair. Henry Altman is chairman this year, but he also has a ranch to look after. What they need is a manager of the fair that will look after the cowboys, horses, and steers. C.B., you could do that! By golly, you could!" said Warren in his abrupt, disarming way.

"Oh, whoa back. I'm still learning. Remember? I'm the new kid in town. Give me some time."

"This is the time to start," said Warren.

NINETEEN

Johnnie Gordon

By spring Charlie often went into the kitchen when the supper dishes were finished and the others were in the bunkhouse playing cards. He enjoyed drinking coffee and talking with Warren. One rainy evening he was feeling particularly blue because he missed Etta and the children terribly. He wished there were some way they could live near him. He felt as miserable as the weather looked and took his time stirring the cream and sugar into his coffee. "Hope my wife and kids are all right. This rain could have them flooded out, and I'd never know about it for a couple of days." Charlie looked anxiously at Warren.

"Reminds me of that blizzard in January. The darn thing kept us storm-stayed three days. Remember how we worried about the dumb calves in the meadow?" Warren smiled. He drank his hot, steaming coffee gingerly, blowing before sipping.

"How could I forget? I couldn't see ten feet ahead when I went to the meadow. Those calves were calm as all get out, chomping on the hay we'd spread for them down in a little snow-filled gully. Above their heads the snow was blown about by a sixty-mile-an-hour gale. Out of the gully the cold cut like a thousand knives. Not even the toughest bronc could face that wind for long. I had to face away even with a wool scarf over my face and hunch over like an old man to walk. But those calves were safe."

Warren put down his coffee cup. "How'd your father come through the storm? Did he lose any animals?"

"Pa didn't lose any cows. His herd's small and he kept a stack of hay for them under a cutbank that protected the herd from the wind. Then, too, his cows are Shorthorns and skinny. They take the cold and wind better than some others."

Warren lifted his cup and looked across the steaming liquid to Charlie. "So—I'd guess your wife is doing just fine during this rainy season. Your father will look after things. We always have a bad rainy spell every spring. Then the weather can get cold again —maybe for two or three days and snow. That's the worst. Wet, heavy spring snow can take a herd down to nothing if they're caught in it. I heard Johnnie Gordon, a Scotchman with the broad *a* dialect, lives north on Horse Creek, right next to your pa's Y6, had bad luck with the January blizzard."

"I remember him," said Charlie. "Asked him if he needed someone to help get his hay in. Gordon said, 'Aye, be brief, I have a living to make. I have not a cent for you to take.' I chuckled over his manner of speech all the way to Cheyenne. That was the same day you hired me. He's not the only one who had bad luck. I heard the Two Bar had calves caught in wire fences. The calves stood against the fence and didn't move. Froze to death. They fell, making mounds of cattle. There was nothing visible but a couple heads when the snow drifted over them. Must have been a mess to get rid of those stinking carcasses when the snow melted," said Charlie, holding his cup for more coffee.

"Smelt stronger than a wolf den when everything thawed. That's one reason I don't like barbed-wire fences. Even Gordon feels the same. He said, 'Barbed wire has its abuses and its uses.' Now, here's an enigma. One day those rotten carcasses smell so powerful, you can't get on the lee side. Then the very next day they've mostly disappeared. Probably wolves, other scavengers, like crows and buzzards. Just when you think you can't stand the mess, it's almost gone. That reminds me of something Gordon said the last time I saw him. He seems to have changed his mind about hiring help. He wanted to know if I could recommend a good hired hand for him. He's in dire need of a foreman. He wants to take down his fence and put up some trees in his meadow before next spring storm hits." Warren watched Charlie's face. "You want to work for Gordon? He's our Wyoming poet and chief storyteller. You and your family could be together." Warren smiled as Charlie seemed to relax. Warren laced his hands behind his head and cracked his knuckles. "Gordon also needs a cook. There's a ranch house. You and your family could live there."

Charlie smiled back. He got up and looked out the window. The rain seemed to be easing up. He felt suddenly cheerful. "Thanks a lot! I'll sure miss you though, Senator. Let's keep in touch."

The two men shook hands. Warren was immediately sorry he'd told Charlie about the foreman's job at Gordon's L5 ranch. He'd lose one of the best men he'd ever had. In his heart he'd known Charlie wouldn't stay with him forever. Charlie was quick to learn, easy to get along with, patient with men and animals, and could do the work of two men.

Charlie was sorry to leave his good friend, but he also knew he'd not stay on the Warren Lodgepole Ranch forever. Next morning he tied his gear onto the back of his saddle and rode home to tell Etta the good news. On the way he stopped at the L5 on Horse Creek to look at the ranch house, where he and his family would be staying.

The house sat firmly on a foundation of wide logs. Its sides were unpainted, weathered silver-gray logs, chinked with white plaster. The roof was gray shingles, steep to ward off snow. Built against the east wall, sheltered from the winds was a shed, more like an enclosed lean-to. Charlie supposed dry wood could be stored in there and venison could be hung and cured, frozen in winter so thin slices could be cut off to fry with breakfast biscuits.

What a delicious sizzling a beefsteak can make on a hot stove! Charlie's mouth watered. When the weather is steely cold and the morning's sun is just a faint orange glow in the east, inside there's warmth and Etta looking after the first meal. Reluctantly he pulled away from his daydreaming and knocked on the open door of the shed. There was no answer, so he went inside the shed and knocked on the back door. It was instantly opened by a wiry man of medium height. His hair was yellow-white and reached to his collar. He had long sideburns that partially covered his ears like muffs. The rest of his face was clean-shaven. "Ah, Mr. Charles Irwin. I've been looking for you ever since I told Francis Warren I need a foreman. You come to work for me, I'll see you get a fair fee."

Charlie could not help himself. He laughed softly. "Yes, I'll take your job. I understand you want a fence removed and trees put in right away and you want a cook. I'll do the trees, my wife will cook."

The men shook hands. Charlie said he'd be back first thing in the morning to begin.

Gordon said, "You'll occupy this house. I'll move to the bunkhouse. I fired four cowboys, couldn't stand their noise. Lost most of my cattle. They were winter killed. All that's left is a pile of hides." Gordon's mouth turned down, and Charlie thought he saw a tear in the corner of the clear blue eyes.

When he left the L5, Charlie noticed the large square box in the creek. He looked inside and saw himself in miniature against a background of deep blue. There was a bucket and dipper tied to the box. It was an ingenious way to dam up the creek into a well of ready water. Along the south part of the yard was the bunkhouse and privy. Charlie noticed a dip in the land beyond and thought it would be ideal for a barn or other sheds and a corral in the center.

Etta was washing clothes in front of the stove. She used a round zinc tub and washboard and homemade lye soap. The tub was perched on a wide board laid between two wooden chairs. At her feet was another tub containing cold rinse water, already full of soaped, scrubbed, and wrung clothes.

Charlie burst into the door, shouting, "We're together! No more separations!" He hugged Etta, feeling her wet hands warm and sudsy on the back of his neck. He lifted her off her feet and swung her around.

"I wish someone had done this to me when I was a kid," she squealed. "What will the children think if they see us?"

"My dear, they'll think I should swing them around next." He put her down and told her the news. "I'm not going to miss the best of life anymore—you and the kids."

Joe had seen his son come up the lane. He left his wood chopping, gathered up the three children, who were feeding the chickens or chasing them to see if they would fly. "Come, your pa's home. Let's see what he has to say."

The two little girls, now two and four years old, climbed into Charlie's lap. Floyd, six years old, dragged a clothesline rope behind him and began to roll it up. "Pa, I put a loop around the rooster today," he said proudly.

"Did I ever tell you what my grandma Rachel did to me for lassoing one of her best laying hens? It's best you practice on bushes and stumps. I'll set up a couple fence posts for that purpose when we get to the L5." Charlie's eyes danced.

"Pa, stumps don't move," said Floyd. "I'm ready for roping moving objects."

"I think I saw some cats around Mr. Gordon's bunkhouse," said Charlie. "Now, get your clothes in a pile so we can pack them in the wagon."

"What about Grandpa Joe?" asked Joella.

"Oh, don't worry about me, child. The L5's not more than four miles from the southwest corner of the Y6. Besides, I have news of my own. Will is bringing his family out as soon as he can find a buyer for his dairy herd."

"Margaret didn't write a word to me!" cried Etta. "I've been writing to her ever since we got here."

"It paid off," said Joe. "Will thinks cattle grow fatter and faster here than anywhere on earth. You accomplished what you set out to do—convince them to join us. They're acoming!"

Etta bit her tongue. Joe was right. Actually, it would be good to have Margaret here. Her face lighted up. "Everybody has good news. I have some news myself. If I don't say anything you'll find out soon enough." Suddenly she became shy and thought maybe she should have waited to tell Charlie when they were alone.

Joe saw her face turn pink and her eyes drop. "Honey, you tell Charlie. I already figured it out when you didn't run fast as an antelope after this here grandson of mine. Write to Ell, so's she can come when it's time." Joe cleared his throat and punched Charlie's upper arm. "Musta been some Christmas Eve you spent here. Nice Christmas present you left," he whispered.

"Pa!" said Charlie, himself turning red. Then he turned to Etta, who was smiling. "When?"

"Early October. I'm about three months gone."

"And you're emptying those tubs by yourself?" He was looking at the washtubs of water.

"Oh, I dip the water out with a bucket like I always do until there's only a little in the bottom before I take the tub outside to dump." Now Etta laughed and looked up. Her laughter sounded like the rippling of the creek behind the ranch house on the L5, bubbly and clear.

Charlie helped Etta rinse, wring, and hang the remaining clothes. He emptied the tubs and set them up against the back of the house.

"I get the wash done twice as fast this way. You're going to be a big help from now on," said Etta.

"Oh, no, just for a few months," Charlie teased.

Etta could not believe the room there was in the two-bedroom cabin Mr. Gordon had built. She especially liked the hot-water reservoir at the back of the kitchen range. There was a heater in the sitting room and doors hung on the openings to the bedrooms, which could be closed off in winter. There was a front door, which was hardly ever used. Outside the front door Etta planted blue-flowering morning glories and forget-me-nots. Gordon said they reminded him of the heather in the old country.

Charlie and Gordon dug cottonwoods from the banks of Horse Creek and planted them on the northeast side of the meadow. The meadow was filled with yellow, red, and lavender wildflowers. Looking at it from a little rise of earth behind the privy, it looked like a patchwork quilt. Gordon's handful of skinny cows would soon grow fat munching this mixture of grasses and green shoots and multicolored flowers.

The final snowstorm in April was a deluge of wet flakes covering everything with a six- to eight-inch blanket quickly. Charlie spread hay on top of the snow for the cattle that stood close to the six-foot-high, freshly planted boxwoods and cottonwoods. "The more hay the fewer hides," said Gordon. While the snow melted into the ground, Charlie and Mr. Gordon went over the L5's books. Charlie was determined to put the ranch in the black as soon as possible. He liked this honest, well-educated, gallant man.

"I expect much and get little," said Gordon. "Maybe if I expect little, I'll get a great deal."

Charlie suggested that they raise Herefords instead of Shorthorns. "I've noticed that the Shorthorns develop tuberculosis easily. It may be some delicacy in their inheritance. Anyway, no use accumulating a lot of veterinary bills." Charlie asked Mr. Gordon to run his few cattle with those of the Y6 so they could be worked as one herd until roundup time, or time to brand or time to sell to packing houses. "Running with Pa's herd may increase yours and his more rapidly. I'm going to have to figure some way of building up your cattle herd. It takes money to buy calves," said Charlie with a sigh, "and your barrel's empty. We gotta close the spigot."

Gordon's blue eyes brightened. "C.B., you go to the upcoming meeting of the Wyoming Stock Growers' Association as my representative. Aye, Senator Warren will be there and some others you might or should know. Though times be bad, this man will thrive, for he has the will to strive."

Charlie had no idea what he was getting into when he went to the meeting in Cheyenne's opera house. The men were seated on wooden folding chairs in the basement banquet room, which was a large rectangular box painted white inside. Charlie first looked at the large, framed pictures on the four walls. They were oils done by contemporary artists, some garish with color, others subdued, a scene along the Chugwater, elk in the canyon of the North Platte, a cattle roundup near Medicine Bow, and snow on the Laramie Peaks. The stockgrowers had no prepared talks. Anyone could get up and say what was on his mind. There were not only cattlemen present, but railroaders, packers, National Forest rangers, and a couple sheep growers, who pretty much kept to themselves.

Charlie could tell from the talks that the railroaders were courting the stockmen's business, hoping for a marriage between ranchers and the freight business.

When Judge Joseph M. Carey, with white sideburns and a white beard, blue eyes, and a nearly bald head, stood up, the whispering stopped. He spoke of preserving the range, especially from overgrazing by both cattle and sheep. He had a fair grasp of how the cattlemen hated the sheep grazing on cattle pastures. He was fluent and was not intimidated nor stampeded by questions from cowboys and ranchers.

Another man got up, adjusted his silver-framed spectacles, and spoke about mavericks, the stray, unbranded animal.

This law that mavericks were the property of the state was new to Charlie. He sat up and listened intently to the rest of the talks.

After the meeting he found Senator Warren talking with Richardson from the Union Pacific. Most of the other participants, a colorful variety of people, ranchers, cowboys, railroad men, the governor of Colorado, meat packers from Chicago and Omaha, feed station and stockyard managers, and men hunting jobs, went across the street to Hank Murphy's Saloon.

Warren was talking about the upcoming meeting of the newly formed Consolidated Cattle Growers' Association, which was to be in St. Louis. "I intend to go and will keep you gentlemen informed of anything new." He also said that he'd heard one of the large ranchers in Montana, Conrad Kohrs, had to dispose of fifty or sixty head of cattle because of turberculosis.

"I been watching the Herefords on Gordon's ranch. The ones that made it through the winter seem like tough, rugged animals. I've advised Gordon to breed them with the few Shorthorns my pa has," said Charlie.

"I'm going to try the same thing," said Warren. "Might eradicate tuberculosis altogether. See, you know as much about cattle as any of us."

"I want to know who is handling the meeting in St. Louis. The Union Pacific was asked, but turned the honor down," said Richardson.

"Oh, some commission firm, Hunter, Evans, and Company. They work for the meat packers," said Warren. "Notice of the meeting came from them."

At the beginning of summer Charlie ran into Senator Warren again. He was buying supplies in Cheyenne. He asked the senator how much the state wanted for mavericks and how the money should be paid.

"As I understand the law, it is clear that the money should be sent to Governor Richards, who then distributes it throughout the state for the benefit of cattlemen. You have some mavericks, C.B.?"

"Well, there are some listed on Johnnie Gordon's books. We ran across some two-year-old steers, unmarked, in the Coad draw, brought them back to Gordon's place. I talked to Mark Coad about them, and together we decided to let Gordon have them, because his winter losses were greatest. I want to know who to pay for those nine steers."

"Have you got the L5 brand on them?" asked Warren.

"Yup, did that after talking with Coad."

"Fine, you've done right for that old poet. The law has to do with roundups. A foreman is supposed to sell all the mavericks to the highest bidder. In your case, no one bid, except Gordon, and he set no price. The bidder puts his brand and/or ear slit on the cattle. Now, if you sent a check to Governor Richards for maverick steers, he'd be so shocked he'd believe you were plumb weak north of your ears—so would I."

They walked across the street and stood under the red and white striped awning shading the window at the Tivoli. Charlie wanted to ask Warren about the meeting in St. Louis, but Warren spoke first. "Let's go in and have a cup of coffee. I want to tell you about the St. Louis meeting."

The Tivoli was a bar and restaurant where organ music was

played most afternoons at four. There were ladies sipping tea at several of the tables.

"Counting numbers of people, that meeting in St. Louis was huge; counting its success, depends on where you come from. Let me explain," said Warren.

"C.B., these Texas cattle aren't ready for the rich pastures of Wyoming or Montana; they have to come up the trail and gradually get used to them. Besides, many have tick fever. I was so disgusted. Those southern ranchers believe in the motto, let the buyer beware. Those men had the audacity to hold up banners during the meetings and pass out paper fliers—all containing one word: *Trail*," said Warren.

"So, they're serious about cutting a wide track from top to bottom of our country? Leaving a scar on the belly of Mother Earth, my friend Red Cloud would say." Charlie felt scorn rise and constrict his throat. He pushed back a lock of sandy-brown hair. "They'll destroy pastures and watering holes. Northerners'll carry shotguns!"

"The Texas cowboys looked for a fight. The northerners said they'd put up fences, charge for crossing their ranchlands and using their watering holes. We held caucuses, argued for a day and a half, until the Texans backed away from the conflagration of our fiery words. Then the southerners turned right around and proudly pointed out that they voted for William Jennings Bryan because he was against cutting a canal through the Isthmus of Panama. They thought that would make us feel better. Can't they see the two cuts are entirely different? That's an example of pure woolly-headed thinking. It turned my stomach."

"Our vice-president, Teddy Roosevelt, lived on a ranch in Dakota Territory. Don't Texans know that? Every cattleman I know is a Republican. Jeems, haven't Texans heard of conservation?" said Charlie.

"They're overstocked. Waste is a way of life," said Warren.

"I hope a wide cattle trail comes to nothing. In another year the Texans will ship stock by rail and vote Republican. It's the only way to go. I wouldn't go on another trail drive—not for all the Shorthorns in Texas!" said Charlie.

Both men laughed heartily.

By the end of July, Will and Margaret, their two children, and their household goods had come by rail to Denver, then north to Cheyenne. They were enthusiastically welcomed by the Irwins. Their baggage and belongings were deposited at the Y6, but everyone stopped at the L5, where Etta had prepared a huge ranch dinner. Joe came in just as Charlie was introducing Johnnie Gordon and the hired hands to his brother and sister-in-law. No one was more surprised than Charlie to see his brother Frank standing with Joe. Frank looked wonderful. "I heard Will was coming here. I wanted to welcome him," Frank said.

Etta seated everyone around the large dining table, which was lighted with lanterns hung from the walls. The children were seated in the kitchen, with Floyd at the head of the small table to look after the smaller children.

There was beefsteak, slabs of baked salmon (from a can), mashed potatoes and milk gravy, wilted lettuce with vinegar and oil, baking powder biscuits and fresh butter, apple pie and coffee for dessert. Everyone spoke and laughed at the same time. The men talked about irrigation. "A little water and the hand of industry moves," said Gordon. Next they discussed the settlers who were moving in close to the ranches. One of the cowboys said, "Settlers are handy with the rope and carry a lightweight branding iron inside their boot. Mavericks will be a thing of the past, same as dinosaurs." Margaret and Etta talked below the men's deep voices and carried on talk about their children.

After dinner the men went to the sitting room. The children were allowed to go outside and play with the kittens. Margaret and Etta cleared the table and washed and dried and stacked the dishes and scrubbed the pots and pans. The dishwater was thrown out the back door on the morning glory vines. The children were called inside while the men went out to look around and get Will somewhat acquainted with ranching in Wyoming. Johnnie Gordon was delighted to show off his new barn and horses and cattle in the near pasture. Frank talked about the settlers who were bringing sheep into cattle country. He was all in favor of sending the herders farther north, into Canada. "Sheep graze the grass so short there's nothing left. Besides, where sheep have been, cattle won't feed, 'cuz they hate the smell of wool and sheep turds."

Charlie told about all the wild turkeys he'd seen on the corral railing early in the morning. The big birds came in to feed on grain that'd fallen from the horses' mouth bags the day before.

Charlie thought Will had become a hail-fellow-well-met, with a breezy nature. He seemed to be an optimist, coated with a humorous varnish, with a twinkle in his eye so that one never knew if he was putting a story over or not.

Will said, "I sold my three dozen black and white Holstein milk cows for forty dollars apiece, and with what I'd saved from working the coal mines, I come here pretty well-heeled. I've got my eye on buying a hundred and fifty Herefords, yearlings, as soon as possible."

Gordon told him to be sure to feed them plenty of hay during the winter. "The more hay, the fewer hides," he repeated to Will. "Better to sell live cattle than the hide. Winters make or break a man here."

With a straight face Will said, "I bucked a couple big snows while mining the Timberline. Once after a chinook the boss sent me to Colorado Springs for supplies. I loaded my packhorse with a dozen quarts of whiskey and a big gunnysack full of bread. When he saw that load, the boss was really disgusted and he yelled, 'How in tarnation we gonna use up all that durned bread?'"

Before dark Charlie hitched two horses to the spring wagon and took his father, Will, Margaret, and little Gladys and Charles to the Y6. Joe had cleaned the ranch house and fixed the loft for the children. They were delighted to sleep *upstairs* with their Grandpa Joe. Will and Margaret shared the big bed built against the wall, with leather lacings stretched tight across the bottom. Will dreamed of a great herd of white-faced cattle getting fat and sleek on the rich Wyoming grasses. Margaret had visions of riding horseback, visiting with Etta, and learning to sew.

Long after the cowboys had gone to the bunkhouse and·Etta and the children had gone to bed, Charlie, Frank, and Johnnie Gordon were up exchanging yarns, telling their thoughts about the Wyoming cowboys.

"The boys I work with on Coble's Iron Mountain Ranch are a devil-may-care lot," said Frank, "roystering, gambling, revolver-heeled, brazen, light-fingered, with a touch of bravado that's really appealing. But there's one who's almost shy. That loner, Tom Horn, is at the IM. Remember when—"

"I know what you mean," interrupted Gordon. "In a herd cowpunchers are mean, but individually they are good workers, genuinely sincere. To know some is an inspiration, to trade with some is an education. If you let any one of them bluff you, your discipline is shot to hell. And those boys move from one outfit to another, free as the wind. Theirs is a kind of nomadic life on the plains."

"Well, I've found that the foreman cannot ever be wrong. That's why everyone wants to be foreman," said Charlie. "That fellow, Horn, he doesn't want to be foreman?"

"No, no," said Frank.

"If a foreman doesn't make money for his employer, his services drop rapidly in value," Charlie went on. "Same as being mayor of a town. You gotta keep the town solvent."

Gordon said he couldn't agree more. It was well after sunup the next day when Frank saddled up and rode off toward Cheyenne and then across the Pole Mountain Road to the IM ranch, where he worked as hard as any other cowboy. He was a born horseback rider. His legs fit the saddle so he had complete control of his horse. As he rode out across the prairie he hummed "Git Along, Little Dogies."

Johnnie Gordon was pleased to have Etta and the children living in his ranch house. He liked to take six-year-old Floyd to the corral when the cowboys were breaking in a new bronc. One morning he told Etta that there were two broncs being broken. "C.B. found one horse down by the wide place in Horse Creek. The other horse must have come back to the drinking hole hoping to find his friend. C.B. got the second horse this morning. They're in the corral together. I have more horses on this ranch than I've bought outright. C.B. and you, ma'am, have brought life back to this place. I'll sell those horses and buy Herefords."

"Oh, Mr. Gordon, let Charlie sell them for you. He can sell duck-down jackets to Mexican cowboys in the middle of a heat wave," said Etta. Her laughter bubbled up to match the rippling of the creek.

Gordon nodded, knowing that Charlie could get better quality and three or four more cows for the strong, beautiful horses than he. Charlie was a master at bargaining. "Let your son come to the corral. He'd enjoy seeing two broncs tamed."

Etta agreed. She and four-year-old Joella and two-year-old Pauline would pick the wild currants she'd seen on the bank of Horse Creek behind the house. The men would enjoy currant jelly on their biscuits.

"Don't let Floyd get in the way. Watch him with his rope. You know he pulled Tom, the cat, out of the cottonwood yesterday. The dog chased Tom up the tree and Floyd chased the dog," called Etta.

Right away Floyd surprised Gordon and the two cowboys by climbing on the back of someone's horse from his high perch on the corral railing to ride around the outside. The boy hung on to the horse's mane and waved with his other hand. A wide grin spread across his tanned face.

"That kid is something," said one of the cowboys.

"He'll be a top-notch rider one day for sure," said the other cowboy.

"I can see it now, a big poster reading FLOYD IRWIN, BOY BRONC RIDER! at the Cheyenne Frontier Days," said the first cowboy, wiping his face on his red bandanna.

Gordon yelled, "Ki-yi-yippy! Ki-yi-yippy-yea!"

Floyd smiled broadly with all the attention. He swung his rope while riding the horse and caught the corral gate post. Gordon sucked in his breath. He thought the boy was going to be pulled from the horse. He wasn't; the horse stopped just in time. Gordon ran and pulled the boy off. "Go back to the house, where you'll be safe, and stay until we get these horses broke. My God, it's a wonder you weren't bucked off or pulled off with your own rope." He sat the boy on the ground and gave him a gentle shove toward the house. "Your father would never forgive me if something happened to you on one of those horses. Don't put your rope around the neck of any of the laying hens either, you hear me, buddy? Your mother'd scalp me for that." Floyd turned and waved as he trudged to the house. He wore boots and Levi's, same as the men. As he got close to the house, he swung his rope around his head and let it land over the head and front paws of the sleeping dog. The dog began to yip and bark loudly. It danced here and there trying to get the rope off. Floyd laughed, tripped, and the dog ran away with the rope trailing behind. Luckily Etta had come from behind the house to investigate the commotion.

"Son, get that rope off the dog. It could choke if the rope ever caught on something. Bring the rope to me. I'll put it up so the animals will be safe for one day at least."

Floyd stomped inside, growling to himself. "Now I suppose I gotta work my numbers?"

"That's right—school time for you and no berry-picking time for me," said Etta.

At the end of August all ranch work came to a halt. It was time for the annual Frontier Days celebration between Tuesday, August 28, and Saturday, September 1. Charlie volunteered to be on the entertainment committee along with Warren Richardson. He was in town every day for a week prior to the festivities. By Tuesday the city of Cheyenne was crowded, and still people poured in on every incoming train and stage. The first excursion train from Denver came in Tuesday morning, met by a large throng and a band. Other bands were stationed at street corners giving concerts. Many settlers came in to spend the morning buying supplies and the afternoon going to the fake shows. The favorite was Bosco the Snake Eater. Cowboys and ranch people also seemed to take a morbid interest in Bosco's handling of the snakes and taking one in his mouth to eat every once in a while.

Charlie stayed in town at the Industrial Club with Johnnie Gordon. Etta and the children came to town for the sights in a wagon with Joe, Will and Margaret, and their two youngsters. The children were wide-eyed seeing vendors up and down the street with brightly decorated canes, tin horns, megaphones, balloons, badges, and flags. The adults were surprised at how quickly these items were sold out.

Blind beggars and other mendicants were plying for money here and there throughout the crowds. Restaurants were packed to the hilt. Etta and Margaret were glad they'd brought picnic baskets, because both overheard visitors say they had been in the city all morning and could not find a place to obtain a meal. The saloons and gambling houses also had long lines of people waiting outside for their turns to get inside.

By eleven o'clock Joe and Will led their group to the shuttle so that they would have a good seat to see the afternoon's events. A streetcar packed to the doors left the Cheyenne depot at 12:15 p.m. for Pioneer Park. When it arrived at the park, the grandstand was already half-full and the bleachers were filling fast. The Irwins had tickets in the grandstand. Sitting high, they could see the roads leading to the park dotted with people, on horseback, on wheels, or on foot. Clouds of choking dust were raised by all the travel, and those on the roads came into the park with their clothes all the same color, alkali gray. The streetcars were run every fifteen minutes by courtesy of the Union Pacific until the last event was staged.

The sports were to start at two o'clock. Owing to the difficulty of getting some judges and officials to the Frontier show on time, the first sport was delayed for about half an hour. Floyd, Joella, and Gladys yelled along with some of the impatient spectators, "You'll have to hurry!" Joe stamped his feet and joined the children's cries. Etta and Margaret tried to hush them.

The first event was the cow-pony race for a half-mile. The purse was sixty dollars to be divided, first place, forty-five dollars, second place, nine dollars, and third place, six dollars. All of the entries were required to carry a hundred and eighty pounds or more. C. E. Thornburg riding Charles Hirsig's horse, Bumskie, won.

Next was the running half-mile, free-for-all, catch weights, with a similar purse. The horses would not line up properly at first. After half a dozen false starts, the horses were allowed to go over seventy-five yards of track. Bob Hilton won on Hirsig's Johnnie J.

The cow ponies ridden by ladies attracted more attention and enthusiasm than any other event besides the wild-horse riding. The distance was half a mile and the purse was twenty-five dollars for first place, fifteen for second, and ten for third. All of the ladies wore divided skirts, and several were rigged up in typical cowgirl style with bandannas around their necks and wide-brimmed hats on their heads. When the horses began racing, the people in the grandstand and bleachers rose as one in their excitement. Etta and Margaret yelled as the ladies rode in reckless fashion and kept everyone breathless by the chances they took.

"Oh, I'd like to wear one of those getups and ride a cow pony like that!" yelled Margaret. "You think I could do it?"

"Of course you can," said Etta. "Look on the program—one of the riders is a Mrs. B. Michaels, and another Mrs. Clara McGhee."

"I mean do you think Will would permit it?" said Margaret.

"Ask him," said Etta.

"I don't care what you do. If you want to do something, go ahead," said Will, not really paying attention to his wife's request, but watching two ladies' horses come down the stretch neck and neck. Fourteen-year-old Jennie Pawson's horse won by a nose. The ovation was thunderous as the good-looking, lithe girl rode to the judges' stand.

The two-mile relay race was interesting to everyone. Each cowboy rider was provided with four horses and rode half a mile on each. At the end of each heat he dismounted, changed his saddle to the next horse, mounted, and rode the next half. There were three entries: Frank Irwin, using horses jointly owned by himself and his brother, Charlie; C. E. Thornburg, using Charles Hirsig's horses; and S. Shirley, riding horses provided by the Richardson brothers.

To the embarrassment of Etta, Floyd stood up and yelled, "Hello there, Uncle Frank!"

Frank waved toward the grandstand. Floyd beamed and waved back. People around Floyd hissed, "Sit down, young fella, so we can see." Etta quickly pulled him down and gave him a fierce scowl.

The three bunches of horses were stationed at intervals of one hundred yards along the track to avoid confusion in changing saddles. In the first heat Frank came under the wire first, but almost lost his head to C. E. Thornburg, who was much quicker at changing saddles. In the second and third heats Frank came in first, and he won the fourth half by fifty yards. Joe clapped harder and longer than everyone around him, saying, "That cowboy's my youngest son!"

When the wild-horse race was called, the crowd had a real sample of wild life in the woolly West. The animals for the contest were provided mostly by the entrants. None of the horses were familiar to the feel of a rope with a cowboy on the other end of it. The distance of the race was half a mile, no hobbling or tying-down of stirrups was allowed. Each rider was given one assistant to help him saddle and bridle his animal. The purse of one hundred dollars was divided into three moneys. The fun began when the first horse was taken from the corral and continued until after the winner of the race had been across the line for some time. Eight riders and eight horses were taken with some difficulty before the judges' stand with saddles and bridles lying on the ground beside them. At the signal the men laid on the leather.

"There's Uncle Charlie!" squealed little Gladys. All eyes turned to Charlie, who was in the middle of the track in front of the grandstand in a grand melee of flying heels and heads, pitching, rearing, biting, kicking horses, and dodging men. The first man to mount, Otto Plaga, was up in less than a minute. His horse gave an exhibition of the real thing in cussedness. Plaga's belt caught on the pommel of the saddle, causing him to be thrown, but he quickly remounted, and soon after his horse settled down to run. The other riders had their share of trouble. The mounts persisted in bucking all the way around the half-mile. Charlie's horse insisted on turning and coming back to the grandstand to give another show of fancy pitching before bucking him to the ground. Cowboy clowns diverted the wild horse so Charlie could hobble to safety. One of the horses could not be saddled at all and finally broke the rope that held it and escaped. The horse was pursued by a crowd of whooping cowboys. Jack Dolan, from Pine Bluffs, won the race; Otta Plaga, from Sybille, came in second; and W. H. LaPash, from Cheyenne, was third.

The program of sports was closed that evening by a realistic imitation of a frontier stagecoach held up by Indians and rescued by the cavalry. This show had been Charlie's idea. Six government mules from Fort Russell were hitched to a cumbersome old

Deadwood coach. A big load of pioneers, who were actually cowboys and cowgirls, completed the equipment. The Indians carried out their part of the holdup in dead earnest. The cavalry had some difficulty in persuading them that a good thing could be carried too far.

As soon as possible after the holdup the crowds came back to Cheyenne for their supper and the open-air ball or the French ball.

Etta was too tired to stay, so she, Charlie, and Joe took all five children back to the wagons to sleep. Will and Margaret stayed for the open-air ball. A large canvas enclosure had been erected that was crowded to capacity by eight-thirty that evening. At that time a vaudeville performance was given, and when it was over the dancing continued until midnight. The weather was excellent for open-air entertainment.

Next afternoon at the Pioneer Park there was Indian foot racing, then Indian horse racing, and bronco riding.

Today Frank was ready to ride John Coble's wild bronco, Steamboat. The horse did not squeal or neigh like other horses, but roared with a loud honking, similar to the low, growling hoots of a steamboat in foggy waters. The horse was pulled in wild on the 1901 spring roundup. It was jet-black with two rear and one front white stocking feet. The fourth foot was coal black. Some cowboys believed that the horse was somehow injured during the gelding process so that his voice was ever after low and hoarse. Others said it was because he was injured when someone tried to pull him with a rope around his neck. Actually he was brought in from the Laramie Mountains by Frank Foss. Foss branded and castrated Steamboat and in doing so let the horse strike its head against the side of a large rock half out of the ground in the corral, breaking a bone in its nose. Foss saw the bone poking out and told Sam Moore to trim the bone. Moore tapped the protruding bone with a fingernail, then, with a pair of snippers usually used on barbed wire, he trimmed the bone so that it was flush with the horse's nostril. "All is well," Moore said. But all was not well. The horse had a strange, loud whistle as it breathed. Jimmy Danks said it sounded like a steamboat. So that became its name.

Steamboat was one of those horses that could never be broken; he was always a bucking bronco. He was destined to become a legend—more famous than most of the men that rode him. The wild and nervous horse was led out into the arena and walked to the front of the grandstand. The crowd roared and whistled as it sensed the power this horse would show in his jumps. Steamboat was blindfolded and seemed to quiet down some. He stood with his feet spread wide as the saddle was put over his back and seemed to squat slightly when the cinch was tightened. Charlie eared down the horse, by holding his head down and pulling on his ears, so that Frank could get in the saddle. Will talked gently to the twitching horse, and when he saw Frank was firmly saddled he nodded to Charlie, who let go the ears and whipped off the blindfold. The two brothers jumped back to the arena railing as Steamboat exploded into long crooked jumps. The crowd gasped as he sunfished and seemed to turn in midair. Suddenly Frank lurched too far to the right. His foot held in the stirrup only a fraction of a second, but long enough to send his body swinging like a pendulum under Steamboat's body. The crowd gasped.

Frank automatically stiffened his body and passed smoothly underneath the horse, but he was kicked by flying hooves before he cleared. This was the single event that established Steamboat's ongoing reputation as a wild bronc. Frank held his head afterward and complained of a headache for a week. Charlie wanted more than anything else to own the wild bronc from the first moment he'd heard its terrifying, wheezing whistle. He'd seen Danks trying to break it. The horse was stubborn and when Danks thought it was halter broke and took it out of the corral to a nearby flat, he found it was a bucker. Steamboat had a special way of throwing himself around with a twist, forelegs going south, hindlegs going north. Danks never could stay on his back. He told Coble, "I can't teach that gol-darned horse a blamed thing."

Coble told him to turn the horse out, as there was no time to fool with a damn bucking horse. Coble wanted to give the horse to the Elks Lodge in Cheyenne. He thought it might be used as a "goat" in their initiation rites or keep the grass around their hall cropped close to the ground. The lodge never took the horse after several members saw it buck Frank off its back to its belly, then the hard ground. Charlie had never been sorry that he later bought Steamboat from Coble.

In the next event Duncan Clark did some fine work in the fancy cattle roping and won a one-hundred-dollar purse. Charlie watched this event carefully. He felt he could give Clark some competition and promised himself he'd enter the steer-roping contest the next year or so.

Charlie recognized the cowboy, Tom Horn, by his mustache and cool, gray eyes. Horn had a group of bronco busters and fancy cattle ropers with him from the IM Ranch. Horn's group won first honors in their riding and roping contests.

Charlie went over and shook hands with Horn. He was in a good mood and said he certainly did remember Charlie. He also said he'd seen Frank, who worked with the same outfit as he, the IM.

"I've never ridden in a roundup with your kid brother, but I understand he's a decent cowpuncher, if he ain't crying about the food, thin blankets in the bunkhouse, and no advance pay. I'll tell you one thing. He sure has guts when he's riding that black outlaw pony called Steamboat. I admired that show!" said Horn. Then he talked Charlie into entering the very next event. A novel contest that Charlie admitted he set up himself. It was called the Rough Riding contest in which men acted as horses. Each man bore upon his back a rider and tried to dislodge his burden. Charlie was one of the horses and Leonard Lynch was his rider. Duncan Clark was a horse with DeWitt Irving as his rider. There were three other horses and riders.

Charlie and his rider, Lynch, won this contest. Charlie did well as the "horse," giving the best stunts, giving out a bunch of high and lofty bucks, a snaky, weaving motion. Lynch did well as the rider, looking like he was lost overboard in a choppy sea. But he hung on like a government postage stamp. He wore a pink shirt and pair of white chaps that were beauties.

Then occurred the most exciting event of that Saturday afternoon. The notorious Pearl Ward and a Denver girl, Buckskin Jimmie, had an altercation over a yellow band around Pearl's hat. "A yellow ribbon brings bad luck to any kind of contest. Not only that, it shows you are chicken-hearted with a yellow streak." There was a fierce fistfight. "Take off that band!" continued Buckskin Jimmie.

"I won't and you can't make me," answered Pearl, who was large, athletic, good-looking, and dressed in bright colors. She swung out with a right fist, then a left on the other's chin. The police interfered and removed the girls amid much cheering and applause. After the ladies' cow-pony race there was a reconciliation and both girls agreed to give an exhibition of fancy riding at the City Park on Sunday afternoon.

A week later at the L5 ranch a couple of the cowboys were training a new cutting horse for the fall roundup. Floyd was back on the top rail, watching. When the training was ended, one of the boys took Floyd in the saddle with him. "Come on, let's you and me see how this horse works, cowboy."

"Yup," said Floyd, "let's see." He put his rope around the saddle horn.

They rode out across the rocky field strewn with green and yellow grass and small yellow cactus flowers growing in clumps. Some cattle were grazing in the open field and some near Horse Creek.

"You see that little white-faced dogie?" asked the cowboy, pointing straight ahead. "We'll get that pretty little heifer away from the herd. Hang on. Here we go!"

Floyd held to the pommel. He watched as the chosen cow dodged and shifted suddenly. The freshly trained horse was ready, as if he knew exactly what the cow was going to do next. His ears worked to and fro, making Floyd laugh. The horse's eyes seemed to flash in the sunlight, and he seemed to be enjoying every minute as much as Floyd. The horse had the cow in the corral in no time. The next cow they worked out was not so easy, and it had no intention of being put into the corral except by ropes. Floyd found that when a cow is determined to duck and twist out of the way, there is little a cutting horse can do with it but run right alongside, turning and spinning as the cow does. The boy gritted his teeth, hung on to the saddle horn, and watched the cow move in a snaky line as it spun. The horse dashed back and forth, kicked up dust on one direction, reared backward, and then fell forward like it was shot from a cannon. Then the horse got behind the cow and rushed it into the enclosure. Floyd relaxed, held up one small hand, and yelled, "Hey — nice going! I'm going to be a steer roper!"

"You bet," said the cowboy, looking played-out himself.

By the first of October, 1901, Ell was at the L5 to help Etta through the delivery of her fourth child. All Ell could talk about was the assassination of President McKinley.

"Why would the president meet his assassin, Leon Czolgosz, in Buffalo, New York?" she asked one evening after supper.

"Why, dinna you understand? That is where the Pan American Exposition was in progress and the president went to see what was there," answered Johnnie Gordon pragmatically, leaning his chair back on two legs one evening after supper. "There is no need to worry. The country has a fine leader in Theodore Roosevelt. This country will have the Panama Canal built and guarantee its neutrality."

"What about those territories we gained from the Spanish-American War? There might be trouble there," said Ell. "Anarchy seems to be a way of life for some these days. I don't want to raise a child during these uncertain times."

Etta gasped in surprise and looked sharply at Ell. "You don't really mean that."

"But I do," said Ell. "There's going to be a war involving more than just little Spanish-speaking countries. The Americans will be involved in a global dispute because of all this unrest by those who wish to dominate. An anarchist doesn't believe in government or laws, but he wants to rule. It's a topsy-turvy mess. It's a convoluted way to reason. I'd like to see an end to it, but I don't." She threw her hands up in the air and let them drop in her lap. "It's no place for a woman of my temperament to raise children." Ell did not raise her eyes to Etta.

"Aye, aye, dear lady, where is your faith? Roosevelt sees all the problems. He'll provide more military training for the United States officers in due course. He's heard severe criticism of the army's performance in that Spanish-American War," said Gordon. "If this country is well prepared there won't be a confrontation; at least if there is, the United States will come out the winner. Dinna wonder why people fear things that are different? They fear ideas, they are suspicious of people that look and behave differently."

Etta cleared the table, washed the dishes, and put the three children to bed. When she came back, Ell, Gordon, and Charlie were still sitting around the table with the kerosene lamp lit in the center. They were talking about men who were different. Gordon was talking in general terms when Etta joined them again.

"Love is perennial, but crime is constant," said the Wyoming poet.

"So that the ranchers are easy prey for theft when their property is scattered all over the county. There are men who are eager to take advantage of low-priced beef and ask no questions about its origin," said Charlie.

"Aye, it's nigh impossible to convict a cattle rustler. Juries are nearly always composed of people who are on the side of the poor settler or underdog as rustlers are sometimes portrayed. We ranchers are villains, even though we may be broke and owing for the cattle we raise."

"Why are ranchers villains? Seems to me you could work together, ranchers and settlers and farmers," said Ell.

"Ranchers came to this area first, and we have something the latecomers want. We have the land they prefer, even though there's plenty still available for homesteading, as C.B. has discovered and is taking advantage of—say, he'll probably have you apply for a quarter section before you return to Colorado. He's smart, you know. He's homesteading in a kind of checkerboard pattern so no one will want those unclaimed sections surrounded by his property, then he can run his cattle over twice as much land," said Gordon, relighting his pipe and laughing and enjoying the pleasant fellowship.

"I never should tell you my plans," chided Charlie, putting a couple chunks of wood in the range to keep the chill off the kitchen as they talked. "If you hear I'm running for mayor of Cheyenne, don't believe it. I've changed my mind."

"Let me tell you about a case that involves me and that fellow, Tom Horn," said Gordon, settling in his chair. "He was hired as a range detective by the Swan Land and Cattle Company—a large consortium, owning several ranches in the area, and all run from corporate headquarters in Edinburgh, Scotland. Horn is different. He's half-Indian and half-French, according to him, and a natural-born sleuth, according to me. He can stalk as quiet as a cat or come out in the open and fight tooth and nail like a man and take the medicine if he loses. He was with General Miles, hunting Apaches, he's run train robbers into the arm of the law, he's a western man, living on the banks of the Rio Grande, deserts of Arizona, prairies of Montana, and now the banks of the Chugwater and Sybille. I don't understand him. He doesn't like living in any kind of house, and a road is useless to him. He can slip into canyons, getting to his destination faster than most by means known only to himself. He has a constitution of iron and the mind of a fox."

Charlie interrupted. "Years ago I lived on the Middle Fork of the Sappa, on a farm, with my folks. One winter a man stopped off at our place with a woman and several kids. The man was Tom Horn. He bought an old horse of ours and took off in the middle of night—one of the coldest nights of the year. I was a curious kid, and as soon as I found he'd gone by himself, I tracked him. I found him holed up in a ravine using the carcass of that old horse to keep from freezing to death. I was astonished."

"That's the same Horn as works for Ora Haley, mainly at the Two Bar and now and again for John Coble at the IM. He knows all the ways of the Apaches. He and Geronimo were thicker than ticks on a hound dog."

Etta set coffee cups on the table and brought in fresh hot coffee and cream and sugar. "He sounds like an interesting character."

"You'll probably hear stories about him yourself. He's a loner, but he also likes to spin tall tales. People love to retell Horn's stories."

"I enjoy listening to your brogue, Mr. Gordon," said Ell huskily.

"Well, this story I'm going to tell isn't short, so there'll be much listening enjoyment," chuckled Gordon, relighting his pipe with a match.

"Jack Madden was a settler who had hauled a wagon load of beef into Laramie every couple of weeks. That Irish chap's stock was two cows and a couple unbranded yearlings he'd lured into his corral. The ranchers knew what he was doing, getting rich butchering someone else's steers. The hides never showed a brand, but they were most often cut strange so as to leave out the mark. He always said that was the way the Irish skinned out an animal, to placate the little people, you know, the elves and such. The sheriff at Laramie said no one could pin a thing on the man unless he could be caught in the act and a brand on a piece of hide could be produced.

"Horn knew that and he also knew that the local juries aren't worth the powder to blow them into perdition." Here Gordon, the gentleman, stopped and nodded toward the ladies.

"I certainly appreciate your high regard for women's sensitivity," said Ell, fluttering her eyelashes.

Gordon beamed and continued. "Last November I was up in the middle of the night, excuse me, can't always hold my water, and I saw Horn riding through my pasture, his Winchester by his side, a blanket behind his saddle. He wore overshoes and an overcoat and carried field glasses. I heard two or three days later that he walked into the office of the Swan and spoke to his boss, Alexander Swan. Nobody had heard him ride up nor walk into that office. Swan, sitting on a chair tipped against the wall, knew that Horn would not spill what was on his mind right off, so he talked about the ranch gossip. A cowboy gossiping can say less but talk longer than any living creature I know. Horn sat against the wall, down on his haunches, and finally he told about his detective work. He'd watched Madden, his wife, and a cowhand, Hugh Dorson, drive a slew of cattle to the Madden pasture. This was no regular roundup, just a gentle nudge up a gully where those cattle were quietly grazing. Since all of the Swan cattle were used to free running, they could be moved easily from one pasture to another where the grass was thick.

"Horn is thorough. He not only watched Madden's pasture,

but he kept an eye on the log shack. Out in the hills there are no curtains on windows and Horn saw that when Madden was doing chores outside, Dorson was inside kissing Mrs. Madden. Each night a cow was cut out from the herd in the pasture and enticed up to the barn door by a pile of fresh hay. The cow was shot, lifted by block and tackle inside the barn. It was butchered and packed into the wagon.

"Alex Swan told Horn to cut his gossip tongue and stay away from drink, but to go to Laramie and find out who was buying Madden's beef. Horn did what he was told, and he also picked up the hide that had been disposed of by Dorson in a little draw behind Madden's place. A horseshoe brand was on the hide. Horn kept the stiff cowhide hidden in the bunkhouse on the IM. After a couple of weeks he added to the hide a dozen patches of hide all with the horseshoe brand. Suddenly one afternoon the boys at one of Swan's ranches noticed that they had another slew of newly weaned calves missing. Horn was told. He took off like a scalded rabbit down the valley past the cottonwood, whose yellow leaves were dropping. He skirted the main road to the Chug. There was no movement of man nor cattle along the Sybille. Horn circled wide around ranch houses and kept his eye peeled for men on horseback or moving cattle herds. He saw nothing, so circled back, finishing the biscuit and bacon rind he carried in his pockets.

"At the Two Bar ranch he unsaddled his horse and took it into the barn. He ate supper, picked up a couple of men, harnessed a team to a wagon, and saddled a couple of horses. The men spread out, rode fifteen miles in two hours. Then, over an embankment they saw a little creek and beyond it was a meadow with a hundred grazing cattle, and there, sheltered by a hill from the southwest winds, was the Madden log shack and barn. Horn took the lead, his Winchester in his right hand. Near the barn he halted and raised his hand for the others to stop. They waited for Horn to go hunched down inside the barn. There was some yelling and a sharp scream and the double doors swung wide open. The boys didn't wait now, they rushed in and found Horn covering Madden with his rifle. Behind Madden was a half-skinned cow, and Madden's wife holding a lantern so that the men could see to butcher."

Etta was wide-eyed with attention. Ell kept her velvet-green eyes on Gordon as though he were the only other person in the room.

Charlie, caught up in this dramatic moment, waved his hands

and said excitedly, "I can just see Horn standing there with his trusty Winchester raised to his shoulder, and the rustler startled, crouching with his bloody knife lowered against the corpse, and his wife, standing like a statue, her dress bloodied and her eyes galvanized in the light of the lamp."

Gordon shook his finger in Charlie's direction. "Aye, but you dinna know the wife wore a yellow rain slicker to protect her dress." Gordon's eyes glistened. "One of the cowboys used his head. He took the lamp and set it outside, far away from the barn. Another tied Madden's hands together behind him. Madden's wife tongue lashed that cowboy with strong, unladylike language until his ears were burned. Horn, with savage stoicism, took the raging woman to the house, which was no more than a poor, one-room log shack. Inside two children lay sleeping on a grimy blanket on the floor. Horn took Madden in the wagon to the Cheyenne sheriff, along with the damning evidence of that bloody, half-skinned cow sporting the horseshoe brand of the Swan outfit.

"Next morning the deputy sheriff went out to the shack and brought Mrs. Madden and the children into Cheyenne for questioning. Then they were released to go back to that dirty, run-down hovel. Madden had to stay in jail to await trial. Of course, he didn't admit he had enough money for his bail. His lawyer took the mortgage on his meager ranch and the effects left in the log house and barn as payment for his fee.

"Hugh Dorson stayed at the Madden place to look after his own interests. Even the severed branch grows again. Life went on. Madden's trial was three months later. I was on the jury."

"I'd bet my last dollar you were jury foreman, Mr. Gordon. Anyone with your intellectual capacity and understanding of people should be," said Ell, licking her lips, ready to say more.

"Sis, you have more wind than a bull going uphill. Let Gordon do the storytelling," said Charlie.

Ell smiled sweetly at Charlie. Then she smiled more sweetly at Gordon. "I can hardly wait to hear the whole story. I love to listen to your voice."

"The case was stretched out over two days and made all the papers. It could have been over in two hours. During the trial the two innocent children held hands and smiled. The judge had more sympathy than justice. Horace was right when he said, 'A jest, a smile, often decides the highest matters better than seriousness.' In his final speech Madden's lawyer said nothing of cattle rustling, only of unculpable children forced by strangers, who could never understand their plight, to attend a trial about matters they could not understand. The lawyer argued that the big ranchers were starving out the little ranchers. He said the big Swan company, in fact, was a foreign company that dared to invade the state of Wyoming. Using that line of reasoning, the lawyer, a pettifogger, reasoned that there could be no crime stealing from foreigners who had no business in the United States anyway. It was all horse sh—horse manure, wet hay. The jury went out late in the afternoon. I can tell you I dinna know what to do. I was sick in my heart. The crime was plain as the brand on the cowhide. The judge went home for supper and about eight in the evening returned.

"I told the other jurors that if they dinna convict, worse things may happen. I told them all ranchers would be losers. As soon as the judge returned I, foreman of the jury, sent word we were ready to report. You know how news spreads? There was a huge crowd inside the courtroom that night to hear the verdict. Our report was that the Maddens were guilty.

"The judge gave Madden a little talk and sentenced him for three years. Mrs. Madden was let off free to raise those two innocent children. Dorson celebrated by going on a three-day drinking spree, which landed him in jail the fourth day."

"What a good story about Wyoming law," said Ell. "I expected a lynching. Honest."

"But that's not the end of my story. The deputy sheriff, an easygoing lad, did not tie the hands of Madden, the prisoner. Remember there was a crowd in the courtroom and a large number of settlers outside in the hall. When the prisoner passed the settlers, an argument broke out between two roughly dressed farmers who acted drunk. The deputy's attention was sidetracked. The prisoner pulled away and went pell-mell down the stairs, out to the main floor. The deputy came to his senses and charged lickety-split after him, but one of the farmers fell in his path so that the deputy went flat on his face. Madden was out on the street, mounted a waiting horse, and rode out of sight.

"A search was started. But no one was prepared to hunt a man at night. Someone tried sending a telegraph message to Chugwater to keep an eye peeled for Madden, but no one answered at the station. Some of the crowd went to Hank Murphy's Saloon to oil their throats and loosen their tongues before they decided how to conduct a search. Horn said something like this to Alex Swan that night: 'Difficulties cause the average man to leave off what he has begun, but a true man does not slacken in carrying out what he has begun. Although obstacles may tower a thousandfold I will succeed in finding the prisoner.' Most of us went home disgusted.

"Next morning the *Cheyenne Leader* carried the whole sordid story of Madden's escape. In time it was about forgotten. An offer of a thousand dollars for his return had been made, but no one claimed it. Some thought Madden teamed up with the Hole in the Wall gang. It was rumored that after a couple of months Mrs. Madden, the two children, and Hugh Dorson left for Laramie. There they took a train headed for Washington or Oregon Territory. Of course the lawyer got the farm, the horses, and the cattle, selling them at a premium to some unsuspecting neighbor."

"Which shows people do what they have to according to their own standards," said Ell, reaching out her hand to touch Gordon. "Marriage can be like a horse with a broken leg. You shoot it, but that don't fix the leg. What happened to Mrs. Madden? I think she's got spunk. Dorson and Madden don't amount to spit in the river."

Charlie frowned at his sister for flirting with old Gordon. Etta poured more hot coffee.

"Now comes more about our friend Horn," said Gordon, keeping the tension high so the women would stay for the end of his story. "One day I met Horn in the Tivoli, where he'd been drinking beer. He wanted to talk. He told me he'd heard of a plot to find Madden. He didn't think anything about it because he himself had looked everywhere he could think of, even going back to the log shack once in a while. But not long after he was riding the Swan line, hunting stray cattle, and he came past the Madden shack. He remembered about the plot, so he tethered his horse and went up to look at the deserted place one last time. But it wasn't deserted; someone was inside.

"Madden was at the rickety kitchen table with his head in his hands. He wasn't armed, so Horn sat across from him and asked what he was doing. The man seemed dazed. 'I'm looking for my wife and kids,' he said. Horn tried to tell him they had gone long ago and it was useless to look for them. 'Old Hugh Dorson's looking after them,' Horn said. That angered Madden and he kicked at the table legs and the wall of the shack, making it tremble as bad as an earthquake. Horn tried to get Madden to go into Cheyenne with him, but he refused. Horn said he'd send someone for him. The man raved and ranted, so Horn left. A couple of days later Horn said he went back to take the man some grub and again talk him into forgetting his wife and kids and going to Cheyenne. He was certain Madden wasn't rustling cattle any longer and thought the most the sheriff would do was credit Horn with bringing back a fugitive and then let the man go. Horn would pick up an easy thousand dollars.

"When Horn got to the cabin, everything seemed deathly still. Only the buzzing of those big green horseflies could be heard with the rushing of the creek water. There was no horse, no saddle, no bridle in the barn. Inside the shack the smell was so nauseous and thick he could cut it with a knife. He found Madden lying on a cot. His gray wool blanket snugged around his chest was dark with dried blood. His revolver lay beside him. Horn said there was no doubt in his mind what had happened. He felt sick at his stomach and he went outside for a gulp of fresh, clean air. He told me he grabbed some dead wood and, without really thinking about what he was doing, piled it inside the open door, lit a match, and numbly saw it flare up into orange flames. He turned, got on his horse, and rode away, not looking back as the whole dry shack caught fire." Gordon sighed and closed his eyes.

Ell sighed. Her eyes did not leave Gordon. Her hand fluttered like an aspen leaf against her blanched throat. "I'll never have kids."

"Jeems, the man lost the reward money. He let it go up in smoke," said Charlie. "He drinks locoweed in his coffee."

"Charlie!" said Etta sharply. "Maybe the man had another goal, other than making money."

"You can be the judge of that," whispered Gordon. He continued in a low voice. "Horn's face was like a mask when he told me the last part of Madden's story. Then all of a sudden something in his face slipped or fell away. I saw a hint of softness. Horn's chin quivered and his eyes were not steely, but liquid, like deep, still water. He muttered. His voice was barely audible. 'That Madden was a dirty rustler, a jailbreaker, but he'd suffered plenty for his crimes. He didn't commit suicide—not really. He was murdered. You know who killed him? I killed him. I told him his wife and kids were with his cowhand, a man he'd trusted. I didn't lay a hand on him, nor point a gun at him. But I put that forty-five slug in his heart, as sure as I'm sitting here drinking beer.' Then his eyes glassed up and his face became brittle again. It was a moment to be remembered. A moment that rarely happens. It stirred my heart. To this day I can see that enigmatic man gaze over my head as if watching something far beyond vision. For just a fraction of a second he'd held himself for my inspection. I was honored beyond words. Horn's hard and thorny as cactus, but there's a soft place deep inside. He only acts cold-blooded as a rattler with a chill."

Six days later, October 6, 1901, Ell asked Charlie to take the three children to Margaret at the Y6 after breakfast. "Etta is having contractions."

Charlie looked in the bedroom before leaving. "I saw you up this morning looking perfectly fine. You sure this is the day?"

"I've had three others. I'd say I'm birthwise." She smiled and grabbed the rags tied to the rung at the head of the bed. She gritted her teeth and grimaced. A low growl grew into a scream that slashed the air.

"Wait! I'll be right back!" called Charlie. He pushed Floyd and the two little girls out the front door. He buttoned the children's coats and pulled their wool caps down below their ears as he boosted each one up in the wagon.

"What's the matter with Mama?" asked Joella. "Is she sick?"

"You dumb bunny. She's having a baby," said Floyd.

"How?" asked Joella. "You said she already had one in her tummy."

Charlie hitched the horse to the wagon and wondered how his six-year-old son was going to unravel Joella's tangled thoughts.

"The baby's coming out. That's why we have to go visit cousin Gladys and Charles." Floyd was practical.

Pauline began to cry. "I wanna stay with Mama!"

"You can't," said Floyd. "Don't act like a baby, because today you grow up. There's a new little baby coming to our house." He sat with his back straight and held the reins until Charlie jumped up into the wagon.

"A noodle baby?" asked Joella, incredulous.

Floyd turned and looked at his sister like she was a hair in his soup.

The sun was bright all day, but the wind blew in clouds by late afternoon. Charlie stayed in the barn and brushed the horses after he'd cleaned out the stalls. He checked over their shoes and mended two of them with the meager blacksmith equipment Gordon had. "I'll get Pa to look over all your horses in the spring. He's one of the best farriers you've ever seen."

Gordon nodded. "C.B., why don't you go up to the house and see how things are coming. You go from one thing to another here, and your thoughts are not on what you're doing. Look, there's a hole in your shirt, where a spark lit. You didn't even see it. Aye, go, lad."

Charlie didn't need coaxing. Inside, he drank a cup of coffee and sat at the kitchen table, hesitant to barge into the bedroom. He could hear Ell talking to his wife.

"I don't know what we are going to do if this baby doesn't come by night. I'll have to send all the boys to the Y6 for supper. What'll Margaret say about that?" Ell laughed.

Etta said something. Charlie couldn't hear because she muttered and groaned. Charlie was no longer hesitant. His wife was in pain, and he wanted to be there to make her feel better.

He saw Ell bending over at the foot of the bed. There were newspapers spread out over the bed where Etta lay. Then he saw Ell's hands move in like the pincers on a lobster. They were red and held tight and rocked back and forth. The top of the baby's head emerged, the hands were out of sight, but the arms rocked gently and skillfully, and one tiny shoulder emerged, then the other slipped into view. Suddenly a wormlike tiny being was in her bloody hands. Charlie could hardly breathe. He didn't move. Ell laid the ugly, glistening creature on the newspapers between Etta's legs and cut the dark cord. She bound it quickly and neatly with a thin strip of torn cloth. She held the baby up to the light from the window. The wormlike being had arms and legs and it cried. The sky beyond was streaked with wide red gashes. Charlie could not tell if the infant was a girl or a boy.

Ell was sponging the baby's face with mineral oil. She wrapped it in a clean rag. Charlie wanted to tell her to wash the rest of the baby. He opened his mouth, his throat was dry. He closed his mouth, and his hands doubled into fists at his sides. Ell was hovering over Etta. She was whispering in staccato bursts, "Bear down! The afterbirth! Atta girl! Good work!"

Etta gasped, then lay quiet, breathing easier, rhythmically, as if asleep. Ell looked up, but said nothing to Charlie standing in the doorway. She did not rouse Etta but packed a wad of cloth between her legs, cleared away the red, soggy papers, and walked past Charlie to put them in the kitchen range to burn. Ell went back to the newborn, cleaning it thoroughly with warm water and mineral oil. She wrapped the baby in a clean, flannel square and laid it in the little wooden bed Joe made for Floyd. The baby was really not so bad-looking.

Charlie began to rock on his feet. He was going to see Etta, to hold her hand and tell her everything was fine. Her face was as white as the bed sheet.

Ell got between Charlie and Etta. She was efficient and knew exactly what had to be done next. She knew that Etta was pale from loss of blood. She looked in her black medical bag on the dresser, took out a darning needle, threaded it with catgut that was being softened in a pan of hot oil on the back of the range. She bent over Etta and deftly sewed a couple stitches in the torn, soft tissue, pulling tight, but not puckering the edges. She pushed the packing back in place and bound it securely.

Etta awoke and feebly felt her midsection. "Where's my baby?"

Charlie was thinking, I'll tell her to name the baby Frank, after my baby brother. Pa's so proud of him. He's finally growing up and going to amount to something. He can sure ride a horse.

"The baby's right here," said Ell. "What are you going to call this cotton-headed little girl?"

Etta reached up for the bundle. "Let me look first," she said softly.

Charlie knelt beside the bed. "This is Frankie," he said.

"Frances is better," Etta murmured.

"She certainly took her sweet time coming," said Ell, sitting in the rocking chair. "I'd say this one is as stubborn as any Texas mule. As far as babies are concerned, I'd call it quits."

TWENTY

John Coble

Three days after her fourth baby's birth, Etta lay in bed watching through the window as the sky slowly became darker. Before supper Ell brought in the baby to nurse. Suddenly Etta could wait no longer. She was bursting with curiosity. "Please, tell me what you mean that you'll never have kids? You love kids. Kids love you."

Ell looked startled. The outside light was a pearly gray. She started to pull the curtain.

"No, don't shut out the twilight and don't turn on the lamp. Talk to me." Etta was propped up by pillows in white, muslin cases. The baby took short audible breaths as it nursed and a tiny fist lay warm against Etta's breast.

"I can't talk about it. I never should have said anything. I talked during a weak moment," said Ell. "Of course, Les and I want—wanted children. It's unfair. It's so hard." Tears filled her eyes and she brushed them away with a corner of her apron.

"Go on—just say it. Tell me. You'll feel better. A woman with your special talents . . . all the medical knowledge you have . . . the compassion, the caring for others . . . you shouldn't be troubled with hard problems. Come on, what's the matter?" Etta put the sucking baby on her other breast. A drop of blue-white milk rolled across the baby's chin. Her vigorous nursing ceased, and she slept.

"Promise you won't say a word to Charlie?" Ell twisted a button on the front of her dress until it lay in her hand.

"Promise, cross my heart, hope to die," said Etta.

"Well—here goes. Les had the mumps when we moved to Colorado Springs. Both sides of his face swelled so he looked like a jack-o'-lantern. His earlobes bent in right angles. He said he felt worse than a calf with the slobbers. I was a young, heartless sap. I teased him, saying I'd married a kid, not a man." Her voice caught. She waited a few minutes before continuing. She began to twist another button, then suddenly stopped and held her hands together.

Etta could see the outline of Ell's face and figure in the deepening gray light. She was a beauty, with a flawless face, deep, green eyes and long lashes, a straight narrow nose above a full mouth that turned up into the most alluring smile, a long slim neck that met strong shoulders. There were dimples beneath those shoulders in the back, especially when her arms swung backward. Charlie and the children had the same kind of dimples. Etta thought them beautiful, a delightful Irwin trait.

Ell was not a simple person, but she had a way of taking the complications out of others' lives and setting their minds at rest. Her hands were warm. Her hands were cool. Whatever the need, Ell could satisfy. She was good with the elderly, her peers, or children.

Etta thought about how old Johnnie Gordon was positively smitten by Ell. But Ell knew her place and how to handle feelings. All the Irwin children loved their Aunt Ell, who named the meadow flowers, let caterpillars crawl in her hand. She ran and sang with the children, but at the same time kept their high spirits in check.

"Then I was embarrassed, disgraced. I was shamed. I could tell no one. I thought it was my fault, that I should have known of some powerful root or bark that could bring him back to normal. I was angry and hurt. I shut Les out. I was scared to death." She pushed a bracelet around and around her wrist. "I was bitter. I thought only of myself, being deprived of sex. Not deprived of love because Les does love me. Marriage is more than sex. But at first I could think of nothing else. I had a home, companionship, understanding, compassion, clothes, the good life, but I was deprived—there were no good times in bed."

"Deprived of sex, no good times? What do you mean?" asked Etta, conscious of the baby's breathing, the laughter of the three children playing outside in the dark. In her mind she saw the three children bundled against the cold, and she imagined Ell in a flannel nightgown, woolen stockings on her feet. A sudden catch contracted the muscles in her chest.

Ell pressed her hand to her forehead. "When Les recovered he couldn't perform — he couldn't — he wanted to — and I wanted to. Oh, God, I wanted to!" Ell sobbed into her hands. Finally she dried her eyes and looked away from the sleeping baby.

"You love him?"

"Yes, I do love him. But I'm bitter. I can't understand why almighty God let this happen to us. Etta, we were perfect together and ecstatically happy. Now making love is as useless as putting a milk bucket under a bull or tits on a boar pig."

Etta wanted to laugh, but something held her back. She said, "Bitterness has added color to your language, for sure. Poor Ell. Poor Les. I'm so sorry. You both must have been humiliated and sick in your hearts."

"I felt deeply hurt. Me, who always had been a healer. I couldn't heal the one I loved most. I was blinded by self-pity. The thought of no sex forever was excruciating. Sex, to me, was a kind of power. Now I had no power over the most important person in my life. Thus, Les was not the only one left impotent. Life was rough as a cob." Her tears started up again.

Etta reached out for her sister-in-law's hand. "You can't fight something like that with tears. Les is still the same person with all the decent attributes you saw when you first knew him. Sex isn't everything. Charlie says, 'If you can't flee, go with the flow.'"

"That's easy for you to say. You don't know what it's like. I tried potions, lotions, massages, sitz baths, magic words and gestures, even prayer. When nothing worked on Les, I was angry, then sad. I felt inadequate and inferior. You have no idea the mortification I went through."

"You're right, I don't know, but I'm not ignorant. Stress enriches life, and you're letting stress ravage yours."

Ell looked surprised. She thought she was telling Etta all her feelings. She thought Etta would understand, not criticize. Tears washed her face. She got up from the rocking chair and went to the window, looking out on the yellowed grass where the children were throwing wood chips at a tomato-can target.

Etta held out the sleeping baby. "Please put her back in the crib." She felt empty without the child in her arms, more vulnerable.

"Why? Why is it so hard for me to deal with?" asked Ell.

"No one knows how to react in a situation until the time comes. Each person is an individual. What did Les do?"

"He took one of the rooms upstairs. He goes to work at his accountant's office every day. He comes home in the evening and eats supper with the men patients I look after. He takes care of my bookkeeping. He advises me about the health-care business. We go out to the latest plays. He is like a wonderful man courting his lady friend. We hold hands."

"Some of the most famous men, Plato, Leonardo da Vinci, Michelangelo—"

"That doesn't make me feel any better—they were homosexuals, not geldings."

"Ell, Les is not a gelding! My God! He's, he's—listen, I don't think it's fair to make a judgment, to put a name on it, except impotent."

Ell twisted her bracelet around.

"Everything you loved about him, except that one ability, is still there."

"Yes, you're right. I know that."

"You know he suffers. You admit you've been selfish and indulgent in self-pity. He'd change if he could. Don't you suppose it's been really hard for him to accept the truth?"

"He knows what he is," said Ell, sighing.

"Do *you* know what he is?" asked Etta.

"Well, he's a man. He's suffered. He's kind, tolerant, and responsible. He's unhappy. He's married and wants to stay with me. He knows his obligations. He's a man with a handicap," she said without hesitation.

"He's more of a man than some we've both seen," added Etta.

"Honest, I can't imagine myself married to any other—yet there's this big gap in my life. I miss sex. I like sex. Is that terribly wrong?"

"I'm surprised at my own feeling. I don't think it's wrong at all. Talk it over with Les. Let him know you love him. Tell him of being unsatisfied, unfulfilled. Every problem has a solution when you think rationally. Your marriage is like a horse with a broken leg."

Ell hesitated then had to smile. "How's that?"

"You shoot it—you haven't fixed the leg."

Neither young woman spoke for a while. Then each looked

up. Ell spoke first. "I have my patients to look after, babies are born, children break bones, get diphtheria, adults have TB, dropsy. Did you know mostly men come to stay at my health spa for rest, hydrotherapy, herbal teas, lotion massages?" Her face brightened. "When those men leave me, I want them to feel a whole lot better. It just dawned on me that I'm going to do whatever I can to make them feel their best. You know what I mean?"

Etta's eyes widened. She put a hand to her mouth.

"Les and I will share everything, except bed. I'll make him happy in other ways. But there's no reason why we both must suffer forever, and by God I won't. I should have thought of that before."

"What about children?" asked Etta, her heart pounding hard.

"Children?" she asked sadly. "I'll come to play with yours and Will's. My men will pay well for what I know about certain plants and human cycles. I'll not be embarrassed by a pregnancy that ties me to some strange man."

Again Etta was shocked by her sister-in-law. She didn't say a word for a moment. Then she ventured, "I wonder what your grandma Malinda would say if she knew? What would she say about using contraceptive knowledge for—uh—you and your men patients to—uh—to have an affair with no intense devotion or attachment. It's—it's sinful. You wouldn't. You are really joking, just to see what I'd say. Aren't you? Your grandmother would be scandalized. She'd say you are bringing a hornet's nest about your ears."

Ell brushed her hand over her silken, strawberry-blond hair. She smiled. "She'd understand. She always said, 'A person does what he has to do. Life is short. Live it thoroughly. Don't keep your head in a sack.'"

There was more silence. Etta had tears in her eyes. "I'm so sorry for you and Les. This is hard to believe. My feelings are all mixed together. It's like looking in the looking glass and suddenly seeing a face you don't recognize. I can't believe what I've heard."

"Look at it this way. There must be others that have had such a problem. Grandma Malinda used to say, 'There's nothing new under the sun when it comes to men and women together.' I'm lucky—Les and I love each other, even if that love is on a different plane nowadays. I'm beginning to think of him not as my Adonis, but as my mentor." She took a deep breath. "Well, little Etta, you know what kind of sister-in-law you have."

Etta pointed to the kitchen. The children were banging on the door to come inside. "I think they're cold. They've been out a long time."

"I'm coming, you little coyotes," called Ell. She let the children in and helped them hang up their coats, caps, scarves, and mittens. Pauline had only one mitten.

"The dog took it," said Joella. "I think he ate it, so no use going to look for it."

That logic made Ell laugh. "Joella thinks like me."

Etta said, "Oh, please, don't tell me that—not today."

Pauline put a cold, chubby hand on the baby's face and instantly the baby woke crying. Ell picked her up and rocked her back and forth in her arms. "Hush-a-bye, sweet Frances—Sweet Frances, what middle name do you have that will last a lifetime —bittersweet lifetime?"

"You give her a middle name," called Etta. "Make it melodic, something unusual. Name the baby before you leave us."

"Get supper first," said Floyd. "Want me to lasso a chicken?"

Two days later Etta was out of bed, doing the easy household chores. Ell was packing her suitcase. She was about ready for Charlie to take her to the Cheyenne depot so she could take the Union Pacific train to Denver, then the Denver and Rio Grande to Colorado Springs. The three older children were watching their aunt Ell.

"Are you going to wake baby Frances to say good-bye?" asked Joella, tossing her long blond hair about her shoulders.

Ell took up the baby and held her high in the air. "I'm going to give her a good-bye kiss even if she isn't awake. And we're going to have a naming ceremony before I leave."

The children gathered around, wondering what their fun-loving aunt would do next. Etta followed them to the sitting room.

"Is this a big ceremony? Should I tell Pa to come in?" asked Floyd.

"No, no, it's just us. Now, watch and listen." Holding the baby in a flannel blanket, Ell twirled around three times and held the baby away from her dark wool dress so she wouldn't be covered with white flannel fuzz when she boarded the train. She looked at the floor and whispered to the children, "Can you see them? All the little people have gathered with us to hear your baby sister's full name."

"Little people? Like the ones Mr. Gordon talks about?" asked Floyd, showing some doubt after looking at the bare floor.

"They live outdoors, but come in for special occasions, usually making themselves invisible to unbelievers. Mr. Gordon told me the most melodic and lovely name he knew. It was his mother's name, Gwendolyn. I do believe it is a favorite among the little people. Ooops!" Ell pulled three-year-old Pauline back beside Floyd. "You almost tripped on one little person. Here's the genuine ceremony: I name this wee lamb, Frances Gwendolyn." She handed the baby to Etta.

"A cup of tea to seal the name giving," said Ell, putting cups on the kitchen table and motioning for everyone to come sit.

"There's no time," said Etta. "Charlie will be in any minute calling, 'All aboard for the depot!'"

"There's time," said Ell. "Charlie needs a hot drink before setting out for Cheyenne. Look out that window. Lazy snowflakes are beginning to fall."

The Irwin-Gordon fall roundup of 1901 brought in more than a hundred unbranded steers, cows, and heifers. Charlie surmised that the animals were caught in a coulee in the area where most of the Irwin cattle range during the winter. They were out of sight so were never found by their rightful owners and probably written off their books by now.

"I don't have any intention of some damned line rider seeing us outlined against the sky or squatting over a lonely campfire with a bunch of mixed, unbranded cattle nearby," said Will. "Let's get these scrawny critters over to the Y6 and slap a brand on them pronto."

"All right. Let's move them out now," said Charlie.

"Afterward, you think we could make one more roundup to see what more we find?" asked Will.

"Nope. We have our own cattle and then some. Don't be greedy."

"Aw, Charlie, if I'm going to raise beef cattle I have to have a sizable herd. I'm not going to run a cattle ranch like some female chicken farm," said Will as he rode around the bunched-up herd, careful not to frighten a skittish cow by talking too loudly or lighting up a cigarette where the cow could see the bright flame or smell the smoke. In the Y6 pasture Will, Charlie, and Johnnie Gordon sorted out the unmarked animals after they had sorted the Y6 brands from the L5.

Will took the young, unmarked cattle for the Y6 brand. Charlie took the rest for Gordon's L5 brand.

Gordon was stunned. He could not believe that anyone would share their cattle herd with him, even if the animals were rangy, wild beasts.

"Listen, boss, I don't think anyone with an ounce of pride would claim them scrawny things right now," said Charlie. "But you and I know that a winter with our main herd, some spring fattening on rich, green grass, and they'll be something fine to sell those Chicago packers. You'll be in the black on your books."

Johnnie Gordon shook his head. He was still amazed. This foreman, C.B. Irwin, had a heart as big as a grandfather bull buffalo. "You're right. Where is my pride? Those scrubs are so thin we'll have to wrap them in extra cowhide to keep them together. But if they fatten up during the spring, I'll sell them. I'm thinking if our Hereford bulls breed with those skinny Shorthorn cows, we'll have something more worthwhile by spring. C.B., thanks for everything." Then he stopped as though something else was on his mind and he didn't know how to say it. "Uh—I'm so curious, I have to ask this. Why did your delightful sister want to know my mother's name—she's been dead six years."

Charlie burst into a fit of laughter. "No offense, sir, but this is the honest truth. Our youngest baby was just given your dear mother's name as her middle name. Didn't Etta tell you? My sister wanted to honor you, and she didn't want you to feel she was in any way—uh—flirting, but that is something she does quite naturally."

"C.B., I was taken by your sister. She impressed me as a competent woman—and intelligent. She honored me. Why, I am flattered. You and your family have wrapped yourselves around my little finger."

"If that's the case, sir, then you get another honor."

"What's that?"

"Put the ear crops on these steers and cows as soon as Will and I get them branded." Charlie chuckled heartily.

Gordon nodded and moseyed off to the barn to sharpen his knife on the revolving, round cement block. He pumped the contraption like a bicycle and lay the knife blade against the spinning cement.

Charlie hired a local rancher's wife, Dora Miller, to come help Etta with the cooking and cleaning for a few weeks. A cot was placed in the children's room for Mrs. Miller, who was glad to have a change from cooking for her man, two boys, and a schoolteacher who rented a room at the Miller place. She said Miss Kimmell, the teacher, would cook, but save the cleaning at her house until she returned. Mrs. Miller was a large woman, with powerful arms and legs, strong shoulders and back, and large breasts. She knew what had to be done and went right to doing it. She peeled potatoes, fried the beefsteaks, and made gravy. She couldn't understand why anyone might want something else for supper. She scrubbed the floors, but could not understand why Etta wanted the window curtains washed and ironed. She was impressed with the books on the shelves in the sitting room and even more surprised to see Floyd read.

"I taught him," said Etta proudly. "He really needs to go to school with a trained teacher."

Mrs. Miller said, "My boys ain't much interested in school, although they're interested in the schoolteacher. Her name is Miss Glendolene Kimmell. My, oh, my, she has the most unusual eyes you ever saw, big and brown and kind of fish-shaped. I told my man, James, 'I think she's oriental somewhere in her background,' he says, 'Those Celestials have all the looks, but they're too small-boned for any kind of work, except book reading.' I used to think she had the loveliest name until I heard what you named your youngest. Say, *Gwendolyn* and *Glendolene* are alike. You know our schoolmarm?"

"No," said Etta, checking the bread she was baking. "Baby Frances was named for Mr. Gordon's mother."

"I had three strapping boys, but never a little girl." Mrs. Miller looked longingly at Joella and Pauline sitting at the kitchen table, stringing macaroni on cord to see who could make the longer chain. "Girls are sweet and docile. I believe they even smell different, like clover honey. Boys smell like cow pies right from the start. Don't you agree?"

During the winter of 1901 Etta had a letter from her sister, Kate. She wrote how their mother and father had sold the Kansas farm and moved with all the young ones to Tonkawa, Oklahoma. Mr. McGuckin found the town needed a Baptist minister. Immediately he found his calling. In a few months he rallied the congregation into donating time, money, and materials for the construction of the First Baptist Church in Tonkawa. The news made Etta feel good. To Charlie she said, "Ma must be so proud. She's always wanted Pa to do something that would be uplifting. Ma never did like living on a farm; she wanted to be citified. I know how she felt, because I miss living in town. I heard some of the ranchers have a house in town for their wives and children to stay in while the young ones go to school. In summer they're all back together on the ranch. Sounds nice. What do you think?"

"I think it takes money," said Charlie. "My dear, there's nothing I wouldn't do for you. First let's get Gordon on his feet, then we'll start saving—"

"You mean we haven't saved anything yet? Where has the money gone?"

"You know."

"No, I don't know. Tell me."

"Well, I sent some to Will and Margaret so they could have enough for their fare here. Then I paid the Wyoming Stock Growers' Association two dollars a head for the unbranded stock we found in the fall roundup. I know Warren told me to forget it, but there were more than a dozen head and I didn't want anyone accusing us of burning rawhide that don't belong to us. We picked up a lot of unclaimed stock, others were just too lazy to hunt for them, or they were gathered by someone working ahead of the roundup. Anyway, they're paid for fair and square. Alice Smith, the association's secretary, said I was the first to get a bill of sale for unbranded stock."

"Charlie, you bought stock for your brother Will and for Gordon, both?"

"Why not? Keeps us out of trouble and they'll each make money on them. Will says he'll put his money on the Y6 books."

"We'll never have enough to get a house in town and send Floyd to school!" Etta cried.

"I said there's nothing I won't do for you. Be patient," said Charlie.

"I hope that Floyd isn't sixteen by then," said Etta with a laugh. The sound was harsh. "Maybe I'll send him to a one-room ranch school."

"There's none close, unless we start our own," said Charlie. "Just have more faith in me. I'll get you what you want soon enough. There's always a way if we don't play leapfrog with a unicorn."

"Charlie, you say funny things." Etta laughed. This time it was a melodious sound. "I can't stay angry with you." She put her arms around his waist and drew him close. "I love you so much. I don't really begrudge Gordon nor Will a few scrubby cattle. After all, I have you and four children who all, like you, have dimples in their backs."

There was a foot of snow on the ground and it wasn't yet Thanksgiving. Etta and Dora, as they now called Mrs. Miller, had cleaned the cupboards and were dusting the books on the shelves. Etta told Dora about her desire to send the children to the school in Cheyenne. "I want them to have the best education possible. If we can't live in Cheyenne, I suppose your Miss Kimmell is good."

"Miss Kimmell is no bigger than you are, Missus Irwin. I'm sure she's fine as a schoolmarm. One of the cowboys from over at the Iron Mountain Ranch is sweet on her."

"Charlie's brother Frank works there, at the IM. It's not him that is courting your schoolmarm, is it?" Etta teased.

"Oh, no. It's another cowboy, Tom Horn. A big man, about as tall as your Charlie, and he wears this little mustache across his upper lip. It looks like a piece of deer moss. He tells her how to be firm with those big kids, especially the Nickell kids. They need discipline."

"Why's that?"

"Missus Irwin, I could write a book on that there subject. Didn't you read the papers about Willie Nickell's shooting last summer, July eighteenth to be exact?"

"No, I don't remember anything like that. Did this Willie shoot well?"

"Oh, don't say that. He didn't do no shooting. He was shot. That overgrown thirteen-year-old was dry-gulched, let me tell you." Dora set her dustcloth down. Tears streamed down her face like a rainstorm hitting the side of a craggy cliff. "Oh, Lord, if you don't know nothing, I have to start way back. So much has happened. You won't believe how people can be—mean—heartless." Her eyes were red and puffy. She blew her nose on a rag she kept in her apron pocket. "Kels Nickell and his dumpy wife, Mary, had a nerve to blame my husband, James, for the shooting of that boy. I'll swear, whoever asks, that James was home, sick with a headache built for a horse, the day of the killing. James, himself, told John Coble he stayed to home that day. Coble came out to ask what we all knew about that trouble."

"Mr. Coble?" asked Etta.

"You know that fine-looking gentleman?"

"No, but I've heard of him. Charlie's brother works for him, like I said."

"Ya, I guess most everyone has worked for him once. He raises mostly horses. Sells them back East as polo ponies. It was ten years ago when Kels Nickell went to John Coble's ranch to accuse him of letting the IM cattle graze in his sheep pastures. Nickell got into an argument with Coble's foreman, George

Cross. Cross told Nickell that it was more like Nickell's sheep
trespassing onto the IM pasture. Everyone knows cattle won't
graze where sheeps've been. Anyway, there was a frightful scrap.
John Coble tried to break it up. A more honorable man I never
met. Nickell has the morals of a hydrophoby skunk. He jumped
Coble like a roadrunner on a rattler and ran his knife into Coble's
stomach—twice.

"Cross brought Nickell into town to the sheriff. Then took
Coble to Doc Maynard's place. This was in the *Cheyenne Daily
Leader*. I can remember James reading it to me as if it were
yesterday. It was hot as ashes in Hades that day. I guess we all
learned Nickell has a short fuse. Poor John Coble carries a couple
of ugly scars on his stomach to prove Nickell's temper."

"Dora, that's a horrid story, an awful way to settle a dispute."
Etta felt unsettled.

"Well, missus, it was that same devil, Kels Nickell, that
caused James to shoot Baby Brother. Honest." Tears again
streamed down Dora's face.

"Dora, you don't have to tell me this. It's too painful. Let's
wash the floor," said Etta, fascinated yet repulsed by the violence
in these people's lives.

"You know, now that I've started, it's better that I finish,"
Dora said, and wiped her eyes on the hem of her dress. "Kels was
one of the first ones in these parts to have the gall to raise sheep
in cattle country. Right off, them sheep grazed over on our place,
as well as over on Coble's and others. James went to Nickell and
told him nice to keep the sheep out of our cow pasture. Kels paid
no attention. He said, 'Mister Miller, I think you're full of horse
manure.' So James started carrying a rifle and swore he'd shoot
every sheep he found on our place."

"Oh, I don't like guns. Did you stop him—your James?"

"Oh, no, ma'am. I don't tell my man what to do, that ain't
safe. Only a fool argues with a mule. Early this spring, when
there was snow on the north side of the hills and in the gully,
James took our precious four-year-old, Baby Brother, out target
shooting. Actually, they went looking for sheep. I don't know if
they found any, but the gun'd been shot. James cleaned the rifle
and showed Baby Brother how to look inside the barrel to see the
crud that needed wiping out. James swears he checked and got all
the shells out. But he was wrong. Accidentally he let the hammer
slam back just as Baby Brother walked up to have a look into that
barrel." Her shoulders hunched forward and she sobbed, with her
hands over her face. Then she looked up and said, "That was the

blackest day of my life so far. That .30-.30 shell smashed into Baby Brother something fearful. He never knew what hit him." She let the tears slide down her cheeks unchecked. "It was Nickell's fault for having sheep in the first place!"

"Oh, my, Dora, I'm so sorry," comforted Etta. "But it's wrong to blame someone else for our mistakes no matter how terrible."

"Missus Irwin, James wouldn't have had that gun unless he was after sheep, and that's what killed Baby Brother. I swear to God, I can't feel any kindness toward the Nickells. Neither does James and our two boys."

Etta gasped. "Dora, don't say that! What about this Willie Nickell that's dead? His mother has a broken heart same as you."

"Oh—on that fateful morning the kid, little Willie, was dressed in his pa's hat and rain slicker on account of the drizzly weather. Folks say he was going to bring back a sheepherder who'd left his pa's ranch the day before. I guess Mr. Nickell had a change of heart and decided to hire the herder and sent the boy to bring him back. Willie brought his horse to the gate, climbed down, and removed the wire loops from the post, took his horse through, and before he could put the loops back he was shot twice. The thirteen-year-old son of Mary and Kels Nickell shot! Now they know what grief is!"

"Oh, my! Who would do such a thing? Who?" repeated Etta.

"Someone who hates sheep. So most any of the ranchers, I'd say. But it don't make no difference; the boy was mistaken for his pa. Remember he was wearing his pa's hat and slicker and riding his pa's big brown horse and the morning light was gray with rain and clouds."

Etta wondered why she was held spellbound by Dora's gruesome talk. She told herself she'd not repeat a word of it to Charlie, but she also knew she'd tell him every word.

Dora could not be stopped. Her mouth was like a windup toy; it chattered until the spring lost its tension. "James and our two boys were taken by the sheriff to Cheyenne. They were asked a lot of questions; stupid, James said, but nobody could prove anything. James wasn't the least bit scared, but the boys were petrified. The varmint Nickell was shot in the arm not more than a week after James and the boys came back from Cheyenne." Dora snickered. "I think Nickell was going to the barn with his little girl at his side to milk his cows. Musta' scared the stuffing out of the little girl to see her daddy curl up, grovel in the dust, because he was shot. And to make matters worse, a couple days afterward some of Nickell's sheep were clubbed to death."

"That poor man!" cried Etta.

"No, he ain't. He buys sheep for two dollars, grazes them for a year, and sells them for ten. He makes money faster than the cattlemen. I can't make myself feel sorry for a man that's lucky he wasn't killed same as his son, Willie, and of course our Baby Brother. The man's well off, if you think how he blamed near ruined me."

"Ruined you?"

"Yes, ma'am. I'm a woman, but I don't want no more children, no more. Children are more heartache than joy. They do as they please, not as you say, and they curse you more times than they praise you. But you love 'em. You don't want one killed. When Baby Brother died, I was no good for nuthin' for weeks."

Etta felt out of sorts by Dora's attitude. She began to scrub the floor herself. Dora began to get the noon meal. Each was quiet with her own thoughts.

During the meal, Dora, who hadn't been to many homes besides her own, and was a bit unsteady about her manners, happened to pour buttermilk in her coffee instead of cream.

"I'll get you another cup of coffee," said Etta quietly. "You're still upset from me letting you talk this morning. It's my fault."

"Oh, no, don't go to any bother for me." Dora blew on the curdled mixture. "I often use buttermilk in my coffee. It gives it a tart flavor."

No one said a word. The cowhands kept their faces steady.

After the men had eaten and left for additional chores, Etta put Joella and Pauline down for afternoon naps. Floyd was allowed to go down to the corral with the men. Etta sat in the rocking chair to nurse the baby, and Dora heated water to wash the dishes.

Dora broke the stillness. "I was afraid your mister was going to ask me why I was talking instead of working this morning." She gave Etta a glance.

"Charlie wouldn't criticize you. He'd leave that to me."

"If he'd asked me I was going to tell him I was working until I got hurt. You see, I was fixing the noon meal and I slipped on the bar of lye soap left on the floor from the scrubbing and wrenched my knee." Dora leered, without a suggestion of a smile.

Etta laughed. "You wouldn't?"

"Yes, I would, but I didn't have time to practice the limp. Say, I've been wondering. Does the mister want another?" She was drying the pewter flatware and nodding toward baby Frances.

"Charlie's good with children," said Etta. "Yes, I think he'd like another boy."

"I knew a family once had five children; three boys, then a girl, then another boy. They was named Matthew, Mark, Luke, Ann, John. You know, most men don't want the consequences. That's a fact. All they want is the fun of acting like bulls. Most are that way. Maybe yours is an exception. An exception is somebody who don't follow the ordinary rules. That fellow Horn don't follow ordinary ways. He told me he left home when he was only fourteen on account of a whipping his pa gave him that laid him in bed for a week." Her eyes squinted and she seemed to wink to the right. "He's sweet on our schoolmarm, Miss Glendolene Myrtle Kimmell—comes to see her. My boys August and Victor have calf eyes for her, but she don't have time for them. I think she likes older men. Tom Horn is ten, fifteen years older than your man. Ah, he's good to look at. He's about six feet two, broad-shouldered, deep-chested, not an ounce of superfluous flesh, with muscles of steel, straight as an Indian, with just a suggestion of a swing or swagger. He might be hard-featured except for his full lips. His eyes don't flinch and can stare anyone down. He's always polite and good-natured. Mr. Coble thinks he's one of the finest cowboys in the country. When he was at our place, he told us about his getting up on the ridge pole of the corral gate and dropping down to the bare back of a bronco as it came out. He had no saddle or bridle, nothing to hold him on except his spurs. That's a wild ride!"

"Tom Horn must be someone important in these parts. Mr. Gordon told a story about him bringing in a rustler."

"Important? I don't know anyone important. Horn's a cowboy with a wonderful shot. He can stoop down while riding a horse, pick up a stone or can, throw it in the air, and hit it once or twice before it falls to the ground. The Indians are said to be afraid of him because he's so quick on the trigger. James sees him riding the line once in a while, looking for sheep or cattle grazing outside their own territory. If he saw someone suspicious, someone moving cattle or burning out brands, he'd have the drop on them. He works for John Coble, who got Nannie E. Steele to nurse him back to health when he came to these parts from the Spanish-American War with malignant fever. Mrs. Steele lives about a mile from the Nickell ranch."

Etta's mind was in a whirl. She could hardly wait for evening to tell Charlie all the things Dora Miller talked about.

* * *

"Women spread stories faster than jam on bread. I swear there's not as much in the newspaper. Did Dora say anything else about Tom Horn? We'll know more about his life than he does himself, if Dora Miller continues to prattle. What else did she say?"

"I've told you every bit." Etta snuggled closer to Charlie. "No, I haven't. I just thought of something else." She giggled and her laughter was like the ringing of tiny silver bells. "She said men are fun-loving bulls."

"Why, that woman talks about everything! I bet she could talk a donkey's hind leg off. Doesn't she ever work!" cried Charlie.

"Sshh! You'll waken the children. Or worse—Dora will hear you. She sleeps with the bedroom door open, just to hear what goes on at night. Floyd told me she snores." Etta giggled again. "I think Floyd will be glad when she's gone and not sharing the children's room."

"I agree with Floyd. The minute you feel strong enough to scrub the floor alone I'll take her home," whispered Charlie, punching his pillow into a ball under his head.

"I scrubbed it myself today," said Etta.

Next morning Dora surprised Etta by saying, "Tom Horn is being questioned about Willie Nickell's death. I'm telling you this for your own good. Most settlers and farmers don't like anything about the big ranchers, including their cowhands. James told me they are looking for something suspicious about Horn, maybe that pins him to the Willie Nickell shooting. 'Horn's as good as any and better than some,' said James. Horn's not new to the law. He was deputy for three Arizona sheriffs, he has no love for sheep men, and even you said he's known for getting rustlers out of the territory. When I get home I'm going to tell James what you said yesterday about him in the company of a rustler. It'll make the case against Horn more air tight. Lock him up for murder." Her voice took a bitter vindictive quality. Etta did not like it. Dora's face was white and her mouth was a tight slash. "I hate the sound of ba-a-a-ing sheep and the smell of sheep dung. But, then, I don't have much use for those swanky big ranchers."

Etta gasped and almost dropped the flatiron. She laid the damp gingham curtain on the board and felt the steam rise against her face as she ran the iron over the material. "Maybe we shouldn't talk so much. This whole thing is awfully confusing to me. In some ways it sounds like a family feud."

"Forgive me, Missus Irwin, I didn't mean you, nor your man

After all, C.B.'s only a foreman. He doesn't run his own place nor belong to the association where the big ranchers are. You've been nice to me and we are friends.

"John Coble's a big rancher. Our schoolmarm told me he comes from a wealthy Pennsylvania family and came out West rather than accept an appointment at the Naval Academy. Can you believe that? He started the Frontier Land and Cattle Company with a hoity-toity Irishman, a Sir, if you please, Horace Plunkett. But the two were wiped out in the horrible winter of eighty-six and eighty-seven. The Irishman went back to Ireland to be some kind of politician, and Coble moved to the Iron Mountain region to start a horse ranch. I think he took in a lot of them wild horses and broke them for his herd. You can do that if you've lost most of your money."

Etta continued to iron, breathing deeply of the hot, moist steam, as if it would stiffen her backbone. "Dora, I have some good news for you."

"Oh, I could use some of that," said Dora, smiling.

"Charlie—Mr. Irwin—is going to give you your pay tonight after supper."

"God bless him. I can use all the money I can get my hands on."

"And he's going to take you back to your family. I'll miss you, but see, I can do lots of work myself now and still look after the children. Floyd can help with some of the lesser chores, like bringing in kindling and setting the table."

Dora looked dumbfounded. "You don't want me no more?"

"Your work is finished. I'm sure your husband and sons will be glad to have you back. Even the schoolmarm will be glad to let you do the cooking," said Etta. "Laws, you were a help to me. You can tell your family that. The cowboys here spoke about the good meals you prepared."

"It was your biscuits, Missus Irwin. But I'll tell James what you said anyways. I've never been away before. My boys, Vic and Gussie, will be happy to see me back. You've been real nice. I hate to leave these pretty girls of yours. Maybe you'll come to visit me."

"Of course," said Etta, feeling an overwhelming fatigue. She wished supper were finished and Charlie were hitching up the wagon to take Dora Miller home.

A week after Frances was born, Frank came to the L5 ranch to borrow Charlie's Henry rifle. "I want to go elk hunting. If I get one, I'll send a roast to you for your supper." Charlie agreed. He thought Frank looked good. He was a little taller and still thin, his face was tanned, and his eyes sparkled.

"The foreman, Duncan Clark, is leaving the IM for Montana. I bet you could take his place," Frank told Charlie.

"I'm here until after spring roundup. I want to be sure Johnnie Gordon is back on his feet."

"Couldn't Will look in on him once in a while? Will could go on roundup with him. My boss, Coble, built a new ranch house. Etta and the kids would like it. The bunks are upstairs on the second floor right now. He's going to build a bunkhouse in the spring. Want me to tell him you'd like the job?"

"What about Pa, doing all the blacksmithing by himself?" asked Charlie.

"Will's there. Mr. Coble has horses, not a lot of dumb cattle. What do you say?" Frank tied the rifle behind his saddle. "Remember those wild horses we broke back in Kansas? You always said you wanted a horse ranch."

"I'll think about it, then this weekend if I've decided in favor of the job and it's still open, I'll ride over to the IM. I'd like to see your spread anyway. Been hearing a lot about John Coble."

"He talks a little funny, but you'll like him," said Frank, letting his horse carry him out to the road near Gordon's place.

Charlie first talked with Etta. She was in favor of the move if there was a raise in pay for Charlie and if there was a one-room ranch school close by for Floyd. Then he talked with his father. "If it's an opportunity, go, son. Don't worry about me. Will and I'll work on this place until you come back and run it yourself." Will promised to help Gordon with his spring roundup. "Maybe you could get a day or two off and come with us," suggested Will. "Then you could be sure Gordon got the right cattle."

"That sounds all right," said Charlie. "Now I have to talk with Gordon."

Gordon surprised Charlie by saying that he himself was contemplating a change. "I've found a fellow by the name of Hunter who wants to buy my place. He's looked at my books and seems satisfied that I have plenty of cattle. To meet Hunter was an inspiration, to make a deal with him is an education. He has some ideas about irrigation."

Charlie said, "Show me an irrigator and I'll show you a worker."

"Couldn't have said it better myself," said Gordon, smiling. "T. B. Hicks at the First National Bank said Hunter had a ranch called TY on the Chugwater in the early days, and now he raises

Herefords on Crow Creek, eight or ten miles from Cheyenne, so he knows what he's doing."

"What are you doing, sir?" asked Charlie.

"I'm going to visit the old country. I think I'll jump on the bread wagon and loaf with the rest of the bundles."

"I'll miss you. Etta and the kids will miss you," said Charlie.

"C.B., the love of your fellow man is the best monument that you can leave behind. If you'll miss me because we were friends, it's enough for me. I know I'll never forget your generosity and kindness. I often see you at work and say to myself, 'My God, there goes a man!'"

"You'll give me a bad attack of swelled head," said Charlie with a chuckle, reaching out to shake Gordon's hand.

"I do have some advice for you, C.B. Don't try to be the Napoleon of the West, but when you get hold of a good thing, freeze on to it. I want you to write to me. I'll leave the address. Write on one side of the paper and both sides of the subject. This country is turning a corner. There's going to be some interesting happenings. More irrigation, more industrialization."

John Coble reminded Charlie of a banty rooster. He was hardly more than five and a half feet tall. He was a neat dresser. His hair was tinted with coal black and neatly cut. He had a short, trim mustache across his upper lip. He spoke with a clipped, aristocratic, eastern accent and used his hands for emphasis. Johnnie Gordon told Charlie that Coble was one of the best cattlemen in Laramie County. Gordon sought out Coble and told him that C. B. Irwin was the most competent foreman he'd seen since coming to Wyoming twenty years ago.

Charlie went on horseback to the Iron Mountain Ranch to seek out the foreman's job. It was an all-day trip. Coble acted surprised to see him, although he'd expected him since talking with Gordon the week before.

Coble waved his arms around, saying, "I daresay, the job is yours, Mr. Irwin. The ranch house is ready for your wife and children to move in immediately. I don't live here at the ranch. I come to help with roundups, branding, breaking the wild horses, and right now I'm working on the new bunkhouse off and on. In the meantime, the cowhands bunk upstairs in the ranch house."

Charlie was grateful for the job and shook Coble's hand. He said, "Thank you. I'll bring Etta and the kids over next week with all our gear."

"Sounds good to me. We're ready for the fall roundup. I've

got to move four hundred cows and steers and about half as many heifers from their summer grazing in yonder mountains to the low meadowlands in the foothills. It's your job to cut out the three-year-olds and take them to the stockyards while they're fat. A hard winter is a killer for cattle. Gordon told me you saved his herd." Coble's brown eyes drilled into Charlie.

Charlie didn't flinch. "Yes, sir. We put a thin, ratty-looking herd on some summer grass, and they're fat and healthy enough for anyone's book."

Etta felt blue whenever she thought of leaving the L5. She'd begun to think of the ranch house as home, mainly because Frances was born there.

The Irwin family occupied the first floor of Mr. Coble's new log house. The entire second story was one large room where all the ranch hands, including Frank, bunked on cots placed side by side. There was a bathroom inside the large wooden house. That is what it was for, bathing. One huge porcelain tub with claw feet sat on oversize bricks. There were galvanized tins used for wash-tubs in the room. Hot water from the kitchen range was carried in buckets to the tubs, and cold well water was used to cool the bathwater to the desired temperature. On Saturday nights there was standing room only while the cowboys waited for their baths. On the average, three to four men could bathe in the same water before it was carried out and the full buckets of water tossed off the back steps. Then fresh hot and cold water was carried in.

Etta made it a policy to keep herself and the children out of the way during the Saturday night baths. She and the children bathed in a washtub in front of the kitchen range during midday, when she could close and bolt the kitchen door.

Etta did all the cooking at the ranch house when the cowboys and chuck-wagon cook were gone. She cooked for the hands left behind to make repairs and do the blacksmith work, while the others were on the roundup.

One morning Floyd slammed the kitchen door and called for his mother, "Ma, I have something to tell you!"

"I'm changing the baby's diaper. Come into the bedroom," she said.

"Ma, the cowboy Mrs. Miller thinks should be locked up for murder is in Pa's crew, one of his hired hands on the roundup." Floyd was breathless.

"What are you talking about? Tell me from the beginning and go slow," said Etta, with a safety pin held between her teeth.

"You know, Tom Horn."

"Floyd, that was a lot of grownup talk you heard between me and Dora Miller."

"Ma, I heard Mr. Coble tell Pa the name of the men who were going on the roundup. He said, 'Tom Horn,' then said, with his hand over his mouth, 'Don't believe rumors, Horn is a good man. He's a square shooter and would never shoot a boy. Rustlers and sheep men respect him, but would sure like to see him move to Montana.'"

"Floyd, you must not listen to adults talking. You carry tales, and that is gossiping. Find your pencil. We'll work on your sums while it's quiet in the house. Go sit beside Joella at the kitchen table. She's writing out the numbers."

"Oh, Ma! I wish I'd fed the horses the sugar lumps in my pocket instead of coming to tell you some news. Oh, crap! Double crap!"

Floyd slid into the chair beside his sister and took one of her pencils, which made her yell.

Etta stood behind her son with a wet washcloth and a bar of yellow soap. She rubbed the cloth on the soap and tilted Floyd's head back.

"I'm washing your mouth of those foul words. Think before you speak," she said quietly, holding Floyd's head firm while she swished the washcloth in and out of his mouth.

Floyd's eyes watered, but he did not whimper nor cry out. Joella watched with a gleam in her eyes. She held the indelible pencil tip against her tongue, making a large purple dot.

Charlie leaned out from his horse to shake hands with the men John Coble introduced. Horn was last and was about as Charlie remembered, a trim mustache, receding hairline to his brown hair, and eyes that pierced through a man like an ice pick jabbed into a block of ice. He was more than six feet tall and weighed over two hundred pounds. He rode a large-chested, sleek brown horse he called E.W. His voice was soft and clear so that Charlie could hear him talk to the horse, but underneath was the sharpness Charlie remembered.

"Horn, you old horse thief! Remember when you bunked at the Irwin place in Kansas, Middle Sappa Creek, you bought an old horse and used its hide for a lean-to?"

Horn pulled out a small sack of tobacco and roll of papers. He rolled a cigarette, all the time looking at Charlie with clear, cold eyes. "Don't ever call me a thief, mister. I remember the episode. That was a lifetime ago."

"You were on your way out to Wyoming, going to work for Swan Land as a range detective or something," continued Charlie. "Is there good money in that?"

Horn took a long pull on the cigarette, glanced at his boss, Coble. "You talk a lot. I'm cowboying, and that's all that's your business."

"Take it easy," said Coble. "I never realized you two met. I guess it was before Horn worked for John Clay or Ora Haley."

Charlie laughed. "All right, past is past."

"You're growed some since the last time I saw you, Charlie. You've got Mr. Coble calling you C.B., so I guess you changed your name since the last time I saw you."

Charlie shook hands with Horn and said, "You call me Mr. Irwin, when you work for me."

John Coble told Charlie that Horn was a good worker and didn't irritate the others with a lot of nonsense talk or any fool practical jokes, as some men were prone to do.

The third night out on the roundup, before getting into their bedrolls, a couple of the men had Jew's harp matches. A tall blond rangy kid, Jim Danks, took the winnings. Then Charlie saw his opportunity and challenged John Coble to a roping contest. "I just got a twenty-dollar bill that says no one can even rope a decent second to me. And if we can get a competent set of judges out of this outfit, I'll wager more because I know I'm tops."

Coble never had one of his foremen challenge him before. He could rope a steer or a horse as well as anyone; therefore, he decided to go along with the challenge.

"Too bad Duncan Clark ain't here," said one of the cowboys. "He was one of the best ropers I ever seen."

Horn stepped forward. "You boys know that I can rope; my bunch of ropers won at the Frontier Days fair. I'll be judge."

"I've seen every Frontier Days fair Cheyenne has ever had. I'll be an impartial judge," said Slim Burke, the range cook. "With me judging there won't be any trouble, because cussing a cook's as risky as branding a mule's tail."

"You boys get your ropes warmed up. Maybe some fancy tricks first, then some calf-roping. See who can bring one down and tie it faster," said Clayton Danks, Jim's brother.

"Suits me fine," said Charlie, pushing his wide-brimmed hat

back on his head. He grinned at his brother Frank, who sat on his bedroll. Frank wondered what had come over Charlie to dare the ranch manager to match rope juggling. Charlie knew what he was doing. He knew that he was the new boy in the neighborhood and he had to prove himself as soon as possible so that the men would respect and obey him.

John Coble already had his calf-rope in his hand. It ran about twenty-five feet in length, and one end was whipped tight to prevent unraveling. An eye was fixed at the other end through which the rope was run through to make the loop. This was the honda.

Charlie checked over his rope. He had rewrapped the honda the previous night, so he knew it was smooth and tight.

Coble began to cast his rope from his hands so that it whirled before it touched the ground. The centrifugal force of the loop distended it so that it was open in midair as it revolved. The friction of the spoke, or free end, against the honda prevented the loop from closing. Coble stood with his feet slightly apart, body bent forward at the waist, then he threw the right hand in counterclockwise direction slightly away from his body, and at the same time released the loop with both hands and held the guiding spoke with the right-hand fingers. He did a flat loop, wedding ring, then a big loop, over his head and around his body. A couple of the boys whistled, the others clapped. Coble was egged on so he made a big loop and stepped in, stepped out, and passed it around his body.

Charlie bit his bottom lip. He was surprised. His new boss, a short man, but strong, was good with his rope. Charlie was impressed and wished he'd done some practicing while on the trail for old man Gordon. Now, here I am, he thought, foreman of another outfit and I have to prove myself. Well—here goes—nothing.

The cowboys chattered about the skills of John Coble. Charlie stood on a flat piece of ground, placed his feet just right, and began a spin just over the ground. A good flat spin, getting into the rhythm of the spin so that he could give just enough push with his spinning hand to keep the loop out without overdoing it. He well remembered the hours of wasted time he'd spent in untangling rope when he first started and when he could not keep the rope dilated and clear of the ground. Charlie began humming. He was hardly aware of the faces before him. He brought the rope up and did the butterfly, a figure eight with a small loop, humming in time to the spinning rope. Then he did the zigzag and ocean wave. If the men were cheering or clapping he was unaware. His concentration was strong. He brought the loop back to his right side by a series of butterflies, and then carried the spinning to the left across his front and over his shoulder so that it rolled gracefully and like a rigid wheel down to the opposite side, then he came down into a butterfly and went into the over-the-spoke trick. He brought the loop between his two hands in such a way that it fell in front of the rope, then caught it afterward with a butterfly.

Horn realized at once how hard this trick was to perform and whistled loudly. Someone told him that the judge should shut up and not influence the voting of the men.

Charlie rolled the loop over his left leg, which was held out straight before him. His hand let go and caught the spoke on the opposite side as the loop fell. He finished off with the rolling butterfly, where the spinning loop was thrown up and over.

Charlie was still humming, and the noise sounded like the drone of hive bees, getting louder and louder, then falling back and becoming so quiet it was almost inaudible, then gradually rising in a crescendo once again until the droning was so loud it seemed the air was in constant vibration. When the last rolling butterfly was complete, the rope went limp and the droning stopped abruptly and Charlie, now sweating profusely, bowed and stood with a big grin on his face.

"Son of a gun!" yelled John Coble. "This man has to enter the fairs. Wow! That was the most beautiful thing I've ever seen."

"Wait a darned minute!" yelled Horn. "We haven't seen the roping yet. Let's see you pull in one of the young ones—a calf!"

Charlie wiped his face with his kerchief and mounted up beside Coble, who was already on his horse. They rode out beside the herd of grazing cattle in the moonlight. The dampness on his skin cooled him quickly and Charlie began to shiver. Coble was first to cast and caught his calf by the two front feet and threw it heavily. Before it could rise, Coble had dismounted and grabbed the hind feet and wrapped a short rope around them. While Coble was standing beside his calf, Charlie looked for a likely place to make his cast. Coble's horse had stuck to the ground but now moved its hind feet around a little. The calf must have seen and it lashed out, pulling loose its hind feet.

Charlie was afraid it would frighten the other animals and start a stampede. Luckily Coble had seen to it that the animal was away from the main herd.

Charlie rode around slowly until he found a calf standing

alone close to some brush. The mother was ten, twelve yards away lying down, but watching. Charlie swung. He talked softly so not to frighten the mother, who was now standing on her feet, but not alarmed enough to bellow or run.

Charlie brought his calf all tied tight and proper over his shoulder so that the boys could have a good look.

"Mr. Coble had his calf wrapped up on my count of four. Mr. Irwin had his tied on my count of five, but it is still tied. You can see it's tied because Mr. Irwin brought it over here on his shoulder for us to examine." Horn could hardly keep his voice controlled.

"Charlie," said Frank in a funny squeaky voice, "you don't have to bring the animal in. That's not in the rules!"

"My God, he's carrying that animal!" cried Jim Danks. "That's a strong man!"

"Hey!" yelled Charlie. "Hold on there!"

Coble and Horn were laughing and pounding each other on the back. Coble pulled out a wad of money, but put it back in his hip pocket.

"I thought Mr. Irwin won both contests," said Jim Danks.

Slim Burke said, "Sit tight and watch."

A pockmarked man rose and walked in his peculiar horseman's gait to the edge of the camp firelight, then ambled back again while the men were bantering and dickering about who had won the show. "Looks like rain," he said. "That ring around the moon always brings rain."

No one seemed interested in preparing for wet weather, so he brought out his bedroll and placed it under a small pine tree that had thick branches on only one side. It was out of the wind and somewhat sheltered from any driving rain, should one come.

Horn asked, "Mr. Coble, how much were you counting on paying anyone that could skunk you with roping tricks?"

"I was promised a cool twenty and decided to add a ten to that," said Coble, with a jolly look to his face.

Charlie looked half-sick. "You boys mean I have to pay this —rotten snake in the grass thirty dollars? That's a month's pay for a good cowboy. You know I won fair and square. What's the matter with your eyes? They crossed?"

"What's the matter with you, Mr. Irwin?" asked Coble. "Don't you have the cash?"

"You'll get your money," snapped Charlie. "But now it's bedtime with us." He felt a little put out with John Coble and wondered where things began to go wrong. He decided it was best if he acted like a proper foreman and thought the incident out alone. "Frank Irwin and Slim Burke are the first guard men. We'll point the herd on a due southerly course and point them up that little divide in the morning. Now get to bed, everybody. We'll come out of this high pastureland tomorrow."

Horn and Burke were talking, and Charlie spoke sharply to both men. "Get to bed, Horn. Get on your horse, Burke."

"We just want to say that as judges for tonight's contest we made a hell of a mistake. It is the new foreman that wins the pot. How about it, boys? Do you all agree?" said Burke.

There were hoots and hollers and shouting with agreement. Coble glared at Horn and Burke, then at Charlie, and handed over his wad of three ten-dollar bills. "I didn't think I'd ever have to let loose of that," he said with a sigh.

"But you knew you didn't win. Your horse moved. Your calf broke out of the pigging string. And you didn't speak up to say so," said Charlie, almost in a whisper. "What kind of impression you think that made on your men? You want them to think you're some kind of weasel?"

Coble turned pale in the firelight. "I'm the boss. No one talks to me like that!" Coble edged toward Charlie. Several of the boys dropped their blankets and were on top of Coble in a second. They held him pinned to the ground. Charlie pulled the men away and helped Coble to his feet.

"I'm sorry about that. I hope you aren't hurt, sir," said Charlie. He turned to the men, who were grinning from ear to ear. "Mr. Coble is the boss and if he wants to punch me he can. If he gives me an order I don't think is right, I'll tell him—if he can show me the merit, I'll follow, but you boys don't argue. Follow orders. Understand?"

There were more hoots and hollers. Coble grabbed Charlie's hand. "I say C. B. Irwin passed the initiation. He's a top-grade foreman. Welcome to the IM. From now on you're in charge of these cowboys. They saw firsthand how you react in a squeeze and how you feel about fair play and discipline. You have our respect."

Charlie's mouth hung open. "My own brother didn't warn me. I ought to wring his neck." He closed his mouth and his eyes glinted in the tiny firelight. Then he said, "I'm sorry I called Mr. Coble a rotten snake in the grass. Actually, right now he's more like a puffed-up frog in a cream can."

Coble waved his arms and bent over in a fancy bow. The cowboys whistled.

* * *

Charlie noticed that most of the men were asleep with their feet pointed toward the dead fire when Frank woke him. Frank said, "Wake up, ol' C.B. and take hold. You're on guard. Slim is calling Coble out."

Charlie groaned and sat up, ready to take his turn.

Frank said, "If you expect to follow the trail, you'll have to learn to sleep fast. Just look at all those smooth white feet; you'd think someone would sleep with his boots on. I guess no one expects Indians to attack."

Charlie poured himself a cup of strong coffee from the graniteware pot sitting on a stone beside the fire. "Coffee's as cold as I am," he said.

On guard Charlie sang to keep awake and to keep the cattle settled. As the two men went around and met, Charlie said, "Is it true Horn is sweet on a round-faced, almond-eyed wench that teaches at the Iron Mountain School?"

The next meeting, Coble said, "Keep a closed mouth, but that's the one. She's smooth to get him. Miller boys came to the ranch to invite him to a supper that she prepared."

Charlie said, "Hope he didn't spill his coffee."

Coble turned back in the saddle and added, "Nope, but he confessed to me that he felt like his collar was too tight."

Coble began whistling and Charlie picked up the rhythm and sang softly. The cows were all bedded down and content to chew their cud.

Then Charlie said, "You have a girl, Mr. Coble?"

Coble answered, "Yes, I do. She is lovely. Wears lavender and reminds me of heather. But I wonder how she feels about me."

Charlie heard Coble sigh as their horses slowly walked past each other. Charlie said, "She invite you to her place?"

"Once or twice," said Coble, slowing his horse. "She showed me her girlhood pictures in an album held together with a big silver lock, like my five-dollar belt buckle."

"That's your answer," said Charlie as they passed by once again. "Could I send my seven-year-old boy to that Iron Mountain School?"

"Certainly. Lots of the ranch kids go. But if he were mine, I'd let him go to the school in Cheyenne," said Coble.

"You and my wife," said Charlie.

When they met again, Coble spoke first. "You don't want your son to be a gristle-headed, barnyard yokel who never stops at the back door to scrape the manure off his boots. Boys need proper training. Don't let him become like the Nickell kids or even the Miller boys."

"I'll think about it and save my pay for the proper school," said Charlie. "You can't force a woman, and she has to think the whole idea is her own." Charlie sang his way past the fire, climbed down from his horse, and gently told Burke that it was time to get up and get more than coffee hot for the boys. A thin line of light was noticeable in the eastern sky. The wind had come up, and the stars were hidden by clouds. By noon there was a steady drizzle and a grayish fog over everything.

The creeks ran bankful, and two or three times they crossed over a small, fast-running creek. The cattle always stopped to drink and the boys had to prod them on.

"What if another spread ran their herd up here for the winter?" Charlie asked Coble.

"That's impossible. We just cut out what does not belong to us when we come back for ours or bring them all in and cut them out as we pass their ranches. Don't worry, by summer you'll know all the brands between here and Medicine Bow."

"Ever run into any Indians?"

Coble laughed. "Nope. They're all on the reservations, my friend."

Charlie told Coble about his experience with the Sioux at Pine Ridge.

"Poor devils, I say."

"You'd change your mind if you ever saw a Sioux riding a good horse."

That night the rain stopped and the moon stood nearly full in the sky. The men did not complain. Their slickers had protected them some, but most slept between blankets and all had a cold supper because dry wood could not be found. The next day was clear. They were back to the meadow, which was protected on three sides by shallow rocky walls and bordered on the fourth side by a small creek so that none of the cows would wander far away. They had picked up a dozen unmarked cows, which were held by a rope and branded while Charlie marked their ears for the IM. Also in the herd were two dark-coated buffalo cows with a young one apiece.

"Leave them be," said Coble. "By spring they may still be here, showing these domesticated beasts where the grass is best."

Etta had sizzling hot steaks and mashed potatoes for the cowboys' dinner, along with milk gravy and biscuits and string beans and raisin pie.

"You feed too good," warned Burke, "and the IM ranch will pick up every stray cowboy that goes through this country."

Etta smiled. She knew what the men appreciated.

TWENTY-ONE

Fire at Iron Mountain

Many a night after the cows were milked and fed and the chores completed, the cowboys sat at the big oak dining table and swapped yarns or played solo, a game similar to bridge, except that one successful bidder alone took on the others, or cribbage, pegging out the scores, fifteen-two, fifteen-four, fifteen-six, or poker, long after Etta cleared off the table. Etta often put a kettle of oatmeal on the back of the stove to simmer all night and be ready for the next morning's breakfast of biscuits, gravy, thin-sliced steaks, fried eggs, thick oatmeal with salt and pepper and fresh butter or thick cream and sugar. Of course there was always the hot black coffee.

Charlie looked forward to the evenings around the table. He kept his mouth shut and let the others talk. He loved to hear the exploits the cowboys bragged about. Most were only half-true.

Horn was that way. He loved telling about how good he was with his Winchester, how he could site a coyote, or even a man, at five, six hundred yards and hit the target midway between the eyes.

"I heard you have a kind of signature or trademark," Charlie said to Horn one evening. "Some say you leave a rock under the head of your victims whether they be man or beast."

Horn colored, rubbed his hands together, cleared his throat, and said, "Boys, if you believe that, you can believe that tomorrow the sky will be green and the grass blue." His eyes seemed to be deep gray with a never-ending bottom, like a deep pit.

Later that evening Charlie and Etta talked quietly. "It's some craziness when neighbor is pitted against neighbor, brother against brother," said Charlie. "Everyone suspects everyone else in this Nickell affair."

"Maybe it's because the papers print a little here, a little there all the time, so's it's even in the big eastern papers," said Etta.

"That's coming from Joe LeFors. He's a tinhorn deputy marshal who thinks if he can pin a murder on some unsuspecting man, he'll get himself a big promotion, even go into politics, have any position in the state he wants."

"I don't like it. It's ugly. Isn't there something I can do?"

"Squelch every rumor. Think in straight lines. Throw cold water on anything that looks like fire," said Charlie.

All the talk about guns and hitting targets reminded Etta that Frank had borrowed Charlie's rifle. "I don't remember Frank bringing the old Henry back after he brought in the dressed venison."

"Sure, he brought it back. It's on the bedroom closet shelf. Go look," said Charlie.

She did and found the rifle. "I feel ashamed of myself. I just don't want Frank to be seen with a gun and have someone accuse him of something he didn't do. Oh, Charlie, times are terrible. Everyone who carries a gun is a suspect."

"That includes about every dadburned rancher in Wyoming!" Charlie's voice boomed out.

Charlie was surprised at the work his father and Will had done to the ranch house on the Y6, a twelve-room, two-story place. Out back was the bunkhouse. The closet, as Joe called the outhouse, was built to one end of the icehouse, about twenty yards from the kitchen door. Will laughed when he showed Charlie, saying that Margaret still had the children using chamber pots because she didn't want to bundle them in coats, hats, and scarves each time they had to go. Not far from the back door was the water pump. Beyond the bunkhouse was the smithy and carpenter shed with all of Joe's tools. East of the huge barn was the chicken house, wagon shed, granary, corrals, and cattle sheds. Charlie suddenly wanted to start work on his own ranch so bad he could taste it.

"I'm coming back here with Etta and the kids just as soon as I can buy some good horseflesh," promised Charlie. "The time will be here soon, you'll see."

Joe's hair was white, but he seemed just as quick and agile as before. He and Charlie rode horseback out to where Bear Creek ran into Horse Creek. The ground was clear of snow in many places where the wind had blown it away. Ahead the hills looked like the long backbone of some prehistoric monster. "That's all ours." Joe waved his arm in a wide arc. "See there, that hill at the end of the range, soft and rounded? I call it Round Top. It's my favorite. It seems to me a sentinel, looking over this here land, a place from where the winds are born and come howling from that round top out across the flat plain. One day I left my bedroom window open and that wind blew everything out the door but my mattress!"

"Frank and I want to come over here on our days off and bring in some wild horses. We'll tame them and bring them in to use as broncos for this year's Frontier Days. What do you think, Pa?"

"I think, do it. But be sure you get paid for the use of your stock," said Joe. "You should watch Margaret ride that big yellow horse she calls Old Gold. She has the fancy notion that she might enter the cow-pony race during the Frontier Days celebration. What do you think about that?"

"I think it's fine. She's trying to prove to herself that she can live on a ranch. She also wants to prove to everyone else that she is as good or better than these other ranch girls."

"What will Etta think?" asked Joe, dubious about his daughter-in-law entering a horse race. "Is she inclined to this modern notion that women can do everything a man can do?"

"Pa, Etta believes in initiative and teamwork. I would guess that when Etta learns Margaret is ready to enter the race, she'll help."

The moon came up, a partial globe at the edge of the horizon. It floated over the dark curtain of night like a split pumpkin rind. It sent down enough reflected light so that Charlie easily followed the roads back to the IM ranch. Charlie thought of Margaret and Etta. They were like blond and brunette sisters. Etta strait-laced as a fine calfskin shoe, usually, and Margaret flirty as an Abilene dance hall girl, at times.

The snow flew around the first of December. There was no letup for a week. When it was finished, the snow was as high as the first-floor windows. The men were kept busy hauling hay out to the cows and horses.

Floyd rode horseback to the one-room schoolhouse. He liked

the schoolmarm, Miss Kimmell. She let the boys chop the firewood and have footraces and rope-spinning contests. There were five boys and eight girls, giving the school the unlucky number of thirteen pupils. For two, three days Floyd could not get to the schoolhouse. Then the winds came and blew harder than usual, making eight- to ten-foot drifts against the house and barn. The roads were generally blown clear of snow.

Etta and Charlie invited Will, Margaret, their children, and Joe to the IM ranch house for Christmas day. Nothing marred the festivities. Everyone, including the ranch hands, enjoyed the dinner of roast pork, beefsteaks, mashed potatoes, gravy, biscuits, canned tomatoes, applesauce, mince pie, pound cake, whipped cream, and coffee.

During the meal Floyd asked, "Why does Ma say, 'Clean your plate before dessert'? If I were a mother, I'd let my boy eat dessert first, then if he still had room, try the other stuff. What if there's a fire while we're eating dinner? We'd have to run out before the best part. If I were boss—I'd make a rule for dessert first." This sense of priority endeared him to his sisters and cousins.

The new year of 1902 was cold and the snow continued to fall so that there were drifts deeper than three feet where protected from wind.

Charlie made sleds for the three older children from the wooden crates the two-dozen canned tomatoes and peaches were packed in when bought from the Union Mercantile. For metal runners that were slick and fast on the snow, he used barrel hoops fastened to long blocks of wood. Etta often went sledding with the children after supper if the baby was sleeping. Charlie talked with the cowboys. Some, such as Jim and Clayton Danks, John Ryan, and Dan Thor, stayed year-round; others came and went with the seasons, working north in summer and south in winter. Tom Horn stayed, but one day told Charlie he was thinking of moving to Montana.

One evening, about the middle of January, Etta was out in the back of the ranch house with Floyd, Joella, and Pauline romping in the snow. She threw snowballs and jumped on Floyd's sled. She let snowflakes melt on her tongue and laughed when her face was wet. She whooped and yelled with her children, pulling each up the small hill. She showed them how to make "angels" in the snow by lying full length on a pristine spot and moving arms from their sides up to their heads for "wings." She had each child put his sled against the back wall of the house before going inside.

Charlie thought that when Etta laughed and played in the snow she was like a precocious child herself. He was sure a stranger would not be able to say for certain she was the mother. She had more life and happiness in her tiny body than any two farm women he'd seen come into Cheyenne for supplies. Etta's cheeks were red as apples and matched the children's.

Inside, where it was warm, she put two chunks of split wood into the fire box of the kitchen range and a pan of milk on top for making hot chocolate. She took her own wraps off. Then she helped the children remove their coats, leggings, scarves, mittens, and overshoes.

"Ma, I want to pass around the cocoa cups," said five-year-old Joella. "I won't spill."

"Girls always want to do this or that," complained Floyd, a year older. "Boy, I'd give Joella whereat. When I hit her with a snowball, she cried. I wish her tears had froze, on her nose, so it glowed like a rose—"

"Floyd, stop!" said Etta sharply. "You put soda crackers on each saucer." She reached into the cupboard for the box of crackers.

"Floyd, you can pour the cocoa," said Joella with generosity.

After their cocoa was finished the children were sent to bed. Each called good night to the cowboys, who were also enjoying the cocoa and crackers.

Etta rinsed off saucers and washed cups and the cocoa pan. Charlie munched on crackers while tucking the children in their beds.

Eventually the cowboys, tired of talk, climbed the stairs to their beds. Etta turned out all but one coal-oil lamp. This last lamp she carried into her and Charlie's bedroom.

"Listen to that wind blow. It's become stronger in the last hour. I've a notion to wear two pairs of underwear and two pairs of socks to keep warm," said Charlie.

The baby began to fret. Etta pulled the crib next to her bed and changed the flannelette diaper, and sat on the bed to nurse her.

Charlie lay back in bed and watched his pixie wife sway back and forth, rocking Frances back to sleep. Charlie lifted his eyes and looked about the familiar room, then something in the doorway stopped his glancing. There young Floyd stood in his long-johns.

Charlie sat up. "You all right, son?"

"I don't like the wind. It sounds like crying. It's blowing smoke from the fireplace back into the house. Smell it?"

"Aw, you're dreaming. Come sit on the bed with me. We'll sing a song while your mother feeds the baby."

Floyd ran across the room and flung himself into his father's lap. Charlie wrapped the dark-haired, slender boy in his big red flannel shirt and softly sang "The Old Rugged Cross." Etta laid the sleeping Frances back in her crib and thought of putting the old pink shawl over the crib blankets. She decided the baby was warm enough. Besides, the floor was too cold to walk on with bare feet, even as far as the closet for the shawl.

The bedrooms were not heated. Charlie carried Floyd to his room off the kitchen. It was meant to be a pantry, but there were not enough hands at the ranch yet to have use for that many stores. Everything could be kept in the kitchen's cupboards, drawers, and bins. Floyd had an iron cot, painted white. He'd asked for that when he saw the cowboys slept in white iron cots upstairs. "I don't want none of sissy feather beds," he'd told his mother. The stairs leading to the cowboys' second floor were outside Floyd's room.

Five-year-old Joella and three-year-old Pauline had thick feather mattresses in the small bedroom down the hall from Charlie and Etta. On the dresser was a pitcher of water and china bowl for washing. Joella's chore was to put fresh water in the pitchers each day. The old unused water was put in the bucket on the back of the stove for dishwater.

"Thank goodness, the cows and horses are close by this winter, with stacks of hay," said Charlie, sliding back into bed. "My feet are ice."

"I know, that's why I moved way over here," said Etta, giggling.

"Hope it doesn't snow tonight. Cows are so dumb, they won't find the hay if it's covered up, even if they walk over it."

"Can't snow, the clouds are high," said Etta. "In the spring could we rent a couple rooms in Cheyenne so that I could move in with the children, then Floyd could go to school? Please, Charlie?"

"You'd leave me here? Who'd cook? Who'd warm my feet?"

"Slim Burke'll come back. He can cook. You don't eat anything but biscuits and gravy, mashed potatoes and beef, and canned peaches. Anyone can fix that. A couple of rocks heated in the fireplace and wrapped in a flannel towel will warm your feet."

"You're hard-hearted, dear. I'd miss you and the kids."

"When you come to town for supplies, or some meeting, you could stay over with me and the kids."

"Couldn't you teach Floyd yourself, just a while longer? Is it that important that he go to school?"

"I bet you that your brother, Will, lets Margaret stay in town with her kids while they are old enough to be in school."

"Ah, green-eyed jealous," said Charlie, moving closer to Etta. "Margaret won't move to town and you know it. She likes the ranch and the horses. She'll send her kids to a one-room school like we have for the Iron Mountain district."

"Jealous? Not of Margaret. She rides horses with the cowboys. She wears divided skirts. I'd really like a house in town so I could dress up once in a while."

"My ma felt that way. Maybe that's why Pa frowns when he sees Margaret climb on a horse bareback and race around the pasture. But Pa likes Margaret. He told me not long ago how good she was taking care of the ranch house and that her cooking has improved. Once you told me you didn't think she could cook even if she set a haystack on fire."

"Oh, Charlie, I remember. That wasn't nice of me. I like Margaret. But still, it's unladylike to ride a horse all day and let the housework go and those kids shift for themselves. I suppose she lets Joe do the cleaning and chase after those two kids."

"Don't be so sharp-tongued," said Charlie.

"I remember when they were married. Margaret was just a child. Not bad-looking, really pretty, but she had so much to learn. I guess she's learned."

"We Irwins know how to find good women," said Charlie, half-asleep.

"I'll make ice cream tomorrow. Floyd can help turn the freezer crank. We'll use icicles from the eaves, so you won't have to go to the ice house." Etta waited for Charlie to notice she'd changed the subject. She heard only his even breathing of sleep. She listened to the short breaths of the sleeping Frances. Soon Etta was asleep.

After midnight the wind blew hard. Fine snow was picked up and moved around against the base of hillocks and buildings. It blew off the flat ground, exposing gray, dead grass. Charlie woke, listened to the howling wind, then gently as possible took his one hundred ninety pounds out of the bed. He didn't want to disturb Etta. The floor was like walking on an iceberg. He scratched his broad chest and listened again. The wind was blowing a gale, screaming around house corners. He pulled on his pants and shirt, wrapped himself in an old blue robe, but still could not stop shivering. He padded out to the sitting room. There was something in the cold air he could not quite identify. He smelled the cold ashes of the fireplace and thought of Floyd thinking the wind blew smoke back inside the house. His nostrils retained the smoky smell of the ashes. He went into the kitchen and lit a coal-oil lamp left on the table. Carrying the lamp he checked to see if Floyd was well covered. Of course he was. Charlie continued along the icy floor to the girls' room.

He looked beyond the half-opened door and chuckled. Joella was sleeping with a wide, pink hair ribbon perched on top of her head. Pauline was snuggled so far down in her covers that it was hard to see her soft, straight brown hair. Satisfied that everyone was all right he went back to the kitchen. Then on some impulse he took the lamp up the wooden stairs. He sniffed the warmer air at the top. The warmth felt good, especially around his legs.

He pushed the door wide open, kept the lantern behind him so as not to waken the cowboys. A table was against the far wall, where the men sometimes played cards or talked before going to bed. The room was stuffy. Charlie thought, six men sleeping can't be enough warm bodies to make the room feel this close. Or can it? Heat rises. The soles of his feet felt warm. He put the low-glowing lamp on the table and bent to feel the floor. He heard John Ryan snore. The floor was warm. That's not right, reasoned Charlie. He ran his eyes over the rough floor planking. Some of the cracks between the boards were wide enough to sweep in all the mud and dirt these men could bring up on their boots. He felt the floor again and moved closer to the wall by the table. There was a blackened pie tin with several old cigarette butts. Charlie wrinkled his nose. He was tempted to dump the mess. A smelly cigarette butt could go down some of the cracks between floor boards easily.

Charlie wondered if the men ever lost anything—like a jack-knife or coins or pocket comb—down the wide cracks. His eye caught something by his foot—a gray-blue wispy tail. He sniffed smoke. Yes, smoke, and it shouldn't be there! He stayed on his hands and knees and smelled along another wide crack. His nostrils felt the sting of acrid smoke and the floor was hot on his knees, right through his two pairs of underwear. His mind could not believe what his eyes and nose told him. He crawled to the far side of the room and found that also unusually warm. Then out of one of the wider cracks came a tiny, thin finger of red flame and his brain knew.

He scrambled to his feet yelling, "Men! Fire! Get out! Fire! The house is on fire! Get up!"

The Danks brothers were up first. Charlie stood by the cots, calling urgently, "Move quickly. There's a fire under the floor boards!" His eyes betrayed his terror.

All six men pulled on Levi's, shirts, grabbed boots, blankets, angora chaps, sheepskin coats, a saddle, a .30-.30 Winchester, anything they saw of value. None were fully awake, but all fully aware of the danger. Orange flame rippled like liquid waves. Charlie dumped the water from the pitchers on the floor and followed them down the stairs.

Clayton Danks went after Floyd. Charlie ran to waken the girls, thinking he'd take them in to Etta.

Neil Clark grabbed Charlie's arms. "You get the missus and the baby. I'll get the children. Jimmy'll get the payroll and books."

Charlie took his sheepskin coat and cap from the hook. He picked up Floyd's boots and his own.

"We'll get pails of water and drown it," said Charlie, going after Etta. He talked to himself. "I'll get an ax and open a hole in the floor. We'll drown her good." He caught a flash of Floyd wrapped in a woolen blanket, carrying a lantern, and a pile of dishes, going out the back door with John Ryan.

Etta rushed to put her coat over her nightdress and overshoes on her stockinged feet. She picked up Frances and went to the closet for the big, pink woolen shawl to wrap around the baby, who had on only a diaper shirt and a long cotton nightdress.

When everyone was standing outdoors, shivering, Charlie yelled, "Why aren't the pails by the water pump? We need to get water on that upstairs floor. Come on!"

Clark took the bucket of warm water off the back of the kitchen stove and ran upstairs. His blue robe flapped around his legs beneath his coat. Frank went into the back shed for a broad-blade ax and a couple of hand axes. Etta dropped the baby in Joella's lap. Joella sat on the back steps as if still asleep, the pink ribbon still in her hair.

"Hold Frannie while Floyd and I pump water!"

Etta grabbed a bucket where several hung on nails at the back of the house. The wind tore at her hair and pulled Floyd's blanket open.

She yelled, "Pull the fool thing closed and don't get wet! I'll pin the blanket so's you can work easier." Quickly she pulled two big safety pins from her coat pocket and tugged at Floyd's blanket.

"Ain't that something pretty," said Floyd, pointing to the flames that were licking out of the east top-floor window. Yellow sap oozed from the pine frames and the lapping flames roared and snapped.

"Take the water inside to the men!" Etta screamed. She put another bucket under the spigot and worked the pump. Her heart was pounding. She was afraid the water would freeze and the pump would go dry. "Fire is the most ugly something on the prairie," she said. She then yelled at Frank, "Hey, drop those axes and take this water upstairs! Don't spill! I know it's heavy, but you can do it!"

"Hey, I'm not six years old!" Frank yelled back.

One of the Danks brothers ran out of the house with an armload of yesterday's baked bread and some kitchen knives. He put it all on a blanket near the bunkhouse, then went to help Floyd carry a water bucket.

Etta pumped water as fast as she could, keeping the buckets filled as they were brought back. She glanced at Joella huddled over the baby and at Pauline huddled against Joella for protection from the wind.

Suddenly the men came pell-mell out of the house, each carrying something—books, a chair, an iron griddle, a clock, a lard bucket, a can of coffee. Charlie held Floyd. He yelled, "We gotta let her go! It's hot enough to singe the feathers off a chicken at the top of the stairs. When the stairs go, the whole place'll go fast. I got the Henry rifle, I'm going back for the baby's crib and your clothes. That's all!"

"Oh, no!" Etta shrieked and grabbed Charlie's arm. "What if the ceiling falls? You'd be trapped. Frannie can sleep anywhere. My clothes aren't important." Etta began to laugh hysterically. She couldn't help herself. The men stared at her. She pointed. "Look what Joella has in her lap. Her big hand mirror! Oh, that is so funny!"

"Lookit Pauline!" cried Floyd. "She's hugging her pillow."

The boys chuckled and looked at the items they'd brought out.

Etta was adamant. No one else should go inside the burning house. "If I can leave my mother's silver brooch," she said softly, sobbing, "which means a lot to me—you can leave the rest of the things. Nothing is worth getting burned for."

Charlie grabbed a bucket and shoved it toward Etta. "We gotta save something for Mr. Coble! Throw water on that half-done bunkhouse, and the barn. Move! Watch out for the hot ash and sparks! Floyd, take your sisters inside the bunkhouse out of this blamed wind!"

"I thank Mr. Coble for putting a roof on the bunkhouse last weekend," said Etta.

"We shoulda' moved in half-furnished or not. Then this wouldn't have happened," said Clayton Danks, grabbing a full bucket of water, passing it to his brother, who passed it on to Frank, who got it to Neil Clark, who threw it on the bunkhouse roof and sides.

After about thirty minutes the line shifted so that the men were closer to the barn. Charlie had a ladder against the barn's side so that he could scramble up and down as the buckets were passed to him.

"Water turns to ice the minute it splashes out," Charlie panted. "But keep it coming!"

Suddenly everything was bright. Brighter than if the northern lights were on full power. The outdoors was lit up like arc lights. The ranch house was a jack-o'-lantern, then it burst into flames from top to bottom.

"Watch the sparks!" repeated Charlie. "Stay away from the house! It's a goner! You can't save her. Save the barn and the bunkhouse."

The men continued to throw water on the bunkhouse roof and the barn walls.

A couple hours later Clark was at the water pump. The handle froze and would not move up and down. "Oh, hell! Fill the buckets with snow and spread on the barn's roof!"

Charlie yelled, "Snow won't stay, the wind'll blow it off! What blamed luck! Kick those burning boards in a pile. We'll melt the snow!"

"Missus Irwin, you go inside the bunkhouse with the children," said Jim Danks.

"But—I can help. Charlie needs—" sputtered Etta, not used to being told what to do.

"Sure, you're needed. But not out here, freezing your a— arms. Go inside and look after the kids."

Etta went. How good it felt inside the half-finished bunkhouse, out of the piercing wind. She heard Joella and Pauline crying softly. "No crying," she said gently. "I'll find a lamp and we'll look around here. I know the men brought blankets somewhere."

"We're sitting on them," sobbed Joella. "And here's the lamps."

"I sat on the bread," said Pauline. Her voice quivered.

Etta lit the lamp from matches in her coat pocket. She thought of the waste of good matches with all the flames outside. She found the round-bellied iron stove and made certain by feeling that it had a pipe connected from the stove to a hole in the ceiling before she broke up an old wood crate and put it in the stove. Here's hoping snow's not packed in the chimney, she thought as she held a thick splinter in the lamp flame. When the fire was blazing, she went outside to bring Floyd in to warm up a bit. "Bring a bucket of clean snow," she said. "I found a sack of sugar and some coffee."

Floyd was not happy staying inside with the women. But he was so sleepy his eyes would hardly stay open. Beside the stove he felt warm and relaxed.

Etta fixed the girls a place to sleep between big sacks of flour and grain that were stored in the bunkhouse. The baby was cradled on a pile of clean hay between two grain sacks lined with a thick quilt. Frances hardly wakened during all the yelling and commotion.

Frank came in for warmth, found some cups and bowls someone had saved from the house. He poured himself steaming coffee. "Goddamn it's cold as hell working with freezing snow water in this bitchy wind." He glanced at Etta and said, "Sorry, I thought you went outside."

"Don't you ever talk that way in front of the girls, nor Floyd either," she snapped.

"I don't have any mittens. My hands are frostbitten," he whined, and held his hands clutched together.

Etta looked at his hands under the yellow kerosene lamp, hoping they weren't frozen. She looked around the long room, bent, and pulled Floyd's boots off. The child was so exhausted he did not open his eyes as his mother took his socks off. He slept with his head on a sack of flour, his back toward the stove. Etta flung the socks toward Frank. "Wear these, but bring them back when you're done. Floyd will need them tomorrow."

"Thanks, Et." Frank rushed from the bunkhouse, his hands in the black wool stockings.

Charlie and Jimmy Danks came in next for coffee.

"I put a lot of sugar in for you," said Etta.

"Don't apologize. It's the best I've had," said Charlie, smacking his lips. "Wind takes heat right out of a body." He sat on the floor with his back against the wall.

Jimmy said, "Yep, fans the flames and blows the snow. My face gets hot and my feet freeze."

"How in blue blazes did this inferno start, Jimmy?" asked Charlie, so tired he could hardly hold his cup of coffee.

"You suspect me?" asked Jimmy, his soot-streaked face peering up into Charlie's.

Charlie looked down and stared a few seconds, resting. His mind was slowly warming up. "You are the one that smokes like a Bessemer converter. A cigarette butt or two pushed between cracks in that floor keeps the room neat, but if those butts are not stone cold—they could smolder for hours, then all of a sudden flare up." Charlie closed his eyes.

"Occasionally I empty the pie tin down those cracks before we hit the hay. Last night we played cards a spell and I got rid of the stinky butts when we finished. You think—maybe—oh, God! It is possible!" His eyes bulged out in terror.

"I don't see another explanation," said Charlie, opening his eyes. "I know you didn't deliberately set fire to the ranch house. Drink your coffee. Go back out there and keep your mouth shut. Don't be a sap. No one set this fire on purpose. It was fate."

Disheartened, the two men went out the door not looking back. Each knew that Etta would not breathe a word of what she'd heard.

Clayton Danks and Neil Clark came in next for their coffee. "This hot coffee has enough sugar to give me the energy I need to climb to the top of that gol-darn barn once more if I have to," said young Clark. "Did you see the wind catch that firebrand and carry it clean over the barn's roof? I used two buckets of snow to get those small fires out caused by flying sparks. Wind blows on top of that barn like it was the highest peak of the Himalayas."

Etta filled their cups twice.

"With your cheeks red and your hair blown around your face —well, it reminds me of a Greek goddess I once saw in a book," said Clark.

"Oh, go on!" said Etta.

"Yes, ma'am."

"Thanks," said Danks. "We'll be in again before dawn." He put his cup on the floor and his arm on Clark's shoulder. "You've a lot of nerve to practice being Romeo with the boss's wife."

Clark turned to Etta before he ducked out the door. "Who expected the night to be like this when we enjoyed cocoa in the kitchen—ages ago, ma'am."

Etta smiled. She felt like crying. John Coble's new ranch house was gone. The men could manage in the unfinished bunkhouse. She and the children would have to go to the Y6 and live with Joe and Will and Margaret.

Neil Clark came back inside. "I just want to say that come morning, I'll milk the cows so your little ones'll have fresh milk."

"That's thoughtful. But it's my job to do the milking. I reckon I can still do it." Etta decided she liked this gallant young man who practiced his courting talk on her.

"You work hard. I'm going to suggest to Mr. Irwin that we take turns with the milking. Women should be admired and looked at."

"Mr. Clark—thank you. I suspect you are rehearsing those words to use on some young lady in Cheyenne." Etta wiped her eyes and smiled.

"In Laramie," Clark said, and went outside.

Thor and Ryan came for coffee and a short rest, then found strength to go out again. Etta watched through the window. She saw the men dump snow on flaming sticks blown near the barn. Then she saw the men turn in unison as a chorus line and her eyes followed theirs. The house roof fell in slow motion and at the same time the second floor pitched crazily sideways and fell into the first floor with a muffled boom and a deafening roar. Sparks flew outward in the shape of a fan with the wind. The roar of the flames was resounding, even inside the bunkhouse. The windows shook as if the air were rent by thunder. When the burning slacked off, the house stood as a skeleton, blackened bare bones with the inside gutted. Only the carbonized first floor walls stood. Then suddenly they, too, were eaten fast by thick yellow tongues that licked out as far as they were stretched by the wind. The skeleton was gone. Only ghostly gray smoke was left. The men came into the bunkhouse one by one. Their faces were dirty from soot and shadowy beards. Two men had burns on their hands. Charlie thought his hands were frostbitten. He had piled snow around the burning house to keep the lower flames and debris contained and not blown from there halfway across the prairie. Frank kept moaning that his feet were blocks of ice.

No one took his coat off.

Jimmy Danks stood beside Charlie. Everyone could see he

was so tired that he could hardly put his hand out to shake Charlie's. "Mr. Irwin, we all thank you for getting us out of there. We'd have burnt when that hellfire broke loose. We'd never woke up soon enough to get to them stairs. Nobody's noticed, but you're a hero."

"Charlie's a person like the rest of us. He did what was called for. I'd have jumped out the window if Charlie hadn't come upstairs," said Frank, who was on the floor with his back against the wall, closing his eyes.

"And broken your head as wide open as any breakfast egg," grinned Charlie, who was utterly exhausted. Everything seemed to go slower than normal. "Tomorrow we have to talk about what we are going to say to John Coble," he said, stretching out on the floor next to the sacks of grain. He held his aching hands in a bucket of melted snow water. He had to grit down on his teeth to keep from crying out, the pain was so bad.

Etta helped Frank put his feet into another bucket of snow water. In a few minutes tears were running down his face. "My God, my feet feel like they're on fire."

"I'm so tired my tongue's hanging out a foot and about forty inches," said Clayton Danks.

Etta knew the men were hurting because of fatigue, frostbite, and burns. She blurted out something she'd heard her own mother say once to her brothers. "Put your warm hands over your ears and hum softly to take the pain away."

Charlie hummed for ten, twelve minutes, then fell asleep. The others tried. Frank pulled his feet from the bucket and slept. He woke and hummed and slept again. Etta put the pink wool shawl around his feet. The others had rolled into the blankets. Etta found a blanket and lay close to Charlie after turning the lamp out. Charlie saw sparks jump from dying embers of the house behind his closed eyelids. It seemed morning came only minutes later. The wind had died down. White clouds ran across the pale-blue sky, their underside planed flat by the wind. A golden glow spread out in long spokes from the horizon as the sun emerged. The air was clear and dry and cold. The blackened snow and charcoal-rectangle remains of the IM ranch house were leftovers from a garish nightmare.

Charlie was stiff in every muscle. He crawled to the window and looked out in the cold, blue dawn. He smelled his clothes strong with smoke and felt a sickness rise from deep within his stomach. He thought if daybreak was so special, it should be scheduled at a more convenient hour.

Yesterday there was a beautiful, useful ranch house. Today's light showed nothing. Worse than nothing. Something that was a blackened mess, that had to be cleaned and scraped away.

All knew John Coble's heart would break. He'd taken such delight in building the ranch house with all the comforts one could desire. He was a bachelor who relied on female advice. Etta guessed that he, along with Neil Clark, was looking for a feminine partner. She thought that Mr. Coble, with his eastern accent, ruddy complexion, and neat attire, was attractive to women. She dreaded the moment he would come to see the ruins of his ranch house. She felt she could never again look at his face without crying. His ranch house had suited her better than any place she'd lived. To her it was not losing a piece of valuable property as it would be to Mr. Coble. To her it was losing a protective shelter, an outer layer that was comfortable and safe as well as decorative.

The snow glistened with the brightening golden light of sunrise as the sun's orb cleared the earth's edge. Millions of glittering crystals almost too brilliant to look at greeted Etta through the soot-stained window.

The children wakened. Etta gave them each a small hunk of bread torn from a loaf that was still warm from being next to Pauline as she slept.

"I'm sure stove up," said Clayton Danks with a laugh. He went out and chopped hunks of meat with a hatchet from the beef that hung in the barn loft. He brought the meat back in a bucket. Etta thanked him and added snow to the bucket before putting it on the back of the stove to simmer. "I'll see what else I can find," said Danks. In twenty minutes he was back with spoons, enameled plates, and a couple of kettles. All were sooty black and smelled of acrid smoke.

"Laws, the scrubbing I'll have to do," said Etta with a sigh.

Danks look disappointed.

"Oh, I don't mind," Etta said quickly. "I'll scrub them and it'll save eating with our fingers." She made her petticoats into dishtowels, washcloths, and diapers.

After breakfast of bread, sweet coffee, and milk the men decided to sort through the ashes, pick out whatever was usable, and store it in the barn. Jimmy Danks hauled all usable logs to one side and chopped some for firewood.

"I hope we find more buckets or kettles for milk," said Clark. "There doesn't seem to be enough for cleaning, cooking, and milking."

"Could we freeze the milk and keep it like blocks of ice?" asked Etta.

"You sure think good, besides looking good," said Clark.

The noon meal was stewed beef and fresh milk. Afterward Charlie and Jimmy Thor rode for Bosler to find Mr. Coble.

Floyd found his stockings under Frank's blanket. He dressed in boots, underwear, and a wool blanket and went out to help the men sift through the ashes and charred remains of the house.

"If you find Mama's silver brooch, put it in your pocket and bring it to me," said Floyd.

Before dark Charlie and Jimmy Thor were back. Their horses were loaded with food supplies along with several faded, threadbare shirts and Levi's. Charlie called out so that even those in the barn could hear, "Mr. Coble's coming here day after tomorrow! He wants to rebuild!" In the meantime they were all to carry on from the bunkhouse as best they could. John Coble said he'd sell beef cattle to raise money to rebuild.

After supper of more stewed beef and bread and some canned peaches Floyd dug deep into his pocket and pulled out Etta's silver brooch. The clasp was melted against the back. "Neil found it," said Floyd.

Etta knew it was silly to be sentimental about a silver brooch, but she could not stop the tears that slid down her face. "My mama gave it to me when I was married. It belonged to her mama," she explained to Floyd. "I'm not crying because I'm sad. These are happy tears."

The men watched the children pass the delicate filigreed pin among themselves as though they'd never seen it before. Finally Floyd said, "I'd like you to wear it."

Etta pinned the brooch to the neck of her nightgown with a safety pin. In the gray twilight the burnished silver looked beautifully fine, dainty—exquisite.

Neil Clark said, "Go for a walk, ma'am, before it is too dark to see. Look in the barn and see all the stuff we saved. Me and the men'll have the dishes done when you get back—the snow water's boiling already. Mr. Irwin, go with her."

Etta had her coat and scarf on before anyone could change his mind.

Charlie was embarrassed by the attention Etta caused by being tearful over a sentimental brooch. He was glad to get outdoors. He breathed deeply of the cold air and felt better. He locked hands with Etta.

"What does that runt, Neil Clark, think he is, running the

foreman and his wife out in the cold?" Charlie growled. He tucked Etta's arm under his own.

"I like him," said Etta. Her voice was warm and rolling like a tiny creek meandering through a meadow in spring.

"I was about to tell you the same. He's right, you know. You've worked as hard as any of the men. You and the kids are going to Cheyenne. I'm going to get a house in town for you."

Etta stopped walking. She couldn't talk. Her throat constricted and squeezed more tears from her eyes.

"Don't cry, dear. I thought about a house in Cheyenne all the way to and from Bosler. Don't say we can't afford it, because I thought about that, too. I'm going to stay here, working for Mr. Coble until he builds a new ranch house and things are going all right for him, then I'm going to work with Pa and Will on the Y6. It's time I started raising my own horses. That's what we came to Cheyenne for—horses."

Etta had her arms around Charlie's wide waist. Her tears spilled on his sheepskin.

"I sure hope those tears are for happiness," he said with his arms around her shoulders.

Etta looked up and smiled. "The children and I will stay at the Y6 until we find a place in town. I can raise chickens and add to our savings." Her throat was open and she wanted to talk.

"Don't count on chickens. We're going to find that place in town right away. Mr. Coble told me about one that's for sale."

Etta felt Charlie's belt buckle press against her breast. "What did Mr. Coble say about the fire?"

"First he was mighty relieved that no one was hurt. He knew the wind was blowing like fury. He suggested a couple of sparks might have left the chimney and hit the roof, or even spit out the fireplace when we were all in bed. I let him talk. He said, 'I've the best bunch there ever was at Iron Mountain. We'll rebuild the house just the way she was.'"

Etta turned and looked at the blackened remains. The only things that could be identified were the kitchen range, tangled iron from the sleeping cots and bedsteads, and the stone fireplace. The sight made her feel half-sick. She turned away to sort out her thoughts quickly. When she took Charlie's hand and looked up into his face her eyes were bright. "That's wonderful! Not the fire, but Mr. Coble and Cheyenne. There's something to look forward to. That old saying is true. Heaven is right next to hell."

A week later Etta sat in the kitchen of the Y6 ranch house to read the papers Joe had brought in from Cheyenne. She was holding baby Frances on her lap. The *Cheyenne Daily Leader* attracted her attention with bold headlines: LOCAL COWBOY CONFESSES KILLING WILLIE NICKELL. She read that Tom Horn was arrested on Monday, January 13, 1902, in the lobby of the Inter-Ocean Hotel in Cheyenne.

The paper said Horn confessed the killing of Willie Nickell to Deputy U.S. Marshal Joe LeFors. Even Etta could figure out that Horn walked into a deliberately set trap. Horn went to see LeFors about the job in Montana. He and LeFors had a couple friendly drinks while talking about the Montana job. Then LeFors began asking Horn about the Willie Nickell killing.

All the time they were talking and LeFors was being so friendly, the court stenographer, Charles Ohnhaus, was in the next room with his ear to the crack in the door, taking shorthand notes! Etta felt her mouth become dry. LeFors had indeed set a trap for Horn.

"It's so unfair!" cried Etta angrily.

"LeFors is desperate," said Joe. "He wants someone to pin the Nickell killing on. And Etta, you're for sure all growed up when you notice life's mostly unfair."

Etta said, "Grandpa Joe, I wonder when Miss Kimmell's coming back? Rumor has it the schoolhouse is closed tight. I wonder if she would lie to give Tom an alibi if he needed one?"

Joe chuckled and said, "Etta, it's none of your business. But I'd guess she would. She's in love with Horn."

Her eyes glistened. "I'd lie for Charlie. But I know positively he'd never commit murder."

"Horn has an alibi. He was in Laramie the day Willie Nickell was shot. People saw him there that evening."

Etta read on. A few moments later she looked up again. Joe could tell she was steaming. Her words sounded like the hissing of boiling water. "You and I and everyone else knows Tom exaggerates when he's likkered. He'll tell how he captured every cattle rustler in the country single-handed. Remember his story about bringing in Geronimo? That's just talk! Now read! Right here! LeFors says Tom bragged about the shot he made at the Nickell boy. 'It was the best shot I ever made, and the dirtiest trick I ever done.' Tom uses better grammar. He's say 'ever did.' I know I have an ear for language." She was so agitated she wouldn't let Joe open his mouth. "Look at this! It says Tom told LeFors the reason there were no footprints around the Nickell gate was because he did the job barefoot! Laws! What boasting!

No one can run around without boots on that cactus- and rock-lined ground. If he were barefoot his feet'd be cut. I know his feet weren't cut. You want to know how I know?"

Joe was curious to hear what Etta had to say.

"Dora Miller told me. She saw Tom and Miss Kimmell in Miss Kimmell's room at Miller's. Dora thought Tom'd left the night before, but instead he'd stayed and in Miss Kimmell's bed." Etta's face was pink. "Dora told me that Tom had big white feet that were smooth as a baby's bottom." Etta wiped her face with her apron and didn't look at Joe. "Well—women see those things. Dora never mentioned if Tom's feet were cut or bruised. She'd have noticed that. She saw his feet not more'n two days after he got back from Laramie. She said they were white and smooth." She rested her elbows on the table.

Joe blinked and cleared his throat. "Etta! Don't go repeating that. You're a married woman!"

"Dora told me. She's married. Being married makes it easier to tell. Do you suppose I could get Dora to tell the sheriff about Tom's big smooth feet?"

Joe stared at his daughter-in-law trying to remain calm, when all the time he was breaking up with laughter at her description of a man's naked feet. "What if the Miller kid is the culprit? Do you suppose Dora Miller's going to testify about Horn's baby-bottom feet?"

TWENTY-TWO

Frontier Days

Charlie told Etta that there was an unwritten story in the Tom Horn–Willie Nickell affair. "It's about the cattle barons versus the sheepherders and homesteaders."

Horn's preliminary hearing came eleven days after he was arrested in the Inter-Ocean Hotel. Rumors ran rampant. No one expected Horn would stay in jail nor be convicted for this crime.

Charlie went to town for supplies once a week on orders from Mr. Coble. Then he went to the county jail. He and Horn sang or talked about many subjects. One day they'd sing all the ballads they could remember. Another day they commiserated with each other about how the country was changing.

The house in Cheyenne that John Coble suggested to Charlie was on a large triangular lot. The right angle was bordered by Eddie and Twenty-eighth avenues. The long side was along Randall. The white clapboard house faced Eddie. When that avenue was later renamed the full address became 2712 Pioneer Avenue. There was a full porch supported by pillars. Inside Etta liked the living room with its wide windows facing the front tree-lined street. Charlie liked the dining room because it was large enough to hold a desk and chair at one end. "I'll keep all the books and papers for the Y6 here. I'll manage the Y6 the way Pa expects and this will be my office." He tried to speak in a calm, slow voice.

Etta was busy examining the two bedrooms, with bath between, which were along the north side of the dining room. Beyond the dining room was the good-sized kitchen with the third bedroom, and a pantry was built along the north side. Going out the back door, Charlie and Etta discovered an L-shaped building. The short side was east, behind the kitchen, and contained a bunkhouse that could sleep six men easily. The long side was north of the house and held six horse stalls and three storage rooms, one for coal, one for horse feed, and the third a tack room, for saddles, horse medicine, etc. Between the house and the L-shaped "barn" was a wide space to work the horses. Behind the barn's storage room were corrals. Behind the bunkhouse was a neat stack of baled hay.

Etta could see right off that she didn't have to coax Charlie to buy this place. He'd already decided it was the place for her and the children. He'd decided he could spend weekends here getting caught up on the book work and working any special horses he might acquire. "The children can walk from here to the Central School."

"Come on, let's go downtown to get the papers on this place," said Charlie. "It's a necessity, not a luxury."

"I'll wait right here on the front porch steps until you come back," said Etta. "I'm going to decide where to plant trees for shade and flowers for color and joy."

"But there's snow covering the yard." Charlie bent to kiss Etta.

"I can see the green grass in my mind's eye."

Charlie waved, climbed into the wagon, and snapped the lines so that the horse trotted toward Cheyenne's business district.

Etta walked around the house and barn half a dozen times, tramping down the snow, imagining what it would be like with the children running around inside and outside.

In two days Etta and the children were moved into the house. On the second day Etta admitted to Charlie that the place was "more than I anticipated even in my wildest dreams."

Charlie went back to the IM as foreman. Floyd was enrolled in the Central School's second grade.

The school was a large brick structure with a yard enclosed by an open fence of round, iron railing. Floyd was impressed by the method of dispensing water during recess. Someone had installed two large rectangular tanks with iron drinking cups chained to the front. "Girls drink from the tank on their side of the playground and boys from the tank on their side," he explained to his mother. "Someone must drain the tanks at night and fill them in the day, or during this cold weather the water would freeze and split the tanks."

Etta nodded agreement. She was sure not many six-and-a-half-year-olds would be that astute. As she hugged him, she gave thanks to God for letting Floyd go to a proper school. She didn't want him to go to a one-room school again, not even the way she had to in New York State years ago, when most of the pupils were McGuckins, her brothers and sisters. She was pleased that the pupils were separated into different rooms according to their grade. What Floyd does is his responsibility and no sister will come home and tattle on his behavior, she thought. That's the way school should be.

One weekend in the spring, before the snow was completely gone, Charlie came home and made an announcement. "I'm going to have a meeting here tomorrow morning. A couple of the ranchers want to come here and discuss the changes that are taking place."

"Who's coming and what changes?" asked Etta.

"John Coble for one is coming and John Clay and Ora Haley. Some of the big ranches are going to break up. They want to talk about putting fences around their pastures—to keep the sheep out."

"Those men are big ranchers—why would they want to come here, instead of the Industrial Club or the Inter-Ocean Hotel, and talk about such things?" Etta clattered the breakfast dishes.

"You should be flattered. They want to see this place. I suspect John Coble wants to see the children. I think he misses having them at the IM Ranch. I know he misses your cooking, dear."

"That's flattery. I want the truth!"

"I have told you all I know. Mr. Coble asked if they couldn't meet here on Sunday morning."

"What if I decided to go to church and take the kids?"

"They'd have to wait until you got back to see you and the kids."

"Charlie, there's one thing wrong."

"No, dear, it's all right. The men will meet here and see all the work you've put into making curtains and decorating this house. They'll be impressed."

Etta scowled. "That's it. What's wrong is the house!"

"I don't understand." Charlie was confused. "There's a living room, a dining room, three bedrooms, a pantry, a big front veranda, a bunkhouse for cowboys who come to town, and six horse stalls—"

"See—most of the decorating has been getting things for the bunkhouse or fixing up the barn. Things you want. Look at the dining room! A desk and chair and papers, but no table with chairs to match!"

Charlie's eyes darted to the dining room. "I told you that was to be my office. There's plenty of room for my desk in there."

Etta wiped her hands on her apron and strode to the dining room. "It's—it's bare! Really, Charlie, you can't have those older, respected ranchmen meet in a place with no furniture. What would they tell their friends? 'Etta Irwin is only a farmer's daughter and her house proves it.'" She was breathless.

Charlie was stupefied. He'd never given it a thought. Etta wanted her house to look as nice and well furnished as any other well-to-do ranch wife living in town. Charlie loved Etta more than life itself. He loved to watch her putter in the kitchen, fly around like a mother hen getting the four children dressed in the morning, send Floyd off to school and the others out to play. Etta always hugged Floyd and at the same time felt under his coat for the hidden lariat. At six years old Floyd was only interested in juggling his rope. It was a hemp lariat Charlie'd bought him and then shown him how to remove the kinks and make it pliable by stretching it between trees. Charlie had shown Floyd how to make the rope waterproof by greasing it with petroleum jelly and equal parts of melted paraffin. Etta scolded them both for spilling hot wax on the kitchen floor.

Etta was small, lean as a whip, wiry. She was vivacious. Charlie could rest his arm on the top of her silky brown hair. "So, that's what this caterwauling is about. This house is not enough; you want furniture and clutter!"

Etta turned and glowered at Charlie. "I do not want clutter! I want good furniture! Someday you are going to be a big rancher, and how you live and entertain is as important as what you do on your ranch."

Charlie stepped back and pushed the hair off his forehead. His brown eyes shone. "I'm not manager of the Y6 yet. My pa is. I am only the foreman at Mr. Coble's IM. But you're right about one thing. I'm going to be big. I'm going to be well known around Cheyenne! I aim to be as important as John Coble, John

Clay, or Ora Haley! Maybe more important, maybe I'll run for public office someday!"

Five-year-old Joella went out on the porch, slamming the front door behind her. Three-year-old Pauline stood next to the front window sucking her thumb and watching her sister. Frances cried out from her crib in the bedroom.

Charlie and Etta paid no attention to the children. They glared at each other.

"You tell your friends to hold their meeting in the Industrial Club until I can get my house furnished properly to have guests." Etta waved her arms around the bare room.

"We can't meet at the club, I'm not a member. Not yet!"

"The others are!" she snapped. "If they need you at this meeting, you can be their guest!" Etta's face was stormy and her eyes glinted like chips of ice.

"Confound it! John Coble's not allowed in the club! Something about him taking a couple shots at a painting—Paul Potter's bull—I told you that story."

Etta's eyebrows went up.

Charlie went on. "Tomorrow morning we're going to have three men here for a meeting. We'll sit around the kitchen table. I suppose they think if some of the larger ranches break up they'll be bought out by sheep men. We're all so against sheep we wouldn't even ride through a flock with a wool shirt on."

For a moment Etta was silent as though gathering more steam. "You act as though the way the house looks doesn't matter. Charlie, it does matter, just as much as how I look or how you look. Do you think all I know is what I learned on that dryland Kansas farm?"

"I think you are jealous. You watched me spend money on the bunkhouse for new cots and blankets and on the barn, and now you think it's only fair I spend some on the house."

Etta was astonished at his words. She blinked. She knew Charlie had dreams of being one of the largest horse breeders in Wyoming. She wanted to do everything she could to see his dream fulfilled. When she married Charlie she knew there would be disagreements, yet she was sure, with understanding and love, the quarrels would dissolve. Etta believed in dealing with everyday affairs in a practical, straightforward way.

Charlie was a dreamer and believed in an idealistic scheme of things. He thought everyone was his friend and in business matters the ranchers all worked together. He wondered if Etta didn't secretly applaud the inferno that took the IM ranch house. When they first came to Wyoming, she'd had her eye on one house or another in town. Had she used Floyd as the excuse to get a house in town? She always said Floyd and the girls had to have the best schooling available. He couldn't argue with that. He wanted the same thing.

"I'm not asking you to spend a lot of money. You can get something on sale at the Cheyenne Furniture. In the long run having a nice place to entertain or hold meetings will make you money. We can invite Senator Warren for supper. Charlie, someday you'll be invited to the Governor's Ball because of your influence on ranching. I know it as well as I know Joella will be in first grade next fall. Look in yesterday's paper. See if there is a ranch auction. We could get a dining room set cheap at an auction. Let's—"

Charlie had a hard time controlling his voice. "Etta, you don't have to buy someone's used furniture. Do you think I can't afford to get the things my wife wants?"

"Charlie, I don't have my head in the sand. I know what it took to get this house. I'm—"

"My wife is going to want for nothing!"

"I want you to let me finish a sentence!"

Charlie's eyes opened wide. His mouth was open, then it was closed and his lips were pressed tight. He turned to the closet for his overcoat and stalked from the house.

Etta was afraid she'd cry if she called out to Charlie. She looked out the window where Pauline was standing. She saw Joella in a coat half-buttoned, a wool cap pulled over her blond hair and no overshoes nor mittens. The child was sliding on a piece of old oilcloth down the front steps into the snowbank beside the walk. Etta saw Charlie bend down to say something to Joella and lay the oilcloth over the porch railing, then turn her toward the front door, pointing to her wet shoes. Then he walked toward town, pulling his muffler up around his ears.

Etta ran out and grabbed Joella. "Young lady, don't ever go out without your overshoes and mittens!" she cried. "You'll freeze!"

At lunchtime Charlie was not home, but a horse-drawn wagon stopped in front of the house. Two delivery boys came to the door. One said there was a dining room table and six chairs in the wagon for Mrs. C. B. Irwin.

Etta was so surprised, her first inclination was to tell the delivery boys they'd made a mistake. The driver showed her Charlie's signed note for the furniture, and she knew it was no mistake.

She showed them where to put the mahogany table and chairs.

That evening she served supper on the table covered with a carefully ironed bedsheet. "My dear," said Charlie, "this room looks like a real dining room. Before tomorrow morning bake some of your delicious cinnamon rolls for our three guests."

Etta was not smiling. She was breathing hard. "Charlie, I'm more than grateful, but you can see I have no proper cloth for the table."

"I don't see that." He went to the coat closet and handed her a large package from the Cheyenne Merc.

Puzzled, Etta took the box and said, "What's inside?"

"Your tablecloth, Mrs. Irwin."

When the three men arrived, Etta had the cinnamon rolls baked and on the dining room table with cups of hot coffee. She used the delicate Haviland china Ell had given her when they lived in Colorado Springs. Etta had fresh cream, butter, strawberry jam, honey, and white and brown sugar.

John Clay said he'd longed for brown sugar in his coffee ever since leaving Edinburgh. Ora Haley said he'd never tasted such good cinnamon rolls, and John Coble kept his mouth full so he couldn't say anything until Etta came to clear the dishes away and the men could have their meeting.

"This is a lovely room. You have wonderful taste. I just noticed that the lace curtains and the tablecloth match," said Coble.

Etta smiled broadly and touched Charlie's shoulder as she left with the dishes on an enameled tray.

"When we leave here it will be like this meeting and conversation never took place, you understand?" said John Clay, pulling at the lobe of one ear.

"Yes, sir," Charlie said. He was going to listen carefully. He was grateful to Etta for taking the children outside. He knew these three men were probably about the most important ranchers in southeastern Wyoming. To have them meet at his place was indeed an honor.

Charlie knew about the range conflicts that were discussed first. There was no secret that the cattlemen claimed the grazing land was theirs. They had been in the territory first. The newcomers, small ranchers, sheepmen claimed there were no legal rights because of prior use and the free public grazing lands were for anyone. The cattlemen were frustrated because the small settlers were becoming more numerous and many helped themselves to the beef of the larger operators. Many accused rustlers were turned loose because of lack of evidence or sympathy for the accused and his family. It was well known that property in both cattle and horses was nonexistent in the minds of the small settlers. Coble, Clay, and Haley wanted no range war like the Johnson County war, but they wanted to explore what could be done to keep the rights of the cattlemen protected by the law. By afternoon they had decided to hire Tom Horn to ride protection for their ranges and pay him as much as the Montanan offered.

"Horn was credited but never arrested for the 1895 murders of two local small homesteaders living near Horse Creek in the Laramie Mountains," said Haley. "He's in jail now and I for one think he's been framed. By George, when he's out and riding the line again for us, he'll sure enough scare the damned sheepherders off!" He lit the cigar he'd been chewing.

"So, we agree to hire him to ride the line as soon as he's free," said Coble. "That's it. All we want for him to do is ride the pasture lines between the Sybille and Chugwater creeks. That territory is big enough to keep him out several nights a month. His reputation will be our success in preventing any more thievery, changing cattle brands, and ignorance of our property boundaries. Sounds good."

The three men shook hands. They shook hands with Charlie. "Thanks, C.B., for giving us a place to meet where we don't raise a lot of questions. Remember, we weren't ever here. You didn't hear anything." Coble spoke in a whisper. "No one's to know Horn's working for three ranches."

The spring brought electrical storms, whirlwinds, hail, and cloudbursts. Then came the hot summer winds from the southwest. Traveling on horseback half a day from the IM ranch to Cheyenne, Charlie brushed passed the willows, reddish brown with sap, that lined the tiny streams. The roadway was fringed with yellow sunflowers and rabbit brush. He and Frank had brought in more wild horses that spring. Charlie was going to send a wire to the office of the Denver Festival of Mountain and Plain and offer to supply them with a dozen bucking horses that year.

During the two-day Frontier Days celebration of 1902, Etta looked after her own four children plus Margaret's boy and girl. She sat with the children in the grandstand.

Margaret entered the ladies' cow-pony race riding her favorite horse, Old Gold. She wore a white divided skirt and a red silk blouse that she'd sewn on Etta's machine. The Irwin children sat on the edge of the wood plank to see Margaret.

She won in fifty-two seconds for the half-mile race. Jennie Pawson in a green shirt was second.

Etta stood and cheered.

Then came the wild bronco race, and Frank Irwin, delicate in appearance but tough as sisal, won the fifty-dollar purse.

One event fascinated them beyond belief. There were fifteen Shoshone braves with ten squaws all the way from the Wind River Reservation, near Fort Washakie, who came out on their favorite ponies, all saddleless, some with rope bridles, some with hackamores, some absolutely bare. All of these Shoshones, in beautiful colored regalia, lined up before the judges' stand. The flag was brought up and dashed downward. The race was on! The ponies were lashed with quirts in order to move them closer to the front. In several cases the long legs of the Indian riders encircled the bodies of the ponies. This race was for a purse of twenty dollars, the winner to receive fifteen, the second best three, and the third two.

Yellow Calf, the Shoshone chief, dressed in jeans, tattered buckskin jacket, and a black wide-brimmed hat with a high round crown, had the best horse, and came under the wire an easy winner. Yellow Calf was not satisfied with the promise of his winnings by the judges and wanted his money as soon as he'd earned it. So before he or his fellow buckskin-jacketed Shoshone contestants dismounted, they were paid in silver dollars.

Next, half a dozen Shoshone braves, with long braids hanging down their chests, came out to the center of the arena and performed a corn dance, or reasonable facsimile. Two of the breechclouted near-naked men, their bodies glistening with goose grease in the sun, beat their hands on taut buffalo-skin drums. The other four danced the heel-toe step and wailed in an eerie, high-pitched keening that seemed to penetrate the innermost soul of all the listeners. The four dancing Shoshones were dressed in decorated breechclouts, moccasins, and beautiful white doeskin shirts, which they believed showed their thankfulness to the Great Spirit for a bountiful corn crop.

The next event was the squaw race, with ten participants. The women were dressed in doeskin tunics that were beaded on the yoke and sleeves and fringed at the bottom. They wore high-top moccasins that reached their knees, which were beaded along the sides and on the tops. The women had only a beaded band or thong tied around the forehead to the back of their heads to keep their hair out of their eyes. When the winner, My Goose, was announced, her husband, Yellow Calf, came to collect the silver dollars.

Charlie, as foreman of the IM spread, had Slim Burke take the chuck wagon out to the fairgrounds and do the cooking for his cowboys who participated in the two days of events. The men slept in the bunkhouse at Charlie's place on Eddie Avenue. Rumor spread fast that C. B. Irwin was a square foreman, one who treated his men well. At suppertime men from other outfits stopped by the chuck wagon that was inside the gate at Frontier Park, to seek out Charlie and ask for a job at the IM that fall.

Charlie already had a reputation for being a strict foreman, but one who never played favorites with his men. Everyone who worked for Mr. C. B. Irwin had to consistently follow the same rules.

In the evening, when the park was deserted except for the livestock and the night watchmen, the Irwin family was with the rest of the merrymakers on the crowded streets, watching the masqueraders and listening to the bands on various downtown corners. There were French balls, cakewalks, and clog dancing. The streets had been scraped, rolled, and covered with canvas for easy outdoor dancing.

Etta carried Frances, who was asleep. The other children were becoming tired and whiny.

"Let's take the children home," suggested Margaret. "After all, I have to get some sleep, too, because tomorrow afternoon after the last show I am to have my picture taken for the paper. Honestly, I was almost afraid to enter the race. I thought I was not strong enough, my horse not ready. And now, suddenly it's over and I'm to have my picture taken so people will know who I am."

"And who are you?" asked Etta gently.

Margaret was carrying three-year-old Charles and holding the hand of five-year-old Gladys. "I'm Margaret Irwin, mother of these two children, Will Irwin's wife, and somewhere in between a person who likes horses and loves to ride. That's not too complicated, is it?"

"Oh, no!" said Etta, boosting Frances to a more comfortable position on her shoulder. "It is exactly what I expected. But I will tell you something in confidence. See these houses with the lights shining out their windows and their closeness to their neighbors? That is what I like. I like my house in town."

"You don't like the ranch?" Margaret was surprised.

"I like it only because Charlie likes it. Charlie is going to come back to the ranch and raise horses. Supplying the horses for the Denver festivities and for this Frontier Days has filled him with enthusiasm for getting back to the Y6."

"Does Charlie know you prefer town?" asked Margaret softly.

"No, I don't suppose he does, but the Lord knows I've given him enough hints. There's the old saying, there's none so deaf than those who won't hear. He won't listen to me. He loves the outdoors, the sunshine, the fresh air, the smell of dust and barnyards, the rippling muscles of a horse running in the pasture, or the knotted muscles of a horse ready to explode as it bucks skyward. I love Charlie more than anything. So I'll manage, and now I have these four children to keep me running from morning until night." Her laugh was lighthearted.

The women put the children to bed and then sat down to talk until the men came in.

"Do you remember when Will first brought me to the soddy in Kansas?" asked Margaret.

"We called you Will's Baby then. The roles seem to be changed now. You baby Will along with your children. He never objects. He likes being pampered," said Etta. "You're the grown-up, Margaret."

Next afternoon Margaret was back in the arena on Old Gold and won the silver loving cup. And late in the afternoon Charlie took Floyd to see the tented exhibition titled "Buffalo Bill."

Buffalo Bill Cody sat regally on the back of a golden palomino. His long yellow hair flowed out from a tooled, leather headband. His performers tumbled and vaulted from one horse to another, spinning around in midair. Afterward Floyd stood in front of the big top and tugged on Charlie's sleeve. "Pa, I'm going to be a roper and trick rider."

"It's hard work, son. Takes practice, every day," said Charlie.

At Charlie's elbow a clear voice said, "The important thing is publicity. Let me present myself. I am the one and only Buffalo Bill."

The man was as tall as Charlie, his face was tanned. His beard matched his long yellow hair and his eyes were as blue as turquoise. Charlie introduced himself and pointed to Floyd saying, "My son."

Buffalo Bill shook hands with Charlie and looked down at Floyd. "Start out with ten tricks. Practice until you never make a mistake. Hire a photographer to take action shots. Send the shots to state fairs, circuses, anywhere that might hire a trick rider.

Wear silk shirts and sparkles, work where the trick can be seen by the whole audience. When you are five years older, come see me. What's your name, son? I never forget a face nor a name."

"Floyd Leslie Irwin, trick roper and rider, sir." Floyd held out his hand.

Charlie gulped.

"Aahh, that's good! Publicize yourself! If you can't believe you're good, who will? Get your name and picture everywhere." Buffalo bent down to put his hand on Floyd's arm. The buckskin fringe on his coat tickled Floyd's nose. "I'll hire you by the tricks you can perform. I'll feature the stunts that are most spectacular. Don't you forget me, Master Floyd Irwin." He shook Floyd's hand.

Most Wyoming cowboys were not overly impressed with Buffalo Bill's trick riders and ropers. They were too familiar with this type of entertainment and most of them could do the stunts he and his performers featured. Charlie wasn't impressed either and vowed that if Floyd performed it would be with new and exciting tricks. What impressed Charlie was the rush of memories and the similarity between his old friend Colonel Johnson and Buffalo Bill. There was a flashy grandeur that was charming—almost enchanting.

The final attraction was an old-fashioned stage holdup by the Indians and a rescue by the cowboys. The stagecoach pulled out and the Indians on spotted ponies ran *kiyi*-ing after it. The Indians were in breechclouts and moccasins and daubed with colored paints and goose grease. In a few minutes the Indians were overtaken by a bunch of cowboys. A noisy, fierce battle ensued and the Indians were defeated. The firing of blanks from the revolvers did not stop until the stagecoach reached the grandstand. Then the audience saw old Chief Yellow Calf and his son stealthily coming behind. Two cowboys swung their lassos and captured father and son. They were hauled up on the cowboys' horses and trotted off to the other side of the arena amid loud applause from the crowd.

Floyd stayed close to Charlie to watch the cowboys pick up their gear after the final act. With ropes hanging from the horns of their saddles and their revolvers in holsters at their hips, they looked like desperados in broad-brimmed hats and angora chaps. In reality, most cowboys were courteous, quiet, and unpretentious, with hearts as big as the broad cattle range that extended from horizon to horizon. Actually their gun was as innocent as their rope. It was ready for an emergency when nothing else would do.

Charlie jostled his way through the crowd to get to the corrals and tend to the animals. The fence was wrapped in orange and black crepe paper, same as most of the buildings and many homes in town were decorated with twists and streamers in the colors of this year's Frontier Days, orange and black. Charlie felt empty all of a sudden. The celebration was anticipated for months and was now nothing but memories. He smiled to himself. All fall and winter he and his family and the cowboys would retell stories about this year's Frontier Days events clear up until time for next year's events.

TWENTY-THREE

Hanging of Tom Horn

That fall Charlie made numerous trips to Cheyenne to see Etta and the children. Both Floyd and Joella were in school. Charlie also came to town to attend Tom Horn's trial. He thought it was the thing to do. He was foreman of the outfit Horn worked for. Traveling on horseback Charlie noticed the small gullies held splashes of red and yellow wild currant and the rosebushes were yellowing. The hillsides were bright with frost-touched golden aspens. He spotted herons in the small creeks and flocks of crows flapping to distant rookeries. He noticed the pungent odor of greasewood and the scent of pine and newly cut alfalfa and native hay. He loved these sights and smells.

Tom Horn's trial began on October 10, 1902. There were more than a hundred witnesses, and the case hit every major newspaper in the West from St. Louis to San Francisco. The courtroom had standing room only during the entire two-week proceeding.

On October 24, 1902, the verdict was in. Tom Horn was guilty and was to hang on January 9, 1903, between 10 A.M. and 3 P.M.

One cattleman commented, "Cheyenne juries ain't worth the powder to blow them into hell." Another said, "When a man ain't good for anything else, he is just right to set on a jury."

Horn's attorneys filed a motion for a new trial in the district court. Judge Scott refused. Appeals were made. A petition of error was filed and a stay of execution was granted, but no new trial.

The winter was hard and feed for cattle and game was covered with hard-packed snow on the range. Before Christmas, Charlie heard rumors of a plot to blow up the jail and set Horn free. He did not believe them. Then dynamite was found concealed in the snow outside the brick wall of the courthouse and a piece of lead pipe was found in Horn's pants leg.

Warm summer winds blew over the prairies sending Russian thistle bounding across the flats and hollows. The stretch of buck fences could be seen for miles; the snow fences seemed to lead nowhere. The air was so clear that mountains far away seemed close, and the stars shone so brilliantly they looked within reach.

Early Sunday morning, August 10, 1903, Tom Horn and a man, Jim McCloud, also on death row, escaped. Horn grabbed a Belgian-made revolver from the sheriff's office as he ran out. He went through the alley, away from the direction in which McCloud rode off on horseback. On the lot across the street from the courthouse was a small carnival. Horn stood close to the merry-go-round and tried to remove the safety on the revolver. He was nervous and anxious. The safety would not slide front or back or either side. It was jammed or locked! He ran over a pile of dirt just as the merry-go-round operator tackled him. Deputy Dick Proctor told him to walk back to the courthouse or else he would fire his six-shooter into his back. Horn felt the muzzle of the gun and walked. It was humiliating to walk in front of the large crowd that had come from various church services and gathered in front of the courthouse, curious to get a glimpse of the jailbreakers. "I hope to heaven McCloud got away," said Horn.

However, McCloud was also being escorted to the courthouse not far behind Horn.

The sun was bright in a cloudless sky that Sunday. Etta walked serenely to church with the four children. Coming home she overheard the buzzing excitement in people's voices as they retold how Tom Horn had attempted to escape. She could hardly wait to tell Charlie, who was at home gathering his gear to ride back to the IM ranch.

* * *

Charlie, on horseback, made a little detour going past the courthouse on his way out of Cheyenne. He noticed a crowd in front of the Inter-Ocean Hotel across from the Union Pacific Depot. He stopped and listened.

The attempted jailbreak gave strength to plenty of gossip in the streets of Cheyenne.

The governor ordered armed soldiers to patrol Cheyenne's streets. A Gatling gun was mounted in the entrance to the Laramie County Courthouse and Jail. A deputy sheriff and guard were at every window. An arc light near the courthouse burning night and day was added to reinforce discouragement of any rumored attack or attempted jailbreak.

A week later John Coble asked Charlie to ride up to the Miller Ranch. He was certain young Victor Miller had shot Willie Nickell and wanted Charlie to convince Miller to make a clean confession.

Coble said, "I've had word from Al Bristol. He used to work for me. Good man. He's always been trustworthy. Bristol said he once caught Victor Miller skulking around the IM's horses in the Wall Rock pasture. The kid climbed over the fence and was near one of my special bred racers. Bristol grabbed the kid by the back of his collar. The kid admitted he was stealing the horse. Bristol growled and scared the kid right down to his toenails. He told Bristol it was he who shot Willie Nickell twice in the back and it was he who put a flat rock under Willie's head, the way he'd heard Horn had done to a couple of cattle rustlers. Said he'd do it again because he hated the whole Nickell outfit. Said old man Nickell had sheep pellets for brains."

"Why, that little cold-blooded son-of-gun!" cried Charlie.

Coble lowered his voice a trifle so that Charlie had to lean forward to hear all he said. "Bristol said he took the kid into Cheyenne for a talk with an attorney, Walter Stoll. The kid was so scared his mouth kept going dry and he shook the whole time. Remember the kid had been in jail not long before on account of shooting old man Nickell in the elbow?"

"He was let go on insufficient evidence," said Charlie.

"Right. Bristol knew Stoll would do nothing about the attempted horse theft, it was his word against the kid's, but he wanted the attorney to take down the kid's murder confession."

Charlie's eyes brightened. "That would be a lucky break for Tom Horn. Sad for the poor kid, though."

"Well, when Bristol took the kid to Cheyenne, the kid denied even being at the Rock Wall pasture. He said he was in Cheyenne the day Willie Nickell was murdered. He even signed an affidavit saying so. It was his word against Bristol's. And for reasons of his own, Stoll believed the two-faced kid."

"You want me to go to the Miller place and get Victor to go back into Cheyenne and confess?" Charlie was dubious.

Coble laughed and said, "C.B., I know your ability to talk a man into most anything. Remember this is going to get an innocent man out of jail. Tom Horn did not shoot Willie Nickell!" Coble's voice went up. He leaned over and put his hand on Charlie's arm. "I want you to tell Victor that you have word that the Cheyenne law officers are on their way out to arrest him. Tell him the best thing to do is to go quietly to town and confess. That way it'll be much easier on himself and his family." Coble paused and looked at Charlie.

Charlie felt his heart pounding fast. This was not the kind of job he wanted to do for his boss. "Mr. Coble, Victor isn't going to do anything I say. Look here, you are the honored, upright, honest, big-time rancher. He'd be more likely to do as you suggest."

Coble turned red, then smiled and picked at the dried grass beside the ranch house step. "I would do it, but I'm taking a lady friend, a special schoolmarm, to Denver, for a performance by Lillie Langtry."

Charlie rolled his eyes. "I didn't know you were courting."

Coble smiled and said, "I know I can count on you, C.B." He shook Charlie's hand, picked up the tether line, mounted his horse, and trotted down the dusty road.

Coble's visit soured Charlie for any kind of work for a week. His mind whirled with thoughts. He never liked to be obligated to anyone, especially someone he worked for. Obligations meant trouble. If he went to the Miller place, one of those boys might have a shotgun aimed on him. They could accuse him of being there to steal horses or rustle cattle. With no outside witnesses he'd be jail bait himself.

Finally Charlie decided to take Neil Clark with him. Neil Clark, blond and raw-boned, was just about the best horseman Charlie had known. The two men rode across the prairie that was filled with *dog towns*. The white-tailed, prairie dogs burrowed holes in the earth for miles in all directions. Each burrow entrance was surrounded by a ring of earth, and as the two horsemen approached they saw the prairie dogs sit on top of the mounds, barking the alarm in a voice similar to a yappy little dog. The prickly pear cactus was flowering, yellow, tinged with a thin line of red on the edge. They rode past black sage with its dull green leaves and oily, pungent aroma. Along the creek bottoms the wild plum and chokecherry were ripe.

The Miller ranch was one of the few that was completely fenced. Dora Miller was out in the yard. She wore her husband's big, black, rubber overshoes. When she walked, the unfastened buckles scraped against each other. She wore a man's red flannel shirt over her long cotton dress. She looked as if she'd pulled a cow out of quicksand. The mud-encrusted cow was tied to a skinny aspen. The cow's legs were spraddled. Its tail was up and it bawled so loud no one could hear himself speak.

"Howdy, ma'am!" Charlie yelled, riding in close. "Your place looks mighty fine!" He tried to sound cheerful. "I could use an extra hand and wondered if your boy, Victor, would be interested! I'd like to talk with him!"

"Oh, no! Vic's in Wheatland doing work for Mr. Clay! But I do wish he'd skeedaddle home and do something about this blamed cow!" Then she recognized Charlie and put her hand to her mouth. Taking her hand away she asked, "Mr. Irwin, there's no trouble, is there?"

Keeping Clark behind him, Charlie said, "Dora, what kind of trouble do you mean?"

"Well—well, you see—you know there are some who'd like to see poor Vic, or my husband, James, in jail in place of that hired killer, Tom Horn! The schoolmarm, Miss Kimmell, she moved away, swore to Sheriff Smalley that James and both our boys were here the morning Willie Nickell was shot!" The cow stopped bellowing. "That schoolmarm was sweet on Tom Horn. You know that. He was with her here more'n once when we was all in town." Her eyes were bright and she tried to smooth her tangled hair.

Charlie wondered why she said this to him. It was something women would gossip about. He nodded and winked. "I guess you could say they were sweethearts."

"More." Dora touched Charlie's leg. "I could tell every time he was here. I kept her room straight and washed them sheets."

Charlie felt his ears burn. He thought that Dora Miller was lonely and that was why she was running at the mouth.

"I heard that schoolmarm warn Tom about Joe LeFors, the peace officer. She told him LeFors had something up his sleeve. Tom wasn't scared of no man and paid her words no heed. So—he's the one in trouble. Isn't he?"

"His trouble seems to be sitting around in jail getting pale and letting his muscle turn soft on account of some weasel who's too chicken to tell the truth." Charlie watched Dora's face.

She looked straight ahead at the sad-looking cow and blinked once or twice. A vein in her forehead throbbed. A nerve spasm made one shoulder twitch. "The Lord takes His own revenge on all critters." She was looking at the cow that had begun bawling again.

Charlie yelled, "I'll put my faith in the Lord anytime!" He tipped his hat and nodded.

Charlie and Clark rode out to the Chugwater Creek with the intention of following it up to Wheatland, hoping to intercept Victor. Charlie knew Dora didn't want him looking for Victor, even though she had not come out and said so. Going to Wheatland was an all-day trip.

They were lucky and found the boy at John Clay's place. Charlie left young Clark to talk ranching with Clay, while he took Victor out behind the barn and repeated the arrest story. He urged Victor to ride into Cheyenne with him and confess before the officers came after him.

"Son, it would be a terrible sin for an innocent man to suffer and be punished for a crime he didn't commit. For a crime that you, yourself, already confessed to. If you don't tell the authorities now, but continue to lie, think how it will weigh on your conscience forever. You'll never be rid of it. It will follow you around and burn like fire and brimstone in your brain. Who really shot Willie Nickell?"

Victor looked pale. Charlie hoped the boy was not going to be sick. "No man has been hanged in Wyoming for the past ten years. And because you won't talk, a man is going to hang."

Victor licked his lips. "Ma told me what would happen if I ever again told anyone I shot Willie. Willie was scum! No better'n his sheep-raising pa. I ain't guilty. If I say I am, my pa will think I'm a yellow-livered skunk. I ain't that! So, like I said, I ain't guilty of nuthin'. I intend to go home, even if there are a dozen law men after me!" He paused and licked his lips again. "I didn't sign nuthin' saying I locked horns with Al Bristol! There's no proof I even talked with him. It's his word against mine. I signed a paper saying I was in Cheyenne when Willie was shot and that I was never at the Rock Wall." Victor was shaking and his face was as white as birch bark. His tongue kept moving and licking his lips, same as his ma's had. "I wasn't there. Must have been some other rustler Bristol talked with. He doesn't really know me. He could have thought it was me."

Charlie had heard enough excuses. He grabbed the boy's arm. His hand fit all around. He squeezed hard. "Did I say anything about Al Bristol and the pasture at Rock Wall?" Charlie's brown eyes had orange flecks, like tiny flames reflecting in them.

"No—I guess not," Victor stammered and kept his head down. A sudden breeze blew his hat to the ground. Charlie thought he saw tears before the boy's hair fell over the pale blue eyes.

Charlie's voice was gruff. "Put your hat on, keep your hair back so you can see me."

Victor pulled his arm free and grabbed his hat. "You hurt my arm bad."

"Your conscience hurts worse, doesn't it? Get on your horse and ride with me straight to Cheyenne and confess. Save your poor ma and your pa, too, an untold amount of grief and heartache." Charlie grabbed the boy's arm again, increased the pressure, and waited for an answer.

Victor looked at Charlie, opened his thin mouth, blinked his watery, pale, fishlike eyes. Charlie could see beads of sweat on his forehead and feel the muscle spasms in his thin arm. He let up on the pressure, expecting the boy to answer in the affirmative.

Instead Victor proved his agility by jerking fast downward, stomping on the top of Charlie's instep and hitting him in the belly with his small, balled fist. He ran out of the barnyard before Charlie could gasp a good-sized breath. Charlie watched Victor mount his horse and ride off without looking backward.

John Clay looked up. "Something sure put lightning in that kid's feet!"

It is a fact that during Tom Horn's riding of the line the stealing of calves practically ceased. But during his twenty-two months in jail, murders and more sheep killings took place. In July 1902, one hundred and fifty armed men stopped fifteen herds of sheep, destroyed two thousand head and scattered the rest, killed one herder and drove out the others. In February 1903 a gang of masked men killed Bill Minnick and two hundred of his sheep. In March, seven masked men tied up a herder, burned his wagon, killed his horses and five hundred sheep. In July, National Guardsmen restored order in Thermopolis, where sheepmen threatened to lynch a man suspected of the murder of Minnick. Most of the perpetrators of these crimes were not found and brought to trial. If they stood trial, they were not convicted.

Some of the witnesses dared not testify, nor counsel dare to plead, because of fear for their lives. Horn was in jail nearly two years and roughly fifty murders were committed in Wyoming then, with no convictions.

It is ironic but true that if Horn were a rustler, he would not be spending his time in jail. The area's cattle thieves regarded Horn as their enemy and they wanted him removed, just as they, along with the big cattle ranchers, wanted Nickell, the area's first sheep herder, out of the country.

It became a common saying on the streets of Cheyenne, "Show me a cattleman who is against Tom Horn, and I will show you a rustler!"

Charlie was upset. He told Etta about talking with Victor Miller on John Clay's ranch.

Etta looked pensive. Charlie liked that little-girl look. She put her hand on Charlie's arm. He liked the feeling of her warmth through his shirtsleeve. "Let's say Tom Horn had nothing to do with Willie Nickell, and Victor Miller nor his pa didn't either— who, then?" said Etta.

"It's a mystery to me! Maybe someone from the outside. I don't know. All I know is this thing has me on edge. I like Tom. I fear the wrong man will hang. Tom is a scapegoat. Tom is so confident that the murderer will step forward and give himself up that he's not worried. Not even nervous." Charlie looked up. "I have a gut feeling that someone could write a letter to the governor saying he was the true murderer and the governor would ignore it."

"Charlie, don't look so down-in-the-mouth. You tried. Forget Victor Miller. Maybe Mr. Coble will think of something else. I heard Coble's personally responsible for hiring the best legal defense for Tom that could be found in the state, Judge Lacey, and District Attorney T. E. Burke. Certainly they will defend Tom. You don't have to worry. So don't take your feelings out on the cowboys."

He got up and she got up and stood on her toes. He bent down and kissed her. "Dear, this whole legal thing has me stymied. Next week I'm going to take another gunnysack of horsehair to Tom for his rope making."

"Try to be more sociable than a rotten tooth." Etta kissed him again.

"Ya! I'll see you in a couple of weeks when me and the boys come in town for Frontier Days." His voice became soft and gentle. "I couldn't live without seeing you and the kids." He gave her a squeeze and went for his coat and hat.

In September the streets of Cheyenne were decorated with orange and black crepe paper streamers for the annual Frontier Days celebration. Thousands of visitors and residents of Cheyenne again thrilled to the cowboys bouncing across the arena on whirling, frothing, wide-eyed cayuses, or racing long-horned steers from the Y6 ranch neck and neck, flying into the air and landing in the dust. The newspapers ignored Tom Horn for a week.

Charlie entered the steer-roping contest. He didn't even come in third. Frank won the quarter-mile horse race. Margaret won the ladies' half-mile race. The Irwin family was beginning to earn a fine reputation among cowhands and cattlemen all around Cheyenne.

A week later Charlie's team of horses and wagon kicked up a fog of dust that floated above the potholed, graveled highway leading into Cheyenne. The dust drifted downwind until it settled on lupines, lespedezas, umbrellalike blooms of the wild buck-wheat, and autumn goldenrod. Charlie barely saw the gray powder on the petals of roadside sunflowers and blades of yucca. His eyes took in the whole spectrum of wildflowers, the tall bluestem grass and the dust all combined. He heard distant cow-bells. The songbirds had already gone away. He thought it was good to see the open space, where the earth met the sky. It soothed his mind.

The air before sunup was crisp. Charlie's breath condensed into wispy fog and so did the breath from the loping horses. Charlie wore his wide-brimmed hat, a sheep's-wool-lined jacket, muffler, gloves, wool trousers, and boots. He glanced at the translucent gray sky. He knew it would turn a tremulous red against the low clouds, as if announcing the coming of a cool, clear blue dawn.

Charlie was on his way into Cheyenne for the ranch supplies. After the wagon was loaded he planned to have lunch with Etta and the children, then go to the county jail for a visit with Horn. He was going to take Horn another gunnysack of horsehair.

Horn had on soft leather slippers. Charlie wondered if he missed wearing boots. Horn's faded blue flannel shirt was clean and so were his brown trousers. His hair had been freshly trimmed and so had his mustache. His face and hands were deathly white, faded from lack of sunshine. "It'll sure feel good to sleep in the hills with the stars overhead once again. Charlie, if anything happens—did anyone think to take my thirty-thirty

Winchester out of Coble's place during the fire?"

"Hey! So, it's yours? Frank put it in the IM bunkhouse. Nobody claimed it. Coble said it wasn't his. Jeems! I should have known! I guess we didn't save your bedroll and field glasses." Suddenly Charlie felt melancholy.

"You and Coble are the only ones who have been in to see me. After I finish braiding all this horsehair I'm going to write some letters. Maybe I'll send you one. If you go fishing send me one that weighs five or six pounds. I'm hungry for fish. Charlie, if anything happens—that Winchester—it's your rifle."

"Hey! What's going to happen? You have the best lawyers in the state. You'll be out before spring roundup," said Charlie.

"Maybe—I keep thinking I could have been killed in that stupid break me and McCloud staged. I was lucky. Luck can run dry, you know."

"Do you know the song the cowboys are singing now?" Charlie wanted to cheer up his friend. "*Life's Railway To Heaven*?"

"No. Do you?" asked Horn.

"Yes. I'll teach you." Charlie sang the sentimental song in his full tenor voice.

Life is like a mountain railroad, with an engineer that's
   brave;
We must make the run successful, from the cradle to the
   grave;
Watch the curves, the fills, the tunnels; never falter, never
   quail;
Keep your hand upon the throttle, and your eye upon the
   rail.

Chorus:
Blessed Savior, Thou wilt guide us till we reach that bliss-
   ful shore,
Where the angels wait to join us, in Thy praise forever
   more.

You will roll up grades of trial; you will cross the bridge of
   strife;
See that Christ is your conductor, on this lightning train of
   life;
Always mindful of obstructions, do your duty, never fail;
Keep your hand upon the throttle, and your eye upon the
   rail.

You will often find obstructions; look for storms of wind
   and rain;
On a fill, or curve, or trestle, they will almost ditch your
   train;
Put your trust alone in Jesus; never falter, never fail;
Keep your hand upon the throttle, and your eye upon the
   rail.

As you roll across the trestle, spanning Jordan's swelling
   tide,
You behold the Union Depot, into which your train will
   glide;
There you'll meet the Superintendent, God the Father, God
   the Son,
With the hearty, joyous plaudit, "Weary pilgrim, welcome
   home."*

"If the governor commutes the sentence to life imprisonment,
they'll move me by train from here to the state penitentiary in
Rawlins. I'll be like a caged bear. There's only one way out. I'm
going for it," Horn whispered.

Charlie saw Horn's intensely piercing dark, almost black, eyes
turn liquid, like deep, still water on a moonless night. Charlie
whispered, "You planning another escape, my friend?"

While Charlie was out of town, his sister, Ell, from Colorado
Springs, had come to visit Etta and the children, as she did every
year about this time.

Etta was amazed that Ell's silky, long hair was no longer the
color of honey, but a soft apricot-orange. The braid encircling her
head was like a bright, double halo that complimented her sea-
green eyes. Ell smelled erotically musky. She wore multicolored
beads like a rainbow around her neck. The brown, slim, pongee
dress daringly showed her ankles below the tiny flounce when
she got off the train. Her high-heels were covered with an apri-
cot-orange-colored silk. Her silk stockings matched.

The redcap, who recognized beauty, carried her bags and hat-
box inside the depot, then asked if he could fetch her a drink of

*Reprinted with permission from: Tom Horn, *Life of Tom Horn*, New York;
Jingle Bob Brand, Crown Publishers Inc., 1977 [James Horan], 1904 [John
Coble], p. 310.

water. The men on the depot's sidewalk stopped to look at this striking, sensual young woman.

"If you are going to help me with commonplace chores, we'd better go home before some gentleman makes a pass," whispered Etta, giggling.

Ell's voice came loud from deep inside her throat. "Yes. Isn't it marvelous how attentive men are? I love it. Does Charlie treat you right?" Her lashes brushed her cheeks when she blinked, which she did a lot.

"Charlie—is just Charlie. I love him. He's old-fashioned. You know, he believes women are complementary to men—a secure comfort men can depend on." Etta leaned near Ell. "Confidentially, he'd be embarrassed with the attention you attract."

"Here's a secret to think about. Mattie Silks was my heroine." Ell had a throaty laugh.

"Mattie?" Etta was puzzled. Ell's perfume suddenly smelled cloyingly sweet.

"A wealthy jezebel."

"Honest?" Etta was glad Charlie was not home. He'd not only be embarrassed, he'd be shocked.

Etta felt a twinge of jealousy because Ell looked lovely even while mopping the kitchen floor. She wore floor-length flowered skirts, crisp, white blouses, and rainbow twists of beads. Ell was not only beautiful, she was also competent. She papered the bedrooms and sewed curtains while Etta prepared meals and looked after the children. Floyd and Joella got chicken pox. When they were nearly well, Pauline and Frances got chicken pox. Then all four had pinkeye. No one thought to call a doctor. Etta waited and if there was no continuing soaring fever, she knew they'd be well soon. Ell applied herb lotions and fed the children bark and root infusions that she said stopped inflammation and fever.

Baby Frances fascinated Ell with an ability to get into cupboards and closets before she was missed. She crawled faster than most toddlers walked. Pauline delighted Ell by watching over Frances like a mother hen. Joella confided in her aunt Ell what the other girls wore to school and what was in their lunch pails, what boys she liked best. Floyd confessed to Ell that he wanted to spend weekends on the Y6 with Grandpa Joe. "I can juggle my rope there without Ma's nagging."

By the middle of October the sun had changed color. It was no longer a great golden globe. As the winter approached, the sun turned to a ball of plasma that was like white-hot silver radiating through the gray clouds. The yellow fluttering leaves of cottonwood and willows had fallen on the creek banks. The wind was cold.

Etta and Ell had canned garden corn, string beans, and tomatoes.

Coble had asked Charlie and Frank to take petitions all over the state for signatures asking the governor to commute Horn's sentence. Coble paid the men's expenses. Everyone in the state had heard of Tom Horn and the murder of Willie Nickell. There were few who believed Horn a desperado or criminal. Charlie and Frank crisscrossed the state from Sheridan to Rock Springs, from Jackson Hole to Casper. They rode the train and hired horses to get signatures from businessmen, churchmen, ordinary citizens, cattle ranchers, sheep ranchers, and thousands of cowboys. The large ranchers were invariably on the side of Horn's innocence and glad to sign. Many added an extra note: "When T.H. was free there was fewer rustlers." "Squatters are the crooks." "Small settlers steal our cattle. Horn can stop the stealing." "Horn's a straight shooter." "Horn wouldn't shoot a kid in the back."

Frank and Charlie avoided the small settlers, as these folks believed Horn guilty of some crime, maybe not the one in question, but something in the past. They were afraid of Tom Horn.

Charlie and Frank had thousands of names and began to feel good about this mission. Back in Cheyenne they filled up on Etta's cooking.

"Dear, can you guess how many greasy spoons we've seen?" said Charlie.

Etta teased, "I can tell by looking. Frank used to be so skinny a strong wind would lift him; now he'll give his horse a swayback. And you, Charlie, will have to get your belt lengthened and send out for special-made pants."

This year Ell had an added mission to her visit. She asked Charlie for money to invest in her earth medicines. "I'm going to be an apothecary and dispense only natural medicines. You know I've always wanted to do this."

"What does Les think?" said Charlie, sipping coffee.

"Oh, pooh—Les thinks I've not quite grown up. He won't allow me another cent to spend on some exciting new herbs from Mexico. Why, some of the teas I make from Mexican yams are as good for animals as for people. A friend was sick with consumption and coughing all the time. He got relief from a tea I made him from yam peelings. Another time I bathed the back of this same friend's collie dog, where it got gouged on some barbed wire. The wound healed clean as morning dew."

Charlie snorted and shook his head. "I'm a skeptic, same as Les. But that don't mean I don't believe in teas. Remember how Grandma Malinda knew a plant for most any sickness—but she stayed in her own backyard. She didn't go off to Mexico. I'd say Les has good sense not letting you spend his money on some fool sweet potatoes. Grow your own. That's a darn sight cheaper."

Ell turned from Charlie and looked at her brother Frank. She smiled and seemed as expectant as a sparrow watching a worm-hole. "You can stop watching me like I have a pocketful of money. I'm plumb broke." Frank pushed his chair away from the dining table.

Etta pulled the children away from their father and uncle so that the two men could deliver their precious petitions to the acting governor, Fenimore Chatterton, who'd taken the job when DeForest Richards died. Charlie and Frank left the house with high hopes that the petitions would convey the message that the ranchers of some account were all in favor of letting Horn go free. Horn cherished life; he lived by the old range code. It was against his grain to dry-gulch a thirteen-year-old kid.

Charlie felt a kind of awe as he hitched his horse to the post and walked up the wide concrete steps of the gold-domed capitol building. He was surprised to see men from the Wyoming National Guard stationed at the entrance. One of the guards stood in front of the door. "What is your business?" He held his rifle across his midsection to block the entrance.

"We have something for the governor. Mr. John Coble telephoned that we were coming," said Charlie. He was astonished that the capitol building was protected. "What's happening? What's the security for?"

"The governor's life has been threatened." The guard took the petitions and asked Charlie and Frank to open their coats. When it was clear that the two men carried no weapons, the petitions were given back and the door opened. There was another guard at the door to the governor's office. Again the men were searched before they could go inside. By now Charlie was keyed up. He had a fleeting suspicion that the governor was overreactive.

"Brace yourself, we might have a hard sell here," Charlie whispered to Frank.

Fenimore Chatterton was a portly gentleman with a broad mouth and nose and tiny, raisinlike eyes. He seemed inflexible.

Charlie did his best. He complimented the governor on the beautiful scenes of Wyoming in the paintings on his office walls. He talked to him about fly-fishing, which was the governor's favorite sport. He talked about how the people of Wyoming believed in the governor, how the constituency regarded him as a fine, upstanding, empathetic representative of their values. "Those people never questioned your integrity, sir. The good people all over the state know you'll do what they desire most. Do you believe in capital punishment, sir?" asked Charlie.

Governor Chatterton took the pages of legal paper with the thousands of signatures, but he would not look them over while Charlie and Frank were sitting in front of his massive oak desk. He said, "No, personally I do not believe in capital punishment. You may tell your fellow cattlemen that a proper hearing has been given Mr. Thomas Horn and the recommendation of the jury must be taken under the law. Good day, gentlemen."

In the foyer Frank whispered, "It seems he's made up his mind. Never interfere with nothing what don't bother him none." A smile spread across his face. "Charlie, you could—"

"Oh, no! Don't even think it. Frank, we've done our part. That governor doesn't believe in capital punishment personally, he said so, but he does politically," said Charlie. He felt let down, deflated as a worn-out bellows.

"Maybe Mr. Coble'll think of something."

"It's too late. Forget it, Frank. If this thing went some other way, someone else would be hanged. Some people won't be satisfied until they have a hanging."

"I need a drink," said Frank. "I'm drier than an empty water barrel."

"Forget that, too," said Charlie. "We're heading out to the IM and getting back to work. Jeems, that Chatterton is pigheaded! I truly believe someone has got to him, paid him off, and scared him to death."

Frank said, "Suppose the governor takes time to look over those petitions and wants to contact us. Maybe we ought to stay in town overnight."

"You're right. Let's go home. Etta'll make us dinner."

For the following week Charlie's mind was in a torment. He couldn't stand to stay in the IM bunkhouse; it was stuffy and he couldn't breathe. He couldn't stand the barn; it was dark and dusty. He couldn't stand the blacksmith shed; it was hot and uncomfortable. The sunshine was too bright. The breeze was too strong. The air too cold.

He wondered if Horn was actually being railroaded. Or was Horn keeping his mouth closed to protect someone? Who?

Charlie was upset. He decided he had to talk with the cattle barons. If Horn was innocent, he should be freed. If there was more than a slight doubt about his innocence, maybe he should be given life in the pen, but not hanged on such trumped-up, flimsy evidence as LeFors's interview. And Charlie had a plan.

"If Horn's sentence is commuted so that he gets off, fine. But if the sentence is changed to life in prison, it's worse than hanging for Horn. Life in the Rawlins penitentiary'll kill him," said Charlie.

Everyone nodded. Their faces were clouded and dark. "There's a chance Horn will get life," Charlie continued. "He'll be put on the westbound U.P. for the state penitentiary in Rawlins. That train leaves Cheyenne in early evening when it's still light. By the time the train hits Medicine Bow, it's dark. We'll have Horn's horse ready, saddled, and carrying his gear. When the train comes through, we'll cause some commotion, stage a train robbery, anything to divert attention, so that Horn can be taken off. He'll get on his horse and head south to Mexico. I'm sure we can pull it off."

"C.B. Irwin!" sputtered Coble. "Why didn't you tell us of this scheme sooner! We'll have to think about this and work out the details."

Charlie went out to see his father. Joe's back seemed to have a permanent curve, like a scythe. His hair was snow-white. His face and arms and hands were tanned. The skin looked like wrinkled parchment flecked with liver spots. Charlie knew Joe would never admit he was slowing down, but Charlie saw how slow he walked and how he'd get caught up in story telling and forget all about blacksmithing or mending corral fences.

"Son, when you coming to stay at the Y6? I can do the work all right, but I don't have the head for thinking that you have," said Joe shaking Charlie's hand. "A family ought to stay together."

"I know, Pa. I'll give it some serious thought," said Charlie, feeling relieved that Joe didn't suspect there'd been talk of buying off Governor Chatterton and stopping a U.P. train in order to get Tom Horn off and on his escape route to Mexico.

* * *

When John Coble came out to the IM ranch to see how the new house was coming along, Charlie put down hammer and nails and spoke first. "Mr. Coble, my father is on the Y6 ranch over yonder on Horse Creek by hisself. It's quite a job for a man his age. I have an obligation to my father. The house is about done here. I've enjoyed working for you. What I'm trying to say is that I want your permission and good wishes to leave as soon as I can. Neil Clark would make a good foreman. Honestly, I mean no offense. I'm looking forward to being my own boss."

"I admire a man that wants to look after his family," said Coble. He extended his hand and spoke softly. "I'm depressed about our friend in the Laramie County jail. The governor hasn't done a thing. I hope he doesn't wait until the day of the hanging to commute the sentence and ship him to Rawlins."

"There's plenty of time. Everything's ready. All I need is the word," said Charlie.

On the 19th of November, 1903, Charlie came in from the Irwin Y6 ranch on horseback. The day was clear and cold. There was a fine, crystalline snow blowing across the prairie. He was surprised to see so many wagons and strange horses tied to the hitching posts in town and strangers walking the streets.

"Hey!" he called to Etta. "You see all those people in town?"

She came out from the kitchen and hugged Charlie, then let him take off his mackinaw and wool cap and muffler. "It's barbaric! I can understand friends of Horn's coming to town, like yourself, but not all these eastern newspapermen and just curious people. It's like selling souvenirs at a funeral. It's a circus. Perfectly decent people coming for a hanging! There's something black, wicked, and perverse in human nature."

"Not in you," said Charlie nipping her ear.

Etta grumbled some about not having room for all the horses. Actually there was plenty of room in the six stalls alongside the house.

After supper Charlie did not go to town with Frank and the cowboys. He did not drink and he did not want to get mixed up with the crowd and the carnival mood. He felt half-sick. His dinner sat heavy on his stomach and he kept wondering how his friend Horn felt. Charlie didn't want to attend tomorrow's hanging. But it was something he had to do. He had to show his respect and friendship for Horn. He had to say his last farewell.

There was a large knot in his stomach. His throat also had a lump that seemed to rub against the larger one.

Floyd coaxed Charlie into going outside a moment to see his latest rope trick. The temperature was near freezing. With a quick wrist movement Floyd brought the loop up, over, and around in front. Then with a rotary motion he let go with one hand and the loop slipped over Charlie's head and shoulders, caught his arms at his sides, and pulled tight around his middle.

"Gottcha!" squealed eight-year-old Floyd.

Charlie growled, then had to laugh. The trick brought back a rush of memories of his own boyhood. He felt better. Then he saw a movement through the bunkhouse window that caught his eye. At first he thought it was only Frank and the other cowboys playing cards around the kerosene lamp in the center of the table. He looked at his pocket watch as Floyd rewound the rope and ran for the warmth of the house. He thought the boys had come back from town early. Then he saw the red dress. Ell was sitting in the midst of the men, a cigarette in her mouth, dealing the cards. Everyone was laughing, having a good time.

He told himself it was not the gambling that bothered him. He enjoyed gambling himself. It was not the cigarette. Ell could do as she pleased. It was the sight of a woman, in a slinky, red dress in the bunkhouse on this particular night. A woman playing cards in a bunkhouse was thought by most ranchers to be bad luck.

That night before he went to sleep he told Etta that he'd called the depot and arranged for Ell's train ticket. "It has to be used first thing in the morning. I'll give her some money for those Mexican herbs she came for!"

Next morning Etta noticed that the men picked at the biscuits. She wondered if it were because their vivacious card-playing partner had taken the five A.M. southbound to Colorado or the impending unlucky hanging that left them quiet as featherdusters.

More snow fell during the night. The air was crisp. The wind blew from the northwest. Horn's lawyers were appealing to the governor at that very moment for a complete pardon or a commutation of the sentence.

"An appeal for a new trial on the ground that the verdict was contrary to the evidence, contrary to law, and was not sustained by sufficient evidence was overruled. Therefore this hanging goes on as scheduled." The governor refused to interfere, no matter how logical the lawyers sounded, no matter how emotional the lawyers became.

The men that left Charlie Irwin's home were subdued as they huddled inside sheepskins and walked quickly in the cold air. Their boots made the snow squeak.

At dawn the funeral bell at St. Mary's Cathedral rang for a long, tense five minutes. Charlie and Frank and their friends walked close together toward the courthouse.

Frank spoke softly, "Jeez, look at all the guards. Over there, on top of the jail's roof, see the rapid-firing guns?"

Sheriff Smalley handed Charlie an envelope, which he opened and read:

Cheyenne, Wyo.
November 20, 1903

John C. Coble, Esq.,
Cheyenne, Wyo.

As you have just requested, I will tell all my knowledge of everything I know in regard to the killing of the Nickell boy.

The day I laid over at Miller's ranch, he asked me to do so, so that I could meet Billy McDonald.

Billy McDonald came up and Miller and I met him up the creek, above Miller's house. Billy opened the conversation by saying that he and Miller were going to kill off the Nickell outfit and wanted me to go in on it. They said that Underwood and Jordon would pay me.

Miller and McDonald said they would do the work. I refused to have anything to do with them, as I was not interested in any way. McDonald said that the sheep were then on Coble's land and I got on my horse and went up to see, and they were not on Coble's land.

I promised to stay all night again at Miller's, as McDonald said he would come up again next morning.

He came back next morning and asked me if I still felt the same as I did the day before, and I told him I did.

"Well," he said, "we have made up our minds to wipe up the whole Nickell outfit."

I got on my horse and left, and went on about my business. I went on as John Brae and Otto Plaga said I did, and on to the ranch, where I got in on Saturday. I heard there of the boy being killed. I felt I was well out of the mix up.

I was over in that part of the country six weeks or two

months later and saw both McDonald and Miller, and they were laughing and blowing to me about running and shooting the sheep of Nickell. I told them I did not want to hear of it at all, for I could see that McDonald wanted to tell me the whole scheme. They both gave me the laugh and said I was suspicioned of the whole thing. I knew there was some suspicion against me, but did not pay the attention to it that I should.

That is all there is to it so far as I know. . . . All that supposed confession in the United States marshal's office was prearranged, and everything that was sworn to by those fellows was a lie, made up before I came to Cheyenne. Of course, there was talk of the killing of the boy, but LaFors did all of it. I did not even make an admission, but allowed LaFors to make some insinuations.

Ohnahaus, LaFors and Snow . . . all swore to lies to fit the case.

Your name was not mentioned in the marshal's office.

This is the truth, as I am going to die in ten minutes.

Thanking you for your kindness and continued goodness to me, I am

> Sincerely yours,
> Tom Horn*

"What are you going to do with that?" asked Frank. "It's Coble's and you read it!"

"I figure it was given to me for some reason. Wait." He recognized George Evans of the *Cheyenne State Leader* and John Thompson of the *Wyoming Tribune*. He showed them the letter and urged, "Make it fast. You gotta get this in the paper and out on the streets before the hanging. A couple of hours at most."

The next two hours were tense. Charlie walked into the outside courtyard and nodded toward Thompson. Thompson shook his head and pointed his thumbs down. Charlie's heart sank to the ground. There had not been time enough to get an extra or even a flier printed before this execution. Oh, double jeems! thought Charlie. A man's life is cut off, thrown away for lack of time! For not moving fast enough!

*Reprinted with permission from: Tom Horn, *Life of Tom Horn*, New York, New York; Jingle Bob Brand, Crown Publishers, Inc, 1977. James D. Horan; 1904, John Coble, pp.283–4.

The men stayed inside the courthouse where it was warm until they were given tiny white ribbons to wear in their lapel and led out to the courtyard. Two companies of the Wyoming National Guard surrounded the courthouse. There were ten armed men around the jail itself. No one was allowed to be on the streets near the courthouse while the hanging was taking place. The governor wanted no attack against the jail to get the doomed Horn out.

Deputy Proctor stepped up to the gallows' platform and in a loud voice began to point out how they were designed by Cheyenne's architect, James P. Julian.

"My stomach's in knots," whispered Frank.

Charlie flexed his knees and breathed deeply the needlelike near-freezing air.

Deputy Proctor paused and looked at the open door of the cell leading to the platform. "All right, we're ready now."

Horn stood up and looked at the cross beam. He was pale from his long confinement in jail.

Charlie's stomach contracted. He swallowed and was acutely aware of his neck muscles. He felt dizzy. His head throbbed.

"Lost his tan," murmured Frank, "and he looks thin."

Horn walked out and seemed to tower above even those men on the second tier of the platform. He was well over six feet tall. His features were sharp and clean. He had a neat, small mustache on his upper lip that was brown and matched his thinning hair. He had on flat, leather slippers, dark trousers, a brown corduroy vest, and a yellow and white striped, soft silk shirt. The collar of the shirt was unbuttoned, showing a red scar on Horn's neck. He brushed cigarette ashes off his vest and glanced back at his carefully made cot where he'd left a braided horsehair hackamore, not yet finished. Horn sighed audibly. Then, chin up, he walked twelve steps, handed his cigarette to the *Wyoming State Tribune*'s John Thompson, and stopped on the side of the gallows' platform. He looked at the group of sheriffs and said to Ed Smalley, "What a scared-looking lot of lawmen. What's making them shiver? Is it the cold this twentieth of November, 1903, or is it fright for what they are to see?" His eyes were squeezed down hard and penetrating. Suddenly his face softened. "Hello there, Charlie."

"Hello, Tom," said Charlie, having a hard time keeping his teeth from chattering as the wind came up sharp and biting.

"You and Frank sing me one of your songs. You can do that?"

"Oh—sure," said Charlie. His knees trembled. "Frank and

I'll sing." He cleared his throat and began to hum. Frank swallowed hard before taking up the tune, "Life's Railway to Heaven." Charlie could not look at Tom, nor at Frank, as he sang the popular hymn. His voice had more than the usual amount of vibrato. After the first verse the words came out somewhat easier, steadier. Their voices carried deep and now unbroken over the entire courtyard. "...never falter, never quail...Keep your hand upon the throttle and your eye upon the rail."

As the two men sang in their rich tenor voices, Ed Proctor fitted the straps that held Horn's arms and legs. Charlie could feel perspiration gather under his arms and in the middle of his back. Tears streamed unchecked down his face. He could not see that there was not a dry eye among any of the men, except for Tom Horn himself. The song was over, Charlie mopped his face with his handkerchief, and the courtyard was deathly still. A light snow was falling.

The leg straps pulled Horn's legs together and he nearly lost his balance. In a jesting tone Horn said, "Seems to me you birds might steady me. I might tip over." Sheriff Smalley and Joe Cahill held his arms, supported him, while his knees and feet were bound together.

Proctor fixed the noose, formed with a knot of thirteen wraps. Cahill pulled the black cap over Horn's head. In a loud voice Proctor asked, "Tom, are you ready?"

Without a moment's hesitation came the reply, "Yes."

Sheriff Smalley sobbed and put his arm over his face, and turned his back toward Horn.

"You can't be losing your nerve, Ed?" said Horn through the black hood.

Cahill and Proctor lifted Horn onto the trapdoor. The only sound was the hissing of rushing water underneath Horn's feet.

Charlie thought the sound of the water went on and on. The gurgling heightened the tense feeling of doom. Charlie could not hold back his heaving sobs. Then suddenly, without warning, the trapdoor divided with a loud crash and Horn's body swung between two halves of the door. The force of Horn's weight on a four-inch by four-inch rod, supporting the door, pressed on a spring. The spring acted on a hydraulic valve which opened and let water run from a container. When the container's equilibrium was upset, water spilled out, tripped a weight, and the trapdoor fell open and Horn hanged himself. There were two, three spasmodic quiverings, then the body went limp in the frigid air.

Thompson of the *Wyoming State Tribune* was first to break the tension. "He was hanged at eleven-o-four. Thirty-one seconds since he was on that damn door! He's fallen nearly four feet!"

Everyone knew after Proctor's explanation of the device that the drop could not be longer, because the full weight of the body would rip the head off.

Charlie let the breath out of his burning lungs. It was an explosive sound of hot, pent-up air.

Etta Mae McGuckin,
eighteen years old.

Charles Burton Irwin.

Kenmore Coursing Club group, 1895. C. B. Irwin is in front with a
spotted dog. Frank Irwin, well-known jockey, is on the left on a
horse. The building in the background is the Sherman County
Courthouse in Goodland, Kansas.

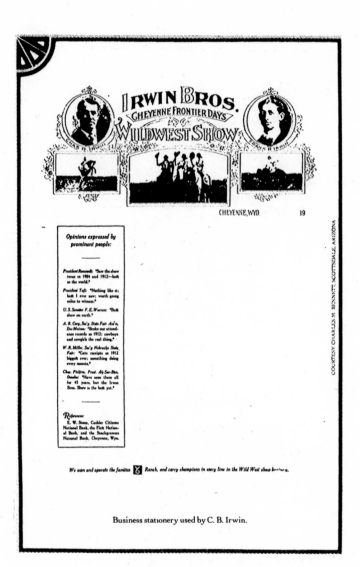

IRWIN BROS.
CHEYENNE FRONTIER DAYS
WILDWEST SHOW

CHEYENNE, WYO.   19

Opinions expressed by prominent people:

President Roosevelt: "Saw the show twice in 1904 and 1912—best in the world."

President Taft: "Nothing like it; best I ever saw; worth going miles to witness."

U. S. Senator F. E. Warren: "Best show on earth."

A. R. Corey, Sec'y State Fair Ass'n, Des Moines: "Broke our attendance records in 1912; cowboys and cowgirls the real thing."

W. R. Miller, Sec'y Nebraska State Fair: "Gate receipts in 1912 biggest ever; something doing every minute."

Chas. Pickens, Pres't. Ak-Sar-Ben, Omaha: "Have seen them all for 45 years, but the Irwin Bros. Show is the best yet."

References:
E. W. Stone, Cashier Citizens National Bank, the First National Bank, and the Stockgrowers National Bank, Cheyenne, Wyo.

We own and operate the famous 😼 *Ranch, and carry champions in every line in the Wild West show business.*

Business stationery used by C. B. Irwin.

C. B. Irwin roping an unruly steer, 1906. This picture appeared in the December 1925 *National Geographic*, page 624.

No. 531—Clayton Danks champion Bronco Buster for 1907 and Steamboat the meanest bucking bronco in the word.

Clayton Danks in angora chaps, and the famous bucking bronc, Steamboat.

Charlie and Etta Irwin's children.
Floyd, *top; left to right:* Joella, Frances, and Pauline, about 1908.

Left to right: Teddy Roosevelt, Buffalo Bill, Charles Hirsig, and Charlie Irwin, Cheyenne Frontier Days, August 28, 1910.

Joseph Marvin Irwin, Charlie's father, and William H. Irwin, Charlie's brother, about 1910.

C. B. Irwin and Charles Hirsig driving a buffalo team during a Frontier Days celebration, about 1910.

ROUTE CARD
Irwin Bros. Wild West Show

June 15-16	Cheyenne, Wyo.
" 17	Sidney, Neb.
" 18-19-20	Alliance, Neb.
" 21	En Route.
" 22	Broken Bow, Neb.
" 23	York, Neb.
" 24	Fairbury, Neb.
" 25	Red Cloud, Neb.
" 26	Hastings, Neb.
" 27	Holdredge, Neb.
" 28	En Route.
" 29	Sterling, Col.
" 30	Ft. Morgan, Col.
July 1	En Route.
July 2-3-4	Ft. Collins, Col.
July 5	En Route.

OFFICIAL ROUTE CARD
—OF THE—
Irwin Bros. Real Wild West Show
Season 1914

Elko, Nevda,	July 13th
Winnemucca, Nevada,	July 14th
Lovelock, Nevada,	July 15th
Reno, Nevada,	July 16th
Enroute	July 17th
"	July 18th
Colfax, California,	July 19th, 20th and 21st
Roseville, California,	July 22nd
Sacramento, California,	July 23rd
San Francisco, California,	July 24th, 25th, 26th, 27th, 28th and 29th

AL. FAIRBROTHER,
Mail Superintendent.

Route cards for the itinerary of the Wild West show.

COURTESY DR J. S. PALEN, CHEYENNE, WYOMING.

Left to right: Frances, Pauline, and Joella Irwin, 1914. The three girls have the same saddles, bits, and headstalls on their horses.

Charlie Irwin in the New York Stampede, 1916.

An advertisement for the Irwin Bros. Cheyenne Frontier Days Wild West Show.
The Wyoming Tribune, Saturday, June 7, 1913, p. 7.

Floyd Irwin on his horse, Fashion, in front of the
Sioux camp outside Frontier Park in Cheyenne, Wyoming.

Buddy Sterling in the driver's seat and Roy Kivett.
Sterling took care of Will Rogers' polo ponies. Kivett was
raised as a member of the Irwin family.

C. B. Irwin (*left*) and the Baron de Rothschild of France, standing beside the Buick touring car and Model T Ford.

The Wyoming
State Board of Child and Animal Protection

Know all Men by these Presents, That I, *F. R. Dildine*
President of *The Wyoming State Board of Child and Animal Protection*, being there-unto duly authorized by the Board of Directors of said Board, do hereby appoint and com-mission _Charles B. Stevens_
of _Cheyenne_ , County of _Laramie_
and State of Wyoming, an *Officer of said Board for the State of Wyoming*.

It is the duty of said Officer to familiarize himself with the laws under which he shall act; to investigate all cases of cruelty to animals, or neglect or abuse of children, coming within his notice; to take whatever action in each case shall best secure the prevention and punishment of cruelty to animals and wrongs to children; to utilize every opportunity to create humane sentiment, and to discharge his duty as an officer of the law and of this Board impartially and fearlessly.

He shall furnish a report of his work to the said Board whenever it shall be called for. He shall have no power to contract debts or incur liabilities for the said Board. He shall remain in office until his successor shall have been appointed, or this commission revoked.

This commission shall be his authority to act for the said Board in all matters herein specified.

Given at the office of *The State Board of Child and Animal Protection*, at Cheyenne, Wyoming, this 4th day of *June*, A. D. 19*18*.

Witness my hand and the seal of the Board.

F. R. Dildine
President

ATTEST: _C. B. Bartlett_
Secretary

E. A. Burke

Charlie was given his commission and star as an officer of the Wyoming Humane Society and State Board of Child and Animal Protection in 1918 and remained an officer for the rest of his life.

Frontier Days Parade on 17th and Capitol Avenue, Cheyenne, in the early 1920s.

Fire at the Tia Juana Racetrack in Mexico in 1924. All the barns on
this side of the railroad tracks were destroyed.

Left to right: Pablo Martinez, a famous jockey, Will Rogers, and C. B. Irwin.

General "Black Jack" Pershing *(left)* and Charlie Irwin.

Douglas Fairbanks, Sr. (*left*), and Charlie Irwin.

Chief Red Cloud and Charlie Irwin with three Sioux women.

PERSONAL

France, April 18, 1919.

Mr. C. B. Irwin,
Cheyenne, Wyoming.

My dear Charley:

I have received your letter of January 1st, and am pleased to know that you are getting on well and thank you for the newspaper clipping which you enclosed.

With reference to your inquiry regarding certain members of this Expedition, it is learned with deep regret that the men you mention met with misfortune in the honorable discharge of their duties, fighting in a noble cause, and I ask that in conveying the following to the respective families, you express my sincere sympathy at their loss.

Private Sidney McIntosh, 122955, 96th Company, 6th Marines, was reported on July 22, 1918, wounded in action, severe, between June 2nd and 10th, and his death was reported February 9, 1919. He was buried in American Battle Area Cemetery in Commune of Boureschès, Department of the Aisne, grave No. 34, marked with a cross. The exact date of Private McIntosh's death and burial, unfortunately, are not available.

As to W. C. Irvine's boy, Flying Squadron, Canadian Forces; records of the American Statistical Section with the British show a Van Rensselaer V. Irvine, 43 Squadron Royal Air Force, missing in action since July 29th. This case is now in the hands of the American Statistical Section with the British to determine the status of this soldier.

Relative to John Hay's boy, of Rock Springs, Wyoming: Records show that Sergeant Archibald L. Hay, 2260715, Company G, 362nd Infantry, was killed in action September 29th and that he was buried October 1st, one kilometer south of Epionville, Cemetery No. 1. Sergeant Hay's grave is marked with a cross.

Reply to your letter has been delayed awaiting additional information regarding Mr. Irvine's boy, but nothing further having been learned to date, I am sending this on now and will communicate anything additional immediately upon its receipt.

With best wishes, believe me, as always,

Very sincerely yours,

John J. Pershing.

A personal letter to C. B. Irwin from General John Pershing.

C. B. Irwin with jockey E. Taplin on Bonnie Kay
at the Agua Caliente track in Tia Juana, Mexico, 1930.

Flood at the Y6 ranch, 1935.

Pine Ridge, South Dakota.
April 3, 1934.

Dear Mrs. Pauline Sawyer:

I am writing this letter to tell you how sorry we felt for my good friend Mr. Charles B. Irwin's death. All the Indians who made good friends with your Dad. Mr. Irwin. felt pretty bad. I know I never will find a better man like Mr. Irwin again. The Sioux Indians will miss him pretty bad. We thought we was going to see him again this year. but I guess we will never see him again any more.

I will always remember Mr. C.B. Irwin like the day I last saw him.

I am hoping you will answer me right away and tell me about Mr. Charles B. Irwin's death. I am anxious to hear about it. The Indians who knew Mr. Irwin lost a good man.

I remain a friend of Mr. Charles B. Irwin and family.   Mr. Charles Yellow Boy.
                              Pine Ridge,
                                     South Dakota.

The above letter to Charlie's middle daughter, Pauline,
from one of the Sioux, meant a great deal to the Irwin family.